THE ULTIMATE EROTIC EXPERIMENT

Subject: Christina North

Question: What does a woman need to totally satisfy her?

Possibilities: Pure love. Anonymous sex. Marriage. Adultery. A superstud lover. An intellectual lover. A psychiatrist lover. A priestly lover. Another woman. A row of different partners. Exhibitionism. Self-gratification. Any or all of the above and even more, each given a thorough testing.

Result: A convention-shattering, shamelessly revealing vision of the wildest sexual possibilities —in a novel that takes you into a future that only the one and only Robert Rimmer could have conceived and vividly brought to life. . . .

Love Me Tomorrow

Big Bestsellers from SIGNET

☐ **COME LIVE MY LIFE by Robert H. Rimmer.**
(#E7421—$2.25)

☐ **THE GOLD LOVERS by Robert H. Rimmer.**
(#Y6970—$1.25)

☐ **THE PREMAR EXPERIMENTS by Robert H. Rimmer.**
(#J7515—$1.95)

☐ **PROPOSITION 31 by Robert H. Rimmer.**
(#J7514—$1.95)

☐ **THURSDAY MY LOVE by Robert H. Rimmer.**
(#E7209—$1.75)

☐ **NEVER CALL IT LOVE by Veronica Jason.**
(#J8343—$1.95)*

☐ **BLACK DAWN by Christopher Nicole.**
(#E8342—$2.25)*

☐ **CARIBEE by Christopher Nicole.**
(#J7945—$1.95)

☐ **THE DEVIL'S OWN by Christopher Nicole.**
(#J7256—$1.95)

☐ **MISTRESS OF DARKNESS by Christopher Nicole.**
(#J7782—$1.95)

☐ **THE WICKED GUARDIAN by Vanessa Gray.**
(#E8390—$1.75)*

☐ **SONG OF SOLOMON by Toni Morrison.**
(#E8340—$2.50)*

☐ **RAPTURE'S MISTRESS by Gimone Hall.**
(#E8422—$2.25)*

☐ **PRESIDENTIAL EMERGENCY by Walter Stovall.**
(#E8371—$2.25)*

☐ **GIFTS OF LOVE by Charlotte Vale Allen.**
(#J8388—$1.95)*

*Price slightly higher in Canada

If you wish to order these titles,
please see the coupon
in the back of this book.

Love Me Tomorrow

by

Robert H. Rimmer

A SIGNET BOOK

NEW AMERICAN LIBRARY

TIMES MIRROR

NAL BOOKS ARE ALSO AVAILABLE AT DISCOUNTS IN BULK
QUANTITY FOR INDUSTRIAL OR SALES-PROMOTIONAL USE.
FOR DETAILS, WRITE TO PREMIUM MARKETING DIVISION,
NEW AMERICAN LIBRARY, INC., 1301 AVENUE OF THE
AMERICAS, NEW YORK, NEW YORK 10019.

COPYRIGHT © 1978 BY ROBERT H. RIMMER

The author wishes to express his thanks to Artists &
Alchemists Publications for permission to quote from
Erotica by Diane Ippolito.

SIGNET TRADEMARK REG. U.S. PAT. OFF. AND FOREIGN COUNTRIES
REGISTERED TRADEMARK—MARCA REGISTRADA
HECHO EN CHICAGO, U.S.A.

SIGNET, SIGNET CLASSICS, MENTOR, PLUME AND MERIDIAN BOOKS
are published by The New American Library, Inc.,
1301 Avenue of the Americas, New York, New York 10019

FIRST SIGNET PRINTING, DECEMBER, 1978

1 2 3 4 5 6 7 8 9

PRINTED IN THE UNITED STATES OF AMERICA

This book is dedicated to the

UNITED PEOPLE OF AMERICA

who in the year 2000 will be

LOOKING BACKWARD

and wondering why they waited so long

to make the inevitable transition

Today

"Must we forever be like children, seeking purpose in the fall of the rain, in the sweep of the wind, in the strike of lightning! Why must we always seek it in ourselves? . . . No, your life has no more purpose than any other beast . . . It has no purpose except as you choose to give it one. I give you in the nature of life itself, in the momentum that keeps it spinning on its course, an unquenchable instinct for self-determination—if you wish to call it that; and in the flesh that accumulates around itself I give you the capacity to learn by experience, and to test your knowledge by experiment."

—Homer W. Smith,
Kamongo

Except for a hospital johnny which I can't keep tied around me, I'm sitting here naked. Outside the only window (barred) in this room, I can see a small green lawn, and a fountain, sprinkling a moss-covered stone Diana and her deer. They're surrounded, and thoroughly screened, by thirty-foot cypress trees—famous guardians of the already dead. Somewhere in back of them is a twelve-foot barbed-wire, electric, chain-linked fence.

I haven't been able to find the eye, but I'm sure that this room is monitored by a television camera. While I'm typing on this typewriter, they're watching me,—"they" being either one or both of my two science-fiction jailers, Drs. David Convita and Max Lebenthal, and maybe their lackey, Rose Plackett, as well.

A few days ago David suggested that I should use the time, "while we're still making final tests," to write my autobiography, an account of my dual life.

"Although we know a great deal about the physical you, Christina," he said, "and we're aware of some of the mental turmoil that you have been going through, your own story of your life could be very instructive, not only for us, but for yourself, as a therapy, to discover your own drives and motivations.

"Maybe I'll write about two freaky scientists who are determined to experiment with the life of a wealthy suicidal woman they've kidnapped and locked up in a remote laboratory somewhere," I told him. But he only smiled and left the room, locking the door behind him as always.

I suppose that while I'm waiting for the opportunity to escape from this nightmare, I might just as well try to squeeze the essence of Christina North Klausner out of the packed tube of her life. A mind-paste blended with pepper as well as mint. What's a more intriguing story than the manic-depressive or maybe schizophrenic life of a former porno

3

writer, actress, and late spouse of a well-known investment banker?

I'm sure of one thing, I can't force the story out chronologically, beginning that Christina was born on April 24, 1947. No—I'm simply going to have to jump in to the "now" of 1980 and try to work back and forth.

◆

As I type, I'm looking at Christina. She's sitting in the third row of a large theater, watching a ballet. Who watches the watcher? Karl, of course! Karl watches everything, including his money and his wife.

I recognize the music, It's Tchaikovsky! It's *The Sleeping Beauty* ballet, the story of Princess Aurora, a virgin princess. The pretty young dancers, none of them over twenty-five, dressed in tights or tutus, their breasts and penises and balls encased in little mounds, are leaping or pirouetting, and continuously assuming the stereotyped gestures of classical ballet.

Sitting between Karl and Christina are two children. They're Karl's children, Michael and Penny. Christina may have borne them, but unless she straightens up and flies right, Karl will probably divorce her and the court will give him the children. I don't understand Christina very well. She's a difficult woman to penetrate. A loner, remote. When I look in a mirror and see her high-cheekboned face and haunted blue eyes staring back at me, I ask her, "Who are you? You poor, sick-looking stranger. You can't be me."

Right now, Christina's watching the dancers impassively; she's not empathizing with them. She knows that Karl thinks she is bored, but it's not that. The ballet makes her uneasy. A long sleep is death. It reminds her of the many times in her life she has wished she could close her eyes and never wake again. While she loves ballet, the story of Sleeping Beauty simultaneously depresses her and makes her feel elated.

If she told that to Jerry Greenberg, her psychiatrist, he would agree. Elation and depression are the seesaw she's chained to. But Jerry doesn't have the faintest idea what makes Christina tick, either. To him, intimations of immortality and premonitions of imminent death, in a physically healthy woman, will be cured on "transference day." On that miracle day, and thousands of dollars later, Christina Klausner will at last be able to view her life from the Greenberg perspective.

4

To hell with Jerry Greenberg! To hell with Karl Klausner, too! If Karl is ever bored, no one will ever know it. Karl has trained himself never to reveal "lower-class" emotions. He has often told Christina that their sponsorship of the ballet is no big thing. They don't have to see every presentation during the season, but he—and she—do have some social responsibility to the arts—and indoctrinating their children.

"Anyway, I enjoy these evenings," he insists. "So will Michael and Penny. This will be their first professional ballet. And it's opening night. All our friends will be there." Ah, that is the real key to Karl's behavior. Karl's friends. They not only confirm his success, but, in Karl's words to Christina, "without each other, we wouldn't exist." Karl is referring to monetary existence, of course.

During dinner at the Parker House before the ballet, Karl has reminded Christina that when he first met her, all she had talked about was the ballet. "You loved it, then, Christina. You told me that you practically lived at the Joffrey or at Lincoln Center during the season. You told me that in your next life you hoped that you were born a Russian. You were planning to become Christina Norkova, the star of the Bolshoi Ballet."

Yes, that was true. Christina is always living in her next life. But she wonders why Karl hasn't mentioned her infamous novel, *The Christening of Christina*. Doesn't he remember that in her novel, and in the porno movie version, Christina retold the Sleeping Beauty story with spindles which actually turn into throbbing penises? But he doesn't mention the past. Nor does she. Instead she reminds Karl that this isn't the Bolshoi or the Joffrey Ballet. It's the Boston Ballet. But Karl knows the qualitative difference. Between his thirty-ninth and fifty-ninth year, he not only had become a connoisseur of the arts, he had become a multi-man. A multimillionaire who can afford the sequential luxury of multi-wives. Six years ago, when Christina became the third female in the changing Klausner ménage, she gradually discovered that if Karl and his wife of the moment weren't enjoying the best (or, at least, the most expensive of everything that man had placed on this earth), other than financial reasons were involved.

The founder and president of the best-managed and most profitable mutual fund in America, The Klausner Fund, made a lot of money, and he spent it. He was successful and rich, he told Christina, because he cultivated the masses.

5

They invested their money with him because they believed in him. He was a success because he had made it a point not to hide himself behind the facade of money. Unlike many of his competitors, he had dared to invade the hinterlands and talk to the Rotarians and veterans and the small businessmen, and he had convinced thousands of them that he was really one of the boys. Investing in The Klausner Fund was investing in America. They believed in America, didn't they? By definition they must believe in Karl. Karl might not be Uncle Sam, but he was Santa Klausner with a bag full of bucks which he paid quarterly to the faithful.

His activities in Boston were equally important. After all, he often reminds Christina, while nine months of the year they live either in West Palm Beach or Villefranche, they are usually in residence at Marblehead from early May to August. In a couple of weeks their sixty-foot Hatteras, brought up from Florida by Captain Fletcher, will once again be moored off the Corinthian Yacht Club. Along with the ballet, it is important that the Klausners patronize local institutions such as the opera; the symphony, and the better hospitals. Even more important than their personal proximity to Boston is the reality. The Klausner Fund has heavy investments in Boston banks, insurance companies, and electronic firms. Christina should understand. The Fund is able to make successful investments because Karl personally knows the high caliber of the men who run these companies, and he watches their management carefully.

Why, Karl wonders, does Christina continuously agonize over money? He was poor once, too. Christina has heard Karl's life story many times before, but he has summarized it again at dinner at the Parker House. Christina's father, Arthur North, an electronics engineer, was earning twenty-two thousand a year when he divorced Grace. And later, as a vice-president of The Klausner Fund until she retired four years ago, Grace was earning forty-five thousand. By comparison Karl's family had been poverty-stricken. His father had been an assembly-line worker, an industrial peasant. All Karl ever learned from him was not to trust anyone and not to follow in his father's footsteps. No one ever got rich working for someone else.

What's more, Christina can stop teasing him. He never was an SS officer. During World War II, he was a navigator with the Luftwaffe. In 1949—when Christina was only two years old—he had saved enough money to come to the United

6

States. He had lived with his father's brother in Milwaukee, where he finally opened a Volkswagen agency on borrowed money. Fortunately, he sold it at the peak of America's enthusiasm with foreign cars. In the process of becoming a citizen of the United States, he discovered that the best way of making money was trading in money. Despite what Christina may think, he is well aware that it isn't money that gives life meaning. It's the power that money confers on its owner. Only the men or women who personally control at least twenty million and can, if they wish, earn a million tax-free dollars annually, have their feet on the rungs of the United States power ladder. Since Karl has approximately one hundred and twenty million, he's on the top rungs.

Christina will be happier if she stops trying to straddle two worlds. America is a class society based on money. Intellect doesn't count. She has proved that to herself. Garbage collectors make as much money as college professors with Ph.D.'s, and a hell of a lot more than poets. Marrying Karl Klausner had been a sound monetary decision. Married to Karl, she has triumphed over her nonexistence as an American peasant. She has joined the ruling class.

Right now Christina is pondering the word "patronize." It's the leit-motif of Karl's life. He patronizes everybody, including his wife and children. It's a safer role to play than simply being human and loving them.

But Christina isn't really angry with Karl. She's sad for him. The poor man has no laughter in his soul. When she reminded him earlier tonight, at home, that he must have married her because the previous Mrs. Klausner probably didn't enjoy sucking Santa Claus's weenie, Karl didn't think that was funny. Especially when she told him, since he was the king of his Wonderland, and he expected queenly attention to his aging prick, that His Royal Highness should remember the queen's cunt. Sucking and licking is a two-way street on which Karl, from the beginning, has erected a one-way sign. All things considered, he should have bought a vacuum cleaner to suck him off. It would have been more efficient, and much cheaper than Christina.

Right now Karl is assuring Penny that when this act is over he'll take her to the champagne bar, and she can have a sip of Daddy's champagne. Michael, who is obviously not enjoying his first exposure to culture, has slid so far down in his chair that his head is resting on the seat. Looking up at the ceiling, he asks Christina if he can buy some popcorn.

7

"No, honey," she tells him, and she can't help grinning. Karl is frowning. He is irritated by Michael's itchiness and his lack of attention. "They only sell champagne and orange juice at intermission."

"I don't like champagne. I'm hungry."

Christina shrugs. "Less than an hour ago, your father spent twelve dollars on a roast beef dinner for you. Why didn't you eat it?"

"I wasn't hungry then."

A very simple answer. Why can't Christina be so direct? Is it true that she enjoys abrading Karl's ego? Not being wholly honest with him makes him flinty. But she really doesn't irk him. The few sparks that she grinds off him usually fall harmlessly to the ground. No one can set the great Karl Klausner on fire that way.

Anyway, in the past few years, if Karl had really ever made any attempt to communicate with her, he would have discovered that it isn't classical ballet she's objecting to this evening. She might have tried to explain to him her fucked-up emotional responses to this ballet. She might have been able to tell him that it really wasn't because, eight years ago, she had written a novel about a modern Sleeping Beauty which sold five million copies in paperback. Long before that the Sleeping Beauty fairy-tale—presumably a nearly universal myth in the human unconsciousness of a young girl sleeping for a hundred years to escape her own sexuality—intrigued and frightened her.

But Karl has no patience with such nonsense. Intuitive or transpersonal thinking is for people who live in societies where they still shit in outhouses. The practical man flushes his excreta directly into the river or the ocean and worries about pollution later, when it becomes a problem. Baffled by Christina's impracticality—"Christina, when will you decide to grow up?"—Karl insists that after they return to Marblehead this spring, she see Dr. Jeremiah Greenberg again.

In a few minutes now, Aurora will dance with her spindle. Christina wonders if Tchaikovsky understood the symbolism of the spindle. Probably not. If he had, Tchaikovsky would have called her Princess Briar Rose. Christina identifies with that name better than Aurora. It was that story, with Arthur Rackham's ominous drawings, that Grace read her when she was a child. When Aurora swoons on the stage, the first act will end. Then Karl will ask her if she wants to join him in the lobby for a glass of champagne. A cultural hangover

8

from another century, when drinking champagne between acts was a genteel tradition done in the company of one's peers. Amusing that Karl, of all people, will join the crunch of several thousand of the proletariat to drink insipid New York State champagne. Their wine cellar in Marblehead has at least fifty cases of Dom Perignon, or Mumms, or Peiper Heidsick.

Of course, the reason is that one corner of Karl's "reality"—his male friends—is in this first-night audience. Never let it be said that bankers and industrialists don't appreciate the arts. They are here, aren't they, sporting their glossy, bejeweled wives? Visual proof of their monetary and hence amatory power.

Alas, Christina has no female friends. Wives of Boston and New York business executives (for that matter, European, too) are wary of her. It doesn't matter. They bore her. Most of them stopped using their brains so long ago, they have atrophied from disuse. All that is left are female robots with dry cunts. Take away their possessions, their children (who can't tolerate them because they too soon will become full-circle reflections of their parents), take away their baubles, bangles, and beads, and there's nothing left.

As for men friends, what irritates Christina is that it never occurs to most of them to mix a little friendship with fucking. Maybe that only happens between young men and women. She remembers Newton Morrow (*Oh, God, Mory, where are you?*) that homely kid she screwed with when she was at Radcliffe working for her doctorate. He tried to be a friend and lover. God, was that only ten years ago?

Except for Hank Hutchings, whom she probably should never have got involved with, Karl's friends tend to be horny male creeps. Long married, many of them have a hard time getting an erection, and when they do, they can't wait to shoot the cannon. They're afraid that their powder may dribble out of the rust holes. Some of them probably would enjoy being whipped. Penance for the whippings they are giving their customers and clients? Does Karl know how many of them have their own videotape of her famous porno movie classic, *The Christening of Christina?* They're not sure whether Christina is a sleeping rose or a slimy garbage pail. Like filthy flies they wouldn't give a damn, anyway, if she really is the latter.

Of course, their plastic, sexless wives have the proper educational credentials—a comfortable bachelor's degree from a

9

substantial woman's college. Before they graduated, some Harvard or Yale man managed to teach them not to faint when they held their first cock up to their lips. After one or two tries, they quickly discovered that it really wasn't necessary to take the throbbing salami fully into their mouths. With a darting tongue, agile fingers, and, at the finale, clenched teeth, they can guide the helpless hose so it spurts its juices on the victim's belly. It's an oral genital routine that works and requires little or no involvement. Christina knows. She's done it. She knows all about many of their friends' sex lives, too. With a few drinks under their belts, many of Karl's frustrated male friends have marveled at Christina's on-screen ability. Karl is a lucky man. They wish that they were married to a cocksucker who could take the whole damned thing in her mouth. God, she even swallows jism as if she loves it—without gagging!

Christina knows their motivations. Shoving their pricks in some complaisant female's mouth, after a hard day battling business dragons, restores their emasculated egos. A few of them actually daydream that Christina is eagerly waiting for them on the parapets of the castle, waving a handkerchief at her clanking knight, and finally, too impatient to wait for her chevalier to undress, will mouth-diddle him through some hole in his rusty armor. It's useless to tell them that not even Karl can command that ultimate male ecstasy. Penis nursing. Nor could Johnny Giacomo, the actor, she had deep-throated in that crappy movie version of her novel.

She finally tells Warren Ellison, one of Karl's business associates, the truth. The big globs of cum dripping out of her mouth and over her face and breasts that he has seen in that movie weren't hot from Johnny Giacomo's geyser. It wasn't cum at all, but a more palatable mixture of sugar, flour, and water—or, when it seemed to be dripping from his prick, and she didn't have to have mouth contact, sprayed-on hand lotion photographed even better. Johnny might have the longest prick ever to appear on the silver screen, and it might have the girth of a donkey's gellung, but when it came to the long pull, it ran out of fluid as quickly as any man's. After they ejaculate, Warren and Karl might only have shrunken peckers while Johnny is still sporting an unruly, soggy hot dog, but Johnny's Schnauser doesn't obey him either.

Christina is really smiling to herself. She doesn't hate men. She feels sorry for them. Most of them don't really want to fuck, or simply hold a woman in their arms as a co-equal hu-

10

man being. All that most of them are seeking, even at the height of their passion, is a warm vagina to disappear back into, or, at the very least, comforting tits, attached to a woman who might not always say it verbally, but makes it continuously apparent. "Mr. Wonderful. That's you!"

———◆———

God, I can't stop watching Christina. She's really a chameleon. Christina One, Christina Two, Christina Three. She takes on the coloration of her environment, but inside she remains herself. Now she is (I am?) watching Princess Aurora dancing with her spindle. Is the spindle, in reality, the male penis? Is the hemp which will prick her finger, in reality, her fear of the ultimate male penetration? Is the wicked Fairy Carabosse's revenge the "curse" of menstruation, handed from woman to woman over the millenniums? Never mind, the Lilac Fairy will redeem Aurora. The Lilac Fairy is changing the Wicked Fairy's curse into a hundred-year blackout.

Momentarily, Christina Klausner is Christina North. Nineteen, not fifteen like Aurora. Next year she will graduate from Radcliffe. She's two years younger than most of her classmates. She's Christina the scholar, Christina the virgin, and finally Christina the bewildered, swallowing a dozen of her mother's sleeping pills. At twenty-four, saved by her mother from her attempted excursion into tomorrow, she is Christina North, Ph.D. (a clinical psychologist). At twenty-seven, shortly after her fuck film is released, she's lying on the kitchen floor beside Johnny Giacomo's gas oven with all the windows closed and the jets hissing their soothing promise of endless sleep.

"You really don't want to die, Christina." Jerry Greenberg is stretched out on an Oriental rug on the floor of his office. His head is propped on a pillow, and he's watching Christina—who is sitting in a lotus posture—through his half-closed eyes. At seventy-five dollars an hour, Jerry's stock in trade is his informality. If Christina wishes, and he thinks it will help her, Jerry has told her that he, too, will be delighted to screw with her. "You really want to be saved, Christina," Jerry is telling her. "Suicide is often a desperate call for help. You were hooked on the adolescent instinct to drop out of the confusion of the world. You needed time to grow up while you were waiting for the handsome prince who someday would save you."

11

Christina is giggling. What crap. She was no adolescent when she was fucking with Johnny and making a porno movie. Too bad she doesn't have an M.D. instead of a Ph.D. Then she could hang out her shingle and give Jerry some competition. She could overwhelm her patients with Freudian symbolism or Jungian myths, just as easily as Jerry Greenberg. But instead she encourages him. Why not? It will be amusing to see whether he will agree.

"Maybe it wasn't a Prince at all that I was waiting for," she tells him. "I loved my father's dork. When I was four, I always tried to catch him in the bathroom and watch him pissing. Grace, my mother, was greedy. She wouldn't let me have it."

Jerry shakes his head solemnly. She has given him the psychiatric clue. "Ah—now we may be moving in the right direction. Next time we'll re-explore your relationship with your father."

On stage Aurora is swooning. The Wicked Fairy reveals that it is *she* who has given Aurora the spindle. Only she's not a she. She's a man! David! Dr. David Convita! They're in the room with the barred window, and he's holding Christina (Aurora?) naked in his arms. She's trying to pull away. But she knows that he won't quit. "You should have gone back to the sources, Christa," David is telling her. "Charles Perrault stole his version of the fairy tale from Giovanni Basile's *Il Pentarmerone*. She isn't Aurora, or Briar Rose, or Snow White—she's Talia. The prince didn't kiss her awake. He was a cunt-happy king who found her sleeping in the palace where her father had left her."

Christina knows all the Sleeping Beauty stories, but she lets David rave on. "Overwhelmed by her beauty," he says, "he undressed her, screwed her, and she didn't wake up. Nine months later she had twins, the Sun and the Moon, and one of them, searching for her nipple, found her finger, and, presto, he sucked out the hemp. Poor Talia. There she was, alone in the forest with two kids to bring up—wondering who the mysterious stranger was who had fucked her and run away."

Although Christina knows she has seduced David, she's not really happy about it. She's done it for a reason. He's the Wicked Witch and she wants to escape his curse. Her only hope is that he will fall in love with her. Despite Oscar Wilde, no one can kill the thing he loves. So she doesn't stop his finger, which is lightly exploring her clitoris and is telling

12

him that her vagina is glistening and ready. While he is talking, he slides deep inside her. What can she do? She can't scream or fight him. She must sigh and pant and seem to be deliciously overwhelmed. Like Talia, who probably wasn't asleep, but knew she'd be raped if she protested, she lets him screw her, but she can't force herself to help him much. Then, suddenly, she's unable to hold back. She climaxes with the bastard. Angrily, she rips her fingernails into his ass and across his back.

"I hate you both," she sobs. She knows her seduction plan has failed. "You and Max are kidnappers. Show Max your bleeding ass. I dare you! He'll kill you. He wants me for himself. All either of you want is your own private sexual slave. This anabiosis stuff is crap. I want to get the hell out of here. Right now. If you don't let me go, I'll escape. Your other zombie, Rose Plackett, will help me. She knows that I'm a prisoner here. When I tell Karl what you and Max have done to me—and whoever else you've kidnapped and are hiding in this building, you'll both be guillotined. Yes, guillotined—not the electric chair. Then, like Salome, first I'll dance with your fucking heads, and then I'll kick them around like soccer balls."

But she can't stay angry with David. He has hypnotized her. She is reminded of *Briar Rose,* a poem by one of her favorite poets, Anne Sexton.

She recites the lines to David, and he is smiling. "Of course, Max and I both love you. We have to love you, or we wouldn't be willing to devote our lives to you. But you've evidently forgotten. Christina Klausner is dead. She didn't die like Anne Sexton with the garage door closed and the engine of her automobile running, or with her head in a gas oven like Sylvia Plath. Don't you remember? You even provided your rings. Your body will be found washed ashore eventually. They found your Mercedes parked near Pier Four."

The curtain is closing. The audience is cheering the swooning ballerina. Karl has taken Penny and Michael to the champagne bar. Warren Ellison, president of the First Merchants Bank, lean, Caribbean-tanned, his black hair flecked with gray—a younger, fortyish version of Karl, slips into the seat beside her.

"Christa, you're ravishing tonight. It's been a long year. I've missed you."

Christina's expression is sardonic. "Your wife is missing you. I can feel her eyes boring into my back."

13

Why doesn't she tell Warren that twice last summer was enough? God, once should have been!

But Warren is holding her hand. "Can I see you Wednesday afternoon?"

Christa suspects that if Warren can't play with her tits, he'll keep a prior appointment to play squash with some male friend. She's tempted to whisper in Warren's ear that she's sick of fucking with aging knights and decaying kings; in the future she's going to bed with a dragon. But alas, that's just the kind of thinking that makes Warren excited by her. Her unpredictability. No one can guess what Christa may say next. She's delightful. She chops up the weeds growing in his stodgy brain.

Then she has a better idea. "Karl is planning to invite you and Betty on a Memorial Day cruise. I'm supposed to call Betty. The Stones are coming, and so are Link and Rita Sevigny. You and Betty will make eight of us. It will be very boring. We'll all get drunk and try to go to bed with each other's spouse. The men are going to work, of course. You'll have to help Karl make the yacht tax-deductible. Karl will bring his twenty-four-old secretary, Lizabeth Geist, along. If I'm not available, you can try your charms on Lizabeth."

"Why won't you be available?" Warren demands.

"I may decide to kill myself. If I do, maybe you'll help me."

Warren laughs. But Christina means it. Being dead is a way to keep her promise to herself. Maybe, if she could really sleep a hundred years, a new kind of prince, brimming over with love and laughter, would kiss her awake.

———————

I'm reading what Christina has written so far. Am I really watching myself, and not Christina? Is Christina really me? If she is, then right now I'm still sitting here in this room with the barred window, looking at the portable typewriter on the card table in front of me. The typewriter is labeled SCM—Smith Corona-Galaxie Deluxe. Jesus, that's America for you. We don't just have galaxies. We have them top drawer and deluxe.

Christina. Get serious. Think about how to get out of this anteroom of hell. Even though they've stripped you, and they've taken your clothes, you can still try to get out of here.

14

Stop kidding yourself. You're not Christ! You haven't had a last supper yet. When you do, no matter what crap they tell you, you're not likely to get resurrected. All you are to David and Max is a human guinea pig. If you think the U.S. Government wouldn't let them experiment with you, you're kidding yourself. Didn't they inject plutonium into terminal patients at Los Alamos to discover whether plutonium caused cancer in human tissues? You bet your ass they did. And they never found the answer. Why? Because the patients died of whatever diseases they already had before they could tell what effect the plutonium might have had. Who authorized that fiasco? Probably the same kind of mealymouthed bureaucrats who are behind this experiment. They're futurists tampering with your future, but not theirs!

God, how time passes! Those plutonium experiments were six years ago. You were only twenty-seven. It was 1974, midway in the sick-sex seventies. Nearly half the male population in the United States saw you naked in that silly movie. Where are the roses of yesteryear? Have they forgotten the Linda Lovelaces and Marilyn Chambers and Christina Norths? Maybe not. If you can get to the Cape highway, the first truck driver who sees your ass will grind his rig to a halt. All you have to do is tell him, "You guessed it, buddy. I'm one of the famous sword swallowers. The one and only Christina North." He'll be so ecstatic that he'll drive you all the way to Marblehead. Years from now he'll be telling his grandchildren, "Yes, by golly—Christina North offered to do 'it' to me, too." With tears in his eyes, he'll tell them that he still remembers your gullet tightening on his erect weapon, while your uvula was tickling his glans!

Don't try to argue with David Convita or Max Lebenthal. Let them fuck you. Don't swallow any of those antimetabolic pills Rose Plackett gives you. In a few days you'll snap out of this lethargy. They can't turn you into a damned lungfish or a hibernating Winnie the Pooh. One day they may forget to lock the door. If they'd only give you a metal fork or knife instead of this plastic stuff, maybe you could pry it open. Then you could just walk out of here. Force yourself. Don't be so goddamned apathetic. If you don't care whether you live or not—at least, the choice of how and when you die should be yours. They haven't just brainwashed you. They're trying to make you the willing accomplice of your own murder!

You weren't so complaisant a week ago. My God, was it

15

only a week ago? Maybe you've been here two weeks, or a month.

An hour or so ago Max Lebenthal, followed by Rose Plackett, unlocked the door, and greeted me with a cheery good-morning. After hooking me up to an EEG machine—maybe my slowed-down brain waves will tell them why I was just lying there instead of screaming bloody murder—Rose left. Pretending that I was still half-asleep, through slit eyes I watched the expression on Max's face as he examined me. He listened to my heart, and then, noticing that my mound was completely exposed below my hiked-up hospital johnny, and that my legs were slightly spread, his fingers traced my labia, trickled across my pubic hairs and navel, and outlined the under curve of my breasts.

Behind his glasses, his eyes seemed wet. "You are a very beautiful woman, Christina." He sighed. "It's strange that you don't care whether you live or die."

"I want to live long enough to get the hell out of here," I exploded. "You and David aren't fooling me. David lured me here with his weird science-fiction crap, but I knew from the beginning that all he really wanted to do was fuck me."

I decided I'd lay it on the line with Max. "In case you don't know it, he's done it already. What are you waiting for? You're next in line." I tried to hug Max, but he pulled out of my grasp. "Please," I sobbed, "if you'll let me go, you won't have to force me, I'll really make love with you."

But Max only shrugged. "You never should have listened to David. Now we've gone too far with you to turn back. I can assure you, however, unlike my confrere, I'm morally unable to have my cake and eat it."

So I know two things. While Max can't avoid thinking of me as a woman, he doesn't approve of David mixing pleasure with business. On the other hand, it's obvious that they can't forcibly detain someone for God knows how long, and then tell the police that it was all a mistake; they are sorry; haven't they finally let her go free? No—that's not going to happen.

Do I really give a damn? The pills and injections they are giving me have chained me to my own inertia. After two current attempts to kill myself, I guess I have proved that I don't want to live. Or Christina doesn't. God, am I crazy? Is there a suicidal Christina and a more sanguine me? In that case, David's proposal to Christina makes some sense. "Since you obviously don't care about your life, Christina, give it to us. We'll care for it as if it were our own."

A proposition like that, after Christina's second suicide attempt in just over a week, has a Mephistophelean simplicity to it. But now that Christina has been seduced and is getting to know David somewhat better than she had anticipated, I think she is becoming a little dubious. Ever since she acted in that porno movie, millions of men have had a magnetic attraction, or phallic affinity, to Christina's lips and mouth. Men are magnetized by her suppliant breasts and the close-ups of her moist, inviting lower lips. They really believe that movie. Christina is really a sixteen-year-old virgin, wearing a flowered dress and big floppy hat, who sings in the choir. Every Sunday she fantasizes her seduction by the Jesus-will-save-you minister.

What the hell difference does it make if David Convita wishes to possess the mythical attributes of Christina's mouth and cunt, and at the same time perpetuate the whole of her for an eternity?

David talks as if he's serious about the experiment. "You have assimilated the antabolones with no contra effects," he tells me. "Now we are giving your body a chance to adapt increasingly to Vitalebens, the more powerful antimetabolite which we have perfected. Your hibernaculum, which I promise we will show you very soon, is completely computer-controlled."

While I gaze at him skeptically, he goes on, "Although there's a growing literature on cryobiology, much of it is very technical, and while science-fiction writers like Robert Heinlein and Frederik Pohl in their books, *The Door into Summer* and *The Age of the Pussyfoot*, have used low temperature to create a kind of suspended animation with reduced, or no metabolism, as pathways into the future, the Russian writer N. Amosoff, who is an M.D., in his book, *Notes from the Future*, has given a very much more thorough analysis of the problems of freezing and thawing human beings or any organism. But all of these writers were speculating. While Max and I have actually experimented with some cryobiological approaches, we're now moving in an entirely new and exciting direction of biochemistry. We're convinced that the only practical approach to a long sleep is with low human temperatures becoming a natural by-product of chemical anabiosis, and not induced by direct freezing.

"So we're moving very slowly with you. Before we move

17

into your final countdown, I hope you'll read some of the books we've been giving you, and that you'll continue writing your autobiography."

———◆———

I guess the best place to begin again with my life is at the ending. The extended Memorial Day weekend begins early Friday morning at the Corinthian Yacht Club, where we meet Warren and Betty Ellison, Henry and Priscilla Stone, Link and Rita Sevigny, and one of Karl's secretaries, Lizabeth Geist. Liz is the only woman aboard (excluding myself) who can wear and is wearing a string bikini. The others will try. Lizabeth looks delectable. The others have been in the refrigerator too long. Their moisture has dissipated.

A week before the cruise, I still hadn't telephoned Rita, Betty, or Priscilla. Karl had invited their husbands, and told them his plans were open-ended. We might sail (there were no sails, of course) as far south as Ocracoke, North Carolina, with stopovers along the way, beginning with Friday night in Nantucket. The boat (Karl never fails to point out that it is a ship) was fully equipped with ship-to-shore telephones. If some of the men were needed, they could fly back to Boston and be in their offices in a few hours. Karl was exasperated with me. Why had I procrastinated for two weeks? Why hadn't I immediately confirmed to the "girls" that I was delighted that their spouses had accepted Karl's invitation? Why couldn't I plan with them—tell them what clothes they should bring, tell them what fun we would have sunning and shopping? Why couldn't I just occasionally act like a normal American woman and enjoy the luxuries her husband had provided for her?

I told Karl that after six years he should stop trying to play Henry Higgins with me. I wasn't Eliza Doolittle. He'd never make me a queen of the North Shore or any place else. I was bad-mannered, and he knew, even when he first met me, that I was anti-social. His friends and their wives aggravated my disease rather than making it better. I didn't tell Karl, but I knew that unless I was half-mulled on booze I could never survive four or five days confined with half-naked, self-satisfied bitches, tanning their expensive skins on one of the sun decks. Even worse would be playing foursomes of bridge with them, or shopping inanely for junk in seaport towns. It would have to be either liquor or grass. If I

18

smoked a joint on the windy deck no one would know. I knew that Karl and his friends had tried marijuana long ago, but they had rejected it. All of them, their wives included, were too verbally aggressive. They could never let go and float away on a euphoric pot trip.

Karl never seems to mind that all of his friends (and mine) aren't really friends. None of our friends really have friends either. We are all surface companions who rarely disclose, even to our spouses, the kind of people we really are. I knew that all of the women played golf together at least once a week. But golf is just another American way of being gregarious with no intimacy. I detest golf. I like to scuba dive or sail a boat. I have had more fun with Karl and the kids sailing around the harbor in our O'Day-sailer than I ever had on his goddamned yachts.

Priscilla's hobby is collecting expensive New England antiques. Rita runs a French boutique in Beverly. Last year Betty was elected chairman of the New England Federation of Women's Clubs. While I would be first in line to snuggle in bed with John Adams or Benjamin Franklin or Thomas Jefferson, if they were to show up, I'm not interested in owning the sinks they washed their faces in or the pots they pissed in. And I don't give a damn about the latest styles from Paris, Italy, Miami, or New York. I like to be naked. When I have to have my body covered, blue jeans and one of Karl's old shirts are as good as anything. As for women's clubs, the creeps who join them are usually fucking around with one extreme or another. They're either raising their own consciousness so they can give their men a hard time, or they're screwing up women's liberation by trying to be "total" or "fascinating" women. An impossible project since most of them really don't like to fuck, and neither do their husbands. Alas, neither do I anymore. The only thing that is holding me together is my childhood daydream.

Maybe, giggly thought, Karl is really the prince who is temporarily croaking like a frog. But I guess not—I've hurled him against the wall enough and he doesn't turn into a prince.

Certainly Warren Ellison, sitting beside me in the stern of the yacht-club launch, knowing that he can't be seen, his fingers snaking along my spine and into the crack of my buttocks, isn't my frog prince, either. I grimace at him, but he only smiles back. Warren is confident. Somehow during the next days he'll create the right environment. He'll isolate me

19

from the group for an hour or two and he'll sink his rod into Christina's shaft. Warren's rod and my shaft will comfort thee. Bullshit!

Chattering gaily, happy to see each other again after a long winter, we are being ferried out to Karl's new Hatteras-built yacht in the club dinghy. It's *our* yacht, Christina! Yes, Karl, I hear your silent reminder. But please stop signaling my weary brain. Karl is telling everybody that Captain Fletcher, "Five Star" (he acts like a former naval admiral) and Timmy Quinlan and his wife Suzie (direct from the Old Country), who function as first mate, deckhands, and chief cooks and bottle washers, are ready aboard and waiting for us. It's a seven-hour trip to Nantucket. We should be there by four o'clock this afternoon.

I'm smiling and talking with everybody, but the real? Christina is in a hateful, sullen mood. I know that Karl is finally reaching the breaking point with me. My obsession with my current painting, and my conviction that if I can complete it, it will be the masterpiece of my, as yet, nonexistent career as an artist, is depressing. Not only to me, but I suppose to Karl. But Karl doesn't understand. Somehow I must make this painting hobby "work." For the first time in six years, I have been overwhelmed, once again, with my hateful, gnawing obsession. I must accomplish something worthwhile in the world. I must not live in the shadow of Karl's or any man's success. I have the education and the talent. Despite what Jerry Greenberg may think, it really doesn't bother me that thus far my only claim to worldly fame is a sexy novel and my ability to swallow a phallus, or write about doing it. None of Karl's friends or my mother seems to understand that *The Christening of Christina* is not a dirty book, and the movie is a great deal more than a fuck film. Even most of the goddamned critics never realized that I was glorifying sex, not degrading it.

Before David Convita trapped me, I was still pushing hell out of myself. I was embarking on a new career. (Not really, I suppose, since when I was majoring in English and psych at Radcliffe, I had crash-studied art.) For good or bad, in the past two years I have completed thirty canvases. Bill Glazer, who owns a gallery on Newbury Street, can't wait to have a one-man Christina Klausner showing. Why don't I insist that I'm Christina North? My paintings are signed that way. And they're good. Maybe even great. I'm sure of it! But, of course, the Klausner name is the magic drawing card. For all

I know, Karl may be subsidizing Bill Glazer. Good therapy for his fucked-up wife. Bill told Karl that the dreamy, erotic qualities of my canvases are unique. I am a modern Maxfield Parrish, painting a semi-abstract, fairy-tale dream world. My paintings have a *Lost Horizon* quality which can only be a mirror of the real Christina. Glazer's full of crap. He doesn't know that I'm not really Christina. I'm impersonating her.

Unfortunately, Karl isn't very happy with the real Christina, who I have to admit is boringly moody, and more often than not, is sobbing, or is hysterical, at her own inability to be as "good" as she knows she is. The truth is that I'm really very self-confident. But like everyone else, I need a pat on the shoulder. Not the whole world, but a few people, maybe only one, who honestly could tell me, "Christina, you're great." Alas, it's obvious from Karl's constant annoyed shrugs and his bitter complaints that for him I'm great but for all the wrong reasons.

"Christa, you must snap out of it," he keeps telling me. "I don't know what the hell is bugging you, but your mother agrees with me. You've got to get a grip on yourself. You're chasing a mirage, a chimera. Your search 'for the real you' is the same crock of shit which most of your generation bought hook, line, and sinker in the 1960s. Stop trying to look up your own asshole. You won't find yourself in your intestines. Why don't you just relax? Try self-hypnosis. Everyday, tell yourself how damned fortunate you are! You can enjoy all the good things. Get it out of your head that I married you because I thought you were a sexpot, or because, like your mother, I wanted you to become a famous poet, or a novelist, or an artist, or a pianist. You're pretty competent at all those things. But you've got to face reality. If you had really wanted to succeed, you'd have concentrated on one thing, and nothing would have stopped you."

Karl is obviously contrasting his dedication with my dilettantism. "Anyway, you were successful once—with that silly book and movie. Did the money you earned make you happy? Hell no, you gave most of it to that Giacomo character. I married you because I loved you. Despite your crazy suicide attempt—threatening to jump off the sixth floor of that fleabag hotel (for which you probably had some justification, if only to escape the urine stink)—and all the notoriety that it got you, basically you seemed to me like a bewildered child. Even now, when you relax, you have a wonderful sense of humor, and you have a keen mind, and a nice body. Why

21

don't you simply enjoy your painting or writing poetry? Stop trying to use your talents as a weapon for self-fulfillment. You've been creative in a more important way. You're the first woman I have ever known whom I wanted to have children with. What's more, you've been a good mother. In the past few years, until the painting bug seized you, you've been reasonably happy. Stop flaying yourself with your wasted education. What's an education for except to make money, or to have enough smarts to enjoy it? You and I can't begin to spend the money I've accumulated. You're better off by far than if you had driven yourself crazy trying to make money or get recognition as a famous poet, novelist, or psychologist."

I suppose I should be grateful that Karl isn't making a point of the fact that I'm not much good in bed, either.

Years ago, during those first few ecstatic weeks, living with him in his apartment in New York, we inevitably exhausted the details of our lives, and who we thought we were, and who the real "us" was, and finally, two months later, when we got married, we were no longer talking our heads off before, after, and during lovemaking. At least, Karl wasn't. Finally, pregnant, without realizing how it happened, I joined the female get-sex-over-in-a-hurry club. But Karl still lives with the illusion that the sight of his rampant prick turns me into a moaning, groaning pornographer's dream girl. He doesn't know that, according to Jerry Greenberg, I'm an impersonator. What the hell, if I can impersonate a great poet, why not a great whore?

Of course, I'm not stupid. Karl's invitation to Lizabeth Geist to join us on this cruise should have been a red-flag warning to me. Despite his excuse that Warren, Henry, Link, and he had a mountain of detail to corral—it would take them at least eight hours to structure their sixty-five-million-dollar financing plan for a new Boston waterfront hotel, and they needed a secretary as they went along, to get the wording in shape, I recognized Liz's style. She's an upward mobile middle-class kid who would gladly hump her ass off, and be a bright, sparkling companion for life, if she could only land a Karl Klausner, or one of his companions. Karl hadn't married his previous wives for better or worse, or in sickness and health. So, why, after six years and two kids, should he begin with Christina?

While I am thinking these thoughts and apologizing to Betty, Priscilla, and Rita for not being in closer contact with them since our return to Marblehead nearly five weeks ago, the club launch arrives at the landing stairs of the yacht. Betty remarks on the clever name emblazoned in brass letters on the stern: *FUND-A-MENTAL, ONE*. The name, of course, is the same as the new mutual fund which Karl had recently inaugurated. Investors in FUND-A-MENTAL, ONE are futurists who will become millionaires, if Karl picks the right portfolio of exciting new energy-oriented companies which are being amply funded by the government in the pursuit of alternate energy sources—from nuclear fusion to photovoltaic cells and solar energy.

Knowing that it will aggravate Karl, and because I am irritated by the presence of Lizabeth, whom the other females are probing, with cool voices and raised eyebrows, as we climb the landing stairway, I tell them all in a loud voice that I tried to convince Karl that he should drop the adverbial ending, and call the boat (ship?) *FUNDAMENT*.

"It's easier to say." Maybe I'm not laughing, maybe I'm sneering, but no one gets the message. I have to explain. " 'Fundament' is from the Latin *fundus*, the bottom, hence, the part of the body that one sits on. In Black Masses in medieval times, instead of kissing the Cross, a part of the ritual was to kiss the Devil's fundament—ergo, his asshole."

Warren is laughing, but the rest of them, including Karl, are smiling painfully. Of course, I should have realized that Betty, Pris, and Rita are the kind of women who don't have assholes. God knows what they call their rosebud when they wipe it or wash it—maybe anus, if they are reluctantly forced to verbalize. Alas, certainly not fundament.

Five Star plans to drop anchor in Nantucket Harbor at four P.M. The men and Lizabeth quickly set up an informal conference room in the main lounge. After I show the women their staterooms—the ship has three, all with showers and a master bedroom—they finally arrive on the top deck, wearing bikinis, with slightly overhanging tummies, and carrying their latest Literary Guild and Book of the Month Club novels, cigarettes, and suntan oil. I watch them lay their expensive flesh carefully in the sun chairs. Prissy wonders if she dares to remove her bikini bra. Five Star and Timmy can see us from the wheelhouse, but I encourage her. I know she is hoping that the men will eventually arrive, and they'll be

23

charmed by her embarrassment, but they'll see her well-preserved breasts. Rita takes off her top. Betty, who is blonde, finds a shady spot. Not to be outdone by Prissy, she removes her top, but she makes sure she's in the shade. She explains that Warren is turned off by women who have white breasts and crotches and behinds while the rest of them is tanned black. They reminded him of white-lipped minstrel niggers. I casually strip, explaining that I agree with Betty. "I'm not the type who can lie for hours frying herself in the sun," I tell them. "My cunt enjoys the fresh air more than the rest of me." They all laugh politely. Rita wishes that she dared to use gutter language easily, as I do.

"You think 'cunt,' don't you?" I ask. "What do you call your snatch?"

Rita shrugs. "I don't think about it."

"What does Link call it?"

Rita looks uncomfortable. Finally she says, "We're all at least ten years older than you are, Christina. I, for one, don't think about sex as much as I did when I was younger."

"I do," Prissy says. "I think of it all the time. Henry calls my vulva his sleepy little pussy. It only purrs when it's full."

"My God!" Betty laughs. "Warren is a once-a-week man. If I want any more than that, I have to read about it." She produces a book, *Emmanuelle II*. "You should write a book like Emmanuelle Arsan, Christina," she says. "Emmanuelle has tried everything."

I shrug. I knew they'd love it if I'd entertain them with my sexual exploits, but I'm not in the mood. "You could use a vibrator," I tell her. "Emmanuelle's problem, and the woman in that other book, who called herself 'O,' is that they thought their clitoris was in their asshole. Unlike Christina, they never discovered that it's really in their throat."

I'm facing them in a sun chair. They are all staring at my crotch—it's hypnotizing them. It's a hissing, open-mouthed snake, spitting at them. They're Eves who have lost their apples (marbles?) in the Garden of Eden. I can't help it, I decide that I should really blow their minds. "I'll tell you a secret," I say. "Karl has it arranged with the guys. The next three or four nights we're going to play musical beds. Each night one of us is going to end up in a triad and compete in a love duet with Lizabeth." Betty is staring at me, astonished. "After the first night it will be an oral Olympics. The winner, the one who finally gets the dork of the night in her vagina, will be the one with the most indefatigable mouth."

24

They believe me. I finally have to admit that I am only kidding, and the conversation turns to other things. I listen while they languidly discuss their travels in Europe last winter. Most European countries are no fun anymore. Inflation and communism are ruining the world—or their children. Betty has three. All married. One pregnant. Rita has two. Prissy has two. None of their children are under twenty. Penny and Michael are five and four. If any of these women was ten years older, she could have been my mother.

Smiling, Prissy points out that when Penny and Michael are a few years older, Christina will calm down. "I mean," she says, "you'll have to be careful how you act, and what you say in front of them. You'll probably decide that you'd better not run around naked anymore. You certainly can't when Michael is fifteen or sixteen."

"You mean he might have an Oedipus complex?" I shrug. "Maybe mothers should teach their sons the act of love. One sure way to brainwash men is to really liberate mothers and let them indoctrinate their male progeny. Anyway, it's too late. I'll never live down my past. Eventually, Michael and Penny will learn that their mother was a cocksucker." I laugh. "On the other hand, if the world is still around by 1990, maybe they'll be teaching kids the joys of oral sex on television."

Damn. I know that I'm drinking too much. Suzie, who keeps flitting up the gangway with sandwiches and fresh fruit Jello, had served me three vodkas and tonic to their one drink, which they are all nursing. Keeping my mouth shut, I once again silently wonder how I got to be me. I really don't need Jerry Greenberg to tell me that I'm a "self-hater."

Jerry's theory is that my mother, reacting to the fact that my father divorced her when I was ten years old, turned me into an overachiever. Through my successes, as well as her own, Grace found a way to vindicate herself. She proved that she was better than most men. Particularly my father, Arthur, who had no real ambition, and was willing to drift through life as a second-rate engineer working for peanuts.

So I had to prove that I loved Mummy best. The only way to do that was to be the most popular girl in school (among the teachers, of course. They were the only ones who counted) and to bring home report cards with all A's—and not to forget to practice "your" piano. "Two hours a day, Christina."

In the matriarchal one-child North household which Grace

created after Arthur had gone—obviously my father never loved me very much; I have no idea whether he's dead or alive—the byword was "don't waste time." The house was littered with inspirational books like *Life Begins at Fifty, How to Live on Twenty-Four Hours a Day,* and, of course, *Elliot's Five Foot Bookshelf of the Harvard Classics.* "The fifteen minutes a day you waste can make you an educated person, Christina."

Evenings, when I had finished my homework, and Grace had returned from her job, she listened to me practice the piano, and daydreamed of the day when Christina's name would appear on the marquee at Symphony Hall. When it became apparent that I enjoyed writing poetry, then she was certain that I could combine the piano with poetry and write complete musicals. I was Lerner and Loewe all in one package. Unfortunately, my poetry couldn't even be sung by a Jacques Brel or a Neil Diamond. It really was too morbid. Anyway, as Grace pointed out, poetry wasn't profitable. The only way poets could become famous was to commit suicide. I knew that without her telling me. I had read everything Anne Sexton, Sylvia Plath, and John Berryman had ever written. I knew Anne Sexton's *Suicide Note* by heart.

If I insisted on writing, then why not fiction—stories? I had a wonderful imagination. I could become a famous novelist. But whatever I did, I must do it better than anyone else. All by herself, Christina North could prove that women were not inferior to men. Grace and I together could prove that men needed us, we didn't need them!

◆

An hour before we arrive in Nantucket, I grind my vagrant thoughts to a halt and announce to the girls that we should root the men out of the salon. The most effective way to do it will be to charge in on them bare-ass naked. For a moment I think Prissy may join me, but she loses her nerve when Betty says, "Not me, my rear end is too fat. I'm not going to jiggle my tits and behind in competition with Lizabeth and Christina."

"That's silly," I tell her. "I'm too bony. When I was twenty-six, I had a hell of a time getting a job as a go-go dancer in New York City. But they'd hire you, right now, in a minute." I meant it. Hundred-and-forty-pounders like Betty actually look better naked than dressed. The extra flesh flows together and isn't compressed in nasty-looking bulges created by clothing.

I can't convince them, but by this time I am drunk enough to do it myself. Naked, I wander into the lounge where the tycoons are impressing Lizabeth with their financial acumen. Big wheels in their smoke-filled room, they are arguing some obscure legal point about the security agreements in their proposed financing. When they see me all their faces, except Karl's and Liz's, light up. "Hallelujah!" Link yells. "Lady Godiva has arrived."

"I got a haircut." I laugh. "So you can see all of the demure maiden beneath her locks. Unfortunately, my sea horse is sinking rapidly off the starboard bow."

Warren joins the insanity. "Stop the ship while we rescue Lady Christina's steed. Where's the rest of the broads?"

"On the top deck, drowning their sorrows because their men put work before pleasures of the flesh."

Karl is annoyed. "Please get the hell out of here," he says angrily. "And put some clothes on before Timmy or Fletch see you."

"They've been spying on us all afternoon," I tell him. "They've been so busy watching the mammaries of upper-class matrons, and hoping your wives would show them their cunts"—Karl is frowning—"pussies, I mean, that they nearly ran the ship aground when we were going through the Cape Cod Canal. Come on, all of you, shuck off your clothes. Enjoy what remains of this balmy afternoon." I flop in one of the white leather armchairs in the lounge and grin tipsily at them.

All of the men except Karl, whose face is flushed with repressed anger, are staring at me as if I am the whore of Babylon. Maybe I am a little crocked. Actually, I'm a female Pagliacci. Crying on the inside, I'm still trying to be the bon vivant wife, and inject some laughter into this moribund cruise.

Karl decides to try cajoling me. "Look, Christa, be a good girl," he says. "We've still got some work to do. When Fletch anchors at Nantucket, Timmy will take you and the girls into the pier. You'll have an hour or so to wander around the town. We have reservations at Skipper's Dock for nine o'clock and supposedly they have a good orchestra. Before we all go ashore we'll have a few drinks. In the meantime, you'd better coast."

I'm dimly aware that I've already exceeded my cocktail

hour quota three hours ahead of time. "Pris and Betty want to go ashore. Rita has gone to her stateroom to relax awhile. Since I can't distract you from your monetary pursuits, I guess I'll have to go to bed and play with myself."

Warren's quizzical expression and raised eyebrows are trying to ask me when *we're* going to play together. Peeved at Karl, I toss Warren a crumb, and at the same time try to shake Lizabeth's aplomb. "Don't wear yourselves out," I tell them. I hold my mouth open, impersonating a sensuous, open-mouthed Playboy Bunny. "At midnight, you can join Lizabeth and me. We're going skinny dipping by moonlight."

Lizabeth smiles at the cheers from Warren and Link, but she's obviously embarrassed. Lizabeth isn't the outdoor-girl type. Men only get to see her bare-ass one at a time, on satin sheets.

Finally losing his patience, Karl stalks across the lounge and yanks me out of the chair. Staring at me balefully he twists my arm behind my back, and with his left hand dug firmly into my ass, he propels me out of the room. "No one is going skinny dipping on the beaches around here," he tells me. "There's a dangerous undertow."

Sobbing, I yell at him, "For Christ's sake, Karl, stop being so practical. We can go skinny walking. None of your friends have to take their clothes off and show their skinny pricks. They can walk barefoot and show their skinny ankles."

Two more drinks and about an hour and a half later, I am lying naked, in a drunken sleep, on our bed in the master suite. Half awake, I realize that Karl is shaking my shoulders and holding me in an erect sitting position. He's demanding to know why in hell I insist on fucking up the whole cruise by drinking myself into oblivion. Aware that the engines were no longer throbbing and the boat is rocking gently on its anchor, I try to stop the room from revolving. I'm dimly aware that Karl is naked, too, and his prick is big and ready for action. Bewildered, with a faint thumping beginning in my forehead, I know I am going to have a miserable hangover.

Karl is kissing my breasts and nibbling my nipples. His finger is bruising my clitoris. "I'm sorry," I sob. "I don't know what in the hell gets into me." I lean against his bare chest seeking his protection. I'm wondering if I am going to pass out. "You can screw me if you don't mind screwing a corpse," I tell him. "I can't help you. I think I'm going to throw up." Remembering a similar high-school response— "Kiss me, nothing makes me sick"—I laugh hysterically.

Disgusted, Karl drops me back on the bed. "For Christ's sake, Christa, it's five-thirty. Shove a finger down your throat and get it over with. Suzie's prepared hors d'oeuvre. We're having cocktails in an hour, and then we're going to dinner. You're going to come, if I have to carry you over my shoulder."

But at eight o'clock, after four Alka Seltzers and several vomiting sessions, I collapse on the floor of the cabin. I am partially dressed in my lime-green pant suit, which is sagging around my knees. I am dimly aware that Karl, fully dressed in a white suit, his thick gray-black hair brushed carefully over his ears, is staring grimly at me.

"I'm ready," I mutter. "Pull up my pants, and help me slip on my jacket. I don't need a bra."

"The hell you're ready." Angrily, Karl lifts me off the floor and dumps me on the bed.

Tears are running down my cheeks. I'm crying not because I'm disappointing him, but because I'm saying good-bye to him forever. When they've all gone ashore, I know I'm going to jump overboard and swim back to Boston.

By ten-thirty I'm a little more sober, but the boat-ship, rocking gently on her anchor, is still making me seasick. And now I'm really depressed from alcohol and self-castigation. I'm convinced that I'm a millstone around Karl's and my children's necks. I'm sure that if I continue to live, eventually I'll disgrace them all, even worse than they have already been disgraced by my lurid premarital life. I decide, Fuck it, I'll stop thinking about it and do it!

I tried sleeping pills when I was nineteen. I tried gas and jumping from the window of a crumby hotel near Greenwich Village, both within two weeks of each other, when I was twenty-seven. In every case, according to Jerry Greenberg, I didn't actually want to die. When I stole my mother's sleeping pills, and later swallowed them on a bus to Los Angeles, I left the empty bottle in plain sight on her bedroom dresser. I turned on the gas oven in our apartment a half hour before I was certain that Johnny Giacomo would come home, and I managed to stay poised on the parapet of that hotel until the fire department arrived with a net, and spread it out six floors beneath me. Like Roo, up a tree with Tigger, I was actually laughing when I jumped.

Jerry Greenberg made me memorize Ted Rubin's words: "*I am because I am.* I exist and need no justification for my existence. The fact of my being is enough. . . . My life, my

29

existence, my being is not predicated on standards, values, achievements or accomplishments. *I am*, not because of the books I write, money I earn, degrees conferred, children I have—I am, with or without these accoutrements."

The song the Beatles sang when I was a kid epitomized it. "I've got a ticket to ride." My ticket is my existence.

The only damned trouble with this all-American pep talk is that my ticket only seems to be valid in the house of mirrors, or on the roller coaster, and the merry-go-round. I am either Christina dizzy or Christina distorted.

If Jerry is right, he's only partially right. Whenever I try, in rational moments, to get at the roots of my despair, I know one thing. I'm not purposely trying to attract attention to myself. Temporarily, I'm so subjectively oriented that I'm really playing a last-thrill game with myself.

Watching oneself on the brink of death is like walking the knife edge of orgasm. If you give in—surrender—you'll lose yourself for a moment. The preliminary—rehearsing in your mind how you'll destroy yourself—is simply an extension of the euphoria of sexual foreplay, with permanent death the potential climax.

Perhaps, if it had been normally cold weather, I'd have thought of some other way, but it is a very-warm-for-May night. Ever since I had read *The Bell Jar*, I had been fascinated with Sylvia Plath's description of her character's attempt (hers?) to swim beyond the point of no return. Two days of a warm southerly airflow has kept the nighttime temperatures close to seventy. A thick sea fog floats over the still, cool ocean water. The water may be very cold. All the better. I won't have to swim too far.

Stripping off the pants of my green suit, which I have soiled with vomit, I'm thinking that when my nude corpse washes up on the Nantucket shores or on the Cape, it will provide local ministers with somber Sunday warnings to their parishioners. Those who live by the sword, etc. . . . BODY OF FORMER PORNOGRAPHIC STAR FOUND NAKED ON BEACH. FOUL PLAY SUSPECTED. Of course, no one would ever conceive of the obvious. Christina decides to leave the world the way she came into it.

I'm halfway up the dimly lighted stairway leading to the salon, from where I'll have easy access to the gangplank and landing platform, when I hear Warren Ellison's voice— "Thanks for the ride, Timmy"—followed by the retreating putt-putt of the outboard on our launch. Warren has come back to the ship alone. No doubt he's determined to have his little rendezvous with Christina. How has he managed to escape the others? The lounge clock points to 10:45. What excuse has he given Betty or Karl to return to the ship so early? What should I do? I can run back to the bedroom and lock my door, but Warren will drive me crazy knocking on it. Who else is on board? Not Timmy. He's running ferry service. Suzie is probably around, but she'll be in the crew's cabin by this time. Five Star? But at night, he never comes below. He has a tiny bedroom on the bridge.

Knowing that Warren will have to walk through the lounge to go to his cabin—or mine—I wait in the shadows. The erotic potential of the moment temporarily overwhelms me. I feel as if I'm hang-gliding, naked with the kite wings strapped to my arms, off a steep cliff. Both orgasm and death await in the ocean below. My "Hello, Warren, looking for somebody?" startles him.

"Jesus Christ," he grunts. "You nearly gave me a heart attack. What in hell are you doing?"

"I'm running naked to God," I tell him. The words, written by Meister Eckhart but being said by Mory—Newton Morrow—have suddenly jumped into my mind, and I'm seeing Warren through a haze of tears.

Mory is kissing my eyes, my nose, my neck, my breasts, and I feel his penis slipping inside me as he says; " 'Knowledge is no particular thought, but rather it peels off all coverings, and runs naked to God, until it touches him and grasps him.' "

Warren, the here-and-now reality, is gradually becoming more accustomed to the darkness. "Why in hell are you walking around naked at this time of night?" he demands, and he grabs me and tries to kiss me. "Thank God—God isn't around," he's telling me breathlessly, while his hands are searching my body frantically. "You'd tempt Him as well as the Devil."

"How did you manage to get back here without them?" I ask.

But Warren isn't answering. He has pushed me onto a couch and he's slobbering over my vulva like a starved man. I'm afraid he's going to literally eat me. Finally, yanking at his hair, I get his attention. "God, it's been a long time, Christa." He sighs. "Nearly a year. I've thought about you constantly. We've got to do better this year."

I don't tell him, but having an affair with Warren Ellison,

31

even being unfaithful for the second time since I had married Karl, hasn't flushed out Prince Desire, or even come close. Tonight I am finally going to stop searching, and maybe, although he doesn't know it yet, Warren is too.

"Is Timmy bringing the rest of them back on the next trip?" I ask.

Warren shakes his head. "They're all dancing. There's a special floor show at eleven-thirty. I told Betty that I was very tired. I was in San Francisco Wednesday. Just got back yesterday. Betty doesn't give a damn. Rita met a clothing buyer she knew from Lord & Taylor's. He's young, bearded, quite charming, and is probably giving her fantasies that she's twenty-five again. Link was telling Betty to stop worrying about her weight, that she's really delightfully plump, and that he's a nineteenth-century man who prefers his women Renoir-style. He was finally dancing with her. Karl has disappeared with Lizabeth. Prissy and Henry have found a common enemy. Their loose friends. They're holding hands." Warren chuckles. "My only friend is back on the yacht, tossing her cookies. Someone had to come back to hold your head." Warren is pulling me by the hand. "Come on. Let's find a bed."

"Take your clothes off here," I tell him huskily. "We're going swimming first."

Warren shivers. "The water's too damned cold. Come on, Christa," he pleads. "We haven't got much time."

I shrug. "Okay, go down and wait for me. I'll see you later." Laughing, I tell him that adultery isn't half so much fun in bed. Karl will fuck there almost any time. "Come on. Stop being so prudish. Take off your clothes and leave them here. We'll tiptoe quietly down the boarding stairs. You first. On the bottom steps, I'll jump in your arms and shinny onto your prick. Then, when I count to ten, joined together, we'll jump overboard." Warren is still dubious, but I can see that I'm intriguing him. "All you have to do is hold your breath. As we go under we'll have a simultaneous magnificent underwater orgasm. Then we'll dry off and do it again, more quietly, in bed."

Warren shakes his head, but I have captured his imagination. Besides, he doesn't dare tell me that at forty-five he's no match for a thirty-three-year-old nymphomaniac. Laughing and kissing him, with a firm grip on his throbbing penis, I convince him that he must descend the gangway backward,

32

step by step. The night air is wet. The only sounds are our giggles, and tiny waves lapping the hull.

I suddenly wonder why I'm standing here naked with a naked president of a Boston bank. A few feet below the low-lying fog, the black water is inviting me to disappear into it. But I stop thinking and slide onto Warren's engorged and upright organ. My legs are clamped around him. His prick is deep inside me; we are ankle-deep in water. His hands are clutching my ass, and he's trying to maintain a precarious balance on the tiny, undulating landing platform.

Then I'm suddenly yelling to him, "I'm coming. Oh, God, Warren, I'm exploding!" It's not true, but Warren is too far gone to know. "Jump, honey. Jump!" I yell. "Hold your breath. We'll climax together." The thought crosses my mind that if I hang on tight enough, I can drown Warren, too.

But Warren is resisting me. For a few seconds we are tottering on the edge. Warren is trying to convince me that I can cool my hots for him without going swimming, and I'm screaming at him that he's a coward and maybe a fag. Then, too late, we hear the putt-putt of the launch.

Timmy's searchlight picks us out. Above all the other voices, I hear Karl yelling, "Jesus Christ, they're fucking together!" Simultaneously, Five Star turns on the ship's floodlights. It's broad daylight. Timmy hasn't reached the landing platform in the launch yet. Still clinging to a bewildered Warren, my legs a vise around his back, I swing all my weight against him and we tumble into the water with me on top, still clutching him.

Of course, even before we tumble in our genitals are no longer joined, but I know that *now* Christina is really in trouble. Karl's yacht may still be floating, but all its passengers have gone aground. The only way out for Christina is to disappear, permanently.

It takes Timmy and Karl a few minutes to get his guests out of the launch. In the meantime, without Warren, I'm doing it. I'm swimming off into the night!

———◆———

Two days later, after dragging him back from his holiday weekend, I'm sitting on the floor of Jerry Greenberg's office. "Karl really isn't angry with you," Jerry is trying to convince me. "He telephoned me this morning from the ship. I assured

33

him that while you are a troubled woman, I'm sure that you and I can work through your problems together."

I know that Karl has told Jerry that I tried to commit suicide. And I'm well aware that if I'm not careful, they can have me committed "for my own good," and I'll be wandering around the corridors of some expensive sanitarium, with all the other manic-depressives, for the rest of my life.

"If he told you I was trying to drown myself, he was wrong." I try not to appear too flustered or insistent. "It's very simple, really. I was very embarrassed. I never intended to screw with Warren Ellison. It was a hot night. I was going swimming to get rid of my hangover."

"They had to search for you for nearly twenty minutes," Jerry reminds me. "You weren't just swimming near the boat. You were swimming away from it."

"I was confused. I didn't know what in hell to say to Betty. How do you apologize to your husband and the other spouse, or convince them it wasn't serious? How do you tell them you both were led astray by your sexual compulsions, but that it was no big thing? That's why I flew back this morning from Newport. I was afraid to tell them I'm no longer blessed with any normal sexual morality."

"You had to face them at breakfast. How did they react?"

I shrug. "Warren and I took the tack that we were really going swimming. Then, suddenly, being naked together, we got carried away. Betty was pretty distant. Most women who catch their husbands in adultery don't have all their best friends along to witness the action. Yesterday, when we tied up at the marina in Newport, I took the simplest way out. I told Karl that I was a little depressed and I needed to talk with you. I told him that he shouldn't make mountains out of molehills. I'm not in love with Warren Ellison. I'm sure that I didn't damage his prick, or he my vagina. Anyway, now, with me out of the way, Karl can play nursery rhymes with Lizabeth. You know, what's good for the goose . . ."

"You aren't jealous?"

"It's an interesting question. I am. But I don't think Karl should be. A rich man who has married three times can marry a fourth. I suppose that's what scares me—not that he may fuck Lizabeth—but that emotionally I can't afford to lose him. I know that I often treat him shabbily, but even when I'm doing it, a part of me is telling me to stop. I know that Karl and my kids are my life raft in a raging torrent. On

34

the other hand, I'm afraid that when I hit bottom, I may drag them all under with me."

Jerry is silent awhile, and then he says, "You've been seeing me for some time. While I haven't pushed it, with your credentials, and background in psychology, I presume that you have made some self-diagnosis of your problems. How would you describe yourself clinically?"

I laugh. "Maybe you're right. I am the product of my mother's conditioning. But in a larger sense, I'm symptomatic of the entire twentieth-century anomie. The subtle but very real machine alienation of human beings. I doubt very much that I can be cured with Freudian approaches. About ten percent of the American population suffer from manic-depressive symptoms sometime in their lives. Every year more than twenty thousand of them take their lives. Several millions more probably contemplate doing it. There's a Dr. Ronald Fiere who wrote a book called *Moodswing*—he thinks that lithium could make the whole world happy and smiling. He believes that the manic side of manic-depression is a thing of the past and so are shrinks like you. Eventually, if we're not careful, we may all have our anti-social behavior modified by Big Brother who loves us. Someone has even suggested putting lithium in our drinking water. One way or another the suicidal will be saved. The worldwide suicide rate is estimated at more than one thousand suicides every day."

I shrug. "What does it prove? The so-called experts think I may have a chemical imbalance in my neuro transmitters. They'd categorize me as a bipolar depressive. All my life I have periods when I fly very high. When I'm at the top of a cycle, and I'm positive that I am God and I can accomplish anything or be anything I wish, even though I'm haunted by the certainty that any minute I will crash back into reality, I don't want to lose those 'highs.' I like them. I feel like a goddess—and I get things done.

"I keep coming to you because I want a cure, not a crutch. We both know you can prescribe some of the tricyclic anti-depressants when I'm depressed or lithium when I'm manic or even electro-convulsive therapy. But so far you haven't. And I appreciate it. All that stuff is like aspirin for a headache. I want to know the cause. I want to transform myself by a sheer act of will."

Halfway through my self-analysis, I am sobbing. "God-damn it, Jerry, I refuse to live my life propped up and held together by chemicals. All I really need is deep human involvement—with Karl, with Michael and Penny whom I love very much, but I'm afraid I'm not a good influence on them—with someone—but somehow that escapes me, too. I frighten everyone away. Anyway, I'm sure of one thing: eating lithium isn't going to change the environment of my life.

"What is your sex life with Karl like?"

"Karl is methodical. He diddles my clit and he sucks my tits, testing with his fingers to see if my cunt is lubricated. Then, when he thinks the machinery is oiled, he comes on top of me. He even tries to last until I come." I'm grinning. "Alas, the poor man never makes it. I'm slow to climax."

"Have you tried any of the female techniques to slow him down?"

"No. Karl thinks all that crap is nonsense. He read an article that it's normal for a man to come a few minutes after he enters a woman. Farting around, waiting for a woman, or, God forbid, extending fucking for an hour or two, is bad for a man's prostate. Karl takes pride that at his age, he can go all night without having to piss."

Jerry displays no reaction to this nitty-gritty revelation. I have a feeling that in the sack Jerry is probably not too different from Karl.

"Tell me about your love life since you married Karl. Who else have you been intimate with besides Warren Ellison?"

"There's only been one other man." I know Jerry doesn't believe me, but it's true. "But I don't want to talk about him."

"Maybe you should. Perhaps he's the key."

Now I'm really sobbing. "Did you read the papers yesterday?"

Jerry looks puzzled and a little dismayed. "You mean the guy who was murdered when he answered his front door bell at five o'clock in the morning? Hank Hutchings? Were you involved with him?"

"Not recently. The summer before last. He was one of Karl's borrowing customers. Hank was a lamb among the wolves. They finally ate him." I shrug. "If you've been reading the rumors, the theory is that Hank was in such financial difficulty that he arranged his own murder." I'm laughing now, deliberately covering the sick feeling in my guts and head. "My fifty minutes is up. You and Karl can stop worrying about me. I obviously will never manage to kill myself." I wonder if Hank had really hired a hit man. How did he contact him? Any of my former acquaintances in Greenwich Village who might have taken the assignment to dispose of Christina had long since vanished.

For the next two days, I'm my own Yo-Yo. I'm bouncing rhythmically on a string, rising confidently to the top at a mere flick of the wrist. But I'm scared that when I lose the motion I won't be able to wind me up again, and I'll just dangle there. Grace, along with Mrs. Steffens, is minding the children. She's surprised to find me back from the cruise so soon and alone. She's aghast when she finds out why. She is panicky for me. Karl will surely divorce me. No man ever forgives an adulterous wife. Why do I insist on defying all the normal sexual traditions? Where have my so-called sexual freedoms—insanities—ever got me? I'm an outcast. Normal women won't have anything to do with me.

"I'm not the only crazy one in this world," I storm at her. There's all kinds of freaks and creeps who you think they're quite sane. You stick to yours and I'll stick to mine. If I hadn't rebelled against your careful imprinting of me, I'd end up just like you. A fifty-five-year-old momma "whose urine would etch glass."

Grace was listening to me open-mouthed. When I was a child and had temper tantrums, she confined me to my room. Now, she squirmed in her helpless silence. "You may have proved you can get along without men, but you sure as hell fawn all over Karl. I'm setting him up for you. He doesn't have to divorce me. He can have me committed. Then you'll have a second chance to nail him to the wall. Or you can be his housekeeper and peek through the keyhole and watch while he screws with Lizabeth—the next Mrs. Klausner. Maybe once in a while he'll even service you."

Grace is mad as hell at me now. "You're a very bad woman, Christina. I'm ashamed of you. You deserve whatever you get. As for Karl—if I hadn't sent him to New York to rescue you from your sex-mad friends, you'd be dead right now."

But I'm not really listening to Grace, I can't stop thinking about Hank Hutchings. I wonder if I should go to the funeral home in Marshfield where he is laid out. Two summers ago, I had spent three or four hours, almost every week, making love with this laughing man, in a Holiday Inn near Plymouth, and now he is dead. I suppose that our "interludes for lovemaking"—Hank's words—could have still been happening, if I hadn't gone overboard and thought that at last I had found

37

my fairy prince. Hank had opened the barred door for me, but he wisely avoided being led into Christina's prison.

The next day Karl and all the others leave the ship and fly home from LaGuardia. Karl tells me he hasn't canceled the cruise to pay his respects to the dead, but because he's worried about me.

"I'm not angry with you, Christa," he tells me. "Actually, Warren getting caught with his ass out—*in flagrante delicto*—was the best thing that ever happened to the son of a bitch. Ever since we elected him president of the First Merchants last year, he's gone through an alarming personality change. He's become a pompous bastard. He sends out a monthly newsletter to all the depositors. *Conversations with Warren Ellison.* He interviews himself as an authority on everything—from stocks, bonds, option buying, to closed-end funds, and, of course, banking and the economic system. But now his wife, his friends, and eventually everybody in Boston knows the truth. Like every male, he's a horny bugger. You took the wind out of his sails. You should have seen his face when we picked you out with our spotlight. It's a wonder he didn't have a heart attack. If it weren't for Hank Hutchings, Judgment Day would have finally caught up with Warren Ellison!"

I'm a little surprised at Karl's reaction. I ask him if it isn't embarrassing for him, too. After all, I'm his wife.

Karl grins. "I haven't lived with you for six years without knowing a little about what makes you tick, Christa. You talk a big game, but you're not promiscuous at all. I figure you did it because you were pissed off at me. It isn't as if either of you looked as if you were enjoying yourselves. Tottering around on a gangway, trying to screw with a woman scissored around you, didn't look very appetizing to me."

For a minute I think Grace is wrong. Karl still loves me. I hug him. "Did you go to bed with Lizabeth?"

Karl has a sheepish look on his face. "I didn't do it for revenge. Call it curiosity. Even with you I often have the feeling that I'm going to bed with a child—my own daughter. But Liz was a mistake. She's a competent secretary with nothing much between her ears. Tits and cunt can't substitute for a mind." He shrugs. "I'll suggest to Warren that he should get her a job at the bank, then she won't be under my feet."

It's obvious that Lizabeth is a minnow who will eventually

38

be swallowed by a shark. But I don't feel sorry for her. "Am I a mistake?" I ask Karl.

He pats my ass. "No, but you're a goddamned enigma."

He really thinks so when I tell him that I think we should go to Hank Hutchings' funeral. "Absolutely not," he tells me coldly. "I trusted Hank. Not only did he screw me financially, but just when I finally had Warren Ellison behind the eight ball—really feeling penitent—scared shitless that I'm going to hold a lifetime grudge against him for fucking my wife—Hank gets himself murdered, and the whole slimy truth about him comes out, and Warren is vindicated. I'm the one who convinced Ellison to loan Hank three million more on that condominium project. Warren never liked him. He actually put it in writing to me that he was going ahead with the additional loan on my say-so and against his better judgment. He felt that Hank lacked creditability. There was something missing in his character. He wasn't really a man's man. Now it turns out that Ellison was right. Half of the supposedly 'confirmed' buyers for the Weatherly Estates condominiums don't exist at all. Hank actually forged about thirty percent of the sale agreements. He was operating on the premise that he'd get by on his good looks. Somehow, he'd sell the place to legitimate buyers before he was in financial difficulty. It's bad enough that I got taken for over a million, but when the news came over our ship telephones, Warren had a hard time concealing his 'I told you so's.' He knew that so far as you were concerned, he was off the hot seat with me."

We are in bed while this conversation is taking place. Suddenly Karl, who has been playing with my breasts almost absentmindedly, gets on top of me. Then, to remind me that no matter what the hell I do I'm really his, he kisses me fiercely, bruising my lips and face. Although my vagina is still dry, and I'm in no mood for lovemaking, he thrusts his prick viciously into me, forcing his way through my resistant labia. He's hurting me, but I don't complain. He's paid a lot of money to own my vagrant cunt.

In a few minutes it's over. I try to go to sleep, but I can't get Hank out of my mind. I remember two summers ago and the long discussions with him, naked in bed in the rented womb of the Holiday Inn. Like me, Hank is on a merry-go-round, trying to grasp the brass ring and never quite succeeding. Now I realize that his laughter and joy were probably a manic cover for the fears that must have obsessed him. Was there a clue in his words, which I remember vividly? "Christa," he would often tell me when our genitals were merged and we were floating together in a sublime detachment, "nothing on earth, after basic food and shelter, should have a higher priority for any man or woman than discovering this serenity, and the joy and the altered consciousness they are capable of giving each other." And his thought brought tears to my eyes and seemed like an echo from my past. Dear Mory, why did I send you away? Why didn't you stop me?

———◆———

Friday morning at breakfast—it's just a week since the start of the ill-fated cruise, I tell Karl flatly that if he won't go to Hank's funeral then I'll represent the family. Karl gets very angry with me. "You stay the hell away from there, Christa. It's a matter of principle. You're a Klausner. The Klausners can forgive a man who makes an honest business mistake, but this man was a crook, and even worse, a coward. If he had come to me or Ellison, and honestly faced the music, we'd have figured a way to bail him out. In certain circumstances, those of us who manage the money should stick together"—Karl grins—"if only to save each other. Hank would have lost his shirt, of course, but we most certainly would have kept him out of jail. Eventually, if he was any kind of man, he could have got going again. But the bastard didn't even have the nerve to kill himself. Instead he hires some thugs to blow his head off."

"No one's proved that," I tell him angrily. "That's a nasty police story to get them off the hook because they can't find who did it, or a motive. I hate you, Karl Klausner, and all of your creepy friends. Two weeks ago at the Marshfield Country Club you danced with Carol, and I danced with Hank, and you were very charming with both of them. I just can't understand how you can make such an about-face. It certainly wasn't Carol's fault. She's the one who has to face the collapse of their lives."

Of course, I don't mention Hank's last conversation with me while we were dancing. "Christa, it's been a long time," he told me. "You were the only ray of sunshine in my life. I don't know how to tell Carol, but I'm really weary of the rat race. Can't we escape and have a few afternoons together?

40

You're the only person I know with whom I can, momentarily, forget that the bells never stop tolling."

But I was noncommittal. I was afraid that my own need to disappear and lose myself in Hank's cheery warmth, and the amazing mutual process in which somehow we transformed each other, would trap me again. Now I wondered why Hank had never fully revealed his darker side to me. With the slight hint about "the bells tolling," hadn't he revealed that we were truly brothers under the skin? I suppose that in any relationship, one person being totally honest and self-disclosing— me—was more than enough. Two manic-depressives, unless they could continuously counterbalance their highs and lows, could never reinforce each other. Now it was finally obvious. Hank lying in a coffin with his head blown off had been groping in the same black, endless tunnel as I.

While these thoughts are coursing through my head, I am still excoriating Karl. "I don't give a damn what you say," I tell him. "I'm going to the funeral. I should have gone to the funeral home, if only to give Carol some support."

And so, not listening to Grace's warnings that I'm playing with fire, and thanking God that today she's finally going home to her own apartment, I leave the children with Mrs. Steffens and I drive my Mercedes to the funeral home in Marshfield in time to join the procession. I no sooner arrive than I'm sorry I came. Carol, sobbing, with her children clinging to her, is grim enough. But when Warren Ellison greets me somberly—he has come without Betty—it suddenly occurs to me that Karl has another reason for not wanting me to appear at Hank's funeral. He knows that Prissy and Henry Stone, and Rita and Link Sevigny, plus the Ellisons, will be there. Everyone on the damned cruise who knew that Karl's wife had cuckolded him would be there, and, even worse, the story was probably spreading like wildfire.

I'm one of the last ones to walk into the funeral home where several hundred people are waiting to hear the minister's dreary words, praising the murdered man. I notice a sudden buzz of interest. The women look smug. The men's eyes glitter. Obviously, Betty, Prissy, or Rita has told the latest escapade of the notorious Christina Klausner. If I were Karl, I'd counteract their nonsense. Tomorrow I'd place an advertisement in the *Boston Globe* advising that Karl Klausner's wife Christina was using her vagina, with his permission, to help him in his business ventures.

41

I commiserate with Carol, and tell her to ignore the rumors. She is sure that Hank was murdered by some contractor he owed money to. She is broke. Her hundred-and-fifty-thousand-dollar home is mortgaged to the hilt, and will have to be sold. The children will have to go to public schools. "Oh, Christa," she sobs, "I'm not like you. I don't know anything. I majored in history and government. After Wellesley, I was going to law school, but I married Hank instead."

Poor Carol. She's forty-two. Once she had a pretty face, but it's getting crinkly around her eyes. She isn't flat-chested, but she's not the milk-fed type. We live in a society where forty-two-year-old widows with no money and three kids exert very little magnetism on the male population, even if they look like femmes fatale.

After the minister has concluded his encomiums, I have two choices—I can either follow the cortege to the cemetery in my car, or I can accept Warren's invitation and ride with him.

The latter, of course, is like tossing a match on the oily, simmering, and insincere greetings that I am getting from the contingent of female mourners. "So nice to see you, Christina. Too bad Karl couldn't come. Is he feeling all right?"

Warren is holding the door of his Jaguar open for me. What the hell. I climb in. "Jesus," he says, as he lines his car in the procession, "you and I are in the doghouse. You should take up wrestling. That was some vise you had me in."

"I hope you spell the word with a 'c' not an 's'," I tell him.

Warren doesn't understand his own pun. He smiles vaguely. "How is Karl reacting?"

I don't give Warren any details about Karl. Just a warning. "Enemies with engorged pricks are easily shot down," I tell him. "Maybe if the women of the world would unite they could go one step further than Lysistrata and insist on coed armies. Fucking someone and fighting him in our brave world seems to have the same connotations. Karl isn't really mad. A prick with his prick exposed is a weak prick. Does Betty still love you?"

"I told you that last summer," Warren says. "Betty and I gave up in bed a long time ago. We think it's easier to live together than to try again. For Betty, appearances are more important than reality. Unfortunately, there were too many witnesses this time. Betty's ownership pride in me has suffered a severe blow."

"If the situation were reversed," I tell him, "you'd be shocked. Your rights of possession would be challenged. If you discovered some flat-bellied, smooth-muscled, pride-of-the-Olympics screwing Betty, you'd choke on the bile regurgitating in your throat."

"I didn't know you were an Olympic contender," Warren mocks me. "But I think I can handle you better than Karl does."

"You weren't doing so well the other night. Why in hell did you keep looking for me? Why didn't you just let me swim back to Boston?"

"Karl looked as if he was going to let you. He was so busy ignoring me and helping the others aboard his yacht that he let Timmy pull me out. Since everyone else was fully dressed, it was logical that the naked satyr go searching for the naked nymph." Warren laughs. "Anyway, to be honest, I needed time to get my bearings. You may have had an orgasm, but I didn't. I was so damned mad at you that if Timmy hadn't been there when we pulled you out, I'd have lashed you to the launch and finished the job right there, under the cover of the fog."

"You look the SM type." But Warren isn't widely read in sexology. I have to explain to him that some men prefer bondage. "They can't get off," I tell him, "unless the woman is tied up and helpless, preferably screaming, while they shove their doughty tool into any handy orifice." I didn't remind him that when I was finally sitting beside him, naked and shivering in the stern of the launch, I suddenly realized I was sitting on the bastard's hand, and he was trying to wiggle his finger along my perineum, or shunt (Johnny Giacomo's more colorful word for the space between a woman's asshole and her cunt).

Our surface banter stops at the cemetery. I'm relieved that Warren isn't angry with me. Not that I really like him or I ever plan to screw with him again, outdoors or indoors, but it distresses me when I know that anyone is irritated or unhappy with me. I don't need any help in this area. I'm surfeited with my own displeasure at myself.

On the way back to the funeral home to get my car, both of us are silent. We are contemplating the pointlessness and shortness of life. Warren wonders aloud how a man like Hank, who was seemingly weak and lacked determination in

43

other areas, could muster the courage to have himself assassinated. Between us, we can find no answer. I leave Warren with a peck on the cheek.

"No hard feelings," I tell him. "Happy hunting."

Yesterday

"Said not the serpent in the old story, 'If you eat of the fruit of the tree of knowledge you shall be as gods.' The promise was true in words, but apparently there was some mistake about the tree. Perhaps, it was the tree of selfish knowledge, or else the fruit was not ripe. The story is obscure. Jesus said the same thing when he told men that they might be the sons of God. But he made no mistake as to the tree he showed them, and the fruit was ripe. It was the fruit of love, for universal love is at once the seed and the fruit, cause and effect, of the highest complete knowledge. Through boundless love man becomes a god, for thereby he is made conscious of his oneness with God, and all things are put under his feet.
It has only been since the *Great Revolution* brought in an era of human brotherhood that mankind has been able to eat abundantly of this fruit of the tree of knowledge, and thereby grow more and more into the consciousness of the divine soul as the essential self and the true hiding of our lives."

—Edward Bellamy,
Equality

On an impulse after leaving Warren, I drive slowly past the salt marshes that gave Marshfield its name. There is no hurry. I can be back in Marblehead in an hour, I am aware that I'm slowly succumbing to a crawling sexual feeling that is suffusing my whole body, making me tremble with my own suddenly overwhelming eroticism. It's as if my subconscious is trying to destroy the memory of Hank's impassive, frozen, undertaker's face. The tingling of my breasts and clitoris are proving that, in spite of myself, I'm still very much alive.

But then, I suddenly remember another reason. Nine years ago this summer, on a warm Memorial Day weekend, Newton Morrow and I wandered together, naked, in these tall grasses. Leaving a rented automobile on a secluded road (we had obtained it for the day by pooling our meager finances), we shucked off our jeans and sneakers and carried them into the swamp, along with a bottle of wine and a picnic lunch we had made together, and, of course, books—particularly *Life and Death of the Salt Marshes* by John and Mildred Teal. Among a thousand other things, Mory was interested in comparing the marshes in New England with those near his home in the bayou swamps of Louisiana.

Breaking a path through the green *Spartina alteniflora*, which was well over six feet tall and felt cool and moist against our bodies, we slipped barefoot into the warm, silty mud. Seagulls went squawking into flight, fearful that we would plunder their newly hatched eggs. Laughing, waving at them, afraid they would swoop down and peck our naked flesh, we tried to assure them that their "Jonathan babies" were safe.

But, alas, they didn't understand. The naked Adam and Eve below them were adventuring where modern men and women, who had asphalted and plasticized their environment, and thought marshes made convenient dumps for twentieth-

47

century refuse, never ventured. Mory and I were returning to our ancestors, whose traces, still existing in ourselves, filled us with inexpressible memories. Our bodies yearned for the seas from which we came.

"In the act of love," Mory told me, after we finally had discovered a large kettle hole filled with murky saltwater and we had tumbled naked together on the soft *Spartina partens* grass, "we'll blend ourselves with the gulls and thrushes and clams and quahogs, and millions of sea creatures."

"And bugs," I added, waving a few curious ones away.

"Bugs?" Mory grinned. "How could they bite us? We're joining their continuous mating dance."

Amazingly, they didn't bite us. Evidently we weren't the most succulent things in their world. Like us, the insects seemed to be intoxicated with the sun and salt and windswept swamp that had existed long before man appeared and will be here long after there is no one left with brain cells to remember that man existed. Lovely, immortal bugs and worms and algae, much of their life still parthogenetic, able to re-create themselves by subdivision, none of them cursed with memory or the knowledge of their own transience, all of them sustaining each other in a joyous life chain.

———◆———

Now, unable to stop myself—it's only one-fifteen and I know that I don't have to be home until four or five—I finally find the road that leads into our special marsh. It really isn't a road. It's a cul-de-sac, surrounded by six-foot grass. Except for a few rusty beer cans and a sun-dried condom, time has stood still here. I'm Chrissy again and I'm twenty-four, and I'm madly in love.

Turning the ignition off on my Mercedes, knowing that I can't help myself, I must once again walk through the grass naked, and feel its sensuous fronds brushing at my body, I sink into the soft mud as I search for a place covered with the silky *Spartina partens,* the low soft grass that Mory and I had made love in for at least the two-hundredth time so many years ago.

My shoes and dress and pantyhose are locked in the car, and I'm heedless of who might see me. Gliding through the shimmering green ocean, turning into a walking mass of goose pimples as the soft, squishy tidewater oozes over my ankles, I finally find a saltwater pool in a sun-drenched clearing.

Kneeling naked to the grass, which forms a soft cushion for my breasts, I gently slide back and forth against it, and then I roll over and feel it deep in the cleft of my behind. I know that I can't stop. I know that I must assuage my crying hunger for a different kind of surrendering love, a love that I have experienced with only one man. My hands, making love to myself, will be Mory's hands. The soft swamp mud that I'm massaging my breasts and vulva with isn't mud in my hands. I'm a female animal in heat, rolling in my Mother Earth trying to return to my primeval essence. Mory is beside me. We're doing it to each other, and we're hysterical with laughter as I slop the mud over Mory's lovely, gigantic erection. I'm turning him into an ancient phallic god with a weapon three feet long.

As I lie here now—feathering my breasts and stomach and labia, feeling my fingers exploring the contours of my ass, holding myself breathless on the edge of a tall cliff and, when I can no longer stop it from coming, wanting to plunge down and disappear into my own orgasmic ocean—I wonder why I have never told Jerry Greenberg about Newton Morrow. I guess that if Jerry could see me now, naked, lost to the world, tears in my eyes as I stare at the blue sky, he would think I was narcissistic as well as a manic-depressive. But he'd be wrong. I had loved Mory. Does love like that have to be fragile and transient? Mory didn't believe it. "All we have to do is never stop running naked to God, Chrissy," he had told me. "If we learn how to do that, we will share our joys and orgasms for as long as we live."

Alas, while I never stopped running, it wasn't toward God, but to old Beelzebub himself. Why, after those idyllic months, my last in Cambridge, before I went through the motions and graduated with the tassel dangling from the right side of my mortarboard—Dr. Christina North, who couldn't even heal herself—did I tell Mory (my intonation made my voice sound just like Grace's) that we should have one year apart to discover ourselves? If there was anything still left to learn about each other by that time, God alone knew what it was. But I persisted. I would go to New York City and work at Bellevue, and Mory could go home to Lafayette, Louisiana and try to appease his daddy. Newton Morrow wasn't going to try to save the world for Jesus. He was going to marry a northern girl who rarely, if ever, went to church. And whether Daddy believed it or not, he was going to become President of the United People of America.

I can see Mory now, with a one-way ticket to New Orleans in his hand, tears in his eyes, telling me, "I really think we should get married first, Chrissy. I hope you're not doing this because of Jennifer. I like Jennifer—I guess I love her a little, too—but I'll always love you first. You'll always be my First Lady."

I didn't blame Mory because Jennifer had occasionally shared our bed. Even though I often wondered if she were better mated for Mory than I was, and I was occasionally mildly jealous of her, I wasn't sending Mory home because of her.

I suppose basically I was motivated by my fear that instead of being Mory's First Lady, I might be the noose that strangled him, or, like a drowning person, I might hang on to him so desperately that I would pull him down along with me.

There were other reasons. I didn't want to be blamed by Mory's daddy because Mory wasn't going to follow in his footsteps. Mory told me that the world needed to be saved— "And that is for cotton-picking sure." But he wasn't going to ask for Jesus's help to do it. "There's too many Billy Grahams, Oral Robertses, Rex Humbards, and Tom Morrows now. When I'm President, I'm not going to save people for Jesus. I'm going to save them for themselves."

But I wasn't listening. I was sending Mory home to explain to his father that his future daughter-in-law believed that evangelists might have one foot in heaven, and they might even provide an inexpensive kind of psychiatry for the masses, but that Grace and I had at least one thing in common: Smiling, haughty men who wore their halo in one hand and their Bible in the other, and seemed to have an inside track to God, made us uneasy.

My doubts were reinforced by Grace's certainty. How could two people as different as Christina North, a poet and a dreamer, and Newton Morrow, a determined political evangelist, make it together? Christina the wife of a minister? God forbid! And, of course, Grace never stopped reminding her daughter that there were hundreds of younger versions of Karl Klausner, whom she was working for—men with much more money and potential than Newton Morrow—ripe for the plucking, across the river (but not into the trees) at Harvard Business School.

50

Whatever the reasons were that motivated me, I'm sure I believed my serious, tearful words. "Mory, it will only be a year," I tried to assure him. "Before you know it, we'll be back together again. I'm counting on you as much as you're counting on me."

———◆———

Now, gasping at my own self-produced delight, wondering if I will try to walk the precipice just once more, drifting along with a few cumulus clouds that are providing a backdrop for my reverie, I wonder where Mory is. He must be thirty-seven. I wonder if he has been as faithful to me in his fashion as I have to him. I wonder if he ever relives his dream about being President of the United People of America with "dear Chrissy" as his First Lady. More likely, Daddy Tom Morrow has submerged him in some law office where he is counsel for the Morrow Evangelical Foundation. Or, God forbid, perhaps Mory has finally changed colors and made his truce with necessity. Perhaps he is an entrepreneur—or, even worse, maybe he's working for one of the large corporations he detested.

One of the reasons I never told Jerry Greenberg about Mory, or, for that matter, never mentioned him to Karl, was to protect Mory's dream from their incredulous laughter. Neither of them could identify with a twenty-nine-year-old perpetual student who calmly affirmed that it was his destiny one day to be President of a very new kind of America.

And I'd laugh at Mory, and tell him that he didn't just want to be President. He wanted to be God. A savior. A latter-day Jesus Christ, who would re-create his people in his own image of a new tomorrow. But my teasing was a loving teasing, and it didn't matter then. Mory could be President Jesus for all I cared, I would help him. My seduction was complete. I was Mory and myself simultaneously. We shared that ephemeral kind of loving that those who "grow up" find unbelievable and irritating. So much so they often succeed, as they did with us, in making the lovers participate in their own self-destruction.

———◆———

The first time that I was aware that Mory existed was in the Harvard Coop bookstore. At least once a week during my

51

undergraduate years at Radcliffe, and when I was working on my doctorate, I'd take a few hours off and poke through the three floors filled with a hundred thousand or more books. Scanning the new titles, often being seduced by the wonders within that their covers extolled, I was entranced by the ever-changing flood of printed ephemera. It was both an aphrodisiac and a chastening experience for me.

I was in love with the printed word. I wanted to join these thousands of authors, all with their particular insights and fictions and fantasies, vying with each other, competing for their brief moment of acknowledgment and human love and attention. Here were millions of words that I could never absorb. No one, in a lifetime, could read anything but a small fraction of the more than forty thousand titles published in just one year. I was driven to be among that number. I wanted to be one of the saints of the English language. I knew it was foolish and egotistical, but I wanted all my written words preserved on paper and in type. Even though few people might actually read my books, I told myself that being a saint gathering dust on a library shelf long after I was dead was better than not being a saint at all. The actuality, of course, when I met Mory, was that my collected poems and a few dozen short stories only existed in long-forgotten issues of popular magazines, or were still in my notebooks read by no one except myself.

Not only was I obsessed by my need for praise and recognition, but I was convinced that one way I might achieve them was to know everything. Like Thomas Wolfe, whose *Of Time and the River* was already covered with dust on library shelves, I was determined not only to read thousands of the new books being published, but I fantasized that if I went at it systematically I could read all of the wisdom of the ages, waiting patiently for me—their priestess—between the covers of a million books in the Widener Library.

If the devil himself had materialized, and told me: "Christina, you can have the trade-off that I offered Faust," I would have eagerly assented. "Take my soul, my tits, my cunt!" Small exchange for a lifetime of omniscience. I, Christina North, at one fell swoop would know everything, past, present, and future. For the duration of my life, before I boiled in Hell, if not a god, I'd be a goddess. The Delphic Oracle herself.

On the other hand, particularly before my final year at Harvard when I met Mory, there were days when I wandered through the Coop as a way of doing penance for the times I had abandoned my intellectual and literary life and joined the Philistines and Epicureans. All my life I have twisted on a spit, revolving over the fires of my schoolmarm brain, only to turn and simmer on the reality of my physical body and appearance, which I could use like a net to sweep in males when I was in the mood.

During my years at Harvard I had been dating, in addition to others, Biff Gaffner, a Harvard Law student, and Harry J. Mitchell, the Third, who was his mirror reflection at Harvard Business School. At times I turned off my brain and joined the ranks of the sophisticated and wealthy Harvard and Radcliffe and Wellesley students who cruised to the best eating places and discos in Boston in expensive foreign cars. I knew the vagina and soft breasts of Christina were the eventual price of admission, but I didn't give a damn. Like tire streaks on asphalt as they accelerated from zero to seventy miles an hour in seven seconds, the temporary ownership of Christina was proof of their existence and importance. Skiing in New Hampshire, Vermont, and Canada with Bill and Harry and other equally financially secure and poised young men; or driving with them to New York City in three and a half hours to see the Joffrey Ballet or the latest play opening; or picnicking at Cranes Beach or Provincetown—naked in motels and on lonely sand dunes, my brain dulled with wine, I tried to abandon my overachieving, fame-seeking brain, and with my nipples hard and my vaginal juices flowing, become some kind of Earth Mother.

Temporarily, I was one of the plebians, or proles, who had leaped over the wall and joined the rich. Like a Roman slave girl, invited to the banquet of my masters, watching the behavior of their emptyheaded girlfriends, I impersonated my betters. Enjoying the luxury of fine cars, old wines, exquisite Continental cooking, candlelight dinners, and erotic bedrooms in country inns, or suites in the Plaza or the New York Sheraton, I vacillated between my two realities, as I did once again years later when I finally married Karl Klausner.

So I slept with Bill and Harry and several others more than once in those years, and they ejaculated in Christina's hand or mouth or in her vagina, but she was detached: a third person, standing beside the bed observing the particular man thrashing up and down on her or moaning beside her; and she kept wondering why she was incable of the surren-

53

der that would bring the shuddering orgasm and momentary escape that she needed so desperately.

After one of those weekends, totally bored by the frenetic chase and the sex, which for Harry was a kind of addictive lust—"I have to marry you, Christina, whether I want to or not, because I never can get enough of your body"—I made up my mind that I was never going to stray again from my self-created convent—the apartment I shared with Jennifer Manchester on Sheppard Street in Cambridge. It wasn't just Harry's or Bill's lack of interest in me as a total person, I was still trying to make up my mind whether I was a fraud, and whether my interest in poetry and music and literature and art, and the world of ideas that I kept trying to shove down Harry and Bill's throats—they were only politely interested—was any more valid than their world of law and business and the domination of their feeble minds by the bottom-line mentality of America.

Thinking these thoughts, I wandered into the Harvard Coop paperback section, halfheartedly examining titles in the new books, psychology, sociology, and literature sections. I was suddenly conscious that I was traveling along the shelves in the same direction as a tall—he was almost six and a half feet—brown-eyed boy with a Sephardic, scruffy beard and a sunflower smile. We had not only bumped against each other several times, but now we were blocking each other's way.

"Why don't we make an agreement?" I finally asked him, certain that he must be a newly arrived Harvard freshman who had probably grown the shaggy crop on his face as a first act of filial defiance and nest leaving. "When you've finished exploring the sociology section, I'll switch with you," I told him. "Then you can have the psychology section to yourself."

He grinned warmly at me. For a moment, I had the uneasy sensation that I was drowning in the loving expression that suffused his brown eyes, and made him look like a five-year-old on Christmas morning. "I'm really sorry," he said, pronouncing it "Ah'm" with a soft southern inflection, "but the truth is that I've been waiting for you to arrive. I usually come here once a week, too. You've missed the last two Thursdays. Last week I put an advertisement in the Boston *Phoenix*, hoping you might read it. It said: '*Blue-eyed female, poet and book lover, who haunts the Harvard Coop bookstore, usually on Thursday afternoons, please call Newton Morrow, Gallatin Hall, Harvard Business School, for impor-*

tant message.'" He shook his head sadly. "I guess you didn't see it."

While I was sure that this refugee from the nineteenth century was some kind of sexually frustrated twerp, I still couldn't reach shore. I was still trying to swim out of his penetrating brown eyes. I learned later that among his other weird accomplishments, including an amazing self-taught fluency in Spanish and Russian—all related to his master game plan—Mory had studied hypnotism. Right there in the Coop, trying to tell myself that this man wasn't even handsome, and certainly was no stylistic match for Harry J. Mitchell, the Third—I was slowly becoming his first willing subject.

Even though I suspected it was dangerous—especially when the sender was seemingly so unsophisticated as to signal his absolute attraction to a woman—I asked the question. "What was the message?"

"I wanted to tell you that I'm in love with you," he said. I'm sure that he was blushing—I was—but the forest on his face was an impenetrable cover. Listening to him, I was suddenly teen-age disoriented. "You see," he continued, "now that I've actually spoken to you, I'm telepathically certain that at last I've found my female counterpart—a woman who is searching."

"Searching for what?" I asked.

"Maybe the philosopher's stone." He was nervously shifting the books he was carrying from one arm to the other. "To be honest with you, I've been in love with you for quite a long time. I saw your picture in the Boston *Globe* four years ago when I was going to Harvard Law. I read about you, and I felt so sympathetic I thought about telephoning you—but I was afraid that you'd think I was some kind of Jesus Freak. Please, Chrissy—"

By this time, I was staring at him dumbfounded. This creep even knew my name. He knew about my first trip to nowhere, which by this time I wasn't even sure that I had actually taken. He was obviously a religious fanatic, determined to save Christina North from eternal damnation.

"Please, I didn't mean to frighten you," he said contritely. "I know this is a strange way to get acquainted, but today I decided that wishing wasn't going to make it so. It was now or never." He was aware that I was uneasily trying to end the conversation without appearing too impolite. "Really, Chrissy, you're not in some dark alley. You're in the Harvard Coop. I'm not going to pounce on you."

I wasn't too sure. He had a hell of a nerve calling me Chrissy. I was certain it would be a long dull day before I ever became that friendly with him. For all I knew, he might be sexually frustrated enough to pull back his coat and reveal his penis pointing at me. I wondered how much more he knew about me. Maybe he had even followed me to my apartment. Maybe he was a poor, sick voyeur who stood on the sidewalk waiting for me to undress—Jenny had warned me I should pull down the shades—trying to catch a glimpse of me naked. At the same time I was thinking, Here is a perfect example for my doctoral thesis. For the first time, I was meeting in the flesh one of those sexually hung-up men who filled the classified pages of the Boston *Phoenix* with their sad cries for a woman to relieve their genital distress. I wanted to tell him that if he went back to his room and masturbated he might feel better. But I was afraid that he might ask me to help him. Though he was still talking, I kept edging away from him, working my way toward the escalator.

Finally we were blocking the aisle in front of the long rack of science-fiction titles. I was trying to repress my maternal instincts, which kept telling me that this poor jerk probably just needed a mother to hold his hand. But I knew it wouldn't stop there. Give this guy an inch and the next thing, he'd want to go to bed with his surrogate mother. But my vanity and curiosity were leading me by the nose. Was he really a student at Harvard Business School? Had he graduated from Harvard Law School? He looked as if he should have been studying agriculture at the University of Massachusetts. I was not only transfixed by his gentle, loving eyes, but I was irritated that he knew much more about me than I did about him. Not only that, he had given me an irresistible challenge. Despite what he had read about me, he didn't believe that I could have such unlikely information as what the philosopher's stone meant, stuffed in my fluffy head.

By now we were definitely in the way of three long-haired science-fiction freaks, who were avidly examining novels with covers of supermen shooting laser guns at bug-eyed monsters in outer space.

"Really, I'm not interested in alchemy," I told him haughtily. I was dimly aware that engaging in a conversation with a guy like this was like letting an encyclopedia salesman get his foot in the door. "The search for the philosopher's stone that could transmute base metals into gold is as futile as the search for Utopias—or writing novels about galaxies that are thirty million light-years away." I gestured at the science-fiction titles. "Anyway, we're blocking the paths of future scientists. They don't know it, but they'd probably be better off reading fairy-tales, particularly 'Jack and the Beanstalk.' "

I had finally worked my way through the crowd toward the escalator. Following me, Mory was beaming. "But that's just what I want to talk with you about. Human alchemy—you and me—combined, we're the philosopher's stone!"

At the narrow check-out counter he got ahead of me, trapping me so that I couldn't escape until he had purchased his books with a Coop charge card. Surprised, I looked at the titles. *Androgyny*, by June Singer, subtitled *Toward a New Theory of Human Sexuality; Erotica*, by Diane Ippolito, and *To Have or To Be?*, by Erich Fromm.

Finally, free at last, ahead of him going down the escalator, I remembered that he had said that he lived in a dormitory at Harvard Business School. As we walked out the front door, I couldn't resist telling him, "I read Fromm's book. When you cross the river, you'd better hide that one. It's all about getting rid of a 'having society' and eliminating big business and going back to a 'small is beautiful' world."

"I know it." Mory was holding my arm altogether too possessively. "That's just what I want to talk with you about. I'm a spy in the house of the Lord. Will you have lunch with me at Grendel's? We have much more in common than you might think."

"What?" I demanded.

"We're both much smarter than our peers."

"Oh, God," I groaned. "Harvard is overrun with gifted students. The problem is that most of us started college before we were properly weaned."

I finally reluctantly agreed to have a sandwich with him, but I told him that I'd pay my own way, and it would have to be a fast lunch because I had a lot of studying to do. Following my suggestion Mory, who was looking at the menu a little bewilderedly, ordered a quiche lorraine. I still didn't believe him when he told me that he was a lawyer. He had passed the Massachusetts bar, and was now in his final year at Harvard Business School. Even if it was true, it seemed obvious that he was monetary light-years removed from Harry J. Mitchell, the Third. He was wearing a ragged sheepskin coat and blue jeans, and I wondered if he could even afford his own lunch, let alone a half-gallon Zinfandel, which he stopped at a liquor store to buy. Grendel's didn't have a liquor license.

He grinned, again guessing my thoughts. "We don't have to drink it all. If you're worried about money, it's all right. Daddy Morrow is a tight old skinflint, but he can afford it. Anyway, he owes it to me. For the past year and a half, I've been his free legal counsel. You see, sometimes Daddy goes too far. He gets so mad, trying to save people for Jesus who don't want to be saved, that he's been known to punch them on the nose, or personally identify backsliders before big audiences and say very bad things about their sick little greedy minds. Since they can't sue Jesus, some of those who Daddy says belong to the Devil try and sue him."

I discovered as we talked that Daddy Morrow—Tom Morrow—*Tomorrow*—was a very popular evangelist preacher in the Southwest. He had seduced several hundred thousand devoted followers who hoped that one day he'd run for governor of Louisiana. They had not only provided him with a New Orleans skyscraper, a printing plant, and a big home in Lafayette, but also with his own airplane, a DC-7. Of course, it was all owned by the Morrow Evangelical Foundation. Daddy was extremely exasperated that Newtie, *Newtomorrow*, was futzing around with the infidel at Harvard Business School. Newtie hadn't yet discovered that all the business case studies in the world couln't butter his bread any better than Jesus could.

As he told me about his daddy, I realized that Mory had a cross to bear equivalent to my mother Grace. "We both need a Simon to help us carry the Cross," I told him. "But what bewilders me is when do you have time to read this stuff?"

Between sips of wine, I was flipping through the books that Mory had bought. "And why in the world does a HBS student give a damn about androgyny?" Before he answered, I told him that I had a friends at Business School—Harry J. Mitchell, the Third, in particular. So far as I could discover, Harry's only reading was the headlines on the Boston *Globe*. "Harry complains that often he doesn't have time for these. Mostly he's completely buried in the avalanche of business case studies that pour out of the bowels of Harvard Business School like continuous diarrhea."

Mory laughed. "H. J. Mitchell is in some of my classes, Chrissy. Do you mind if I call you Chrissy? Friends and enemies call me Mory."

What could I say? No one had ever called me Chrissy. I

wasn't even sure I liked the diminutive, and Mory was much too intense. I had a feeling that he was a human time bomb. If I weren't careful I might set the fuse, and he'd blow up in my face. But my damned mother instincts were working against me. What could I do? All the time he was talking to me, he was lapping me with his eyes and wagging his tail like a stray puppy dog who had found a new friend.

Mory told me that Harry was a typical second-generation HBS student. He had been cloned from his old man who, I must know, was chairman of the board of the Mitchell Companies—a conglomerate that old man Mitchell had put together and one of the top five hundred companies. "I don't know how a clone is in bed," Mory said, "but afterwards he must be pretty dull."

He was grinning at me, obviously trying to determine from my reaction whether I had actually gone to bed with Harry. "Of course, while there's no assurance that the original brains will be replicated, a clone's libido is probably still intact. On the other hand, there's no assurance that H. J. Mitchell's daddy had any brains to begin with. He may be a clone himself that was derived from an advanced computer system."

It was obvious that Mory was quite aware that I dated with Harry Mitchell and was out to destroy him. On my last date with Harry Mitchell, when I told him that I was forsaking all others temporarily for Mory, I got Harry's incredulous summation of Newton Morrow. "Jesus, Christa, don't get involved with that weirdo! He's a complete egomaniac. He'll probably graduate *cum laude* without cracking a book, but he's just a Louisiana hayseed. He insists that people like him are going to pull the throne out from under us unless we roll up the sleeves of the capitalists and help make them workingmen, too. In the New Tomorrow world he's always spouting about, he not only plans to do away with the banks, the life insurance companies, and the stock market, which he says are already outmoded, but he's going to show the workers themselves how they can own all the businesses that are left. When one of the professors told him that he sounded like a lineal descendant of Karl Marx, Morrow told him quite seriously that he was a reincarnation of Edward Bellamy. He was born on the same day that Bellamy had died, and he was intellectually committed to making Bellamy's 'Great Revolution' a reality."

But Harry was too late. Even though I managed to resist Mory for approximately twelve days after that lunch, I knew that I was hooked. I not only enjoyed his mad conversation, but I was entranced that he could harangue me on one wavelength while on another he was telling me subliminally, "Chrissy, Chrissy, I love you."

"You have to understand," Mory responded to my question about androgyny, "that as a little boy, I was imprinted with girls. There were no boys my age in the neighborhood where we lived, and I have three sisters. By the time I was five or six, I had fondled and kissed all my little girlfriends' genitals, and they had kissed and tasted mine. What's more, we knew instinctively that our parents wouldn't like what we were doing—including watching each other pissing and shitting—so we were smart enough not to tell them." Mory laughed. "Occasionally I see those girls now, and they're very grown up, with breasts and everything. A couple of them are in Daddy's Flying Choir, singing sexual hosannas to Jesus. When I remind them of the innocent fun we once had, they look at me, horrified. They have brainwashed themselves. What we did as children never really happened." Mory was smiling, enjoying my eyebrow-raised reaction to his story. "Anyway," he continued, "my sex life ended abruptly long before my teens. A few years ago I went to bed with a girl to whom I was briefly engaged, and in the interim there were a couple of others on a very transient basis, but during the past two years I haven't met a woman who would even know what androgynous meant, let alone ask me why I read such a book—and I'm sure they would think that June Singer means by androgyny some delirious HBS-Avon-Gillette-Revlon world where the men wear perfume or drown themselves in after-shave lotion or dress like women to compete with the females. So I have resigned myself to a world of wet dreams."

I couldn't suppress my surprised grin. Here was a man I had met less than an hour ago who was telling me openly about his sex life. "Most men would deny that they have a strong balancing female component," I told him, "and I suppose most women are afraid to reveal their masculine tendencies. Maybe the truth is that both sexes are a combination of each other."

Mory agreed. "So far as I can determine, no male teaching or attending Harvard or Harvard Business would admit to harboring any female characteristics. If he fails to finish the year without a strong bottom line, a good executive might feel like shedding a few tears, but the directors or stockholders better not catch him wiping his eyes. Competitive business, underwritten by patriarchal biblical codes and modern law, is like cutthroat competitive sports—they're among the last strongholds of male machismo. Only the male who denies his Yin can prove his superiority over the female."

As I listened to Mory ramble on, I felt as if I were being entertained with a shaggy-dog story, or in truth that maybe he had just been released from the psycho ward of some local hospital. Especially when he told me that in 1992, when he would be fifty, he was planning to run for President of the United States. On his second try in 1996, he was sure that he'd be elected. "The future is very exciting, Chrissy," he said. "Some people, like your friend H. J. Mitchell, think I'm a Trojan Horse, or a fifth columnist, who has insinuated himself into Harvard Business. But it's just the opposite. I'm one of the few people alive who has the perspective to save capitalism. The enemies of capitalism are the old-time capitalists themselves. We must create a people's capitalism. The people of the world are approaching a new crossroad. You and I can help them pick the smooth highway instead of the slough of despond."

"How do you know they'll buy your pilgrim's progress?" I asked him sarcastically. Once again I was feeling leery. Sane people may know they're Napoleon, but they don't talk about it. "What party is going to nominate you? You'd scare the shit out of both the Democrats and Republicans."

"I'm going to organize the liberal wing of the dying Republican party, and combine it with the millions of people who are weary of big government. My slogan will be, It's not what you can do for your country, it's what your country *must* do for you." Mory laughed. "Which is to make it possible for everyone to live a full, happy life."

It was obvious that Mory's ego was considerably stronger than mine, but I knew that on a lesser scale, I was driven by the same kind of insane vanity. Mory knew that I had graduated from Radcliffe *magna cum laude* when I was twenty, and that my poetry had been published in *Harper's* and *Vogue*.

"But I finally faced reality," I told him. "I finally realized that I wasn't going to set the world on fire. I'm not going to become a great poet. I'll probably even be a mediocre psychotherapist. If my mother hadn't tried to relive her life through mine, I'd have gone to college, graduated, got married, had children, and been one of the contented of the earth."

Then I told Mory something I never admitted openly to anyone, even the psychiatrist who had taken care of me—and even Grace, who pretended that it really never happened. "In the summer of my junior year, I was pretty screwed up. I was living with my mother, who had been temporarily transferred to New York. She got me a job in the New York office of The Klausner Fund. My friends all lived in the Village or had migrated into loft apartments on Houston Street. Most of them were mediocre artists, actors, or unpublished novelists and poets, but they were so sophisticated, and exuded so much self-confidence, that I felt hopelessly inferior. I bought a ticket on a Greyhound bus for Los Angeles. After an hour or so, I swallowed a dozen sleeping pills. I had emptied my mother's supply. I figured that eventually someone would find me—sleeping permanently." I smiled at Mory through my tears. "That's the missing part of the story that wasn't in the *Globe*. I thought you should know. I'm not really your dream woman."

As he listened to me, Mory had a dreamy, loving look on his face. I wondered if he was suddenly going to come around to my side of the table and try to hug me.

"Many years ago," he said, "I wrote a novel, *Doctor Heidenhoff's Process*. It was about a suicidal woman." Mory's eyes were a twinkling question mark. "You didn't happen to read it, did you?"

I shook my head, vaguely wondering how a man who had spent the past five years either in law school or business school had found time to write a book. I wasn't aware until nearly two weeks later that Mory was coolly telling me that he was a reincarnation of Edward Bellamy, and that the "many years ago" that he had supposedly written this novel were actually nearly a hundred years ago.

"The heroine, Madeline Brand, was very much like you," Mory was saying. "She was the prettiest girl in a small town in western Massachusetts. All the young men wanted to go to bed with her." He laughed. "Since my novel takes place in the nineteenth century, obviously my young men didn't dare evoke this thought. But one young fellow in particular, Henry Burr, was very much in love with Madeline. Madeline thought that he was a little too poky and prosaic. She rejected his advances and ran off to Boston with a very smooth-talking new man in town, Harrison Cordis. Beneath his pleasant exterior, Harrison was a dastardly villain who assured the virgin Madeline, if she went to bed with him, he most certainly would marry her, and make her a respectable woman.

"Poor Henry. Even though Madeline had run off with Harrison, he still loved her. In a few years he became very wealthy, but he was still obsessed with Madeline. Madeline's mother told him that Madeline had been seen in Boston, and Henry went in search of her. A few weeks later, he discovered her living alone in a boarding house, contemplating suicide. Although she isn't pregnant, Harrison has taken her virginity and she is a ruined woman. Even if Henry is willing to forgive her, which he is, she can't wipe out the memories of her sinful past. She can't marry Henry because she is no longer the virgin bride that he deserves.

"At this point in the story," Mory went on, "I invented electric-shock treatment. I introduced Doctor Gustave Heidenhoff's process, which was a galvanic shock treatment to obliterate certain memories. Doctor Heidenhoff proposed that eventually the mental physician would be able to extract a specific recollection from the memory, just as one pulls a tooth. He solved Macbeth's question, 'Canst thou not minister to a mind diseased; pluck from the memory a rooted sorrow; raise out the written troubles of the brain?' "

Listening to Mory, a little exasperated, wondering what all this nonsense had to do with me, I shrugged. "Doctor Heidenhoff's process won't work with me. I'm not a virgin, and I don't have any guilt over my sexual sins."

"Nevertheless," Mory said, "it's your memories—memories from a previous life you have lived, a theory being explored by some therapists who believe in reincarnation, and early imprinting by the person you were in a previous life—their image of something you were supposed to be, or accomplish, and haven't, that has made you suicidal."

Mory went on, "Dr. Heidenhoff also points out, 'I break for the weak the chain of memory which holds them to the past; stronger souls are independent of me. They can unloose the iron links and free themselves. Would that more had the need for wisdom and strength, thus serenely to put their past behind them, leaving the dead to bury their dead, and go blithely forward, taking each new day as a life by itself, and reckoning themselves daily newborn even as verily they are!' "

"All right," I said, wondering what devious thoughts in Mory's brain were motivating this conversation, and if he really believed what he had said about reincarnation. "I under-

63

stand Doctor Heidenhoff's process. I'm more interested in what happened to Madeline. Did she live happily ever after with Henry?"

Mory shook his head sadly. "Unfortunately, when I wrote the book, I was more cowardly than I am now. Doctor Heidenhoff's process was actually Henry's dream. Before Henry got a chance to convince Madeline of his merits, she sent him a note. 'I do truly love you,' she wrote, 'but I could not be happy with you, for my happiness would be a shame to the end.' Madeline killed herself."

Mory reached across the table and touched my hand. "That's why I almost telephoned you, Chrissy. I wanted to tell you to stop imitating Sylvia Plath or Anne Sexton. I wanted to tell you that you could be better than they were. You could be anything you wanted to be. You didn't have to commit suicide to become famous. What good would fame do you when you were dead?"

I stared at him angrily. "I don't know if I like you."

We had finished lunch. Mory was still sipping his Zinfandel.

"I'm being honest," he said. "Your poetry is morbid. It's filled with death allusions. Your short stories tell me more about the other side of you—a bright, laughing Chrissy." Smiling, telling me that he had a photographic mind, he suddenly quoted from a short story I'd had published in the *New Yorker* a year before. " 'The whole of me wonders at my body. It has outgrown my brain. I'm liquid sexual Jell-o trying to find the mold of a man to flow into. I'm a trembling leaf. I'm a wind-tossed daisy. Rich color communities saturate my brain. I'm a sacred tree. I'm worshiping myself at some ancient Asherah. It's June, and I'm the summers that used to be. Wind, sky, clouds, the beginning of catalpa blossoms, are liberating my mind from an earth-bound, seed-filled, hungry-to-mate body. My mind is unhitched from its anchors. Soon, maybe I'll sail into the night . . . but then, last night I dreamed that I threw my cat out of the window. It was only a seven-foot drop, but the conscious act was shrouded with malevolence. . . . I live in a world of unfinished prospects. I have a laissez-faire mind.' "

As Mory was quoting from my story, I knew that here in this restaurant, separated by the table, he was actually making love to me. "You see, Chrissy," he said, "you didn't know it when you wrote that, but you were inside my mind, too. The only difference between us is that I'm not sailing into the night. I know where I'm going. But I can't get there alone, either."

But I wasn't too happy with Mory's reaction to my poetry. I picked up Diane Ippolito's *Erotica* and flipped the pages. I had read these love poems before, a little shocked, knowing, then at least, that I could never have written such blatantly sexual poetry. Not only would Grace have read any poems I had published, but up to this point, in my twenty-fourth year, I had never, even in bed with any of the men I had known, been able to evoke my sexual feelings or needs, let alone write them on paper.

Determined not to let Mory overwhelm me, I told him if he was going home to masturbate while he was reading Diane's poems, he might as well hear a woman read them to him. It was three-thirty on a bleak rainy afternoon and the restaurant was long deserted. Jennifer had told me that she wouldn't be home until seven or eight. I could have invited Mory back to our apartment, but not only didn't I dare, but I was a little angry with him. Spurred on by the Zinfandel, I picked up *Erotica* and skip-read it to him across the table in my most sultry voice.

" 'You press both hands to my inner thighs/ then let them rise to my throbbing cunt/ the musk of your sweat/ your semen mingle and intoxicate/ I am blood/ I am the first moment of breath/ Rocking your movements to mine/ I hold your penis still/ Moving my cunt over it/ letting the juices come/ I am astride pouring my cunt over you/ shaping myself to your undulation/ Before we are done, I will know you dancing to my body/ caught under but joyously bearing/ Before we are done I will know you like heady woodsmoke/ Lowering again close over you/ I soak your penis/ you tap/ press/ tap quietly at my nipples/ you yield to me/ form under me/ and I carry you like a ripple/ and now I love to play/ knowing that the spasm is only a breath away/ knowing that I have no power, nor do you/ There is only this game/ a thrusting into air as children/ do in swings/ resting their grip/ testing the desire to rejoin space/ testing the love of earth/ which pulls us just as/ dangerously close to the edge.' "

I looked at Mory, and I blushed. This was crazy poetry to be reading to a stranger in the middle of the afternoon in Harvard Square. Mory touched my hand, and there were tears in his eyes. "Chrissy," he said. "I need to test the love of earth—and be a child with you. Do you dare?"

———◆———

Mory began his campaign to achieve "the very necessary blending with Chrissy" with a daily morning and evening telephone call. The Friday morning after our luncheon, the telephone rang at seven-thirty. Jenny answered on her bedroom extension. I picked up the phone and listened groggily after I heard her yell that it was for me.

"Wake-up call, Chrissy." Mory sounded unbearably cheerful. "I love you. I talked to you all night, but you didn't answer. It was very lonesome."

Despite my insistence that I hadn't answered him last night because I hadn't given him a second thought, I hadn't even told Jenny about him; despite my furious "This is a hell of a time to telephone anyone," or my calmer, "Thank you for a nice luncheon, Mory, I really enjoyed it, but I'm going to be very busy right through the holidays, and there is really no time in my life for Newton Morrow. Why don't you just accept it? We are ships that passed in the afternoon"—it was no use. Despite every weapon I could muster, Mory persisted.

Even though I tried to convince him that my head was never on straight in the morning (he finally delayed his morning calls until eight-thirty), and that in the evenings he was interrupting my work on my doctoral thesis, Mory simply ignored my cold brush-off.

"We're the missing half of each other, Chrissy. I'm sure of it. It's not just genital. My brain is in love with your brain."

"If you love my brain," I told him, "stop jarring it. It was a very peaceful, cud-chewing cow brain until it met you." Of course, that wasn't true, and it was just the kind of talk Mory loved. The only sound way to escape him was not to respond to him at all.

Finally, when I refused to answer the telephone, Mory enlisted Jennifer's aid, and she soon became his enthusiastic supporter. "I don't know what your Mory looks like, but he's not only delightfully batty, he's a charmer on the telephone."

She laughed. "He tells me that he's a reincarnation of Edward Bellamy, who wrote *Looking Backward*."

"He tells everybody that," I groaned. "Maybe he is, beard and all."

"He thinks that as a future lawyer, I should read Bellamy's

66

Equality—and so should you. Since it's out of print, he made two Xerox copies and asked if he could bring them over tomorrow. Who the hell is Edward Bellamy?"

I shook my head violently. "If he comes, he's all yours. If he ever gets inside the door, he'll never leave. Bellamy was a writer who lived in Boston. Some critics thought that he was the lineal descendant of Nathaniel Hawthorne. Bellamy died about seventy years ago. In addition to *Looking Backward*, a Utopian novel about the United States in the year 2000, he wrote among other things a sequel to it called *Equality*. Mory says that it is a much better book than *Looking Backward*. I've never read it. Mory not only believes that he's the spiritual descendant of Bellamy, but he told me that he has only a quarter of a century left. He says that before he's fifty-five he's destined to be President—not of the United States but of the United People of America. Single-handed, Mory is going to initiate Bellamy's Great Revolution—if they haven't confined him in a nuthouse before that."

But before two weeks had passed—during which Jenny shared Mory's calls with me via our separate bedroom extension phones (we'd had them installed so that we could monitor the lies we told our male friends and their reactions to them)—I knew I was slowly capitulating. I was intrigued by Mory's belief in reincarnation and the futility of suicide. Mory insisted that killing myself wouldn't solve my problems. He told me that unless I went all out and achieved Brahma in this lifetime, my fate, like that of all humans, was to be reborn again endlessly until I made up my mind to find Nirvana.

"We can do it together, Chrissy and Jennifer," he told us, "in this lifetime—and we'll never have to be born again!"

Neither Jenny nor I could tell when Mory was serious, or whether he was just playing with one of the weird mutations that were forever tumbling out of his brain.

"Our present incarnation is a giant step in the right direction," he said. "While neither of you has yet discovered who you were in your previous life, you should understand how and why Edward Bellamy has subsumed me. In the nineteenth century he transformed his life energy in words which were preserved on the printed page. Like seeds looking for a place to germinate, they floated around for a half century. Just as the existence of human beings on this earth, given the necessary chemical environment, was a statistical certainty—just as the energy which combined to make you and me (and the billions of those who are alive now, or who lived and died

67

before we were born and have been continuously transformed back and forth between matter and energy)—just as that energy will be the fundamental essence in the universe even after all human beings have disappeared from this planet—so, the energy that was Edward Bellamy, against seemingly impossible odds, found the neurons that comprise the brain of Newton Morrow and was born again."

Sitting on the edge of my bed, I could watch Jenny across the hall listening and shaking her head in wonder and amusement as Mory expounded his theory of death and rebirth. "What does Daddy Morrow think of your ideas?" she asked him.

"Oh, he agrees. Absolutely." Mory laughed. "Jesus saves—because, if you'll let him, he, too, is endlessly reincarnated in you."

After that phone conversation, when Mory finally agreed to stop talking—we all had to study some of the time—Jenny was laughing hysterically. "Sister Christina"—she touched my hand as if I were a novitiate—"I'm going up to North Conway for the weekend with Jerry Miner. I think you'd better give up. Invite Brother Jesus Bellamy for the weekend. You're absolutely safe. He'll talk you into an orgasm without even touching you. What's more, he may be able to give you saner perspectives on life than either Freud or Jung."

I had a date with Harry Mitchell on Saturday, but Friday night I was free. Mory walked the nearly three miles from Business School through a November blizzard to our third-floor walkup on Sheppard Street. A shaggy, brown-haired, bearded snowman with fiery brown eyes greeted me when I opened the door. Shivering for him and for myself, I toweled his head dry while he unloaded the tote bag he was carrying.

"Here's a jug of Chianti to mellow us," he said, handing me a half-gallon bottle. "The records are recordings of Bob Harrington, the Chaplain of Bourbon Street; Daddy Morrow; and Jack Van Impe. They're all crusaders for Christ. I thought you might like to compare their various styles. This stack of four hundred and twelve pages is a Xerox copy of Bellamy's book *Equality* that a clerk friend of mine who works in the mines of 'B' School ripped off their copier for me. For contrast, here's a couple of books on the Federal Reserve—this one denouncing the Federal Reserve System's manipulation of our money supply would have delighted me when I was Bellamy—the other book is simply a history of banking." Mory's eyes were searching the apartment. "I'll put

68

them both in the bathroom next to the toilet. I have an exam on world monetary policy on Monday. But the most time I plan to allot to these books is a fifteen-minute Saturday or Sunday morning flip-through when I'm taking a crap."

I stared at him crossly. Spending an evening listening to evangelists quoting biblical chapter and verse or screaming about Jesus, or listening to Mory read Bellamy's book, which was probably so out of date that no one had bothered to reprint it, didn't jibe with the erotic candlelit, soft-music environment I hoped I had created.

"I didn't invite you for the weekend," I said. "I told you very emphatically that if you wanted to share spaghetti and meatballs with me, you were welcome. I told you that you'd have to leave early. I have a lot of reading and studying of my own to do tomorrow."

"I remember." Mory was staring down at me like a jolly giant who was wondering if I were edible. "But it's a terrible night outside. I'm hoping that you'll change your mind. I promise, if you'll let me sleep in your bed with you, even though I most certainly will have a big erection, I won't try to make love to you."

Mory opened his bottle of wine and poured us each a glass. "I brought over a magazine that I borrowed from Bud Jamison, my roommate. I wanted to show it to you. It's filled with naked women." He grinned at me ruefully. "You might as well know the truth, Chrissy. The only woman I was ever in love with didn't really enjoy sex. I remember once when I asked Rose Anne to let me look between her legs—maybe even let me kiss her a little—she thought I was quite perverted." Mory shrugged. "You probably know a lot more about men than I do about women. They have a name for guys like your Harry Mitchell and that fellow you date at Law School, but I wouldn't want to tell it to you."

"I probably know the word you're thinking," I said bluntly. "Cocksman." I said the word coolly, determined to shock Mory. I wanted to convince him that I wasn't predestined to be his First Lady.

Mory looked as if he might burst into tears. I got the impression that the Chrissy he had created in his mind was a virgin, or that at the very least he hoped that I wasn't too sexually experienced. I wondered how he expected me to react to the pictures in the magazine. Did he think they would excite me, and make me an easy conquest?

Determined to cool him off—and certain that after I had

fed him I'd find some way to give him a hurried exit—I decided to be as blunt as these inanimate women in his pictures would have been if he had ever met them. "As I've already told you, I'm not a virgin," I said. "I've done just about everything you'll see in those magazines with more than one guy. It was really a big bore." I was exaggerating my sexual know-how considerably, of course, but I was sure that Mory would have been surprised and shocked even by a truthful report of my dispassionate sexual life before I knew him.

"I guess the truth is that I'm undersexed," I said. "I've never admitted it to any guy before, but I've never had an orgasm." I paused. "But don't get any ideas. I'm not interested. I've had guys work on me all night and nothing happens."

I was of two minds as I spoke. I wanted to frighten Mory away, and I wanted to convince him that I was a typically pragmatic woman. I wanted him to think I was as uninterested in the male sex drive as a street prostitute in the Combat Zone. At the same time, somehow I was wondering and hoping that he might pierce through the stripped-down, sexually mechanical world that I was beginning to believe was the nature of things.

To my surprise, Mory understood. "I feel sorry for the women who pose for these pictures, Chrissy," he said. Sitting beside me, he turned the glossy full-color pages of the magazine. A very pretty naked woman in her twenties was posed on her knees with her buttocks in the air. The photographer couldn't have been 6 feet away from her behind. The face of a man protruded between her legs. His tongue was on her labia. She was completely exposed and vulnerable. In another picture, her ass and the tiny hairs clustering around her clean pink asshole and growing in profusion around her labia were nearly life-size. In another picture, she was lying on her back, holding her vulva open with her fingers. She smiled, open-mouthed and vacantly, at the camera. Her breasts were a soft cascade on her chest. In other pictures, she was holding and sucking a guy's penis.

Mory shook his head. "I suppose for most guys, me included—and for boys in their early teens who have never seen a woman naked, and wouldn't dare to ask a woman to show herself like this—these pictures serve some purpose. If the guy wasn't there between her legs, they might be considered anatomical. But what bothers me is what's in the minds of the man who took these pictures or the publisher who produced the magazine or the guys who buy it and look

70

at them. They all seem determined to make the ineffable mystery of the female so commonplace that she's comparable to an inanimate carcass hanging on a meathook in cold storage.

"Don't get me wrong," Mory added. "I don't object to photographing the female and the male naked—but I get angry at the stupidity of the people, men in particular, who simply turn females into cunts, things they shove their pricks into. Humans become objects with whom one never experiences the tear-blinding realization that this is a total woman, this is a total man, and that he and she, with their absolutely lovely genitals, the means through which they can blend themselves with each other's body, are such a miracle that I want to kneel down and pray and put my face against the female's genitals. I want to kiss them, and thank God for this amazement. My objection to these pictures is my objection to a dehumanized world where television and the shadows on the tubes and the color-separated dots have replaced the warmblooded reality."

I couldn't help it. Suddenly I knew that I loved Mory, too. And I was so carried away with him that after a second glass of wine, my hunger assuaged with the cheddar cheese and crackers I had served, I doubted if Mory was ever going to get the spaghetti and meatballs.

He was grinning at me, but there were tears in his eyes. "What I can't understand, Chrissy, is not that you've screwed with guys like Mitchell—but how you could spend entire evenings with them. Maybe it's because I'm a few years older than a lot of the future captains of industry at 'B' School, but Bud Jamison, my roommate, buys five or six of these beaver magazines a month. He's engaged to a girl who's in her last year in Wellesley, but I have a feeling that she isn't anywhere near as real or as intrinsic to Bud's life as the mergers and acquisitions, or the intricacies of financial statements, and, of course, ultimately, bottom-line profits. You marry a guy like Bud or Harry, Chrissy, and you're going to be mighty damn lonesome. The only thing they'll ever read a few years from now are their own interdepartmental memos and the stock-market page of the *Wall Street Journal*."

I was smiling, and I wasn't pulling my hand away from Mory, who was playing with my fingers as he talked, but I couldn't help teasing him. "You think all my friends are bottom-line freaks," I said, "but when I told them about you, they cracked up. They think Daddy Morrow has the best racket of all, saving people for Jesus. Completely tax-deducti-

71

ble. Marching them down the sawdust trail with his hands in their pockets, your daddy lives as high off the hog as the president of General Motors. You told me that your daddy has his own airplane. How did he get that?" I chuckled. "I'll bet your daddy doesn't feel all sad and quivery inside when he sees a naked woman with her ass in the air. After he's finished shoving his thing into her, he probably feels very penitent and wants to tar and feather her."

As I should have known, Mory was exhilarated by verbal conflict. "Sugar pie," he said, "I'm not singing any hosannas for my daddy, either. You're right, he may not earn as much as the president of General Motors, but he makes as much as the President of the United States. The problem is that my daddy has a capitalist mentality, too. Daddy Morrow talking up a Jesus storm, or praising the Lord who isn't paying any attention to him or the problems of the world, is equivalent to Buddy Jamison's daddy, who cures people's arthritic and sexual problems with *Nori*, iron spelled backwards, or helps them escape into a dream world with *Nitey-Night* tranquilizer pills. Together, hundreds of thousands of these kind of daddies, who dominate America, create the kind of society where women become sexual objects, and grit their teeth and stick their behinds in the air, or dance nude in smoke-filled, liquor-saturated barrooms because they are still slaves to the money economy that these Big Daddies control. I told my daddy that one day someone who really loves women, and doesn't worry so much about Jesus, is going to come along and free the slaves."

Mory stopped talking for a second and stared at the red wine in his glass, conjuring up worlds that he was not able to communicate to me. Finally he said, "You can help me, Chrissy. We'll praise the Lord and pass the love ammunition. We'll erase both my daddy's kind of world and Buddy's daddy's kind of world from human consciousness. Loving men and women, caring men and women, men and women who are taught how to really like each other and enjoy each other—men and women who have learned that their sexual yearnings, their genetic need for each other's flesh, is the true center of their lives—are the kind of people who will finally dare to open up their arms and, unafraid for the first time in their human history, embrace each other and accept each other for what they are."

Mory smiled at me sadly. "I guess you know, Chrissy, that

72

I'm making love to you the only way I know how—with words."

I couldn't help it, I kissed his cheek. "There's worse ways," I whispered.

He kissed me, and I shivered. I didn't know whether I liked his soft, hairy feel or not. Most Harvard Businessmen wore their hair short, and shaved. Once again, with the amazing empathy that always existed between us, he guessed my thoughts. "You don't like my beard," he said with a big grin. "When I was Edward Bellamy, back in the late nineteenth century, I wore a beard."

I knew that he was probably teasing me to go into details on his previous life, but I ignored the challenge. "Edward Bellamy didn't plan to be President. The last bearded President was Benjamin Harrison."

Mory was laughing. "You're absolutely right, Chrissy. In my present incarnation as Newton Morrow I haven't kept up with the changing manners of the twentieth century. What's more, I've been denying both my and Bellamy's androgynous nature."

I wasn't sure that I understood what Mory meant, but over my protests he insisted that I find scissors and a razor. Tears running down my cheeks, I told him that I was sorry, I really didn't mind his beard, and if it was Bellamy's beard I couldn't cut it for him, anyway. He finally wrested the scissors from my grasp and I watched him while he hacked his fur away. He told me that he needed me for his mentor. Obviously, since it wouldn't be long before women were contending for the presidency of the United States, he couldn't go around looking like a male gorilla. It was time that he stopped hiding his female component behind a beard and let his dual nature shine through.

Finally, since the damage he had done was irreparable, I helped him trim the forest down so that it was shaveable. As I watched him before the bathroom mirror, stripped to the waist, his clean face and chin suddenly became so young and vulnerable I wanted to hug him.

"You've been hiding the wide-eyed boy behind a mask," I told him.

"Living in a jungle with tigers and lions, I felt safer if I looked ferocious, too," he said. "Now that everyone can see the naked truth, I'll probably lose presidential credibility. You might as well know the rest. I'm a sexual mess. I can't just screw with a woman and walk away." Mory laughed at my

73

confused expression. "Oh, don't worry—I'm not a homosexual. I don't mean 'can't,' I mean I haven't—because I don't want to. You see, Chrissy, I believe that sexual intercourse is just one aspect of a total mutual mental surrender. Unfortunately, I can only do that with a mental equal."

"Thanks for the compliment," I said. "You're probably deluding yourself. How do you know, even if you make that surrender with someone like me, I won't eventually, in the words of that song, 'Walk all over you'?" There were tears in my eyes. "I guess what I'm trying to tell you is that I'd be afraid to come on mentally naked with any man. I'm sure he'd end up thinking I was a prime candidate for psychiatric treatment."

We were back in the living room drinking a third glass of wine. I knew I should be heating up the spaghetti and meatballs, but neither of us seemed to want the interruption of food. I knew this was prelude. Mory was sexually starved, and for the first time in my life I really wanted a man to take me in his arms.

Not actually believing I could do it, wondering if Mory was going to read Bellamy's *Equality* to me all night, I finally made the overtures. Kissing Mory's lovely clean cheeks, wanting to press his face against my breasts, I told him that I guessed I owed him something for sacrificing his hirsute manliness to my whim. My lips were suddenly all over his face and chest and stomach. I slipped my hand under his belt and held his big penis, and I whispered, "Let me ride on your joy stick to oblivion."

Amused by my simile for his penis, Mory struggled out of his pants. I told him that I had read the words in a porno novel, and that his penis pointing in the air really did seem like a very happy fellow.

"Help me wash him," Mory said.

Naked in the bathtub shower, we knelt and soaped each other's genitals and each other's behind and asshole, and we kissed and laughingly admired the soapy wetness of each other's nether parts.

Amazingly, Mory was right. He had a female sense that paralleled mine. Naked in my bed, we were each other's hungry child. Searching his body with my lips and tongue, I was sobbing my joy at the fragility of my lover's body. I counted his bones, laved his belly and pubic hair and testicles with my tongue. And he curled into me like a friendly caterpillar, his mouth tenderly searching my delta, his tongue sliding over my labia, and perineum and tickling my rosebud with a delicate affection that was close to adoration.

For the first time, I really wanted an erect penis in my mouth, and I discovered that it was warm and independently animate on my lips and in my throat. And while I knew that Mory couldn't withstand this loving assault, I couldn't stop. Gasping how sorry he was that he couldn't last, he overflowed. Laughing, I was aiming his milky white stuff at my mouth and lips and breasts so that I could taste it, and it kept shooting over my eyes and cheeks. And then I tumbled on top of him so that he could share his warm soup, which was in my mouth and on my lips, with me. His penis was still so hard that it was slithering inside me, and then I was riding it, screaming, sobbing, ecstatic with the realization that I really could reach an orgasm.

Gasping in his arms, reveling in my *petite mort*, I felt Mory kissing my neck, and his fingers, like erotic feathers, brushing across my buttocks. Finally, gently parting the cleft of my behind, he laughed and tickled my rosebud, and he asked me if I was anally erotic. Obviously, I was without ever having been aware of it before, because his fingers on my anus were making me excited again.

"Damn!" he said, as his penis slid out of me. "If I were a yoga, I'd teach my silly prick to obey me. He really wants to stay inside you forever."

"Don't worry." I smiled at him. "I really like him little. Now he's in my power." To prove it, I lifted his sweet, limp weenie. Remembering the pictures in the magazine that Mory had brought with him, I turned north to his south. Before I took his deflated penis in my mouth, I told him, giggling, "I'm not competing with those women in the magazine, but now you can see the 'me' that no one in the world has ever seen before. I'm probably not very pretty this way, but what you see is all yours, very much alive, and probably pretty ugly."

But Mory disagreed. He could see my dangling breasts, and he described me for me. "Such perfect skin—not a blemish," he said. "God, Chrissy, you're Grecian-statue perfect."

"You missed the mole under my breast."

"No, I didn't. I kissed it a minute ago," he said. "Oh, Chrissy, you have such a strong, firm behind. You're just as pretty going as coming! Your sweet, soft bush, the very pretty lips of your vagina, your clean, wrinkled asshole, all have a warm, ethereal look." He buried his face in my flesh, and I heard him chuckle. "Altogether, they're saying, Kiss me, kiss me, kiss me! Never stop!"

I could feel his tongue slowly tracing circles around my labia and moving very close to my anus. Gasping, I was unable to continue my deliberate up-and-down encirclement of his penis, which once again was slowly gaining strength and beginning to stand alone.

"I read in one of those porno novels about what you're doing. It's really terrible, Mory. You'd better stop!"

"I can't." Mory sighed. "I'm a suppliant at the altar of love. I'm becoming you. Chrissy, you have a most lovely body."

His tongue traced the entire length of my vulva and rosebud. "If my daddy really understood religion"—Mory's voice was muffled by my flesh—"he'd know how close to God I am now. This is much more sensible than eating the bread and drinking the wine. Kissing you, I am you. Kissing me, you are me. The actual and symbolical taking of each other's flesh is a joyous way of giving each other temporary possession. It's totemic magic. By tasting each other's body, we become each other and whatever God may be."

Now I was only partially hunched over his face, comfortably lapping the length of his penis. "What you're doing is called a rim job. I read it in one of those books." I giggled. "I never knew that I was actually an anal-erotic character, too."

I twisted slowly out of his embrace of my behind and kissed him from his navel to his mouth.

"I know what you were thinking," he said suddenly. "It's as though your mind spoke to me even though your lips and tongue didn't move."

"What was I thinking?" I demanded.

"You think it's terrible that you let me kiss your behind, and you're wondering if it tastes terrible in Mory's mouth."

Not knowing what to say, I grinned at him. "Maybe it isn't sanitary?" I finally whispered. "Doctors tell you that you can spread germs from one place to another. Women always wipe front to back."

Mory's penis was inside me again. "Honey, I never kissed a woman's behind before," he said, "but an hour or so ago, I just washed your rosebud. Anyway, I couldn't help it, I love all of you."

I was floating again. Pierced by Mory's penis, I couldn't believe it, but once again I was on the verge of a climax.

What had happened to the cold, sexually detached Christina North? How could I let myself be so helpless, so needful? Why was I so suddenly secure that I dared to surrender myself over and over again to this man who was almost a stranger?

Oh, God, I really loved this crazy guy. "Do you want me to kiss your rosebud, too?" I asked him. "I will! I want to! Do you want to stick your big prick in my ass? If you want to, you can. Honey, honey, honey, I'm yours. Even if you're Edward Bellamy, I'm yours! Whatever you are or want to be—even if it's a silly damned President—I am!"

"Rosebuds are for kissing, not fucking," Mory said. "All I want to do is to stay happily lost in your vagina for the rest of my life . . . or at least until we fall asleep."

"Don't you want my spaghetti and meatballs?"

Mory shook his head. "No—I'll have a light breakfast, after which, still inside you, I'll spend tomorrow with you in bed. When I finally have to come out Monday morning—since I can't detach my penis and leave him inside of you permanently—you'll probably be so numb you'll think he's still there."

"Of course, this is totally an illusion," I told him. "It works now because I'm twenty-three and you're twenty-eight. We find each other's lean, tight-assed, flat-stomached bodies very erotic. You certainly wouldn't want to kiss my mother's behind. Her ass is soft and flabby and vastly overfed. If you stuck your face in Grace's rump, it would disappear."

"You're absolutely right!" Mory was captivated by my hilarity. "And that's something else we must do. When I'm President and you're First Lady, we're really going to liberate women—from overeating, too."

———◆———

After that night, except for an occasional visit to remind his roommate that he was still alive, Mory in effect moved out of his room at Harvard Business and lived with me and Jenny in our two-bedroom apartment.

Jenny was intrigued with Mory, too. When he finally became our regular breakfast and supper companion, she discovered that among a thousand other crazy ideas that he was always casually dropping here and there was the plank in the platform of his future political party. It was going to be a populist party, which Mory said would elect him President. The plank, only one of many other inflammatory planks, would demand a complete rewrite of the Constitution, which the United People would then adopt. There would be no more states in the United States, since Mory was going to do away with the inefficiency of them, too.

Jennifer was studying constitutional law, and her biggest dream was that when she graduated from law school she would get a job in the offices of one of the Supreme Court justices. While she agreed with Mory that the Constitution might be outmoded, she disagreed with him vehemently on the necessity to rewrite it. According to Jenny, the myth of its infallibility was the only glue that held the country together. She got involved in such extended arguments with Mory that occasionally she ended up in bed with us. Still unable to shake the defenses of the imperturbable *"Presidente,"* giggling, we all made love together.

While it was a few months before I shared Mory with Jenny, for some reason whenever we made love together it was never orgiastic. Mory told us that it even reminded him of himself when he was five years old. Once again he was playing naked with little girls and they were playing with him. I was never seriously jealous of Mory and Jenny. It wasn't only Mory's assurance that I was his First Lady, but I was certain that it was true. And Jenny and I agreed that while Mory might not appeal to most women, he exerted a magnetic attraction on females like us. Was it because he was so totally sexually naïve? A throwback to a generation of men who enjoyed women? Partially, I suppose. But it was more than his obvious joy and wonder, and even a kind of awe-struck delight with our bodies—Mory actually enjoyed the female mind, and ours in particular. Since I loved Jenny's brains, too, how could I deny her—or him—the other's genitals?

Lying in my bed, we encompassed the world and time. "You and Jenny are much more practical than I am," Mory told us. "I don't believe that women are necessarily more pragmatic than men, but over the centuries of male domination the male has forced the female to face reality. Foolish men—chasing rainbows, fighting wars, playing Icarus roles and flying too close to the sun—have never fully understood that the continuous first order of genetic priorities is to escape from our island selves and merge with each other. The only way any man or woman can do that is male to female, female to male—knowing, sensing, caring, feeling, and learning how to simultaneously blend into each other's flesh and mind.

"Only when we teach a whole generation," Mory told us, "how to enjoy a continuous flesh wonder toward each other, and all that implies, will we become fully human. Millions of men and women now alive, and billions not yet born, are ready, or will be ready, to climb to a whole new level of human consciousness."

Because loving Mory meant loving Edward Bellamy, in self-defense, I reread *Looking Backward,* discovered *Equality,* and became fascinated with the excerpts from Bellamy's unpublished notebooks in Arthur Morgan's biography of him.

Although Mory could never be pinned down as to whether his beliefs in reincarnation were literal or figurative, and he vacillated between personal rebirth and a Buddhist conception of a continuous life and death, he often coolly referred to Bellamy's ideas and books as if he personally had been intimately involved with them, and was now, in this incarnation, being given a second chance to bring them to fruition.

In my triadic relationship with a live man and his former spirit, I couldn't help being intrigued by Bellamy's, Mory's, and my need to express our unique worth. In his journal of his twenty-second year, Bellamy expressed, as he would many times in his life, his continuing sense of failure: "Yes, I am indeed sorely weary and sick at heart. I am not what I counted myself. I had thought myself to be something greater than other men, and find that I am but after all a mediocre person. Well, then, I'm weary and could wish to die, for good and all and over with it." As I read these words, shivery with identification goose pimples, I wondered if some weird fate had brought Mory and me and Bellamy together, or if Mory and I were a total reincarnation incorporating Bellamy between us.

I asked Mory, if he were really Bellamy, why this time around he was so self-confident.

Mory only laughed. "I didn't believe that when I wrote it—and neither should you. When you think that way, it's just self-pity at not being recognized by your fellowmen. This time around I have more patience. The die is cast. I have twenty-four years left to turn my social theories, which everyone said were Utopian when I wrote them a hundred years ago, into reality."

Jenny kept warning me that Mory was a cross between a loving evangelist and a slick carnival hipster, and I'd better be careful, or I'd be seduced by my own Bellamy-Morrow daydream. I was creating my own metamorphosis that transformed them both into gods. The way I was reacting, I'd end up in Mory's personal sideshow attraction. "See the Liquid Lady—transformed into jelly by love."

I knew that Jenny's sarcasm was tinged with admiration. It was obvious that Mory had infiltrated her defenses, too. When I told her that if Mory became a nuisance I'd meet him some other place, and it wasn't fair because she never brought any of her male friends back to the apartment and to her bedroom, Jenny just shook her head.

"Bringing a guy here and involving him in my private life, is a commitment that I don't want to make yet. Mory is your red wagon. But I'd miss not finding him here, sprawled on the sofa, or tripping over the books he always is lugging and strewing all over the floor, or trying to inveigle you or me to read."

It amused Jenny to retaliate at Mory's invasion of our privacy by wandering into the bathroom when he was taking a piss, or sitting on the edge of the bathtub, engaging him in a conversation on some legal problem that she was studying, while he was sitting on the toilet, his jeans around his legs. Mory, not embarrassed a bit, became the prosecution or defense attorney as the case demanded.

"To be honest," Jenny told me, "I'm enjoying our triad. Even though it irritates Jerry Miner when he thinks I may be sharing your southern cracker, I refuse to turn the apartment into a ménage à quatre."

I guess that I could write a book about my joyous, laughing, loving, mind-boggling months with Mory, but my perspective would be repetitious. I'd be trying to recapture over and over again the bubbling sublimity (a contradiction in words? No, definitely not!) of our moments together. And always interlaced with our silliness and sheer hilarity, and our enjoyment of the lovely mystery of our flesh commingling, was the impact of Mory's probing mind. We were twin maniacs surrounded by the spirit of Bellamy. Mory, intent on assimilating all knowledge so that when the time was appropriate he would be ready to be President; and I, still convinced that the more I knew the more likely that one day I would write the perfect story or poem, or find a key to the inner reaches of the human mind that surpassed Freud's or Jung's—and, of course, in the process, I'd be applauded by an adoring world. What did it all matter? I couldn't face that question or really answer it.

———◆———

I wonder again if the reality of the world has finally whipped Mory into line, or worse, if like me, he has totally given up. What would he think if he knew his Chrissy cared so little about what happened to her that while she was writing her autobiography—a fare-thee-well world—two mad scientists, Convita and Lebenthal, were planning her New Tomorrows in another century. I suppose that in the past years I could have easily found Mory. But then I married Karl and Mory was a closed book that I was afraid to open again.

Lying naked on the marsh grass where we had made love so many years before, I remember one of our afternoons together. While my seminar schedules were erratic, and I was spending most of my time working on my doctoral thesis, I usually returned to the apartment by three-thirty. Mory was often there before me, or he would arrive within an hour. If Jenny hadn't come home, we'd often lie down in my bed, and more often than not our never-ceasing conversation, while we kissed and touched to emphasize our ideas, would become an aphrodisiac, and we'd make love for the second time that day.

But one afternoon in May I opened the door and found Mory standing stark-naked on the four-foot-in-diameter oak coffee table that Jenny and I had found in a second-hand store and had cut down to coffee-table height. His penis was pointing at Jenny who, sitting on the sofa, was listening to him. She was wearing panties but nothing else. Laughing at my surprise, she invited me to join Brother Mory's prayer meeting.

Mory wasn't a bit embarrassed. "Welcome, Sister Chrissy," he said, ignoring my what-the-hell-are-you-two-doing expression. "You're just in time for our talk about Jesus, brotherhood, Solidarity—as I used to call it in the nineteenth century—and the Cons-tit-tution of the United States."

I managed to suppress a nasty flare of jealousy. While Jenny and I had tumbled together naked with him in my bed, our lovemaking had had a silly kind of spontaneity. Now, I suddenly wondered if I could ever tolerate Jenny having Mory all to herself.

"Remove your blouse and bra, Sister Chrissy, make yourself comfortable. Let your tits experience this warm spring air while I dedicate them to Jesus. After I'm elected President, and we are sleeping together in the White House, Sister Chrissy, the first order of business will be to present the people of America with a new Cons-tit-tution, which will not only improve our daily lives, but will help us achieve the brotherhood and sisterhood that has escaped us for millenniums, and would have made us all much more loving and better in bed with each other."

"Don't lose your cool." Jenny grinned at me. "I've got a date with Jerry later," she explained. "I was having a quick nap when I heard Mory arriving. He was talking to himself. I heard him in the shower, declaiming against the madness of the world, and then he was haranguing his image in the mirror while he shaved. Since he was evidently rehearsing his presidential campaign speech, I told him that I'd be happy to be his audience."

"How did he get that?" I pointed at Mory's semi-erection, which was once again elevating slightly as he realized that he would shortly have an enthralled audience of *two* almost-naked female acolytes.

Jennifer laughed. "When he talks about the Cons-tit-tution, Brother Morrow becomes a very erotic man. He gets excited all over." She smiled conspiratorially at me. "He's been talking for the past hour. He got so wound up in his oratory, he dropped his bath towel. His thing was pointing at me. Honestly, Chrissy, I couldn't help it. I kept thinking if I shook it a little, he might shut up."

"Don't you worry, Sister Chrissy," Mory said. "You are the First, and only, Lady who ever gave your friend and mine any peace of mind." Mory stared at his penis. "Yes, the poor thing does have a mind of sorts. Praise the Lord! But even if we live a hundred years, Sister Chrissy, he's yours, first and forever. Sister Jenny understands. Sister Jenny and I are good friends, but there is only one Sister Chrissy. I'll love her until I die. Amen. As you can see, I'm a little wound up this afternoon. I've been experimenting with the old sawdust-trail kind of rabble-rousing that my daddy is so good at. Maybe when I run for President, I'll mix a little religion and politics. Keeps the people more interested to talk about hell and damnation, which they don't believe in, than to rave on about present reality, which they can't do anything about. So if you'll be quiet and join Sister Jenny on the couch, Brother Morrow is about to give you both the most important message of your young lives."

Reassured, I undressed and got a jug of sangria out of the

refrigerator. Mory maintained his coffee-table platform and didn't stop talking.

"It's too bad there's no brothers in the congregation this afternoon," he was saying when I joined Jenny on the sofa, clad as she was. "But I must admit that I'm happy about that, because this is the most fascinating and just plain exciting audience that a preacher ever tried to save for Jesus.

"In the early 1930s, long before you ladies were born, and even before Brother Morrow saw the light of day, President Franklin Roosevelt appointed several advisers who were referred to as his "brain trust." Among them was Rexford Tugwell, who had been professor of economics at Columbia. Like my doppelganger, Edward Bellamy, whom the business community referred to as an impractical dreamer, Tugwell believed that traditional democracy and government planning had better learn how to walk hand in hand, or democracy itself wouldn't survive. The doctrine of competition which was embedded in the American psyche, and the John Locke—Adam Smith philosophy of a world that was up for grabs by the elite, whose property, ill gained or otherwise, should always be protected by the government—Tugwell believed that these concepts combined to emerge in the Constitution of 1787 as "constitutional checks and balances." They have not only screwed up the country ever since, but they never have really constrained the congressional, executive, and judicial branches of the government. One or the other is always trying to grab power from each other. They finally become responsive to the people only when their heads are in a guillotine—usually of their own making.

"The result has been to divide authority, stalemate creative action, and preclude accountability. In addition, the Constitution of 1787 created a government concerned with special interests instead of national concerns, and it entrenched a government that finally has become a government by executive order, with departments and agencies which are probably constitutionally illegal. But no one has the guts or money to challenge their existence, even though most of them aren't responsive to the people's needs or their legitimate demands."

Mory was smiling beguilingly at us as he spoke. His voice had a compelling, reassuring tone, and his brown eyes were flaming with inspiration. He was the teacher who not only propounded the problem, but who the students were confident would propose the solution. By confusing contrast, he also looked like a big kid who needed his mother to put her arm around him and praise him and hug him. No wonder Jenny couldn't resist grabbing his penis. I wanted to kiss my smart-ass baby from head to foot!

"Many years later," Mory was continuing, "Tugwell proposed that the Constitution should no longer be amended, but that it should be completely rewritten, and made to express the realities of the twentieth century as best we could do at any particular moment in time. Over a period of years, working with the Center for Democratic Institutions, Tugwell has prepared many versions of his Constitution.

"Ha-ha! I see Sister Jenny shaking her head emphatically—no! Let me remind you, Sister Jenny, that the Constitution of 1787 was written by men who, even then, agreed that it was the best they could do under the circumstances. It wasn't a sacred tablet handed down by God to Moses. Most certainly, in their wildest nightmares, the signers never anticipated a presidency as powerful as it became under Richard Nixon, or a federal government which now employs more people than the total population of the entire thirteen states. The delegates at Philadelphia represented a population of less than three million people!

"Sure, eleven years before they had agreed that all men are created equal, but they knew in their hearts that a new aristocracy was already building its foundations in America, based on the ownership of land."

Mory grinned. "In my other life I wrote the story of Shay's Rebellion. I told the true story in my novel *The Duke of Stockbridge*. I suggest you read it. As Edward Bellamy, I was one of the first to point out the economic origins of our Constitution. It simply added up in those days, as it does today, that equality belongs to those who have the power of money, or the control of the land, or the capital machinery of the country. The rest of the 'equal' citizens of this new nation, even though they weren't fully aware of it, gradually became the agricultural or industrial slaves. They had no choice except to work and be paid at the whim of those who had stolen their birthright. Tom Paine shouted, 'The birth of a new world is at hand. We have it in our power to begin the world all over again!' Unfortunately, no one was listening!

"And keep in mind, Sisters, that even after months of wrangling, and all kinds of compromises between those who wanted strong state governments and those who wanted some semblance of a government that wasn't a complete anarchy, the delegates left out the entire Bill of Rights. Not that it really mattered. Today, the changing day-to-day meaning of the Bill of Rights is in the vacillating minds of the legal profession and the Supreme Court. Interpretation of the first eleven Amendments reflects the moral and ethical twisting and turning of our Chief Justices over two centuries. And you wouldn't have had a Bill of Rights at all if it hadn't been tacked on by the state conventions and finally ratified two years later. But it didn't include any voting rights for your great-great-great-grandmothers.

"The fact is, Sisters, that the men who wrote the Constitution—which by some mystical thinking is still supposed to be a perfect conception, and is supposed to guide this country for centuries to come—didn't believe that women had very many rights, anyway. Today, two hundred years later, millions of those old-time patriarchs still don't feel very happy about an Equal Rights Amendment."

Mory paused for breath. "Even though he doesn't seem to give a damn, praise the Lord, Sisters! How many still glad you came? Raise your hand! Sister Jenny, do you have a question?"

"No, just a statement," Jenny said. "There's too many judges and lawyers and businessmen who have a vested interest in maintaining the past. You're pretty naïve. You're tampering with their wealth and property. They'll howl you down. A dirty Commie-Red. At least, if you ever do run for President, I beg you, don't try to change the Constitution at the same time."

Mory chuckled. "The rules of the ball game are a-changing, Sister Jenny. The people of America are beginning to understand that they can never resolve the problems of the twenty-first century with a basic charter written by men of the eighteenth century. Perhaps, the men who wrote the Constitution really did believe that all men are created equal. One thing is for sure, they didn't arrange the game so that equality lasted. You stop being equal in the United States from the day you're born to median-income-level peasants. The delegates in Philadelphia looked upon their new nation as the starting line in a new race—winner take all. What difference did it make that those who brought up the rear weren't equal anymore? The winners would give them jobs, and pay them for what they were worth—worth being calculated on the productive value of the particular land and machinery that consumed their energies.

"Could these men, who lived two hundred years ago,

conceive of the United States as it is today? When they were arguing in the hot summer months in Philadelphia, Indians were trading at an outpost called Detroit. Ohio and Kentucky, and most of the states up to the Mississippi, were peaceful forests where even God himself could take a nap and never hear a human sound.

"How could these men dream of an Industrial Revolution, or of the upper-rich-class population of less than five percent of America that grew out of it? How could these men envision a world where millions of men and women live and die in cement jungles? How could the delegates at Philadelphia, all of whom had a one-to-one relationship with the earth, all of whom had cleaned the black earth from under their fingernails—Sisters, I ask you: How could these men, who long ago turned to dust, write the laws that you and I must live by?"

"Weren't they reincarnated like you?" I asked timidly.

Mory beamed. "Right, Sister Chrissy. Absolutely right. And many of them are now on their third or fourth reincarnations. Unfortunately, they are still emulating their forebears. So, I ask you. How can these men, if their minds have remained stultified in the past, guide the people of America? The people who, by the year 2000, will be close to three hundred million strong. A joyous mixture of ethnic groups that didn't exist at all when those delegates were in Philadelphia."

Mory bounced off the coffee table. Bending over us, he swept his face across our breasts, kissing them enthusiastically in succession. His saluting penis was too great a temptation. I stuck my half-emptied glass of sangria over it. Mory yelped at the sudden coolness, but his prick didn't go down and it dripped wine all over my panties. Jennifer was laughing hysterically, both at Mory's reproachful look and at me as I pulled off my panties, wiped his dripping member, and kissed it.

"I'm sorry, Brother Mory," I told him, "but I don't see how you can continue this very interesting discussion with such pressure in your water hose. It's either going to explode lengthwise and ruin our rug, or it will grow so heavy it will tip you forward. You'd not only tumble off the coffee table but you could break your head and your jamoke as well!"

"Sister Chrissy," Mory said, "I don't know whether your remark is prompted by your horniness or a general boredom with this very important subject." He grinned at Jennifer.

86

"Obviously, I can't satisfy one member of my congregation and leave the other uneasy and dangling."

Jennifer shrugged. "I certainly have no long-range designs on your handsome male body. And there's no doubt in my mind that Chrissy not only found you, but that you probably deserve each other. On the other hand, while my legal mind has forced me to follow your arguments and listen to your insane thesis very carefully, I must admit that, like Chrissy, I've been unable to keep my mind off that pointer of yours. I've been wondering how it could keep wagging at us while your mind was presumably elsewhere. I was even wondering if the incredible was going to happen and you might have an intellectual orgasm without benefit of hands or a vagina." Jennifer stood up and stripped off her panties. "As with Sister Chrissy, you've started my vaginal juices flowing. What are you going to do about it?"

Laughing at Mory's momentary consternation, I was totally *not* jealous of Jenny. I couldn't help myself. The thought of the three of us tumbling together suddenly made me feel very erotic.

"This indeed is a puzzling situation." Mory grinned. "But as your future presidential candidate, I must learn to roll with the punches and meet any situation head on. If the good sisters will accommodate Brother Mory, he will attempt to resolve the strange gnawing sensations you are experiencing in your genitals, and then afterwards we can return to the primary agenda of this impromptu meeting."

I noticed that Mory had finished his glass of sangria and the afternoon sunlight was reflecting on the cheap crystal cutting. Flicking a sharp rainbow of light across our eyes, he was suddenly speaking to us, as we sat on the couch, in a very much more subdued voice. His words brushed across our eardrums like an audible caress.

"I told Sister Chrissy, many months ago," he said, "that way back in my law school days I dabbled in hypnosis and studied with a medical doctor who was an expert in the art. I have found few occasions to practice it except in the form of self-hypnosis, which incidentally is a very useful adjunct to the art of Tanta, or the ability to indulge in extended sexual intercourse without losing one's seed."

As Mory spoke both Jennifer and I were aware that he was reflecting sunlight to create a rhythmic, metronomic-like glitter back and forth across our eyes, focusing our attention. His words continued with the same drone, with no variation

87

in pitch. "I'm appalled," he said softly, "when I look at your lovely bodies, the perfect flow of your breasts, as you drift into a dreamless sleep, and I see the tender, almost-separate identities of your aureolae and your soft pink nipples, which seem to be watching me as intently as your eyes are watching me—I am appalled that those silly forefathers of ours who wrote the Constitution never really appreciated the delectable minds as well as the bodies of their women. They never listened to Abigail Adams, who stated the obvious: 'If you are to have educated men you must have educated women.' But now, dear Chrissy and dear Jennifer, I am happy to see that you are no longer resisting with your lovely minds but instead they have become one with your bodies. The wine you have drunk is making you pleasantly euphoric. You are falling into a deep, deep, sleep. Sleep . . . sleep . . . sleep."

Later, when we compared notes, Jennifer and I realized that we were only dimly aware that Mory had told us while he was talking to us that no hypnotist could make a subject do anything that was against his or her will. But he knew that both Chrissy and Jennifer wanted a loving man to kiss their vulvas, and then very, very slowly insert his penis into them, one after another, so that they might reach several blissful orgasms.

"That is what you want, isn't it, Chrissy? Isn't it, Jennifer?" And we nodded and listened. "So now if you will arise from the couch, and walk over to the pillows that are scattered in the corner, I will be able to help you." And we did. "And now, if you will place two of them on the floor under your buttocks, Chrissy, and you will do likewise, Jennifer, and you will lie on them with your legs opened, Brother Mory will kiss your lovely nether lips and try to assuage the hunger of these poor, unthinking creatures who have been neglected this afternoon."

As we lay there with our eyes closed Mory had two suppliant slaves at his command. "As you know," he told us, "the lovely key that opens the door to the deep, warm wells beneath is your clitoris. You both have such lovely vulvas, delicate as butterflies about to take wing. It is difficult to know where to begin."

I could feel the tip of Mory's tongue feathering the hood of my clitoris. Slowly, teasingly, back and forth, and then gradually more insistently searching and capturing the little devil. Then he left it momentarily to attend Jennifer, and all the while, as he moved between us, he described and compared our clitorises and labias and the warm, soft fragrance of our vulvas. He kept spieling a continuous euphony of loving silly talk—asking our genitals, as if they were individuals, if they were ready yet for the joyous penetration that would soon be forthcoming.

He didn't have to ask. Both Jennifer and I had peaked so rapidly that within a few seconds after he entered first me and then Jennifer we climaxed. Moving easily from me to Jennifer and back, leaving one of us still panting and moaning as he carried the other over the brink, Mory was the master of his harem, holding our asses tight, kissing our breasts, and leading us up higher and higher in a lovely slow torture of his flesh probing ours.

Had he really hypnotized us? I don't know. All that I'm sure of is that the living-room clock had moved forward about forty minutes when he finally told us to please take our seats on the couch once again and commanded us to wake up.

And to our amazement his damned penis was still erect! Whether we actually, or by mental insinuation had had orgasms, nevertheless our yoga President hadn't climaxed yet! When we asked him how he could still have an erection, and why it seemed to us that no time at all had elasped, he grinned at us and said: "I told you that it was a very puzzling situation." He looked at his penis. "The better part of valor seemed to take care of the momentary problem but save the big event for Chrissy. Only a very strong yoga could do that, believe me! Now—to get back to our meeting. Sisters, history moves inexorably—not in a circle, but in a slowly rising line toward a world where freedom and responsibility and equality are in a perfect balance. In the confusion of our day-to-day world, it's often difficult to detect this inchworm creeping toward the future, but coming events cast their shadows before. A new kind of human being is emerging from the old womb and is demanding to be counted. The tiny newborn's heartbeats finally became audible in the early 1960s in America. When this new American finally found his voice, he rebelled against the nationalism and trumped-up patriotism of leaders intent on fighting one more useless war. Unbelievably, the rebellion succeeded, and provided fertile soil for a growing number of men and women who were standing up against the tide of consumerism and telling us that we must discover new social goals aimed toward a life-oriented society instead of a quantity-oriented society. No longer could we afford to devote our lives to achieving an ever-increasing gross national product, or spend two-thirds of our incomes on consumer goods.

"Other men and women, by the thousands, were demanding that we stop drifting, and insisted that we make reasonable plans to achieve a future where all human beings could spend a portion of their lives in creative work that confirmed their dignity and worth as men and women. A world without futile hot wars and cold wars, or frenzied cutthroat competition that was turning our lives into a dreary, idiotic routine of work-work-work; buy-buy-buy; consume-consume-consume!

"Others, not realizing that history is an inchworm, were heralding the future as if it had already arrived. 'This is the Age of Aquarius,' they shouted. Or Consciousness III, or the Greening of America. And they dreamed the future. But it wasn't quite ready to be born yet. A few million couldn't do it by themselves. We needed tens of millions to band together in Common Causes.

"But don't think it's a lost cause! Those people of the future America are out there—right now! Thousands of groups and organizations are searching for a new tomorrow that no leader, as yet, has been able to clearly define for them. From nude beach advocates trying to legislate the human right to be naked where it is convenient to be naked; to humanists trying to explain that a world without a personal God is still an exciting, here-and-now, viable world; to human-potential groups trying to discover the many mansions of human consciousness; to hundreds of thousands of those who are daring to experiment with new ways of loving and living together while they search for viable alternatives to monogamy and the nuclear family. All of these people are deep undercurrents which are slowly building up to the surface of the ocean, until one day, in a new coalition of human solidarity, they will thunder on the beaches of our New Tomorrow. A few million of these loving people without portfolio and no franchise are already a bigger ripple than most people realize. They are a warm pink glow on the horizon, presaging the day of the New Sun that will soon rise on the New Tomorrow."

Mory had delivered his sermon with the spellbinding aplomb and conviction of an old-time preacher. Both Jenny and I were captivated—ready to raise the flags and start marching.

"Hear! Hear!" Jenny yelled. "Hail the New Sun—Newton Morrow! I can't wait. When are you going to usher in the Golden Age?"

"With your help, Sister Jenny, and yours, Sister Chrissy, the New Tomorrow will be here sooner than you think. With the unintended help of President Nixon, the American people finally woke up. They realized that they had to pay attention. The Big Brothers were lurking in the forest ready to eat all the Little Red Riding Hoods in one big gulp. Hopefully, the next President will help cut the government jungle down to size. Hopefully, he will realize that a truly democratic country, based on much greater economic equality of its citizens, is the only path into the future.

"Before the year 2000—in my new incarnation as Newton Morrow, the Great Revolution that I predicted in my book *Equality*, without bloodshed, will have transformed the country!"

Mory was waving his arms up and down. "Sisters—with your help I'm flying! I'm counting on you! When the time comes, together we will lead the people out of Egypt. Sisters—"

"My God," I interrupted, "I don't know whether you're crazy or on speed. I'm devouring your words, but I don't even know what the hell you're driving at! First you're talking about the Constitution, and then some fairyland where we can all pick daisies together. When and if you follow your daddy's advice and stop studying and get into politics, you better not try saving the people of America for Jesus. Not with your testicles and penis hanging out. You'll be assassinated before you've finished your first speech!"

Mory laughed. "Aha, the sister in the balcony thinks Brother Morrow is a sinner and a Communist, just because he's preaching to her in his birthday suit. When they hung poor Jesus on the cross, I'm sure that they weren't so fastidious. In those days they didn't cover a traitor's genitals with a loin cloth. And I'd like to remind you, Sister Chrissy, the real sin in this world is not our genitals, but our egos, which overwhelm us! We're afraid to let go. We're afraid simply to be. We must 'have'! Having is a cheap way to achieve the ego identity we are so afraid of losing. Remember what Meister Eckhart said: 'Knowledge is no particular thought, but rather peels off all of its coverings and runs naked to God, until it touches him and grasps him!'

"Having an affinity with the Buddist mind, Eckhart also said: 'I pray that God may quit me of God.' That day, Sister Chrissy, will come to pass when we have finally chartered a

91

new society, and written a new Constitution which really spells out our hopes and dreams for a New Tomorrow.

"But to answer your question more specifically, when I last made my appearance in this world as Edward Bellamy—"

"Oh, dear," I sighed. "I should face reality. I've been screwing with a poltergeist."

"Worse," Jenny said. "Mory hasn't told you who he was before he was Bellamy. My bet is he was Jesus, and this is the Second Coming." She squeezed my arm. "For you, anyway."

Mory ignored us. "In the late nineteenth century, though I had never read Karl Marx, I was his contemporary. Like him, I assumed that the state would wither away. Thus a hundred years ago, when I was writing *Looking Backward*, and later *Equality*, I failed to anticipate that private capitalists wouldn't give up easily. I assumed that the profit system would come to an end by the year 2000. I thought that buried within its laissez-faire philosophy was its own death wish. I never dreamed that private capitalism would become so desperate to save itself that it would underwrite social security, pension systems, and finally a welfare state.

"In my Bellamy incarnation I was intent on eliminating the profit system and creating public capitalism. I was on the right track. But I didn't define carefully how my new system would come into being, or how the transition could be achieved.

"Thus, my former theories must not only be elaborated, but in the twenty-first-century solution which I am proposing, I will make it clear that the kind of public ownership that I am advocating is not the Socialist party solution. I will never put the capital and machinery and land of this country into the million-creepered hands of a blind, anonymous, stumbling, unfeeling, computerized robot that nationalized industry and a socialist government would be. And though I was once fascinated with a concept of national industrial service, in this incarnation, seeing where the Pentagon mentality has taken us, I must make it clear that the hundred billions we spend on defense each year will be very rapidly eliminated. Both the socialist route and the military route to New Tomorrow are worse than the private capitalistic system that I inveighed against in *Equality*.

"Most of my nineteenth-century conclusions were reasonably valid, especially the belief that we must all have greater monetary equality. That can easily be accomplished within reasonable parameters without destroying human initiative. But it will only begin with a New Constitution which will create a total people's environment that minimizes, or eliminates, federal control, and offers a unique new kind of profit system which forces all citizens—by social edict, not by governmental regulation—to assume *equal responsibility*. Amen. Praise the Lord. I see some empty seats down there. Some of the congregation are getting itchy bottoms. Sister Jenny, I need your presence for a few more minutes."

Mory paused and took a long swallow of sangria. "While I'm catching my breath, Sister Jenny, will you please tell Sister Chrissy some of the highlights of the Tugwell Constitution? While Sister Jenny has told me that her professors look upon Tugwell's Constitution as a Utopian daydream, I am not intimidated. When you're finished. I will explain to both sisters how the Morrow Constitution improves the current Tugwell revision."

"I love you, Mory," Jenny said, "but none of us is going to live long enough to see a Tugwell Constitution or a Morrow Constitution. You're going to have to face reality. Why don't you admit that you aren't running naked to God, either? You're just hypnotized by your own ego."

"Ah, Sister Jenny," Mory said sadly, "let me remind you of one of Jesus's parables—*Matthew* 13:31. 'The kingdom of heaven is like to a grain of mustard seed, which a man took and sowed in his field. Which indeed is the least of all seeds; but when it is grown, it is the greatest among herbs, and becomes a tree. So that the birds of the air come and lodge in the branches thereof.' All you need, Sister Jenny, is faith—tiny as a mustard seed. Praise the Lord!"

Jenny shook her head at me, but couldn't help laughing. "There are smaller seeds than a mustard seed, which proves the Bible can't be fully trusted. But I give up," she said. "Tugwell's latest version has twelve Articles, beginning with a Bill of Rights *and* Responsibilities. Article Two refers to the New States. Each New State would comprise no less than five percent of the population. Article Three establishes an Electoral Branch with an Overseer who will supervise all elections.

"Article Four has a Planning Branch with a National Planning Board appointed by the President and fifteen members, each with terms of one to fifteen years, to provide an annual rotation of one member. Article Five concerns the presidency. The President would be elected for nine years.

93

There would be two Vice-Presidents, one for Internal Affairs and one for External Affairs. They would have Chancellors who would replace the presidential Cabinet. After three years, the President can be removed from office if he is rejected by sixty percent of the electorate. Article Six would create a non-elected Senate. It would be composed of former Presidents, Vice-Presidents, Chief Justices, Overseers, Chairmen of the Planning Boards, and former governors, as well as various former officials appointed by the President. Their term is for life. Article Six also details very comprehensively the responsibilities of the House of Representatives, which is the original lawmaking body, elected by the New States.

"Article Seven establishes a Regulatory Branch with a National Regulator of Economic Affairs appointed by the Senate. The Regulatory Board charters all corporations and enterprises as well as performing a host of other functions that are no longer left to what some economists think is the superior wisdom of the marketplace. Article Eight establishes a Judicial Branch and details the functioning of this branch. The rest of the Articles go into details of national and state functioning which are not spelled out by the Constitution of 1787. A final Article details how this miraculous change in government, economic, and social policy will occur." Jenny grinned. "It's some mustard seed!"

"Thank you, Sister Jenny, the revisions which I'm making," Mory said, "offer the name Commonwealths as a more descriptive and appropriate name than the New States, since all national wealth will be a common pool shared by all. These Commonwealths will completely eliminate the names of the old states. The people of each Commonwealth will decide by popular vote the name which they wish to adopt for their Commonwealth. Assuming that a merger of Canada and United States must eventually occur in the twenty-first century, I'm projecting a total population of approximately four hundred and fifty million United People of America. I'm excluding Mexico temporarily, but my population projection not only includes Puerto Rico, but assumes that all of the offshore islands in the Carribbean and the Bahamas will together comprise one of the new Commonwealths. The Tugwell-Morrow Constitution, of course, is not an immutable document. It will be amended, and if necessary rewritten, many times.

"For the moment, I have prepared a map of the entire area, which will, at the beginning, consist of fifteen Commonwealths with an approximate population in each Commonwealth of thirty million people. Each Commonwealth will have its own Governor elected by thirty Regions within each Commonwealth. Each Region will have a population of one million people. Each Region will have ten City Communities with approximately one hundred thousand people, and every City Community will have five hundred local groups of two hundred people called Associates.

"Every man, woman, and child in the United People of America will be an Associate in his government, with a direct link and responsibility up and down the pyramid. The families who comprise these Associate Groups will be monogamous family corporations, or group family corporations.

"Each Community, every three years, will elect twenty-five officials in an open public election. In descending order of the votes they win, the first will be automatically elected to the House of Representatives of the particular Commonwealth. Each Commonwealth will have two hundred and eighty-five elected officials. The next twelve elected by each City Community would automatically become President and Vice-President of the particular Region, and Regional Representatives; the lowest twelve would automatically become President and Vice-President and City Community Councilors. Fifteen members of the House of Representatives in each Commonwealth will be elected *by their members* to the Congress of the People. The four hundred and fifty Congressmen will elect, from their number, the President and Vice-President of the United People of America. He or she will have a term of office equivalent to the Representatives but, of course, can be reelected by his or her peers triannually."

I was bewildered. "Just how do you plan to be elected President?" I demanded. "By the Congress of the People? You may only be President for three years."

Mory laughed. "You're quite right. But you understand, to bring about the Great Revolution and the New Constitution, I will have to go through the insanity of one final election by a popular majority of the people. Once I'm finally elected, whether I remain President is not of great import. The office of President will no longer be a position for self-glorification or power-seeking. The men elected to Congress who will elect me, or one of their peers, as President, will be professionals who are just as capable of being President or running any of the appointive offices, or running any of the agencies, depart-

95

ments, and commissions of the government, and they also would be elected to these various posts by their members.

"Keep in mind, Sisters, that my revisions of the Tugwell Constitution are largely in the area of the presidency and the structure of the Commonwealths and the elective process. Otherwise, the Tugwell Constitution is an excellent beginning charter for a New Tomorrow.

"My concept of the presidency is that the man who is elected to this position by the Congress must be a philosopher-statesman. He must be totally interested in the sum total of human problems, and he must be constantly proposing new ideas and legislation to improve the National and the Regional Commonwealth Governments' responsibility to the individual. You must keep this in mind, too. The governments' responsibility to the people is even greater than the people's responsibility to their governments. Leaders of modern democracies, along with totalitarian leaders, seem to have forgotten the principle of 'advise and consent' ultimately belongs to the people themselves. The new ship of state will no longer have a Great Father at the helm. The President will be honored because he is a human being with broad perspectives seeking answers to human problems."

"Hurray!" I yelled. "I was beginning to wonder when you were going to have time for the First Lady. As one of your constituency, I insist that going to bed with me is a first order of business."

"Amen. Praise the Lord, Sister Chrissy. We don't even have to vote on that!" Mory stepped off the coffee table and flopped between Jennifer and me. "But you've missed an important point. While I could be unseated as President, I would then become a Senator for life."

"Oh, God," I groaned, "you'd still be blowing bubbles. In your New Tomorrow, when do you have time make love?"

Laughing, Mory calmly stretched out naked across our legs. " 'He who kisses the joy as it flies, lives in eternity's sun rise,' " he said.

Trying to slide out from under him, Jennifer held his penis. "I'm not sure how you seduced Christa and me a little while ago," she said, "or how you managed to survive with this creature still ready and able, but it certainly deserves some kind of accolade." She gave Mory's penis a kiss, and then evidently feeling a little oral herself, she gave it a quick, deep suck. "This is a historic moment." She chuckled. "Now, if you ever do become President, I'll write my autobiography, and tell the world that when President Morrow was a young man, I sucked his prick, and it tasted delicious!"

"Praise the Lord." Grinning, Mory lurched out of our mutual embrace. "Sorry to stop you, Jenny, but the future President was about to erupt. The first amendment to my New Constitution will be to allow every male the final death test. If he doesn't respond to the ministrations of two lovely women, then he's ready to be buried. Save me, Sister Chrissy, I'm not ready for my next reincarnation yet!"

Disappearing into the bathroom, Jennifer yelled at us, "Please, you two, finish in Christa's bedroom. If I keep Jerry waiting too long downstairs, he's sure to barge in up here. If he ever suspected that I had kissed the President's dingus, he'd be sure that I was crazier than both of you."

———◆———

The tall marsh grass is casting warm summer shadows across my naked body. Lost and lonely in my memories of Newton Morrow, I wonder if Mory still thinks he's Edward Bellamy. God—he only has twenty years left.

Today and Tomorrow

In time it should be possible to synthesize a variety of antimetabolites so that we will be able to bring almost all metabolic functions to a complete halt . . . Artificial hibernation enhanced by antimetabolites should allow humans to have their metabolism reduced by two orders of magnitude (1/100th of normal) for extended periods. . . . The direct enzyme antimetabolites would bring cellular functions to a halt. The heart would not beat, and there would be no electrical activity in the brain coordinating the various organs. . . . It is doubtful that metabolism could be suppressed completely through chemical anabiosis, so temperatures below 0° centigrade without freezing would be useful . . . the combination called super-hibernation would not halt all biological change. Diffusion and random molecular change could damage parts of the cell membranes. . . . Therefore, super-hibernation might require brief periods of periodic arousal. . . .

—Robert Prehoda,
Suspended Animation

Back home finally—it's four o'clock—I'm feeling subdued and a little depressed over my remembrance of things past, and I'm trying to forget the unfinished feeling I always have when I masturbate. I slip quietly upstairs to my bedroom before Michael and Penny see me. The shower washes away the Marshfield salt and mud still clinging to my breasts, behind, and vulva. I'm supposed to be ready to go to dinner with Karl at *Maison Robert* at eight. Karl will be home by seven, Jenny O'Donnell, our chauffeur, will drive us back to Bolton. In the meantime, Penny finds me in the bathroom and asks if I will take her to the library. The library is only a few miles away. I can't refuse the beseeching, needful expression on her skinny face. Grace told Karl that at five years Penny is not just our child, but she's a duplicate of her insecure, introspective mother at that age.

I hug her and she asks me why I am crying, and I tell her it's because I love her, and I tell her to find her brother and we will most certainly go to the library. A few minutes after we arrive I have picked out a pile of Doctor Seuss picture books for Michael, and Penny has found a book, *About the Sleeping Beauty,* by P. L. Travers. Will I read it to her?

The book makes me feel uneasy, but we take it home. Of course, I know why I'm suddenly jittery. I'm aware that one day, too soon, I may have to explain to Penny and Michael—before their friends tell them—why their mother has written such a "dirty" book as *The Christening of Christina.* But it isn't a dirty book (I remind myself). It's a lovely story of a young girl reveling in her newly discovered sexuality, who then is overcome by fear—not because she really believes she is evil, but because her mother and daddy and friends, and the Evil Witch, or the Thirteenth Wise Woman, convince her that the spindle (penis) she has never really known but dearly loves, will harm her.

Sipping a Jack Daniel's on the rocks, reading the book to

101

Penny (Michael is quickly bored), glad that Grace isn't around to moralize about my drinking, pleased that Mrs. Steffens is delighted that I'm being a good mother—she has vanished somewhere in the house—I read Penny P.L. Travers' re-creation of the Sleeping Beauty story. I am fascinated, and Penny is entranced. But suddenly I know that I am too involved. I'm being too introspective. P. L.'s version of the story is transformed to a mythical kingdom replete with a Sultan and a Sultana and all the *Arabian Nights* trappings. The Sultan sounds just like Karl. When the Twelve Wise Women whom he has invited to Princess Rose's christening bless her with such intangibles as a life of joy and contentment, he whispers to the Sultana, "I'm astounded. Not a penny piece? Good temper, health, peace and joy, and not a single jewel? No bags of gold, no marble mansion? Poor child. She'll be as poor as a mouse."

Penny is ecstatic because she knows, of course, that the Princess isn't really going to die at all. All she has to do is sleep a hundred years and she'll be born again. When you're only five years old, what's a hundred years? Hell, when I was Penny's age, I knew for sure I was going to live a hundred years at the very minimum.

By five o'clock, I know that I've drunk too much. I've got to slow down. I have to shower and dress for dinner with Karl's new partners. Bill Adams and Fred Bradford, the male spouses of our proper Bostonian friends of the moment, have joined forces with Karl temporarily, for the purpose of buying all the shares in a closed investment fund which has a liquidation value at least 20 percent higher than its market price. If they consummate the deal, which involves several hundred million dollars, within the next three weeks our heroes will split approximately thirty million among them. The men promise us (Mary and Charlotte and me, their wives), while we drink cocktails before dinner, that their "wrap-up" will only take twenty or thirty minutes. We can listen and learn—and then they will descend from their thrones, put aside mundane monetary affairs, and be lively companions to their lovely wives.

Topping three Jack Daniel's before dinner with three glasses of a thirty-five-dollar-a-bottle Chateau Margaux red wine which the haughty waiter assures Karl is an excellent vintage, I exchange a million superficialities with Mary and Charlotte. In fact, I am a model citizen throughout the entire evening. Finally, dizzy from the drive back to Marblehead, at twelve-thirty I'm tottering, but safe, in our bedroom. Then Karl makes the mistake of asking me if I had a nice time with the Bradford and Adams women.

"I was bored shitless all evening!" I yell at him. "Why did you have to drag your wives along? Why don't you play your little boys' games and leave me out of it?"

"I'm sorry," Karl tells me, and with his calm response proves what I already know—that I'm being unnecessarily bitchy. "I really didn't care about Mary's or Charlotte's reactions, but I had hoped that you might find the inside workings of this maneuver rather fascinating. You always preach to me the merits of curiosity, but you won't exert yourself to understand the Philistines."

"Because I can't believe that you're for real!" I scream. "You tell me that you can make ten million dollars overnight by a shrewd kind of foresight, and nobody gets hurt. I may be stupid at economics, but a million poor schmucks are paying and don't even know it."

Karl shrugs. "People involved in this deal aren't your precious lambs. They're wolves we caught napping."

But that isn't what is really bothering me. I can see Hank—his eyes shot out and his head perforated with bullets—under the lid of his closed coffin. I try to verbalize it for Karl.

"I'm horrified by the contrast," I tell him. "You tell me that in less than three weeks, with very little effort, you're going to be ten million dollars richer. If Hank Hutchings killed himself, it's because he was broke. But even worse, all the time we were eating dinner, telling the waiter that our two-hundred-dollar dinner was not up to their usual standards, millions of the four billion or so people on this planet are starving to death." By this time, I'm a sobbing drunk with the beginnings of a thumping headache.

Karl is only half listening to me, but I'm too wound up to stop. "Why don't you face it, Karl? Divorce me. I'm hopeless. I'm too provincial to be the wife of a rich man. I'm really the sow's ear branch of the North family. You can't make a silk purse out of me."

By this time, I am naked. Using the furniture and walls and door frame to support myself, I stagger into the bathroom. Opening one of the drawers below the bathroom sink, searching for my toothbrush, wondering if I'm going to throw up, I discover a bottle of Darvon sleeping pills. A few days ago, I had read in the *Wall Street Journal* (a goldmine of trivia) that twenty-eight tablets is a lethal dose. Suddenly I'm sober. Why not? There isn't one damned good reason why I should live, and a million why I shouldn't. My hopelessness isn't Karl's fault. Sometimes I really love him, particularly, like now, when I have bewildered him beyond belief. How can I explain to him that I have to kill myself simply because I know that I can't finish my current painting? It's a noose around my neck. I can't make it work, and the reason is simple. Like everything else I try, I'm suddenly positive that it's only half-ass accomplished. I'm just not good enough to be whole ass. While I'm thinking these thoughts I swallow twenty-eight pills, two at a time, with a water chaser, and then take four more for good measure.

When I wander into the bedroom, wondering what I'm going to look like dead, Karl is propped up in bed reading his *Wall Street Journal*. Like Somerset Maugham's Reverend Davidson, he shakes his head sadly at his Sadie Thompson, and tells me he hopes that tomorrow I don't have a big head.

With my knees bent and spread, I sob, "You better hurry, Karl. This is your last fuck. You'll never forget it. It's a snuff fuck. You can screw me while I'm dying. If you can last long enough, I'll give you a rigor mortis orgasm. But be careful that I don't trap your penis, or they might have to bury you with me."

"Damn it, Christina." Karl sighs. "I begged you not to drink so much. You know that I detest maudlin women. Why do you have to spoil a nice evening? I already complimented you. You were a perfect lady. I was very proud of you. So why are you acting this way now?"

"Because I hate Christina Jekyll, and I hate all your creepy friends. None of them know how to let go and have a good belly laugh. I'll bet none of them yell or scream or faint when they have an orgasm. Like you, when your buddies ejaculate and catch their breath, they smile politely at their plastic-doll bed companions and tell them, 'Thank you, dear, that was nice.' Then they immediately finish off the evening reading their Bible, good old Wastrejo."

Karl still hasn't taken off his trousers. "You better hurry," I warn him. "After tonight you'll have to roll up your *Journal* and stick your prick, as well as your head, into it. I won't be around."

When he comes out of the bathroom demanding to know if I am just trying to get his ass, or if I really have swallowed that whole bottle of Darvon pills, I shrug and tell him to stop

104

wasting time. It finally penetrates his mind that his drunken and unpredictable wife actually may have done it again. While I'm yelling and protesting that I really don't give a damn, I want to die, and he's better off without me, he wrestles my flaying arms into a housecoat, and fireman carries me to the garage.

"Let me go!" I scream. "I'm not worth saving." But Karl has propped me up in the death seat of his Silver Cloud Rolls-Royce and fastened me with a seat belt. Beside him, a broken and bent-over drunken U, I keep muttering insanities at him while he drives seventy miles an hour through surburban streets to the Saugus General Hospital.

———◆———

By Saturday morning, when Karl visits me in the hospital, the quiche lorraine, the ragout of lamb parisienne, the Jack Daniel's, the Chateau Margaux, vintage 1971, and the Darvon pills have been pumped out of my stomach. Though I feel as insubstantial as my own ghost, once again I have been saved.

At Karl's urgent request, and obviously a substantial sum of money, Dr. Philip Leonard, head of a clinical group specializing in "depression," has driven from Hartford and talked with me for more than an hour before Karl arrives. A gentle white-haired man in his fifties, he explains that no one is sure of the basic causes, or how to cure, the kind of bipolar depression I am experiencing. It seems to be caused by changes in the central nervous system's catecholamine metabolism. Catecholamines are chemical substances which are released from the nerve endings and function as neuro transmitters. The major metabolites of norepinephrine in the brain appear to be relatively low during periods of depression. Often the imbalance can be ameliorated by anti-depression pills. If I will stay on a high-dosage regimen for a few weeks and then turn myself in for lithium treatment, my troubles will be over for life. I can stay out of psychiatric wards, and I can stop worrying about electroshock therapy. With my training, I obviously should realize very well that controlled lithium treatment isn't dangerous. It produces the same effect as the trycyclics, especially controlling the manic side of my personality, which is always eventually counterbalanced by deep depression.

Karl is very gentle with me. The concerned expression on his face, and the realization that he isn't really angry with me, releases a flood of tears. "I really love you, Karl," I tell him. "I hate myself for causing you so much misery."

I promise him I won't ever do such a silly thing again. He tells me that no one, not even Grace, or the children or anyone who'd been on the cruise, is aware of my suicide attempts.

Everyone who was on board, including Warren (Karl has evidently brainwashed him), knew that Christina was crocked. After failing with Warren, she was trying to seduce the sharks. But no one thought I really had "swimming to Boston" on my mind. Of course, I scared everybody to death, but the whole business happened because I had drunk too much.

"And, of course, you were mortified." Karl flushes and changes the word to "embarrassed." "As you damned well should have been at being caught with Warren Ellison.

"But you don't have to worry about that. This isn't the nineteenth century," he assures me. "Most of our crowd have had their little sexual flings, including me." He kisses my cheek. "I love you, Christa. I guess sometimes I react to you like a father, but bear with me. Give me six months to untangle myself and we'll take a long vacation in Spain or Greece."

Karl is happy when he leaves the hospital. I've promised him that when I come home Monday I'm going to be a new Christina. The Andrew Wyeth Christina, crawling toward Christina's ramshackle house, and never reaching it, no longer exists. She has arisen from the long grass, and embracing the sky, is leaping in slow motion until she merges into the arms of her lover and savior. Karl and I will be merged for infinity on Keats's Grecian urn.

Of course, I don't tell Karl the unerased questions that keep sneaking around in my head. Why is it so immoral to decide that one no longer wants to live? Why are men so impelled to legislate their fellowmen's morality?

I finally fall asleep. Then, suddenly, I'm awake. My watch tells me only a few minutes have passed. A man is sitting beside my bed. He's watching me with a bemused expression on his face. He is very precisely dressed in a black suit and a white French-cuffed shirt. His blood-red tie matches the red stones in his cuff links. The coruscating flashes of a similar stone on the ring he is wearing on his fourth finger reflects in the light on the bedside lamp, and flicks monotonously across my eyes. His eyebrows are bristly and nearly form a V at his

106

nose. His black hair is carefully trimmed, and his pointed black beard has an unreal quality. I wonder if they are actors' accessories, pasted on his face, which he may suddenly rip off in great disdain at the part he is playing, while he coolly reveals the real man underneath. I wonder if I'm dreaming him. His heavy-lidded almond-shaped eyes give me a shivery feeling.

"Good evening," he says. "I'm David Convita."

I have a presentiment that I should ring my call bell and summon a nurse. He sees me fumble for it. Anticipating me, he briefly puts his hand gently over mine. "Don't be alarmed. I'm an M.D. While you're not my patient, I've taken the liberty of visiting you."

My digital watch tells me that it's well after midnight. It's an odd time for a doctor to come calling.

"If you're another damned psychiatrist," I tell him, "please go away. I'm a psychologist myself, and I've analyzed myself and been analyzed by too many shrinks already. I'm sure, Dr. Convita, that there's nothing you can tell me about myself that I don't already know."

I know that I'm not being very friendly, but I doubt that any normal doctor would be visiting me at nearly one o'clock in the morning. More likely, he's some character from the psycho ward who has discovered that the former Christina North is aboard, and he's planning to climb into bed with her and get his.

"Really," I tell him very gently, "I wish you'd leave me alone. It's very late, and I haven't been feeling well."

Convita is smiling. "You can call me David," he says. "I understand your natural uneasiness. I'll only stay a few minutes. Let me assure you that you're not hallucinating and I'm not the Devil, or any other ogre who you may be conjuring in your mind. I'm not a psychiatrist, either. My only interest in Freud's theory is in an idea expressed in one of his early lectures. I believe that he stated that 'our relationship with the world, which we entered so unwillingly, seems to be endurable only with intermission; hence we withdraw again, periodically, into the condition we experienced prior to our entrance into the world; that is to say an intrauterine existence.' "

Convita, touches my hand gently. "Sleeping, we return to the primal warmth and darkness and absence of stimulus. According to Freud, 'Every time we awake in the morning, it is

107

as if we were newly born.' Freud even suggested that perhaps one-third of each of us has never been born at all."

His eyes are twinkling. He knows that he has captured my interest. "My colleague, Max Lebenthal, and I are very fascinated with this human phenomenon. Assuming that sleep is a form of personal dying, which each of us must do every day to survive, Max and I have gone one step further and are investigating the potential of extended sleep or hibernation, or aestivation as it is called for spring and summer withdrawal."

I am beginning to make a vague connection. The reason for Convita's interest in me is that I have been playing with death, too. I wait for him to evoke it.

"If you think about it, Mrs. Klausner," he says, "in many other societies suicide has often been looked upon as an honorable act. I don't have to remind you that the Japanese pilots who committed hara-kari in World War II by dive-bombing out troops and carriers became national heroes. In ancient Rome and Greece many of the leaders, such as Hannibal, Brutus, Cassius, Cleopatra or Lycurgus, Cato, Zeno, and Socrates (who didn't have to drink the hemlock), used suicide as a saner solution to their problems than 'taking arms against a sea of troubles.' In fact, viewed from the perspective of the disaster that he finally created, Hamlet would have probably benefited his constituency more by 'not being' than 'being.'

"In our opinion, since the Western world is becoming more receptive to the idea of beneficent euthanasia with every passing day, we may soon enter a new world where those who can't adapt to this mechanistic world or force it to conform to their necessities, or are unable to control their 'future shock,' may discover cheerful ways to eliminate themselves. In the coming years, many people may even become heroes or heroines by volunteering their lives in service of their fellowmen."

This strange man is watching me intently as he speaks. "I know that you have been through a very traumatic experience, Mrs. Klausner, and I don't want to tire you so late in the evening, but my colleague and I have a gambling proposition which we, and several others working in the same areas, are offering to carefully selected people, like yourself, who are vacillating between living and dying."

He is silent a moment, evidently trying to anticipate my reaction. "If, of your own free will, you would assign your living body to us, we believe that through a process of chemical anabiosis we have nearly perfected, we can induce prolonged periods of hibernation equivalent to deep sleep, with no physical damage to your brain or body. We are confident that we can maintain this low metabolic state for periods of up to twelve months, and probably much longer. Not only that, but combined with hypothermia, or low-temperature maintenance of the body, we are proving that we can reduce human metabolism approximately ninety percent. In effect, your mental and bodily processes would cease. On the surface, you would seem to be dead, but in actuality you would be in a state of suspended animation."

Before he finishes speaking, he takes my hand, and I'm trapped by his opaque, staring eyes, which seem to have the same reddish cast as the ring on his left hand that he is now moving slowly and is flashing hypnotically across my eyes. I'm partially aware that while he was talking he has been using the trick of concentrating my attention on a glittering object. But I don't have strength enough to look away. I'm watching him open-mouthed, and I'm frightened not just because I'm entranced by his intensity, but because I'm not really shocked by the insanity of his proposal.

"I gather that you're trying to tell me that I can have my cake and eat it." I try to look away from him, but I can't. I try to sound sardonic. "Are you telling me," I ask him, "that with your assistance I can sample death, and if I don't find it comfortable, after an agreed-upon time you'll revive me? Then, I can decide whether I want to make it permanent?"

He chuckles. "You might call it a kind of Suicide Underground—an alternative to either life or death."

"It sounds more like the deal that the Devil offered Faust's girlfriend, Marguerite."

"You have a nice sense of humor," he tells me. "Perhaps a better analogy is that you could try the glove on and see if it fits. But we've talked enough. You can sleep on the idea, Christina. Relax and drift off into a lovely floating world." His voice was like a gentle caress. I can't take my eyes off his flashing ring. "Now you're going to sleep. Monday, the day after tomorrow, you'll be released from here. You'll return to your home in Marblehead. You will tell no one about our little conversation. Tuesday morning, at nine o'clock, you will telephone me. You will call my number, 471-8583. Now, before you go to sleep, repeat what I've just told you . . ."

Slowly, I hear myself repeat his words. He closes my eyes

109

with gentle fingers. "I will invite you to lunch in Boston, and you will tell me, 'Of course I'll come, David. Of course I'll come. . . . Of course I'll come.' "

———◆———

Of course, I can't help myself. David has given me a post-hypnotic suggestion. I'm even quite aware that the compulsion to telephone him goes beyond any natural curiosity. While I'm in fairly good equilibrium, flying neither too high nor too low, I'm consciously trying to stay out of my studio and leave that damned painting alone. I must stop trying to be what I'm not. I may empathize with *"Christina's World,"* but I'm not an Andrew Wyeth or an Edward Hopper or even a nouveau Maxfield Parrish. I'm Christian Klausner, mother of two children, wife of Karl Klausner who, if given the choice, would prefer that his wife dabble with her minor talents, but not take them seriously, or maybe even join the ranks of the idle rich and be thankful that she doesn't have to make a living as an artist or a poet or a novelist or a psychologist, or even a cocksucker.

David's phone number is a long-distance call. A woman answers. Is it his wife? No. She sounds too efficient. "Dr. Convita will be with you in a moment." She must be his nurse.

David wonders if I can drive to Boston. I assure him that I can. He tells me that he will meet me at Pier Four in the cocktail lounge at twelve-thirty. Before I leave, I'm about to tell Mrs. Steffens, who is taking the children to the beach, that I'm having lunch with a Dr. Convita, and that I'll be home long before Karl arrives. Then I suddenly decide that neither Karl, nor Jerry Greenberg, nor Dr. Leonard would approve of David or any of his fascinatingly morbid ideas. (As I type this, I suddenly realize, though I wasn't consciously aware of it at the time, that I was still reacting to David's suggestion, and I had burned my bridges behind me. I had left no traces. There's one exception. My long-distance phone call to the Cape will be listed on the telephone bill. But I'm sure Karl will never connect it with my disappearance. David has kidnapped me, and I no longer exist.)

But then I was thinking, So what can happen? I'm going to meet a man in a crowded restaurant. After lunch, and an hour or more of his really crazy conversation, I can bid David Convita good-bye forever.

110

By a quarter of one, I'm sitting with David at a table overlooking Boston Harbor, and he's telling me how delighted he is to be having lunch with such an attractive companion. He explains that Max Lebenthal and he have a laboratory on the Cape near Camp Edwards, but for the past two years they've been so busy working on a special, federally financed scientific project that they've been living like recluses in another world.

"A future world, you might say." David is holding up his glass of water. "Max and I are cryobiologists. If you stop to think about it, water is man's most amazing cosmic gift, or perhaps the truth is vice versa. If you subtract about thirty-five percent of your body weight, the remainder of each of us is held together by water. Yet, we scarcely know whether the essence of a person is the water or the remaining few pounds of chemicals. Not only that, when man can really control water, desalinize it at will, or separate it easily into hydrogen and oxygen, we will turn the earth into a Garden of Eden."

Unlike most men I know, David seems to have the intense, probing kind of mind that I find irresistible. He dares to ask ultimate questions and seek ultimate answers. "But water isn't what makes us male or female," I tell him. "The real mystery is in those few pounds of chemicals. And you're overlooking the long-term reality—sane or insane, the lives we all live are written on water."

David is smiling. "Since every material thing resolves itself into neutrons and protons and finally energy, both the water that holds us together and the handful of critical chemicals are constantly appearing in new guises. All of us are composites. Billions of us have lived and died, but none of us has totally vanished. You and I are a million-year-old mixture. Obviously, the act of suicide is an impossibility. The *sui*, or essence of us, never dies."

"Maybe you're right," I tell him wearily. "But I've failed at everything that I've tried, including killing myself."

"Failure implies some social concept of success," David answers. "If I remember correctly, you were a very successful porno star. You wrote articles and shocked hell out of people by saying that you had overcome your earlier Puritanical sexual morality and your WASP conditioning, which you blamed for your suicidal tendencies."

He chuckles. "You evidently accomplished this by the simple process of opening your mouth and sucking male cocks. You even wrote an article, which was published in one

111

of the psychological journals, affirming the theory that most men and women grew old faster than they should because they repressed their continuous human needs to suck and taste each other."

"I see that you've thoroughly researched me." I'm staring grimly at a freighter in the harbor, passing by our window, and I'm wondering why I don't tell David that reminding me of my past makes me very uneasy. "Maybe the truth is that I've gone far beyond being a simple manic-depressive. Maybe I'm a hopelessly crazy schizophrenic."

David shrugs. "Most psychiatrists play the politics-of-therapy game. If they were really interested in curing human psychological problems, they'd admit the truth. The only correct approach is to create a new tomorrow, and eliminate the kind of world that once made one in ten Americans occupants of psychiatric wards and insane asylums. And despite lithium, we're a long way from resolving the kind of psychologically inhuman world we have made. Eventually, we must create better environments. New tomorrows where people can live more creative lives, and not measure the value of their creations by how much they will bring in the marketplace. You could live to enjoy that kind of world, Christina."

As we eat lunch, David's emphasis on "new tomorrows" reminds me of Mory and brings tears to my eyes, but I refuse to reveal my thoughts to this man who once again is exerting an hypnotic effect on me. David keeps telling me how much he'd like to have me meet Max Lebenthal. He wants to show me their laboratory. "We can be there in an hour," he tells me. "Since our work is subsidized by the government we're practically inside Camp Edwards and the Army base. We'll introduce you to Pluto, our dog, who has been successfully maintained in hypothermia for two separate six-month periods, and Aqua, our calico cat, who has just finished her first six-month cycle. We'll show you innumerable fish, mice, and insects we have super-cooled, who have survived beautifully. Now we're moving beyond hypothermia into a chemical approach to reduced metabolism. If you decide to join us, it could give you another, more fascinating, option."

The option, of course, is really the Hank Hutchings option. If I can't take my own life, I can hire an assassin, or give myself to one. Scarcely aware that I'm eating Boston scrod and sipping white wine, I can't help toying with the damnable idea. But I'm only half listening as David explains that their project is related to manned space trips to Mars and Venus and beyond, and that the potential for human interstellar travel already exists, particularly if the human-discomfort factor can be resolved. "Controlled anabiosis," he is telling me, "is the only logical solution to the boredom and confinement of travel into other planetary systems. Eventually, completely self-contained space vehicles equivalent to ocean liners will be developed. People traveling intergalactically—human lifetimes away—will live and die on these ships, and new generations will be born as the voyagers search for new worlds. But that may be five centuries from now. Right now, relatively, we are in the fifteenth century. The first Christopher Columbuses in space must be hibernators."

"But why are you experimenting with potential suicides?" I ask him. "It seems to me that if you'd publicize your experiments, you'd have thousands of volunteers. As you've suggested, it could be a new fad. A new way of becoming a national hero or heroine. Lucky winners would get the biggest prize of all. They'd be born again in the next world. Men and women in prison for life could be offered their freedom in another century. Old people, who are going to die in a few years, anyway, would get a chance to take a peek at tomorrow. There are thousands of people like the astronauts, or mountain climbers, or professional soldiers, who live their lives challenging death."

David shakes his head. "None of these people you mention would like the odds. While we've made extraordinary progress, Max and I estimate our chances with human beings surviving and adapting to the antimetabolites that we have synthesized, and still being alive if they are frozen and then thawed twenty, fifty, or a hundred years from now, are nearly zero for freezing and about fifty percent for hibernation. That's why, thus far, we have experimented only with short periods of low-temperature hibernation, using perfusion and blood replacement with cryoprotectants which we have developed. Prior to our successful—but as yet unreported—experiments with Pluto and Aqua, two scientists, Smith and Lovelock, froze golden hamsters, which are hibernating animals and have a high resistance to cold injury. They were frozen in a liquid bath by direct immersion at minus five degrees centigrade. After varying lengths of time, none so long as we have attempted, they were thawed by radio-frequency heating. Artificial respiration was used during the thawing process.

"When more than fifty-five percent of their body weight

113

was frozen," David continues, "none of the hamsters survived, although they temporarily resumed normal breathing. Ice formation injured their eyes, lungs, stomachs, and intestines."

David is paying the check as he talks. "Come on, Christina. It's a nice afternoon for a ride. Come and take a look. I'll have you back here by about five-thirty. You'll be safely home by six-thirty."

"Really," I demur, "I can't. As you must have guessed, I'm on tricyclics. I'm supposed to take three pills a day. I left in such a hurry this morning that I not only forgot to take my pill, but I didn't bring any with me." I wasn't lying. At least momentarily, I was willing to go along with Dr. Leonard and any treatment that would let me swim over my self-created hell.

"What are you taking?" David asks.

"Amtryptyline," I tell him.

"No problem." He asks the waitress for a paper cup so that we can take some water with us. "In my bag, in my car, I have a similar anti-depressant." He takes my hand sympathetically. "We certainly don't want you to lose any ground."

Following David to his car, I wonder why I don't just tell him that I think he's crazier than I am. I'm even wondering if the whole mad idea of offering a potential suicide the direct challenge of giving up her own life isn't something that Karl might have cooked up with David to jar me into sanity. I've always thought that Karl is the kind of man who, if you held a pistol to your head and threatened to pull the trigger, would challenge you to go ahead. But Karl couldn't be calling my bluff. Hadn't I proved to him that I wasn't bluffing?

Still, it's one thing to think so little of your own life that you are willing to kill yourself. At least then, when you finally do it, even though you might have considered it many times, the act is spontaneous and impulsive, and it's too late to retreat. It's something else again to give your life to a stranger on the chance that you may discover what it is like to be dead or to live into another century.

In his station wagon, in response to David's request, as I swallow the pill that he's taken out of his medical bag, I point out my Mercedes, and then I wonder why he has asked me where it is.

"Just didn't want you to get tagged," David tells me. "You're all right. No one will bother your car for a few hours on the pier."

In his car I ask him, "Why don't you confine your experiments to older people? The way many of them have to live today, without families, without much hope of any kind, confined in nursing homes or senior citizens' centers, thousands of them would probably volunteer. You'd be giving them a socially approved way to end their lives. They're living with one foot in the grave, anyway. A lot of them might like to try hibernation for as long as a year. It would give some sense of purpose to their lives."

"About fifteen years ago," David says, "an area of cryonics—freezing the dead, against some future day when they might be thawed, and cured of the diseases, such as cancer, that were slowly killing them—received international publicity. There still are a few cryonics societies left. A very fascinating man, Robert Ettinger, founded the movement. He wrote a book, *The Prospect of Immortality*, about some aspects of it. While there are only a few cryotoriums left in the United States where a body can be frozen, according to Ettinger membership in the society is still growing. As far as we've been able to determine, there are only twenty-four bodies now being preserved in the United States in cryonic suspension. Keep in mind that these people were legally dead to begin with. No one has tried to thaw them. In our opinion, when and if they do, the subjects will be quite dead. The process that has been used involves blood replacement with a cryoprotectant, a solution like glycerol, similar to anti-freeze. The corpse is placed in a Thermos-shaped capsule and is frozen to minus three hundred degrees centigrade with liquid nitrogen. The liquid nitrogen must be replaced continuously. I suppose, if you were a President or a dictator, or a famous sex object, you might like to have your body preserved for posterity." David chuckles. "If you were female, anyone who decided to fuck with you would freeze his putz off."

I am watching the hot asphalt Cape highway—a long ribbon stretched interminably before us—and I'm wondering why I don't tell David to turn around and bring me back to Boston. Or if he won't do that, I can demand that he simply let me out of the car. I'll hitchhike back. He knows I'm angry at the innuendo about sex objects, but he skips along in his dissertation.

"Joking aside," he says, "we're certainly not interested in freezing anyone who is already dead. But you must remember that we live in a world where only the society itself, acting through its courts, has the legal right to take another

115

person's life. The law would probably interpret the hibernation of a living human being, even if that person were willing, as servitude or selling oneself into slavery."

I shiver. "To be quite honest, David, the whole idea leaves me cold, and that's no pun. On the premise that I may eventually kill myself, you're asking me to be one of your laboratory animals. In between my hibernations, if they're successful, you may even promise to let me out of my cage temporarily. I suppose since I'd be an easily available 'sex object,' if you felt like screwing me there wouldn't be much I could do about it. Among other things, you'd have your own captive sexual slave. If I screamed too loudly, you'd simply shove me back into hypothermia until I cooled off, literally or figuratively."

"I might be tempted," David says, "but the truth is that taking a woman against her will has never appealed to me. Without an actively cooperating woman, sex is a bore."

"That's another problem," I tell him. "I don't seem to have a very strong will when I'm with you. I'm easily hypnotized, as you've already proved. Even right this minute, I'm of two minds. I feel this conversation is silly, and that I should be honest with you. I don't give a damn about your experiments or your laboratory. Yet, right now, I'm suddenly feeling very lethargic. I don't care whether Christina or hell freezes over." The thought crossed my mind that the supposed tricyclic pill he has given me shouldn't give me this detached feeling. I wonder in a desultory way whether he has drugged me or hypnotized me again.

David is responding to my sexual fears. "Christina, I may not have had as lurid a sexual past as you seem to have had, but I have been married. My wife divorced me because she couldn't tolerate my scientific obsessions, which interfered with our home life and our togetherness. But before marriage and after, I've had no difficulty in finding attractive bed companions. While I find you sexually appealing, my prime interest in you is exactly the same that I have with any woman or man of your relative age. Our goal is to outwit human death. We and many other scientists have proven that we're on the right track with animals. Now, without getting involved in a nationwide discussion of the morality or immorality of our experiments—you must already be aware of the problems caused by doctors who have attempted well-meaning euthanasia, or abortions past certain prescribed months—we are quietly contacting people like yourself who will trade a 'now'

116

they are no longer interested in for a future time where they may discover a more simpatico world."

David is driving faster. He sounds as if he's trying to convince himself. "Several years ago," he tells me, "before we received 'no questions asked' government funding, the multimillionaire, Tom Gates, who died a few months ago in Texas, offered to set up the Gates Foundation with a fifty-million-dollar funding. The sole purpose of the foundation would be to perfect the freezing of human beings, in the hope that they might be revived in a hundred years. The old man was seventy-five at the time, and in reasonably good health. When Max and I told him that we would be interested, if he would work out the financial details as fast as possible, and consign himself to us while he was still alive, he was a little shocked. He agreed, but he wanted a written guarantee that he would be thawed in one year to see if we really knew what we were doing." David laughed. "Since that time, we have moved far beyond super-cooling into chemical anabiosis and mildly low temperature maintenance of the human body as a more feasible way of guaranteeing longevity."

"You keep telling me that there is no guarantee."

"Of course there isn't. There was no guarantee that you'd be saved from your various suicide attempts."

"I wish that I hadn't been," I tell him, and I can't hold back the tears flooding my eyes. "I'm an embarrassment to my husband and my children. No one needs me in this world."

"You've been playing footsies with the 'savage god'." David's voice sounds cruel. "Most people are quite shocked when someone prefers to annihilate himself than live. Today, we even question God when human life is cut short, before its normal statistical longevity. No matter how bad it may get, we're supposed to have the guts and moral fiber to live it through to the end. A few weeks ago a sixteen-year-old girl, standing on the portico of her church, kept the priest and the parishioners at bay by threatening to slash her throat with a penknife. She had already cut her jugular vein, and her wrists were bleeding profusely. While the police and the priests tried to talk her into surrendering, some of the crowd were exhorting her: 'Go ahead. Kill yourself and get it over with!' They hated her because she could no longer cope with the world and wanted to die."

"She sounds like a good prospect for you," I tell him bit-

117

terly. "When do I get to meet the other members of your Suicide Underground?"

David chuckles. "Too bad we can't publicize the name. I'm sure we'd have hundreds of applicants. To our knowledge, there are only three other laboratories in the United States working on this project. We meet every six months and discuss our progress. We are behind two of the others, who already have eight volunteers in hibernation."

David is slowing the car down. Suddenly, he abruptly turns off the highway onto a sandy road.

"We don't advertise that we are here," he says. The opening to the road is nearly obscured by a thick growth of scrub pines. The transmission of the car scrapes against the dune and grass growing between the ruts. A tangled forest of creeping vines, thorn-laden bushes, and stunted pines brush against the windows of the car.

Fighting a dull torpor which is slowing down my responses, I scream, "You said that your laboratory was on the Army base. Where in hell are you taking me?" I suddenly wonder if I've gone joyriding with a maniac. I wonder if David is going to stop the car, drag me out, and rip off my clothes. I can see myself running naked through the briars trying to escape him. My breasts and belly are lacerated and bleeding. "I'm not Princess Briar Rose yet!" I yell, and I'm opening the car door and about to leap out, when we bump to a stop in front of a twelve-foot-high chain-link fence, topped with running barbed wire.

As the gate slowly opens in response to an electronic signal from David's car, he soothes me. "Christina, I told you that this is a top-secret project. We aren't located directly on the Army base for security reasons."

While I'm belatedly and foggily wondering why I'm so special that I'm invited to see the inside of a top-secret government installation—I'm sure to tell Karl, and he'll tell his friends—David is explaining that the laboratory grounds are located on approximately four acres which are fully protected from intruders by the fence, which is electrified. He drives his car about a quarter of a mile beyond the gate and parks in front of a low brick-faced building which seems to be about fifty thousand feet square and is covered with trumpet vines bursting with orange flowers. Six other cars are parked in front, facing the building. The laboratory suddenly doesn't seem so formidable. But when I step out of the car, I'm unaccountably wobbly on my feet. "I must have been sitting too long in one position," I tell David as he gently takes my arm. I'm still wondering why in hell I've let myself be driven ninety miles from Boston to see some damned scientific laboratory, buried deep in the forest on the Cape. Then I have a sudden frightening presentiment. David not only believes what he has been telling me about preserving and extending human life for many years, but he's quite mad. His obsession leads him to believe that the combination of my suicidal tendencies and the fact that I've written a novel about the Sleeping Beauty legend makes me a prime candidate for his version of the story of Princess Briar Rose.

Shivering at my thoughts and the sudden coolness of the air-conditioned interior of the building, which makes me wonder if I'm entering my own future crypt, I'm still disassociated, and feeling strangely feeble. I'm unable to evoke the scream of terror which is trying to worm its way out of my churning intestines. Through the window wall we are passing, I have glimpses of several men and women wearing white coats, and cages of hamsters and mice, and scientific instruments of all kinds, and I can see my contorted face, but I can't seem to release my suppressed yell of fear.

David is guiding me down a rug-covered corridor at the back of the building, and then he opens the door into what seems to be a study. Three of the walls are lined with books. A sliding window wall looks out onto a trimmed green lawn with a stone fountain in the center surrounded by cypress trees.

A tall, skinny incarnation of drawings that I have seen of Don Quixote, with receding sandy hair, and cheeks sunken around protruding facial bones, stands up from behind a large mahogany desk and greets me. "I'm David's partner, Max Lebenthal," he says, and his next words confirm my fears. "It's delightful to have the famous Sleeping Beauty join us in person. I remember your movie. While this is no castle in the forest, I think you may find our laboratory quite interesting."

I'm hearing him, and although I'm not dizzy, I know that I'm wavering, I'm finding it increasingly difficult to stand up. David is holding my arm firmly. I have the strange sensation that everything I'm hearing, or saying, is in slow motion. I feel as if I have been smoking marijuana. Time has slowed down. A minute lasts an hour. I manage to look at my watch. I can't believe it. It's only three-thirty! Has only an hour and a half passed since I got into David's car? I get a grip on myself. "I really haven't much time," I tell them. "David promised me that he'd have me back in Boston by five-thirty."

"She's had one Vitaleben," David tells Max. "Her doctor prescribed Amtryptyline, but she just started the regimen the day before yesterday. She forgot to take it today."

David motions me toward a leather couch. Gratefully, I slump onto it. "You didn't give me Amtryptyline in your car." Suddenly, I know damned well that he has duped me. Whatever he gave me, it wasn't any tricyclic anti-depressant pill.

David anticipates my question. "With your background in clinical psychology, though you never practiced psychiatry, I presume you know that tricyclics take a few weeks for a build-up before they work. In fact, no one knows exactly why they work with some depressives, or why lithium calms the manic phase. The pill that I gave you is not a mood elevator per se, it's a compound that Max and I synthesized from the brain cells of hibernating animals. A well-known cardiovascular surgeon, Henry Swan, tried this successfully a number of years ago. He worked with the brains of lungfish, which can hibernate up to two years. Swan's experiments with rats proved that the chemical which he called antabolone reduced the rat's metabolic rate. Our synthesis is more complicated. It will slow down your total metabolism about fifty percent for about twenty-four hours. Your calcium metabolism of course, is likewise reduced. There's an interesting by-product to our experiments. In 1955, several doctors working in a metabolic unit of the Payne Whitney Clinic, who were studying the biological aspects of psychiatric disorders, discovered that calcium is a nervous-system 'sedative.' Fluctuations in the amount of calcium at the cell membranes affect the flow of substances in and out of the cells—for example, the influx and efflux of sodium ions."

David is holding my hand, feeling my pulse. "We'll give you an interesting book to read by Dr. Frederick Flach, *The Secret Strength of Depression*. Flach will give you some background on the role of calcium loss in aging, which Hans Selye insists accelerates the aging process by activating the removal of calcium from the bone."

I'm understanding David, and although I'm still not percolating very well, I manage to yell, "You son of a bitch, I'm not reading anything you give me! You've been experimenting with me already. You won't get away with it." I'm sobbing, and tears are pouring down my cheeks. "My husband will sue you out of existence."

Max looks a little perturbed, but David smiles at him reassuringly. "It's too bad that Vitalebens aren't patentable. Unfortunately, they contain no new chemical combination. Otherwise, we could take our discovery to one of the pharmaceutical companies. A possible side effect of the lower metabolism induced by these pills is a total elimination of bipolar depression. Max and I could become rich men. But you don't have to worry, Christina, Max and I have taken Vitaleben over fairly long periods with no apparent harm. And they may give the patient a longer life in the bargain."

Max is nodding happily at me. "You must understand, Mrs. Klausner, that we're only part way to our goal, which is to successfully slow human metabolism to about ten percent of normal."

"I'd rather be crazy than be a vegetable," I manage to say. "You know goddamned well that right now I'm terrified. My whole body is screaming at you. Your fucking pill is worse than chloral hydrate. If you gave me a mickey, at least I'd be unconscious." I am stumbling for words for the sensation I am experiencing. My mind is a motion picture whose frames are turning so slowly that when I initiate a potential action, the integrated sequence catches up with it so slowly that the response flutters off into nothingness. Although my speech sounds quite normal to me, I feel as if I am trembling with fear, but before I can transform the fright into a muscular reaction, I lose interest.

Meanwhile David, determined to indoctrinate (brainwash) me, picks a book off Max's desk. "Here's a very interesting overall survey for laymen by Albert Rosenfeld called *Prolongevity*. We hope that you'll read it, Christina. With your background, and our direction and guidance, we know that you're going to become increasingly interested in extending your own life-span."

Once again, while I'm listening to David read from the book, I wonder if this is all some kind of cruel joke that Karl is playing on me. I've been kidnapped by maniacs who are trying to convince me I can live forever, while all I've been trying to do is to die today.

David is calmly reading to me. " 'For a long time biomedical scientists believed that almost any slowdown in the rate of life processes was accompanied by a slowdown in the metabolic rate . . . it has been axiomatic that the life-span is inversely proportional to the metabolic rate. And so it is on a species basis. The shrew with a high-burning rate dies in a year or two, while the Galapagos tortoise, with a slow burn, goes on for a century or two. The hummingbird has a very high metabolic rate, but it keeps itself going by 'hibernating' every night—slowing its motor down to a slow idle, as it were. Bats have to do that for twenty hours of the day. But it does not hold for individuals within a species.' "

"You see," Max interrupts, "the conundrum that we are trying to solve is the intermix between high metabolism, hibernation, and lower-than-average body temperatures. As Bernard Streger pointed out some years ago in *Medical News:* 'The question is whether long-lived people have slightly lower than average body temperatures. A few degrees centigrade drop in body temperatures could add something like fifteen to twenty-five years to human life! But, of course, that is difficult and costly to maintain.' "

"Max is experimenting with himself in all directions at once." David says. "He sleeps naked with a thin blanket with the temperature at fifty degrees, and using McCay's work as a basis—McCay doubled the life-span of rats by reducing their caloric intake—Max is able to survive on about a thousand calories a day, which, unfortunately, may induce higher metabolism rather than lower. So there's obviously many other factors in combination with lowered metabolism that create greater longevity or slow down aging."

"Please, both of you, I beg you." I'm sobbing and I'm nearly hysterical. "Let me go. I don't want to be your human rat in a cage. If you do that to me, I'll really kill myself. Please, for God's sake, take me back to Boston. I promise you I won't breathe a word about this to anyone."

Max looks questioningly at David, but David shakes his head in an emphatic no. "It's too late, Max. We can't turn back now. I told you that she and Rose Plackett are about the same size. If I get Rose back to Boston by four-thirty, Rose can drive Christina's Mercedes to that boat rental place in Saugus. She should be there by five. I've rented a Boston Whaler already. I'll meet Rose near Egg Rock. We'll capsize the boat Rose has rented, get Rose back into her own clothes, and we'll be back here by eight. They'll find the Mercedes by tomorrow or the next day at the latest. And that will be that. The pattern will be obvious. It's the kind of thing Christina might do, anyway."

Max shudders. "This isn't the way we planned it. You convinced me that, like the others, she'd be amenable, and she'd be happy to join us."

David shakes his head again. "What has motivated those who have joined us already is open to question, and you know it. Rose is our only real convert. We really need more time to study the suicidal syndrome." He laughs grimly. "Maybe the very thought of what we are offering is shock therapy. I don't have all the answers. According to Werner and Stiles, they've had one-hundred-percent enthusiasm. Before we take another voyager into tomorrow, we'll have to review their approaches."

"The others have chosen people like Rose," Max tells him. "She has no family. No friends. That makes a difference. We've given Rose someone who cares about her—us."

"You!" David says. "She adores you." He sits down beside me and holds my hand. The bastard is staring at me with an intense, loving expression. I can't look away from his burning eyes. "You can stop worrying, Max. Christina will come around."

I'm listening to this conversation with muted anger. I even think I'm capable of getting up and running out the door, but I still don't seem to have the energy. I'm some kind of tranquilized zombie, and then David proves it.

"We need to borrow your clothing, Christina," he says, and he gently wipes the tears from my cheek with his handkerchief. "We'll get you some others later." As he talks he unbuttons my blouse, takes it off, unhooks my bra, removes it. Then he unzips the trousers of my pant suit. He gestures to Max, who pulls them off, while David lifts me slightly off the couch. Blushing, if he had any blood in his face, Max slides off my panties. I'm stark-naked. David, holding my hands again, looks at me approvingly. "You really are worth preserving, Christina," he says. "It's fortunate you wore a pant suit today. It didn't occur to me until right now, but it would be inappropriate to be renting an outboard wearing a dress."

"I'm not renting any outboard," I mumble, and I can't stop crying. I hear my voice as if it belongs to someone else.

"We need your rings and your watch, too," David says. "Take them off and give them to me."

And I do it! At the same time, I'm telling him, "Let me go. You can't do this to me. You can't do this to me."

"We're not doing anything to you yet," David says. As I stumble toward the door, still with some conviction left that I must escape, he takes me in his arms and kisses my cheek. "In a few days your understudy, a woman about your age who died a few weeks ago, is going to commit suicide for Christina Klausner. Long live the new Christina!"

◆

During the week my two jailers and Rose Plackett usually all arrive together. They take small samples of my blood for their analyzer. Then either David or Max remains, often for as long as an hour, and talks with me—or tries to cajole me into believing that what they are doing is for my own greatest good.

According to David, they have perfected a computer analyzer based on ultraviolet spectroscopy. Working with very small samples of my blood, they can measure and monitor more than a hundred biological changes taking place in my body.

Max tries to assure me that they are proceeding very carefully. Before they actually put me into some kind of low-keyed hibernation, they are building a complete biochemical profile on me. Gradually, as I realize that I am never going to divert Max sexually or use sex as a means of effecting my escape, I discover that he is more of a scholar than David, and less of an opportunist. While they both keep promising me that I will eventually see their laboratory, they have never let me out of my room. I'm certain that not only don't they want me to know in advance what is actually going to happen to me, but they don't want me to see that the building already houses quite a few voluntary (?) formerly suicidal hibernators.

While I can't pry much out of Max about his life, I know he is more than fifteen years older than David and that he has been married for thirty years and has four children. I also know that Max would be happier if I were a willing subject. He has spent many hours trying to convince me that he and David are not going to let me die. I am going to be one of the first human beings to *experience* death—actually stop living for a while—and then be born again.

He tells me that if he were younger, and if he didn't have such a commitment to finding the answers *now*, he'd take a hibernation break himself. "Just think, Christina," he says, "long after David and I are dead, you will be alive and enjoying the world of 2030. You might even be alive a hundred years from now, and you'll still be a young woman of thirty-three."

He ignores my observation that humans in 2030 or 2080—if they had been permitted to make their own choice—might have preferred to have vanished from this earth.

He believes that, given the choice, most people in reasonably good health would always prefer life to death. "You have to understand that we are only incidentally cryobiologists," he explains. "We are primarily gerontologists working with the amazing and involved processes of human aging. We're not alone in this field. David has given you a good layman's survey, *Prolongevity,* by Albert Rosenfeld, which I hope you have read."

I have, first in a desultory way, then I became fascinated by the inevitability of biologists discovering the answers to death. When they succeed, I wonder if they won't mess up the world more than the nuclear bomb has.

But Max only shrugs. "Rosenfeld points out that all biologists have a common conviction that there does exist within ourselves an identifiable 'clock of aging'—a genetically determined program that dictates how we will age and die, and the rate at which this will occur, and that we have an excellent chance of discovering the location (there may be more than one) of the 'clock of aging,' as well as the nature of the operating mechanisms, and how to interfere with them to our own advantage."

Thinking I may discover more about Max if I keep him talking, I surprise him by telling him that I know the bare outlines of some of the biologists' theories. There is Robert Kohn's cross-linkage theory. Supposedly, adjacent molecules become coupled, and the cell's enzymes can't break them apart, thus gradually causing old age. Cross-linkage could occur in the protein enzymes or in the nucleus of the red-blood cells, or in the DNA, or in its transmitters, RNA's. And there is Leonard Hayflick's theory of cellular aging, with the human cell containing its own irreversible clock. We are composed of mitotic cells that continue to divide as the body lives, and post-mitotic cells such as the brain cells and heart cells that divide only once, and have self-destruct calendars built into them. Or there is Donna Dencla's belief that aging is hormonal in nature, and the clock of aging resides in the

125

brain, and the thyroid gland which produces thyroxine, which is the great god of life, controlling the metabolic rate and the speed at which cells burn their fuels and consume their oxygen. Dencla believes that there is a blocking hormone (Deco—the death hormone) that prevents cells from using this thyroxine.

I can't help laughing at the pleased expression on Max's face. "And there's Denham Harman's theory that all cells produce a quantity of free radicals which fuck their way into union with other molecules, screwing them up completely, and inevitably causing an aging effect."

I can tell from Max's expression that he doesn't approve of mixing human sexual terms with his biology. "All these damned theories, and yours, too, run counter to Nature's plan. Attempts to counterbalance inevitable aging and death with antioxidants and chemicals ranging from thyroxine to Vitamin E are dangerous. You'll screw up the whole planet before you're through. Human beings should continue to evolve in a continuous life-and-death cycle. That way, working with statistical averages, normal genetic mutations can occur which will improve the species. You and David are bio-lunatics. I don't believe in God—or you—but when man fucks around with his worm's eye view of things, he sure as hell is going to end his world with a bang."

But Max only smiles at me benignly. "Man can't leave well enough alone because he never knows where 'well enough' begins or ends. Right here in our laboratory we are learning enough to create *self-induced* genetic transplants. Ultimately, we may be able to simulate them chemically. If we discover the perfect activator, your cells may never wear out. In fact, there is no reason why our cells couldn't go on forever. You could remain Christina—thirty-three and beautiful and in good health—for several centuries, and then, if you get weary, you could choose your time to die."

"Goddamn it," I tell him, "I've already tried to choose my time to die, but I'm surrounded by interfering morons. The thought of becoming a living Rip Van Winkle horrifies me."

But neither Max nor David even listens to such objections. Max has evidently reported some of this conversation to David, who tells me, "We're not really searching for the Holy Grail, Christina. Right now, we believe we have in our hands an intermediate solution. We don't know how to stop active cellular aging—man may never learn how—but we are on the verge of an exciting breakthrough. We believe that we can achieve complete anabiosis and stop all human processes without cellular damage for as long as twenty years."

David has brought in a cloth-covered cage. He takes it off the floor and puts it on my bed. I shudder when he removes the sheet. The cage is filled with two-foot-long snakes. They are brown or reddish and marked with bands that form X's or V's. Their long tongues are snapping angrily at the walls of their glass prison. "They're adders," David says. He lifts one of them out of the cage. "They'll bite, but their poison is rarely fatal to humans. "We import them from Scotland. At nine degrees centigrade, they hibernate in caves or hibernaculums. They've been known to hibernate as long as two hundred and seventy-five days." David laughs. "You have more in common with these little devils than you may realize. Vitaleben, to which you're adapting very well, is partially synthesized from their brain cells, and from those of the African lungfish. We believe we have the perfect thyroxine."

Interestingly, in the past few weeks, instead of being depressed or even completely manic, I've been experiencing a subdued sense of elation. Subdued is the keyword. I'm no longer out of control. I'm not vacillating between extreme highs or lows.

David tells me that my average body temperature, over the past two weeks, has been running 86° F. instead of the normal 98.6°. Yet, I'm able to function mentally and physically without any difficulty, and even though my skin must feel quite cool to others, I'm not cold or shivery. Whether my changed mental outlook is due to the antimetabolic injections, or has been induced by a growing curiosity to actually see the laboratory, I'm not sure.

But since last night—Christ, I think it was last night—when I finished *Notes from the Future*, whatever curiosity I might have had about their experiments has been considerably dampened.

In Amosoff's novel, the hibernation procedure is described in some detail—as it is in Robert Prehoda's book, *Suspended Animation*. But if anabiosis could be achieved, there are at least a hundred other procedures involved, including removing waste products with kidney dialysis machines, keeping the heart from fibrillating before it reached 60° F. both during freezing and thawing, plus general asepsis in the intestinal region and in the oral cavities, and much, much more. All of which, in my opinion, would simply reduce the human body to a robot mechanism. Is that the future I'm headed for?

◆

I think I'm slowly regaining my sense of time reality. I have a sensation that I've been on a long, long voyage. Sitting here at this table, trying to type the continuing saga of Christina, I think that I typed, "Long live Christina!" But I'm sure that can't be true. Yet everything seems to be where I left it last night. The table near my bed has the same pile of twenty or so books on biochemistry and cryobiology that Max and David have given me to read. Yet, though the room seems unchanged, I seem to be waking out of a dream that was—is—Christina.

I've been reading over these manuscript pages, and I must admit that they are a horrible mishmash. Past and present are still blending in my mind. I must fight it. I must complain to David. This cheap sulfite paper he gave me is already turning yellow. It will never last a hundred years. Big joke. Neither will I. If I don't stop hallucinating, if somehow I don't merge the present, past, and future of Christina, I can easily diagnose my own finale. I'll tumble into a hopeless state of insanity. Damn. I'm not sure that it was this morning, maybe it was yesterday, or one or two days ago? Anyway, I had a vague sensation that Rose Plackett or someone was leaving a breakfast tray near my bed. Then she was gone—a minute? . . . an hour? and I woke up screaming. The tray was there with orange juice, cantaloupe, toast, butter, and coffee, and on it was the first newspaper I've seen since I arrived here. The paper looked as if it had been saved for the junkman, but then someone had decided that I might like to see it and had neatly refolded it. I don't know why. I haven't read it yet. The problems of the world don't interest me. First, I have to assimilate my multiple selves and the recurring dream I'm having—or is it reality? I almost prefer not to write about it. While I'm dreaming it, I'm me—and I'm me watching me again, and it terrifies me. But right now, force yourself! Whatever you are typing this minute, Christina, isn't present. *It isn't present!* Dream or reality, everything you are writing *has* happened to you. Maybe. . . .

But I close my eyes, and they're sitting beside me and I'm lying in a shallow crib. Sometimes I think one of them is David. At other times I'm sure that they're total strangers.

128

They are watching me with worried expressions on their faces. They turn me gently from side to side. They massage me with loving hands. They all wear skintight skullcaps. But even when they all seem to be strangers, I'm not afraid of them. Why do they care for me so much? Do they love me?

I'm too weak to raise my head, but when I stare upward through the misty pale blue light, I can see the vague reflection of a naked woman. She's wearing a skintight skullcap, too. Beneath her breasts, and issuing from her arms, neck, and legs, are connections of thin tubing which seems to flow into the side of a transparent shell. She's being fed intravenously. Is she dying? Is she me? The expression on her face doesn't change. If she's me, why can't I tell them? My brain is laughing at them. Why is it so important that I be kept alive? I want to die.

They speak so softly to each other. Their words have a familiar sound, but no meaning. I have a feeling that I'm in a strange country whose language I have heard before, but then I'm floating in a churning ocean, and I can't resist the currents drifting me toward a wild, chaotic whirlpool. My tiniest thought is a splinter, cresting for a moment on a wave, and then disappearing into the endless angry water. I feel anxious. I want to cry. I know I have misplaced something. I see it for a moment. A huge gothic house on the top of a hill surrounded by an iron fence. I run toward the entrance. It's open! But just as I get there a heavy, spiked gate crashes in front of me. I'm on the outside screaming, clinging to the gnarled cast iron, tears running down my cheeks.

"You bastards! You fucking bastards, let me in."

My mind is screaming, but no sounds are coming from my mouth. My computer is running without its software. I'm sobbing my dismay, but there's no change in the passive image that I see stretched out above me. Days, weeks, months, maybe even years, are passing, but I continue to lie here. There is no night or day, only this floating, misty blue light, and loving strangers peering at me endlessly. Are they doctors? Why are we all wearing these skullcaps? Are we swimming in the deep ocean? Are we wearing caps to keep our hair dry? Do we have hair? Ah, I remember! Getting hair wet. Going swimming. Drowning! No—God, no, I don't want to think about swimming.

I'm sure that one of them must be David, but he has no beard and he seems to be older, like Karl. Oh, Jesus. Not Karl. He's the Yang that has no Yin. This man likes me. He is very constant. Sometimes through the blue fog, I think I see tears in his eyes. When his fingers massage me they search my flesh. Are they asking tentative little questions? Does he love me? Who is he? Who are they?

One of them is a woman. Is it Rose? Rose Plackett, my jailer? As they swirl past me, I catch glimpses of the shifting curves of their bodies. Their clothing, shaped either like shirt tunics or jump suits, seems to be transparent. Or am I dreaming? Do I really see through the cloth which floats over breasts and buttocks, over triangular mounds of pubic hair and penises? They are all erotically beautiful.

Oh, please, I beg you. Tell me. Who are you? Who am I? Why am I lying here in this half-open womb? Womb? The word floats lazily through the cells of my brain. When will they sever the multiple placentas and force me to be born? It's too late for labor. Do it now! Cut through the soft flesh of the belly that envelops me. Release me! My mind is an abandoned house with the doors and windows nailed shut. But inside the house I can hear muted stirrings. Inside, strangers with cold eyes are peering through the slats at me. Why don't they let me in? It's cold out here. I'm shivering. What are they whispering to each other? Oh, God—I'm freezing. Oh, God—please tell them to let me inside where it's warm.

Suddenly, I have a strange feeling that they can understand my thoughts. Occasionally their words—unspoken—pour over me as they watch me. They're not really words. They are floating images, pictures. I merge into them, and I'm no longer tossing on a frenzied ocean. I'm lying naked on the edge of an incoming tide on a warm summer day, and the ocean is tasting my body with tiny little tongues.

Over and over again their soothing water image absorbs me. . . . I'm being caressed by infinity. I surrender. I open my mouth and I try to speak, but no sound emerges. There are no words between us, but somehow their deep assurances permeate my brain. "We're receiving you," they seem to be saying. "We're receiving you. Your brain is alive. Don't give up. Keep trying. Your thoughts are water. Let them flow around the rocks in the stream. Be patient. You have world enough and time. We love you!"

Maybe I'm not dreaming this. Maybe I'm only being dreamed. Maybe I'm a dream of this special man who has immersed me in an oily bath. A woman is helping him. They're turning me over. They're carefully exploring every

130

contour of my body. They seem delighted with me. I'm their child. Somehow, I must tell them. I love you. I love you. I reach up with my hands, and I touch their faces. I'm sobbing. Yes, it's me. I can hear me! I'm screaming my delight and wonder. Oh, God—they don't understand. I'm being born, but I'm frightening them.

"David." I hear the woman's voice for the first time. Or is it her voice? She seems to be talking with her eyes. She's telling my special David to quiet me. I hear her mind saying, "She recognizes you, David. She's picking up our waves."

I stare at them. Their mouths aren't moving. They're communicating with me by flooding my brain with ever-changing images. In his mind, David is holding me in his arms. He's kissing my cheek, his hand is holding me at my center, cupping my vulva, while he gently kisses my breast. But actually he's only sitting beside me. The woman is aware of David's image. She's not angry, but she seems dubious. Now David is telling me without words that soon we'll be talking. Why do I need to talk when I can hear his mind so clearly in my mind?

"Please," I beg him wordlessly. "Who are you? Who am I? Why can't I remember? What's happening to me? Am I dying?"

"No. No." Their messages come back together. "You're not dying. You've sensed it already—you're being born. You are reincarnated. A young woman. We know many things about you. But not all. You've been asleep for a long, long time. Now you must regain your mind. It will be easier for you if you try to gradually recapture the person you were, rediscover yourself. Who you were is only the first phase. One's identity viewed from the macrocosm is everybody's identity. When you discover who you were, the next phase is learning who you will become. The whole world is waiting, Christina."

My mind is asking, Is it you, dear prince? How long you have kept me waiting. I smile and then I wake up.

<hr>

Jesus Christina Christ. If I'm ever going to absorb the shadow, let alone the substance of what has happened to me, I guess my only hope is to try to remember the scenario step by step.

When I finally unfolded the newspaper—the Boston *Globe*—which Rose had left on my breakfast tray, the date October 10, 1980, confirmed my guess. Today was Saturday!

This had to be yesterday's newspaper. A Saturday *Globe* wouldn't be delivered on the Cape this early in the morning. As I slowly added the days which had elapsed, I couldn't escape the shuddery question. Had I really been Max and David's prisoner for over four months? I scanned the headlines. CORCORAN MURDER TRIAL GOES TO JURY. PRESIDENTIAL ELECTION STILL IN DOUBT. REPUBLICANS SHOW NEW GAINS. RUSSIA DENIES SUPPLYING AIRCRAFT ONCE AGAIN TO EGYPT. SO HAS THE UNITED STATES.

Americans and Russians provided the armaments so that the rest of the world could kill off their surplus populations. As Thoreau had pointed out nearly two hundred years ago, reading newspapers only resulted in a time-wasting repetition of man's insanities.

And then my eyes froze on a headline at the bottom of page one. BODY OF CHRISTINA KLAUSNER, WIFE OF WELL-KNOWN BOSTON BANKER AND MUTUAL FUND SPECIALIST, WASHED ASHORE YESTERDAY. Sobbing, I read the story of my own death.

While it had been presumed that the former Christina North, who had married Karl Klausner in 1974, had drowned in a boating accident off Egg Rock on June 3rd, her body had never been found. She had rented an O'Day sailer from the Mantori Marina and Boat Rental, presumably for a short pleasure sail up the Saugus River, and off the Lynn and Marblehead shores. Although the sea had been relatively calm, and the boat was equipped with an outboard which she could have used if she had problems returning against the light offshore breeze—nevertheless, tacking toward shore, she had apparently capsized.

On June 4th, Christina's Mercedes had been discovered parked near the boatyard. When he saw her photographs, Jack Mantori told her husband that he was sure, although she was wearing sunglasses, that it was Christina Klausner who had rented his boat. Christina's body had evidently only partially submerged, and had been kept floating for four months by the strong sea currents. Her features were badly eroded by the sea and natural deterioration. Karl Klausner identified his wife by a ten-carat diamond ring he had given her, her wedding ring, and a diamond-studded digital wristwatch. Despite her early history of several suicidal attempts before their marriage, Karl Klausner insisted to reporters that he and his wife had been very happily married, and that Christina enjoyed her life as mother and had adjusted very easily to the world of wealthy jet-setters. The Klausners had homes in Villefranche and Palm Beach as well as in Marblehead. Klausner told reporters that Christina loved to sail, and that she handled small sailboats like an expert. According to Karl Klausner, her death absolutely couldn't have been premeditated suicide. Christina had drowned in an unfortunate accident. Beside her husband, Karl, Christina left her mother, Grace North, and two children, Michael, four, and Penelope, five.

Of course, that wasn't the whole story. Enterprising reporters had exhumed their morgue and filled most of one of the inside pages with a complete and lurid review of the life of the once-notorious Christina North, who had graduated with high honors from Radcliffe as an undergraduate, and four years later had earned her doctorate in clinical psychology. Although she had never practiced psychotherapy, two years later Christina had published a sexually oriented autobiographical novel (they didn't say pornographic), based on The Sleeping Beauty legend, about a young girl's sexual awakening. A year later, when Christina starred in the X-rated movie based on the novel, the book had climbed onto the best-seller paperback list and stayed there for six months. As an undergraduate, she'd had poetry published in several well-known magazines. Her collected poetry was not well known, and had been privately published after her marriage. The book had been received, in poetry circles, with some praise for Mrs. Klausner's potential. Before her fatal accident, Christina had embarked on a new career as a painter, but none of her paintings had ever been exhibited.

No big encomiums or eulogies. Those were for dead heroes. Christina was a Fourth of July rocket, and not even a very good one. Lighted, she had risen a few feet off the ground, and then phutzed back to earth. When Christina was assembled, the manufacturer's inspection team had taken a day off.

Actually, when I stopped sobbing, what irritated me even more than the newspaper story was that neither David nor Max had had the nerve to tell me in person that my suicide was now a fait accompli. Technically, Christina no longer existed. Their faithful hound-dog bitch, Rose Plackett, had not only been agent provocateur in my suicide, but this morning she had brought me the newspaper telling me of my demise.

I suddenly realized that I was no longer depressed. I not only wasn't personally playing footsies with death any longer, but I was no longer quite so apathetic. I knew that I must break out of this prison and escape from these lunatics. Neither Max nor David was going to lose any sleep if Christina died. I was just another laboratory animal, one grade above a mouse or hamster and only a little more difficult to procure. The big difference was that I wouldn't flush down the disposal so easily. They'd have to cut me up first, or bury me.

I was going to escape. I still didn't have the faintest idea how I was going to do it, but I was sure that Saturday was the best time. Was it Saturday? I had no calendar, but I was vaguely aware that every four or five days, a couple of days went by and neither Max nor David visited my room. Rose brought my meals and there was little or no conversation between us. These days must be the weekend.

If today was Saturday, I might never get this chance again. I tried to stop my mind from wandering. I was sure that I must be very, very close to the day that the flame of Christina would be turned down—perhaps forever.

I knew that my body was tolerating the Vitaleben injections, but this morning, sitting on the toilet in my windowless bathroom, and for the first time in weeks having a fairly solid bowel movement, I suddenly realized that I was wearing two-inch bandages encircling both my arms and across my insteps. When had they put those on me? I couldn't remember. Were they to heal my veins, which looked worse than a junkie's from all their injections? But I didn't have time to worry about that.

Trying to get a grip on my vagrant thoughts, I realized that there was another reason that I was sure that it was Saturday. Weekday mornings I was aware of the automobiles arriving, and I could hear the technicians who worked in the laboratory exchanging early-morning greetings with each other before they entered the building. This morning it was so quiet I could hear the bluejays singing outside my window. When I looked through the window bars, the courtyard seemed the same, except that the fountain was not flowing, and it occurred to me dimly that the statue of Diana and her deer seemed much more weathered and covered with moss than it had been.

Since I was sure that it must have been Rose who had delivered my breakfast, there was a good possibility that she and I were the only human beings in the building. I tried not to think of who, or what, might be in the subterranean cellars. Because I usually asked whoever appeared first what

134

time it was, I knew that Rose must have arrived this morning between eight-thirty and nine. I was sure that I had been dawdling, trying to hold myself in focus, for two or even three hours. It was obvious that I didn't have much time left before Rose returned with my lunch.

Rose was usually very distant with me, and I couldn't get her to tell me how in hell she had gotten involved with these madmen. David told me that she was a registered nurse, and like me she once had been suicidal. Her entire family—her husband and two kids—had been killed in an automobile accident, and she had been driving the car. Her mother was in an asylum. Her father was dead, and her husband's relatives blamed her for the accident and hated her. She had no one in the world who cared whether she lived or died. With complete access to hospital pharmacological supplies she had nearly succeeded in killing herself, not once but on three different occasions. Then David and Max had "saved" her.

As David pointed out, Rose had more justification for joining the Convita-Lebenthal team than I had, which meant that unlike me she could be given greater responsibilities. Not only was she taking the Vitaleben injections, but according to David she was looking forward to her super-hibernation. In the meantime she had become a valuable and trusted assistant.

A few days (weeks?) ago, I had finally inveigled her into a conversation, and since then she had become even more remote. Even though she is a little heavier than I am, and looks as if she could easily knock me down, I think she's afraid of me.

"I'm going crazy confined in this room!" I had yelled at her. I pointed out the window. "It seems to be a beautiful day. Why can't I sit out in the courtyard and get some sun?"

"The sun's rays aren't good for you," Rose said. I noticed she speaks in the same not-quite-there way that I know I do. It must be those damned injections.

"I don't give a shit whether they're good or bad," I told her. "Find David or Max, and tell them if they don't let me out of this room, I'll kill myself."

"You've already committed suicide, Christina." She smiled. "Someday, you'll completely forget that you had self-destructive tendencies. You will be one of the fortunate ones. You will read your own obituary and be happy that it didn't happen."

"You crazy bitch," I told her, "do you call what you are

135

doing living? Why don't you admit it? You and I are their fucking guinea pigs. Max may be telling you that he loves you, or maybe he's even screwing you, but one of these days, he and David will shove you and me into their computer-operated life-support systems. With a tear in their eyes, they'll wish us bon voyage—into some future garbage pail . . . Please," I begged her, "let's both walk the hell out of here while we've still got a chance."

But the poor dimwit, who even before Max and David seduced her probably only had half a functioning brain, which they have already expropriated, only shook her head sadly.

"I'm happy here." She stared at me vaguely, evidently wondering why I wasn't.

"Goddamn you!" I yelled, and I flung the soft plastic knife, fork, and spoons that they give me with each meal at her. "Maybe I can't kill myself with these, but if you don't tell Max or David to come here *right now,* I'll suffocate myself with this pillow."

Rose evidently believed me. She gently but firmly extricated the pillow from my fists.

"I don't need a goddamned pillow," I told her. "If you don't tell Max or David to come here immediately, I'll shove this fucking johnny down my throat."

I purposely kept swearing because I guessed that it horrified Rose. David had told me that while Rose was obviously in love with Max, she was, in her words, a "respectable woman." Max was married. Which meant that Rose would never try, as I had, to lure him into the sack.

"None of the doctors is in the building." Clutching my pillow, Rose had backed toward the door. It was the first time I knew that David and Max actually lived somewhere besides this laboratory. "Dr. Convita could be anywhere." Rose shrugged disapprovingly. "He's divorced, you know. In the summer, he used to live in a shack on the dunes near Truro. Now he lives with a woman in some kind of commune."

This had ended the conversation. Rose departed finally, tossing my pillow on the foot of the bed and telling me to behave myself. I guess she had decided that if I really wanted to kill myself, she couldn't stop me. I had heard the key turn in the lock behind the closed door.

If I was right, and today was Saturday, the only thing I had working for me was surprise. The door of the room opened in. I knew that Rose unlocked it from the outside with one of the keys that she carried in her uniform. If I stood behind the door when she arrived with my luncheon tray, then before she was fully aware that I wasn't in her usual line of vision, and that I wasn't lying on the bed or typing or sitting on the hopper in the doorless bathroom, or sitting in the Boston rocker, which was the only other chair in the room, there was a good chance that I could shove her hard enough so that she'd lose her balance.

I needed some kind of follow-through—some kind of weapon to smash her on the head with when I had her down. But there was nothing loose in the room, or in the medicine cabinet, and there was nothing that I could unscrew with a plastic knife. There were books, but you couldn't knock a person out with a book. Then I saw it. The perfect cudgel. One of the rockers from the rocking chair. I was barefoot. I couldn't kick it off. I worked on it for a long time, but I couldn't loosen it. Then, delighted that my brain was still functioning creatively, I noticed the metal uprights in the hospital bed. Using the supports as a lever, and tottering around with the heavy rocker, I finally pried one of the rockers loose.

Flaying the air with my rocker, I was momentarily a female Genghis Khan sweeping out of the mountains and decimating his enemies. Any flesh that I connected with was going to feel as if it were being severed with a scimitar. In the mood I had worked myself into, I didn't care if I broke the bitch's head. Rose had had the effrontery to be my suicidal stand-in. Now I'd be hers, and I wouldn't need some damned corpse they had exhumed and dumped into the Atlantic to finish the job.

The coup de grace dawned on me when I saw the pat of unused butter on my breakfast tray. Using a paper napkin, I carefully oiled the floor where I was sure that Rose would have to step before I gave her the big shove.

I had no idea of the actual time, but I knew I had to get into position so that I could hear Rose when she unlocked the door. I leaned against the wall on the opposite side of the door. The minutes seemed to be drifting into hours. I began to feel dizzy. I knew that if she didn't arrive pretty quickly, I'd end up the blob on the floor, not Rose. I wondered if she had forgotten me, or if I had miscalculated. What would I do if she arrived with David or Max? When she finally opened the door, would I still have the strength and determination to attack her? If I didn't actually knock her down on the first try, what then? She might wrench my weapon out of my hand. If she did, she'd be angry enough to beat the shit out of me.

These gloomy thoughts were pounding through my head when I heard the key turn in the lock. So that I could push her with both hands, I had put the piece of the rocking chair on the floor beside me. Holding my breath, I picked it up and waited. The door opened slowly. As Rose stepped into the room, I knew that she was hesitating. She didn't see me, but she was walking forward, saying softly, "Christina? Christina?"

Screaming like a banzai attacker, I lunged at her. The tray that she was carrying flew up over her head. Her shoes slid on the greased floor, and she landed with a heavy one-two thump, as first her ass and then her head banged against the asphalt tile. I stood over her brandishing my weapon. Dazed, pathetic, almost in shock, she stared up at me. There were tears of fright in her eyes. I had done it! To my amazement the tables were completely turned. I was the avenging deity.

"Please, Christina, for God's sake," she whimpered. "Don't hit me. I'm still recovering. I don't want to die." She tried to turn on her side and push herself off the floor.

"Don't move!" I yelled at her. "If you try to get up, I'll split your skull open." I knew that I was play-acting. I was hyped up by my own sheer nastiness. I was watching myself, in the role of a demented female, starring in a television or movie drama. My harsh words sounded as if someone else were saying them.

"Give me your keys, you bitch," I told her. "And don't make any false moves, or I'll kill you. Strip down. You wore my clothes. Now I'm going to wear yours." I let her sit up, threatening her that if she didn't stop procrastinating and arguing with me, and if she didn't take her damned clothes off, I'd bludgeon her to death. Watching her, it crossed my mind that she wasn't wearing her usual white uniform. Except for the material itself, her outfit was styled like the parachute-jumper playsuit that had limited popularity a few years ago. I was dimly aware that I had seen garments like it before. Then I remembered that the people in that damned recurring dream that I had been having wore similar clothes. Whatever the material was, it was semitransparent, and it seemed out of character for Rose. Not only that, but she was wearing it open down the front, nearly to her navel. The cloth clung to the curves of her breasts and the contours of her stomach. Even the triangle of her pubic hairs was faintly visible. The one-piece suit ended just above her knees. She was wearing sandals and no stockings.

As she reluctantly wiggled out of the playsuit and was finally naked, I suddenly remembered myself as Christina in Johnny Giacomo's movie. Only then it was I, the virgin princess Christina, being forced to undress while the mother of the prince prepared me for my deflowering—not by the prince but by some of her slobbering courtiers who would try to turn me into a whore unfit for her son.

Shaking the memory loose, I discovered what seemed to be a beeper in the pocket of the garment which Rose finally handed to me.

"What's this for?" I demanded.

Rose was hunched over sobbing into her knees. "That's so Dr. Convita or Dr. Thomas can contact me," she sniffled. "I don't live here. I've been coming in weekends to make your meals."

I wondered who Dr. Thomas was, but I knew that now wasn't the time to get into conversation with her. "What do you do if it this thing beeps?"

"Please, Christina . . . you don't understand what has happened to you. You're being dehibernated. You don't have to escape. In a few weeks David will let you go. Look at me, I'm proof of it. I'm on my own."

I stared at her angrily. "You're their goddamned robot pimp!" I yelled. "Don't give me a lot of crap. Just tell me how to use this thing."

"It's not like the beepers that you knew," Rose muttered. It's similar to a personal citizen's band radio, or like your own mobile telephone. You can receive and talk on it directly to the person whose signal you are coded with."

I didn't understand what she meant, and in my hurry to lock her up, and get out of my prison, I failed to ask her the key questions. When and why did David, or anyone else, signal her? What would happen if I didn't respond to the beep and answer it?

"Please, Christina," Rose was beseeching me, "you're not ready for discharge yet. Many of your cells aren't completely reoriented. I beg you, lie down on your bed. Let me go. I won't tell them what you've done. Please, Christina. David cares for you very much. He wouldn't want anything to happen to you. Let me get up, then we can talk. I'm not angry with you."

I wasn't about to believe that Rose would suddenly become

139

my friend if I let her get off the floor. I was edging back to the door, getting ready to slam it closed and lock her in, when she screamed, "Christina . . . you can't possibly get out of here! The fence is laser-controlled with an electric beam."

"Where's the goddamned circuit breaker?" I waved the rocker in her direction. "I'll turn it off."

Rose stared at me wildly. But she didn't answer. She was obviously frightened. "I can't tell you where it is—no matter what you do to me. Whatever you do—" she was sobbing again—"I beg you—don't touch anything electrical in this building. There's too many lives dependent on the electric current. And you could electrocute yourself."

I knew that I was wasting too much time. Even if I actually beat Rose with my scimitar, I was positive that she'd never help me escape. They had thoroughly brainwashed her. "Stay right there on your ass," I told her. "Slide over to that far wall. Don't get off the floor until I've locked this door. If you do, I'll bash you to a pulp."

I backed out of the room, pleased with my television-gangster language. In another second Rose was locked in, and I was bursting with laughter at my own daring. I smoothed Rose's playsuit over my hips, still surprised by the strange material, which adjusted to my smaller frame. The garment reminded me of a television commerical advertising pantyhose. A model is walking away from the viewer, her ass bobbling suggestively. Finally she turns, looks over her shoulder at whoever is watching her, and says breathlessly into the camera something like, "They make me feel as if I ain't wearin' nothin'." Sick! I was sure of one thing, my new outfit left no doubt in the owner's or viewer's mind.

A digital wall clock inside the first door I opened leading into the laboratory read 1:36. I remembered Rose had said that she came here weekends. Was it Saturday or Sunday? It was too late now to ask her. I had only one goal—to find the electrical controls for the fence. With the electricity turned off, I could walk through to freedom. Then I'd run like hell through the woods to the highway, and before the day was over, give Karl, my loving husband, the shock of his life.

To my surprise, most of the laboratory was a miniature zoo. There was cage after cage of mice, rats, hamsters, and guinea pigs, and entire areas devoted to insects and microbes and snakes, and in one section, deep pools with turtles and large fish, several of which I recognized as carp. They reminded me of Huxley's character J. Stoyte in *After Many a*

Summer Dies the Swan. He lived on a diet of carp, hoping to absorb their longevity. I suppose I had expected some kind of Frankenstein-type laboratory with boiling vials and tubes of effervescent chemicals, but the entire floor was as sedate as a hospital or pharmaceutical-company laboratory. Even an amateur could quickly guess that the scientific focus was a continuing study of the longevity of living creatures.

Running wildly from one end of the building to the other, searching along the outer walls, I couldn't find any electrical controls or circuit breaker for the building. In the L where my room was located there were four more empty hospital-style rooms, and one that was decorated with several water-color paintings and a bookcase with a few books. I assumed that was Rose's room. There were no fuses in any of the rooms.

Then I remembered that David had told me that the building had three underground cellars. The laboratory was their public face. I was sure that somewhere, belowground, were living creatures—human beings—frozen or hibernating. Prisoners that David and Max had seduced or kidnapped for their experiments. I opened every door I could find looking for a stairway, but there was none.

Time was running out. Panting, wondering if I would collapse from the continued exertion, hoping my pounding heart wouldn't jump out of its rib cage, I opened the front door of the building and ran toward the fence. Maybe the electricity hadn't been turned on. But then I noticed a sign: KEEP OFF. U. S. GOVERNMENT PROPERTY. THIS FENCE PROTECTED BY LOW-VOLTAGE LASER BEAM.

Sobbing, dejected, I stumbled back toward the building. Then I noticed a strange automobile parked a few feet from the entrance. It was shaped like a clear plastic egg, split lengthwise. It was much wider than a normal small-sized car. It reminded me of pictures I had seen of an automobile designed by Buckminster Fuller way back in 1930, which could get 50 miles on a gallon of gas. Four people could easily sit side by side on the front and back seats without crushing each other. I could see a steering wheel inside. The dashboard panel only had a few unfamiliar instrument controls. Centered at the windshield level was what seemed to be a small television screen.

It occurred to me that if I could drive the damned thing, I could smash it into the electrical fence. The tires would insulate me. If I could open the fence even a crack, I could slide through without touching it. But the curved, clear sliding panel door of the strange automobile was locked, and I couldn't open it with any of Rose's keys. Rose probably knew where the right key was, but I was afraid to unlock the door and try to force her to tell me.

Back in the building, I remembered the library-office where David had brought me the first day I had arrived. The keys to the car might be there. Happily, the door was unlocked. The room hadn't changed much. It was still lined with books, and evidently was still being used by David and Max as a study. The mahogany desk was strewn with papers diagraming some biological processes. Gasping and sweating—I hadn't stopped running since I'd escaped from my room—I flopped in the chair in front of the desk and yanked open one drawer after another, searching for keys or God knows what—maybe even a gun to kill David and Max with, should they arrive.

Strangely, I had no desire to kill myself. But I was beginning to have a hopeless feeling that all my effort was in vain. I'd never escape from this damned prison. Before the day was over they would have captured me, and I'd be back in my room waiting for the inevitable.

Tugging on the handle of one of the bottom drawers, I suddenly realized that it was locked. I tried to pry it open with a letter opener that I found on the desk but the opener snapped in two. I discovered a heavy cable under the desk going directly into the floor, and I was sure that it must contain the electrical controls of the building. I needed a screwdriver, or a thin piece of strong metal, to wedge it open.

Back in the laboratory, ripping desk drawers open and screaming my frustration—precious time was fleeting—I finally found a metal file. Wedging it into the desk, I broke the lock, and sure enough, what seemed to be a control panel slid out. It had one switch-lever. Was this the electrical control to the fence? I lifted the knife-switch. Nothing happened. Then I noticed that the entire wall of books opposite the desk was slowly sinking into the floor. Behind it was the metal door of what turned out to be an elevator. I had found the way into the basement!

Just as the elevator door was opening in response to my push on the outside button, I heard the beeper. It was buzzing insistently in the pocket of Rose's garment. I wondered if I could control the panic flooding me. What should I do? I was familiar with beepers. Karl had one that he carried on

142

the golf course—in case a financial crisis occurred in one or another of his dealings. His beeper required him to contact an answering service by telephone. According to Rose, this one would put me in direct contact with David, or whoever was signaling.

I knew that if I didn't answer, it might alert someone. Trembling, I pushed the button marked RECEIVE.

"Checking Rose," a voice said, and I knew it was David's. I fumbled with the gadget and finally pushed a button marked SEND. How would Rose respond? "Everything is fine, Dr. Convita." I tried to imitate Rose's voice, which is higher pitched than mine.

I pushed the RECEIVE button, and I was choking with fear. "You sound strange, Rose," David said. "My reception isn't too good. Is Christa all right?"

The bastard. Christa was practically having a heart attack. "I just brought Christa her lunch." I told him. "She was reading."

"What time did you check the hibernaculum?" was David's next question.

"I'm going to do it now," I responded. Though I didn't realize it then, that was the wrong answer, and my question, "Where are you?" compounded the error.

"You know damned well where I am, Rose." David sounded very upset. "Check back with me at the usual time. Closecom." The last word evidently meant that David was through talking. I wondered vaguely what the regular time was that Rose should check back, but I knew damned well that neither she nor I was going to do it.

It occurred to me that David might be on the Cape. Maybe only a few miles away. If Rose (or I) didn't check back, he could be here in a few minutes.

I had to find the electrical controls. There were three buttons on the elevator control. I pushed number one, and the elevator descended and opened on a corridor facing into a clear glass window. I suddenly realized that I was looking into a large, completely equipped hospital operating room. The door was locked. None of Rose's keys fit the lock. A dim light suffused the room. I could see what appeared to be electrical connections on the far wall, but it would have taken a sledge hammer to break the protection of the glass window wall, or to smash the metal door leading into the room.

This room obviously represented the first stage. Here was where David and Max's suicidal volunteers were prepared for freezing or hibernation. I had a strange déjà vu feeling. Somewhere, in another life, I had been in a room like this.

Back in the elevator, I pushed number two, and the door opened on a similar corridor facing into a room filled with computers. The door of this room was locked, too.

Certain that the bottom floor must be the hibernaculum, I was slowly turning into a moaning lump of jelly. It took all my strength to push the final button. The elevator door opened on a third room, similarly constructed. Behind the clear window wall, the room seemed to be immersed in a softly lighted pale blue floating fog. As my eyes adjusted, I could see row after row of cigar-shaped, clear plastic caskets, each held aloft by two metal-jointed arms protruding from the floor that were very slowly oscillating, turning, and vibrating the tubes. Hypnotized, suffused with a sense that I had been here before, I tried Rose's keys in the door. It opened. Dazed, nearly swooning, I wandered between the rows. Inside each tube, suspended midway between the top and bottom, was a naked pale pink human being. Their eyes were closed, but their faces held the suggestion of a faint smile. Extruding from their arms, necks, chests, and legs were plastic tubes connected with U-shaped plastic shunts joining the vein and artery tubes. Each person in his or her own acrylic casket was evidently connected to the side wall, which was covered with hundreds of instruments. Among other things, I was vaguely aware that the blood circulation, heartbeat, respiration, and temperature within each capsule were being monitored.

Identification strips had been inserted into the separate panels. I read a few of them in a state of shock. "Mary L. Phillips, Born May 31, 1958. Hibernated December 6, 1988. Thomas M. Sacerosa, Born February 16, 1952. Hibernated April 6, 1985. Henry M. Bergson, Born July 16, 1957. Hibernated August 12, 1983." There were nineteen bodies in the room, eight women and eleven men, all between the ages of thirty and forty, all with hibernation dates extending into the middle of 1990. Were these people David and Max's suicidal volunteers? Were they frozen solid inside their capsules? Were they dead or alive? The significance of the dates on the panels slowly penetrated my consciousness, but as if I were in the early stages of a nightmare. I hadn't yet woke up screaming.

I tried to read the controls on the various panels. The internal body temperatures of most of the bodies were given in the metric system, but they were somewhere between 5° and 10° centigrade. The heartbeats were one or two a minute. For a few seconds I was immobilized between sheer terror and curiosity. These people weren't dead. But they weren't alive, either! They were zombies, and I was destined to join them. Screaming, I ran to the elevator. There was only one way to escape this charnel house. Somehow, I had to force Rose to open that gate.

When I unlocked the door, she was sitting on the bed wrapped in a blanket. I waved the rocker at her. "I found the hibernaculum." I tried to restrain the hysteria in my voice. "If you don't open that gate and drive me out of here, I'm going back down in that elevator and smash those capsules to pieces. Where are the keys to that automobile?"

"They're in the room at the end of the hall." Rose was sobbing. I made her walk in front of me, and she tripped on the blanket she had wrapped around herself.

"Drop that damned blanket!" I yelled at her. It tumbled at her feet and I was staring at her naked behind. "I'm warning you, Rose," I told her. "If you try anything funny, I'll really beat you to a bloody pulp."

Two minutes later we were inside her car. Looking pathetic and fragile, her large breasts rubbing against the steering wheel, Rose whimpered, "We don't have to crash the gate, Christina. The electronic gate control is right here on this panel."

The car started without a sound. The gate was slowly opening. Then to my horror, as if I were staring into a mirror, an automobile exactly like the one we were in appeared on the other side of the gate, blocking our way. A tall, gray-haired man got out. He was wearing a loose-fitting, semi-transparent jump suit—similar to Rose's. He walked toward us, a grin on his face. I could see his penis and balls vaguely shrouded behind the material. Grabbing my rocker, I slid out of the car and ran toward him brandishing it. Whoever the bastard was, I'd slash him across the groin. If he wouldn't let me go, I'd kill him!

As I swung, he ducked. A second later I was lying on the sand underneath him, screaming helplessly, as he smiled at me.

"She doesn't understand, David," I heard Rose say. "She thinks it's 1980. She doesn't know that it's happened to her already."

The man—it couldn't be David—was clean-shaven. His

face, though ruggedly handsome, had the lines and creases of a man in his fifties.

He pulled me to my feet. "You're a little premature, Christa," he said. "Your sweet sixteen-year *rebirth* party was supposed to be about two weeks from now—in September. Welcome back to the world. It's Saturday, August 24, 1996. If Max Lebenthal were here, he'd soon be able to wish you, 'Happy New Year, 5756.' "

———◆———

As I walked back to the laboratory between the naked Rose and this man who called himself David, the neurons firing at each other in my brain created a no-man's land. My left brain kept telling my right, Play it cool. Don't be frightened. This is one of your early-morning REM dreams that seem to last two lifetimes, but actually only take a few minutes. Go along with these dream people. The truth is that you're in your own bed. Karl is sleeping next to you. If you slide your feet across the arctic area between you, you can wiggle your toes into the cleft of Karl's naked ass. But don't do it! Not yet! If you force yourself awake now, you'll never know what happens.

Rose was trying to assure me that she wasn't angry with me. David was telling Rose that after they checked out the laboratory and hibernaculum, we could drive back together to Mashpee. "Jagger Raynes and Zara Schmidt are 'coptering down this afternoon," he said. "You'll meet all the shareholders in Love Group #317865, Incorporated." His arm was around me, and he was caressing my back, evidently trying to dispel my confusion.

"Really, Christa," he said, and he quickly snuggled my cheek, "I'm not an ogre about to eat you. In a few days we'll drive back to Boston, and I'll take you shopping for new clothes. I'm sure that our corporation, which isn't too rich, will approve an expenditure of at least a thousand dollars." David laughed. "Unfortunately, the money won't buy much. One thing that you're going to discover, which hasn't changed: The rumor of middle-class affluence is still the biggest con game in town. We're all broke. The median income is now forty-five thousand dollars a year, but the dollar in comparison with the 1980 dollar is worth about thirty-two cents."

David patted Rose's naked behind, and she grinned back at

146

him with a very loving expression. "All of this means that on a summer day like this, we save our clothes, and enjoy one thing that's still free—the air blowing around our genitals. Anyway, See-Thru jumpsuits like the one you took off Rose are cheap. There's a winter version which comes in various colors. In the winter, they're made of Thermo-Dactyl material—it helps to retain your body heat—and covers your wrists and ankles. They're equivalent to walking around in long underwear. But they fit skintight, like ballet leotards, and they make us all—tall and skinny, old and plump, young and nubile—feel erotic toward each other. Of course, only the lecks wear them. We're not sure yet whether you'll turn out to be an ik—in which case the fashion world of Paris, Japan, Italy, New York, take your pick, is still alive and thriving."

While David was talking, he was checking the building, and we waited while Rose unearthed a lab technician's coat. Wearing it, when she bent over, the lower curves of her buttocks were occasionally exposed, but then, it occurred to me, so were mine, and not just the lower curves, but my whole ass, in what was evidently a lower-income economy garment.

I was conscious that David was either holding my hand or my arm, or gently caressing my behind—particularly as we descended in the elevator to the hibernaculum. Then I screamed. I didn't want to go into the mausoleum ever again. Maybe he was worried that I might go into catatonic shock, or that I'd fall groveling on the floor, frothing at the mouth, but he seemed determined that I must somehow cope with this underground graveyard filled with lost souls.

Shuddering, I let him lead me up and down the aisles between the rows of clear caskets. I was unable to keep my eyes off the serene, placid, recumbent statues of suspended flesh. They were all pale, pale pink, floating in soft blue clouds. I suddenly realized that the breasts of the women and the penises of the men were trembling ever so slightly. All of these bodies were controlled by some external machinery that was not only circulating plasma in their veins but was vibrating and turning their bodies in very slow motion.

I was unable to choke back my hysterical sobs. David took me in his arms for a moment. "Dear Christa," he said softly, "you must understand. You've *been* here. You never have to come back. Your hibernation is over."

Slowly, I was beginning to understand. The dream I had been having of being reborn had actually happened. I had

147

been reliving one phase of the dehibernation process. At the same time, my feeling of terror was turning into dull anger. The inescapable truth was that I had been kidnapped by demented scientists who had chained my body to a crap table and tossed the dice. Win or lose—it made no difference. There were more Christina Norths than there were gamblers, anyway.

Finally, back in the acrylic automobile which David had arrived in—virtually a prisoner between him and Rose—not giving a damn about David's explanation that the laboratory now had its own fail-proof, nuclear-powered generating system, and the hibernators, three floors underground, were safe for at least fifty years, I finally exploded.

"You fucking son of a bitch!" I yelled, as he turned off the dirt road onto the highway. "If you really are David Convita, and you've kept me a prisoner for sixteen years, I'm going to kill you, if it's the last thing I do."

"Unfortunately, Christa," David said, "despite the publicity given to cloning humans in the late nineteen seventies, we haven't successfully cloned anyone yet. All you have to do is look closely at me. I'm the original David Convita. And you can see that unlike you, I'm stuck with my aging body." He was smiling, and he didn't seem the least bit perturbed by my threat. "When we last talked together *verbally*—without benefit of the brain caps which we were experimenting with when we began to dehibernate you three weeks ago—I was a very much younger man." David explained that brain caps were primitive at this point but eventually were expected to facilitate complete nonverbal communication between the wearers.

Except for the familiar intensity of his hypnotic expression, I still wasn't sure. He no longer wore the black beard which had modified his slightly thrust-forward chin. His hair was still thick, but was more white than black. And as I had noticed earlier, the creases around his mouth, and the slight sag of his lantern jaw, indicated the face of a man in his middle fifties.

"If you really are David Convita," I told him, knowing it would be futile to demand that he stop the car and let me out on the highway, "how old are you, and why isn't she—" I gestured at Rose—"as old as you are?"

"I'm fifty-six. Technically, I suppose, you're forty-nine, and Rose is fifty-one. Actually, in terms of physical aging, as you can see in the rear-view mirror, you're still only about thirty-three and Rose is about thirty-five. For the past sixteen years, like those people you've just seen in the hibernaculum, we've maintained your metabolic rate at less than ten percent of normal."

Staring at myself in the eight-inch-high mirror that curved over the front windshield from one door to the other, I was astonished to see that not only had the haunted, bony look disappeared—my face was a little fuller than I remembered—but my light brown hair was cut in a Dutch boy style exactly like Rose's.

"Who in hell chopped up my hair this way?" I demanded. "I may still be thirty-three, but I don't look like me."

Rose smiled. "You're a leck now. Leck women don't bother with hairdressers."

"What are lecks?" I asked. Temporarily, my curiosity was subduing my anger. "Why is that you know more about's happening than I do?"

Watching David's expression in the mirror—aware that the road seemed empty of the usual Cape traffic on a late August weekend—I could see his eyes squeeze together in what seemed a fleeting expression of guilt.

"We'll tell you about lecks later," he said. "Let's say for the moment that Rose was a more willing accomplice than you were. Because of her nursing experience, we decided to dehibernate her first so that she could help us with other 'returnees.' When I brought you to the labs in June of 1980, Max was very angry with me. He wanted me to let you go immediately. Even after you had more or less given us your clothing, and you were fully aware that we were going to fake your suicide—even after you had signed a release—which, of course, wasn't legal at the time—giving us the right to experiment with your body, Max was very uneasy about you." David sighed. "The truth was—*is*, if you like—Max realized that I was too much involved with you as a person.

"Sixteen years ago, during the first few months that you were with us, I kept encouraging you to write your autobiography. I was intrigued that the Vitaleben, as it does with most manic-depressives, was gradually stabilizing you. Max was afraid that I was falling in love with the 'real' Christina."

"Were you?" I asked, and I noticed that David's voice seemed a little husky with emotion.

He touched my hand and grinned at me. "Of course I was. I'm in love with Rose, too, and every damned female in that hibernaculum—as well as a half dozen or so that we lost."

149

"Lost?"

"You and Rose, thus far"—He paused, and I wondered
fleetingly what he meant by "thus far"—"are the first two
who have survived. We used a different technique on the
eight or nine people who preceded you. In those days, we relied more on external hypothermia than on self-induced temperature reduction. When we thawed them, they died within
a few months. It was just as well, because they had suffered
brain deterioration."

"You might as well know," Rose said, "that you and I are
the first who seem to have suffered no cellular damage."

"But David just said 'thus far,' " I said grimly. I wondered
abruptly if I would slump over in the seat, dead at last, or
whether my brain, which suddenly felt as if it were pushing
against my skull, would disintegrate and I'd start to babble
like an idiot.

Dave sensed my shock. "There are four others in the country whom we are pretty sure that we can dehibernate in the
next year or two with no physical damage. They were hibernated using the original Vitaleben formulas and techniques.
In the past five years, with vastly improved biochemical techniques, we are much more certain that we can successfully
hibernate and dehibernate anyone within a maximum fifteen-
year period."

David shrugged. "We've learned the hard way, through
trial and error. As Rose is aware, particularly because she as-
sisted in your dehibernation, we brought you out of it on a
celgo-gaski—that's a wing and a prayer in Loglan, a new language that the lecks are crazy about. You'll learn about the
lecks and iks later, but right now, you should keep in mind
that sixteen years ago, while you were dubious, Rose was
quite willing to experience the trade-off. You should never
forget that. If Max and I hadn't played God, in all probability you'd both be dead by now."

"What do you mean by trade-off?" I guessed that David
was avoiding explaining his qualifying "thus far," but since I
was gradually accepting the fact that dream or not, I wasn't
waking up, I was beginning to find it fascinating. "Where's
Max Lebenthal? I want to talk with him. I trust him more
than I do you."

I was aware that David was driving at a fixed rate of
speed, and that the automobile which was now in front of us
and the one behind—both of the same general style—were

both maintaining a distance of about fifty feet between us. I learned later that all electrics, as well as automobiles that run on ethanol, an alcohol fuel made from human waste and garbage, were computer-controlled vis-à-vis each other. In heavy traffic conditions the distance between cars could be minimized to ten feet, and on crowded highways—which were infrequent—double and triple lanes were permitted, but no automobile passed another, and all speeds were laser-beam controlled.

"Max died two years ago, June 8, 1994," David said. "He was about seventy. He probably could have lived at least fifteen more years—the average life-span has now jumped to seventy-eight—but he had used his own body to test his changing theories of human longevity. Most of them were wrong. Before he actually died, we could have hibernated him, but Max felt that his job on this earth was completed. That's the hibernation trade-off, of course, not only to return to earth in a new era but to prolong your total life. Eventually it may become a global obsession."

David continued. "Nearly twenty years ago, when Max and I joined this NASA project, it never occurred to us that the handful of us who were involved weren't working in our own private vacuum. We should have known better. Breakthroughs in scientific discovery generally occur in various parts of the world at the same time. Independently of any government projects, several biologists, working for the major pharmaceutical companies, have discovered hibernating activators similar to Vitaleben. They even improved those that you and Rose received.

"The enthusiasm for possible hibernation has been aggravated by a continuous, and thus far unsolvable, worldwide economic depression, which began in the eighties. Most sociobiologists are finally agreeing that the nature of man in any historical era is directly conditioned by, and is the product of, his economic environment. Fortunately, millions of people have established *kitsa*—humans making love and caring for each other—as a first priority of human existence. For millions of others, the kind of monetary pressures we are still all living under has become a terrible day-to-day struggle. So the trade-off may become a gamble that millions of people may be willing to take.

"At least a dozen major corporations are ready to go into the hibernation business. *Beginagain, Newlife, Manrise*—to

151

name a few—are all subsidiaries of the major energy companies. Presumably, for a one-time investment of fifty thousand dollars of our highly inflated dollars, within the next year or two, anyone will be able to trade off fifteen years of living now for fifteen years in the future. Some of the newer companies plan to offer two-year Hibernation Trade-Offs to prove that hibernation really works. The heirs of a fifteen-year hibernator would automatically be covered by a two hundred thousand dollar insurance policy. If you don't make it, your heirs may have money enough to help them survive fifteen years from now."

David sounded cynical, but he was grinning. "This is only one of the problems in the brave new world which you've returned to. Obviously, if all the people who are anxious to be hibernated survived, and they were all dehibernated at the same time, they'd create entirely new population problems. Of course, there are arguments both ways. Hibernation of a few million people—taking their chances that they may never come back to active life—would balance the population growth, which, I'm sorry to tell you, is now running very close to predictions. There are at least five billion people alive on the earth today, a billion or so more than there were in the late 1970s. Space travel isn't about to solve the problem. Only about ten thousand people are living in space stations, and there about six hundred on the moon. The only way the government can spend more money on space exploration is to do away with tax slavery and turn us all into direct slaves doing whatever the masters in Washington think is best for all of us."

David's cool, philosophic amusement was making me angry. "I don't give a damn about your financial and political problems," I said. "I'm interested in *me!* If I'm really not dreaming and you really have tampered with my life, then you are no better than the Nazi war criminals."

"You can sue me if you want to." David was smiling. "I'm afraid no one will be interested. You're alive, aren't you? The sixteen years we deprived you of haven't been that great. Anyway, most of the older generation have forgotten World War II and the Nuremberg Code. The Nuremberg trials took place a half-century ago. Today they are as meaningless as the Code of Hammurabi. The theory that the voluntary consent of the human subject is absolutely essential for human experimentation, or that a human being might not have been

152

"so situated mentally" to exercise free choice—or the entire concept that "no experiment should be conducted where there is a priori reason to believe that death might occur"—none of those precepts corresponds with the facts of life today. In a state of hibernation, for example, no brain activity or heartbeat is discernible. Based on your 1980 definitions, hibernators could be pronounced legally dead. Thousands of those who will presumably exercise free choice in the next few years and will have paid for a fifteen-year hibernation may never be revived. Yet, the waiver of responsibility that the individual would sign completely absolves the companies who perform hibernation—in perpetuity. Eventually, if the hibernation mania actually becomes a way of life, the legal problem will have to be decided by the Supreme Court.

"One of the arguments against legalizing anabiosis is that it will invalidate life insurance contracts. The current proposal is that any life insurance policies of hibernators that aren't issued by one of the hibernating companies would automatically be canceled." David laughed. "Some lawyers are already arguing that hibernation for anyone past fifty years of age should not be permitted. Others are proposing that the age limit be set at sixty-five, plus a certificate that the potential hibernator be in good health. Amusingly, most of the people who have expressed interest in hibernation, and presumably have already volunteered, are past sixty. If the whole hibernation business is finally legalized and the hibernators survive, beginning about 2010 a very large old-age population is going to be dumped on the world."

David shook his head. "One thing hasn't changed. Most people don't give a damn about the future. Politically, hibernation might be a godsend. The old social security and welfare programs have collapsed. The older generation is temporarily being completely subsidized by negative income allotments, which are taxed directly out of current income. The truth is that it would probably be cheaper to support people in suspended animation than to keep them fully alive."

David laughed grimly. "As you can see, we no longer have to depend on suicidal people for hibernation experiments. In fact, there are serious proposals that one way to resolve the high cost of maintaining those who have committed crimes against society would be to hibernate them involuntarily—and send them off into space. If they survived, they could

153

colonize some planet in interstellar space. On the other hand, many people think that hibernation may ultimately turn out to be an unexpected form of euthanasia. Obviously the younger generation, which is presently greatly outnumbered politically, but eventually will be in control, will find a way to solve its problem. One way to get rid of a horde of old people would be to turn off the electricity in the hibernaculums." David paused. "And they might not even have to do that. At the moment, despite all the publicity and medical guarantees that extended hibernation is a reality, you and Rose are top secret. You are the only two people who have been successfully hibernated and dehibernated. The fact is that you were originally scheduled for a twenty-five-year hibernation, but our failure rate at several installations had us worried. No one can be sure of the success percentage rate for at least ten years, and even then the statistics won't be projectable, because the techniques are improving."

Listening to David, I was too stunned to respond. Either Rose was already a complete zombie, or she was reacting the way I was. She had said little or nothing as David drove toward Mashpee.

"I'm sure that none of this really is happening," I told David. "My mother, and then Karl, always told me that the reason I had nightmares was that I read too much, and the undigested garbage circulating in my brain cut loose at night."

As we turned off the highway onto a private road, I could see, ahead of us, a large Dutch colonial home, sitting on a cliff that overlooked the Atlantic Ocean. The water, a shimmering blue carpet, extended to the horizon beneath a cloudless sky. Near the home was a perpendicular tower about fifty feet high with a canted, revolving mirror, which I learned later was a solar-power generating system for the house.

But I wasn't listening as David tried to explain that no single family could afford a home like this. It was owned collectively by his Love Group. I was staring at him with tears in my eyes. "You're like every man who ever said they loved the 'real Christina,'" I told him. "They were all full of shit. They loved themselves first, and better. It really hasn't bothered you very much that I might have died. Rose and I, and all those others in that crypt of yours, are simply human guinea pigs."

"Guinea pigs don't commit suicide," David said gently. "I

don't want to keep reminding you, Christa, but based on your past histories, and your personal unwillingness to consent to chemical behavior-modification techniques, you and Rose, and those you've seen in the hibernaculum, would in all probability be dead anyway."

Tomorrow

Your observations on the cause of death, and the experiments which you propose for calling to life those who appear to be killed by lightning, demonstrate equally your sagacity, and your humanity. . . .

A toad buried in the sand may live, it is said, until the sand becomes petrified; and then being enclosed in stone it may still live for we know not how many centuries.

I have seen an instance of common flies preserved in a manner somewhat similar. They have been drowned in Madeira wine, apparently about the time when it was bottled in Virginia, to be sent here (to London). At the opening of one of the bottles, at the house of a friend where I was, three drowned flies fell into the first glass that was filled. I having heard that drowned flies come back to life in the sun, proposed making an experiment upon these. . . .

In less than three hours, two of them began by degrees to recover life. . . . I wish it were possible, from this instance, to invent a method of embalming drowned persons, in such a manner that they might be recalled to life in any period, however distant; for having a very ardent desire to see America a hundred years hence, I should prefer an ordinary death, being immersed with a few friends in a cask of Madeira, until that time, then to be recalled to life by the solar warmth of my dear country. . . .

—Benjamin Franklin, From a
letter to Jasques Barbeu Duborg
(London, April, 1773)

As we drove up the winding private road to the house, David said, "For as long as you wish, you and Rose are welcome additions to our family. You'll not only see a Love Group intimately interacting, but we hope you'll enjoy this new kind of expanded family life. In less than eight years, since family incorporations were legalized, over thirty million Americans have joined together in Love Groups or Care Groups in various forms.

"Many of the Love Groups, like ours, as distinguished from Care Groups, are an incorporation of four couples and their children. The goal of this new-style family is to try and maintain approximately a ten-year age separation between the pair bonds. Paul and Carol Thomas, whom you can see down there working in our garden, are in their seventies. The most important fact that brought about the final legalization of Love Groups and Care Groups is that we do not depend on senior citizens' centers or nursing homes. We're committed to take care of our own—without any government subsidy. Paul and Carol are the only members of our group who are legally married. Ruth Wirtz and I are the next oldest couple-bonding, and then comes Jag Raynes and Zara Schmidt, who are in their middle forties, and finally Chandra Convita—my daughter by my first marriage—and Ralph Skolnick, who are in their early thirties. Jag and Zara have two kids, seventeen and fifteen, and Chandra and Ralph have two youngsters, who are eleven and thirteen. This weekend, when we'll all be together, with you and Rose there will be fourteen of us." David chuckled. "We're an old-style pioneer family, except that here there are no patriarchs or matriarchs—we're all androgynous."

David stopped his car next to a similar one in the driveway. "You're going to discover that for many of us, the sham morality of the late seventies and early eighties has given way to a new kind of joyous sexual honesty. The continuous struggle to survive financially, in a world that is plagued by worldwide inflation, unemployment, and taxation, has created a new sense of human solidarity and community and sharing. There are millions of what the sociologists used to call the middle class who have reached out to each other and are creating a much more loving interpersonal world. In the process, these new-style families have become a potent political force. With a little bit of *gutca*—luck—we hope in this election year that we'll get rid of our beneficent dictator, President Jason Kennedy, and his capitalistic, fascist cohorts who are running the country." David grinned. "But we'll tell you all about that later. Right now, I want you to lie down for a while and simply float. If you think it's a dream, you can keep dreaming it."

I slid across the wide front seat and I followed Rose out of the car. Waiting for me on the other side, David took me in his arms. "I may not be your prince," he told me softly, "but I really do care for you." He kissed my forehead. "You've been my Sleeping Beauty for sixteen years. The first night I talked with you in that hospital room, I fell in love with your brain. I wanted to reach into it and somehow turn off all those sad, hateful thoughts you were constantly having about yourself. I wanted to set you free to live. We can thank whatever gods may be watching. You have no brain damage. So far, you're *gudvalda*. You're doing fine. If you'll follow instructions, we'll jump the 'thus far' hurdle. You have entirely new options. You can still kill yourself, of course. Or if you finally come to detest the world you've returned to, you can try a second round of hibernation. Or you can live out your life and die naturally between 2050 and 2060, a lovely old lady in her eighties or nineties."

David waved at the naked, barrel-chested, bearded, gray-haired man, and the thin, gray-haired, and equally naked woman, who had stopped cultivating their rows of green tomatoes and beans and cabbages and were walking—almost running—to greet us. They grabbed Rose's hands and mine, and seemingly delighted with our existence, forced us to dance in a circle with them on the lawn. While we were twirling, I kept telling myself, Christina, this isn't real. You can wake up anytime that you want to. In a few minutes you'll be telling Karl how you dreamed that you had been hibernated, and then you were revived, and a happy old man and his wife danced a jig with you, and Karl will shrug and he'll tell you to stop reading so damned much nonsense and give your brain a rest.

But dream or not, it wasn't ending. Good or bad, I was being forced to dream it out. Dancing with all of them, I was laughing hysterically. I tried to avoid staring directly at Paul's penis, which was bobbing up and down in a bush of gray-black pubic hairs, or at Carol's slightly sagging breasts and the wispy gray hair no longer covering her vulva. They brought the dance to a stop and both of them hugged me.

"You must be Christa," Paul said. "Welcome to our Love Group. Now we are twice blessed. When you and Rose were young women, I was in my late fifties. Too bad I didn't know you then."

Carol laughed. "Paul forgets that when he was fifty-six, he was still old enough to be your father."

Walking with us into the house, Paul held my hand. "At least you're too old to be my granddaughter." Grinning, he pointed at his slightly elevated penis. "Happily—given the appropriate visual and mental stimulation—the old boy can still lift his head and look around."

I was about to tell Paul that my husband Karl was fifty-nine, and then, with a hollow feeling in my stomach, I realized that if this wasn't a dream, Karl would be seventy-five—or dead!

Paul was telling me that I was more beautiful now than when I had made my movie, *The Christening of Christina*. "It was run on Channel sixty-nine a few weeks ago. *The Christening* appears on the *Sekci* channel regularly. *Sekci* is Loglan for sex. You were quite a technician—orally." Paul laughed. "The iks still watch that stuff, but those of us who live in Love Groups prefer the flesh-and-mind reality of each other."

I guess I was a little shocked. Had sixteen years of hibernation made me sexually frigid? "I remember Christina North," I said. "Her movie wasn't really a porno movie, but it doesn't matter. That woman may look like me, but I'm not her." I sighed. "I really don't know who I am. Who are the iks?"

Laughing, David led us through a large kitchen to a room that was carpeted with pale green foamy material. It had a pile deeper than any broadloom carpeting I had ever walked on. Except for fifty or so huge pillows, all covered in different-colored materials, the room was empty. One wall was a window wall overlooking the ocean. Two of the other walls

161

were covered with pictures, framed and unframed, and the fourth wall was a 6 by 8 foot screen shimmering with a kaleidoscope of ever-changing color patterns. I learned later that this was Life-a-Vision, a completely contained television screen that was only an inch thick, and gave access to a hundred channels, ten of them located in foreign capitals of the world, including Moscow and Peking.

David told me to stretch out on the floor. Carol and Paul brought us all tall glasses of cold root beer which they had made themselves. Paul told David that he would drive into Hyannis and get Jag and Zara and their *nirbo*—children—about five. Chandra, Ruth, Ralph, and Gale and Delight who, David explained, were Chandra and Ralph's children, were all down on the beach.

"I want to keep Christa out of the overhead sunlight," David told them. "We'll take her down to the beach later. You've been eating solid food for ten days, Christa. Your stomach and intestines are functioning beautifully. You may not have noticed it, but you've had no meat or fish. They're still available, but hamburger is four dollars a pound—and only the rich-iks can afford steak or roast beef. Lobsters and shrimps are mostly fond memories."

Rose, who had stayed in the kitchen, appeared with a plate of lettuce and tomato sandwiches. "The bread is soybean bread," Carol said. "We grow the beans and make the bread ourselves. Your lunch has more proteins and less calories than the former McDonald's and Burger King's hamburgers."

"Inflation has wiped out most of the fast-food franchises," David said. "But we have community co-op restaurants, which are much more fun."

Although I suddenly realized that in our See-Thru jump suits we were all practically as naked as Carol and Paul, I was no longer tense. My dream wasn't turning into a nightmare.

"You still haven't told me who the iks are," I said.

"Way back in 1972 or 1973," Paul said, "an anthropologist, Colin Turnbull, I think his name was, wrote a book called *The Mountain People* about a Ugandan tribe called the Iks. Although it's spelled 'iks,' the pronunciation is 'eeks'. They were formerly nomadic, but when Turnbull discovered them, the Ugandan government had forced the Iks to become farmers. They never adjusted to their new environment. They turned into a totally selfish and loveless people. They would shit on each other's doorstep. They laughed when their neigh-

162

bor was in trouble. They'd eat alone so they wouldn't have to share their food. They'd fuck and then turn away from each other. They'd snatch the food from the mouths of old people and abandon them to starve when they couldn't get their own food. As soon as their children could walk, they'd turn them out to forage for themselves. And they never sang or danced." Paul grinned at David, evidently waiting for his permission to continue.

"I don't want to overwhelm you, Christa," David said. "Let's just say for the moment that one of our current presidential candidates had a book published a few years ago. He revived the concept of the iks. He divided the population of the United States into four basic categories. The poor-iks, the rich-iks, the lecks, which is short for intellectuals, and the blanks, who are all those people who were undecided in the national opinion polls you used to have. It is his opinion that the poor-iks and the lecks must combine to save themselves, or we'll all be slaves to the rich-iks, and kept in captivity by the blanks." David chuckled. "Nobody paid much attention to his book until the present campaign started, but now, suddenly everybody is demanding that everyone else stand up and be counted."

David suddenly leaned over and kissed me on the mouth. "We don't know yet, Christa, whether you're an ik or a leck."

"Right now, I want you to lie here quietly and rest. You can feel that we have no air conditioning, but there's a breeze off the ocean. One of us will stay with you, but we won't talk."

"Who will stay?" I asked.

"Whoever you wish."

I grinned. "You."

When the others had left, David slipped off my jumpsuit and his, and held me naked in his arms. "Thank you," he said. "I thought you might hate me."

"I do," I said, "but what can I do about it? I'm not real. I'm your creation. I'm totally dependent on you."

"You won't be when the world knows that you exist. When the media discovers that you have been hibernated for sixteen years, and that you are alive, healthy, and have physically defied time, you'll be famous. All the hibernation companies will try to hire you as their chief promotion manager. You'll give the hibernation craze a new injection of insanity."

I shuddered. "You'd let me do that?"

"Eventually, someone who has been hibernated will. You

can't blame them. It's still a cash-in-on-your-fame society. Overnight, you'd be a rich-ik."

"What about Rose?"

David shook his head. "It won't be Rose. But it may inadvertently have to be you."

"Have to be?" I stared at him incredulously. "You just said I was my own person."

David kissed me. "Please, Christa, you should rest. Whatever happens, you'll have the choice."

"Oh, God—God, God!" I sobbed. "This is completely insane talk. You seem to think that I should be delighted to be alive, or to be still young while all of you have aged normally. I don't even want to ask you about my children, or if Karl and Grace are still alive. I'm no better than a Rip Van Winkle. Anyone I might have known in 1980, including you, has continuity. I'm not only phased completely out of this strange world—I don't understand your crazy language or your new inventions—but I'm totally alone. Somehow or other, you expect that I'm going to embrace all these strangers, your so-called family. But what I really keep thinking is that as soon as I get my bearings I'll scream it from the rooftops. You forced me to be hibernated. That should be a criminal offense even today."

David kissed my breasts. Though I inched away, his fingers gently feathered my clitoris. "Are you having any normal sexual sensations?"

"No! Goddamn it! Why should I? I'm too damned confused and angry to feel erotic. Besides, I *don't* love you!"

David laughed. "You probably do, Christa. But you won't be able to admit it to yourself for a few weeks. Not until you've accepted the fact that the past is past, and you are alive—thanks to me. And you still are a very beautiful woman. While we're on the subject, I don't want you to have intercourse with me or anyone else until you've had your first period. After that, if you haven't left us, I'm sure that all the male penises in our entire Love Group will be happy to assist you in exercising your vaginal muscles. You can begin to experiment by stopping and starting urination, then you can try squeezing your finger." David smiled. "In a week or so, after you've had your first period, I'm sure that you'll find it more fun to practice squeezing the real thing."

"I don't believe what I'm hearing," I said. "It sounds by implication as if everyone spends their spare time screwing

164

themselves into oblivion. Next you're going to tell me that although I'm actually forty-nine years old, I can get pregnant."

"You're not forty-nine, you're thirty-three. Biologically, thirty-four or -five at the most. The sixteen years' slowdown in your metabolic rate has added about a year and a half to your age. You most certainly can get pregnant. I should warn you that although there are now male contraceptives, voluntary sterilization via vasectomies or tubal ligation is the most popular contraceptive method. On the other hand, lecks use no contraceptives at all. We simply use our brains and avoid penetration when a female is ovulating."

"You must be trying to change the population balance in your favor." I laughed. "If taking no chances makes me an ik, then I'll show my colors now." Again the memory of Michael and Penny flashed vividly across my mind, but asking about them somehow was equivalent to admitting that all this was actually happening, and that I was really lying naked in the arms of the man who had ended my former life.

"You don't have to worry," David was saying. "In these sixteen years, we've developed an entirely new approach to premarital sex education, which even most of the poor-iks approve. Abortion as a form of birth control in the United States could disappear by the end of the century."

David paused. "I'm still talking," he said, "and I really want you to have a nap."

"I can listen and sleep, too."

"All right. First, we have convinced millions of people, young and old, that oral sex, eight or nine days a month, without any chemicals in the female vagina, and a nice clean penis, is a very lovely substitute for penetration. Second, intercourse just before and during menstruation, when many women are quite erotic, is widely approved. Third, millions of males have learned how to control their own ejaculation, not only as a mutual source of delight for their partner, but as a precautionary method during female fertility. Finally, we've developed a simple vaginal smear so that any woman can tell in a matter of two minutes whether she is ovulating. In addition, except for small pockets of resistance in backward groups of Jesus followers, who probably don't have the problem anyway, and with the enthusiastic support of the Catholic Church, we have practically eliminated all venereal disease. Everyone is now required to have a six-month venereal-clearance check-up with their doctor or clinic. Before they hop into the sack with each other, strangers show each other their clearance certificate which, like a license to drive an automobile, has one's current photograph on it.

"While we still haven't solved the economics of greed," David went on, "we are slowly learning to mesh the explosive advances in biochemistry with a new kind of caring human being. For example, in the late 1970s people were disputing whether abortion was a victimless act. A nine-week-old fetus had a brain and various organs. Had it acquired a right to life? On the other hand, with later developments that have occurred in recombining genes, we now can predict that the average human life, for those born in this decade, will be at least eighty years, and two percent of those will live beyond one hundred years. Many years ago Leonard Kass, a well-known biologist, suggested that 'seeing nature as a mere material for manipulation and exploitation and transformation' was nowhere near so dangerous as the 'erosion of our ideas of man as something splendid or divine, and as a creature with freedom and dignity.' "

David stopped talking and brushed his lips across my breasts. I opened my eyes, saw his erect penis. Smiling, I held it gently.

"I thought you were sleeping," he said.

"Maybe I was, but keep talking. Your words are become part of this silly dream." I closed my eyes again. "Your penis feels real enough."

In an even softer voice, as if he was resolving the conundrum for himself as well as me, David continued, "Almost simultaneously with the discovery of how we could prolong human life, questions were being asked about the right to die. Sixteen years ago, the question turned on the old ethical-moral axis. If we give human beings an honorable and socially approved way to end their lives, do we create the environment for negative euthanasia? The potential existed, and still does, that discriminatory killing of old people would become an accepted way of life. More than a million people, half of them past sixty, who have tried to buy the future through hibernation, would be taking that risk. On the other hand, we've made the first breakthrough. It's now possible to grow human embryos outside the womb. Several hundred thousand children who are alive and well were embryo transfers. We've stopped asking whether the embryos grown *in vitro,* and were never implanted, and were washed down the sink, had the right to life.

"We've arrived at the future predicted by Bentley Glass, fifteen years ago, who said, 'No parents in the future will have the right to burden society with a malformed or mentally incompetent child.' Today, chromosome studies of fetal cells taken from the amniotic fluid are one hundred percent reliable. Abortions are performed routinely to eliminate fetuses that would develop into physically or mentally handicapped children."

David's voice died out. We lay beside each other silently, stretched out indolently on the foam carpet, our legs supported by foam pillows, while the warm summer air gently searched my vulva and breasts, and David's penis shrank to a warm, comfortable sleeping mouse in my hand.

I knew David was right. The excitement and fear charging through my brain for the past few hours had exhausted my body. It scarcely seemed credible that just a short time after escaping from my prison, I was lying in the arms of my former jailer, and was, if I understood 1996 definitions, actually enjoying kitsa, a non-goal-directed lovemaking, with him.

Maybe there was some truth in the version of the Sleeping Beauty story where Princess Talia was raped and didn't even know it. At the moment, a serene smile on her face, Princess Christina was suppliant and dreamy enough not to have cared if David had physically penetrated her—but, of course, he wouldn't, Christina must wait for her first period.

Beside me, David's eyes were closed. He was encouraging me to sleep, but I was afraid I might disappear once again in "caverns immeasurable to man," and this time the long sleep might turn into the full-blown nightmare which I was sure was still lurking in my mind.

I remembered the summer before I went back to my senior year at Radcliffe. Grace had sponsored my first European tour. London, Paris, Rome, Athens—all the cities as I arrived in them confronted me like huge jigsaw puzzles that somehow I must assemble in my mind, and master within a day after I had arrived. Frantically taking buses, taxis, subways, and city tours to all points of the compass, I tried to absorb each city and become as familiar and at one with it as a native who had lived there all of her life. But it was to no avail. I departed as I came, a bewildered foreigner.

Now, it wasn't just a city. I was a stranger in the world that never knew I had once existed, and couldn't have cared less if it had known. It was a chastening antidote to my former need for fame and my dreams of immortality. If I had been Cleopatra or Virginia Woolf or Marilyn Monroe or

167

one of my former heroines, Sylvia Plath or Anne Sexton, instead of Christina North, or her married version Christina Klausner, it would have made no difference. If there was a moral to my story—and I always liked morals—it was to accept Emily Dickinson's homily: "This is the Hour of Lead/ Remember if outlived/ As freezing persons recollect the snow/ First—chill—then stupor—then the letting go." Either that, or I could listen to the pragmatic lady who also resided in my brain: Make your truce with the twentieth century, Christina, it's almost over. Live it up, baby, face the reality, the world can get along without you very well.

Then a shuddery thought crossed my mind. If this weird transition had actually happened, I could never go home again. There were no bridges connecting me to the past. How would Penny and Michael, or Grace, if she was alive, react to a Christina whose mind had been blanked out since 1980, and, giggly thought, probably looked not that much older than her children? Blood wasn't thicker than water. The raging torrents of the river of time couldn't be spanned. Strangely, I could think these thoughts without feeling depressed. For the first time in my life, I had become completely detached. I was Christina Past watching Christina Present. I awoke from my reverie to find David gone, and a naked boy about ten years old sitting on a pillow, staring at me. For a moment I thought he was Michael and that my dream had finally ended, but then he smiled at me and said, "Grampy Dave said to stay with you. He's gone down to the beach. I'm Gale."

I couldn't help laughing. The man who had snuffed out my life was a grandfather. The world was still prosaic enough to recognize its progeny.

"You're prettier than the Sleeping Beauty," Gale said. "Could I touch your breasts?"

I was a little astonished. "How old are you?" I asked, suddenly wondering if, in this world, kids made love when they were still in their puberty.

"I'm eleven," Gale said.

"Does your mother let you touch her breasts?"

Gale laughed. "Sure, why not? Sometimes Delight, my sister, and I jump in bed with Chandra and Ralph, and Chandra hugs us and snuggles us against her breasts. If they're making love, and don't want to be bothered, sometimes Ruth or Carol or Zara will snuggle with me—or Delight pretends

168

that she's a woman and hugs David or Ralph or Paul or Jag—or even me."

"My God." I still didn't believe my ears. "How old is your sister?"

"She's thirteen."

"What happens if you get excited?" I demanded. "Like now!" I pointed at Gale's little penis, which was sticking straight out from his hairless belly.

"Nothing?" He smiled. "What's bad about that? It feels nice. I know that I'm not supposed to put my penis in a woman's vulva or make love until I'm seventeen. Then, the leck *nirbos* go to Premar for four years, and they sleep together and they learn how to make love and live together."

I was getting intrigued with this conversation with an eleven-year-old. "What if you can't last until then?"

"You mean if I get so excited that I can't wait?" Gale shrugged. "I suppose I can masturbate." He held up his penis and examined it thoughtfully. "When I shake it around I can do it, but it's not so great. I'm too young. Delight says she did it to herself. She has a clitoris. It's like a penis hidden between her legs." Gale grinned. "I guess you have one, too. Delight says she's tickled her clitoris, and it felt very interesting. But she's decided to wait until she can do it with me or some other *nirbo*. Grampy Dave and Ralph told me that when a man is about seventeen, and from then on, he can stay inside a woman for a long time—and it's very nice."

Laughing, wondering how this world, where fathers and mothers, and brothers and sisters, seemed completely in tune with their own sexuality, came to be—I hugged Gale against my breasts. His tongue flicked across my nipples, and then he swiftly kissed my cheek. I had evidently passed the test. "Thanks, Christa," he said, "I like you. Do you want to go swimming?"

"Sure," I told him, "I used to be a good swimmer. But your grandfather mentioned that I wasn't supposed to go out in the sun."

"You're not, not unless you've had melanin injections—like me. If you haven't, you can use Desola. Wait until I get Ralph or Grampy Dave." Gale dashed out of the room, and I heard him yelling over the cliff, "Christa's awake! She wants to go swimming."

My own words were still echoing in my head. "I used to be a good swimmer." For a moment I was Christina Past, en-

169

twined with a naked man, jumping off her yacht, ready to swim from Nantucket to Boston.

When David appeared, I was wiping tears from my eyes. I told him that I was plagued by ghosts. Remembrances of things past might be a problem with hibernators that he had not envisioned. I tried to smile at the naked man who had arrived with him. *"Loi, Kristas."* To my surprise, without introductions, this tall, skinny stranger embraced me and kissed my cheek. The sun warmth of his flesh against mine was fleetingly erotic. "Welcome to the world, and particularly our Love Group. I'm Ralph Skolnick." The aura given off by his crinkly brown eyes and the pleasant smile on his lips wasn't confined to his face. His stubby penis and his testicles—in fact, his whole body—seemed to absorb me in their laughter. At least, I had one thing in common with 96'ers. On days like this, I had never given a damn whether I wore clothes or not. But, of course, in that past world, I was the crazy Christina, with no moral sense. With the exception of Newton Morrow, whom I suddenly remembered with a momentary deep feeling of loss, I had never been able to enjoy the total body unity of a man's face and his genitals.

"I hope that you won't mind if I Desola Christa," Ralph was saying to David, "she's *bilti*—means beautiful." He grinned happily at me.

"Ralph can't wait to get his hands on you," David said.

"Neither could your grandson." I followed them to the front lawn of the house, which overlooked the ocean. "Gale just kissed my breasts." I looked at David with raised eyebrows, but he seemed unconcerned. He winked at Gale approvingly.

I shook my head in wonder. "My God," I said, "maybe it was people like me who are responsible for this. Everyone used to tell me that someday I'd have to account to my children for the sex-obsessed world that I had helped create with my book and movie. Maybe it's a good thing, but it never occurred to me that ultimately children would imitate their parents from an early age and would become sex-motivated, too."

David was opening a bucket of what seemed to be a pale blue grease. "This is homemade Desola," he said. "Paul and I make it at the lab. The commercial variety costs about three dollars an application, so a lot of people, like Ralph and me, are trying melanin injections, which may or may not create skin cancers. Most of the women won't take a chance, so they

170

have to wear Desola. Since Ralph is so eager to touch you, he's elected himself to do the job. You must be covered from head to foot. Desola dries immediately into a very thin, flexible, aerated skin cover. It washes off with a thin solution of alcohol and water. When Ralph finishes with you, you'll be a pale blue lady. You won't be alone, most of the women on the beach are pale blue, too."

David added ruefully, "Our generation was responsible for a lot more serious problems than facing up to our inherent sexuality. The aerosols and fluorocarbons that we so freely used in the sixties and seventies diffused the ozone layer. Today, the actinic rays of the sun are much more dangerous than they were sixteen years ago. Our weather patterns seem to be changing, too, and we have longer, humid summers which extend late into October."

Ralph carefully slopped the stuff over my back. Working his way down to my buttocks, he kept talking as he smoothed the stuff on my skin. "You may find it difficult to comprehend, Christa," he said, "but most of the lecks have discovered how to merge their sexuality with a new kind of transcendental religion called Unilove. The whole concept of Unilove and a joyous, laughing interrelationship of human beings with each other and the universe itself—a religion of solidarity—is closely tied in with most of the Love Groups in the country. The Church of United Love, or Unilove, as it's popularly called, started out as an arm's length branch of the Unitarian-Universalist Association. At last count, it had ten million active members. It's not only attracting most of the younger generation into its fold, but it has forced Catholics, Jews, and Protestants into a complete reassessment of their theological foundations. I'm sure that David will take you to services, which are held in most Unilove Churches on Wednesdays and Sundays. You'll discover that the Unilove concept embraces a very open sexuality. Yet, in contrast with the sick-sex world of the late seventies and early eighties, many of us are very much more Puritanical about human sexuality. At the same time, we're very much freer in terms of our fully evoked sexual feelings, which we recognize and express with delight as a part of our continuing life needs from cradle to the grave."

Ralph paused. "Bend over, Christa, I want to Desolarize your anus and *konbi*—vulva."

"Why?" I demanded. "I'm not going to spread my legs or reveal my asshole to the sun."

Ralph chuckled. "I know it, but I enjoy looking at you and touching you, anyway."

Shrugging, I bent over and grinned at him through my legs.

"You see," he said, and I could feel his fingers in a soft, greasy caress of my anus and vulva, "this is a very good example of what I've been telling you. Sixteen years ago, instead of playfully caressing a woman's vulva—with her permission, of course—I'd probably be staring at four-color photographs of the *konbis* of bored women who held them open for my inspection.

"All of those magazines went out of business nearly ten years ago. They couldn't compete with the real thing on Life-a-Vision. We now have round-the-clock three-dimensional screwing on Channel sixty-nine. But the latest surveys reveal that lately both the poor-iks and rich-iks find Channel sixty-nine boring. The lecks are confident that eventually the services in the Unilove Churches, where you can enjoy live human beings seeking a reunification of their total human sexuality, will eliminate Channel sixty-nine, too."

"I'm sorry, but I'm really bewildered," I told them. "Despite the one movie I made, which I still insist wasn't totally a porno movie, I lived in a world where a lot of people believed—or pretended to believe—that when a man got married, he could never caress another woman." I laughed. "And, of course, vice versa."

"It was an unrealistic world," David said. "We no longer repress our joy at the amazement of each other's flesh. And we no longer have to get married and divorced again to experience more than one loving person. The lecks, at least, have eliminated the confusion of adultery and the back-street world of mistresses and secret affairs. We've made one of Abraham Maslow's discoveries a way of life. Many years ago, he said: '. . . it is not the welfare of the species or the task of reproduction, or the future development of mankind, that attracts people to each other. The love and sex life of healthy people, in spite of the fact that it frequently reaches great peaks of ecstasy, can, nevertheless, also cheerfully be compared to the games of children and puppies. It is cheerful, humorous and playful.' "

"Chandra and I were bonded in a Unilove Church," Ralph said. "While friends of ours played a Mozart quartet, the minister celebrated our merger with a sermon based on Allan Watts' writings. Naked together, we made love for a half hour without ejaculation, while our friends and relatives watched."

Before he slopped the Desola over my breasts, Ralph pressed his face gently against them for a few seconds, and then he quickly kissed them in succession, and finally nuzzled my belly and delta. Laughing, he pointed to his penis. "As you can see, my *pingu*—penis—is erect. The essential difference between the kind of sexual world that millions of us have literally created, and the world you knew, is that although I am partially aroused, and presumably could have kitsa with you, and you might be agreeable to experiencing it with me, at this moment my sexual playing with you is not goal-oriented. I'm simply expressing, through touch, my delight that you, a woman, exist.

"Unlike the people you wrote about in *The Christening of Christina*, or the people who still make porno movies today, we have discovered that the human orgasm, climax, Big O, and all the nonsense of vaginal and simultaneous orgasms, and the curious, totally objective ways that your writers recommended to achieve these, completely missed the point. Once you've discovered the deep subjective joy in your sexuality and can confidently express it in happy love play, the greatest human delight is in prolonging and enjoying the sexual energies flowing through your body. No matter how old you may be, you are transformed. The male is bursting with seed, the female is fresh-turned earth. Before they eventually merge—disappear into each other and become one with the total unity of the cosmos—they can dance together and warmly lust for each other, without purpose, but simply become joy itself in their own existence."

Ralph did a mock bow before me. "For the moment, dear blue lady, my sermon is finished. Let's go swimming."

I plunged my hand in the Desola and, to David's delight, quickly swabbed Ralph's flaring penis.

"Okay, friend," I told him, "now I want to hear you explain your blue *pingu* to your wife."

David was hilarious. "It really does look as if you dipped it in a blue lady, Ralph."

Leading the way, assuring me that Chandra would be delighted when she saw him and met me, Ralph guided me, with David behind us, down a sandy path, curving through dune grass, that led to the beach about 300 feet below us. As far as I could see in each direction, naked or partially naked people were playing in the sand, or swimming and sailing

173

small beach boats. The outer Cape water was calmer than I had ever remembered it. Slow-gathering waves rolled unhurriedly to the shore.

I asked David if the words they kept using—Loglan—were from a language like Esperanto. I remembered reading that in the 1920s a great many people thought Esperanto was going to become an international language.

"Loglan is considerably different from Esperanto," David said. "The theory behind Loglan, which is closely related to normal speech patterns and has a vocabulary based on the common elements in eight languages—English, Mandarin Chinese, Hindi, Russian, Spanish, Japanese, French, and German—is that human beings could create a more powerful linguistic instrument, and might, in just a few generations, create much greater common understanding and a world point of view by increasing the powers of the human mind to express both rational thinking and human emotions."

"Quite a few of us are learning to speak it fluently," Ralph said. "I work for IBM. Along with several other companies, they've perfected dictating equipment that will transcribe the human voice directly from tapes to a computer, or a typewriter, without human interception. Loglan is audio-visually isomorphic—" Ralph grinned—"which simply means that spoken words go into written words in just one way, and vice versa. English, or any other language, would not only limit machine vocabulary, but no other language has the metaphonic capability of Loglan. In addition, when Loglan is spoken onto tape and is mechanically transcribed, it's practically error-free. Many of us believe that Loglan will become a second world language, not only because of its computer capabilities, but because it helps expand human consciousness.

"Loglan was created by James Cooke Brown nearly fifty years ago," Ralph continued. "He believed that the rational power of the human animal is conditioned by the linguistic game, or the particular language which a human is taught from childhood. The structure of each person's language determines their world view, and sets the limit at which one person can communicate with another. We're hoping that within the next two generations, we may break through the language barrier that prevents the people of different nations from really understanding what each other is talking about."

We had finally arrived on the beach. Two naked women, both of them as blue as I was, were walking toward us. "Ralph has been explaining Loglan to Christa," David said.

He gave them both a quick hug. "This is Ruth and Chandra. *De sicni merfu mi ice da detri mi.*"

"*Mia clivu tu.*" Ruth, a smiling, blue-eyed woman, with short-cut black hair, and Chandra, with the face of an Italian madonna, said the words almost simultaneously and were laughing and hugging me affectionately. "David just told you in Loglan that I am almost his wife," Ruth explained, "and Chandra is his daughter. *Mia clivu tu* means we love you. We didn't expect you for another two weeks."

"Don't let them bewilder you," Chandra said. "For most of us, the fun of Loglan is to expand the English vocabulary. Many of the words, because they have sounds or meanings that are common in all eight languages, are easily learned and are very familiar. Another thing that makes Loglan different from any other language is that whether the word is a noun, a verb, adjective, or adverb, the Loglan word doesn't change its basic formation. *Clivu,* for example, is always the same word, no matter how it appears in a sentence. The entire burden of Loglan logic and grammar is carried by about a hundred little words. The simple tenses, for example, are conveyed by three words: *pa, na,* and *fa. La Kristas fa clivu la David, La Kristas pa clivu la David,* and *La Kristas na clivu la David* translates Christa loves David, Christa loved David, and Christa is loving David now."

Chandra suddenly noticed Ralph's blue penis. "Did Christa give you a *blanu pingu?*" she demanded.

"Only in self-defense," I said. "I hope you're not angry."

Chandra shook her head. "I'm delighted. *Pingus* are for holding!"

I sat down next to Ruth on a foam blanket which they had spread on the sand. "Maybe you'd better teach me the Loglan word for afraid of, or just plain frightened," I whispered. "I still can't believe this is happening to me, and it doesn't seem possible that in just sixteen years, people have learned to be so sexually at ease with each other. Sixteen years ago, a public beach like this on the Cape, with everyone naked, happily playing together, would have been inconceivable. All that we had managed were a few nude beaches in Truro and San Diego that were in constant trouble with the police. Of course, you could go to islands like Guadeloupe or the Riviera and see "topless" women, but both they and the men always wore the bottom of their suits. Even more amazing to me, is how all of you manage to live together in a communal home.

How do you manage to casually exchange bed partners without getting jealous of each other?"

Ruth grinned at David, who was lying horizontal to her vertical, and on his belly, was partially stretched across her legs and was smiling at me while she caressed his behind. "I'm afraid that David really hasn't revealed the true state of the nation to you. You should know that not everyone agrees with the way we live."

"I've been taking a step at a time." David slid across Ruth's knees and squeezed between us. Chandra and Ralph were now at the water's edge, tossing what seemed to be a large Frisbee among Gale, Rose Plackett, who waved at me and I noticed was also dyed blue, and a skinny, dark-eyed girl, with a good bush of pubic hair, but not fully matured breasts, who had yelled, "Hi—I'm Delight," at me and gone on playing.

David was telling Ruth, "Paul and I had planned to give Christa at least a full week of briefing, as we have with Rose, before she encountered the world." David flicked his hand gently over my delta, tweaking my pubic hairs almost unconsciously. He grinned at me. "But Christa is a very much more aggressive female than Rose. If I hadn't arrived at the lab, by now she'd be in Boston, threatening to chop off Rose's head with a rocker unless she drove her to Marblehead." David watched for my reaction to his clueing.

"All right," I said with tears in my eyes, "I suppose I have to face it. Where are my children? Is Karl alive? Is my mother alive?"

"Your children have grown up, Christa," David said. "Penny is twenty-one. She's married to a rather conservative and wealthy lawyer, Thomas Muir. I'm afraid that Muir is a rich-ik." David squeezed my hand. "Hold your breath. Like me, you're a grandparent. You have a granddaughter—named after you—who is two years old. Penny is living in your former home in Marblehead."

"Oh, my God, this is crazy! I simply can't believe it."

"Michael is twenty," David continued, "he's starting his first year at Harvard Business School, and he's the apple of his daddy's eye."

"Karl is still alive!"

"Indestructible is a better word," David said, "and so is your mother, Grace. They live in a cooperative penthouse apartment in New York City."

"They're married?"

David shook his head. "No, I believe Grace functions as Klausner's personal secretary and man Friday. After your body was found, Karl married Lizabeth Geist. He divorced her in 1985. In 1987, he married his fifth wife, Barbara Mason. Her claim to fame was several prominent Hollywood actor-director husbands, and one movie, in which, like you, she performed some erotic love sequences." David chuckled. "Evidently Karl had fond memories of you."

"You mean she was a porno star, too?"

David shook his head. "About 1987 the distinction between movies that were termed X movies and R movies more or less vanished. Explicit genital and oral sex was incorporated into R movies when the story line warranted it. Most of the church groups finally gave up. Naked men and women making love together is finally considered a normal human activity, which can be enjoyed as a participation sport or by empathizing with others who are enjoying the act of love."

Trying to conceal my tears, and the fear of seeing my children and Karl and my mother again, I jumped up and ran into the ocean, surprising myself, as I dove under and then came to the surface, by swimming easily. If I really had been hibernated for sixteen years, my brain was still able to coordinate my physical body. The big question mark was whether it could absorb the future shock.

David had followed me, and was now swimming alongside me. Finally, treading water, he held me in his arms and kissed me. I could feel his penis against my legs. I knew that Ruth and Chandra must be watching us from the beach.

"I love you, Christa," he said. "Don't be afraid. All of us care for you."

"How can you love so many people?" I demanded.

He grinned. "If I remember your autobiography, when you were younger you didn't think loving was impossible."

"Unfortunately, I grew up and learned differently."

David had pulled me back so that we were walking on a sandy underbottom, but the water still covered our shoulders. I could feel his hand cupping my vulva, and I stared at him with tears in my eyes. "Did you ever see the opera *Tales of Hoffmann?*"

David nodded.

"You're Spalanzani, and I'm Olympia, your mechanical doll. Wind me up and I'll sing my little song, and dance for you."

David laughed. "You're safe. Until Hoffmann arrives and

you get wound too tight. Anyway, I'm not Pygmalion, and you're not my Galatea. I'm Convita. Translate that and you have the essence of the new Christina."

"What does Ruth think about me?"

"Tonight you'll sleep with us, and I'm sure you'll find out."

———◆———

Early Saturday evening, while the disappearing sun turned the sky and cumulus clouds rosy pink, and the ocean horizon slowly merged with black nothingness, we climbed the curving, sandy path up the cliff back to the house. David, Ralph, and Paul, joined by Jagger Raynes, a flaring-nostriled, laughing black man, joyously washed down their blue ladies. I was the especial object of Jag's attention; he sponged off my Desola as carefully as Ralph had applied it. He was delighted to discover that Christa, David's "bird," had nearly escaped from her gilded cage.

Zara Schmidt, a tall blonde woman, watched him sponge me down. She introduced herself as Jag's PB—pair bond— and told me that Jag and she were the mother and father of the two handsome coffee-colored youngsters, Liana and Raynor, who were watching us, and who didn't seem to mind that Jag—naked, of course—was massaging me gently, with more affection than the washdown required.

"I hope you realize," he told Liana and Raynor, who I'd found out earlier were fifteen and seventeen years old, "how unique a person Christina is. I told David a few weeks ago that if you were willing to reveal your existence, Zara and I hoped that you would talk with some of our graduate students at Boston University. Once we've briefed you, we're sure that you'll have a perspective on the world of 1996 that those of us who have actually lived through the past sixteen years can't possibly have."

"Jag and Zara teach a PASE seminar," David said. "It's a synthesis of psychology, anthropology, sociology, and economics that is gradually supplanting the former independent approaches. Jag and Zara teach the course on a share-the-job policy that many schools have initiated to keep pair-bond teaching teams employed."

Jag nodded enthusiastically and ruffled Raynor's curly hair. "Look at my son, Christa," he said. "He's completely entranced with you. Ray starts Premar in September. We haven't asked him whether he's made love with a woman. The theory is that he shouldn't until he starts Premar."

Zara laughed. "I'm sure he'll try to go to bed with you, Christa," she said. "Right now he seems about to ask you if you're his fairy godmother come to life."

Raynor smiled at me. "You can see, Christa," he said, "parents are just as boring as they always were!"

"Amen," Jag said. "One of the things that I hope we can accomplish, while the contrast is fresh in Christa's mind, is to get her reaction to Love Groups and Unilove, as a contrast to the sexual environment of sixteen years ago that she was familiar with."

"We are the crucial part of the changing world," Liana said. "We were discussing you, Christa, last week, and David pointed out that while your daughter, Penny, is only about six years older than I am, her educational and sexual background is probably very similar to your own."

"What Liana is telling you," Zara said, "is that with us you're living with people who represent only one dimension of the world of 1996. While the estimates are that there are upwards of thirty million of us who think along the same lines, we're still a vanguard. The total population of the United States is close to two hundred and seventy million people. The majority of the people, the iks—rich and poor— are much the same as they were in your time."

Jag agreed. "The point is that if the lecks were as relatively strong in 1980 as they are now, Christa, you might have found identity and self-preservation with a more life-sustaining group of people."

At the moment, I was grasping the implications of what Jag was telling me—or that he knew about my former personal life. We had drifted into the kitchen by now, and all of them, children included, were setting up a huge circular pine table for dinner, and piling on it big dishes of rice, vegetables, bread, nuts, raisins, and bottles of wine. When we were finally seated, and the dishes were being passed around, Ruth explained, "There's no meat. Most people today think it's a terrible waste of protein to feed it to an animal, kill him, and then eat his flesh. We still consume enormous quantities of chicken and fish, and while shellfish is still very expensive, it looks as if fish farming may become a huge industry." She smiled. "When you meet your husband again, I'm sure that if you want a steak or roast beef, he'll have plenty of it. In the meantime, you'll get more than enough protein from this diet."

They didn't give me time to think of when and how I was going to meet Karl again. The whole atmosphere of dining together was such a spirited intellectual exchange among the Love Group adults and children and their two guests that it made the kind of food that one ate insignificant by comparison.

David told everyone that this was my first day and he would leave it to me if I was too tired and would prefer to stop receiving such continuous input. I assured him that I was exhilarated, and, anyway, I was afraid to be alone with my thoughts—and fears.

"I really haven't told Christa how Love Groups and Care Groups are formed," David told everybody around the table. "As she begins to understand the economic environment of 1996 better, she'll realize how continuous inflation has forced people, as it was already doing in the late 1970s, to pool their resources, share automobiles, and abandon their hopes of ever owning their own private quarter acre in suburbia. Instead of trying to hack it alone, and living in small apartments or townhouse clusters, millions of us slowly became aware that having four couples and their children, people like us, share a summer home like this, or our combined apartments in a high-rise in Boston, was simply a saner way of economic life—floating with the tide rather than fighting against it."

"Love Groups are a clear illustration of how sex and family styles," Zara said, "reorient the industrial and political direction of a society. The iks are only now learning that Love Groups and Care Groups are totally opposite responses to big business and big government. While on the communal, on the microcosmic level, they're a pooling of larger forces than the vulnerable one-husband, one-wife family, on the other hand, they are a fiercely individualistic response to the human depersonalization that has been created by an all-powerful state and a capitalistic industrial system. Love Groups are dedicated to the idea of protecting their particular individual members from ever becoming dependent on an anonymous bureaucracy. If we win this presidential election, we'll eventually create a totally new economic system that will permit individual Love Groups and Care Groups, among other things, to provide their own total social and medical security."

180

"I think you should give Christa a demographic rundown on the United States as a whole," David said. "It'll help give her perspective."

"We now have approximately eighty-eight million households in the United States," Jag said. "The government still includes single households in that total. Excluding about twenty-two million single households, we have about sixty-six million two-or-more-person households. About forty million of these two-or-more-person households are still monogamous. There are about fifteen million nuclear-based, with a husband, a wife, and two or more children below the age of eighteen. Altogether, they comprise about one hundred and eighty million human beings. Approximately three million households are now either Love Groups or Care Groups, and they comprise a total of about thirty million adults with four or more children below the age of eighteen. Approximately one-third of the households are two adult households with no children at all, comprising about thirty-six million adults. Other combinations of Love Groups, which the Census Bureau doesn't count, are *pingu-pingu* groups and *konbi-konbi* groups and variations on these, which are composed of two or more lesbian women, or two or more homosexual men."

"Let's see," David said, "what have I overlooked? I didn't mention that prostitution with state-supervised homes has been legalized in thirty-nine states. Women, and *men,* who work in the state homes must take several courses in interpersonal and sexual behavior, and they must qualify for their jobs by passing a fairly easy examination. They're paid fifteen dollars an hour for an eight-hour day—about equal to what a skilled construction or data-processing worker can earn, and they're not required to service more than four members of the other sex in any one day. Incidentally, the word prostitute is rapidly disappearing. These people are referred to as sexual companions, and the supervised houses where they work are called companionship homes. There's also a thriving business in state-registered sexual companions who maintain their own offices and provide sexual variety for higher-income monogamous couples. These companions, who must be licensed therapists as well, charge much higher prices or what the traffic will bear, and they're mostly used by rich-iks, and by lecks who don't live in Love Groups."

"Good God," I said, "what's happened to the old church morality? Why aren't the orthodox of all religions up in arms?"

"There's still a lot of rearguard fighting," Chandra said. "But the sexual evolution that has been taking place at least since the beginnings of the Industrial Revolution is slowly creating a totally new kind of humanity, and in the process, a new kind of politics and economics."

"Let's say," Paul said, "that millions of us are rediscovering our common humanity."

"*Ua*—Loglan for okay—Christa," David said. "I think with this background, we can show you why Congress finally revised the tax laws and is making it possible for a monogamous family, or a group family of up to four unrelated couples, who had previously been married monogamously, or who had been living together without legal ties, to form family corporations managed by the stockholders. Historically, as David Snyder, a well-known futurist, pointed out more than sixteen years ago, 'The concept of an intergenerational family economic unit is not new. From ancient times, until the Industrial Revolution, and the development of the limited-liability corporation (*circa* 1650), the family was the basic unit for economic production and the accumulation of wealth.' Finally, in 1968, Robert Rimmer proposed, in his novel *Proposition 31*, that the State of California could set a precedent and legalize the incorporation of up to three families. Later, in 1976, as politicians and educational leaders became more aware of the continuing disintegration of the American family, Sol Tax, Professor of anthropology at the University of Chicago, proposed that Congress and other lawmaking bodies should authorize a new type of legal entity— family corporations which would be voluntarily chartered, and would, initially, extend vertically over generations, with new members acquired through birth and marriage."

"You have to understand, Christa," Jag said, "that the great hope for the utilization of the family corporation, even in those days, was that eventually it would be able to take over many of the social services and welfare services being provided by an anonymous and bureaucratic government.

"The main impetus behind the present legislation was the final breakdown of the social security system and the inability of the younger generation, which has declined in number, to carry the taxation burden of the over-sixty-five population, which is steadily increasing. You can see, from a social standpoint, the only logical solution was to give the family totally new kinds of underpinnings. Otherwise, total social collapse wasn't far away."

"The new corporate family law permits a monogamous family to incorporate if it has at least one child. Other family corporations, including former ménage à trois, and various equal or unequal distribution of adult males and females, up to a total of eight, can now be chartered. For the purpose of incorporation, an adult must have passed his or her thirtieth birthday."

"Are the children stockholders?" I asked. Looking around the table at the smiling faces of these people, I was slowly moving from the belief that this might be a dream to the hope that it was a reality.

"That depends on the adult incorporators," Jag said, "and, of course, the type of family corporation they set up. Obviously, in Care Groups, the people are all of the same approximate age and there are no children. Using our Love Group as an example, the four children are equal shareholders. The value of their shares when they leave this family corporation is an equal pro rata share of the net worth of the corporation at that moment. For example, our Love Group has a net worth of approximately four hundred thousand dollars. Keep in mind these are 1996 dollars, which have much less than half the purchasing value of a 1980 dollar. Thus, when Raynor, who will probably be the first to leave us—within the next four or five years—if he left us at the moment, would receive, roughly, about thirty-two thousand dollars, or one-twelfth of our net worth."

"But I don't understand," I said. "Why would Paul and Carol, or even David and Ruth, who have no dependent children, be willing to share a portion of their net worth with Jag and Zara and Ralph and Chandra, who do have children?"

"It's a two-way street." Carol laughed. "While we originally pooled our resources with the children as well as the adults, eventually this corporation, or the total family, will take care of us."

"You should understand," Ruth said, "that most Love Groups, unlike monogamous corporations, don't maintain their stability by incorporating the younger generation of children into their particular Love Group. Eventually, the children of our Love Group will create, with others, their own corporation."

"You see, Christa," Raynor said, entering the conversation for the first time—he had been staring at me with a warm look of devotion that was almost embarrassing—"when I or my sister or Gale or Delight leaves this corporation, we won't

183

get our share of the net worth immediately—not until our shares are sold to someone else."

David laughed. "That won't be too difficult. The reason, Christa, is that our style of family corporation, which is popularly called a Love Group, is permitted a great many tax advantages. Hopefully, the eight of us will provide for our total social security. We also maintain an approximate ten-year age separation between the couples. Chandra and Ralph, as well as Paul and Carol, are relative newcomers to this corporation. When we first incorporated, there were only four of us. Myself and Ruth, and Zara and Jag. At the time, Raynor, Liana, and Chandra were much younger and were our dependent children. To improve our tax situation, we needed Paul and Carol on the high side. They joined us about five years ago. When they became thirty, Ralph and Chandra joined us on the low age side—thus completing the corporation."

"Children don't usually join Love Groups in which they've been raised," Paul said. "For the most part, it's more comforting to incorporate Love Groups with new people than with relatives."

Chandra tweaked Paul's beard. "He means by 'comforting' that the younger women in this group go to bed with him regularly."

Paul smiled affectionately at everyone. "Of course, that's a good-will aspect that isn't revealed in the net worth of the corporation. Something else that isn't revealed by monetary figures is the family security. If I should die first, Carol has a home and loving friends, and, in all probability, if she wishes, an occasional younger male bed companion."

"I'll cheer to that," I said. "That's really women's liberation." I couldn't help smiling. Obviously, a loving woman in her early seventies, if she could find a Love Group like this, didn't have to renounce her sexuality. "What happens to your shares when one of you dies?" I asked.

"They revert to the corporation," Carol said. "If either Paul or I die, and the other is in reasonably good health, the shares can be sold to a widow or widower of approximately the same age—of course, the survivor would have to approve the new shareholder."

"And if you're not healthy, or don't want a new companion, what then?"

"We continue to live with our good friends until we die. Since we now have the legal right to die whenever we wish, you may be sure that none of us will permit ourselves to end our lives in nursing homes or become unusual burdens to the other incorporators."

"The corporation can also sell the shares of any of us who die to another person of the other sex," Chandra said, "and, of course, with the eventual deaths of Paul and Carol—their leaving us would open a position for a new couple in their early thirties. At that point, David and Ruth become our oldest members, and Ralph and I would probably be in our forties."

"How do you ever find four loving couples who can get along with each other?"

"Life-a-Vision," Jag said. "Many of the specialized channels also run get-acquainted programs. It's possible to appear on a program which would be viewed by people with similar interests. The fee is fifty dollars, which eliminates curiosity seekers. For this sum you and your husband, or your pair bond, or you alone, can appear in a one-way conversation, naked if you wish. Your name is not given, but you can tell prospective viewers all about yourself. The challenge is to really do this in a kind of defenseless way and not conceal aspects of your personality which a particular person might find disagreeable. The purpose of the exposure, of course, is to discover an existing Love Group, or Care Group, or find people who are interested in forming a new corporation."

"Jesus," I muttered, "it still seems unbelievable to me. I can accept the validity of Care Groups or a group of older people joining together to keep out of senior-citizen centers. Some people were doing that in the late 1970s, but they weren't Love Groups. Tonight, David has asked me to sleep with him and Ruth." I smiled shyly at Ruth, then stopped for a moment, interrupted by their enthusiastic applause. I continued, "While I'm not supposed to make kitsa—there's your silly Loglan word—until I have a period, Ruth has already told me that she is happy that I'm not angry with David, and she hopes that we will make love together soon." I shook my head. "Zara has suggested that before the week is out, she would be delighted if I sleep with Jag. Before she and Jag leave for Europe, she's going to bed with Ralph. Chandra told me that when that occurs, she probably will sleep alone, but she's welcome to snuggle with Paul and Carol or even go to bed with David, her father, and Ruth. I'm afraid to ask who the children sleep with, or whether Chandra has actually made love with her own father, but what I would really like to know is how you plan who sleeps with whom! Why don't you get jealous? How in hell can you all interact with each other every day without having terrible blow-ups? Why aren't the various females in this group ready to tear their husband or another pair bond apart?" I laughed. "When I was last alive in this silly world, everybody was fucking around with everybody else, but everybody got mad at each other. Half the time we hated each other, and when it got too bad, we divorced each other and tried all over again. Either I'm dreaming this, or you're all goddamned saints!"

Almost everyone at the table was laughing at my explosion. "We forgot to tell you one other thing," Ralph said. "While we've all enjoyed kitsa with each other, most of us have friends in other Love Groups, too, and occasionally we exchange homes for a week, and enjoy ourselves with four additional friends of the other sex!"

"Don't you ever need to be alone?" I demanded.

"*Ia! Ia! Ia!*" they all said almost simultaneously. Ruth smiled at my blank look. "*Ia* means yes," she said. "But we've learned how to enjoy each other's aloneness. We live in a much more crowded world than it was sixteen years ago. It's obvious that we're going to live in an even more crowded world. While we must share our space and our material possessions, good friends and lovers learn how to share each other's silences, too. It's something many of us learned for the first time in Unilove—the Church of United Love—and we certainly want you to experience this new approach to the Ultimate, which as much as anything else makes living in Love Groups viable."

———◆———

Ruth and David's bedroom was on the second floor of this old colonial house. Off the upstairs hallway, there were three other adjoining bedrooms, and two more over the garage, where Gale and Raynor and Delight and Liana slept. All the bedrooms had been repartitioned so that each couple had approximately a 20 by 20 foot living and sleeping space. Each room had an air mattress supported by a frame that held it about a foot off the floor. The mattress was big enough to sleep four people comfortably without physical contact, unless they wished it. All of the rooms had adequate closet space for the few clothes that the Love Group members owned, and all of the rooms had a writing table, two reading chairs, and huge collections of books, which overflowed book-cases and were piled randomly throughout the rooms.

Paul told me sadly, "Read-a-Film books and magazines, which can be run off a page at a time on your film reader, or transmitted over Life-a-Vision, will eventually supplant the printed book. There are no hardbound books being produced. When you try the Read-a-Film holder, you'll discover that you don't turn the pages, and, of course, you can't write on them, since there aren't any. People like me, of the old school, find it difficult to maintain a dialogue with the author." Paul shrugged. "It's supposed to be progress."

"One advantage is that you can put an entire library in a few drawers," Carol said. "While this is a fairly large house, we have much more space in our Boston apartment—sixteen rooms altogether. We have plenty of room. At least, we would if Paul could resist collecting old books"—she squeezed his arm affectionately—"and would stop overflowing them into my privacy room."

"When you live with us in our Boston apartment," Ralph said, "you'll see that we have organized our space differently. One of the larger rooms is a communal bedroom where each pair bond has their own bed. The young people all have their own single beds."

I looked at him, astonished. "You mean you all sleep together?"

Jag grinned and answered the unasked question that was jiggling through my mind. "We don't make kitsa together. Our communal bedroom is for sleeping. Of course, some nights when we all *bedgo* at the same time"—Jag chuckled—"there's a Loglan word that's quick and efficient—we often end up talking together for an hour or so. Incidentally, during our bedroom talk and dinner talk, we always attempt to incorporate the young people's points of view and bring them into the discussion."

"Our Boston apartment follows the more conventional Love Group housing arrangement," David said. "Our corporation owns the apartment. All of us, including the young people, have our own privacy rooms where we keep our personal things and pursue our personal interests. Each of us can invite others to our privacy room to talk together, or to watch a particular *telvi* channel that those in the communal gathering room may have decided against."

David smiled. "I shouldn't forget to tell you that an invitation by an adult, to another adult member of the other sex, to

187

visit one's privacy room on a particular evening—an invitation which can be declined without any ill feelings—often is a way of asking another person if they'd like to spend an evening enjoying kitsa. Ultimately, without any structure or particular planning, within any three-to-four-week period, we all share ourselves with each other in a one-to-one intimacy that is sexually oriented but doesn't necessarily involve penetration or orgasm."

"David's saying that while we often frolic and play erotically together as a group," Chandra said, "in the act of love itself, we are seeking a personal intimacy that transcends our separate selves and often gives us a sense of merger with the essence of all life itself. Group sex isn't conducive to this deep, interpersonal blending."

I was still trying to assimilate Carol's statement about the size of their apartment. "How do you afford sixteen rooms in Boston and this summer place, too?" I asked.

"A good question," Ralph said. "We couldn't, if we weren't functioning together as a total economic family. The sixteen rooms were formerly four separate four-room apartments. When we purchased one-half of the entire floor in our apartment building, which overlooks the Charles River, the building owners were very happy to remodel for us. By recombining the space, eliminating separate kitchens and dining areas, and deciding that we could get along without separate bedrooms and individual one-couple living-room areas, we were able to create much more personal privacy space than any of us ever had before."

Ralph smiled. "Paul collects books; my privacy room is loaded with mini-computers and computer peripherals. Carol has joined with some of the other tenants in the building, and they have a huge woodworking shop in the basement. What I'm trying to point out to you is that we haven't sacrificed our individual interests. We've learned how to merge our privacy needs with the joy of community in our bedroom, playroom, and dining room."

I was still a little horrified. "I don't think I could adapt to sleeping in a barracks," I said. "What if one of you snores or has a cold, or feels like reading in bed?"

"We can always sleep alone in our privacy room," Chandra pointed out. "Sometimes two of us sleep together, especially after kitsa, when it's nice to fall asleep with a friend."

"As for snoring, our biomedical technology has solved

188

that," Paul said. "It can be eliminated by a simple operation performed with a local anesthetic. The common cold is also becoming a thing of the past. Most of us take very effective anti-cold injections which keep our blood corpuscles in fighting trim."

Preparing for bed, we performed our nightly ablutions in one of the two upstairs bathrooms. *Po studu* and *po pictu*—shitting and pissing—were done alone or in company with whoever wandered in and out of the bathrooms. I noticed that Ralph and Paul, rather than aiming at the toilet, actually sat down to *pictu*. "An old Turkish custom," Paul explained. "When you're older, you can't always hurry your urine."

Ralph wondered if I had noticed that the toilets contained no water for flushing. "This is a clivis multrum. They originated in Sweden, and were available in the late 1970s, but most builders and architects ignored them. They save ten thousand gallons of water per person annually. Just as important, sewage is not dumped into the oceans and rivers. In the basement, there's a purification unit which recycles the dish water, laundry and bath water, and we use that for the old-fashioned New England vegetable garden that Paul and Carol are in charge of."

"What happens to the shit and piss and garbage?" I asked, staring into the toilet, which unlike the toilets I had known had no water in it. It was simply an open pipe leading into the darkness below.

"They drop into a container in the basement," David said. "A pipe running from the basement to the roof exhausts the surplus gases. It has three compartments, an upper one for toilet wastes, a middle one for kitchen wastes, and a lower one for storage of nutritive salts and humus, which are the final decomposed products."

"You start off with a layer of top soil along the sloping bottoms of the clivis multrum," Paul said. "That provides the bacteria which, along with the bacteria in your feces, aids the decomposition.

"It works very well in the country and suburban areas. Instead of wasting our shit and garbage, we end up with about seventy pounds of fertilizer per person every year. Unfortunately, like solar heating, adaptation to urban housing built in the last fifty years is very slow. But in the major cities, it's only a matter of time before all human waste and garbage is converted into ethanol. Alcohol-driven cars are already competing with the electrics."

David and Ruth and I were finally alone together. I was stretched out naked in bed, with David lying between Ruth and me.

Ruth offered me my own blanket. "David can stand cooler body temperatures than I can," she explained. "He's convinced that learning to sleep cooler is a way to increase longevity."

"Why bother, if eventually anyone can be hibernated so easily?" I asked.

David shrugged. "Only the poor-iks or rich-iks are interested in that kind of longevity."

"Obviously," I said grimly, "in your hands, I was a rich-ik who had no choice."

David kissed my lips. "Christina, that was different. When Max and I began working on hibernation, we didn't know that eventually, like everything else in the consumer-oriented capitalistic system, hibernation might become commercialized, too, and sold as a new way of achieving Nirvana." He grinned. "But no political discussions tonight. I just want to lie here and enjoy both of you. This is very sensuous. It isn't often that I'm alone in bed together with two loving women."

Ruth, who was lying half across David's body, kissed him. "If you want kitsa, I'm sure Christina wouldn't mind."

David laughed. "There you are. In spite of what Jag told you, sometimes three of us combine—occasionally four—and we make love together."

A vivid picture of Jennifer, Mory, and me in bed together streaked across my mind, but it was a memory that disappeared like a flash of lightning. I wondered if David had read about the three of us in my autobiography, but I didn't dare ask him. "I thought I was supposed to wait for my period," I told David as he pulled me into his embrace. I was lying almost cheek to cheek with Ruth. "You are," he said. "But making love together is snuggling together, too."

So, with our bodies entwined, our flesh identity lost, our heartbeats and breathing becoming almost one rhythm, we lay together for a long time, and I knew that, with Ruth's help, David had penetrated her, but neither of them made any effort to climax.

"I still think that I'm dreaming," I whispered into David's neck. The room was suffused with moonlight that I had seen sparkling on the black water below the house before I lay down. "I never read any stories about a future that was like this," I said.

Ruth's lips brushed across mine. "There's very little science fiction being written now. It's no longer possible for most of us to bury our heads in the sand. Fantasies about witches, or sharks, or demon-obsessed people, or monsters flying in from outer space, or interstellar warfare seem totally ludicrous. Since 1990, unless you pool your resources with other couples, food, clothing, and shelter, the basic necessities, absorb almost all of a family's income."

"As Jag and Zara will tell you," David said, "their students can't believe it when they discover that from 1970 through the early 1980s, most people were not only financially better off than we are, they were also completely oblivious to the wolf knocking on the door. Yet, they must have had some intimations of the future. They were on the biggest mass escape flight from reality that has occurred in human history. One writer described the period as the 'age of sensation.' Not only was there an endless outpouring of science fiction, but there were floods of catastrophe novels, and novels based on demonology and witchcraft. At the same time we were deluged with films and magazines and novels that reduced human sexuality to the boredom of pistons shooting sperm into greasy vaginal pumps.

"If none of that worked, then there were Disney Worlds and Adventure Parks, marijuana and alcohol, upper and downer drugs. Finally, a lot of the population was hooked on the human-potential escape routes. Everything from primal screaming to meditation to transactional analysis to EST, which tried to convince you that people were total 'assholes' and 'full of shit.' It was all part of the same search for meaning in a cold, relentless world.

"Jag's theory is that some of this response was due to the built-in repression of a patriarchally conditioned society. The male was still trying desperately to prove his power and infallibility in a business world and in a home environment where he had been reduced to just one more computer number. We're not much better off today. No society of people who really believe that warm, caring human loving should be at the top of all social priorities would ever permit the masochistic, sadistic drives and sick needs for personal assertion which are still the basis of the whole unrestrained competitive mechanism we live by."

By this time, Ruth was lying between David and me like a luscious filling in a warm sandwich. She asked me if I was sleepy, and when I assured her that I wasn't, she joined David's verbal ramble.

"David probably hasn't told you what I do for a living. Three days a week—not in the summer—I teach sex education at Boston University to future public- and private-school teachers. The rest of the time, along with Carol, who's a full-time householder, and Chandra, who works at South Caribbean Foods three days a week—the three of us form the home nucleus of our Love Group, and provide an adult base for the children when they're home from school. The importance of family households is now recognized by the government. In the financial records of our corporation, which we must maintain, Carol, Chandra, and I are paid at the rate of five dollars an hour for general household work. In some Love Groups men assume these duties, and they're paid at the same rate."

"I don't understand your pair bond commitment," I said. "I realize that you're not married in the old legal sense. What's your responsibility to each other?"

"Theoretically, we have none," David said. "But we really like each other. That makes for a friendly mutual commitment with more depth than most marriages. Anyway, in case you're worried, we're both legally divorced."

"We were divorced before we met each other," Ruth said. "Nearly ten years ago. I had two children, girls, with Ed Rutledge, a man I met in college. While the words weren't popular then, I guess our basic problem was that I was a leck and he was an ik. This was finally underlined in court by a judge who refused to give me custody of the girls because I had joined David and was living in a Love Group. The judge's belief, which still dominates fifty percent of judicial thinking, was that this isn't a sound environment in which to raise two females."

Ruth laughed. "Hilda and Lorrie, my children, are in their twenties now. When we're in Boston, they practically move in with us. Daddy Ed married again. He lives monogamously with his second wife, but evidently their home environment is nowhere near so stimulating as our Love Group's.

"So, you see, we are making some progress. While David is right about the bad shape the world is in economically, you're going to discover that in the West, at least, the last vestiges of the male-dominated world are rapidly disappearing. I told my

192

students that to gain perspective on the past, they should read Arthur Clarke's *Childhood's End*, and particularly his *Imperial Earth*. In all of the science fiction novels of those years, whether they were written by Arthur Clarke, Robert Heinlein, Ben Bova, Isaac Asimov, Frank Herbert, Poul Anderson—you name them, the male heroes ran not only the Earth but the planets and space with very little sexual help from their female friends. In the year 2276, Clarke's hero in *Imperial Earth*, the cloned son of Malcolm who runs the planet Titan, which is one of the moons of Jupiter—despite the fact that on the cover drawing he appears as a kind of man that women presumably fantasize about—actually, he is one of the typical asexual heroes of the future. Although Duncan presumably lives in some kind of open marriage, his relationship with his wife never involves joyous kitsa. What's more, he manages to survive a full year after his return to Earth with only one vaguely described sexual encounter with his lifelong dream girl. When it finally does happen, the whole kitsa business is quite disappointing to Duncan."

Ruth giggled. "I remember in the late 1970s that men were so insecure sexually, so frightened of the new, liberated females, that sadistic pictures of women shown bound, gagged, whipped, chained, or even as victims of murder or gang rape, began to appear on record-album covers and in magazine layouts, and in department-store windows. Women were shown in magazines like *Playboy, Penthouse, Hustler,* and others with their legs splayed. The defenseless but uppity woman was put in her place as a sex object. Of course, the whole thing was a pathetic cover-up. The female no longer believed in the image of the male superman. The truth was that he didn't have any in-bed prowess. He was a quick ejaculator with no staying power."

David laughed. "Keep in mind, Christa, Ruth is telling you about the world sixteen years ago. Some of us in the older generation have made the transition to the new world."

Since I guessed that David had been inside Ruth's *konbi* for at least an hour, I couldn't deny that. "Before I go to sleep," I said, "I'd like to ask you something that has nothing to do with sex. Is there any oil or natural gas left? At dinner, Carol pointed out that here in your summer home you cook with solar energy, but since you don't live here in the winter, you don't heat the house. You mentioned that some late 1980 automobiles, which I saw on the road coming here, were the last of the gasoline-driven cars. One of the reasons I ask is that all I ever heard Karl Klausner talk about was how wealthy he was going to be because of his widespread investments in other energy sources."

"You should understand," David said, "that our entire approach to energy and the conservation of fossil fuels has changed drastically in sixteen years. After a big burst of enthusiasm for developing our coal resources, it became apparent that nuclear fission and breeder reactors, though they might be risky, were the only sensible intermediate solution. The long-term problem was to conserve the world's oil resources, not for consumption in automobiles, but as petroleum feedstocks which are crucial to the production of hundreds of thousands of manufactured items as well as pharmaceuticals and some of our basic synthetic foods. As a result, we've cut back on petroleum usage for heating and locomotion to such an extent that there is probably enough, with new discoveries, to last us a hundred years or more.

"By converting fully to nuclear power for electricity, plus alcohol, and solar power, especially for hot-water heating, coupled with widespread use of heat pumps for home heating, plus natural gas and water from very deep wells in geo-pressured zones that exist in more than forty-five countries, our energy crisis has simply become a personal liability. Combined costs of energy now absorb a high percentage of family income, and are closely tied into the vast unemployment and the ever-increasing inflation that we've been living with since the 1980s.

"The combination of forced conservation and high energy costs has reached into every facet of living. It's responsible for the widespread development of Love Groups. It's created a worldwide movement among the people in developed nations to live lives of 'voluntary simplicity.' At the same time, it's diverted energy development from reliance on 'hard energy'—energy produced by huge power complexes—to 'soft energy.' Within the next ten years we'll have a number of power plants producing electricity from nuclear fusion. Unlike nuclear fission, which burns uranium and produces radioactive waste, nuclear fission joins together light atoms such as hydrogen. The fusion of the energy in deuterium and tritium, which are easily extracted from water, for example, will produce from one gallon of water the equivalent of three hundred gallons of gasoline. The days of nuclear fission are coming to an end. But Amory Lovin's concept of 'soft energy,' that he proposed in the late 1970s, is also becoming a way of community development. As Lovin pointed out nearly thirty years ago, the growing dependency on complex power systems made societies totally vulnerable to complete disruption. Normal breakdowns, or a few discontented people, could disrupt the entire country. The only way to prevent such occurrences was to go in the direction of 'soft energy'—or accept further erosion of civil liberties.

"So, even with nuclear fusion a reality, Lovin's 'soft energy' —which really means developing all kinds of energy sources on a 'small is beautiful' basis, with local power sources of all kinds controlled by small communities—is the way that the world is still moving in 1996."

David smiled. "One thing that you'll discover, Christa. Because of the high cost of alcohol and electric storage batteries, together with the virtual disappearance of gasoline for pleasure vehicles, no one goes pleasure driving anymore, and many families have been reduced to one automobile to get the best income producer to work. Everyone else uses public transportation. Electric cars, Trics, are the only automobiles permitted in the cities. They are publicly owned, but are private transportation. Trics are one- and two-passenger cars with a very small amount of trunk space. They literally line the sidewalks of the inner city. When you find one with its flag up, it's available. You insert your commuter travel card to activate both the engine and the computer-controlled time charge. You press your personal identification number on the car's calculator. The time that you use a Tric is metered while the computer-activated flag is down. If you wish to park the car, and reserve it, you simply push the reserve button. When you're finished with the car, you push the release button, which turns up the flag, indicating it's ready for the next user.

"Eventually, you receive a monthly Tric charge for your use of the inner-city automobile. Each city has an Inner Tric Zone of about five to ten miles in diameter. If you take the car beyond the Tric Zone it belongs to, the price per mile increases."

David grunted. "If you're a rich-ik or a politician, you get to use interurban rental Trics. The Tric that we drove you here from the lab in is an eight-passenger rental Tric, and ordinarily rents for fifty dollars a day." He laughed. "We have this Tric as a government-employee fringe benefit. Mostly, they're used by Love Groups and families traveling together."

"What about the United States and the Communist nations?" I asked.

"We're still living with the curse of a world stockpile of a hundred thousand atomic weapons, and we're still arguing what to do with plutonium and the waste from nuclear fission. But there is some very real hope that if a new President is elected, we may consummate a world agreement to launch the entire nuclear armaments of the world into orbit around the sun. We have the capability to do it. While space travel hasn't moved anywhere near as fast as people thought it would in the 1970s and 80s, there are about ten thousand people living, if you can call it living, on space stations."

David yawned. "If the world collapses in the next few years, it won't be for lack of energy or because of a nuclear war, it will be because our government, and our business establishment, are still controlled by men like Karl Klausner and Jason Kennedy. They refuse to admit that a mixed capitalistic and welfare society can't exist simultaneously or that Adam Smith's concept of the 'invisible hand' controlling the marketplace no longer exists. The leaders of the United States, who are still trying to make a world based on private capitalism function, are violating human trust and making a mockery of the Declaration of Independence and the Constitution of the United States."

Laughing, Ruth squeezed my hand. "David sounds as if he's running for President himself. As you'll discover in the next few days, you've been adopted by a very politically oriented family."

◆

Reflecting the truism that the best way to understand your own culture is to try to teach it to a stranger—in the days that followed I not only became the Love Group's favorite pupil (even more than Rose Plackett, I suspect), but each night I slept with a different combination of them. Seventeen-year-old Raynor hoped that I would stay with them forever, and that before he began Premar in the fall, he might practice kitsa with me.

My first nights with the Love Group, I didn't sleep very well. It wasn't because we were three naked adults in bed together. More likely it was because my brain had been imprinted with the fear of sleeping. I still had an uneasy premonition that once again I might return to a long sleep.

Did it matter? I didn't really know. Living suspended for sixteen years gives one a new perspective on being born and dying, which, when you really think about it, are simply opposite sides of the same coin. I wondered if Rose Plackett shared my feelings. We were both strangers in this world, but Rose seemed to be more complacent. Hibernation hadn't flattened out the eternal question mark that had always been a part of my brain function.

As the days passed we all played together, and we were never at a loss for words, talking and comparing information incessantly. I knew that I was trying to avoid facing whatever the reality was, but it was too obvious to ignore. No dream persisted forever. Somehow, I had actually survived sixteen years of hibernation. But I knew I couldn't stay here with this group of people permanently.

Perhaps, as all of them insisted, their Love Group would always be my center, a certain place where I always knew I could find love and affection in the world. It was more than most people had. But they agreed with me. Eventually, if only out of natural curiosity, I had to try to go home again. Although it was obvious that I never could really reinstate the past—nor did I want to—I had to see if some of the threads of my old life were still dangling. If they were, I'd probably pick them up, if only to see where they might lead. I supposed that I would have to support myself, too—but I had no idea how, unless as a sideshow specimen: "Step right up, ladies and gentlemen, see the living Sleeping Beauty. Here she is, the woman who slept for sixteen years and once again is ready, eager, and willing!"

I was beginning to suspect, too, especially because there were no newspapers or news magazines in the house, and also because the occasional attempts of the young people to "show Christina Life-a-Vision" were temporarily diverted, that there was something the Love Group was keeping from me until they thought I was better prepared to accept it.

During the week—Wednesday, I think it was—they finally turned on the Life-a-Vision screen. All of us, except for Chandra and Ralph, who had returned to Boston, were lying or sitting on the floor of the gathering room. We watched a full-length modern ballet, *Send in the Clowns*, written to Stephen Sondheim's music, which I remembered had been part of a Broadway musical more than sixteen years ago. I looked on in sheer amazement as the dancers, in lovely color, seemed to float free of the holographic screen and to be actually dancing, life-size, on the floor in front of us. The dancers seemed so real that to the amusement of the young people particularly—I couldn't stop myself—I walked toward them, and experienced the eerie sensation of not touching living bodies but passing my hand through shadows.

"You'll gradually understand, Christa," David said, laughing at my chagrin, "that the combination of big screen and holography—or third dimension—plus national cable television, which now has over a hundred channels, has completely fragmented the television audience. The total time human beings spend viewing television is probably even greater than it was twenty years ago—if that's possible—but the audience is now divided among over forty commercial channels. In addition, there are thirty-five subscription channels, twenty educational channels, and two gambling channels. Many channels offer two-way computer interaction between teacher and pupil, or the gambler and the state-authorized gambling channel. On the Massachusetts channel you match your gambling instincts against a continuously changing computer 'seed' number. You can play against numbers or more conventional slot machines, all of which appear on your television screen. You receive your winnings by check, and you're charged monthly for your losses.

"Plus that, we have ten overseas channels, which relay programs from the major cities of the world by satellite. The loser in this total television process has been the old network-type television, which formerly could command prime-time audiences. You'll remember that occasionally they numbered more than eighty million viewers. This rarely happens today. It's become such a major problem to reach a majority of the American people via Life-a-Vision that many public officials and educational leaders are proposing that Channel One be set aside as National Purpose Television. The proposal is that on Wednesday nights, at least once a month, for three hours of prime time, no other channels would be permitted to televise."

"You mean that everyone would be forced to listen to government propaganda?" I asked. "That really sounds like 1984!"

"Not forced to listen, and it wouldn't be government propaganda," Jag said. "You wouldn't have to turn the program on. The assumption is that if there were nothing else to watch on a particular Wednesday evening, a larger portion of the great American public might be weaned into greater involvement with their society. In the process, they might become more responsible voters, and hopefully, more people would become involved in local and national matters than do now. In the last national election, thirty percent of those who could vote *didn't*. Even a small fraction of those non-voters, had they voted, could have given the government of this country an entirely different direction."

"The proposal is," Zara said, "that the money that would be required to run Channel One would become a fixed part of the United States budget, but no federal officials would have any control whatsoever over the channel."

"Christa won't really appreciate the importance of the Channel One concept," Paul said, "until she realizes the wild competition that exists among the hundred channels which are now competing for the viewer's time. To lure a large audience today, sponsors of particular television programs must spend hundreds of thousands of dollars advertising on most of forty different commercial channels, trying to convince people to watch their particular forthcoming programs. This is the only way they can capture attention from other programs which are being just as widely advertised. The potpourri program channels like NBC, CBS, and ABC no longer exist. Today, commercial television channels confine themselves strictly to one area, like news reporting, sports, the arts, movies, children's programs, technical subjects. There are channels which are continuous two-way talk shows. There are contest channels, and purchasing channels which offer the public every kind of consumer product. If you wish, you can order thousands of items by telephone and have them delivered to your home from warehouses and local shopping centers."

Paul laughed. "On top of that, there are many other specialized channels offering just about every subject you can think of. Cable television really caters to the joy of living in a pluralistic society. But at the same time, it's created an even greater headache. No one can unify the millions of tiny islands existing within the system, which are often oblivious to overriding social problems. More than ever, the United States is without any central social purpose or national direction. All of this, of course, underlines the necessity of Channel One, or something similar to it, if we're to prevent a total disintegration of the country."

"Don't forget the subscription channels, Paul," Carol said. "They compete with the commercial channels, too. No commercial advertising, other than the promotion of their own programs, can be sold on subscription channels. To clear a particular subscription channel for viewing, all that you have to do is dial the channel number on your telephone. The computer connected to your telephone will measure the time that you keep the channel open for your viewing. In addition to all these channels, there's a picture-phone channel you can use for personal phone calls, and there are video discs and cassettes which can be run on Life-a-Vision. The cassettes can be rented or purchased outright, and many are available in libraries.

"Channel sixty-nine, *Sekci*, is a subscription channel, but it isn't permitted to advertise its own programs, except with the printed title of a particular movie, and one- or two-sentence descriptions which can only appear in print on the screen. The only censorship of Channel sixty-nine is the cost of its programs. You are billed twenty-five dollars an hour to watch Channel sixty-nine, compared to a dollar-fifty a viewing hour for other subscription programs. No sexual violence, or sexual fantasies involving bondage or discipline, can be shown on Channel sixty-nine. But you can watch as much kitsa, oral sex, and group sex, *nudje kitsa*—sick sex—as you wish. Porno cassettes are available to play through the telvi, but few people buy them anymore. There's plenty of opportunity to watch live, dyadic lovemaking.

"In addition to channel sixty-nine, you can often see live sexual performances on stage, particularly where they're a natural evolution of the plot. Regular television movies often show kitsa in detail, but the emphasis is on a total aesthetic effect rather than the mechanical details. Of course, the popularity of Unilove Churches is that they incorporate live sexual loving into most of the ballets and dance sequences which are a part of their services. And there's usually any number of willing Participants who reenact extended ritual sexual intercourse—sexual meditation—during the Unilove Services."

Jag said, "Finally, there are Slice of Life theaters, which are the remains of former shopping-center moving-picture theaters. The theaters are very friendly. You sit at tables facing the screen in very comfortable chairs. The only problem is that the movies are mostly psychological, and often the interaction among the actors is so involved, or so intellectual, that it requires discussion to understand them. The theater owners employ young college students as discussion leaders, and a part of the price of admission is for wine and a wide variety of food."

"Slice of Life movies are becoming very popular," Zara said. "They create a temporary group relationship, and since they operate in a time frame of three or four hours, they don't involve the risks of a Love Group or Care Group.

"Even subscription television is experiencing diminishing audiences, which now rarely exceed five million people. The search for live interchange is counteracting the glamour of television ghosts. In addition, televised sports events don't attract the same percentage of viewers that they used to. There's a growing worldwide interest in creative coed participation sports. Community teams of men and women compete against each other, playing volleyball, softball, modified soccer, and basketball on the grounds of nearby shopping centers or in high school buildings. They entertain hundreds, sometimes thousands, of community friends on evenings and on weekends. Games between live community coed teams have done their share in cutting down television audiences."

"All of this has had an interesting side effect, Christa," David said. "Right now, we're in the middle of a very important and decisive election for President of the United States. Despite the very different choices that are being offered by two of the candidates, millions of people are pursuing a 'live today, tomorrow we die' philosophy. None of the candidates believe they are reaching more than thirty percent of the eligible voters by Life-a-Vision. Many people feel that no matter who is elected, the old-style competitive capitalistic system is doomed, and we are on the verge of a dictatorship, hopefully a benign one.

"As a consequence, even though this could turn out to be the last direct election of a President, and the present states in the United States might be eliminated and recombined into regional governments, all of the candidates have been forced into grass-roots barnstorming of the country. They've been shaking hands with the individual voters in every town, city, and hamlet. The unbelievable amount of effort that they are putting into their campaigns not only reveals the sheer stupidity of these old-style presidential election campaigns, but underlines the necessity for concentrated Channel One programing, if the presidential candidates are to be heard at all."

"What you seem to be saying," I said, "is that most of the people in the country don't give a damn who is elected."

David grinned. "Let's say there are too many millions of blanks who don't care. But millions of iks and lecks, for the first time in many years, are fighting each other from very clearly defined and opposite positions. I've requested the Hyannis Communications Center to make a special run for us tomorrow night on Life-a-Vision of the second in the three two-hour Presidential Conversations." David, who was sitting near me, rubbed my back gently. "Brace yourself, Christa. If a former friend of yours, Newton Morrow, wins this election, this may be the last time anyone ever sees one presidential candidate trying to upstage another on television. The program we're having rerun appeared live two weeks ago. There's one more coming up before Election Day. All the candidates are hoping to double their viewing audience. But so far, even though Newton Morrow is very charismatic, and Kennedy and Manchester are good-looking people and audience spellbinders, they haven't found the *tocki*—key, or gimmick—that attracts the masses. Of course, in this last Presidential Conversation, Morrow appeared naked with members of his Love Group, but, unfortunately, it wasn't announced in advance. Who knows, you may be the *tocki* that does the job."

Staring at David unbelievingly, I completely missed the implications of his last sentence. Had I really heard him right? Had he said Newton Morrow? It couldn't be! Once again I had an overwhelming feeling that all this was a dream.

"For God's sake, Christina, what's the matter?" David asked. "You look stunned."

"I am. I thought you said Newton Morrow."

"He did," Paul said. "You heard him correctly. When the program is run tomorrow evening, you'll not only see your Mory, but your friend Jennifer Manchester and our current President of the United States, Jason Kennedy, both being brought to their knees by New Tomorrow."

A picture of Mory standing naked on our coffee table flashed across my mind. Oh, my God. If this wasn't an absurd dream, that was twenty-five years ago! But I couldn't stop Mory's voice whispering in my head: "Honey, when I'm President, you most surely are going to be my First Lady." The remembrance of things past was so vivid it brought tears to my eyes, and I started to sob. Both Carol and Ruth tried to comfort me. "We've all read your autobiography," Ruth said. "All of us understand how close you once were to Newton Morrow."

"You bastard!" I screamed at David. My mind was a floppy disc. A searching recording beam was trying vainly to find the correct data and feed it onto the tube in bright, flashing letters. What had I written sixteen years ago about Mory or about myself? "Owning my body wasn't enough," I sobbed, wrenching out of David's grasp. "You had to expose my mind to everybody. Who gave you the right to let anyone read my autobiography? You've all told me that this is a Love Group. The truth is that I'm just an archeological specimen you've dug out of the past. All of you are happiest when you're observing me under your microscopes."

"That's not true," Jag said calmly. "We love you very much, Christa. Your biography isn't public property. David shared it with us because we all feel responsible for you—and to Rose. Everyone in this room cares for both of you, because in a very real sense, you and Rose are David and Paul's children. We are the only people who have read your manuscript. If your autobiography ever becomes public property, or if you want to use the miracle of your rebirth to help Newton Morrow, that will be your prerogative. We love you, both Christa Past and Christa Present. And our love is nonjudgmental."

"I can assure you of one thing," Zara said. "Although none of us here know Newton Morrow personally, we're convinced, based on his writings and public speeches, that when he discovers that you're alive, he most certainly will want to see you again."

"I telephoned Chuck Holmes, his campaign manager," David said. "Morrow is in California at the moment, but he's scheduled to speak at the Topsfield County Fair, about twenty miles from Boston."

I shook my head violently. "He won't want to see me! I'm sure that Mory lost faith in me twenty-three years ago, after he found me dancing naked in a go-go bar and discovered that I was living with Johnny Giacomo." I grinned sadly at Jag. "You can't correlate the missing part of my life with the world today. Too much time has passed. Really, it was quite degrading and not worth talking about. The two years I spent in New York were a slow-motion act of self-destruction."

Tears were still running down my cheeks. "I'm sorry," I said, trying to restrain my sobs. "I know I'm overreacting. The whole affair happened in another lifetime. Mory and I are as unreal as Antony and Cleopatra. Mory was lucky. If he had married me, I would have sucked him into my

Stygian nothingness." In the back of my mind, I was still trying to assimilate the other name—Jennifer Manchester—that David had mentioned. "Anyway, I'm glad that Mory married Jenny."

David put his arm around me. "Sweet pilgrim—you're really making progress. You're no longer plowing up to your knees through the slough of despond. You've simply got to accept the amazing reality. You've been born again. Most of the old actors you knew are still in the wings. Some of them are on the stage, but it's not the same theater or even the same play. Newton Morrow didn't marry Jennifer Manchester. She's running *against him* for President. There are rumors that years ago they were sexually involved with each other, but nobody has been able to substantiate them. Your autobiography is the first clue to their former relationship. We can assure you, for reasons you'll soon discover, that the information will remain in this room."

"Is Mory married?" I asked.

"Morrow lives in a Love Group with Adar Chilling," David said. "Adar is the founder of Unilove." David smiled at the sad look on my face. "For what it may be worth," he added, "while Morrow and Adar are formally married, they live in a Love Group. As you've discovered, that gives them a wide latitude of sexual freedom. By a lovely twist of circumstances, which I'm sure that Newton Morrow will appreciate, you may become the leading actress in a whole new play."

I shrugged despondently. "I still feel like Rip Van Winkle—figuratively, too. Rip me open and there's no heart or guts left. Rip me open and you'll hear the Vitaleben hissing out of your rubber-doll woman."

Ruth hugged me. "Don't underestimate your importance, Christina. David hasn't told Morrow's campaign manager that you're alive. But I'm sure when Newton Morrow sees you in the next few weeks, your existence may force all the other actors, including Morrow himself, to learn new lines."

"If you're planning to bring Mory and me together again," I told them, "please, I beg you, don't alert him in advance. I want to think about it. I doubt if he even remembers his First Lady." I started to cry again. "Honestly, it's all wrong. I don't think I should ever see Mory again. It wouldn't be fair."

Jag patted my arm affectionately. "Whatever you decide, Christina, you should have all the pieces of the puzzle to play with. We don't know whether your husband, Karl Klausner, is sexually active, but he is most certainly politically active. His number-one target for total extinction is Newton Morrow. In the next few days, you'll understand why. This is Morrow's second try for President. He ran on a third-party ticket in 1992. The UPA, his party, the United People of America, nearly cost the Democrats, and Jason Kennedy, the election by splitting off approximately five million votes. Jason Kennedy is Karl's fair-haired boy. Another old friend of yours, Warren Ellison, is now Secretary of the Treasury. About once a week, he issues a new scare scenario predicting the total collapse of the United States if Morrow is elected President."

It was slowly penetrating my mind that Mory was fulfilling the prediction he had made so long ago, and I remembered his confident smile when he coolly insisted that when he was President, he was going to create a new Constitution. But the information input was too great. It would take time before my brain could correlate the fact that Mory's and Karl Klausner's paths had crossed, and that they were at opposite ends of a political spectrum that could no longer be defined as "right" or "left."

Attacking the ramparts of both big government and big business, waving the torch for a new kind of capitalistic socialism, Mory was saying, "A plague on both your houses."

Once again I was sobbing, and I was dimly aware, too, that Mory would no longer be the young man that I had known and loved. He was fifty-four years old, and I—my God, who was I?—if I could trust the mirrors, I still appeared to be about thirty-three. If this was reality, Mory was nearly old enough to be my father.

Tears running down my cheeks, I told them, "I really don't think that Mory should know that I'm alive. I'm not the Chrissy he knew, I don't even know whether I'm still a manic-depressive. God knows, I should have more reason to be suicidal now than I ever had before. I'm afraid I'd be more of a hindrance to Mory than a help. I'm not a political person."

I was remembering Mory's sad expression when we finally had parted the second time. Neither of us believed my promise that all I needed was a few more months. Twenty-three years ago—in another lifetime—I had told Mory that when I finally got "my head on straight," I would really come to Louisiana and marry him.

"Mory has every right to detest me." I shrugged at the dis-

205

appointment on their faces. "Since you all know so much about me already, I suppose I might as well tell you the rest of the story." I smiled through a blur of tears at Gale and Delight and Liana and Raynor. "I'm not sure that it's a story for young people, so block your ears if it disgusts you."

We were all still lying randomly on the foam-carpeted floor in the gathering room. Wearing a See-Thru dress that Ruth had given me, and nothing else, my head and feet propped on cushions, I knew my vulva was on casual display. I was vaguely aware that the breasts, deltas, penises—as well as the ears attached to the heads of my 1996 friends—were all waiting to hear my story. I couldn't help smiling. "Despite the book that I wrote," I told them, "and the movie I helped Johnny Giacomo make, I was never *resfu claso*"—I grinned—"see, I'm picking up Loglan words—I was never naked with people where being naked together was warm and friendly like this. The Loglan words *clivu*, for loving, and *clivi*, for life, seem to express your unity. In the 1970s, the people I was naked with had one purpose in mind. We were using each other's bodies to make money. Pumping and sucking at each other while the cameraman poked his lens a few inches away from our slippery genitals or concentrated on the females' mouths engorged with bursting penises, we had shut off our minds. We were totally unaware of each other as persons. The women rarely had orgasms. Even the men, when they ejaculated, might just as well have been masturbating, for the amount of empathy they had with the female. Like prostitutes with their customers, we did the job we had to do, and kept our thoughts on the money we would bring home to our pimps.

"In my case, though I was living with Johnny, I had a different pimp. Mine was the bitch goddess, success. Winning the game—'making it'—which Grace had tried to instill into me from childhood as the first purpose of living. 'Making it,' no matter how, finally had become a way of life for me. When I finally saw Mory again—it was two years after we had kissed each other good-bye at Logan Airport—I had nearly forgotten our fervent assurances that we loved each other, or that I'd always be his First Lady. I assumed that he had followed me to New York because he had read my novel, *The Christening of Christina*."

I sighed. "I suppose in one sense, I had won the prize I was searching after. My book was an instant success, and I was finally sharing some of the sick kind of fame that the media delightedly dishes out to those who dare expose themselves and challenge old-fashioned morals. Unfortunately, when the sideshow pitchman finally handed me the stuffed animal that I had worked so hard to win, it wasn't the cuddly teddy bear I had wanted. It was a mangy, moth-eaten, fucked-out tiger.

"In August, 1973, nearly broke, the advance money on my novel having disappeared into the movie that Johnny had convinced me we should make, I was dancing on a platform in back of the bar at the Cafe Breche, a topless, bottomless bar a few blocks north of Wall Street. *'Breche,'* incidentally, is French slang for the vulva. My specialty, which attracted a lot of men from the financial district, was not only nude dancing, but sexy versions of hillbilly songs like "Cocaine Bill and Morphine Sue" and "Frankie and Johnny," which I sang in a low, husky voice while I flipped my hips sinuously and occasionally spread my legs to give the leering faces below me a view of the split beaver they had paid to see. The sea of faces below me had no individuality. They could have been grinning monkeys or people from outer space. I was only partially aware of the alcohol-urine smell permeating the smoky air. My body didn't belong to me, or to my sad audience. My brain was trying to figure out why I had let the thirty-five-thousand-dollar advance for my book slip so easily through my fingers. I knew that Johnny had seduced me into making the film with him, not because he loved me, but because, according to him: 'We're both very pragmatic and we both want money even more than fame or infamy.'

"Then my eyes suddenly focused on the face of a man sitting at a dimly lighted table opposite the bar. It was Mory, and he was staring at me sadly, shaking his head like a tolerant father who had discovered his daughter playing with herself. I nearly panicked. My fifteen minutes of this particular hour was nearly over. Dolly or Snooky, or one of the other girls, would quickly replace me in the never-ending display of female flesh. For the first time since I had sunk into the sleazy, grimy fleshpots of the city, I was overwhelmed with a feeling of shame. How could I face Mory? What could I say to him? His sweet Chrissy, telling the audience to have 'a little sniff on me,' was obviously a sexual degenerate.

"I knew that Mory must have come from our—my (I paid the rent) loft apartment on Houston Street—Soho—a few blocks from Greenwich Village. Johnny must have told him where I was. I had left a little after noontime to escape three of Johnny's Mafia friends and two of their girlfriends who had arrived to shoot a few scenes for a porno quickie movie that Johnny was making on his own. As usual, before they got down to business, the cameraman and his assistant were enjoying the vacuum-cleaning mouths—never the vaginas—of the female stars of their future film. I had reminded Johnny, for the hundredth time, that I was through subsidizing him. He could pack up today and get out of my apartment. He could screw the whole damned world for all I cared, but I wasn't giving him another cent to make films. Maybe I had sucked his twelve-inch prick and let him shove it into me so the whole world could watch us. But it wasn't going to be a way of life for me. We were broke again. The movie based on my book hadn't even been distributed, and we hadn't received a dime from it. As far as I was concerned, any future relationship between us was going to be strictly monetary. Mainly, I wanted to get the money back I had sunk into the movie.

"Johnny had hugged me when I tried to squirm out of his embrace, as he always did during these fights. 'You've gotta have patience, Christina,' he would tell me. 'We can't quit now, and let our film dribble away in a few raunchy theaters. If we can control the distribution ourselves, we both can make a million. You were right. With your knowledge of psychology, and my flare for directing and producing a movie, you and I have produced the first intelligent porno film. Everyone who's seen it is very excited. It's going to make a lot of money.'

"By this time, although I was usually still screaming at him, or trying to extricate myself from his iron grasp, Johnny would be kissing me and trying to undress me. 'We're really beautiful people, Christina,' he'd say. He would release his penis from his pants, a trick of his when I was angry with him, and it would point at me like a huge rocket about to be launched into outer space. 'Christina, stop worrying. With your face and body, and my magnificent gellung, we're sure to be famous.' He would hold up his penis, expecting me to grab it, and when I'd ignore him, he would say, 'The whole world is going to appreciate this magnificent tool, even if you don't! We're really going to be famous.' In the meantime, he kept trying to reassure me. If I'd just be a little patient, and I'd keep picking up a few dollars dancing, together with the money that he and his friends were making selling porno loops to the Times Square trade, we could hang on and we wouldn't get screwed out of our movie.

"All of these thoughts were careening through my brain as I fled the stage of the Cafe Breche. How could I ever explain to Mory why I had never answered his letters, or why I had disappeared from Bellevue? How could he ever understand that the years I had spent at college learning a profession were down the drain? I was totally unsuited to be a therapist or clinical psychologist. Dr. North was in a worse mental muddle than most of her patients. I knew that Mory must have telephoned my mother. Totally disgusted with me, Grace had probably given him my New York address. No doubt she had mentioned that I'd had my telephone disconnected. I had finally refused to let her, or her emissary Karl Klausner, harass me with their incessant phone calls, or listen while they tried to convince me there were more proper ways to set the world on fire than writing pornographic novels or dancing naked in barrooms.

"In the dressing room, flinging my ninety-dollar Diane Von Furstenberg green-jersey wraparound over my naked body, I knew there was no escape. I had to confront Mory and listen to his bereavement over the decline and fall of his First Lady. While I was being paid fifteen dollars an hour for one fifteen-minute exposure each hour, I was supposed to stay on duty from one until around seven, when the second shift arrived. Dancers were forbidden to sit with the customers, and, of course, were not supposed to solicit them. When I opened the dressing-room door, Mory was already on the other side, towering over the fat manager, Nick Cappola. Nick was threatening to have the bartender, who doubled as a bouncer, throw Mory out.

"Ignoring Nick's warning that I was working, and couldn't peddle cunt on his time, and his angry: 'I don't give a damn whether you've written a book or not; there's plenty of other dancers where you came from'—I grabbed Mory's arm and led him out to the street. He was wearing a rumpled seersucker suit, a white shirt with a black string tie. He was carrying an umbrella and a book. All that he needed was a black felt hat and he could have doubled for an itinerant southern preacher. The sun was breaking through the sullen black thunderclouds. Tiny jets of steam sizzled off the wet asphalt. The temperature was a sticky one hundred degrees Fahrenheit."

I grinned at my 1996 audience, who seemed to be following the story of my former self with a great deal of interest. "I guess you call it Celsius now, but I never could figure out the metric system.

"Walking beside Mory, neither of us knowing where to pick up the threads, I was trying to decide whether I should invite him back to my apartment. I wondered whether Johnny and his crew had left. Finally, I timidly told Mory that he looked very fit and healthy, and that I was sorry that I hadn't answered his letters. 'I'm really sorry. I meant to write. I loved you. I guess I still do,' I told him. 'You knew that I was pretty mixed up. As you've seen, I still am.' I told him that I thought it would be better if I found out who I really was before I involved him in my misery. 'You can see that my search hasn't proved very much,' I told him. 'The only thing I'm happy about is that I didn't drag you down along with me.'

" 'Look, Chrissy,' he said, 'when I telephoned your mother and I found out where you were living and what you were doing, I told her I didn't give a damn. And I didn't care whether you were living with some creep named Johnny Giacomo, I still loved you. I told her that I knew you had written a best-selling sex novel, and that I enjoyed your book.' Mory had his arm around me by this time. 'I told her that I was coming to New York to take you back to Louisiana, and whether Daddy Morrow liked it or not, I was going to marry you.'

"Mory hailed a taxi. 'We're going to LaGuardia and get an eight o'clock flight to New Orleans.'

" 'Mory, I can't!' I sobbed, and I waved the dubious taxicab driver away. 'Not like this. The only damned thing I'm wearing is this dress. Besides, you really don't know me. You don't know that I've made a movie with Johnny Giacomo. When you see me on the screen, screwing with him, sucking him off, you'll want to throw up.' I was really sobbing by this time. 'Don't you understand, I'm not your First Lady. I'm not the Chrissy you knew. I don't know who Chrissy is or whether she ever existed, but whoever I turn out to be, I'm not very nice. If you're ever going to be President, you don't need Chrissy the albatross around your neck.'

"We were waiting for a light to change in our walk to nowhere. Oblivious to the people watching us, Mory pulled me into his arms and kissed me. 'Damn it, Chrissy, I need you. I'm running for state senator. I'm not going to lose because you're my wife, I'm going to win, because both of us are very interesting and controversial people. I'm reaching our generation, and I'm going to reach all the young people and get them to the polls. They'll like you. They'll like us. We haven't got our heads stuck up our asses like the older generation. I don't give a damn what you've been doing. I've got a good friend, Adar Chilling. She's starting a unique kind of church.'"

I smiled at my listeners. "Perhaps it was the Unilove religion that you've been telling me about. Anyway, Mory wanted me to meet Adar. She had read my book. Together, they were certain that I had used my novel as a kind of confessional. Because of my mother's influence, I had inevitably degraded myself as a sexual woman."

"'But now you've done it,' Mory insisted. 'Very few women have ever revealed the Earth Mother aspects of feminine sexuality so completely.' He reminded me that the first day I had met him, I had read part of Diane Ippolito's *Erotica* to him. 'You told me then that you could never write such revealing poetry. But you did it—even more defenselessly—in prose. And it's only the beginning. Adar needs you, and you need her, to give direction to each other. She's got the money power of the Marratt Foundation behind her. The religion she's developing was originally conceived by her father, Mat Chilling. When she gets it established, it will be the cornerstone of a new era in human sexuality.'

"But I wasn't really listening to Mory. I kept trying to see myself through his eyes, and the reality wasn't pretty. 'Did you see what was going on in my apartment?' I demanded. 'That should have turned you off.'

"Mory laughed. He pointed to the World Trade Center a block ahead of us. 'Lewis Mumford called those buildings some of New York City's dinosaurs. Since they aren't petrified yet, maybe we can find a place to sit down in one of their bellies. You can be sure,' he said, 'that I'm not going to stop talking until I've convinced you that it doesn't make any difference whether I'm in orbit in relationship to you, or you're in orbit in relationship to me. The sun would be nothing without the planets in its system.' Mory grinned. 'Besides, I want to read you something from a book I wrote in 1873—*Miss Ludington's Sister*.'

"'Oh, no!' I shook my head in mock dismay. 'Not Bellamy again.'

"Mory was delighted that he had jarred me out of the morbid rut of my thoughts. I couldn't help smiling at him. 'I'm really glad that Edward Bellamy is still your doppelganger.'

" 'Have you read this book?'

"I shook my head. 'I think you wanted me to, but I was too busy working on my thesis.' I pointed to an entrance to the World Trade Center. 'We can take an elevator to the top. The view of Manhattan is worth seeing. Maybe it will be cooler up there.' I didn't tell Mory that more than once, sitting in the open-air pavilion, one hundred and ten stories in the sky, I kept wondering if I could outwit the engineers who had designed this useless beanstalk. My plan was to climb down on the parapet a few feet below and dive off into the air—an angel without wings. The splutter I would make when I landed obviously wouldn't compare with King Kong's. Anyway, most of the time I felt so insignificant that I was sure that I would evaporate on the way down. Standing in line, waiting for the elevator, I reminded Mory that he hadn't answered my question.

"He shrugged. 'No one answered your bell when I rang it. I finally walked up five flights and pounded on the door. A tall guy, stripped to the waist, who looked as if he made a living pumping iron, seemed very irritated by the interruption. When I told him that I was an old friend of yours, he explained that he was God's gift to the porno film industry. He'd be happy to compare penises with me, and if mine qualified, he'd offer me a job on the spot. According to him, the leading man had just shot his wad. Unfortunately, the cameraman had missed the eruption. Now, though he had been worked on by two expert sword swallowers, he still couldn't get it up again. Time was money. With simple editing, no one would ever know whose prick was whose. The only question was, could I get it up?'

"I couldn't help smiling. 'That was Johnny, all right.'

" 'Are you in love with him?' Mory asked.

"I shook my head. 'Somewhere underneath the tough facade, Johnny's just as insecure as I am. Maybe we propped each other up for a while. Maybe he's just someone I can rub Grace's face in. As you know, she's the only person in the world who knows what's right for me. According to her, you were an obsession that I fortunately managed to rid myself of. She reluctantly agreed that I should work at Bellevue. "Try family counseling for a year," she told me. "Karl says it's as good a base for a woman as any. But it's not home base for you, Christina. If you use Karl's contacts in New

York, within a year you'll meet people who really live at the center of things. Just remember one thing, Christina, marriage to the right man doesn't tie you down the way it did in my generation. You can still pursue your own interests. Eventually, if you marry a man like Karl, he'll encourage you to be a person in your own right. Men at the top enjoy a wife who is popular and excels at something on her own." ' I giggled, and told Mory, 'Johnny Giacomo, of course, isn't the right man, any more than you are.'

"We had arrived at the observation floor of the Center. Somehow, talking with Mory again momentarily wiped out the past months. Once again, instead of being an amalgamation of jiggly breasts and genitals, I was a thinking brain. As we wandered past the exhibits describing the origins of world trade, I was captivated by Mory's enthusiasm and the driving curiosity which still fueled his mind. He was still absolutely certain that his destiny was to bring Bellamy's Great Revolution to fruition.

" 'Listen to this, Chrissy,' he said, pointing to an exhibit that detailed the story of money. 'There's the basis of my proposal for a new kind of corporate capitalism.' He read the exhibit aloud, heedless of those who gathered to hear him.

' "In the future, money may well disappear. Computer jargon for a credit card number is 'an economic integrated integer' which can be fed into a computer's memory to keep track of your purchases. Just as bank checks superseded the payment of large amounts of coin and currency, we are now entering an economy in which the exchange of money can be replaced by 'automatic computer accounting.' Soon gold will become primitive money. Wallets will soon be obsolete. Electronic money transactions will occur at the speed of a computer's pulse. In place of money will be an extended, computerized bookkeeping system which will instantly record your purchase. You will not have to touch a single piece of paper. . . ." '

"I shuddered. 'No, thanks,' I told him, and grinned at our circle of listeners, 'that's not my kind of world. It's too mechanical—human beings would simply be extensions of the bank and the government. There'd be no privacy.'

"Later on our tour, we examined the exhibits predicting the future through the year 2100. According to them, by the year 2000, man would be colonizing the planets, there would be artificial intelligence, wireless energy, global libraries, and telesensory devices. A hundred years later, hibernation for in-

213

terspace travel would be a reality. There would be interstellar probes, gravity control, robots, contact with extraterrestrials, control of heredity, travel at near the speed of light, mechanical educators, planetary engineering, climate control, world brains, and finally, in 2100, meetings with extraterrestrial objects.

" 'The word objects summarizes it all,' I said. 'A hundred years from now, people won't be meeting people, but objects will be meeting objects. There's nothing in their predictions of the future about people learning how to love people better.'

"We finally took the escalator to the open-air pavilion on top of the building. Mory was grinning at me wryly. 'Is that what your movie-making is all about?—teaching people how to love each other?' he asked.

" 'Oh, God, no! Maybe it started that way,' I said, 'but it got sick. A kind of leprosy took over.' I was trying not to cry. 'Don't you see, Mory, that's really the problem. Like the rest of the world, I'm completely screwed up, and getting more so. When I started to write the story of the Sleeping Beauty in modern terms, I tried to capture the lovely, romantic idealism of a young woman dreaming about love—and the prince who would rescue her, but then, somehow or other, like some of the versions of the fairy story itself, my book was deformed by some kind of internal sickness.'

"On the top of the building, we sat on a bench. Between the two rivers, miles below us, as far as we could see, Manhattan Island was sweltering. The sun was trying vainly to penetrate a thin haze of air filled with microcosmic particles of burned oil and rubber. While the existence of people down there could be deduced from the erections of silent stone and glass buildings, glittering but non-orgasmic, beneath the impassive, blazing sun, the reality of human life was still problematical. It was four-thirty in the afternoon. Only a half-dozen or so people had left the air-conditioned comfort below them. Sapped by the heat, they were wandering desultorily around the open-air top of the building. There was no moving air, just steamy, oppressive heat. We were biological specimens trapped under a magnifying glass in the blinding glare of the afternoon sun.

"To protect us from the sun, Mory opened his umbrella. 'Chrissy, let's stop wasting time,' he said. 'I love you. Let's pick up my suitcase at LaGuardia and fly home.'

" 'Oh, God, Mory,' I told him, and I hugged him, 'I love

214

you, too. I really want to—but I can't do that to you. Don't you understand? I still haven't found myself, and in the process, I seem to have sunk even lower. I've screwed and blown a dozen men in the past six months. I've cheapened the act of sex, devalued it—I've taken all the wonder and loss of ego out of loving and tossed it in the mud. I'm not the Chrissy you knew. I'm a slimy, infested garbage pail.'

"Mory held my hand and stared at me with a sympathetic expression on his face. 'You mean you have VD?'

"'I couldn't help laughing. 'Not yet,' I said. 'I still have some brains left. What I'm trying to tell you is that I'm not and never have been your fantasy of an innocent, virginal Chrissy.'

" 'This reminds me of some Victorian drama,' Mory said. 'You're trying to convince me that you're a tainted woman. I don't care what you've done, Chrissy. Even venereal disease is curable. Your flesh penetrated by male flesh, your mouth holding a male penis, doesn't mean that your body, or your mind, is corrupted forever. I think your problem is not that you're seeking fame or the power of money, I think you're searching for some kind of anonymous lover. The roar and the applause of the crowd prove you exist, but don't force you into any kind of real intimacy. You never have to expose your real self.'

" 'I have, with one person—you,' I said, 'but it always worried me. If you married me, you might be saddled with an emotional cripple.'

"Mory opened the book he had been carrying, and as always when he told me that he had formerly been Edward Bellamy, his voice had a laughing, teasing, I-know-you-don't-believe-me-but-it's-true quality. 'Ida Ludington's sister was her former self.' Mory was grinning. 'All you have to do, Chrissy, is rewrite this book and give it a little horror twist, and you'll be famous without writing pornographic fiction.'

"Mory smiled and continued, 'When Ida Ludington is in her old age and has become very ugly, *her former self*, a beautiful twenty-year-old woman, comes back to life. Naturally, Ida is very much in love with the girl. Of course, the young woman is no longer her, but is simply one aspect of her former life.'

"Mory chuckled. 'I wrote the basic philosophy behind Ida Ludington's story in 1873, when I was twenty-three. It's in an essay called *How Many Men Make a Man?* I pointed out then that "the unit of humanity is commonly considered to be the individual; this being the name given to the complete organism of the genus homo during the entire period of its growth, maturity and decay; during its seven ages of puling infancy, boisterous childhood, sighing adolescence, ambitious and fiery manhood and womanhood, staid maturity, the lean slippered pantaloon of age, and finally the mere oblivion of second childhood. . . ." I asked if it weren't possible to show that the individual is capable of disintegration into an indefinite number of nonidentical personalities . . . and, if so, can the memory of previous personality states be said to be essential to the sense of personal identity? Despite the intensity of our present experiences, looking back across the gulf of years, we feel most strongly how utterly gone are these past selves. In bidding adieu to old friends, you bid them an eternal farewell. Although, after a few years, you may meet again, your old friend is another person and so are you. Our grief for the dead is largely based on the same illusion. We mourn a friend dead years ago; and yet we must know, recognizing the changes in ourselves, in the meantime, that this friend, as he then was, would no longer be our friend, quite as he used to be.

"On the other hand, I asked, in my book *Miss Ludington's Sister*, are our past selves soulless? The individual, in its career of seventy years, has not one body, but many, each wholly new. Shall we say that only the soul of old age survives? No! No! The Creator does not administer the world on such a niggardly plan. Either there is immortality for all of us which is intelligible or satisfying, or youth, manhood, womanhood, age, and all the other persons who make up an individual live forever. One day, our past selves will meet and be together in God's eternal present. . . . It's the long procession of our past selves, each with its own peculiar charm and incommunicable quality, slipping away from us as we pass through life, and *not* the last self that the grave entraps. What shall it avail for the grave to give up its handful if there be no immortality for this great multitude?'

"I listened to Mory, both bewildered and entranced. 'Are you trying to tell me that even though I can't figure out what makes the self of the Christina who is sitting here right now tick—that one day Christina Future may simultaneously have to live with Christina Past? God, if you're right, and I have to go through that, I think I'll shuck off this dress, crawl over that railing, and fly naked to God—right now!'

"Mory followed me to the railing, and silently held his

216

arm around me as I stared at the parapet below us. I wondered what it would feel like to leap off and smash physically instead of mentally into the uncaring world.

" 'Rather than jump off,' he said, reading my thoughts, 'perhaps we can find ourselves by blending ourselves.'

" 'Why not?' I laughed, but I couldn't shake a hollow, empty feeling inside me. We were standing near a far corner of the building. Facing away from the few people who were looking across the twin tower of the Center, I flicked the sash that held my dress together. The hot sun seared my breasts and stomach. From the rear I knew that I still appeared to be dressed. I was like a confused male flasher, naked under his coat, exposing himself. Partially turning toward Mory, I told him, 'I'm not running naked to God, but I'm standing naked before Him. Go ahead. Make love to me.'

"Delighted with my insanity, Mory leaned back against the railing. His hands traced the contours of my vulva, and then he gently held my breasts and bent over and kissed them. 'No one seems to be interested in what we're doing.' He laughed. 'It's not the best place in the world, but I'm willing to begin here—just as long as it's only a beginning.'

" 'I'm sorry, Mory.' I was suddenly crying and trying to tie my dress. 'You can see that the only self of Chrissy that's left is a whorish self.'

"Mory kissed my face and held me naked against him. He reopened his umbrella and held it behind me. 'I wouldn't call it a whorish self,' he said. 'Rather a joyous, fun-loving self.' Laughing, he warned me that he couldn't hold the umbrella and take the initiative. 'The people over there may guess what we're doing, but they can't actually see us,' he said.

"It was my move. I unzipped his zipper and held his penis. . . ."

Suddenly conscious of my audience, who had been following my story with warm, sympathetic expressions, I was embarrassed. I stopped talking. "That was the last time I saw Newton Morrow," I finally said.

"But what happened?" Liana asked breathlessly. "Did you and Mory actually make love right out there in front of everybody?"

I shook my head. All their faces showed the same disappointment. There had to be more to the story. "People haven't changed much," I said. "I think all you really want to know is whether a possible future President screwed a woman on top of the World Trade Center."

"Not really." Jag laughed. "We're sure that Morrow would have. He's the first man who ever ran for President who's made it clear that loving is more important than acquiring."

"Mory was too tall." I couldn't help smiling at my memories. "Even bending his penis down toward me, it scarcely fit between my legs horizontally. The only way he could have gotten inside me was for me to shinny up on him."

"Indian women did that with their lovers." Ruth smiled. "Their lovemaking was immortalized in stone in the temples at Konarak centuries before Christ."

I grinned. "Of course I did. I encircled him with my legs for at least a minute. Then we heard indignant gasps from across the pavilion. We were shocking some senior citizens."

I couldn't help it. The tears flooding my eyes poured down my cheeks.

"Did you fly back to Louisiana with Mory?" David asked softly.

"No, we went to a hotel, and stayed there two days. Oh, God—don't you see, I really loved him. But I was positive that whoever I really was, wasn't good for him. I proved it months later. Karl Klausner found me in a fleabag hotel on lower Fifth Avenue. He finally talked me out of jumping into the nets the firemen had stretched out, but as David discovered later, even after six years, I was still living in a mental jungle." I wiped the tears from my cheeks. "It's silly to cry about the past. All that happened a lifetime ago. If this is reality, I really should be crying about this." I sighed. "At least I hope that Mory, or Bellamy, was wrong about the immortality of one's various selves. I'd hate to have to live with *that* Christina as my sister."

◆

Later, in bed with Zara and Jag—Jag, naked as we were, was lying between us—I noticed that his penis, which was at least six inches long when it was quiescent, seemed to have grown another inch in length and had a magnificent circumference of at least an inch and a half.

Laughing at Jag, Zara held it up straight and said, "See what being in bed with the famous Christina North does for a man."

Jag grinned at me. "It's not just your physical beauty,

Christina. Call it the effect of a triple amazement. You, quite literally a creature from a world that no longer exists, are here in our bed. Technically you are forty-nine, but you are physically and biologically almost the same age as Chandra. On top of that, having read your autobiography, and watched your movie several times on Life-a-Vision, I feel as if I know you almost as well as any woman in this Love Group."

I laughed. "Don't judge me solely by that movie. When that was made I couldn't have told you who the real Christina was myself."

Zara leaned over and quickly circled the glans of Jag's penis with her tongue then, smiling, she asked me if I'd like to hold it. "Good Lord," I said to Jag, who was grinning at us like a caliph in some ancient seraglio, "with this cannon you must be the prized bed guest in your Love Group. If you are alone with Ruth or Carol, does it grow this big?"

Jag's big brown eyes flashed merrily at me. "Chrissy, the secret to a man's sexual enthusiasm is not because the woman is a stranger, but because of the adoration in the eyes of a woman who he knows cares about him. I love Carol and Ruth and Zara and Chandra. Each of them in very different ways is a loving person and is unafraid of her own sensuous feelings. As they convey their eroticism to me my brain responds instantly."

Jag pointed at his penis, which I was still holding. "My brain as well as your fingers tell me that you are a loving caring woman by the gentle way you are holding me."

"It just occurred to me," I said, "I haven't held any man's penis for sixteen years." I was going to tell him that I hadn't tasted one, either, but that seemed superfluous. I did remember that David Convita's penis had been the last one I'd held. Then the silly thought crossed my mind: how many men's genitals had I touched in my lifetime? It was more than just a fast tabulation of my sexual life. I kept wondering if my brain was really fully functioning after so many years of inactivity. I couldn't remember too well any of the male penises I had known prior to Mory's. There must have been about ten of them. Then another ten when I was involved with Johnny Giacomo. But after I married Karl I had been a good girl, relatively—only Hank Hutchings, Warren Ellison, and finally David. A grand total of twenty-five? But of all of them only Mory, and possibly Hank Hutchings and David Convita, had penises which still blended in my mind with their faces and their total bodies. The rest of them were simply connectors or horns made for blowing—which their owners often preferred. "Giving head" was the term they used then, and if their owners didn't care if there was a maternal instinct in my gentle sucking—any anonymous mouth going up and down on their protuberance would do.

I kissed Jag's penis gently and let it go. "Too bad that I'm not a sexually active bed guest," I told him.

"That depends on how you define sex," Zara said. "I asked David and Paul this morning why they insisted that their female hibernators must wait until they menstruate before resuming sexual relations. They told me that they just wanted to be sure that there had been no ovarian damage and that you could actually get pregnant again. In addition, as you know, most of us lecks don't use any artificial birth-control methods, so until you are on your cycle no one is sure whether you're fertile or not."

"My God!" I couldn't help laughing. "On that score you can tell David and Paul they don't have to worry. I wouldn't get near them, or any six-foot pole like this, unless I knew I was absolutely safe."

"What Zara is telling you," Jag said, "not too subtly, is that we often make love without penetration. If you wish, either one or both of us will be delighted to help you discover whether you are still orgasmic."

Zara grinned at me. "I'll defer to Jag. I love you, but for the most part I'm still quite heterosexual. Anyway, he's had many good female teachers."

I shook my head. I knew that I was orgasmic, all right. Holding Jag had excited me, but I wasn't at all sure that I wanted to climax while Zara watched me. Except with Jennifer and Mory—God, that seemed like a hundred years ago—I had never gotten involved in group sex. Then, sensing that Jag was disappointed, I said, "Okay, let Jag kiss your vulva while I explore his penis. It may surprise you, but I have never made love with a black man."

I kissed Jag on his lips, and smiled at him. "Besides, I'm curious. I'm not sure that I can open my mouth wide enough to get this one in!" I didn't know whether it was the right thing to say, but Jag seemed delighted.

"As you will discover," he said, "the lecks have made great strides in eliminating the stigma of intermarriage. At the same time, while black men and black women are no longer

220

so hung up on their "roots" or maintaining that "black is more beautiful" than the blending of white and black genes—nevertheless, total, loving acceptance by a white man or woman, still reaches some inner recesses of our brains and creates its own eroticism."

Zara smiled. "I think Jag means that if you are in love with a person of another race it is not in spite of his or her color, but because, like everyone else, he or she is a loving person."

I slipped between Jag's thighs, and Zara lay crosswise to him with one leg under his head and one loosely across his chest. And then, amazingly, as I slowly slid my tongue down his penis and toward his balls, I knew that I was becoming very excited. Jag's staff had a proud independence from his body. A black tower that belonged to some Nubian king. Kissing Zara, as I kissed him, he was obviously both an ecstatic worshiper and worshipee.

Long ago, when I had been with Mory, I used to ask him a million questions while we were in the act of loving. Did he enjoy me touching him this way?—kissing him or sucking him that way? Sometimes he'd tell me that we didn't just have sex together—we had verbal intercourse. Now, with Jag, the memories flooded back. I had learned long ago with Mory what most women of my generation had never learned—the sheer excitement of arousing and controlling a man with one's mouth and fingers as he lay there in helpless ecstasy reveling in your touch. Not that a woman should ever turn her mouth into a substitute vagina. Neither should usurp the other's sexual function. Even if a woman can take a man's cock deep into her throat, even if she has numbed herself with cocaine, she still can't shake her head the way she can her ass. A mouth can never flex and snap like a woman's pelvis and give a man the feeling that she is milking the dear sweet thing straight down between his toes. At least, that's what Mory told me.

While a man can thrust and shove in a woman's mouth—face fucking, Johnny Giacomo called it—in order to continue to contain him she must let him be the aggressor. Sadly, that may be why some men enjoy oral sex. The woman, with her hair and head in his hands, loses her identity. All she is is a manipulative object with a hole in it.

I knew the moment that I began teasing Jag's penis with my tongue that he understood this. I kissed him softly south-

221

ward to his testicles, and then I sucked one of them very gently. A little further down I nipped the curve of his ass, and then I slowly dragged my tongue from the edge of his anus to the top of his penis, stopping here and there to nibble on his thighs. His flesh was warm and sweet, and when I shifted position so that my behind was practically resting on Zara's thigh, I felt his fingers, gentle as warm air, exploring my clitoris and caressing the individual hairs on my vulva. Holding his penis erect, very slowly, I let it slide into my mouth until it fully engorged my throat.

Zara, who had turned over now and was watching me, shook her head in disbelief. "My God, Christa, I never thought it could be done. Not all the way."

I gave Jag's shaft three quick strokes down to his balls while he moaned with pleasure. I realized that I was panting—not from containing Jag's penis but because of his insistent, affectionate hands on my vulva.

"Quickly," he said to Zara. "I want to climax inside you. I can last until you come along with me."

By some miracle we all climaxed together. When I finally caught my breath, I told Jag that while I had never learned to swallow a man's jism, he could have come in my mouth if he had wanted to.

Jag shook his head. "I prefer mutual orgasm inside a woman. I love you, dear Christa and dear Zara. I'm glad you're both alive in my world." Zara was still on top of him and he was joined to her. He kissed my lips, and the three of us lay in silent contentment for a while. Finally Jag said, "While I'd enjoy snuggling with both of you all night, it's still early. Before you see Mory on his rerun of his Presidential Conversation tomorrow night, you should read a good chunk of *Looking Backward II.*"

"Did you say *Looking Backward II?*" I stared at him, open-mouthed.

"Morrow published *Looking Backward II* in 1994. The book is not only an extension of Bellamy's ideas in *Equality*, but it proposes a New Constitution very similar to Morrow's ideas that you reported in your autobiography. In addition, it proposes a whole new approach to government and how a people's capitalistic society can be achieved. He also has drawn the battle lines by dividing Americans—and most of the Western world—into iks, lecks, and blanks. He believes that the poor-iks and lecks will combine on November fifth to elect him President. Right now, it's a toss-up between him and Kennedy. A great many of the pollsters believe the election hinges on how many votes Jennifer Manchester corrals and whether she takes them from him or Kennedy."

I still hadn't assimilated the fact that Jennifer—God, she must be nearly fifty years old—was running against Mory. "I suppose by now Mory has stopped telling everybody that he is a reincarnation of Edward Bellamy."

Jag was lying naked on the bed. Zara was snuggled against him. They were a lovely contrast of black and white flesh. Jag shook his head. "Not at all. A great deal of his political appeal is that millions of people really believe that he is a re-incarnation of Edward Bellamy." Jag laughed, and with the hand that wasn't holding Zara, he gently caressed my thigh. "Amazingly, Morrow's belief in reincarnation is giving people a new perspective. Back in your day, a black man sent everyone searching his roots. Somehow Americans, black and white, got the idea of roots confused with a more loving past and a more joyous communal existence. But searching in the past doesn't create the groundwork for a new future. A few blacks may have found their roots, but despite the floods of white tears that were shed over that television drama, there was no stampede to transplant blacks into white suburbia. On the other hand, Love Groups and interracial marriage and a belief in New Tomorrow, plus Morrow's certainty that he has discovered his former self, are doing more for both blacks and whites than digging into pasts that no longer exist."

I was puzzled. "What has reincarnation got to do with it?"

Zara grinned at me. "If you're born again, like Newton Morrow, you may discover that instead of being a sacred cow in your previous existence, you might have been a black person—or, God forbid—you might be a black person the next time around. Remember, while your Mory has an evangelistic background, his God doesn't wear a beard and sit in Heaven watching over things. Morrow tells everybody that being born again and again and again makes much more sense than hibernation. Instead of hibernating and waiting for a future in which you would occupy the same old body, when you're born again, you make an all-out effort to find out who you were formerly. The rebirth is God's way of purifying you, so that eventually you can rejoin the eternal flow of *clivi-clivu*."

"I really can't believe it," I said. "It doesn't seem possible that Americans would buy such a daydream."

"The reason they are buying it," Jag said, "is that no one knows for sure whether he may be right. One thing is certain: Morrow has made all of Bellamy's books—which have been republished in either book form or in microfiche, Read-a-Film—top best sellers. *Looking Backward* and *Equality* and Bellamy's *Religion of Solidarity* have sold over twenty million copies. Bellamy's novels, *Doctor Heidenoff's Process, Miss Ludington's Sister,* and *The Duke of Stockbridge,* have sold in the millions, and Morrow's sequel, *Looking Backward II,* is proclaimed by all New Tomorrow believers as the book which will change the direction of the civilized world for centuries to come."

I couldn't help it, I was crying again—this time happily. By sheer persistence and absolute confidence that he was a first-string Messiah, Mory had done it! He was a Pied Piper with half the people of the United States dancing merrily behind him toward the Golden Age.

"I think we should try to give Christina some background on our total political and economic situation," Zara said. "When you finally watch Life-a-Vision, all you'll hear about is the Big Limbo, which is the popular expression for the continuing economic problems that the world is facing. The allusion is an analogy. You can't dance under the limbo stick of both inflation and unemployment without falling flat on your back. While Morrow has characterized the people in this country as iks or lecks or blanks, it's a typically popular but inaccurate generalization. Many lecks are not particularly intellectual or bookish. Many iks are quite brilliant. Unfortunately, they have a seventeenth century philosophy about the ownership of wealth. A rough dividing line between iks and lecks is one's annual income. Keep in mind that today the median and poverty income levels have merged. Today, poverty level is close to fifteen thousand dollars annually. As a rough figure, those with incomes of one hundred thousand dollars or more tend to be iks, but many of those who are in the poverty-median income levels still believe that this is the promised land where, by some miracle, the poor can become rich. These are the people that Morrow has classified as the poor-iks. Even now, nearly two hundred years after the beginning of the so-called Industrial Revolution, most of them have never understood that despite the hoorah about high income taxes, which were supposed to redistribute the wealth, the *real* income-producing wealth of this country is still owned by less than five percent of the total population."

"You have to understand, too," Jag said, "that those who are in the upper-income brackets, which run, in today's dollars, from two hundred fifty thousand dollars to a million dollars or more annually, are still pursuing life-styles that are very similar to the way upper-income people lived in the 1970s and through the 1980s. For those who have the money, it's an 'after me, the deluge' world. Today, most of the rich-iks marry and live monogamously, but more than fifty percent of them have been divorced and remarried at least once. They can't believe that people who live in Love Groups or Care Groups can let go of their egos or share themselves with each other, both economically and emotionally. Their biggest luxury is still 'the luxury of their integrity.' No matter who it hurts."

"Of course, Christina," Zara said, "the tax advantage of pooling income to achieve fuller lives was one of the big contributing factors to the growth of Love Groups and Care Groups. Morrow's big hope is that there are enough of us to create a strong political bloc. But no one knows for sure yet."

She turned to Jag. "I think Christa should be given some background on what's happened with the various political parties, or else she won't understand how Newton Morrow has been able to drive in the wedge of his United People's Party. The old Republican party is nearly defunct. By and large, the rich-iks have solidified behind the Democratic party.

"While we teach the general subject," Jag said, "we won't blame you if you get confused. In actuality, the present Democratic party has two faces. It claims to be a people's party, but it's actually dominated by big business and the bankers. Neither Jimmy Carter nor any of the Presidents who followed him were able to scale down the size of the Federal Government. It has even greater centralized power than sixteen years ago. We now have a national debt which is a trillion dollars. No one has figured out yet how to combat the continuous inflation. Price increases have been running around twelve percent annually. To try and reduce unemployment, government has gone into the business of providing 'socially necessary jobs' on a big scale. On the other hand, while the business managers scream and tear their hair out in newspapers like the *Wall Street Journal*, and excoriate the politicians, you have to understand that most of the federal projects have been instigated by the business managers themselves in a desperate attempt to save the old capitalism.

225

"The philosophy of these men hasn't changed since Franklin Roosevelt discovered the way out of the 1930s depression with the John Maynard Keynes illusion that the government could prime the economic pump by deficit spending.

"The basic underpinning of the United States' economic growth for the past fifty years has been the trillions of dollars that have been spent on war, or arming for war. Making weapons and manufacturing automobiles for obsolescence are the only ways that the present capitalistic system can survive. Today we're still making the weapons, but a good portion of our economic trouble right now is that long ago we stopped manufacturing ten to twelve million automobiles a year. No one has figured out yet how to employ the millions of people who made them or serviced them.

"Whether they're far-right Republicans or whether they're hiding behind the welfare socialism of the Democratic party, those who still own the wealth in this country are fighting a last-ditch stand." Jag grinned and nuzzled my cheek. "Unfortunately, most Republicans and Democrats don't understand the distinction between welfare and well-fare. Even if Morrow is elected, you can be sure that those who are still the power behind the throne, those who own the country's banks and life insurance companies and most of the industrial establishments, will try to stop New Tomorrow—or any takeover by the United People of America."

"Another thing that may confuse you," Zara said, "is that in a very amusing way, Newton Morrow uses the theories of the old right-wing Republican party as one of his prime weapons to create his New Tomorrow. I'm sure that when you first hear Morrow's speeches, or when you read some of *Looking Backward II,* you would think that men like Karl Klausner would approve.

"Morrow is campaigning on a platform which, among other things, proposes to create a country 'of self-determining citizens,' a society of people who really believe in competition, who believe that hard work should be rewarded, and a society of people who don't believe in government handouts. Morrow believes the only way to stop the encroachment of the Federal Government is to reduce it by one half. He is proposing to do away with pensions, social security, welfare payments and Medicare payments, and to throw the responsibility for their well-fare back on the people themselves by creating a Federal Government that is in economic partnership with the people but on which they can't lean—at least, not too heavily. Sometimes, when you listen to Morrow, he sounds as if he dredged his philosophy up out of history books written by Coolidge-Hoover Republicans.

"But then he flips the coin over and tells you that when he's elected President, he will wipe out the national debt, and propose a New Constitution that will eliminate all the fifty-three states and put in their place fifteen governing Common-wealths. To top it off, and prove that he isn't seeking personal power, if he is elected, this will be the last national election for the President. He cheerfully admits that within three years, when the New Constitution is ratified, he himself may no longer be President. But what really scares the business and banking community is his proposal to eliminate all private banks, the present Federal Reserve system, and all life insurance companies, and within eighteen months after election he promises to establish a true workers' capitalism. The people of the United States would not only own all the industry and service businesses in the country, but, in addition, they would be direct shareholders and receive annual dividends from the profits of a super-corporation which Morrow calls the United People of America."

Jag bounced off the bed while Zara was talking, and I heard him clattering down the hall. He returned in a few minutes with a book which he handed to me. "I knew Paul would have a copy of Morrow's book. Here's *Looking Backward II*, Christa," he said.

While Jag and Zara were obviously tired and wanted to sleep, they assured me they wouldn't mind, since they knew I was very exhilarated by Mory's book, if I read for a while before I went to sleep.

Mory's picture, in full color, was on the back cover of *Looking Backward II*. I couldn't stop staring at it. His hair was a thick, rusty gray. His face had become lean, hard, and angular. The fiery intensity of his brown eyes hadn't diminished. The photograph was a holograph-type print, and with the extra dimension, he magnetized his viewers, and probably would have made most of them uneasy, except that he was smiling. His smile, merged with his obvious basic determination, gave his face a warm, fatherly expression.

Facially, at least, my Mory was no longer a brash young man. He was the symbol of a loving, caring father. I could almost hear him whispering to me, "Sister Chrissy, you're a

227

lucky woman. You've got two men in love with you, me and the ghost of Edward Bellamy."

I read as much of the book as I could that night in one vast gulp—not fully understanding it—trying, at the same time, to bridge the years and once again achieve the marvelous rapport I'd once had with this strange man.

The book began with an amusing interweaving of Bellamy's life and Mory's. "Whether you believe in personal reincarnation does not concern me," he wrote. "The truth, of course, is that as Newton Morrow, I do not have the same body I had when I appeared on this earth as Edward Bellamy. But one's essence—his soul, the irreducible energy that comprises the essential me who was Edward Bellamy, and no doubt the same essence which has experienced rebirth many times prior to Bellamy's appearance on this earth—that energy cannot disappear. Nor can the energy that is the essence of *you* disappear. The only difference between you and me is that by constant search and a modicum of luck, I have rediscovered my Bellamy essence. No one who has lived on this earth ever dies. We are ceaselessly reborn. Whether you wish to believe this or not does not matter. Like it or not, it is your cosmic destiny. Should you become interested in who you might have been in centuries long past, you may, as I have, rediscover your former self. But even if you don't, the search through the thoughts of thousands of minds that have preceded you will establish your consanguinity with all life.

"But," Mory went on to explain, "this book is not about your past or your future—it's about your *now*. When I wrote the first *Looking Backward* and finally an even more detailed sequel, *Equality*, I pointed out that 'the duty of society to guarantee the life of the citizen, implies not merely the equal distribution of wealth for consumption, but its employment as capital to the best possible advantage *for all* in the production of more wealth.' As I pointed out: 'The old ethics absolutely ignored the social consequences which result from an unequal distribution of material things. We now live in a world where everybody absolutely depends on total economic sharing of income producing machinery and property. The old ethics of property ownership overlooked the whole ethical side of the subject—namely, its bearing on human relations. All human beings are equal in rights and dignity. The only defensible system of wealth distribution is one which permits

228

an equal sharing of the income from the land and machinery and our heritage from past centuries—all human inventions which belong to no small group of individuals, but to all of us.' "

New Tomorrow

The cornerstone of our state is economic equality, and is not that the obvious, necessary, and only adequate pledge of these three rights—life, liberty and happiness? What is life without its material basis, and what is an equal right to life but a right to an equal material basis for it? What is liberty? How can men be free who must ask the right to labor and to live from their fellow men and seek their bread from the hands of others? How else can a government guarantee liberty to me save by providing them a means of labor and life coupled with independence; and how could that be done unless the government conducted the economic system upon which that employment and maintenance depend? Finally, what is implied in the equal rights of all to the pursuit of happiness? What form of happiness, so long as it depends at all upon material facts, is not bound up with economic conditions; and how shall an equal opportunity for the pursuit of happiness be guaranteed to all save by a guarantee of economic equality?

—Edward Bellamy,
Equality (1897)

We spent the next day on the beach again, discussing Mory's book.* I told the Love Group while I had stayed awake most of the night reading *Looking Backward II,* I'd still appreciate their help so that I could really understand Mory's economic proposals. "For example," I said, "he says that everyone will have their own individual Capital Account with the People's Government. Somehow, each individual's earnings will be reported into this Capital Account. Remember," I laughed, "what little I know about economics I learned from Mory, and that was a long time ago."

"Let me try to explain it to her." David smiled. "If a biologist can explain Morrow's proposals to a psychologist and we both end up understanding them, then maybe Morrow really can win. Basically, Christa, his theory is that instead of a small percentage of the people controlling the capital of the country, we should go all the way and create a profit-oriented corporate society. Morrow begins with a Federal Government which would be run on a profit-making basis and would pay dividends to all the shareholders—who are the people themselves. A total corporate society would involve every citizen in at least three overlapping corporate communities. First, there would be the corporate Federal Government, and then the corporation which the individual worked for, and finally a family corporation. Each individual would be a shareholder in one of these separate corporations, which are interlocked with each other.

"To really appreciate what Morrow is driving at, you have

* Throughout the following thirty-two pages, in an ongoing way, as she gradually assimilated his ideas, Christina summarizes Newton Morrow's basic economic plan for a New Tomorrow. While most readers in the year 2000 will find this overview easy to understand, if you prefer to follow Christina's story to its climatic conclusion, skip to page 265. However, depending on the time frame in which they are reading this book, many readers will find the "how-to's" of people's capitalism quite fascinating, controversial, and easy to comprehend.

to understand what has happened in the economy in the United States and much of the Western world since 1980. First, we have a continuing and insoluble unemployment problem. This has been caused by two interacting forces.

"One of the interacting forces which created the present unemployment mess was the population increase. We now have forty-five million more Americans than there were in 1980, and a continuing demand for more jobs to keep them employed. If the total potential work force were fully employed, it would mean creating thirty million more jobs than were available in 1980. Many economists insist that we have actually created more jobs. The problem is that there simply is a limit beyond which job creation cannot go.

"Morrow believes that millions of jobs have been permanently lost, in both the industrial and service areas, by the unrestrained forces of a capitalistic system which is not owned by the people themselves. In addition, a social ethic has been drilled into the people for hundreds of years—that it is immoral to be socially 'useless.' The Puritan work ethic still dominates our society. But the never-ending capitalistic demand for greater productivity, to lower costs and improve profits, has finally created its own destruction. The old capitalism has never been able to propose any other solution to restrain inflation except the so-called laws of the marketplace working in combination with greater productivity, which presumably would spread the labor costs of any product over many more units and thus keep the price down. Nobody listened to economists like Louis Kelso, who in the late 1970s was insisting that the productivity of capital equipment—the tools and machinery of the society—far exceeded the productivity of increased human sweat and effort.

" 'Man's machines,' Kelso said, 'are an extension of himself. Each working person should personally own a portion of this machinery in the form of legal stock ownership, and each individual should be able to personally share in the earnings from the machinery or capital piece of the pie, as well as the smaller portion of the pie that his brain or brawn provided.' Kelso proposed Employee Stock Ownership Plans, which would have eventually transferred the ownership, and he wrote books telling how to create eighty million capitalists. But very few of the old-time capitalists were listening, and if they were, they weren't sharing their wealth—not if they could help it.

"On top of this lack of understanding that the old-style

capitalism of bottom-line profits for the few wasn't working anymore, the drive for greater productivity culminated with the Japanese, who in the past fifteen years have developed the computer-automated factory to a fine art. Incredibly complicated operations have been computerized beyond anything you would have imagined in 1980. If the figures for the Gross National Product, which is now close to seven and a half trillion dollars, are restated in 1972 dollars, the present GNP is approximately two trillion. Considering the population increase, the actual physical output of goods and services has remained constant and requires far less human labor than was used in 1980.

"Instead of facing reality—that material and social growth has obvious limitations—(when one row of people in the audience stands up in order to see, the row behind it will have to stand up, too, and finally the whole audience is standing instead of sitting comfortably)—instead of searching for a new kind of society where a smaller portion of the labor years of every man and woman was for the common welfare, the Kennedy government, and every government since Jimmy Carter was President, have chased the rainbow of full employment. They've continued to try to create a society where everyone from eighteen to sixty-five could get a job. Actually, what is meant by getting a job, is being forced to work in order to survive. One must either be employable, or be supported by transfer tax payments in the form of welfare or social security.

"As a result, over the past six years alone, the Federal Government has spent close to five hundred billion dollars directly subsidizing jobs. And this does not include how many trillions of dollars have been spent, over the past half century, creating jobs in the so-called defense industries. Manufacturing weapons for human destruction, creating a death arsenal that continuously becomes obsolete, has been the only way the old capitalistic system could keep people employed. Of course, the whole process automatically creates huge profits and wealth for the few people who control the capital equipment to make the armaments. At the same time, it provides the rest of us with the illusion that our work is really socially valuable, or that we really should believe in some kind of insane work ethic that tries to convince us that somehow we can increase our personal productivity indefinitely.

"Not only have we wasted irreplaceable raw materials, but we have never faced the reality. Millions of jobs have been

235

created, not because people want to work at useless and un-fulfilling tasks, but because this satisfies the approved Christian-Judeo work ethic. No one could conceive of a society where less than half the people working, at any one time, could very well have provided all the basic necessities, and an abundance of luxuries for themselves as well, and simply passed off the surplus to those who didn't 'work' at all.

"No presidential candidate except Newton Morrow has ever asked the basic questions: How can a capitalistic society be reorganized to retain some of the advantages of humans competing with each other? How can humans work together, not for self-destruction or total destruction of each other? How can human beings be given monetary recognition for human excellence exemplified both by the interpersonal value of the products they help manufacture for each other, as well as for wisdoms and skills they can transmit to each other?

"Morrow has shown us how a capitalistic society can be reorganized so that it isn't rooted in the sterile soil of wasting human lives and energy. He has projected a workable, competitive economic system that will produce automobiles, refrigerators, televisions, and thousands of other products that are designed to last at least twenty-five percent of a person's lifetime—products that haven't been purposely designed to wear out in a few years, simply to keep people employed. In addition, he has created the groundwork for a society which doesn't have to spend billions of dollars annually producing weapons of destruction in order to transfer money and keep people working.

"Production of goods simply for the sake of profit is no longer a feasible way of life. But, sadly, we still have dreamers in the White House, like Jason Kennedy, who believe that an economic society can be 'fine tuned' to maintain a balance between full employment and mild inflation. As a result, our national debt has increased to a trillion dollars today. The current annual payment in interest costs on this debt in 1996 dollars is close to one hundred billion dollars." Jag grinned. "Morrow's solution is to simply wipe it out—cancel the debt! And eliminate all the banks and life insurance companies, along with the stock market." David laughed. "Not to mention such small things as the various Klausner Mutual Funds."

"I'm glad Mory still believes in the hereafter." I sighed. "He sounds like one of the early Christians. Unless Karl has changed, he and his gladiators will feed Mory to the lions."

"Maybe," Jag said, grinning, "but times have changed. Millions of the hoi polloi are willing to try anything to break their economic chains. To give you an idea of the current cost of living, a first-class letter requires a seventy-eight-cent stamp. One day in the hospital costs close to a thousand dollars. A loaf of bread costs two dollars and ninety cents. Since 1980, the average increase in the cost of all food items is nearly five hundred percent. Many manufactured products are one hundred and fifty percent to two hundred percent more costly than they were in those already-inflated times. For the past five years, after an average five percent increase, inflation has continued at a twelve percent annual rate. Wages and salaries have also gone up, but they lag far behind. Even worse, the relative percentage of individual income that is spent on energy, the cost of gas, electricity, and oil has increased nearly ten times. The average income earner is spending so much money on transportation and keeping warm, and lighting his home at night, that he has very little left for so-called 'discretionary spending.' This has created an inevitable round robin. As a result, there is much less demand for thousands of products that people can live without, such as furniture, rugs, lamps, ornate clothing, books, television, recorded Life-a-Vision tapes and discs, and many, many others. Consequently, the manufacturers of these items continue to employ fewer and fewer people.

"Interestingly, the government has lowered the taxes on whiskey, tobacco, and *ganja,* which is now imported in quantity from the Caribbean islands and Mexico. Someone up there in Washington wants to help people escape reality. The unpublicized reports are that the use of heroin and cocaine— which are now available through drug-treatment centers—has, after many years of decline, suddenly started to increase again."

"I'm still trying to understand how Mory's people's capitalism will work," I said. "Years ago, it wasn't easy to tell whether Mory was joking when he proposed that the only way to bring the United States into the twenty-first century was to write a New Constitution. Assuming that he is elected, how could he bring the United People of America into existence? I can't figure out how you're going to give every man, woman, and child his own personal bank account."

"You have to understand," Zara said, "that computer technology has developed at a tremendous rate. What can be accomplished with computers today far exceeds the possibilities

237

of even twenty years ago. The bubble and charged-coupled memory systems, used in computers today, store over one hundred thousand bits of data in a square-inch package, and they operate seventy-five times faster than the floppy disc systems. As Morrow explains in his book, we have the capabilities not only to eliminate the necessity for money, except in small transactions for convenience, but even more important, to put the entire money flow under the control of a central banking system. In the process we can eliminate inflation and control the whole cycle of savings and investments in capital equipment. Morrow is proposing that all monetary transactions, made either by individuals or corporations, would simply become additions to, or subtractions from, an individual's or a corporation's Capital Account with the United People's Capital Corporation."

David explained, without my asking, that the bubble memory system had bits stored in the form of magnetic bubbles, which moved in thin films of magnetic material. A bubble represented a "1" in computer language, and the absence of a bubble meant a "0." The bubbles measured about 5 microns across—or a millionth of a meter, and they appeared, disappeared, and zipped around the surface of a crystalline chip. "They were in a developmental stage in the late 1970s," David said. "Today their capabilities are almost beyond comprehension."

"Leave computer memory systems alone," I sighed, "I'm bewildered enough about the idea that everybody would have their own bank account with the government. It sounds like the final invasion of privacy."

"You have to take the concept one step at a time, Christa," David said. "The basic idea is to create a people's capitalism which would cut the present governmental functions—state, local, and national—almost in half, and at the same time eliminate the deadening and impersonal effect of bureaucracy. The government's prime function in a people's capitalism 'is to supply the economy with as much money as needed.' Many years ago Eugen Loebel, a much-neglected economist, in his book *Humanomics,* proposed the elimination of *all* taxes except a skim tax at the point of final purchase. Morrow has carried this concept several steps further.

"First, you have to believe, as Morrow does, that our country belongs to the two hundred and seventy million or more people alive in it at this moment, as well as those who will be born into it each day in the future. Once you accept that

238

premise, it's possible to think in terms of the United States as a People's Corporation in which all the people are equal shareholders. The value of their shares, stated in dollars, becomes each person's beginning Capital Account. Theoretically, from a Marxist point of view, it might be possible to say that the people also own the means of production. But Morrow wants to accomplish that transfer in such a way that we won't end up with a Russian-style socialist government, which is worse, if that's possible, than the government we now have.

"His plan is to preserve the vitality and competitive aspects of the private, corporate, industrial, and service system. Working with a New Constitution, he proposes that all land, privately owned or publicly owned, would revert to the United People's Capital Corporation. Privately owned buildings, machinery, or whatever else privately owned that was on top of the land, would remain in the hands of private corporations.

"The total land value, divided by the total population, would then be *arbitrarily* established at thirty thousand 1972 dollars per person. The Transition Period, as Morrow envisions it, would take about two years, but when Transition Day finally occurred, the thirty thousand dollars would be credited, in full, to every person eighteen years of age or over, and a pro-rata share, or a one-eighteenth portion for every year of life a person had lived who was not yet eighteen, would be set up in these particular accounts."

"It sounds quite insane to me," I said. "I don't see where the thirty thousand dollars per person comes from, or how you value the land. A great deal of land in this country is practically worthless. Some is desert, some is swamp, and some of the land, on the other hand, is very valuable—like the land under New York City, for instance."

"You missed the word arbitrary," Zara said. "The beginning Capital Account requires some basis in reality. The reason for basing the Capital Account on land is to give each person a sense of ownership and immediately transfer a minimum monetary ownership in the country to each citizen. The land would actually be owned by the people, and would be rented to the current owners. The per-acre land-rental tax, whether the land is located under Times Square, or is a cattle ranch in Montana, or a desert in Arizona, will be the same land-rental dollar amount per acre. Rental payments on the land are one of the three sources of revenue to the United

People's Capital Corporation. Actually, this will be a relatively small source of revenue, since the real value of land rental and common land ownership will be recouped from each person's Capital Account by FIST, a floating, instant skim tax, which would eliminate all other taxes."

I still couldn't encompass the magnitude of Mory's proposals. "Are you telling me," I asked, "that there would be no corporation taxes, no income taxes, no state taxes, no property taxes, no sales taxes, none of the hidden taxes on things like gasoline, alcohol, and cigarettes?"

"*Ta dreti*—you're right," Jag said. "FIST would eliminate them all. FIST, in reality, is a variable sales tax that would be readjusted monthly by the UPCC and would be applied to all purchases recorded through each person's Capital Account. The tax would be collected automatically by computer at little or no cost. You can compare that with the cost of collecting just one tax still in existence—the income tax— which now costs the taxpayers more than a billion and a half dollars annually just to collect. As you can see, this form of tax collection would save the combined federal, state, and local governments three or four billion dollars annually. Of course, it would eliminate income taxes, which, with their loopholes, have always been designed to benefit the rich, and keep the control of the wealth in the upper five percent of the population. You can see that Morrow is working toward a greater equality in income distribution."

"I'm really getting bewildered," I said. "You'd better go back to the individual's personal Capital Account, which you say would be taxed for every purchase. Do you mean that no actual money would be used? What will happen when people have used up all the money in their beginning Capital Accounts?"

"People will still continue to work, Christa," Zara said, laughing. "Let me see if I can explain to you. I'm teaching Morrow's theories to a lot of young people. If I can make them understandable to you, I'll know I'm making progress."

"You mean because I'm stupid?" I asked a little angrily.

"No—because you've been a Sleeping Beauty, and you haven't been exposed to the continuous debates over Morrow's proposals." Zara hugged me. "Remember, Christa, you come from a rich-ik background, so in a sense, if we convince you, we can feel that we are making progress.

"You see, in addition to each person's beginning thirty-thousand-dollar Capital Account (or a pro-rata share of that amount, if the person is under eighteen), each person's weekly earnings would be credited directly to his own personal Capital Account, which would be maintained on computers in one of the fifteen Regional UPCC Computer Centers. These Computer Centers would be located in each of the Regional Commonwealths. Regional Centers would handle all inter-region and intra-region transfers. If you made a purchase over twenty dollars, you would use no money. You would have your own Lifetime Capital Credit Card. Your purchase would be recorded electronically in your account within a few seconds after you made it, as a deduction from your Capital Account. Incidentally, by dialing your Regional UPCC Center with your Lifetime Capital Credit Card account number, anytime you wished you would be able to obtain a printed read-out of all the transactions in your personal Capital Account.

"On transactions under twenty dollars, you would use paper money and coins, just as you do now, and you would obtain these from cash dispensers similar to those that were available at some banks in the late 1970s, in amounts up to one hundred dollars. To obtain cash, you would insert your Lifetime Credit Card into the cash dispenser, and the transaction would be recorded and deducted from your account. Since the FIST tax could not be applied on individual cash transactions that you ultimately made with this money, the FIST tax would be applied immediately on the cash dispensed from your account.

"Keep in mind, too, that the FIST tax would include a varying monthly percentage which would be calculated to meet all federal, state, and local monetary needs. In the 1980s, the total cost of running all governments was about eight hundred billion dollars annually. Now these costs have risen to close to two trillion dollars annually. In the 1970s and 1980s, social and welfare costs, supported by the taxpayer, plus transfer payments in the form of social security, Medicare, *et cetera*, accounted for about half of the federal budget."

Zara paused. "Now, listen closely, Christa, because what I'm going to tell you is one of the most controversial aspects of Morrow's proposals. He plans to put almost all of this tax expense back on the people, and at the same time reduce the total cost of all government (including military defense, which would be cut back to fifty billion dollars annually) to less than two hundred billion dollars annually, stated in 1972 dollars."

"Good God," I said, "if there's no social security or Medicare or unemployment insurance or welfare or food stamps, how will millions of people survive?"

"Because they would be able to pay their own way from two additional sources of income which would be credited to their Capital Accounts," Jag said. "Both of these proposals have the rich-iks up in arms. Coast to coast, they've been financing huge 'No Newt To-Morrow' rallies, and they are going all out to try to convince the people that if they don't stop Newton Morrow, there'll be no tomorrow at all!" Jag laughed. "Karl Klausner is only one of the country's millionaires who are predicting the total collapse of the United States if Morrow wins."

"Obviously, none of you believe that Karl is right," I said. It was crossing my mind that if I ever saw Karl again, I would have to take a stand, one way or the other. "Just what are these new sources of income?" I asked.

"The first source is tied in with the FIST tax," Zara said. "The tax would be calculated so that the UPCC would run at a profit. Morrow projects a total tax on purchases which would not exceed forty percent. He believes that, very quickly, this tax could be brought down to twenty per cent. The relatively low FIST tax would bring in sufficient money to run *all* governments—local, state and national—and leave all annual dividends for each citizen of at least two thousand dollars. This 'profit' would be credited quarterly to each individual's Capital Account. Keep in mind, while this is a tax on individual purchases, the cost of everything that you'd buy would be very much cheaper. Corporations would no longer pay purchase taxes on any item that enters into the manufacturing process. None of these taxes, nor former corporation income taxes, would be passed along to the consumer. Morrow projects that the cost of any item, stated in 1972 dollars, will be at least one half; or stated in 1996 dollars, will average one hundred and fifty percent *less* than we now pay.

"You should keep in mind, too," David said, "that the individual 'profit' projections, which are credited to each person's Capital Account, are based on the excess income received from the FIST tax, the land-rental tax, and a heavy tax on all corporate income which is earned *outside* the continental limits of the United People of America. Also, Morrow is proposing to the Canadian people that they merge with us into a United People of America Corporation and create at least

Wait'll you taste Kent Golden Lights.

© Lorillard, U.S.A., 1978

100's
only 10 mg. tar.

Kings
only 8 mg. tar.

Taste 'em. You won't believe they're lower in tar than all the brands on the following page.

Kent Golden Lights: Kings Regular—8 mg. "tar," 0.6 mg. nicotine;
Kings Menthol—8 mg. "tar," 0.7 mg. nicotine av. per cigarette, FTC Report August 1977.
100's Regular and Menthol—10 mg. "tar," 0.9 mg. nicotine av. per cigarette by FTC Method.

Compare your numbers to Kent Golden Lights.

100 mm Brands	MG. TAR	MG. NIC.	King Size Brands	MG. TAR	MG NIC
Kent Golden Lights 100's*	10	0.9	**Kent Golden Lights**	8	0.6
Kent Golden Lights 100's Men*	10	0.9	**Kent Golden Lights Men.**	8	0.7
Benson & Hedges 100's Lights*	11	0.8	Kool Super Lights*	9	0.8
Vantage 100's*	11	0.9	Parliament	10	0.6
Benson & Hedges 100's Lights Menthol*	11	0.8	Vantage	11	0.7
Marlboro Lights 100's*	12	0.8	Vantage Menthol	11	0.8
Parliament 100's	12	0.7	Salem Lights	11	0.8
Salem Lights 100's*	12	0.9	Marlboro Lights	12	0.7
Merit 100's*	12	0.9	Doral	12	0.8
Virginia Slims 100's	16	0.9	Multifilter	12	0.8
Virginia Slims 100's Menthol	16	0.9	Winston Lights	12	0.9
Eve 100's	16	1.0	Belair*	13	1.0
Tareyton 100's	16	1.2	Marlboro Menthol	14	0.8
Marlboro 100's	17	1.0	Kool Milds	14	0.9
Silva Thins 100's	17	1.3	Raleigh Lights	14	1.0
Benson & Hedges 100's	17	1.0	Viceroy Extra Milds	14	1.0
L & M 100's	17	1.1	Viceroy	16	1.0
Raleigh 100's	17	1.2	Raleigh	16	1.
Chesterfield 100's	18	1.1	Tareyton	17	1.
Viceroy 100's	18	1.3	Marlboro	17	1.
Kool 100's	18	1.3	Kool	17	1.
Belair 100's	18	1.3	Lark	18	1.
Winston 100's Menthol	18	1.2	Salem	18	1.
Salem 100's	18	1.3	Pall Mall Filter	18	1.
Lark 100's	18	1.1	Camel Filters	18	1.
Pall Mall 100's	19	1.4	L & M	18	1.
Winston 100's	19	1.3	Winston	19	1.

*FTC Method   *FTC Method

Kent Golden Lights.
Full smoking satisfaction in a low tar.

Source of tar and nicotine disclosure above is FTC Report August 1977. **Of All Brands Sold:** Lowest tar 0.5 mg. "tar," 0.05 mg. nicotine; **Kent Golden Lights: Kings Regular**—8 mg. "tar," 0.6 mg. nicotine; **Kings Menthol**—8 mg. "tar," 0.7 mg. nicotine av. per cigarette, FTC Report August 1977. **100's Regular and Menthol**—10 mg. "tar," 0.9 mg. nicotine av. per cigarette by FTC Method.

three additional Regional Commonwealths. This would bring our population to well over three hundred million."

Once again I was confused. "Are you saying that if Mory's plan was in operation, and I were born in the first year, that I would have as much as thirty-six thousand dollars in my Capital Account when I was eighteen?"

"Maybe more," Zara said, "because, in addition, while you would not join the Central Working Force until you were twenty-five—and you must leave it after you are fifty—you are always permitted to work in the Secondary Working Force, at approximately one-third the minimum-wage rate."

"You mean that no one can work before they are twenty-five, or after they have passed fifty?"

"No," Jag said, "anyone can work after they are fourteen or fifteen, and when they have passed fifty. There will be millions of subminimum-wage jobs. But you should understand that Morrow is really proposing that no one has to work unless they wish to. And, in addition, in most cases, if they do work in the Central Working Force for the twenty-five-year working period, they'll have enough money in their Capital Accounts by the time they are fifty so that they can live very comfortably, and not have to work in the Secondary Working Force. But leave that aside for the moment. Morrow goes into some depth on these proposals in the second Presidential Conversation. The answer to your question about the amount of money in your Capital Account is yes. Depending on your annual dividend from the UPCC, you would have more than enough money at the age of eighteen to pay for your education, and at the same time, you would have the option of working in the Secondary Working Force to supplement this money. Since no interest is paid on money in anyone's Capital Account, in all probability you would join the Secondary Work Force, especially so because all education after high school would be structured around a thirteen-week alternate work-study cycle until you were twenty-five.

"But to get back to an individual's Capital Account from birth. Except for medical costs and post-secondary education, until you're eighteen your parents would pay for your food, clothing, and shelter. No parent would be permitted to make withdrawals from a minor's Capital Account without a counter-signature from a UPCC official, or a hospital official in the event of major medical expenses."

I couldn't help laughing. "If I'd had thirty-six thousand

dollars when I was eighteen, I'd have spent it all in the first year that I finally got my hands on it."

"No, you wouldn't," Zara said. "For one thing, you'd have to pay for your own education, and you wouldn't have any vast earning power, except for UPCC dividends, and subminimum wages in the Secondary Work Force, which you could earn under the four-year alternating work-study program."

"Morrow's proposals resolve the total educational conundrum," David said. "Until a person is twenty-five, a new-style education after high school will become a way of life for most young people."

"You mean that you would have to go to college whether you wanted to or not?"

"No," Jag said, "a people's capitalism has more freedom than any of us ever had or will have under our present welfare capitalism. If you don't want to go to college, you can use your Capital Account to travel, or you can just loaf, or you can join the Secondary Work Force and earn a little additional money until you're twenty-five. Obviously, however, when you are ready, if you want to work in the Central Work Force, you'll have to have some job skills, since most unskilled work will be done by the Secondary Work Force. Consequently, most young people will be very happy to get as much post-secondary education as they can absorb, to develop the necessary skills to join the Central Work Force. But this six-year educational period isn't just to develop vocational skills. Concurrently, young people will be exposed to their entire cultural heritage, and learn how to live and love, too."

"I think Mory's too idealistic," I said. "It really sounds like Utopia. Most of the people in this country are probably no more competent than they were sixteen years ago. Most people have to have a Big Brother to take care of them." There were tears in my eyes. "Even me. My only problem was that I got the wrong Big Brothers." I stared at David. "Maybe even including you, too, David Convita!"

David was amused. "I wasn't your Big Brother, Christa, but I do hope, as time goes by, that you may find I was a good friend. Anyway," he said, "I'm sure that your Mory will love to discuss social responsibility and his new morality with you. He never misses the opportunity to harangue people with what he calls the need to rediscover a new personal, moral, and ethical responsibility, and rebuild our individual strength. He believes that big government, and the Big Brother and Great White Father mentality, have completely

244

eroded the human spirit and are obviously very close to eliminating most of our remaining personal freedoms."

I couldn't help smiling. It was obvious that Mory was still an evangelist, too. "Jag said that there were three sources of income credit to everyone's Capital Account," I said. "You've mentioned each person's personal earnings and the FIST distribution—what's the other source?"

"You're going to hear more about that in the Presidential Conversations," Jag said. "I think you must already realize, from reading *Looking Backward II*, that Morrow's approach to community is to expand the concept of the group-owned corporation on three levels—the personal, the governmental, and the commercial. The commercial level is simply that all corporations in the future would be owned by the people, and since there would be no taxes, other than FIST and the land-rental tax, every corporation, which would be chartered by the Federal Government, must earn a ten percent profit—fifty percent of which would be paid quarterly to the employee owners in the form of dividends. The other fifty percent would be used for capital investment."

"You mean that General Motors and Exxon would be owned by their employees?" I demanded. "My God—now I know why Karl Klausner and Warren Ellison are scared to death of Mory. Even Johnny Giacomo wouldn't like him."

Zara laughed. "Remember, Morrow is convinced that he's the man who is going to achieve Bellamy's equality for the United People of America, and, eventually, for the world. You really should reread Bellamy's *Equality*. It's a lovely American Utopia. Bellamy proposed a world where there are no income differences. Morrow tells everyone that in this reincarnation he has changed his mind. Total monetary equality isn't essential, and at this time in man's history it won't produce a sound, achievement-oriented society. On the other hand, Morrow has scaled down the division of the monetary pie so that no citizen of the United People of America would ever have more than one-million 1972 dollars in his *personal* Capital Account. If he built it any larger, the UPCC would simply skim off the surplus and it would be returned to the people as a part of the total economic pie."

Later, as we continued discussing Mory's proposals in the gathering room, Ruth, finally interrupted us. "*Ua*—okay, that's enough." She was holding a hookah. The pipe bowl was aglow. I recognized the sweet smell. Ruth kissed my cheek. "It's marijuana." She laughed. "We grow it ourselves. It's per-

245

fectly legal to grow it, or give it away, but it's a major crime to sell it. Take a puff, your battered mind needs a rest before you see and hear the Presidential Conversation."

———◆———

As I learned later, each of the Presidential Conversations was held in the environment chosen in sequence by the contenders. The first one had been in the White House, and the second one, which was being rerun for me, had been held on the grounds of the home in which Mory and Adar Chilling lived with their Love Group in Carmel, California. Where Jennifer Manchester would hold the Third Presidential Conversation had not yet been announced, but it would take place on October 23rd. There were no moderators to these Conversations, and no live audience, except the television-camera people. Each contender could speak no more than five minutes, and was clued by an off-camera timer.

Before the program started, David told me to watch the opening carefully. "The candidate whose chosen location is being used," he said, "is given the opening five minutes. When Jason Kennedy started the series, he sat with Morrow and Manchester informally in the Oval Room. Jason Kennedy is very glib. His basic campaign is built around the proposal that the real Golden Age is just around the corner. According to him, if we rock the boat now, and chase after Morrow's New Tomorrow, we will not only never reach New Tomorrow in our lifetime, but we'll disrupt the economies of the world for centuries to come. Incidentally, Kennedy is fifty-six. He's been married twice. He's not related to the Massachusetts Kennedys, but he has obviously traded on their name. He has five children, two by his present wife, Debbie. The youngest, Judy, is eighteen, and lives in the White House."

"Unlike the children in Morrow's Love Group," Ruth said, "Judy Kennedy is going through college in the old-style premarital tradition. She has a female roommate, and although she has been photographed with many different men friends, supposedly she's had no sexual experience."

Once again, when the holographic Life-a-Vision screen was turned on, I gasped. The illusion of depth, and the feeling that we were practically sitting in the backyard watching people swimming naked in a swimming pool, created a strange emotional intimacy. As the television camera panned the pool, I recognized Mory swimming, and then tossing a water ball around with a group of teen-agers and older people, some of whom were sitting naked on the edge of the pool. After all these years my heart was beating quicker, and I knew if Mory was in the room I would run to him and throw my arms around him.

"That woman you see with the short-cut graying dark hair is Adar Chilling," Paul Thomas said. "She and Mory are married legally. They're in the same age position in their Love Group as David and Ruth are in ours. There's an older couple in their late sixties who are also married legally, Henry and Emily Adams. Adams is a banker and thoroughly in agreement with Morrow's theories. If Morrow is elected, Adams probably would become President of the United People's Capital Corporation. This is giving the opposition quite a bit of ammunition. Their premise is that a Love Group in control of the White House, and operating from significant Cabinet posts, would create a new form of monarchy. Morrow argues that his New Constitution makes that totally impossible."

"Who else is in the Love Group?" I asked. And then I wondered why I felt a sudden sense of relief and hope when Zara answered, "There's a young couple in their late twenties. They are Spanish in background, from Puerto Rico, and don't seem to be active politically. Of course, they're a terrific political asset. Morrow speaks Spanish fluently, and can reach more than twenty percent of the present American population in their own secondary language. The other member is Morrow's campaign adviser, Chuck Holmes. That's him—swimming in the pool. He's about forty. His wife divorced him four years ago, and he never remarried."

While Zara was giving me this background, the camera had moved around the pool and closed in on Jennifer Manchester and Jason Kennedy, who were fully dressed in bright summer clothing, watching the activity in the pool. When Mory finally climbed up on the pool ladder, the television camera coolly examined his naked body, while he shook hands with Jennifer Manchester and Jason Kennedy and finally sat down, naked, in a pool chair between them.

Kennedy, with raised eyebrows and a sardonic expression, said, "I realize that it is Newton's option to speak first in this second Conversation, but I hope that our viewers will recognize that they are watching a history-making event. For the first time, in the 1996 elections, a Utopian candidate for

247

President has appeared naked on television." Jason chuckled. "While, obviously, many of Newton's constituency enjoy displaying their bodies publicly, I hope that most of our viewers, who are probably not so disposed, will be able to concentrate on what we are all saying, and not become too bemused by the candidate's genitals."

Mory smiled affably into the camera and said, "I told Jennifer and Jason that in this second Conversation, I hoped that we would bare ourselves, literally as well as figuratively. When they arrived here this afternoon, and found our family swimming naked in our backyard pool, I asked them to join us, but, sadly, they declined. Of course, Adar and I, and other members of our Love Group, realize that many millions of Americans, despite the rapidly changing views of most churches and synagogues, still feel very uneasy when confronted with the naked human body. However, since I'm now sitting down, I'm certain that the cameramen will cooperate and focus on my upper torso and ignore my genitals, which are only trained for nonverbal communication, anyway."

"While neither Jason nor I agree with your daydreams for a New Tomorrow," Jennifer said, "and, obviously, Jason as a big government-oriented Democrat, and I as a conservative Republican, are poles apart, I think this afternoon we should take some time to see if Jason and I, and millions of Americans watching this program, can understand how your Great Revolution and your New Tomorrow will affect their lives."

I listened to Jennifer's beautifully modulated voice, and memories of Cambridge flooded my mind. Jennifer wore no makeup and her hair was graying, but she had aged beautifully. She was slim, and her big brown eyes still dominated her face, and she looked at Mory with the same gentle smile that I remembered from years before, when Mory was lying in our arms, and he was calling us Sister Jennifer and Sister Chrissy.

Jennifer was continuing. "I believe," she said, "that in our first Conversation, Jason explored rather thoroughly his belief that the present business cycle has finally 'bottomed out,' and within the next few years, with the manufacture of cheap electricity and hydrogen by nuclear fusion virtually a reality, we are on the threshold of a total world of material plenty that some of the futurists like Herman Kahn prophesied so many years ago."

"I agree, Jennifer," Jason said, "I think it would be instructive for Newton Morrow to explain Bellamy's, and his, Utopia

248

to the television audience." Jason smiled. "My feeling is that his explanation will contain the seeds of its own destruction, and make us all even more wary of the cataclysm he would set in motion if he were elected President."

I listened intently as Mory went over the basic points of his New Tomorrow, which were essentially those I had read in *Looking Backward II* and discussed with the Love Group. Jason's and Jennifer's retaliatory arguments consisted largely of doomsday reactions.

As Mory spoke, Jason kept shaking his head incredulously, and Jennifer listened with an expression of wide-eyed doubt. "It's obvious," Jason said, "that you are planning to eliminate a great many jobs. In your New Tomorrow fantasy world, there will be no union representatives and no unions. Total government employment will be cut by millions of employees. There will be no insurance agents. There will be no insurance companies. There will be no bankers, no bank employees, no stock market, no stockbrokers. It's obvious that if Transition Day ever became a reality you would add twenty million to the unemployment rolls."

Like a teacher explaining how two and two really makes four, Mory smiled patiently at Jason. "You've forgotten that on Transition Day, everyone under twenty-five and over fifty will automatically be dropped from the employment roster. They will have their own beginning Capital Accounts, will receive an annual dividend in their Capital Accounts, and can, if they wish, work in the Secondary Work Force.

"Since the total employable population—those between twenty-five and fifty years of age—will only be approximately one hundred and twelve million people, at times this work force may be insufficient to produce a satisfactory Gross National Product. So we have introduced the concept of extending the legal working age, as the need arises, to fifty-one, fifty-two, and up to fifty-five years."

"Unemployment will never be a problem in America again," Mory went on. "In addition, the United People's Party faces reality. We face the fact that while the environment of work can be improved, most work in modern industrial society can never be fully creative, and hence, humanly satisfying work. Work, for most people, is not an end, but a means of survival. So we not only propose to reduce the total working years, but for the twenty-five years that people—those who wish to—work in the Central Work Force, the work week will be thirty-two hours, with a month annual va-

249

cation, and a sabbatical-year vacation, at corporation expense, every seven years."

"You make the statement 'wish to work,'" Jennifer said. "I presume that you are implying some people in this twenty-five to fifty-year age group won't work at all."

Mory shrugged. "We assume that a small percentage of people will try to live off the money they receive quarterly from the UPCC. If they wish to try to survive on a below-poverty level income of between two thousand to five thousand dollars annually, they are welcome to try it, with no social disapproval whatsoever."

"What about mothers supporting young children, and people in this group who are physically unable to work?"

"They can form Love Groups," Mory said, "or Care Groups, and with their combined income, we are sure they will survive quite well."

During this interchange, Jason's expression had changed from one of smiling disbelief to anger. "What happens to people who spend their entire Capital Account?" he said. "What happens to people who don't save it for the years when they aren't permitted to work?"

Mory smiled. "Obviously, we won't let them starve. But we expect that any person who is eighteen years old on Transition Day will have a beginning Capital Account of approximately thirty thousand dollars. The next seven years of combined service work in the society will probably deplete one's account to somewhere between twenty and twenty-five thousand dollars. For the next twenty-five years, UPCC dividends will add a minimum of fifty to a hundred thousand dollars to his account. We are proposing that the lowest-income worker in the Central Work Force will receive a minimum of fifteen thousand dollars annually, and another few thousand dollars, in dividends, from his corporation. If he saves ten percent of this, he certainly should be able to put aside an additional two thousand dollars a year, and will have another fifty thousand dollars in his Capital Account, or a total of a hundred to a hundred and fifty thousand dollars, when he or she is fifty. Keep in mind that whether people are married monogamously, or live in Love Groups or Care Groups, they will have very little child-support cost. The combined Capital Account of a monogamous couple, by the time they are fifty, should be well in the area of three hundred thousand dollars or more. A Love Group corporation or a Care Group corporation of eight people, who live together for the full

250

twenty-five years, and have worked in the Central Work Force, would have a total of two million, four hundred thousand dollars in their personal family corporation."

Mory laughed. "Obviously, those who are provident will inherit the mansions and the yachts of the former rich. The big difference, of course, is that they will have to share them."

David turned the Life-a-Vision screen off.

"But we haven't finished," I said, trying to shake off the hypnotic impression of being actually present at this Conversation and to regain the perspective of the thirteen of us flopped, comfortably naked or partially dressed, around the room. "I want to hear the rest of it."

"You will in a few minutes—we're taping it this time. I just wondered if it was coming through to you."

"Most of it. But I still don't see how Mory could make all these changes without a constitutional amendment. When I was last alive, groups had been trying for years to get a majority of the states to ratify the Equal Rights Amendment. It seems to me that Mory's proposals could get tied up in congressional committees for years to come."

"You'd better reread the early parts of your autobiography," Jag said. "Morrow has already drafted his New Constitution with the help of a Committee of 100—men and women who are lawyers, educators, and small businesspeople, as well as men and women from various political and religious backgrounds. They have everything to gain by most of Morrow's proposals. Morrow's thesis is that if sixty percent of the registered voters vote for him, he'll put the New Constitution into effect immediately. Then, both the economic and political directions he is proposing will be legislated over a period of eighteen months—or longer, if necessary."

"Can he get elected by that much of a majority?" I asked. "And if he doesn't, then what? Anyway, if he only has a sixty percent majority, he could divide the country into two warring camps."

"He's already done that!" Ruth reminded me. "He's labeled all of us as being iks, lecks, or blanks. Morrow knows that his only hope is that poor-iks will join with him—and with us, the lecks. Keep in mind, Christina, that middle-class America is really the poor-ik today. Millions of them, living in nuclear-family style, have been badly hurt by inflation. Even more desperate are those couples, or individuals, in their sixties who were counting on social security. Morrow's Capital Account proposals are very appealing to them. Thus far, as

251

you've heard in this Presidential Conversation, both Jennifer Manchester's and Jason Kennedy's basic counterattack is either ridicule or a continuous campaign to frighten the voter. They've mounted a multimillion-dollar campaign to convince the people that if Morrow is elected, the country will become a second-rate Communist nation within a few years."

I shook my head. "I don't understand what is motivating Jennifer," I said. "Years ago, I knew that she and Mory argued continuously. But Jennifer was quite liberal then. I can't picture her as a Republican, running against Mory. It's beyond belief."

"Jason Kennedy people evidently think so, too," Zara said. "As we've already told you, they keep trying to spread the rumor that Jennifer is sleeping with Morrow, but no one's been able to prove it. When they're not face-to-face in public, Jennifer spends most of her time offering herself as the 'Sensible Candidate.' She refuses to admit that she can't win. But we're hoping that the people who vote for her will be those who are fed up with Jason Kennedy. If she could slice Kennedy's lead over Morrow, which was close to four million votes in 1992, when Morrow ran against Kennedy, then Morrow could get elected. But not by his sixty percent majority. Remember, this is a direct election. The electoral college was eliminated in 1984."

"Mory's biggest danger is *zafca*—bad luck," Paul said. "So far there have been two assassination attempts. One bullet grazed his chest. There's a rumor that some of the Secret Service, under orders from Warren Ellison, aren't watching him, or the crowds, too carefully. Morrow is barnstorming the country in one of those Heli-Homes that Winnebago and Sikorsky Aircraft introduced in the late seventies. It's a sitting duck for high-powered rifles."

David turned the Life-a-Vision back on.

"I suppose that you are aware that there are over one hundred and ninety million people in the country whose ages run between eighteen and one hundred?" Jason Kennedy was asking Mory sarcastically. "Did you ever multiply that by thirty thousand dollars?"

"It's over five trillion dollars." Mory was smiling broadly.

"That's two-thirds the Gross National Product in 1996 dollars," Jason said. "Gross savings of all people and corporations right now is only three hundred billion. Seriously, Morrow, I don't know why I'm sitting here listening to such mad ravings. Eventually, with that much savings, plus another half billion or so in your so-called Capital Accounts, owned by people under eighteen, you'd have over six trillion dollars. That kind of money pressing against the reduced production you would have with your greatly reduced work force would set loose an inflation that would destroy the value of the dollar overnight."

Mory shook his head. "At the ten-year six percent inflation rate, and the past five-year rate of twelve percent, the purchasing value of the 1996 dollar, compared with the 1980, will be one hundred percent less by the year 2000. Keep in mind, Jason, that approximately six trillion dollars will be the entire financial stimulus to the economy. Individual citizens would be permitted to borrow from the UPCC in emergencies and for special purchases, or in instances when the UPCC wishes to stimulate a particular industry, but there will be no other source of borrowing or credit expansion based on future earnings. And there will be no finance companies, or banks, or department stores charging eighteen percent interest. The individual and corporate Capital Account backlog is the economic dynamo. In point of fact, the people won't spend six trillion in any one year. When the UPCC is in direct control of the entire savings of the people, government will, for the first time, be able to assume its most important basic function—namely, to keep savings, consumption, and necessary capital investment in balance. When the people of America realize that they're in direct control of their own money, and are dependent on it for their needs and luxuries, they'll quickly learn to moderate their spending in certain areas to keep prices level. They won't want ever again to lose the purchasing value of the money they've worked so hard to save. By contrast, the over-fifty population in the United States today, who tried to save their money in the form of life insurance and savings accounts, have been royally cheated by a continuing succession of governments that have destroyed the value of the dollars they worked so hard to put aside.

"Another thing you should keep in mind, Jason, is that the UPCC which would replace the Federal Reserve system, is independent of all political influence, and even more importantly, cannot be influenced by national and local banks and life insurance companies, since they will no longer exist."

Jason shrugged. "While this is supposed to be a three-way conversation among presidential candidates, I am convinced that the best thing Jennifer and I can do for the American people is to let you rave on. Go ahead, Newton, tell them the biggest daydream of all. You are not only going to take away billions of dollars of life insurance from our citizens, which they have saved in order to protect themselves in their old age, or to leave to their children, but on your so-called Transition Day you're going to eliminate all their bank accounts and savings and all the stock ownership that millions of hard-working American citizens now have directly or through their pension funds. I'm sure that when the good citizens of this country realize that their pension funds will also disappear, they will join me, not in laughter, but in general dismay that anyone with such insane ideas could have received a nomination for President of our beloved country."

Mory smiled. "You keep forgetting, Jason, that we're going to give every citizen a Capital Account. In addition, during the first twelve months of Transition Period, all Americans between twenty-five and fifty years of age will be quickly reemployed at wages not below a median annual dollar value wage of fifteen thousand dollars a year. On top of that, they will be equal shareholders in the People's Corporations that they work for."

"What happens to people who have large amounts of savings?" Jennifer demanded. "And what about the money that people now owe? Are you canceling all debts?"

"No, we are not. But the fact is that most of the people in the United States today live monetary lives that are only one or two paydays away from complete bankruptcy. They have no savings, no equity in anything, no net worth. Our Transition Period plan, which is very carefully outlined in my book, *Looking Backward II*, proposes that within six months after my election, every man, woman, and child would file a very simple registration form with the UPCC listing their total net worth. Net worth is the current market price of certain assets, such as your automobiles, insurance policies, stocks, bonds, house, boats, diamonds. From this figure, you subtract your debts and you end up with your net worth. Ownership of land can't be included in your net worth since all land will be owned by the UPCC.

"Once each person's net worth is established," Mory continued, "and keep in mind that equity in private home mortgages *will not* be included in net worth, each individual's debts will be subtracted from his total net worth. Exclusive of federal, and state debt, and mortgages, the per capita debt is currently about three thousand dollars, and that is a very crude figure. Obviously, many low-income Americans who

254

are heavily burdened with installment debt could have beginning Capital Accounts of less than thirty-thousand dollars. In rare cases, people can borrow up to eighteen thousand dollars from the UPCC, at three percent interest."

"People who pay rent and don't own their homes should be up in arms against you," Jennifer was shaking her head. Her facial expression seemed to be a combination of derision and affection. "In effect, you are giving home owners an additional unreported net worth. What compensates the majority of Americans who don't own their own homes?"

Mory smiled. "On Transition Day the UPCC will assume all home mortgages. Where mortgage payments now include local tax payments, and interest charges, both of these will be eliminated. New mortgages payments will be deducted monthly. But mortgage payments will be deducted with the FIST tax applied. Rental payments will be deducted *without* a FIST tax. Deductions will be made from each person's Capital Account. Note that I emphasize *each*. If homes are owned jointly by one monogamous couple, they will each receive an equal deduction from their Capital Account. Since many homes may be mortgaged to Love Groups or Care Groups, they could apply for a pro-rata-share deduction from each of the Capital Accounts of the adult members of the group. Obviously, present homeowners, as well as future homeowners can own their own homes. If their home is sold, the total sale price would be credited to their Capital Account on an equal basis. As for relative equity between existing homeowners and those who don't own homes, that will remain an individual, or a couple, or a group decision. If they can afford to buy a home they can do so, and UPCC mortgage loans will be available." Mory smiled. "Many of us remember Proposition 13 and how, eighteen years ago, the voters of California gave the politicians their first warning. Not only will we eliminate such inequities as income tax and interest deductions for mortgages, but there will be no property taxes and no income taxes. The floating instant skim tax, FIST, will take care of all federal and state revenues. Big government will no longer have such a long leash or spend your money so inefficiently. But it is not the United People's Party program, and never will be, to strive for perfect monetary equality. Just as now, some people will be better off economically than others, but the gap will be considerably narrowed."

"That's putting it mildly," Jason said angrily. "In every century, this country has been built by a few men and women who were willing to work harder than most, men and women who devote twelve to eighteen hours a day to their professional and business lives. If they make more money than other people, they're entitled to their wealth and what it will buy. Your insane program will make it impossible for the leaders of this country, the men and women who keep us on track, to maintain their style of life. You will completely eliminate all human success drives and initiative."

"Jason is right," Jennifer said. "But our viewers should understand that if you could take all the wealth away from the top five percent of the population who have it, and you could distribute it to the rest of the several hundred millions who don't have it, their individual financial gain would only amount to a few hundred dollars, and, at the same time, the wheels of industry would stop turning."

Mory grinned. "I know it astounds Jason when I mention my previous Bellamy life on this earth, but I'd like to refer our viewers to the last chapter in Bellamy's book *Equality*, which he called Kenloe's 'Book of the Blind.' Kenloe thoroughly answers your objections to a society which would presumably lack monetary incentives, and answers those who purport to believe that equality would make us all alike, or that equality would end the competitive system to our disadvantage, or that equality would discourage independence and originality."

Mory paused. "I usually refrain from evangelist techniques of hurling biblical chapter and verse at my listeners. But if you don't wish to read Kenloe, via Bellamy, then I offer you Zachariah, Chapter Eight, Verse Ten, as a cogent commentary on our world today: '. . . there were no jobs, no wages, no security; if you left the city, there was no assurance you would ever return, for crime was rampant.' Or Lamentations, Chapter Five, Verse Four: 'We must even pay for water to drink; our fuel is sold to us at higher prices.' "

Jason shrugged. "I think that millions of good Christians, Jews, Mormons, and Moslems who are watching us may wonder how Tom Morrow's son ever got associated with a religion called Unilove, which condones live fornication in its services—but I prefer to continue in the good American tradition that a man or woman's religion is not the issue in this, or any, political campaign.

"I'm much more concerned that if you were elected, some Ayn Rand character like John Galt might actually come to life and convince those who are responsible for the current greatness of this country to leave America forever."

"It may prove to be the reverse," Mory said. "More likely, we'll set a brain exchange in motion with the rest of the world. Those whose cranial gifts to their fellowmen can only be measured by the dollars they receive can emigrate to more supportive countries.

"But I do agree with Jennifer. In the late nineteen seventies, about two hundred thousand people had a net worth of one million dollars or more. In twenty years that figure has tripled, largely because inflation has made a million dollars easier to obtain. But even today, counting peripheral dependents, less than one percent of the people have any real wealth. Stated another way, the upper one-fifth of the population receives fifty percent of all the income of this country and owns more than half of all the private wealth in this country, and this percentage hasn't changed for fifty years. Despite Jason's emphasis on hard work or greater merit, many of these people, including Jason himself, never personally earned most of those riches. They inherited their wealth, or married the owners of it.

"If I'm elected President, we'll reenfranchise the American people. We'll give them a new sense of personal involvement and commitment in the business, the politics, and the ownership of their country. On Transition Day, the richest men in this country will have a maximum Capital Account of one million dollars. In addition, there will be millions of Americans whose basic monetary picture will not change. They will have Capital Accounts equal to whatever their current net worth may be at the moment, plus the original thirty thousand dollar individual distribution that would be made after Transition Day. The big difference will be that a majority of Americans, who at the moment have no net worth whatsoever, will have a minimum Capital Account and purchasing power of approximately thirty thousand dollars."

Mory grinned warmly at the television cameras, and the sense of his personal presence—as if he were speaking directly to me and we were in an intimate embrace—was so strong that I shivered.

"Despite some of the polltakers who believe that I am rapidly losing votes to you and Jennifer," he continued, "I wouldn't count your chickens yet, Jason. If I'm elected, nine of the ten million dollars of net worth you have reported to the American public will be skimmed off by the UPCC. On

257

the other hand, when I have restored the purchasing power of the dollar to its 1972 level, you'll be able to buy four times as much with what you have left!"

"You keep talking about the new people-owned corporations," Jason said. "While I fully understand what you're proposing, you seem to have been a little vague about their function, both in your book and in public discussions. Presumably, your people-owned corporations must make a net profit of ten percent on sales each year, with three-year averaging possible, otherwise their federal charter would be revoked and the individual business would be forced to liquidate. The stockholder employee would have no equity when that happens, but I suppose that doesn't matter, anyway. No competent people could be hired to run these companies, anyway. Not when they're paid at the same rate as the janitor who sweeps the floors."

"Jason," Mory said calmly, "the people you're talking about don't run a company—a total work force runs it. A small group of people lead a company. In the past, there have been good company leaders and bad ones, as there will be in the future. It is not the intention of the United People's Government, and it never will be, to set maximum wages. The president of General Motors and his operating and staff executives can be paid any salaries that the board of directors, *elected by the stockholder workers,* approves. Conceivably, the president of General Motors could be paid a million dollars, or more, annual salary. His only problem will be that when his salary exceeds a million dollars, the FIST tax will skim off the excess."

Mory laughed. "Of course, he can try to spend it and accumulate things or material possessions in excess of the value of his Capital Account, but his incentive to do so will be counteracted by the FIST death tax. No one will be allowed to transfer property or a Capital Account to heirs or beneficiaries during his life or at death in excess of one hundred thousand dollars. The next generation will live in a society where each person starts his race toward the million, if he or she is so inclined, on a fairly equal basis. Incidentally, if a company fails, in an average three years, to make a ten percent profit on sales, whatever cash net worth remains in the company would be distributed on a pro-rata basis to the employee stockholders."

"There's an important point that you keep overlooking," Jennifer said. "I think Frank Travers, head of the CIO-AFL, is right, but rather than state his objection in his terms, I'd like to put it in the words of a man whom you admire and who is obviously a guiding light of the Church of United Love. His name is Wilhelm Reich, a man like yourself, who tried to wed sex and politics, nearly fifty years ago. In his book, *The Mass Psychology of Fascism*, he says: 'The socialization of social means of production will not be topical or possible until the masses of working humanity have become structurally mature, i.e., conscious of their responsibility to manage. The overwhelming majority of the masses today is neither willing nor mature enough for it. Moreover, a socialization of the large industries which would place these industries under the sole management of the manual laborer, excluding technicians, engineers, directors, administrators, distributors, is sociologically and economically senseless. Today such an idea is rejected by the manual laborers themselves.' "

"As you pointed out," Mory said, "Reich lived and died nearly fifty years ago. The words 'manual laborer' and 'blue collar worker' that were popular in the late seventies are no longer applicable. If the American worker, whether he is still engaged in some manual work, or is a technician, is permitted to, and can, elect a President of his country, or a governor, or any local official—he is perfectly capable of electing a board of directors to run *his* corporation without the intervention of union middlemen as barnacles on the ship of *his* corporation. One of the basic problems of this country, both in business and particularly in government, is that hundreds of thousands, maybe even several million people, in the twenty-four to sixty-five age bracket, have also discovered how to live as parasites on the system, and they are expending little if any real work effort. Many of them have actually shipped their oars and stopped rowing the boat. During—"

"If you are captain of the boat," Jason interrupted, "they won't have to worry about rowing, they'll spend their lives bailing."

"In any event, they'll be doing something," Mory said, his eyes twinkling. "During the eighteen months preceding Transition Day, during which our trillion-dollar national debt will be canceled, and all functioning of the country's banks, finance companies, life insurance companies, and the investment market will be taken over by the UPCC, the value of all privately owned stock in all publicly owned corporations will be credited to the owner's Capital Account at a per-share value of the stock that existed on January 2, 1994, two years ago.

All publicly owned stock held by any institutions will be canceled. Stock in private corporations will be valued on a pro-rata share of the net worth of a particular corporation at the same 1994 date. The cash value will be credited to the Capital Account of each particular owner. Of course, all monetary values in this liquidation in excess of one million dollars will be skimmed off by the FIST tax."

"Then, as I understand this daydream," Jason said sarcastically, "everyone who works for General Motors, or any other corporation, will wake up on Transition Day morning and find a share of stock under his or her pillow."

"Essentially, you're correct. On Transition Day every corporation in the United People of America will be federally chartered, and each and every person working for a corporation will receive one share of his or her company's stock. This stock will be voting stock, nontransferable. It cannot be sold. On an employee's death it will revert to the corporation. If a person changes jobs, his or her stock will also revert to the corporation. Whenever an owner's share reverts to the corporation, he or she will receive a pro-rata share of the *excess* in value of the net worth of the corporation on the day it was received, compared with the day he or she is no longer in its employ. With a thousand-dollar limitation, *lesser* net-worth valuations will be deducted from the individual's Capital Account. The ownership of the stock permits each person to elect the officials of the corporation and participate in a quarterly pro-rata share of the dividends of the corporation. As we've discussed, every corporation must make a ten percent profit on its gross sales, and every corporation must distribute fifty percent of this profit to the employee stockholders."

"What you're saying—and I think it should be made clear," Jennifer said, "is that no matter who the employee is, whether he's president or janitor, he will receive only one share of stock in his corporation."

"Exactly," Mory said. "For the first time in the history of the world the real wealth, the income-producing wealth of the capital equipment and the machinery, will be equally owned by every citizen who is working in industry or a service corporation. Beyond that, the UPCC and the government are only concerned that a particular corporation makes a ten percent annual profit. Obviously, it must do so within general guidelines that do not create ecological damage, or endanger the health of its employees, or the health of the public to whom it sells its products—or, as in the case with marijuana, tobacco, alcohol, and other similar items, the public must be fully warned of the inherent dangers. But the UPCC will be completely uninterested in old laws such as anti-trust, which will vanish from the books. If two corporations merge and dominate a particular market, or if one is able to undersell all others and captures all the market, the benefit is to the people as a whole, since any corporation that exceeds a ten percent profit will have the excess skimmed off its Corporate Capital Account in exactly the same way it is skimmed off the individual's account.

"Whatever money a particular corporation requires for expansion, machinery replacement, new product development, new buildings, will be generated by the fifty percent of the profit that isn't distributed to employees. Old corporations that have insufficient retained earnings, and new corporations with reasonable chances for successful earnings, will be able to borrow from the UPCC on maximum ten-year loans at three percent interest. If the directors of a particular corporation wish to distribute more than fifty percent of the profits in any one year, that decision must be made in the light of their own corporate planning. Retained corporate earnings will earn them no interest, but could tide them over lean profit years, since it would be permissible to divert retained earnings to bring lower profits in a particular year to the acceptable ten percent level. Obviously, skilled business management will be just as necessary as it is now."

"But it won't be so well rewarded," Jennifer said. "It really is a fantastic daydream, Newton. If you really are a reincarnation of Edward Bellamy, you should, at least, be acclaimed for designing a new Utopia."

"An achievable one," Mory said.

"Let's hope not," Jason said. "The consensus is that Utopias would be dull places to live. You keep talking about corporations, but millions of people now in business are not incorporated. What about them?"

"Alas," Mory said sadly, "I really wish that you'd read *Looking Backward II*. During the Transition Period, the only people who won't be required to incorporate will be professional people, people who are in business as single persons, and government employees. Professional people could be manufacturers' representatives, teachers, politicians, authors, actors, and the few doctors, lawyers, dentists, who practice alone—but not ministers, rabbis, and priests. Individual

261

churches or synagogues must incorporate and be run at a profit. Since they will have little or no expense, except building maintenance and land rental, and no taxes, they should be able to make the necessary ten percent profit, which on the past principle of separation of Church and State, can be distributed, one hundred percent, in any way the church directors, who would be elected by the church or synagogue members, may decide.

"You see, Jason and Jennifer, we believe that the corporate form of endeavor is the best way for two or more human beings to conduct their affairs. Keep in mind that there will be no taxation on corporations. Any former companies or partnerships or individuals that wish to incorporate into profit-making corporations will simply require an easily obtained federal charter.

"The prime purpose of all corporations, whether there are two shareholders or more than twenty thousand, will be to make a profit and distribute it to their shareholders. All corporations, except family corporations, will be required to prepare a social audit. The concept of *The Social Audit for Management* was developed by Clark Abt, in his book of the same name, many years ago.

"Basically, in addition to its regular balance sheets and operating statements, each corporation, regardless of size, will provide the stock and the UPCC with a social audit that will evaluate in full detail its career advancements in the form of increased pay, the cost of its employment layoffs, the value of unpaid overtime work, its equality of opportunity for men and women, as well as various racial groups, its investment in training, its contributions in the form of new inventions, processes, management techniques, its investment in buildings and machinery, its consumption of energy, and its effect, if any, on environmental pollution. There are many other social areas that particular corporations may affect."

"Really, Newton," Jennifer said angrily, and it was impossible to tell whether her dismay was real or assumed, "this entire discussion is so far beyond belief, and any possible reality, that I want you to fully understand that I'm only asking the following question because I want to expose the total economic insanity of your party's program. You have overlooked a very critical point: The United States is not alone in this world. Thousands of foreign investors all over the world own all, or portions, of many of our corporations. In addition, we have an annual foreign trade in excess of one hundred fifty billion dollars. Without the sale of our goods to foreign countries, this country's economy would totally collapse."

"First," Mory replied very calmly, as if he were explaining economics to Sister Jennifer many years ago, as we all lay in bed together, naked, "we import more goods than we export. Our trade balances, for the past ten years, have been unfavorable. Over the past twenty years, our ability to export against foreign competitors, who have developed manufacturing techniques just as sophisticated as we have, has diminished considerably. For a long time we outproduced the world agriculturally, but Russia has finally narrowed that gap. The basic difference in the price of most commodities, now that the Western and a good part of the Asian world has caught up with us, is the cost of labor—plus our own internal very high operating costs.

"Under the United People's Government, despite our higher labor costs, American manufactured products will be equal to or lower in price than foreign products. First, because they will no longer reflect the taxes and inefficiencies of a gigantic government complex; and second, because the work ethic and skills and drive of our new stockholders employees will let us outproduce the slave wages of some foreign countries.

"On the import side of the ledger, I have proposed that when the United People's Government is functioning, any foreign manufacturer wishing to sell his products to the United People will be able to do so freely, with no tariffs. But in the future, to keep our own manufacturing establishment on its toes, foreign manufacturers will have to submit to the United People's Trade Commission a detailed breakdown of their manufacturing costs. Where foreign labor costs constitute the differential in the foreign price of an item that is competing with an American-made item, the United People's manufacturer will be given a subsidy, which will be reviewed annually, to equalize his labor cost with the foreign cost. The foreign manufacturer will then compete in the American market on a quality or charisma basis, and not on price.

"Beyond that, the United People's Government will not interfere in any world trade, nor will it set arbitrary tariffs on particular items. However, when it comes to multi-national corporations, because we are basically opposed to this kind of growth, which has thrown the balance of power in the world to a group of several hundred world corporations and their executives, and because actions of these people and their corporations are uncontrollable by any kind of democratic government, we will not permit American-based multi-national companies (which will lose much of their power, anyway, when the American-based multi-nationals are employee-owned) to include in their national profit figures any profits or gains made in foreign manufacture of products sold in the United People's Commonwealth. Nor can they include any profits made in their foreign operations. American manufacturers manufacturing abroad and reselling the foreign-made products in the United People's Commonwealth will also be subject to the same labor-cost controls as foreign-based manufacturers.

"I haven't answered your question about foreign individuals, or foreign corporations that own stock in American-based corporations. The answer is obvious. Their stock ownership will be paid in American dollars."

"Which won't be worth the powder to blow them to hell," Jason snorted.

"On the contrary," Mory said, "when the transition is completed, we expect that the American dollar will quickly become the most stable currency in the world, because we will eliminate inflation and unemployment while we retain the drive and enthusiasm of a people's corporate capitalism. I predict that within a quarter of a century, people's capitalism will embrace the entire Western and Asian world."

"I'm glad that you mentioned that," Jason said sarcastically. "I think the American people should know that *Looking Backward II* has been translated into Russian, where it is an all-time best seller. Perhaps many of them don't realize also that Newton Morrow speaks fluent Russian and has spent many months in the Soviet Union." Jason stared into the camera with raised eyebrows, leaving the obvious, unasked question to be answered by the viewers.

"I see by the monitors," Mory said, "that we are approaching the end of our air time. You both have been very kind to let me explain many of the details of people's capitalism to our viewers. I would like to give you both the opportunity to close this Conversation and use the remaining fifteen minutes in any way you wish—without rebuttal from me. Afterwards, I hope you'll both join us for a swim in our pool."

Mory laughed, again in a gentle, captivating, teasing way that convinced me, and I'm sure millions of his viewers, that Jason Kennedy and Jennifer Manchester could pose no questions that he couldn't answer. "One other thing, I'm sure that many of our audience are well aware that Soviet Chairman Alex Lubayov and I are good friends. I have spent several weeks every year for the past five years, as a guest at his home near the Black Sea. Alex's problem with *Looking Backward II*, and the entire concept of people's capitalism, is that millions of Russians are so captivated by the idea of a United People of America, and believe that is the kind of society that Karl Marx intended when he wrote *Capital*, and not the government-controlled socialistic state that finally emerged, that they hope they may create the United Soviet People. It's too bad that in my other life, I didn't meet Marx. As Edward Bellamy, I might have started him on the right road a hundred years ago!"

By Monday, the last day of the Labor Day weekend, most of the Love Group had gone to Boston, including Jag and Zara, who would be flying to Europe in a few days. Carol, Paul, Rose, and the children had stayed behind. Raynor followed me about adoringly, still hoping that I would allow him to practice kitsa with me.

David and Ruth were leaving for Boston today. David promised me that the following Friday he would fly back to Hyannis and drive me to Boston.

Before they left, David and Ruth told me that school would start in a week. After that, by the first of October, except for Paul and Carol and Rose, who would live in Mashpee to be near the laboratory until the cold weather set in, the rest of them would move back to their Boston apartment. Although David was confident that I was *dgela*—in good health—while he was gone Paul would take me back to the laboratory, where I would be given a thorough physical examination to make sure that physiologically, at least, I was functioning perfectly.

Evidently thinking that he was giving me something to look forward to, David also told me that Bill Westwood, a friend of Chandra and Ralph's, had three reserved seats for the No Newt-To-Morrow rally being held at the Boston Astrodome on Friday, October 11th. "They expect an audience of close to ninety thousand, and, of course, the rally's televised by the Democratic party. Ralph and Chandra want to take you with them."

David dropped this bomb before my reaction to his earlier revelation that he was sending me back to his laboratory had sunk in, and then he added, "Jason Kennedy won't be there, but Westwood, who's head of the Massachusetts Democratic campaign to reelect Jason Kennedy, not only wants you and Ralph and Chandra to come to the rally, but to join him at a cocktail party in Warren Ellison's suite at the Hyatt-Pilgrim Hotel before the rally."

David was rattling on, scarcely looking at me. "Ellison and Manchester are the featured speakers at the rally. You'll have a chance to meet both of them. Obviously, when they see you, they're going to get the surprise of their lives."

Finally, as he became aware of the shock and fear on my face, David's smile faded. He put his arm around me uneasily. "Of course, Christa, if you'd prefer not to go, or even meet them, it's perfectly all right with us. We're not forcing you."

"I damn well think you are," I said angrily. "You just told me that I have to go back to your prison where you kept me for sixteen years, and now, none of you can wait to see Warren Ellison's reaction when he finally discovers that Christina Klausner is still alive. You know damned well that within a day after Warren sees me, Karl Klausner will be sending his flunkies up to Boston to take your circus freak off your hands." I couldn't control my tears. "I suppose you have no choice—after all, I'm a disruptive force in your Love Group."

Ruth, who had just come downstairs with her suitcase, heard me and put her arms around me. "I guess it hasn't gotten through to you, Christa. No woman in this group is jealous of you. When you can make love again, you can share the men in our family with us—for the rest of your life, if you wish." She kissed my tear-stained cheeks. "We love you, Christa. If, finally, you don't love us, or wish to broaden your life in this new world of yours, you can join another Love Group, or, if you prefer, you can live singly, or you can live monogamously." She added soberly, "Whatever you do, I'd give it a lot of thought before you tried to live with a man like Karl Klausner again. Or Warren Ellison, who's a widower."

"Get it out of your head that you're some kind of circus freak," David said. "You and Rose are very important scientifically, as I've told you before. Everyone is talking about the future possibilities of hibernation, but you two are the first living human beings who can prove that it's possible to survive extended hibernation. Of course, the reality of Rose's previous existence will be difficult to substantiate. She had no relatives or friends when she was hibernated, and obviously, some people are going to say that it never happened to her. But your existence, as the wife of Karl Klausner, is well documented."

David could see that I wasn't too happy with the implications of his words. "Christa," he said, and hugged me, "no one is going to publicize you against your will. If you prefer, and I'm sure that I can speak for Newton Morrow, too, you don't even had to admit your former identity. If you wish to change your name, and never see your former friends or your children again, we can start by getting you a new social security number. They're not much good anymore, but they give you an identity, and from there we can get you a driver's license and charge cards."

"You're very good at that kind of thing, aren't you?" I said sarcastically, remembering the story of my drowning in the Boston *Globe*. By this time I was crying, mostly because I was really frightened about going back to the laboratory and seeing that subterranean basement filled with slowly turning bodies in their hibernaculums. "How do I know you aren't going to start me with Vitaleben, or some other damned thing, and put me back to sleep again?" I demanded, and then, realizing how silly I sounded, I sighed. "Anyway, I'm not afraid to meet Jennifer Manchester—after all, I haven't seen her for a very long time. She won't remember me. But Warren Ellison knew me, just like I am now. Less than two weeks before I disappeared, we went swimming together." I couldn't help smiling through my tears. I was sure that Warren Ellison would never forget that evening—or, as Secretary of the Treasury, want to be reminded about it.

David hugged me. "I love you, Christa. Believe me, none of us here are ever going to let you go to sleep alone again."

Ruth was grinning at me. "David is trying to tell you that not every man in his fifties is lucky enough to find Talia, the Sleeping Beauty, on his doorstep!"

I couldn't help smiling. "Not just Talia," I said, "I'm Briar Rose." Then I had an inspiration. "In one of the German versions of the fairy-tale, she was called Dornroschen. You can introduce me to Warren and Jennifer as Talia Dornroschen."

David nodded agreement. "Anyway, if you should ever have to prove that you actually are Christina Klausner, you can do that, too. When you go back to the laboratory, remind Paul, and he'll give you your personal handbag. There's even a few hundred dollars still in it, but they won't buy you very much now. Your picture on your driver's license doesn't look a day older than your thirty-third birthday, April 24, 1980, when it was taken."

"I'm surprised that you didn't drown my pocketbook, too," I said sarcastically. "That would have gotten rid of all the evidence."

"I suppose we should have. But at the time, all we needed were your rings and your watch. I'm sorry you had to lose your diamond ring, but I'm sure that when Karl buried your body, he didn't leave it on your finger!"

◆

Ruth and David were taking the Heli-Bus service from Hyannis to Boston. David told me that the two-hundred-passenger Heli-Buses serving Cape Cod, the Berkshires, New Hampshire, Vermont, and Maine, after several stops en route, finally deposited their passengers in twelve different landing places surrounding Boston. From these terminals, a few miles from the center city, they could easily rent a Tric and drive to their personal destinations. Heli-Buses, serving all the major cities, had eliminated the necessity for long commuter driving between the suburbs, and actually had extended the options for country living.

"The Heli-Buses, with personal Tric rental both at departure and destination points, are cheaper for all travel in intermediate distances," David explained. "Despite the federally subsidized Work For America program, which now employs nearly half a million people in road repair, and largely because of inflation, only basic national and state highway systems have been maintained. Most feeder roads, and many small-town and city roads, as you will discover when Paul takes you to Hyannis, are in bad shape."

After Ruth and David left, Raynor and I got into a long conversation, and I finally agreed with him that there was no good reason why I couldn't sleep with him that night. Two in bed were better than three.

Smiling feebly at the boyish look of adoration on his face, and encouraged by Carol and Paul, I followed Raynor to his room and slipped out of my See-Thru jump suit. Snuggling beside him, holding his face against my breasts, I told him that I hoped we could just lie quietly for a while.

"My breasts feel a little swollen," I whispered, "so kiss them gently. I think that by morning I'll have my first period in sixteen years."

While Raynor caressed me as if I were a new found and lonesome kitten, and he, the new owner, floated in a euphoric realization of his fantasies, I gently held his penis and let my mind wander. Even though earlier I had been angry momentarily with David, convinced that eventually Rose and I would end up museum pieces as testimony to his and Max Lebenthal's genius, my feeling of depression hadn't lasted. In a very real sense, I seemed to have been born again. Even though I couldn't comprehend half of what I had been hearing or experiencing, and despite the ever-ready tears that were constantly brimming in my eyes—tears mostly of bewilderment—I was sure of one thing. Finally, for the first time in my life, I wasn't fighting against my environment. And I was vaguely aware that my "death and resurrection" were giving me a new objectivity.

I knew, too, that the world of 1996 still wasn't the best of all possible worlds. Although lecks in Love Groups, like this one I was living with, had made significant progress in smoothing the "me first" waters of interpersonal relationships, I was sure from what I had heard about the poor-iks and the rich-iks—a world I had yet to encounter—that most men and women were still trying to solve the basic human problem. People were so immersed in their own ego—as I had been most of my life—that they couldn't comprehend the ego needs of those close to them. Nor could they give "the other" the kind of reassurance and confirmation needed to expand their potential.

It was obvious that Mory was still living in some very idealistic world. Creating a totally new sexual, economic, and political environment seemed to me as impossible of attainment in the twenty-first century as it had been in the seventeenth. But for the first time in my life, I realized fully that the unquenchable dreams of men like Mory were infinitely more exciting to me than the realities and sandcastle achievements of men like Karl.

I was no longer driven to be somebody. My former obsession to be famous, or even infamous, seemed totally ridiculous. What if I had achieved the fame that I had coveted for so many years? Would it have mattered as a sop to my personal ego? Rather than the simple personal enjoyment of creating a poem or finishing a painting that I was involved with, I had really been seeking the roar of the crowd. At last, for the first time in my life, I was enjoying "nowness" with no interest in the past. As for the future—after I had watched Mory on Life-a-Vision, the twenty-three-year hiatus in our lives had vanished. While I could see that Mory had aged, I was once again hearing him as the vibrant and joyous man I had known. And secretly, I guess, I was praying that somewhere in his life there was room for Chrissy, his First Lady. Mory was standing behind me as I stepped on the first rung of the ladder into the world of 1996. If the ladder didn't give way under me, maybe I could climb to the top, and this time—with Mory?—really enjoy the changing panorama. Or was I still daydreaming?

Lying beside Raynor, still holding his penis, which had grown lovely and big in my hand, I tried to reflect his joy and the expression of awe and wonder on his face as he examined by body. Basking in his compulsive male need to taste female flesh, I kissed his clean young body—hairless, except for his pubic hairs, which I ruffled with my fingers when his penis was dancing over my face.

I felt like a young mother, alone with her male baby, kissing him from head to foot as she patted him dry after a bath, and surreptitiously—laughing as she did it—blowing on his tiny penis, or taking it gently between her lips. Feeling guilty, but delighted at the approval of her male child for more kisses that shook his entire body with laughter. Do all mothers—at least a few times—imprint their male child's genitals with a loving mother's kisses? God, that was more than twenty years ago. I was still sure that it had been a healthy response between a mother and her child. I never did it in front of Karl, and I never told him about it. I was afraid that Karl would think that I was a very evil mother. Had I told him that I had kissed our son's penis, he would have equated my silly, loving attention to Michael with my movie reputation as a phallic sword swallower.

Kissing Raynor's penis now very gently, not knowing how to answer his question, "Are you crying, Christa?"—I was— "Why are you crying?" I told him that I guessed that it was because I was premenstrual, and very often, unless they had pills for it now, that made a woman feel moody and a little unstrung. But, of course, the main reason was my uncertainty about finding my way back into "real" life. I was sure that in the coming years, whatever they might be like, I would always be plagued with the question: Would it have mattered, anyway, if I had died in the hibernaculum, or if David and Paul had been unable to revive me? I wanted to tell Raynor that maybe dying and being born again was an experience that would transform and diminish the ego compulsions of any man or woman, and probably might make them more joyous and loving creatures to live with. But how could I communicate these thoughts to a young man, only seventeen years old, floating in the ecstasy of our flesh contact?

To divert his attention from my *il penseroso* happiness, I asked Raynor how he, such a handsome young man of seventeen, presumably at the peak of his sexual powers, had managed not to be "involved" with girls up until now. "When I was your age," I told him, "girls thirteen and fourteen were making love with boys—and often getting pregnant in the process."

Raynor laughed. "A lot of them still do. But most leck *nirbos* are brought up differently. Boys aren't isolated from girls. Right through our teens we grow up playing with them. When we're very young, we're told that the greatest joy in life, the way we will find *Lo Grandi*—that's a Loglan word for the divine, or the God essence of each other—is by blending our bodies. But while our bodies may tell us that we are ready to do this before we are seventeen, we should wait—because our minds aren't ready.

"Since we aren't permitted to use any contraceptives before we're seventeen," Raynor added, "I guess you might say that we're conditioned to wait, because we don't want to conceive children. Jag explained to Liana and me that having sexual intercourse is similar to obtaining a driver's license. While every young person could learn to drive an automobile long before he is eighteen—maybe even when he's twelve years old—most of us never try to do it. We're content to wait. We know we can get our driver's license at eighteen. Most of the leck *nirbos* know that they will continue their education after seventeen in a premarital learning school, and when that happens, they will learn how to enjoy *kitsa* with many different people."

"It looks to me as if some things haven't changed." I said, shaking Raynor's penis affectionately. "Evidently, when a male is in this state before he's seventeen, he only has two choices—he can masturbate or have wet dreams."

Raynor grinned. "No, there's another way. I told you that
271

young *nirbos* grow up playing with each other. In leck homes, we see each other naked from the time we are babies. We see the girls' breasts growing, and they see our pubic hairs sprouting. Most male and female *nirbos* take dance and ballet classes together. In many of the story dances and ballets, we dance together, naked. The girls are delighted when the boys get erections, and our teachers tell us that we can *plici* kitsa—play kitsa—if we wish. Most of the girls are delighted." Raynor leaned on his elbows and stared at me. "You don't understand, do you?"

"I do," I said. "You mean you can play at kitsa, but I can't believe it! You're telling me that young leck girls are taught that it is a very nice thing, if they want to make love with a boy to do it with their hands or their mouths, but not with their vaginas."

"And we can return the *donsu*—gift," Raynor said.

Laughing, telling him that I might turn out to be a leck, I gently took his penis in my mouth and slowly circled the tip of his glans with my tongue. While I was nursing his penis, I was thinking that maybe men and women are making some progress. At least I was no longer physically alone. Obviously, many of the men and women in Raynor's generation were delighted with such a lovely, proud, helpless, filled with women-need wonder as the erect male penis, and its friendly receptacle, the female vagina, guarded by pouting labia and a trembling clitoris—a magic cave willing to open for Aladdin on a minute's notice.

Flooding Raynor's mouth with his own jism, which I had held in mine as he ejaculated, I was momentarily overwhelmed, by the realization I had been fantasizing. Raynor's penis in my mouth was actually Mory's penis. For a moment, I was twenty-four again, and I was Chrissy, in love. But slowly the blizzards of memory stopped, and I was left with the "snows of yester-year."

◆

Late Wednesday afternoon, after my physical examination, which was conducted by a staff of young men and women at the laboratory, and supervised by Paul Thomas, who I suddenly realized was, like David, a doctor of medicine and evidently a well-known gerontologist, we drove back toward Mashpee.

"Your heart, lungs, kidneys, liver, you name it, Christa, are all in good shape," Paul said. "Even Al Webb, who did your gynecological examination, was amazed. After two children, and sixteen years of hibernation, you have the vagina of a twenty-year-old." Paul laughed. "But you've got one problem. Even Al wonders what it would be like to make love with you."

"You said 'even.' " I smiled. It was impossible not to respond to Paul's jovial laughter. "Does that include you, too?"

"Of course"—Paul looked at me sadly—"but alas, I am forty years older than you are, and by 1996 standards, I am a little plump!"

I squeezed his hand. "Actually, Paul, my favorite Shakespearean character was Falstaff. Your age, and the laughter that always seems to be bubbling within you, seduces me. If Carol doesn't mind, I'd enjoy making love with you. But I wish you'd give it to me straight. You said that I was in good physical shape, but you didn't mention mental. I have a feeling that's what David meant when he said I had survived thus far."

I wanted to tell Paul that I had a feeling that lovemaking with him would be a gentle thing, but despite the night I had spent with Raynor earlier in the week, and the fact that my menstrual flow had stopped, I wasn't sure I was really responding as a complete female. I told Paul that he seemed to fit the image of the father I had never really known, and that he might be disappointed in me. All I really wanted was to be caressed, and soothed, and to disappear in the loving arms of a friend and protector. I needed a friend in bed who understood that I was still vacillating between fright and wonder at my new reality.

Paul held my hand. "I told Carol this morning that if everything went well, I might take you to one of the Unilove churches. Tonight, at the Hyannis Church, they're scheduled to do a ballet based on Edward Bellamy's short story 'To Whom This May Come.' The church will be crowded, but I think we might be able to squeeze in. Believe me, Christa, I understand the turmoil that you're going through. Even if the physical dangers of hibernation are resolved, the mental readjustments, after dropping out of the world for many years, may be even more difficult. Despite thousands of volunteers ready to try it, no one seems to be paying much attention to what it means to stop living for an extended period. If you had lived normally, you would be nearly fifty years old. You'd still have your place in the shifting scenery of life.

You would have had continuity of environment and friends. Now, you can't help but feel that you are a strange piece, looking for a jigsaw puzzle that no longer exists."

"It's even worse than that," I said. "You see, in addition to my lost sixteen years when I was sleeping in your hibernaculum, the six years when I was married to Karl Klausner today seem totally unreal to me—especially so because I seem to have returned to a world that's dominated, or at least invaded, by Newton Morrow, the only man I've ever loved."

Paul nodded understandingly. We had turned off the highway, and he was driving slowly between deep potholes and over sunken areas of roadway on one of the side streets leading into the town. "Main Street is better," he said, "but not much. Automobile and truck production is down to a total of about eight million units annually—most of them Trics for local use. Because of greatly reduced automobile mileage, the mileage tax on Trics nowhere near supports the astronomical costs of road construction and repair. Only the cross-country highways, and streets and roads in the main cities, are being maintained. Kennedy has promised direct federal road aid to the small towns and cities if he's reelected."

"From what David told me," I said, "it looks as if most people can no longer afford to drive long distances. Do people drive cross-country, or to Florida, like they used to?"

"Eventually, driving more than five hundred miles out of the main metropolitan areas will be equivalent to crossing parts of the country in a covered wagon," Paul said. "The Heli-bus, Tric rental combination will finally eliminate the need for personal travel on cross-country highways. The Federal Government's venture into the passenger rail business—Amtrak—failed in the eighties.

"But don't get the idea that people aren't mobile. If anything, they're even more so. The cost of heating single homes is so high that millions of people who live in the North will do everything possible to escape to the warmer states and the Caribbean in the winter. It's cheaper to go south than to heat some of the old-style homes like our Mashpee ark. Another thing, Christa, the almost-total rent-a-car concept has not only eliminated owning automobiles for most people, but also has pretty much wiped out the joyless cross-country driving on super highways that we grew up with."

As we drove into Hyannis, I suddenly realized that not everyone wore See-Thru dresses or jump suits. In fact, on the crowded sidewalks, See-Thrus were in a small minority. Many of the women wore loose-fitting, short, mini-skirtlike pants that rode high on their buttocks but concealed their pubic areas. Some of the women wore similar-style skirts, with ribbons of cloth that encircled their breasts, covering them, or crisscrossing seductively just across their nipples. Other women wore longer skirts, although still above the knees, and open at the back, revealing white ruffled panties. The buttocks of some women were almost totally naked from the rear, with brightly colored cloth running the length of the clefts of their behinds, emerging in front in the form of a halter and skirt that completely concealed their breasts and vulvas.

"It's obvious that there's a lot more interesting and sexy clothing around than these semitransparent peasant dresses and jump suits," I told Paul. "I want a dress like that!" I pointed at a woman walking by the spot where Paul had just parked the Tric. She was wearing a knee-length, iridescent pale red and yellow skirt, slit on each side to her waist. As she walked by us, I could see flashes of pale orange, very brief panties covering her pubic area and arching over her buttocks. Her blouse wasn't transparent, but it hung low, supported by her upper arms, and it just barely covered her nipples.

"She's a rich-ik," Paul explained, laughing. "That outfit probably cost over two thousand dollars. I guess what we've failed to make clear, Christa, is that the middle 1990s are somewhat like the 1960s. In those days, the younger generation all wore blue jeans. The girls wore their hair down to their waists, and the guys let their hair grow long and wore beards to distinguish themselves from what they then called the establishment.

"Today, while you can't always tell a person's relative income by the clothes he or she wears, and lots of the poor-iks and rich-iks wear See-Thrus, the lecks popularized them, both as a protest against the high cost of clothing and as a distinguishing garb."

Paul added neutrally, "I'm sure that in the next few weeks, if you want to reveal who you are, or who you were, and the fact that you have actually been hibernated for sixteen years, one of the incipient hibernating companies, which are waiting for a final okay form the Federal Drug Administration to test the new hibernating chemicals on human beings, will hire you for ther public-relations department. Then you'll be a rich-ik and can afford to dress like one."

We were walking toward what Paul said was a former

275

moving-picture theater, a Cinema One and Two combination that had been vacant for years, and now, like thousands of others throughout the country, had been remodeled into a Unilove Church. My mind was only half assimilating what Paul was telling me, because I had suddenly realized that I might not be a rich-ik by today's standards, but I wasn't poor. Two years after I had married Karl Klausner, I suddenly remembered, I had rented my own safety-deposit box in the First Merchants Bank in Boston. God—that would be twenty years ago! I remembered how surprised I had been when a lawyer who had ended up in control of a distributing company that had acquired my movie, *The Christening of Christina,* telephoned me, and told me that he had a check for me. Three hundred and thirty thousand dollars. It was for my share of the earnings of the movie, plus a buy out of future rights. Johnny Giacomo had agreed to the sale. A week later, after a "shopping trip" to New York to close the deal, back in Boston, in bed with Hank Hutchings, I told Hank that if my life with Karl went bust, I wanted to have my own "walk home" money. I told him about my newfound fortune, and offered to invest in his condominium project. But he had only laughed and told me that there were some risks he never took with women. His advice, since he believed inflation was endemic in the monetary system, and because I obviously didn't need the money, was to buy gold—not for delivery, but for resale in the indeterminate future. The certificates which I would receive would be equivalent to warehouse receipts and would represent actual gold bullion that would be held for me in one of the Federal Reserve Banks. Without ever having to physically take possession of the gold, I could trade in it and sell my gold when and if the price went higher. Although gold was then selling for $190 an ounce, Hank was convinced that it was the only sound long-term investment. "In ten years," he told me, "it will be selling for three hundred an ounce. None of the politicians can control inflation."

On Hank's advice, I put my certificates for one thousand seven hundred ounces of gold bullion into a safety-deposit box, and to eliminate any annual rental billing for the box, which might have fallen into Karl's hands, I paid five hundred dollars for the box as a rental in perpetuity. The only way Karl could have found out about the money was if he had found my key to the box and traced it back to the First Merchants Bank. The key? God, what had I done with it? Then I remembered. I had taped it into the back of one of my books of poetry in my library in Marblehead. I had at least twenty duplicate copies of the book stacked on one of the bottom shelves; I occasionally gave a copy to someone who thought Christina North had been a great poet.

According to David, Penelope still lived in the house. That meant that she must have loved the old New England atmosphere of the home, and, hopefully, since Penny had enjoyed being read to when I had last known her, she had learned to enjoy reading by herself and had kept her mother's library intact. If she hadn't, the key to the vault was obviously gone, and so, probably, was my secret hoard of money.

Not daring to ask Paul what the price of an ounce of gold might be today—I still couldn't think 1996 without feeling bewildered—and, at the same time, wondering if Karl might have found my safety-deposit box anyway—how long could a box lie dormant after a death as well publicized as mine had been?—I finally forced my mind back into the groove of Paul's conversation.

"While we've mentioned the Church of United Love, which most people call Unilove," he was saying, "I don't think you're aware of how deeply this new religion has taken root. Unilove is a mixed ball of yarn, a religion of many colors. Unilove members are striving for the same kind of separate identity as Catholics or Jews or Protestants. Their twice-a-week services are constantly changing and are created under the auspices of the Mother Church, whose headquarters are in Carmel, California. The services are designed to meld the Participants, who are the Unilove congregations, and the Celebrants, who are the Readers, the Dancers, and the Orchestra and the Choir, into an overall erotic glow, and, hopefully, give everyone a momentary touching of base with a kind of cosmic consciousness. In many of the services, they manage this in such a way that ultimately the Unilove Participants find that their entire approaches to life and sex and human loving assume a new perspective that dominates their whole lives."

Paul was holding my arm as he guided me through the crowds of people and pointed toward the church, which was a few blocks away. "Incidentally, you should understand, Christa, that the Reader Celebrants are a male and female pair-bond team. They usually have a background in psychology or psychiatry. They're full-time employees of each Unilove Church, and are available to all members of a particular

277

congregation for no-cost consultation on any problems. Their Friends-to-Lean-On services are very popular.

"With your background and training and physical beauty," Paul commented, "you could very easily qualify as a Reader Celebrant."

I shook my head. "I think I'd have to go back to school again. Sex and loving have moved into a whole new and different dimension, and I'm not sure how the puzzle fits together yet, I can't even advise myself what I should do with you—or all the rest of your Love Group, including the children, who want to enjoy kitsa with me."

Paul laughed. "The joy of kitsa is the joy of friendship. Some friends are passing friends; some friends are friends for life. Your own telepathy tells you whether someone is simply an acquaintance, or a person you might really want to share two intimacies with."

"Two intimacies?"

"Your brain and your genitals. You can have one without the other, but then it's not kitsa." Paul pointed to a line about a half block ahead of us. "Services begain at seven o'clock. They're standing in line already. You know that the Unilove Churches, which are individually incorporated, are the spiritual brainchild of Adar Chilling, combined with the financial and promotional genius of Newton Morrow. In addition to this church in Hyannis, there are at least thirty others on the Cape. At last count, there were more than twelve thousand Unilove Churches across the country. Within ten years from its inception, this has put Unilove Churches about fourth in number with actual churches, behind Catholics, Baptists, and Methodists. The Unilove services have also been seen by millions of non-members, and the actual membership of the Unilove Church in the under-forty age group constitutes more than sixty percent of their membership, and is growing rapidly.

"One big reason for their appeal is their live story-dance services which are not only sexually open, but offer a possible repertoire of several thousand ballets and story dances, with new ones being continuously devised by local churches and members of various groups. Some groups, who have perfected a particularly popular story dance, often travel to other churches all over the United States. In a sense, Unilove services arc a modern version of the traveling storytellers and mendicants who entertained villagers many hundreds of years ago with their stories and myths. The interesting contrast is

278

that despite the seeming realism of Life-a-Vision, millions of people are bored with it. They prefer the warm rapport of live performance. One of Morrow's theories is that Unilove has only began to explore its potentials. He believes that if he's elected President, millions of people in the Secondary Work Force will become actors, dancers, and musicians, who'll not only entertain each other in nationwide music, drama, and religious festivals, but who'll provide a strong economic foundation to balance against the material production of the Central Work Force. At the same time they will create a new kind of Gross National Product which is not based on human consumption of manufactured goods."

We were standing in line now, inching toward the entrance. Paul was smiling. "There's only about two hundred people ahead of us. Admission is eight dollars, which is about three-fifty in 1980 dollars. The church income supports the building. Unilove Churches pay regular property taxes.

"The average church takes in about eight thousand to ten thousand dollars a week. Some of the excess income, which is averaging about one hundred thousand dollars annually for each church, is loaned to the Mother Church at very low interest rates, and is available to groups who wish to establish Church of United Love corporations in their particular communities.

"I don't know whether anyone's told you, Christa, but Unilove members, and the individual churches, have not only provided the basic financing for Newton Morrow's campaign, but they're the backbone of the United People's Party. Eventually, you must read Adar Chilling's book, *Unilove*. It's partially autobiographical. Adar's father, Mat Chilling, was an evangelical minister. During World War II, before he became a captain in the Air Force, he ran a tent show in Miami, which he called 'Seek the True Love.'

"I never saw one of the shows, but evidently Mat Chilling raised his audiences to a fever pitch with a sermon based on his new beliefs, which were enunciated in Ten New Commandments—one of which proclaimed that 'Man is God. The only God you will ever know.' The climax of each evening came with a dimming of the tent lights, and a moment of total darkness. Then Cynthia Chilling, Adar's mother, appeared totally naked. She was standing on a platform which rose out of the center of the stage, and was bathed in a warm spotlight. Keep in mind, this was 1943—fifty-three years ago. In those days, the only live nudity anyone ever saw in the

279

United States was in burlesque houses. In those days, burlesque strippers wore pasties over their nipples and shaved their vulvas, and they were constantly being arrested for 'lewd and indecent exposure.'

"Obviously, Mat Chilling's nude wife contributed to the phenomenal success of the tent show. The detailed philosophy didn't appear until after World War II, when it was published in a book called *Spoken in My Manner*. Mat's thesis was that the human body, and humans, following his lead in a new kind of sexual communication and loving, could become God made manifest. Unfortunately, his book was not published until after his death in a tragic automobile accident."

"I read Chilling's book when I was in college," I said, and I was suddenly very interested. "No one paid too much attention to that book until the late 1960s. Then, suddenly, everyone was reading it. I remember that it was published by Yale Marratt, and an organization he established called Challenge, a Foundation. Isn't that right?"

Paul nodded. "Yale Marratt, and his two wives, were trying to legalize bigamy in the State of Connecticut."

I laughed. "I vaguely remember Grace reading about it to Daddy. It was in the newspapers. She was horrified."

"Yale Marratt finally won the battle, but it was many years later. A ménage à trois finally became a legal relationship in 1988. Anyway, after Mat Chilling's death, Cynthia married Yale Marratt, and then they both discovered that his previous Hindu marriage to a woman named Anne Wilson, a Red Cross girl Yale had met in India, was legal, and she had borne Yale's child." Paul was smiling. "As you can see, Adar Chilling's family background ultimately bore fruit in Unilove. Adar and her stepbrother, Yale Richard Marratt, were brought up first in a ménage à trois. Later, when Anne married again, and there were other children, Anne and her new husband and Yale and Cynthia formed a group marriage. Yale, Anne, Cynthia—all of them are still alive, living in Connecticut in a Love Group. The Marratt Foundation dispenses millions of dollars annually in educational grants. Newton Morrow completed the circle by insisting that Yale Richard—Richie, as he is popularly known—be nominated as his running mate for Vice-President. By that time, Newton Morrow had married Adar Chilling, so that Richie is his brother-in-law. So, for the first time in the history of the United States, we have a political party interwoven with a new-style family grouping and fully endorsed by a powerful religious group."

Paul shrugged. "Of course, some people refuse to call Unilove a religion. Morrow sidesteps the whole issue by simply pointing out that his New Constitution would make it impossible for any religious group to dominate the country. Unless, of course, the philosophy of that group finally became the basic philosophy of the society itself. Morrow is only too happy to argue that over a period of a few centuries, that is exactly what happened in the United States and much of the Western world. The basis of our politics and economics is a hardheaded, ulcerous, Protestant ethic and morality, and a success-oriented God. Fortunately, this concept never fully dominated the more palatable, loving, and amendable Catholic God, who can forgive sinners, and give them endless second chances to find themselves.

"While Mat had planted the seed, it didn't germinate until many years later, in the 1980s, when a group of four people, Hannah and Ezra Parsons, and Jud and Ariel Manace (The Manpars) tried to build a church based on Chilling's ideas. Approximately at the same time, a new-style Catholic Mass had been developed in Montreal by a Jesuit priest, Father Jesonge Lereve. Overall, both of their religious approaches were based on returning live theater and celebration to its original home, the Church. The Manpars' church, which, after Chilling, they called 'Seek the True Love,' was predicated on a return to sex worship. Their original church is still functioning as a Unilove Church in Storm Haven, Connecticut.

"But the idea of returning the structure of religious worship to the 'joyous celebration of man and woman, and human sexuality' didn't find the right soil until 1985, when Adar Chilling published her book, *Unilove*. She combined her family and religious background with her early career as a dancer. As a young woman, she had been a member of The Performance Group, and had appeared in Richard Schechner's production of *Dionysus in 69*, which was a continuously improvised drama based on a play by Euripides, *Bacchae*, in which birth rituals and several other scenes were performed totally naked, on stage, by a group of young performers, among whom was Adar Chilling. Schechner had written, as early as 1967, that 'an expressive society would have need neither for pornography nor oppressive controls. Replacing them would be celebratory sexual art and expression: the phallic dances of the Greeks, the promiscuity of the Elizabethans. . . . We are beginning to understand the difference between masturbatory and celebratory sex.' "

The line had started to move more rapidly toward the entrance of the church, and Paul apologized for his extended monologue on the background and attributes of Unilove. "You should understand, Christa," he said, "that I'm one of the few of my generation who sensed that you were trying to express sexual loving in the celebratory style in your movie. You were ahead of your time. Unfortunately, most of your audiences ignored the larger significance of your retelling of the Sleeping Beauty legend." Paul smiled. "Even more fascinating is that you are reliving at least a part of your own story."

We had reached the entrance. Over the former marquee of the Unilove Church was a fifteen-foot sculpture of a beautiful man-woman figure of Adam Kadmon with undefined facial features. It welcomed the world below it with outstretched arms. One palm was open; the other lightly held a formless piece of clay, with the words "Let *us* make man" inscribed on it. The figure had long hair, full female breasts, and what Paul called the Yesod, or Foundation, which, at the crotch of the sculpture, represented the male penis penetrating the female vagina.

"Adar has stated in her book that the many symbols used in Unilove Churches are not for worship, but simply to serve as reminders of the fundamental androgynous male and female unity," Paul explained. As we followed the people through the lobby, Paul pointed to wall paintings showing the Yang-Yin symbols, the uroboric snake, swallowing its tail, the Ardharmarisiva, hermaphroditic image of Indian gods Siva and Parvati; and I Ching symbols; and, to my amazement, a painting of Christ, in several panels, showing him producing a woman from his side, and then having sexual intercourse with her while Mary watches.

"That painting is an interpretation of a Gnostic document called 'Little Interpretation of Mary,' " Paul said. "Carl Jung called this the great truth. The *anima* and the *animus,* the male and female principle, is constantly interacting simultaneously in each of us. Jung explained the meaning of the Gnostic gospels' interpretation of human beginnings with Christ's statement to Mary in John Three: Twelve: 'If I have told you of earthly things, and you do not believe, how can I tell you of heavenly things?' According to June Singer, whose book *Androgyny* was very influential on Adar Chilling and

Newton Morrow, by his actions 'Christ is not only playing the role of Creator God in Genesis, he is also demonstrating his androgyny in a powerfully dramatic way.'

"Basically," Paul continued, "with Unilove, Adar Chilling is restoring the ancient religions of the world, all of which were aware of human duality, and she is freeing them from their male, Christian, Moslem, Judaic, patriarchal domination."

Paul kissed my cheek. "Forgive me, Christa, but you've been listening to me like a wide-eyed child. Your expression makes me want to hug you."

To my surprise, there were no conventional seats or pews inside the church. Surrounding three curves of an elongated oval stage were soft-carpeted tiers that extended to within 6 feet of an oval ceiling bubble that conformed to the size of the stage, and was at least 30 feet above it. Creating somewhat the effect of a rose window, the bubble had evidently been impregnated with colors that let the natural light of the sky come through it, thus creating shifting color mood changes across the stage and over the faces of the congregation, all of whom could see each other, as well as the stage below them.

Paul and I threaded our way among smiling people up the rising tiers, which were about 2 feet high and 3 feet deep. When we finally found a place to sit, I sank into the springy material and was suddenly aware that the seating had been designed to create an intricate sense of body intimacy with people above us, alongside of us, and below us.

Paul pointed out that not all Unilove Churches looked like this. "They conform to the architecture of the particular building which each church owns," he said. "Some churches are actually former Unitarian-Universalist and Congregational churches, which have been adapted. But Adar Chilling says in her book that her early acting experience with The Performing Group, which originally acted in a remodeled garage, convinced her that the seating in a living theater or church should be designed to create audience involvement with each other, and with the actors, the dancers, the singers, and the musicians.

"You should understand, too, that Adar danced with Maurice Bejart's Ballet of the 20th Century. Bejart was a French-born choreographer who used the dance to express mystical experience, the ideal of human brotherhood, and the efficacy of ritual. Some of his ballets are still performed in Unilove

283

Churches. The erotic element in live theater and ballet can be traced back to the Greeks, and much later to Isadora Duncan and Nijinsky, who were among the first to dance naked! It emerged once again in the late 1970s with Bejart and other choreographers."

Paul smiled at me. "Actually, Christa, chronologically, you are only a year or two younger than Adar, so you are probably familiar with the popular cabaret-type nude shows that appeared in the late seventies, like *Oh! Calcutta!* and *Let My People Come*. They were creating an inevitable future environment for the remerger of sex and religion."

As the church filled to capacity, I was gradually discovering that the action on the stage was only one dimension of the service. Already a live six-instrument orchestra, and a choir at the far end of the oval, were playing and singing what seemed like an Indian raga, but with a less monotonous and more erotic sound created by the human voice. As they played and sang, the individual musicians and singers were being televised in a shifting three-dimensional image on a hollow circular screen which was about 4 feet high, and was suspended about half-way between the bubble roof and the stage below it.

"There are four cameramen, who monitor both the stage actions and the Participants, who will engage in extended sexual intercourse during the service. The cameramen will reinterpret the total action of the service on separate levels of consciousness." Paul pointed to three contour chairs wide enough to accommodate two sleeping human beings. "You can't see the fine wiring from here," he said, "but each meditation chair in this particular church is suspended from the ceiling. As you will see, at the beginning of the service, when the three participating couples are sexually joined, the chairs will be raised into the bubble, where the separate couples will remain and lose themselves in sexual meditation throughout the service. Intermittently, the cameramen will watch their bodies and the ecstasy on their faces, and televise it for us in new, loving, creative mixtures on the circular screen.

"Relax, the service is about to begin." As Paul spoke, the natural overhead light slowly dissolved into a misty yellow-orange cloud that enveloped the stage and the audience. Then, like a slowly evaporating fog, it cleared slightly. Standing in the center of the stage, appearing at the same time in multiple images on the screen, were a naked woman and three couple groups, each comprising a naked young man and woman. Each couple stood near their contour chair, forming the tips of an undefined triangle, with the single woman in the center.

The ages of the three couples were difficult to estimate. Paul thought they were probably between twenty and thirty-five, and were pair bonds who were living together in Love Groups. But he wasn't sure of that, because the demand to be Participants during a service in a Unilove Church, and enjoy sexual meditation, was so great, both from members and non-members, that waiting lists, in most churches, were for six months or longer.

I asked Paul who the woman in the center—the female Reader—was. She was about 5 feet 6 in height. Although she seemed in excellent physical shape, and she was very lushly feminine, with full breasts and a slightly rounded stomach, I guessed that she must weight at least 150 pounds, and she was not young.

"Her name is Deborah Tighe," Paul whispered, and then, anticipating my question, he said, "She's fifty-two. She's been the female Reader for this church for several years."

As he was speaking, a naked gray-haired man, identified by Paul as Stephen Flexner, Deborah's pair bond, joined her on the stage. Gently, he cupped her face in his hands, kissed her lips, and then he kissed her breasts. Finally, kneeling before her, he put his face against her stomach and vulva. While he was doing this, his loving gestures were being duplicated by the male axis of the three couples forming a triangle around them.

While he was kneeling before her, Deborah spoke. She had a tender smile on her face, and her delicate voice, evidently picked up by hidden microphones, flowed over the audience. "Many years ago," she said, "one of the first writers discussing the dual nature of men and women, June Singer, said: 'Every naked woman incarnates Prakriti, the female element in the original divine, creative process. In approaching the naked woman, the yogin'—a man who wishes to find divinity together with this woman—'must look upon her with the detachment and awe one feels in contemplating the mysterious secrets of nature, the wondrous ability to bring forth creation. Unless'—during his contemplation of the naked woman, and hers of the naked man—'one feels the presence of the Divine that is about to reveal itself, there will be no rite, only a secular act. The woman—Prakriti—is to be transformed into an incarnation of Satki. As the woman becomes the goddess, the
285

man must become the god. The two will join as father-mother of the world.' "

As she finished speaking Stephen, simultaneously with the three Participant couples, slowly rose to his feet, and Deborah reciprocated his worship of her by kissing his face and cheeks and chest. Finally, sinking to her knees, she kissed his penis, which immediately erected under the touch of her lips. As he spoke, the cameras projected all of them in interchanging images on the circular screen, which now was slowly revolving.

"Welcome to Unilove," Stephen said. "Unilove is a way of life that encompasses the religions of many long-forgotten worlds. Like Tantra, which shows the way to self-enlightenment, Unilove reveals to each man and each woman his or her total involvement with the vast-scale cosmos—God, if you will—operating within the tiny macrocosm of our individual lives, while simultaneously this ultimate Divinity embraces each and every one of us.

"In the words of Ajit Mookerjee, 'Tantra'—as does Unilove—'views the human body as the physical substratum to highest awareness, and the raw material for further transformation, where even conjugal love and sex are considered a means to supreme joy and spiritual edification. . . . Similarly important are Tantra's concepts of the polarity principle, determining the relationship between a man and a woman. A creative interaction, in which the conflict between the outward and inward of head and heart can be resolved.' In the tantric method, which is a cornerstone of the Unilove approaches, 'the female force is all-important since it offers the key to a creative life in the act of living it. The preponderance of masculinity with its aggressiveness and relative lack of feminine qualities'—suppressed by centuries of male-oriented religious conditioning—'has created an imbalance in today's society. To experience the basic sensation of being "I" in its totality is to equilibrate the two opposites, masculinity and femininity. In tantric terms, it means a synthesis, a development of the femininity within each one of us. The higher our spiritual evolution, the more feminine affirmative will be our level of consciouness in relationship to the masculine negative.' "

"My God," I whispered to Paul, "I wonder how Karl, my husband, would respond to that?"

Paul chuckled. "In horror—but don't worry. Men like Newton Morrow are as much a creation of Unilove, as they

286

are creators of it. The kind of government and economics we get are the kind we ask for."

As Stephen was finishing, the male member of each of the participating couples lay down on the contour chair nearest him. All of the males had erect penises. Slowly, the lights dissolved the contours of the stage into a soft orange-yellow fog. The penises of the male Participants were being lovingly laved by the tongues of the respective females, who were crouched over their companions' bodies with their vulvas a whisper touch away from the males' lips. Slowly the chairs, continuously watched by television cameras, ascended through the misty light into the bubble, and the entire church was bathed in a dark purple light, which was so visually impenetrable that I could scarcely see Paul sitting beside me. While the orchestra played, the chorus sang what I immediately recognized as the "Return of Persephone" from Stravinsky's musical drama of the same name. The circular screen came alive again with intermixed holographs of the Participants lying quietly together, serene in their mutual absorption with each other and the Divinity which they were sharing.

Like everyone else in the congregation, I was overwhelmed with a warm, erotic feeling. The music, the lighting, the choir, had integrated us. After about fifteen minutes—while everyone in the audience, still bathed in a deep purple light, seemed to be lost in his or her own reverie, and I (as I'm sure were many of the others in the audience) was responding to my man's reverential touching of my body, and I was kissing Paul almost in a trance—the center screen slowly darkened. Once again Deborah's voice, a husky whisper, filled the church. A misty light pinpointed her. She was now standing naked on a podium that I hadn't noticed before, which was high above the circular screen at the far, straight end of the oval stage.

"The other Reader, Stephen, is on a podium opposite her," Paul whispered. "It hasn't been spotlighted yet. During a story dance like this one, which has a verbal accompaniment, they act as responsive readers. Of course, in many ballets the story is evolved entirely through the dance itself."

"We love in a world where our scientists may be on the edge of a breakthrough in mind reading," Deborah was saying. "In the past few years, using brain caps, we have discovered that we can often discern the mental images of another person. Nearly one hundred years ago, a man whose name will be familiar to most of you, Edward Bellamy, envisioned a world where some men and women had learned telepathy without mechanical assistance. This evening, with our dancers, we will tell you much of this story in Bellamy's own words. His lovely short story, 'To Whom This May Come,' is a manifestation—as is much of his writing—of the Unilove concepts. We particularly hope that you will enjoy the final Love Dance, a pas de deux, which was personally choreograped by Adar Chilling."

The spotlight on Deborah disappeared. An ominous clap of thunder shook the building. White flashes of light danced through the church. Even before the male Reader—Stephen—spoke, I think all of us in the congregation were conscious of ourselves both as separate individuals and, momentarily, as a unified whole. Certainly, as the dance continued, I was transformed. For a moment, I actually became the dancers—particularly the female in the pas de deux. At times, while Stephen and Deborah spoke responsively, they remained unseen on their dark perches. At other times, they would appear in an aura of misty light that picked them out of the darkness and accentuated them as physical beings. While the orchestra was playing the choir was singing a chorale that I discovered later had been written especially for this ballet.

Stephen's voice, in the darkness, over the music:

It is now about a year that I took passage at Calcutta in the ship *Adelaide* bound for New York.

Deborah's voice, slightly trembling, with the choir singing the dialogue:

Three days later a terrible gale struck us.

Stephen's voice, meshing with torrential orchestral music:

All around us and astern and far out to sea was a maze of rocks and shoals.

Deborah's voice, still bodiless:

Presently the ship was struck and almost instantly went to pieces.

Stephen's voice, hopeless:

I gave myself up for lost, but later recalled being
thrown with a tremendous shock upon the beach.

Below us the stage gradually becomes discernible in an
early gray morning light which is slowly being suffused with
the rose-yellow warmth of a rising sun. A man, naked except
for wet black knee breeches of the kind that would be worn in
the eighteenth century, rises to his feet. Bewildered, he dances,
a forlorn, lonely dance.

Deborah's voice, plaintive:

When I awoke the storm was over but I saw no ves-
tige of my companions.

Stephen's voice, surprised:

I was not alone, however.

As he speaks a group of twelve male and female dancers
dressed in colorful translucent clothing leaps onto the stage;
the males doing jetes and grand jetes, the entrechats; the females swirling and pirouetting, in a rollicking, joyful dance.
Smiling, the shipwrecked voyager dances from one to the
other, his mouth moving silently in an obvious attempt to
communicate with them.

Stephen's voice, surprised:

I addressed them in English, in French, German,
Italian, Spanish, Dutch and Portuguese, but they listened to me in unbroken silence.

Deborah, still not visible, as the laughing dancers continue to
dance happily:

It was as if they had agreed not to give me any clue
to their language.

Stephen, still not visible:

Could it be that these people were dumb? My resort
to sign language overcame the remnant of gravity in
that group.

The dancers, leaping happily over each other, doing handsprings and somersaults, are scarcely paying any attention to the voyager.

Deborah, distressed:

> Just when my bewilderment was verging on exas-
> peration . . . a little elderly man confronted me
> and addressed me in English.

The dancers suddenly stop dancing and form a semicircle around the voyager, and an old man who has limped onto the stage.

Stephen, still not visible:

> His voice was pitiable, and had all the defects in ar-
> ticulation of a child beginning to talk.

Old man, from the stage, in a husky voice, over the diminished orchestra:

> I extend you a cordial welcome to these islands. My
> countrymen hope that you will pardon their uncon-
> trollable mirth. You see they understand you very
> well, but they cannot answer you.

Voyager, from the stage, his voice curious and wondering:

> Do they think it so amusing to be dumb?

Old man, as the dancers, smiling, are once again dancing informal pas de deuxs:

> Their inability to speak should not be regarded as
> an affliction. By the voluntary disuse of their organs
> of articulation, the people on this land have lost
> the power of speech.

Voyager, bewildered:

> But you have just told me that they understood me.

Interpreter, his voice over mysterious Oriental music:

> It's you they understand, not your words. You must
> know that these are the islands of the mind readers.
> Three centuries before Christ they were soothsayers

290

and magicians who were banished from their land by one of the Parthian Kings of Persia. Finally, after a long sea voyage, they arrived in these islands. For many generations the power of speech remained voluntary, but gradually their voice organs atrophied. Now, it is solely for the purpose of communication with shipwrecked strangers of talking nations that my office of interpreter still exists.

As he finishes speaking the old man, smiling, limps off the stage. The orchestra slips into a Greek sirtaki rhythm. Dancing affectionately near him, the dancers surround the voyager, but he keeps dancing away, obviously frightened.

Stephen, still not visible:

I was panic-stricken . . . it was as if I were suddenly naked among strangers. I wanted to run and hide myself.

Immediately, in response to his thought, the dancers fling off all their clothing and dance around him naked, amusing him by their actions, which assure him that being naked is delightful and nothing to fear. The female dancers are very erotic, moving their hips in a slow copulatory motion. Gradually, the stage light obscures all of them in an orange-yellow fog. For a few seconds the stage becomes completely dark, then, as the lighting turns to an early evening sunset, the voyager reappears alone, dancing.

Deborah, suddenly visible, naked in a misty blue light, high above the stage:

Slowly, I discovered that when the knowledge of my mind was overlooked by others it operated to check thoughts that might be painful to these people.

Stephen, across from Deborah, also visible, naked in a misty blue light:

In all my life before I had been very slow to form friendships, but now after I had been here three days in the company of these strangers of a strange race, I was devoted to them.

291

While this and the following dialogue is being spoken by Deborah and Stephen, four of the dancers, two males and two females, still naked, dance an extended adagio while the choir sings the dialogue as it is spoken.

Deborah, still visible:

> It was impossible not to be friendly. The peculiar
> joy of friendship is being understood by a friend as
> we are not by others, and yet being loved in spite
> of understanding.

Stephen, still visible:

> From these beloved friends, I first learned the un-
> dreamed possibilities of human friendship. Who
> among those who hear me has not known the sense
> of gulf that exists between soul and soul who have
> mocked love! Who has not felt that loneliness
> which oppresses the heart which loves it best?
> Think no longer that this gulf is eternally fixed:
> . . . Like the touch of shoulder to shoulder, like
> the clasping of hands, is the contact of their minds
> and their sensation of sympathy.

Deborah, still visible:

> In common with the rest of the mind readers my
> friends had no names. Names are, of course, super-
> fluous for people who accost one another by an act
> of mental attention. Thus, any comparison of their
> characters would be confusing rather than instruc-
> tive to those who hear me.

Stephen, still visible:

> The self-consciousness of knowing that my mind
> was an open book has disappeared.

Deborah, still visible:

> I learned that the very completeness of the dis-
> closure of my thoughts and motives was a guarantee
> that I should be judged with a fairness and sympa-
> thy such even as self-judgment cannot effect.

292

Stephen, still visible:

How shall I describe the delightful exhilaration of
moral health and cleanness, the breezy oxygenated
mental condition which resulted from the consciousness that I had absolutely nothing concealed?

Deborah, still visible:

Will you not agree that the curtained chamber of
your mind where you may go to grovel, out of the
sight of your fellow, troubled by only a vague apprehension that God may look over the top, is the
most demoralizing incident in the human condition?

Stephen, still visible:

Think what health and soundness there must be for
people who see in every face a conscience which,
unlike our own, they cannot sophisticate, who
confess one another with a glance and shrive with a
smile.

Deborah, still visible:

Let me now predict, though ages may yet elapse
before the mutual vision of each other's mind is
perfected, and the veil of self is pierced, then shall
the divinity of each of us no longer be a coal smoking among ashes, but a star in crystal sphere.

The stage darkens for a moment. As the stage lights return,
the orchestra is playing a classical waltz. One by one, the female dancers, still naked, dance demurely, but joyously, with
the voyager, who is now also naked.

Stephen, no longer visible:

With my first venturing into the society of these island people, I had begun, to their extreme amusement, to fall in love with the women right and left.
It was difficult to believe that the melting emotions
which I experienced in their company were the
result of the merely friendly and kindly attitude of
their mind to mind. I had to adapt myself to a world

in which friendship being a passion, love must
needs be less than a rapture.

As Stephen finishes speaking, one of the dancers—a strik-
ing, full-breasted, dark-haired woman of about twenty-two,
her hair cut short in the familiar leck Dutch boy cut—suddenly detaches herself from the other females. The orchestra
picks a sparkling polka combined with a Latin American
rhythm. The woman dances around the voyager doing grace-
ful entrechats and tours en l'air.

Deborah, not visible, her voice light and laughing:

When he first met me we were in company. All
but he had read my thoughts, and they watched me
with moistened eyes. I knew that he felt my mind
brooding upon his. And he understood that between
mind readers, who will be lovers, there is no woo-
ing, but simply recognition.

Stephen, not visible:

To my amazement, my love, in whose society I was
almost constantly, had not the least idea of the
color of my eyes, or whether my complexion was
light or dark. Of course, as soon as I asked the
question she read the thought in my mind. It is by
the mind not the eye that these people know one
another.

Deborah, not visible:

Slowly, my voyager is beginning to understand that
the absolute openness of our minds and hearts to
one another makes our happiness far more dependent on the moral and mental qualities of our companions than their physical. A woman of mind and
heart has no need of beauty to win love in these islands.

Stephen, not visible:

While these islanders make a little account of physical beauty, they are a singularly handsome people,
doubtless, in part, due to the absolute compatability
of their temperaments in all their marriages, and

the inevitable reaction upon a body of a state of
ideal mental and moral health.

Deborah, not visible:

My lover knows that I know all his thoughts and he
fears that I rejected the sensuousness of his passion
for me. But gradually he understands by virtue of
our communing minds an ecstasy more ravishing
surely than he ever tasted before.

As Deborah's and Stephen's dialogue continues, the music
becomes more erotic. Finally, all but two dancers have left
the stage. The pas de deux continues. The dark-haired
woman gradually becomes more seductive, teasing the voyager by holding her breasts out to him, swinging her pelvis in
a humorous bump-and-grind dance, doing slow-motion handsprings before him which reveal her vulva, and a hilarious
waddle across the stage that fully reveals her buttocks.

During the dance her fingers lightly flit across the voyager's
penis, and during the rest of the responsive reading, the two
dancers continue their spellbinding pas de deux, which can
have only one ending.

Stephen, not visible:

The ache at the heart of the intensest love is the
impotence of words. My passion was without this
sense of loss, but I realized the high communion
which my sweet companion sacrificed for me. That
I should ever attain the power of mind reading developed by these people was out of the question.

Deborah, not visible:

My lover has yet to understand that we hold mind
reading desirable, not for the knowledge of others it
gives its possessors, but for self-knowledge which is
its reflex effect. All I see in the mind of my lover is
a photograph of my own character. Therefore,
seeing myself in a mirror, I am compelled to distinguish between the bodily self my lover sees, and my
real self which is still within and unseen. Mind
readers seeing their mental and moral selves reflected in other minds as in mirrors learn to recognize

each other's essential identity and bearing—the noumenal self for which the mind as well as the body is but the garment of the day. We learn to be lords of ourselves.

As Deborah is speaking the voyager and his island lover are now dancing a mutual, caressing dance of love, fondly touching each other's body. The female leaps into the male dancer's arms, from which position, suspended by the voyager, she slowly sinks to the stage with her back supporting her. As the television cameras pick up the expressions of ecstasy on their faces, she rises into the voyager's arms. He slowly enters her body, and they climax in what is obviously a very real mutual orgasm.

The stage darkens and the Participants are lowered to the stage as the choir sings a reprise of portions of Deborah's and Stephen's dialogue.

———◆———

As we walked toward the Tric, Paul held my hand, and asked why I was so quiet.

"I guess that I'm falling in love with your world," I said. "Some of it, at least, is no longer a brash, uncaring world. A new light is shining in its eye. But it's still shy and timid, 'standing on the threshold of a New Tomorrow,' as Mory said in his book." I smiled at Paul through the tears in my eyes. "I'm in love with Bellamy, too, and Mory, and those dancers, and the orchestra, and the choir, and the nice feeling that Unilove gives me . . . and"—I grinned at him—"I'm in love with you. You are going to sleep with me tonight, aren't you? You're the only person in your Love Group I've propositioned."

Laughing, Paul squeezed my hand. Beside him in the Tric as he drove toward the Cape highway, I told him that I felt like a young bride going on her honeymoon. Tonight, for the first time in sixteen years, I was going to have sexual intercourse with a man; his penis would actually be inside me.

"I hope that you really like to make love," I told him, enjoying the twinkle in his eye and the sharp profile of his bearded face. "Some women only have one or two death-defying orgasms. Maybe mine aren't so violent, but I used to be capable of twenty or more."

"With your husband, Karl Klausner?"

"God, no." I was about to tell him that Karl was too old, and too intent on his own quick ejaculations, and then I remembered. Even if he didn't look or act it, Paul Thomas was seventy-three! According to his own calculations, biologically he was forty years older than I was. Chronologically, twenty-four years older. Karl had been twenty-six years older than I was. In our last years together—probably partially my fault—Karl had turned into a once-a-week lover. Even then I sensed that he only achieved a good orgasm with me with an underlying feeling of wanting to hurt me. He took his sadistic business world to bed with him. Often, my behind and breasts and stomach had black and blue marks where he sank his fingers into me, more in anger than in love.

As we entered the traffic-control pattern of the Cape highway, which automatically maintained our distance between cars ahead of us and behind us, and steered the car if you wished, Paul turned the dashboard television to a station that was broadcasting color music—shifting patterns of erotic colors that followed the tempo of the music. He set a computer on the dashboard and told me that it was about twenty-five miles to the Mashpee turn-off. "It will buzz about a mile before we arrive there," he said.

Then, he showed me a feature of the Tric that I had been unaware of. He pushed another button, and the entire, very broad front seat slid forward a few inches, and at the same time the back seat folded down and merged perfectly with the back seat. Paul flopped back against some pillows in the back seat and we were lying on what had turned into a king-size bed. He laughed at my bewilderment.

"One of the comforts of the new world on long journeys," he said, as I snuggled beside him. "Unfortunately, in the vernacular of your day, you lucked out. Your companion is as old as Father Time."

I grinned and kissed him, enjoying the rough feel of his neatly trimmed beard on my face. "You don't understand that expression," I told him. "Actually, as you used it, it means that I'm in luck, not out of it. Anyway, I wouldn't worry if I were you. I made love in automobiles in my youth a couple of times, but it was never like this." The interior of the Tric, with shifting colors and music from the television, had been transformed into a voluptuous, swaying love chamber. I slid my hand inside his jump suit and found his penis. It was still a soft little mouse, but it was stirring. "How long before the buzzer rings and time runs out?" I asked him.

"It will be about twenty-five minutes before the driver takes control again." Paul smiled. "Both of the Tric and his body!"

I laughed. "That's not long enough, but it's a good beginning." I slipped out of my See-Thru dress and undid the jump suit. "When you finally have to jump back behind the wheel can you drive this thing naked?"

"Sure, why not?" Paul let me help him out of his jump suit, and he stretched out on our Tric bed.

"You keep saying that you are too fat," I said, feeling his belly and kissing it. "But I've watched you at the house when you were naked. Actually, you have a very heavy beer-barrel chest."

Paul chuckled. "The trouble is that my stomach never learned where my chest stopped."

"Anyway," I told him, and I could feel his penis slowly rising in my hand, "you're not like some fat men. Your belly is very firm, and you're still accessible down here." I shook his penis affectionately. "You don't have to look in a mirror to see if it's still there."

Paul took me in his arms and held me gently against him. I had the strange sensation that I was a very young girl, and I had just climbed into bed with Daddy. Paul wasn't just any man. He was my father. The father I had never really known. I felt deliciously incestuous.

His hand was ruffling through my pubic hair. "Lord," he sighed, "I'm still amazed that you don't seem to have lost one pubic hair in the process. It's as bountiful as an eighteen-year-old's." He laughed. "One thing that an old man like me is conscious of, as well as of my own diminishing erectile ability, is that most women past fifty slowly become pretty bald down here."

"Men lose the hair on their heads," I said laughingly, enjoying his tender explanation of my vulva, "and women lose the hair on their crotches. God in his wisdom knew what he was doing. Would you enjoy sleeping with a baldheaded woman? Anyway, what's so great about female pubic hair?"

"It excites the male," Paul said. "It never ceases to amuse me that some women shave their pubises. They don't seem to realize that their pubic hair rubbing against the male's groin, and merging with his pubic hair, excites a man, and that when a man first buries his face in the female's lovely forest, and later, in the act of coition, actually feels it, like a thousand tiny needles piercing his own pubic hair and titillating his

298

flesh, it creates a special kind of ecstasy that can be achieved in no other way."

Even while he was speaking Paul's face was nestled between my legs, and then I told him I wanted him inside me. He supported himself over me. The gentle rocking of the Tric, and an occasional bump as he hit a rough spot in the road, kept his penis trembling maddeningly on the lips of my vagina and the edge of my clitoris.

"Dear one . . . please," I moaned. "Come all the way inside me before I burst." And when he did, and I felt his penis hard but questioning—not demanding—moving slowly but insistently inside me, I screamed, "Oh, Paul . . . Paul! Thank you. Dear God, thank you. You feel so good." I climaxed, and then immediately I climaxed again. "Oh, honey, can you last?" I whispered.

Paul smiled. "I'm not God, but one advantage of age is that when a penis gets up it doesn't have to hurry. If its owner wishes he can keep it up, with occasional help from his friend, for hours and hours."

"When the buzzer goes off where are we going to continue this?" I sighed. I was afraid that we might have to go back to his bedroom and Carol would be there. How could I make love with him when Carol was lying beside us? What I wanted, when neither of us could stay awake any longer, was to fall asleep in his arms and wake up and make love once more at sunrise.

Paul read my mind. "We could sleep downstairs in the gathering room, or since it's such a balmy evening, if you wish, we can carry an air mattress down on the beach. The moon will be high by one o'clock. If you fall asleep I promise to watch my Sleeping Beauty so that no harm will come to her." He looked at me wistfully. "As a matter of fact, ever since Max Lebenthal died, I have watched you in your hibernation chamber, fallen in love with you and prayed that you would survive."

"Since you really are responsible for me," I said, "I agree. I want to sleep on the beach, but only if you can stay inside me all night."

Paul laughed. "Right now, I'd take bets that I could."

"That's great. Because my vagina has been seriously neglected for sixteen years."

Later, naked on the beach, with a blanket to cover us if we needed it, after we had played together in the water, I sucked Paul's salty penis big again, and with the moon above us I sat on top of him while he carefully guided it back into its nest. We were soft gold creatures of the night. Beneath me his body was a firm, rippling wave. In between extended orgasms that left me sighing, we talked about sex and my amazement that a man in his seventies could be so virile.

"You forget that your world was terribly youth-oriented," Paul said. "With the dropping birthrate and greater longevity now it seems antediluvian that most of the faces and bodies in your movies and on your television were those of people twenty-five or under. Presumably, sex stopped somewhere between thirty-five and forty-five. It was shameful to admit to one's children, even when they were in their twenties and thirties, that their parents in their fifties and sixties, and even those poor souls confined in those horrible institutions called senior citizen centers and nursing homes—thank, God, they are rapidly disappearing—were all potentially fully active sexual creatures and could enjoy making love until their final orgasm with death."

Paul kissed my breasts, and I reveled in the strength of his hands, first grasping my buttocks with a finger tickling, and then pressing deep into my anus when I climaxed, and then afterward, as I lay panting on top of him, I felt the feathery touch of his fingers on my back and down and around the cleft of my behind. When I wasn't climaxing I was trembling in euphoric ecstasy. I was a girl! I was a woman! I was loved! And I realized, as he talked to me, that it was a two-way gift. Love Groups had made it possible for young lovers to enjoy sex in the arms of older, more temperate friends, and for old lovers to enjoy the special bliss of knowing that they could not only arouse their young lovers but enjoy the wilder, more passionate surrender of youth. When it came to loving, I was on the threshold of a new world where "passages" no longer meant mental disruption and readjustment, but where instead all living pivoted around the joy of men's and women's sensuality from birth to death.

◆

Two days later, I kissed Paul, Carol and Rose good-bye and drove back to Boston with David and Gale, Delight, Liana, and Raynor.

I told David that I felt like an astronaut returning from outer space—I was wondering if I would survive the splashdown and reentry into the ocean. David's amused answer was that returning space travelers no longer landed in the ocean. Reentry, after a voyage to the moon, or return from one of the satellites, was equivalent to landing at a commercial airport.

Sensing my reaction to the variety of high-style clothing that I had discovered was still available, Ruth had sent back with David "a Boston ik-dress" and underclothing that she had taken the liberty of picking out for me. I was pleased, although I was sure that the style was not one I would have chosen for myself. The dress was designed so that a very brief orange-yellow flaring skirt was attached to a narrow strip across my midsection. This widened into a transparent halter that covered my breasts but clearly revealed my nipples. If I bent ever so slightly at the waist, the skirt rose high over most of my buttocks, which were suggestively covered by matching underpants, cut very high and revealing most of both cheeks of my ass. I had to admit that the dress was even more sexually erotic than the See-Thrus, which only gave an intermittent display of one's naked body and had the effect of a stop light blinking in the darkness.

"Ruth thought you might prefer not to identify yourself as a leck," David had told me. Paul and he had been casually lying on the bed in Ruth's room waiting for me to get ready. They watched me, naked after my shower, cautiously put on the new clothing while I surveyed the final effect in the mirror. I was getting used to my bangs, and I knew without asking that despite the dress, my Dutch boy hair style, from what I had seen in Hyannis, was also a leck identification. I was sure of one thing: The woman in the mirror might look like the sister of the woman in the photograph on my sixteens-year-old driver's license, but she seemed less tortured and more subtly erotic than I had been.

Both Paul and David were evidently pleased with the ik version of Christina. "The dress is a young woman's style," David assured me. "Even today, although most lecks and rich-iks refuse to go the way of all overeating flesh, not every female over thirty would be able to wear a dress like that. You're absolutely radiant, Christa. I envy Paul that he was the first to enjoy kitsa with you."

"My God," I exploded at Paul. "Isn't anything private in this crazy world? You, and I suppose Raynor, too, couldn't wait to tell David, could you?"

Paul chuckled. "David has a scientific interest in you, as well as an emotional one."

"I suppose that David even has asked you if I was orgasmic," I said angrily. "Damn you both! I'll tell David right now. I enjoyed every minute of my last two nights with Paul. You should be able to do half so well."

David smiled at me sadly. "I love you very much, Christa. But I know that I'm at a disadvantage with you. You don't trust me."

"Why should I? I haven't forgotten that among your other tricks you're a hypnotist, too. I remember the night that you found me in the Saugus Hospital. That night I really thought you were the devil himself. You completely stunned my poor screwed-up brain. You even convinced me—your prisoner—to write my own autobiography. You made me such a willing slave that I couldn't wait for the times that you deigned to fuck me."

David laughed. *"Diprin*—precious one—you're right. In those days I was arrogant. If a person like you wanted to throw her life away, I saw no reason why she (or he) couldn't consign her body to scientific investigators. I guess I still don't. But you trapped me. During the months before you went into final hibernation I vacillated many times. Every day, as you wrote it, I read your autobiography, and discovered the basic you—what Morrow might have known as his Chrissy—surfacing between the lines, and I was in love with you. All you needed was a *fremi*—a friend to lean on. But it was too late. By the very act of kidnapping you, I had made friendship and love impossible."

For the first time I saw tears in David's eyes. "I really love you, Christa—but one thing that anyone learns who lives in a Love Group is that we're not in competition for each other's love. I hope that in the coming weeks, should you decide to have kitsa with me, we'll both enjoy the experience. A lovely bridge that will join our separate selves for an hour or two—and not, by comparison, as strangers fucking."

"I thought you never used that word."

"We don't," David hugged me. "I wasn't sure that you understood the difference. Even sixteen years ago when we made love, for me it was kitsa, not fucking. I hope you understand."

"I'm beginning to." I smiled at him, and quickly nuzzled his face. "Maybe, like a Unilove Participant, I'll even be able to adore and be adored. Maybe I'll even go to bed with you in church!"

When we were finally in the Tric, and on the Cape highway headed toward Boston, I told David that Ruth had been very nice to buy a dress for me, and I really appreciated it, but that it disturbed me. "I hate like hell to be dependent on all of you—or on anybody, for that matter." I told David that maybe my continuing need for recognition—fame or infamy, it hadn't mattered which—had been because all my life, even with Johnny Giacomo, I had been dependent on people I hadn't wanted to be dependent on. First on Grace, who had tried to own me lock, stock and barrel, and then on Karl Klausner, who almost did.

"The couple of hundred dollars that you found in my pocketbook when you hibernated me," I told him, "had been there for months. The wife of Karl Klausner never needed money—just about anything I could dream of was available on credit. But much of my spending wasn't for pleasure. It was an act of defiance to see how far I could go before Karl protested." I sighed. "He never did, and I guess I resented that, too. Anyway, that's the way I feel now. I'm dependent on you, and my whole nature cries out against being beholden to anyone.'"

David, who was now steering the car in computerized control vis-à-vis the cars ahead of and behind him without necessity to watch the road too closely, grinned at me. "While you may not realize it, Christa, that very American feeling is the core of Newton Morrow's political philosophy. He'd probably agree with you, at least on the level of economic dependency. Basically, his proposal to redistribute the economic wealth of this country, and give every individual his own Capital Account, is an attempt to restore the old-time frontier independence. He's trying to restore what is fundamentally a rich-ik approach to life. Much of the money and power drive of men like Karl Klausner originated with the very human need *not* to be subservient—*not* to have to beg for their bread. Unfortunately, the only way they could achieve these goals was to force economic slavery on the rest of us. It makes the rich-iks very unhappy when men like Newton Morrow remind the people that relative monetary equality and personal independence are part of the same equation."

While my jumbled thoughts were chasing each other around my brain trying to link with David's perspective, I once again remembered the gold bullion I had bought.

David was saying, ". . . of course, monetary independence is only one side of the coin. There's really no such thing as personal independence. We are all dependent on each other;

303

maybe we really only exist when another person confirms our reality with his or her love. Anyway, you should——"

Laughing excitedly, I interrupted him. "I just remembered, I may have money of my own. At least, I think I have."

David smiled indulgently. "You mean a personal savings account? Remember, Christa, you were declared legally dead. Karl would have inherited your estate."

I couldn't restrain the triumph in my voice as I told him about my safety-deposit box, and the gold bullion I had bought twenty years ago.

"Do you mean that you actually put gold bars in a safety-deposit box?"

"No, silly," I said, "they would have weighed over a hundred pounds, I had receipts for the purchase. I bought seventeen hundred ounces of it. I could have claimed delivery, if I had wanted to. When you buy gold that way, the actual gold is held in one of the Federal Reserve Banks, I think."

David was staring at me with new respect. "My God, Christa, you were a very devious woman. What if you had really died? No one, including your children, would have ever known about the money."

"They didn't need it—but I might have. As it turned out, now I really do need it." I shrugged. "Anyway, maybe it's too late. After sixteen years, Karl probably found it."

"Don't worry about it." David smiled. "You really don't need to be rich."

"Don't be too sure," I said, and there was no humor in my voice. "I'm not really sure that I believe all this leck crap. Maybe I have greater affinity with Jason Kennedy and the Democrats. If that should be true, then I don't want to have to go crawling to Karl to borrow a few million."

David laughed. "Quite practical. Did you keep the key to your safety-deposit box in your pocketbook?"

"No. But the first day you brought me to Mashpee, you told me that my daughter Penny was living in our old home in Marblehead. Sixteen years ago, all my books were there, over three thousand, in the library. On one of the bottom shelves I kept some copies of my collected poems. I taped my safety-deposit key in the back cover of one of the books."

"So, after we drop the children off in Boston, I suppose you can't wait to drive to Marblehead." David's tone was sarcastic. I could tell that he wasn't very happy with my new-found wealth, or my reaction to it.

I shivered. "God, no! I'm not ready to face Penny yet. Maybe she hates me. A mother who committed suicide isn't a very nice heritage. Anyway, maybe she's an ik."

"What do you care?" Gale, who along with the others in the back seat had been listening, joined the conversation. "You just said maybe you weren't a leck."

"Maybe I'm not," I said a little angrily. "Maybe I'm just me. I'm not too happy with Newton Morrow's idea of categorizing people by the amount of money that they have."

"Not money," Liana said. "Brains."

David chuckled. "Liana's right. There are a lot of very wealthy lecks. Yale Richard Marratt—Richie—Mory's running mate for Vice-President, is worth at least sixty million dollars. Challenge, Incorporated, the foundation that his father started, is one hundred percent behind Mory, and it has close to two billion dollars in assets."

"I never heard of any rich people who gave their money away, if they could help it," I said skeptically. "Anyway, maybe if you're that rich you can afford to be a liberal. What happens to Challenge, Incorporated, and all that money if Mory is elected President? I'll bet they've figured out some way to exempt foundations."

David shook his head. "All the Marratts and Adar Chilling are well aware that a People's Foundation for Grants and Endowments will replace private foundations. Any money required by corporations, groups, or individuals for private research and development in business or education would be supplied on application to the People's Foundation—after careful review. The total amount available would be equal to a five-year average of all grants and endowments, public and private, since 1990. The budget for this agency would become as large as necessary to facilitate economic growth and encourage scientific breakthroughs in any areas that were approved by a majority of the United People's representatives who would be elected from each Commonwealth."

"I really don't give a damn what happens to private foundations," I said. I noticed that we were arriving on the outskirts of the city. From a distance the profile of Boston looked just about the same as I remembered it. There didn't seem to be any additions to the twelve forty-to-sixty-story towers that had been built by insurance companies and banks in the 1960s and 1970s. The basic difference in the surface life of the city was the helicopter activity and the thousands upon thousands of plastic bugs—Trics—that were bustling
305

through the streets in all directions, most of them with one occupant.

"What happens to the Prudential and John Hancock towers and all those bank buildings, if Mory gets elected?" I asked.

"Those buildings still make it quite obvious who controls the money, and who the rich-iks are," David said. "Morrow hopes the cities will become cultural and educational centers. Boston has been on the way to becoming that kind of city for the past sixteen years. Most of the manufacturing businesses moved out long ago. Morrow has suggested that former bank and life insurance buildings, which dominate the skylines in most cities, could be turned into housing for students. Remember, with employment in the Central Work Force not available to citizens under twenty-five, the student population of the country will triple. If those buildings aren't converted into housing, they'll become museums inside and *out*. New buildings more than ten stories high have been illegal since 1988."

I pointed to the First Merchants Bank building, where I hoped my safety-deposit box still was. "At least I'm glad to see that Warren Ellison's bank is still there. Do you know what gold is selling for?"

David grinned. "I've been afraid to tell you. Last I heard, it was selling for more than nine hundred dollars an ounce, and was expected to break one thousand dollars, especially if Jennifer Manchester or Jason Kennedy is elected President. Everyone has lost faith in our inflated dollars. You may be worth close to two million dollars, Christa, but if you really have that much money, you'd better hurry and spend it. If Morrow is elected, he'll take half of it away from you."

"You sound as if you might be a rich-ik, if you only had the wherewithal." I was trying to tease him. "Anyway, even though the money may not be worth that much, if I get my hands on it, I've decided I'll give you and your Love Group half of it for saving my life."

David smiled. "That's encouraging. I'm glad you're happy to be alive. But you're still confused. We'd never be rich-iks, we'd simply be rich-lecks."

————◆————

My first Saturday in Boston, we—Chandra, Ralph, Ruth, David, and I—explored the city together. There were few new buildings or expressways that I hadn't seen before. But the core city, with no trucks permitted on the streets except between one P.M. and five P.M. on weekdays, and with former roads and streets that had been turned into tree-lined walking lanes, seemed to have a new ambiance. Many squares and plazas were overhung with clear pneumatic bubbles that could be lowered during cold or rainy weather. Scattered underneath them were open-air sidewalk restaurants that offered the joys of people-watching for entertainment.

Tremont Street, opposite the Boston Common, had disappeared as an automobile throughway. The familiar pneumatic roof was suspended about 20 feet in the air over a half-mile-long block. Underneath it were thousands of tables and chairs, served from food-and-drink islands from which waiters and waitresses provided table service. Itinerant musicians, small orchestral and mime groups, and acting groups wandered through the area and performed on fifty or more circular stages which had been built about 4 feet above the ground level so that the various audiences sitting at tables could watch, and when the particular performance was over, contribute to the hat-passing if they wished.

"When I was last here," I told them, trying to remember the ravaged, honky-tonk look of the street, "people were afraid to walk in downtown Boston at night. It seems like a more joyous city."

"It could be, but it isn't yet," Ralph said. "Many of the thousands of people who are here night after night are seeking the comfort of people-closeness. It's the only entertainment that most of them can afford."

"Christa has to understand the background," Ruth said. "During the past six years, the permanent unemployment problem has grown so bad, particularly among the younger generation, that millions of them feel that they have been born into a world which is *no kerju*—not caring about them. Remember, too, the birthrate has dropped. The huge postwar generation that was born in the late 1940s and early 1950s dominates the country today. Through the late 1980s, the crime rate soared. Much of the vandalism and bombing of public buildings was the inevitable reaction of the dispossessed minority—the young people. Then the older generation retaliated. The death penalty for murder was restored in every state, and made operative for many crimes against property and persons."

"But what really stopped crime in the streets," David said, "and finally ended the muggings and hold-ups, was a combination of the legalization of drugs, like cocaine and marijuana, and easygoing drug-treatment centers, which supply those who are hooked on addictive drugs. Along with legalized prostitution, these new approaches drastically undercut the profits of crime. Finally, there was the legalization of the civilian stun gun."

"What's the stun gun?"

"They were available in the late 1970s," Ralph said, "but they were restricted to police use." He gestured toward a man sitting with a woman at one of the tables we were passing. They were both wearing dark red See-Thru jump suits. "Despite their clothing, they're probably not lecks," he said, "but you can see that they're wearing stun guns. Many people wear See-Thrus at night because they're available with a stun-gun pocket. The gun can be aimed without removing it from your clothing. If you fire a stun gun at an actual or probable assailant, you'll hit him with an electrical charge which, at a distance up to fifteen feet, will lay him flat on the ground and paralyze him for a half hour or more. If he has a heart condition, or some other medical problem, you might even kill him."

"Why aren't you carrying them?"

Chandra laughed. "Actually, only so-called responsible citizens can buy them, and they can only be obtained through a police station. But so many people carry them that the probability that you might be carrying one protects you. Stun guns have practically eliminated street crime, but they've given the legal profession a whole new source of revenue. Presumably innocent citizens are constantly suing people they claim shot them with stun guns."

"Another thing that has reduced social aggression is C and C." David pointed at some of the tables where people of all ages were drinking from tall glasses filled with a pink liquid. "C and C is a carbonated drink containing a little cannabis and coke—cocaine. Millions of people drink it. It's legal, and cheaper than alcohol. It gives you a quick high followed by a euphoric don't-give-a-damn feeling that lasts about an hour. You don't become belligerent during or after the high, and you can perform broad mechanical functions, like driving a Tric, without too much loss of ability, but until the effect wears off you become a repetitious and generally boring companion. Because it makes you feel like a rich-ik for the first hour or two after drinking it, a lot of people call it the Kennedy-sponsored tranquilizer. Before he was elected, Jason's

308

second wife was a large shareholder in one of the many soft-drink companies that make it."

At the Love Group's apartment Saturday night, I accepted David's invitation to join him in his privacy room, assured by a laughing Ruth that after sixteen years, David and I certainly deserved a few nights together to get reacquainted. Finally convinced by Chandra that she and Ralph would make sure that Ruth wasn't neglected, I lay naked on an air mattress, on top of David, and told him that a Love Group was obviously a man-created womb, a place where you could escape from a world that was still pretty sick and confused. I was going to say "fucked up"—but somehow or other in 1996 the expression seemed very dated.

Practicing tiny, wavelike undulations of my pelvis, which Adar Chilling, in her book, *Unilove,* calls the key to sexual meditation, and squeezing my vaginal muscles ever so gently on David's penis, which was deep inside me, I giggled into his ear, "I'm sure this is better than drinking C and C. How'm I doing?"

"You're a quick learner." With his eyes closed, David was smiling happily. "You're ready for sexual meditation anytime."

I snuggled my face against his. "How long can you last?"

"If you keep floating my penis in the lovely waves of your flesh, and we both become very conscious and concentrate on the rhythm of our hearts beating in unison, I can stay inside you for an hour or two."

"Without coming?"

"I am coming—into a complete unity with my loved one."

"I mean ejaculating."

David kissed me. "If we talk, and we don't drift immediately with each other into another consciousness, one of two things will happen: I'll get so interested in our conversation that the blood will flow out of my penis into my brain and eventually you'll have to kiss me alive." David was grinning at me. "That should be no problem. In your other life, apparently, you were an expert in penis resuscitation."

Laughing, I attempted to strangle him, and we rolled off the mattress. When we were rejoined finally, David continued, "Or we could immediately go to work—sex still being a form of work for most of the iks—and reach a climax. After-

309

ward, we could go to sleep and thus avoid further mental communication, or simply because we had nothing to talk about. Or, if you wish, and most women do, you can float in and out of as many climaxes as you wish."

"You mean that you could bring me to an orgasm and not ejaculate at all?"

"With your careful cooperation. If you were intent on having me climax with you, I probably couldn't last. In Unilove, both the male and female are fully aware of the female's orgasmic potential. They *both* enjoy her orgasm. Since the male can easily learn to maintain his erection while they float freely together, lost in the female's ecstasy, their total joy becomes an integral part of sexual meditation. Eventually, when the female wishes, *she* can bring the male to a climax, which then is often simultaneous with hers, because by this time the female has fully lost her identity and is perfectly responsive to the source of her delight."

I listened to David, astonished. "Do you make love with all the women you know this way? Do all Uniloves enjoy sex like this—as if it were a way of life, instead of a human compulsion?" Having asked the same questions of Paul, I could anticipate David's answers, but I still couldn't believe them.

David was smiling. "I don't know about all Uniloves, but I can assure you that we're not alone. There's millions of us. None of us who have learned the secret of Unilove could be involved very long with men or women who hadn't discovered it, too—or were afraid to explore themselves together as fully realized sexual creatures. That's what Unilove is all about. Unlike many religions, as you've just said, it's a way of life. A male and female joining their bodies for a few hours becomes a wonderful daily escape, for both of them, from the mundane world. Unlike most human activity, this kind of human blending is devoid of a man-conceived purpose."

David rolled me over, and I was underneath him. I could feel his penis in a lovely tentative search of my labia which seemed to last forever. Not until I was in gasping climax did he thrust very deeply, but when he did, almost immediately I climaxed again. Gratefully, I sobbed my release. Tears of happiness were flowing down my cheeks.

When I caught my breath, I smiled at him through rainy sunshine. "Thank you, dear one, *diprin*, that was most lovely. I'm sorry that I've been so fretful."

"I understand." David's penis was still deep inside me. "There's been a lot of talk about reincarnation, but you're feeling as if you have literally returned from the dead"—David laughed—"and now you're screwing with the devil who snuffed out your life."

"Not anymore." I laughed also. "I love you, David, but I'm afraid to admit it—because I'm not sure what loving involves in 1996."

"Simply daring to be whoever you really are," David said, and we lay quietly for a long time. Still inside me, he held me in his arms, his leg under my hip, his face against my breasts.

"The trouble is that I can't quite believe that this is reality," I whispered. I was both ecstatic and sad at the same time. "I keep remembering Rip Van Winkle. He slept for eighteen years."

"Then he became a complete bore. He told the story of his long sleep in the Kaatskills, over and over again, to anyone who would listen."

"And no one believed him," I said. I had an uneasy presentiment that when I finally got the courage and telephoned Penny, she wouldn't believe me, either.

◆

Monday morning at breakfast, hugging Ruth, I tried to thank her for the two nights I had spent with David, and to express how much I cared for all of them. I asked if David, since he was the only one who seemed to be free, could drive me to Marblehead.

Amused, Ruth assured me that David's time wasn't hers to keep or give. "We all love you, too, but David is, to use his own words, in direct charge of your reentry. Paul has assumed responsibility for Rose Plackett."

"Ruth is telling you," David said, "that until you are fully readjusted, I'm at your beck and call." Unsaid was the obvious. David was still afraid of losing me to some unforeseen emotional breakdown.

When all of them, except David, had left for work or school—Raynor was packing and getting ready to leave for a Premar commune in Saint Louis, and would be gone before Jag and Zara returned from Europe—I asked David if he would find the Muirs' telephone number. In a few seconds he was punching out the number on what he called a calcuphone. It didn't televise pictures, but it could be used for on-

311

line transmission of words and numbers, as well as serving as a personal calculator.

"She may ask if you have a picture phone, and if you do, to turn it on." David smiled. "You can be truthful. We don't. Even with a telvi transmission, they're too expensive for lecks."

A woman answered. "Yes, Ms. Muir is here. Will you turn on your picture phone, please?"

I told the woman—obviously a maid or housekeeper—that I only had a calcuphone connection.

"Whom shall I tell her is calling?"

"Talia." Tears in my eyes, I struggled with the answer. "Talia Dornroschen," I said. "I'm a friend of Penny's mother."

There was a long silence. Finally a pleasantly husky voice responded. This woman talking to me was my daughter. For a moment, I was afraid that the choking sob gathering in my throat would make it impossible for me to answer.

"Yes?" she said. "This is Penny Muir. I don't think Mrs. Lawlor got your name."

"I'm Talia Dornroschen," I said. "Many years ago, when you were very young, I knew your mother quite well. I've been away a very long time."

"My mother is dead." Penny sounded just a little bit irritated. Why was a stranger—a friend of a mother whom she had long forgotten—bothering her? "My mother drowned in a sailing accident many years ago."

"I know that." David was patting the tears dripping down my cheeks with a tissue. "For a few years in Cambridge and in New York City, your mother and I were very close friends. I even stayed overnight with you when your grandmother was living with you." The moment I said the words, I knew I had gone too far. All Penny had to do was to telephone my mother and she would confirm the nonexistence of Talia Dornroschen.

Penny was evidently digging in the same vein. "You must have known Karl, my father." Penny still sounded dubious, but it was becoming obvious that, if only as a gesture of politeness toward her dead mother, she'd have to invite me to her home or else find a spontaneous excuse to get rid of me. "Karl is in New York City now. My grandmother is in France. We're expecting them for a visit in a few weeks. Maybe you could visit us then."

"I really don't want to impose on you," I said, and my nervousness wasn't simulated. "But I have a friend who could drive me to Marblehead today. After today, I'm not sure how long I'll be here. I really would like to meet Christina's daughter. You were only a child when I knew you."

"I don't remember you." I heard her sigh, and then, after a long silence, she gave up. "Well, all right. You can come for lunch. But this afternoon, I have to take my daughter to her pediatrician."

Even before I hung up, I thought that I might faint. "I feel sickish," I told David. "I don't think I can go through with it." Poor Rip's words tumbled in my mind, and I repeated them to David. "God knows I'm not myself," he had said when he returned from the Kaatskills, "I'm somebody else—that's me yonder—no—that's somebody else got in my shoes, I was myself last night—but I fell asleep on the mountain, and everything's changed, and I'm changed, and I can't tell what's my name, or who I am."

Before we left, David offered me a tranquilizer, which I refused. "While I enjoyed kitsa with you," I told him with an affectionate grin, "I'm still wary of Dr. Convita's medicine." But an hour later, when we were driving through the familiar Marblehead streets, and past the harbor, I become so agitated that I was on the verge of telling David to turn around and go back to Boston. My mind was a centrifuge, whirling with unmeldable questions. What would Penny say when she saw me? If she didn't recognize me after these many years, should I tell her bluntly that I was Christina, her mother, or should I wait for her reaction?

"You'd better write the script as you go along," David said, empathizing with my thoughts, as I pointed to the familiar circular drive that curved in front of the house. Near Marblehead Point, on a rocky ledge, the house overlooked the harbor and the Atlantic Ocean.

As we walked toward the front door, David tried to reassure me. "I know that you're nervous. But you really appear much more self-controlled and mature than you did sixteen years ago." He squeezed my hand. "Actually, after sleeping for sixteen years—somehow or other you've acquired the look of a princess—a kind of royal bearing which becomes you. Your hair style abets the illusion—it's like a medieval princess's. If your daughter remembered her mother at all, it will be as a different, more distraught woman."

It hadn't occurred to me when I decided to wear my pale green See-Thru, rather than the dress Ruth had bought me—I was beginning to enjoy the feeling of nakedness that wearing only one piece of clothing gave me—that the dress would immediately identify me in Penny's mind as a leck. From the appearance of our former gambrel-style Colonial, onto which a new wing had been added, making it look even more elegant and upper income than I remembered it, it seemed unlikely that Newton Morrow would be welcome here.

A gray-haired woman—evidently Mrs. Lawlor—opened the door. Examining us suspiciously, she led us into the living room, and told us that Ms. Muir would be with us in a few minutes. Nearly overwhelmed, trying to shake off the feeling that I had merely gone shopping a few hours ago and had just returned, I noted the few changes in the room. The twin 9 by 12 foot Sarouk Orientals which Karl and I had chosen before we were married, were still on the highly polished oak floors. My Steinway was in the same position, facing the room on an angle, so that when I played it, I could enjoy watching my guests. While some of the chairs and one couch were new, they all seemed familiar. For a moment it was 1980, and I expected Penny or Michael to come bouncing into the room demanding that I take them to the beach, or sailing, or to the market.

The last painting I had finished but had never been happy with, hung over the fireplace. A woman in filmy white gown was stepping out of the sea in the moonlight. Her face was anguished. Behind her, on the black water, was an empty rowboat. I remembered Karl's bewilderment when I had told him the title: "Crossing—from Nowhere to Nowhere."

David pointed to an oil portrait that hung on a far wall. "Was that you?"

"Karl wanted it painted for our first anniversary," I said numbly.

David shrugged. "Don't expect her to rush in and exclaim 'Mother'," he said dryly. "You're still Christina, but transformed somehow. More blithe."

Knowing that he was trying to sedate me with hypnotic words, I was scowling at David when Penny walked into the room leading my granddaughter by the hand. Mrs. Lawlor was behind her, hovering uneasily in the background.

"I'm sorry to keep you waiting," Penny said, "but Christy is being tyrannical today. She refuses to have a nap." Penny looked at me warily, and I could see recognition and doubt flickering across her face. She was taller than I, and she wore her sandy hair, which was lighter than mine, long and flowing

314

on her shoulders. She had my dark blue eyes and full lips, but her jaw was like Karl's, honed and Germanic. She was a beautiful fraulein in complete possession of herself.

She watched me a little apprehensively as I picked up my granddaughter, who fearlessly snuggled against my neck. Almost stuttering, trying to smile at Christy through a film of tears, I managed to say, "This is Dr. Convita, who drove me here. I'm Talia Dornroschen."

I kissed Christy's cheek, and trying to seem gay and lighthearted, I told Penny what a beautiful child she was. "She looks very much like your mother," I said, wondering if Penny would see the resemblance between us.

Christy seemed to be delighted with me. She was babbling happily, and I gathered that she wanted me to see her dolls. But unlike her daughter, Penny was unrelenting. I remembered the same expression on her face when she was a child and we forced her to say hello to guests she didn't want to meet. Now, she looked so constrained that I wanted to hold her in my arms, too, and tell her that I loved her.

"After you phoned"—Penny's voice was cool and she sounded very unfriendly—"I telephoned my father." Penny hadn't invited us to sit down. Standing uneasily in the middle of the room, we were like suspicious alley cats encountering each other for the first time, the hair raised on our backs. "My father said that he'd check with Christina's mother, Grace, when she returned from France, but he had no recollection that my mother ever had any close women friends. Actually, although I was a child when she died, I've always felt that my mother wasn't a very social person."

I nodded. "That's right. She never overcame a basic feeling of inadequacy—that she was a failure. She was a manic-depressive, and often she was suicidal."

"But she didn't kill herself," Penny said determinedly, as if her words made it true. "She drowned in a sailing accident."

Oppressed by the unrelieved tension, David was shifting from one foot to the other. "Do you mind if we sit down?" he said finally. "Talia is a patient of mine. She's been through a very long physical and mental ordeal. She shouldn't be under stress."

Reluctantly, Penny gestured toward several wing chairs, and sat down in one herself. Mrs. Lawlor was standing near the hall door as if she was expecting someone else to arrive.

"I'll be quite frank with you, Ms. Dornroschen," Penny said. Her voice was icy, but her eyes never stopped searching my face. She seemed to be fighting against recognition. "It would be strange enough that a friend of my mother sought her out after so many years, but your name makes me feel very distrustful. Talia was one of the names of the Sleeping Beauty. When I told my father your last name, he told me that it was German. He translated it Briar Rose, which I'm sure that I don't have to tell you is another name for the Sleeping Beauty. He insisted, since I had made the mistake of inviting you into this house, that I should have police protection. My husband is in New York at the moment, with my father. He telephoned the Marblehead police. I expected that they would be here before you arrived."

Even while Penny was speaking the doorbell rang, and when Mrs. Lawlor opened it, two young men dressed in white See-Thru jump suits appeared in the front hall.

I heard David groan. "At least they're lecks," he said. By this time I couldn't help it, I was sobbing.

"You can search us." David stood up and walked toward the men, who didn't touch him. They could see that his jump suit had no stun-gun pocket like theirs. "We're unarmed," he told them coldly, and I knew that he was trying to restrain his anger. "This was to be purely a social visit. Perhaps we should simply leave, Talia."

Sighing, Penny waved the policemen out of the living room. "I'm sorry we alarmed you," she said. "These people probably mean no harm. They'll be leaving in a few minutes. Would it put you out too much if you waited outside in your Tric?"

"Really, Ms. Muir," one of them said, "if this man and woman have invaded your home, and are here against your will and are annoying you, why don't you simply tell them to leave now? We can't stay here all day."

"My husband shouldn't have phoned you," Penny said. She seemed uncertain, but she ignored Mrs. Lawlor's obvious disapproval. "I'm sorry we bothered you. Please leave. We'll be all right."

Staring warningly at us, they finally left with the admonition that if Penny needed them, they would be nearby. I was trembling with fright, and Christy, who had sensed the tension between us, hung on to me like a long-lost friend. "Daw, daw, see my daw," she said.

"She means her Raggedy Ann doll," Penny said, smiling for the first time. "It's her favorite. Christy really seems to like you."

"I'm her grandmother!" I sobbed.

From the expressions on Penny's and Mrs. Lawlor's faces, I wondered if they were going to call the police back.

"It's quite true," David said. Without going into much detail, he told Penny that sixteen years ago I had agreed to participate in one of the first experiments in hibernation. "Your mother is something of a pioneer. She and one other of our patients are the first human beings that we know of who have survived a long hibernation."

Penny listened to David with tears in her eyes. Distraught, she was wavering between belief and doubt. "I'm sorry," she said finally, after looking at me silently for nearly a minute. "I won't deny that you look a little like my mother. But many people resemble each other. Really, Dr. Convita, your story is quite incredible. My mother would be much older than this woman. I went to my mother's funeral. I know where she's buried."

"That woman wasn't your mother," David said. "I'm sure that we can prove it to you. Show her your 1980 driver's license, Christa."

I fumbled in the shoulder bag that Ruth had given me, and handed Penny the license.

"That's my mother's picture, but what does it prove?" Penny sat down beside me on the couch where I had slumped despondently after the police had left. "I'm sorry—whoever you may be. But nothing you're saying rings true. I know that, presumably, animals of all kinds have been hibernated. The news media is constantly televising and writing lurid stories about hibernation. Supposedly, when the Federal Drug Administration gives the approval, no one will ever have to die. They can be endlessly hibernated, while they wait for a better world." Penny shrugged. "Even my father, who's seventy-five, is very much interested in the possibility. But his medical friends tell him that the possibility for survival is very dubious. If he were hibernated, and he survived, he'd have irreparable brain damage. If that's the state of the art in 1996, it seems very unlikely that sixteen years ago anyone would have had the medical knowledge to hibernate you, or that you would have actually survived. Not only is it completely beyond belief, but it's even more improbable that my mother would have consented."

"It's worse than that." Mrs. Lawlor finally voiced her disapproval. "I don't care what they tell you, Ms. Muir. You'd better be careful. They're lecks. They've got some trick up their sleeve."

Penny nodded. "I'm sure that you're both aware that the presidential campaign has divided this country. When strangers arrive here wearing leck costumes, we can't help but feel suspicious—especially because my father, Karl Klausner, and my brother, Michael, have been very active in the nationwide effort to stop Newton Morrow. I can't help but feel that you may have other motivations for being here."

"Like what?" I demanded. I was suddenly irritated by the Klausnerlike attitude that dominated my daughter's thinking. I was thinking that I should have stayed alive, if only to have prevented Karl from molding two duplicates of himself.

"Like kidnapping!" Penny replied, and then suddenly she burst into tears. "Oh, please—Talia, Christina, my mother, whoever you are, I'm sorry. You see, both my father and my husband are always telling me that I'm too trusting. I guess that the truth is that I'd like nothing better than to believe you. I really don't care whether you're a leck or not." Impulsively, Penny put her arm around me for a second, and then quickly withdrew it. "You're just too beautiful to be evil," she said, tears streaming down her cheeks.

"I love you, Penny," I said, and I was feeling very hopeless. "Maybe we can never bridge the past. Maybe it's just as well. I might be just as bad an influence on you in 1996 as I was in 1980."

Then, remembering one reason I had come, I told Penny that in the corner room overlooking the ocean, there used to be a library. As I said it, I guessed that she was probably thinking that criminals, bent on some nefarious purpose, would have thoroughly researched Christina's life. "I kept duplicate copies of my books of poetry on the bottom shelves."

Clearly trying to accept the reality of me, though her mind kept rejecting such fantasies, Penny answered, "My mother's books are still there. When my father married Lizabeth Geist, Liz wanted to open up the walls and put in picture windows, but he told her that someday, when the world finally realized Christina's talent, he was going to give her books and paintings to Radcliffe."

I asked Penny if I might look at the library. Dubiously, she led us into the book-lined room. It hadn't been changed at all. My mahogany desk was still in the corner by the window. Mory might have said that right now a former self of Chris-

318

tina could be sitting at the desk staring pensively at the ocean. Christina's sister. If she were there, she wasn't visible.

Suddenly, seeing myself objectively and smiling at the lovely human futility of my fame-seeking, I asked Penny if the world had recognized Christina North yet.

"Not for her poetry or paintings, I'm afraid." Penny smiled. "She wrote a novel—a kind of women's liberation look at the Sleeping Beauty legend. It's still listed in the card catalogue at the library."

My eyes were searching the shelves where I had kept the copies of my books of poetry. They weren't there. I pointed to a shelf that held some unfamiliar books, and asked Penny if she knew where Christina's poetry was kept.

She opened a cupboard and handed me five of my slim books of poetry. "When Tom and I reopened the house three years ago, there were only five copies left. Daddy used to give the books to people who seemed interested. I put these away for our children—and for Michael's."

"Do you like my poetry?" I was slipping open one book after the other, looking in the back covers. Searching for the key, I suddenly didn't care whether it was there or not. You can't go home again, I kept thinking. You'll never find the daughter you abandoned, nor your son. There was no key.

Penny wasn't accepting the fact that it was my poetry. "When I was younger, I didn't like it. It seemed too morbid. Too self-centered. But later, I realized that Christina's poetry is a great cry for the love that she never managed to find."

"Maybe she didn't know how to give love," I said. I hugged Christy, whom I was still carrying, and gave her to her mother.

"My grandmother tells me that sometimes I act very like my mother. She means that I don't respond well to her, or any women." Penny sighed. "I guess that a lot of men loved my mother. Warren Ellison told my father that he adored her. In fact, it was after Warren and Karl came to dinner last spring that I decided to put Christina's books away. Warren was looking through the library, and he found them. He asked Karl if he could have a couple of copies."

I could visualize Warren nervously flicking through my poetry. No matter what he had told Penny or my father, Warren never read anything but business books or trade journals. But my poetry probably reminded him vividly of his third and last fuck with Christina. The Scotch tape with which I had sealed the key into the book had probably dried out. The

319

key might even have dropped into his hand. I could imagine his, and Karl's, complete disbelief when they opened my safety-deposit box and discovered my secret hoard. Gloomily telling myself that I might be alive but the chapter of my life called Christina Klausner was closed forever, I asked David to take me home. Home? Where was that?

Penny seemed relieved. She didn't follow through with her luncheon invitation. "I'm really sorry," she said at the door. "I want to believe you. I feel very emotionally involved with you. Perhaps you and Dr. Convita will come to dinner when my husband returns. I'll invite my brother, Michael. Where should I contact you?"

"I'm not sure where I'm going to be." I snuggled Christy's cheek. Her hand was still trustingly in mine. "I'll telephone you. Could I ask you one thing?"

Penny looked at me sadly, expectantly.

"Do you go to church?"

Penny was puzzled. For a moment she hesitated, then she said, "Yes, quite often. Tom and I don't agree on religion. I'm a Unilove."

Sobbing, I hugged her. "Maybe way back then, when I should have been, I really wasn't your mother. I'm glad that we have something in common."

When we were in the Tric, driving back toward Boston, David squeezed my hand. "One of the problems you have to contend with, Christa, is that you're much prettier than your daughter, and you're only twelve years older."

I was feeling too sad to argue with him.

———————◆———————

When Ralph told Chandra and me that his friend Bill Westwood definitely wanted the three of us to come to Warren Ellison's suite at the Hyatt-Pilgrim for cocktails before the rally, it hardly bothered me that Warren would have been alerted, either by Karl or Michael, that some woman was impersonating Christina Klausner. I was completely unnerved, though, at the prospect of meeting Michael, whom I was sure that Penny had told about my visit. Ralph had explained that Michael was very active in the Massachusetts Democratic campaign to reelect Jason Kennedy. He would be on the speaker's platform at the rally. I told Ralph that I really wasn't sure that I could handle an encounter with my son, ever—and especially not confined in a room with a gathering of upper-level Massachusetts politicians and business executives who were giving Jason Kennedy their all-out support. While I had never been a very political person, the coalition of Democrats and Republicans seemed unreal to me. Would Jennifer Manchester be at the cocktail party, too?

Ralph assured me that neither Jennifer nor Michael would be in Warren's suite. "Ellison isn't scheduled to speak before nine-thirty. He'll be followed by Jennifer Manchester. I think she's staying at the Boston Sheraton. According to Bill Westwood, Michael is coordinating the rally, which begins at eight o'clock at the Astrodome. Michael is in charge of the entertainment. Owners of the Astrodome donated the time to the anti-Morrow rally. Admission price is $15.00 which can be donated either to the Democratic or Republican party. The Astrodome holds ninety thousand people. To fill it up, they're offering two hours of entertainment by top comedians, singers, musicians, and sports celebrities. Most of them are supporting Kennedy, but whether they're for Manchester or Kennedy, they have one thing in common—they are totally against Morrow." Ralph added, "Some of these entertainers earn over a million dollars annually. You can see why they are *firpa*—frightened—by Morrow.

"As for the Republicans, when the Democrats hung onto the Presidency in 1980, they had usurped most of the Republican programs. Liberal Republicans, whether they admitted it or not, were Democrats. The Old Guard conservative Republicans, the rich-iks, never could understand that they had no political strength left. The Libertarian party tried to become a third party, but they were regressive. They were trying both to eliminate big government and restore a laissez-faire capitalism. They refused to admit that private ownership of the wealth of the world was an historical social phase that had served its purpose.

"All the Republicans can possibly do in this election is to stem the Morrow tide. The only power they have left is to be middleman on the seesaw. Many of those who still vote Republican aren't too happy with Jennifer. They would prefer to have her pursue a harder line against both Morrow and Kennedy. No one really knows, but the Democrats obviously hope that a vote for a Republican candidate is an alternative vote against Morrow. Incidentally, Jennifer's running mate for Vice-President, Robert Lee, is black. He was formerly a senator from Georgia. However, most of the pollsters believe that the black vote will go solidly for Newton Morrow."

321

Chandra told me that we would be sitting in special reserved seats on the ground level, a few yards from the circular platform that would be erected for the rally. "We haven't told Bill Westwood or his pair bond Janice Bradford anything about you, except that you're a friend of ours. If you don't want to meet Michael or Jennifer, you don't have to. In fact, if you wish, we can leave before the rally is over."

"I'll go to the cocktail party." And then, teasing all of those who were listening to our conversation in their communal bedroom, I said, "I guess I have to go to the rally to discover whether I'm an ik or a leck." I grinned. "Or maybe I'm just a blank."

I was thinking, too, what if Warren Ellison had found my key, he'd be the one person in the world who could prove that I was really Christina Klausner. I was suddenly anxious to observe his shocked expression when he saw me.

While Ralph and Chandra seemed a little dubious when I told them I wanted to wear a See-Thru, instead of my ik dress—they had decided that they weren't going to identify themselves at this particular gathering as lecks—they finally agreed that it might be amusing, especially when I told them that the combination—me, plus my dress, might make Warren speechless for the entire evening.

"Bill probably won't mind," Ralph said, "but you have to understand, Christa, that wearing a See-Thru to a cocktail party in 1996 is equivalent to wearing blue jeans in 1980."

"Don't worry about it," Chandra said. "Janice will approve of you. She refuses to commit herself. Half the time she tells Bill that she's going to vote for Morrow, and then she becomes apprehensive. She's afraid that Morrow's faith in the people is too idealistic, and there are too many idiots who couldn't function without a Big Brother government to take care of them."

"I don't understand how you and Chandra can be invited to a Stop Morrow rally," I said, "or even why you would want to be invited. Aren't you voting for Newton Morrow?"

Ralph laughed. "We've known Bill and Janice for five years. We never let politics come between us. Politics aside, many Democrats live in Love Groups. Occasionally, Chandra sleeps overnight in Bill's group's apartment, and when we can stop arguing, Janice and I enjoy kitsa together. Anyway, the reasons we're going to the rally is to keep an eye on the enemy. Also, while Boston has always voted solidly Democratic—especially if you have a name like Kennedy—no one is sure whether the huge student population won't manage to infiltrate the Astrodome and try to shout down the speakers. The student population throughout the country is solidly behind Morrow. So it could be an interesting evening."

When we arrived on the thirty-ninth floor of the Hyatt-Pilgrim—according to Ralph, the last building in Boston, completed in 1990, which exceeded the new height regulations—Warren's suite was already overflowing with exuberant men and women trying to get the ear of the Secretary of the Treasury. Surprisingly, while there seemed to be no lack of alcoholic camaraderie, very few people were smoking.

"Like automobiles," Chandra told me when I commented on it, "tobacco is another American institution that is no longer providing the hundreds of thousands of jobs it used to. While Jason Kennedy doesn't smoke, he continuously points out that the average American's improved health from kicking the habit has contributed to unemployment. A state like North Carolina, for example, is a disaster area."

If I hadn't already seen Warren on a Life-a-Vision news program, I wouldn't have recognized him. My former lover's hair was now so black and lush that it had obviously been stitched on his balding pate. Unfortunately, his thickened features, blubbery chin, and the deep crevasses around his mouth belied his youthful hair, and gave him the intractable, unyielding look of an elder statesman who was secure in his belief that God was not only on his side, but that God's words issued from his mouth.

Taller, at six feet two, than most of the admirers surrounding him, Warren looked uneasy when he spotted me. While Chandra was introducing me to Bill and Janice, Ralph had ferreted his way through the crowds to the bar, and returned with a drink that he assured me was not C & C, but a new pink vodka drink that contained only about 20 percent alcohol. Relative to the inflated cost of other liquors, it was an inexpensive and very popular drink.

Glass in hand, I edged into Warren's group. "There's no question," he was saying, "that Morrow has strength in New York City and Los Angeles, but there's nothing to fear. By November fifth, he'll have both feet in his mouth. Yesterday in Springfield, he was sucking his toe when he admitted that his government wouldn't be too sympathetic with people who wasted the money in the insane Capital Accounts that he's going to give everybody. He implied that a few thousand

323

starving citizens, who had spent their money unwisely, might become an object lesson for the rest of us. He didn't quite say, 'Let them eat cake,' but that's what he meant. Believe me, underneath his fatherly smile, and his I-love-everybody act, Morrow is a ruthless dictator. The only way he can make his New Tomorrow work is to get rid of more than half of the people in this country. Millions of Americans are getting the message loud and clear. They know that they'll end up in concentration camps, or being ruthlessly liquidated, if Morrow is elected. When I was a young man, they used to say, "There ain't no such thing as a free lunch." The Democrats may have been unable to stop inflation, but most workers' incomes have kept up with it. I can tell you that if everyone gets thirty thousand American dollars handed to him on a platter without working for it, the dollar won't be worth the cost of the paper it's engraved on."

While he was speaking, Warren was watching me with a deep frown etching his face. Finally he said, "If you'll excuse me, it seems that a Morrow adherent has infiltrated our gathering—or perhaps that young woman over there simply feels more sexually available wearing a See-Thru." Everyone laughed as he took me by the arm, declaiming loudly, "Maybe if this young woman will listen to me, I can make her see the error of her ways."

Warren ushered me past a surprised Ralph and Chandra. Nodding briefly at Bill Westwood, and gripping my arm tightly, he led me down the hotel hallway. He opened the door of a nearby room and pushed me in ahead of him. "All right, young woman, I've heard all about you. You and a male friend of yours had the cold nerve to force your way into the Muir home. Who the hell are you? Why are you claiming that you're Christina Klausner?"

I smiled at him coolly. "Warren, I *am* Christina Klausner, and you know it!"

"For Christ's sake," he exploded, "don't give me that bullshit!"

I knew that Warren was trying to cover his shock and complete bewilderment with harsh words and a callous bluffness that he thought might unnerve me.

"Christina Klausner died sixteen years ago," he said. "I went to her funeral."

"Did you ever see her body?"

"There was no face left. She had been in the ocean for months."

324

Enjoying the slow game of showdown, I said, "The body in that coffin wasn't me, Warren."

"I don't give a damn whether it was Christina or not. You most certainly aren't Christina Klausner."

"Why not?"

"Look at yourself in the mirror," Warren was smiling triumphantly. "Christina would be nearly fifty."

"Didn't Penny tell you that I was hibernated for sixteen years? My body metabolism practically stopped. I presume that you're familiar with hibernation."

"The whole hibernation business is a futuristic daydream," Warren said angrily. His face was mottled with bright red spots. "I'll give you an inside tip, young woman. The Federal Drug Administration is never going to permit the use of hibernating drugs or techniques."

"Once you told me that you loved me, Warren." I spoke in a purposely husky and seductive voice that I hoped he was gradually remembering. "How could you ever forget jumping off Karl's yacht with me, while we consummated our last fuck? I'm sure that your wife and Karl have never forgotten it." It was a low blow, but Warren, glaring at me like a lion with a mouse under its paw, deserved it.

"My wife died eight years ago," he said coldly. "I don't know what kind of blackmail you're up to, but what happened that night became common knowledge in Boston society. Anyway, you can't make political points with that old chestnut. I'm going to give it to you straight. If you don't stop whatever you're up to, Karl Klausner will have you arrested for impersonating his wife and attempting fraud."

"I'm only too happy to stay out of Karl's life and yours," I said. Then, crossing my fingers, I played my trump card. "All I want is the certificates you and Karl stole out of my safety-deposit box."

I had hit a home run! I could tell by the astonishment and flicker of guilt on Warren's face that he had found my key.

"I don't know what the hell you're talking about." The tone of Warren's voice was no longer so confident. He ignored the insistent knocking on the bedroom door, and an annoyed voice telling him: "Mr. Ellison. Mr. Ellison. It's nine o'clock. We have to leave for the Astrodome. You're speaking at nine-thirty."

"You know that I'm Christina." My voice was adamant. "The moment you found that key, you knew that it opened one of the safety-deposit boxes in your bank. Only two people knew about that box. Me and Hank Hutchings, and Hank's dead." I laughed sarcastically. "You can tell Christina's dear husband that not only is his third wife alive, but that she wants her money."

———◆———

We drove to the Astrodome in rented Trics. Temporarily separated from Bill and Janice, I told Ralph and Chandra that I felt like an actress who was appearing in an extemporaneous drama for which there was no script, and neither the actors nor the audience knew the ending. While I had obviously scrambled Warren Ellison's brains, I was positive that he didn't believe that I was Christina Klausner.

I suddenly wondered whether it mattered. I certainly didn't want to resume married life with Karl. I was sure that he and Warren had opened my safety-deposit box. I knew that I probably would never get my money. Not unless I was willing to crawl into bed with the master and beg. I wondered if at seventy-five years of age, Karl could still get it up. If he couldn't, neither tears nor contrition nor my thirty-three-year-old body would entice him, anyway.

My only choice was to accept the hospitality of David's Love Group as long as it lasted. But I still couldn't believe that an extra woman—or too much concentration on a particular woman—wouldn't turn the best of Love Groups into separate warring factions. I wasn't even sure that I could adjust to the less possessive sexuality of 1996, although the truth was that "until death do us part" had never been an integral part of my scheme of things, or for that matter, of millions of those who were alive when I disappeared in David's hibernaculum. Perhaps the loose reins of pair bonding, contrasted with formal marriage, give individuals sufficient commitment and interpersonal security without the ownership chains of marriage. Maybe the Love Group itself, surviving above the individuals, was the rock one could swim to if he or she was foundering.

One thing I was sure of. If hibernating ever became a way of life, hibernators would quickly discover that, like dying, hibernation broke the fragile human connection. I was certain that if I met Michael tonight, I would be as threatening to him as I had been to Penny and Warren Ellison. As for Mory—God, I didn't even want to think about an encounter with him. Why should he care whether I was alive or dead?

In pursuit of my evanescent ego, I had rejected Mory's love as thoroughly as I had Karl's.

Ralph drove the Tric into a circular garage surrounding the Astrodome, and we watched it disappear on a computer-controlled belt that would park it, and bring us another when we left. I told Ralph and Chandra that while I'd like to see Michael from a distance, I was really quite squeamish about meeting him—or Jennifer, for that matter. If I was introduced to him, most certainly I wasn't going to try to prove that I was Christina, his mother. For the rest of this evening, and maybe forever, I was Talia Dornroschen.

The huge round Astrodome had been built in the early 1990s, in a former area of decayed housing a few miles from the core of Boston. "Six years ago," Ralph said, "you wouldn't have dared to walk around here during the day, let alone at night. It was called District Two on the police maps. It had more poverty and human degradation than any other area in Massachusetts. It accounted for more than a third of the murders, rapes, muggings, robberies, and assaults that took place in the city."

As we walked toward one of the Astrodome entrances, I asked them what had happened to the people who had lived there. "They've moved closer, or they're living in the ring of suburbs that surrounded the old city. Whenever they're evicted, they create poverty and ghettos somewhere else. Until Newton Morrow came along, human equality was still predicated on millions of people existing in human garbage dumps. During the past fifteen years, an interesting reversal has taken place. The core-city areas now have better apartment housing—much of it was expropriated from the former poor—and more community ambiance than the perennial low-income high-rise apartments that they've built on the outskirts or in the suburbs."

Near the entrance of the Astrodome, hundreds of young people had formed a long human tunnel through which it was necessary to pass to get into the lobby. While there was no screaming or yelling, most of them seemed pretty grim. Many of them were selling candles and exhorting us to "light a candle for Morrow." Others carried signs. MAKE SURE TO-MORROW COMES! THE GOING GOING GONE GENERATION SUPPORTS MORROW! BY THE YEAR 2000 WE'LL ALL BE UNEMPLOYED! MORROW WILL SUPPORT OUR PARENTS SO WE DON'T HAVE TO! $30,000 OR BUST!THE RICH-IKS MASPI! Ralph chuckled at that one. "It means the rich-iks suck!" He pointed

327

to another sign with Loglan words. YOU ARE LOPO STOKAMPA!
"It means that *you* are the struggle."

Some of the youngsters were waving us to hurry or we'd
miss hearing Secretary of the Treasury IK-son, who had just
entered the arena ahead of us. I still couldn't understand why
the demonstration was so low-keyed.

"The reason is standing behind them," Chandra explained,
and she pointed to at least a hundred men and women wearing See-Thru jump suits with stun guns. "As you can see, the
police are here. Some of them are probably sympathetic with
the *nirbos*."

"No one under thirty can own a stun gun," Ralph said.
"There's a black market, of course, but if you get caught with
one that isn't registered, you're in for real trouble, and that
applies to any hand guns. The only revolution that will ever
occur in America will be at the ballot box. The basic theory
hasn't changed. You can speak as harshly as you wish against
the government, but if you raise your hands to strike, you'll
probably get them cut off."

Inside the arena, we could see and hear thousands of
people cheering, with only a few scattered boos. Warren Ellison and Governor Fauci of Massachusetts had just mounted
the center platform. Before we were led to our seats, we
passed through a metal detector monitored by two policemen.
"There's security guards on every access aisle," Ralph said.
"Occasionally they uncover a stun gun, or small arms—but
what they're really looking for are Voice-Amps. They're
about the size of a cigarette package, but they amplify the human voice twenty times more than the old bullhorns." He
grinned. "An aggravated student audience might take it into
their heads to outtalk the speakers!"

We slid past earlier arrivals into our seats, which had been
erected in the center of the arena, about 35 feet away from
the speakers' platform. Chandra pointed out Jennifer Manchester. She was mounting the stairs to the platform, and
waving to a group of people seated just below us. For a moment her eyes caught mine, and I joined with the others and
waved good-naturedly at her. Then a delayed reaction occurred. She stopped and said something to a man following
her. He looked quickly at me and shook his head. When she
finally sat down in an empty seat next to Warren Ellison, her
eyes kept flickering over me, a puzzled expression on her
face. While I was aware of her watching me, I avoided looking directly at her. I wondered what was going through her

head. I guessed that I was a long-forgotten face, a name and a memory that wouldn't jell in her brain. Even if she finally identified me as a possible look-alike of her apartment mate, that was a quarter of a century ago, and she would have to shrug off the resemblance as pure coincidence. I looked too young.

I told Chandra my thoughts, and she laughed. "She probably thinks that you're a friendly Boston Republican—someone she's met before—a party contributor. You're probably driving her crazy, because she can't remember your name." But then I was no longer worrying about Jennifer. At a signal from a young man who had been sitting next to Warren, the orchestra, identified by Ralph as the ELP's Babies—presumably the children of Emerson Lake Palmer—an eighty-five-piece group whose instruments were each hooked independently into the amplification system—reduced their volume so that he could be heard.

I listened to him with tears in my eyes. No one had to tell me that he was Michael Klausner—my son.

"For the next five minutes," he said, "before we listen to Secretary of the Treasury, Warren Ellison, and our lovely Republican candidate, Jennifer Manchester, who has so graciously agreed to add her voice to the growing anti-Morrow tide, the ELP's are going to play an original Colormuse composition, 'Space Love,' which will be projected over the full dome of the Astrodome. As you may know, the unique glass of this dome can be controlled so that it becomes a mirror, or it can be made opaque, translucent, or completely clear. 'Space Love' will be followed by brief talks by our distinguished guests. When they have finished, Bob Dines, the famous comedian, will continue as master of ceremonies. Bob has several surprise celebrities from the sports and entertainment worlds, who will appear later. The ELP's will conclude the evening program with another fifteen-minute coordinated Colormuse offering."

As Michael was sitting down, Ralph quickly explained to me that laser-light shows, which originated in the late 1970s, had culminated in Colormuse, a popular new mass art form that created a hypnotic alternate-consciousness effect on many viewers. Colormuse was also used in many Unilove Churches, which had bubble roofs, in order to create a feeling of cosmic blending. Even before the dome lighting had been turned off completely, red, yellow, blue, and green laser difractions raced around the dome in ever-changing patterns against a total, slowly changing, subdued kaleidoscopic projection that enveloped the entire audience of nearly ninety thousand people in a huge, living umbrella.

As the strange beat—I found out later it was called chug—grew in intensity, or diminished to a whisper, the color patterns evoked the music in erotic embraces or frantic splashing of color which exploded over the ceiling a thousand times more effectively than a fireworks finale. The total effect of music combined with color gave the viewer a curious sense of self-detachment. It occurred to me when the arena was once again normally lighted that while it might not have been intentional, five minutes of Colormuse became a subtle kind of brainwashing. The combination of music and moving color separated you from yourself and your normal flow of consciousness and made you ready for any kind of input.

Once again Michael, boyish in his enthusiasm, sandy-haired, nearly six foot tall, was talking to the audience. "Wasn't that great?" And they agreed with a huge roar of approval. Standing on the middle of the platform, he spoke to them with a Harvard accent that put an "r" on words that ended in "a."

"We hope that you've enjoyed the show thus far," he said, and as he spoke he slowly turned in quarter circles so that he was facing at least a fourth of the audience. "There's much more to come. But despite Newton Morrow, nothing is quite free in this world, so now you have to pay the piper for a few moments"—there were groans from the audience—"but we promise you, the speeches are going to be short and simple. I'm sure many of you remember Robert Frost wondering whether the world would end in fire or ice, and he came to the conclusion that if it had to perish twice, ice would suffice. When I was a child, my mother taught me some rhymes about ice. One of them was the shortest and most famous political speech on record. 'Ladies and gentlemen, take my advice. Pull down your pants and slide on the ice.' "

Michael waved happily at the roar of laughter. "But there's another one—in fact, a lot of them about Simple Simon, who learned the value of a penny, or who slid on the ice before the ice would bear him. And there's old Mother Goose's admonition, which evidently nobody ever taught Newton Morrow, 'If wishes were horses, beggars would be kings.' Tonight, because there are so many Americans who are apparently willing to slide on thin ice, with or without their pants, or who believe what Newton Morrow gives, he won't take away the day after election—if he's elected, which I can assure you he won't be—tonight we are joining here to listen to Secretary Ellison and Jennifer Manchester reaffirm a basic American principle. The only thing which will save America is a free competitive marketplace and a society where each person can rise to the top by his or her own hard work. Years ago, when the Democratic leaders discontinued price controls on every form of energy, they proved the theory conclusively. Today, we all may pay more than we used to for electricity and storage batteries and oil, but no one is afraid that we are not going to have enough energy to keep us out of trouble. And because the Democrats have encouraged the competitive spirit and created the all out government funding for it, by the turn of the century nuclear fusion will be commercially possible. The by-product of fusion, cheap electricity and hydrogen fuel, is going to turn this planet into a Garden of Eden, not just for the people of America, but for every human being on earth. The gross human product will triple. There will be no have-not nations or have-not people. A few years from now, when we read about the reduced material-growth theories of men like Newton Morrow and his predecessors for the past twenty years, we will consider them the mutterings of maniacs.

"Before I turn the platform over to Governor Tom Fauci, who will introduce Secretary of the Treasury Warren Ellison, I want to point out that tonight is a political first. For the first time, a prominent Democratic leader and a Republican candidate for President see eye to eye on one thing. On November fifth, it will not only be good-bye Morrow, but good-bye to his style New Tomorrow."

When Michael sat down, his eyes, which had been probing my face when he was turned in my direction, were now fixed intently on me. I was so uneasily aware, first of Michael's glances, and then of Jenny's, that I scarcely listened to either of them declaim against Mory when they spoke. Michael seemed to be trying to reach me telepathically. I couldn't make out his garbled message, but it seemed to be a loving one. Had Warren told Michael that he had talked with me? Warren had arrived only a few minutes before us, so he probably hadn't had time. If he was aware that I was in the audience, he was ignoring me. But I was certain that Penny, at least, must have told Michael about her strange visitor. Whether Michael believed her or not, his almost-continuous absorption with my face seemed to reflect no anger. On the contrary, while I had no idea whether I might be misreading his expression, he made me feel as if I were a beautiful stranger he had seen at a distance in a crowd. By his eyes alone, he was trying to communicate his need to know me, to talk with me. The déjà vu feeling that enveloped me suddenly made sense as I realized that Michael was watching me the same way Mory had, long ago, when he first took me to lunch in Harvard Square.

Jennifer's surveillance of me was much less intense. She seemed bemused, as if she was trying to exhume some long-forgotten memory from her past. When she spoke to the audience, she projected a cool, laughing personality, which after the brain-crunching tension of Warren's hateful words (he had implied that crucifixion was too good for Newton Morrow, the self-appointed Messiah) was a pleasant relief.

"I'm not ready to light a candle for Newton Morrow," she said, smiling, "but I am glad to hear that the Morrow candle-lighting ceremony is helping the New England bayberry candle industry. While it is a happy symbolism to try and connect the lighting of bayberry candles with the Pilgrims, and with a 'small is beautiful' cottage industry, it wasn't until 1989 that a method of cultivating and harvesting bayberries was finally developed that made it practical to produce bayberry candles and sell them at prices that would compete with petroleum-based products. One of my fears of Newton Morrow is that he is so imbued with old Schumacher's 'small is beautiful' philosophy and 'right livelihood' that if we followed his drummers, we'd soon be picking bayberries by hand again and employing human beings to do work—just to keep them busy—that could be done better by computers."

Jennifer went on to compare Democratic efforts over the past sixty years, beginning with Franklin Roosevelt, to use deficit spending to control the economy, with Republican attempts to balance the budget, stop government spending, and let the people themselves, rather than the bureaucrats, spend us into prosperity.

"Now, more than sixty years later," she said, "the Democrats still create huge unbalanced budgets that crowd our private spending and force us to live with Big Brother government. By now they are trying to blend these approaches with the Republican alternatives, and at the same time insist that somehow the marketplace is the best regulator of human activities. The truth is that today neither party is certain, nor are their economists, to what extent fiscal and monetary policy, or spontaneous public spending, affects real output and employment or actually contributes to more inflation."

Jennifer concluded that while she couldn't endorse Jason Kennedy's monetary program, she was quite certain that Newton Morrow's proposal for people's capitalism was simply pie-in-the-sky daydreaming. Then she said a curious thing, which brought frowns from Governor Fauci and Warren Ellison and just about everybody on the platform. "However, I want the people of America to know that as a Republican in the liberal tradition, when it comes to reducing big government and providing the environment for a new generation to enjoy their independence as free and equal citizens, while I may not agree with Newton Morrow's methods, I do believe in the principles, if they are achieved in the Republican way."

When Jennifer finished—even before she reached her seat—the entire Astrodome was suddenly plunged into darkness. I wondered if ELP's Babies were about to play an unannounced Colormuse number. The windows of the Astrodome were clear. For a moment, thousands upon thousands of us were sitting in total darkness. A full moon, clearly visible above the Astrodome, provided the only light in the arena. As the audience began voicing its impatience, four male voices, speaking in unison from opposite perimeters of the Astrodome, dominated all other sounds. They were using Voice-Amps, which they had apparently spirited past the metal detectors. "Please don't panic," they said. "With the unplanned cooperation of ELP's Babies, we have turned off all the Astrodome lights. After we have lighted candles for Newton Morrow, and they have burned for a full two minutes, the lights will be turned on again."

"My God, the *nirbos* did it!" Ralph, standing beside me, was enthusiastic. "And the children shall lead ye," he marveled, as candles suddenly flickered all over the arena. "There must be ten thousand of them. That's a damn good percentage of the audience."

Backlighted by the moonlit night, the candles created an eerie religious feeling, which was slowly counteracted by a mounting tension that crept through the Astrodome like an evil presence. Evidently Michael realized that the crowd would need an injection of humor to keep it from rioting. Using the stage amplification system, which was still operating, he addressed the audience. "Hi, this is Mike Klausner. If the person sitting next to you is holding a lighted candle, don't blow it out! Keep cool! Congratulate him! We're all impressed. We don't know how the Morrow supporters managed to coordinate this little spectacle, but the result is impressive. The management of the Astrodome may even begin holding candlelight services in the future. In some religions, they light a candle for the dead. Morrow's may not be dead yet, but we can assure you that on November fifth Morrow's candle will sputter and go out forever."

As Michael finished his speech, the lights came back on, and the ELP's began playing chug to the enthusiastic screams and approval of the crowd. Political animosities were forgotten. "Chug is the *sonda*—sound—of the nineties," Ralph shouted in my ear. "The music is composed by a computer. A synthesizer feeds the sounds of the individual instruments into the amplification system, and mixes them. If you want to leave before you go deaf, it's okay with us."

As we edged toward the aisle, I saw Bill and Janice waiting with Michael. Jennifer was standing behind them. I knew that I was trapped. I noticed that Warren Ellison and his political entourage had left the stadium the moment the lights came on. At least, I didn't have to face him again. Several men, who I discovered later were Secret Service men, were standing protectively near Jennifer.

Bill introduced Michael to Chandra and Ruth, and then, laughing, introduced me to Michael. "Talia Dornroschen, the woman you're so anxious to meet. I guess I don't have to warn you that she thinks she's a leck," Bill said.

Smiling, Michael took my hand, which I hadn't offered to him. "Jennifer Manchester and I just discovered that we do have something in common," he said, and beckoned to Jennifer. "We both have a feeling that we've met you somewhere before."

Bewildered, wondering why Michael was concealing his obvious knowledge—either Warren or Penny must have told him that I was claiming to be his mother—I nodded at them. "I guess I have a common face," I said. "Many people have told me I look like someone they know."

"You remind me of a friend I lived with in Cambridge many years ago," Jennifer said. "You wear your hair differently, but facially she could have been your twin sister. I was wondering if she might be a relative of yours. Her name was Christina North."

Michael's dark blue eyes were suddenly bright with tears.

"That's very odd. Christina North was my mother's maiden name."

"I'm sorry to disappoint you," I said, trying to keep my voice steady. "Unfortunately, I have no sisters, younger or older. My family never lived in Cambridge."

I kept wondering why Michael didn't confront me with my visit to Penny and ask me why I had claimed that I was Christina Klausner. When he said nothing about it, I was certain that he thought I was a fraud, and was determined to lead me on until he discovered what motivated me.

Jennifer bid us good-bye. "I'm sure that *my* Christina would never have appeared at an anti-Morrow rally," she said. "It's been nice to meet you, Ms. Dornroschen. I hope, at least, you are one leck who decides to vote Republican."

Michael seemed disappointed. "Warren Ellison invited you to the lobster buffet at the Hyatt," he said. "He'll be really unhappy if you don't join us." Michael was speaking to Jenny, but his eyes were supplicating mine. "It's early—I'm finished here. As you can hear, Bob Dines is taking over. I'd like to invite Ms. Dornroschen and her friends to the buffet, too."

Jennifer smiled. "I really don't think a Republican should break bread with Democrats, but since it's lobster, which only Democrats can afford these days, how can I refuse? Tomorrow on the news services they will announce, 'Jenny Manchester takes Democratic bribe—she cracked lobsters with the Secretary of the Treasury.'"

Michael said wryly, "It will help make up for your pledge of allegiance to Newton Morrow. Your common cause with him on big government didn't make Tom Fauci and Warren Ellison very happy."

Assured by Bill Westwood that Ralph, Chandra, and I would be Kennedy converts before the evening was over, we walked with Michael to the entrance of the Astrodome, and all seven of us piled into an eight-passenger Tric that Michael summoned from the parking garage.

Twenty minutes later we were sitting at a round table in the revolving top-floor roof-garden dining room at the Hyatt-Pilgrim. Jennifer was joking that Newton Morrow must be with us in spirit. All the tables were dimly lighted by bayberry candles encased in hurricane lamps. Above us, a pale moon was glowing in the clear, bubble-proofed sky.

Unlighted Boston buildings, which we could see from our table, pierced the sky like dead relics from another world. When I commented on the darkened city, Chandra told me that city-lighting regulations prohibited all lighting above the street floor after seven P.M. in office buildings. "Many of the restaurants use candles or very subdued lighting," she said, "not just for romance, but to keep their electric bills down."

Jennifer heard our conversation. "You sound as if you're talking to a visitor from another planet," she said. We had all been served huge lobsters from the buffet and had returned to our table. I was relieved to discover that Warren was sitting at a table which was separated from ours by a small circular dance floor. He seemed preoccupied with his group and totally unaware of me.

"I've been in Europe for the past ten years." I hoped that my lie jibed with whatever Ralph had told Bill and Janice about me.

"Energy costs in London, Paris, Rome, Athens, you name the cities, are much higher than in the States," Michael said. "Not only are most of the European buildings dark, but hundreds of streets aren't lighted." Sitting across the table from me, he was enjoying my confusion. Then he asked me to dance. A band comprising a pianist playing what sounded like a John Cage-style tampered piano; an electronic drum that was evidently programed to play any beat; and two bouzoukee players, seemed to be improvising what I guessed was a modified chug rhythm. I didn't know how to dance to the music, but I wanted to escape any further inquisition by Jennifer. And I had a sudden irresistible urge to hold Michael in my arms.

"Well, Mother"—he grinned at me with raised eyebrows when we reached the dance floor and he took me in his arms—"you certainly have aged well!"

I didn't know how to answer him. But finally I couldn't help myself. "Michael, I really am your mother," I blurted out. "Twenty years ago I nursed you, and I changed your shitty diapers. You were my baby boy, and I loved you very much."

Shrugging at this insanity, Michael coolly ignored my words. "My sister, Penny, is in a complete funk about you." He paused and stared at me. "And so am I—but for very different reasons."

336

"What reasons?"

"You're very beautiful. I've never been so compulsively attracted by anyone. I'm damned sure that you're not my mother, which is fortunate, because I'm in love with you."

"Really," I told him, tears in my eyes, "you are being quite schoolboyish. I hope you don't go around trying to convince every strange woman you may take a liking to that you're in love with her. Two hours ago you didn't even know me. Anyway"—I tried to sound gay and lighthearted—"I'm an old lady. I'm thirteen years older than you are."

"How do you know how old I am?"

I kissed his cheek. "Let's say that it's a good guess."

"It really wouldn't matter to me if you were old enough to be my mother," he said. The band had stopped playing. "Please"—he gripped my arm—"I have a room in the hotel. I know it's crazy. I won't push you for sex. But can we stay together tonight?"

I couldn't help smiling. In my previous life, I had been a clinical psychologist. Were Michael and I about to reenact the classical Oedipus story? I was sure of only one thing. If I were Jocasta, and I succumbed, I'd do it deliberately. I'd know that the man in bed with me was really my son. While I was very sure that I wasn't going to bed with Michael, I had a strange feeling that although Michael might not be able to evoke it, he knew instinctively that he was trying to seduce his mother.

I squeezed his hand. "I'll think about it," I told him as we returned to the table. Then I excused myself to go to the ladies room.

Smiling, Jennifer trapped me. "I'll go with you. You may need a guide. Not only have the lights gone out in the city, but some male-female privacy has disappeared in public toilets."

"She means that many of the new toilets are unisexual. It saves building costs." Chandra didn't realize that my ignorance of current mores sounded strange to anyone listening.

Entering the toilet, followed by Jennifer, I was wondering how I could escape further discussion with her. I noticed that the male urinals were separated by a wall from the compartments. Trying to locate an empty stall, I had a fleeting glimpse of men urinating. A man walked out of one of the compartments, nodded briefly at us, and disappeared. Without bending down to see if the occupant's sex was revealed by their footwear, it was impossible to determine if one's companion in the next stall was male or female.

I was pressing against the door of the recently vacated compartment, hoping I could close it after me and escape Jennifer, when she grabbed my arm.

"Okay, stop the crap, Christina," she said. "I don't know how you managed to maintain your girlish good looks, but I'd never forget your husky come-hither voice. I know that you're Christina North."

"You're quite mistaken," I told her angrily. I had made up my mind that handling Michael the rest of the evening was enough of a problem without having an alumni reunion with Jennifer. "My name is Talia Dornroshen."

"That may be the name you're using," Jennifer said. "I don't care what you call yourself. Where have you been? There were newspaper stories about your supposed drowning. What really fascinates me is who did the job on your face?"

I looked at her, bewildered. "I haven't the faintest idea what you mean."

"Where you had the plastic surgery . . . recaptured your youth . . . got rid of the old-age lines and creases."

"You're being ridiculous."

For a moment a flicker of doubt crossed Jennifer's face. Then she shook her head decisively. "You're not fooling me. I can still hear you saying, 'Mory, Mory, I love you.' Why didn't you marry him? That's what I want to know. Why didn't you ever answer my letters? I know that you wrote a porno novel and that you finally married Karl Klausner. God, I don't know how you could have gone to bed with him. Is Mike Klausner your son?"

"I'm really sorry." I was trying to conceal the trembly feeling that was slowly unhinging me. "You should have read your alumni news. As Michael will tell you, his mother, Christina Klausner did indeed die in a boating accident sixteen years ago."

I should have remembered that Jennifer wasn't a person to be sidetracked. Before I could stop her, she had grabbed the hem of my See-Thru dress and was trying to yank it over my head. Struggling against her sudden attack, I slipped on the shawl Ruth had given me to wear, and fell on my knees. The loose-fitting See-Thru swept over my head and I was crouching naked in the men's-ladies room. Cursing Jenny, yelling that she most certainly wasn't acting like any presidential candidate that I'd ever vote for, I swung at her. A man, trying to walk between us, grinned at me appreciatively. "Sorry to interrupt a toilet romance," he said, and disappeared into one of the compartments.

Staring at me triumphantly, Jenny handed me my dress and watched me slip it over my head. "Sorry, Christina, I wanted to be sure. I don't know how in hell you've maintained a twenty-five-year-old body, but that dime-size mole that Mory used to call your 'sexy trademark' is still under your left breast. You're Christina, all right, and now you can stop denying it."

I wasn't very happy with her. "Damn you anyway, Jenny Manchester. You'd have been in a hell of a mess if you had been wrong and ripped off the wrong woman's clothes."

Jennifer told me to hurry and piss. When I finished, she was waiting. "Christa, I'm sorry." She hugged me. "Way back then, I really loved you." She followed me into the hallway. Smiling at last, I reminded her, "You loved Mory, too. Why didn't *you* marry him?"

Jennifer shrugged. "Maybe I wanted too, honey. But you branded him for life. I know for a fact that even before he merged with Adar Chilling, he tried to find you." She looked apprehensively at two women staring at us curiously. "We can't talk here, Christa. The enemy is all around us. Will you meet me tomorrow at the Boston Sheraton? I have a suite there." Jennifer ignored my surprised reaction. "Believe me, I'm probably taking a wild gamble, but I have a feeling that since your body hasn't grown old, your brain, hopefully, has remained young and vibrant, too. Anyway, while you were dancing, I questioned Chandra. She wouldn't tell me very much, except that you were most certainly a Morrow enthusiast." Jennifer laughed. "All I'll tell you now is that years ago, Mory seduced us both. Tomorrow, Columbus Day, he's speaking at the Topsfield Fair. I want you to meet him."

"How can you be seen with him?" I was slowly waking up from my silly daydreams of a loving reunion with Mory to the cold reality. In the quarter century since I had seen him, Mory most certainly had been in love with more women than his once-beloved Chrissy.

Jennifer was hugging me. "If you'll come with me," she said persuasively, "you'll find out. There's a great deal about the campaign I want to discuss with him. For one thing, I want him to be more careful. He doesn't seem to worry that there's quite a few million people who wouldn't give a damn if he was assassinated." Jennifer shrugged. "Hopefully, we'll fly to Maine and spend a few days with Mory and Chuck Holmes, his campaign manager. If worse comes to worse, we can go to bed with him together." Jennifer grinned. "We've done that before. Anyway, you don't have anything to worry about, the sexual odds are on your side. As anyone can see, I'm an old lady." In a strange reversal, with her arm around me, Jennifer seemed like a mother protecting her daughter. "Honey, I can't wait to see Mory's face when he sees his Chrissy. Tomorrow, you can tell me how you did it."

"I'll tell you now," I said smiling. "They didn't know when they buried me that Dracula had been dining on my blood. You'd better watch out, Jenny, vampires climb out of their graves when the sun goes down, and they're always looking for new victims."

———◆———

While Bill and Janice were dancing, and Michael and Jennifer were circulating around the other tables talking with assorted politicians, I told Chandra and Ralph that I was still vacillating, but that in all probability, before the night was over, David's "bird" was going to try her wings. If I crashed or I couldn't get off the ground, I hoped they'd take me back into their nest. Their Love Group was my only family. I loved them all, particularly David. They could reassure him I wasn't the least bit suicidal or depressed. On the contrary, I was beginning to enjoy the new perspective on death and life, and the bustling inanities of living, that my rebirth had given me.

"If, in this brave new world," I told Chandra with a little grin, "you can occasionally spend the night with your father, why should I deny myself? Anyway, Michael is positive that I'm not his mother. I'm really the Sleeping Beauty, and he has arrived in the forest to awaken me."

"Just be careful, Christa." Chandra gestured across the dance floor where Michael, to my shock, was talking with Warren Ellison. I could see Warren glancing surreptitiously in my direction. "Michael is a rich-ik. He's in his first year at Harvard Business School. We're not worried that you'll buy his political philosophy, but keep in mind that the breed hasn't changed sexually, either. They fuck. They ridicule kitsa. They haven't time for love play or things like Unilove. For them, none of that is the real world. Unilove is for romantic lecks. Just make sure of one thing—that Michael has a TR implant."

Chandra explained that TR was a time-release male contraceptive. "It's a testosterone derivative that's implanted subcutaneously. We've told you that most of the lecks prefer not to use contraceptives. They don't even have vasectomies or tubal ligations. They learned how to avoid conception and plan their child-bearing. But the motto of many rich-ik males is fuck and run away." Chandra laughed. "So they can live to fuck another day. Just keep in mind that you still live in a world where at least half of the males don't want too much involvement with the female beyond the necessary but temporary assuagement of their sex drive and recurring domination needs."

Before Michael finally detached me from the group at our table—Jennifer had left a few minutes before—Ralph prepared the way for me with Bill and Janice. "Mike has discovered that Talia is an old friend of his father's. He wants to have a long talk with her and see if he can convert her to the Kennedy camp."

Michael offered no excuses. When he returned to the table he grinned and said, "Talia and I will see you good people later. Thanks for coming." He took my arm proprietarily and guided me toward the elevators. "They know that we're going to sleep together." I told him. I was so *nervo*—jittery—that I was on the verge of telling him that I had changed my mind.

"Is going to bed together bad?" Michael asked. "It's a nice way for strangers to get acquainted."

In the elevator, I asked him point-blank what Warren Ellison had said about me.

"He told me to watch out." Michael laughed. "He's afraid that I might have to call the management to help find a strait jacket for you. He told me that you really believe that you're my mother."

Michael was leading me down the hall toward his room. With his arm around me, before he opened the door, he kissed me. "I told Warren that I didn't care who you were, but I was positive that you weren't my mother."

"How?"

Michael laughed again. "Is a mother likely to be only thirteen years older than her son? Would a mother who looked like you go to bed with her son?"

I laughed, too. "She might—if he looked like you and she got the invitation. Is that all Warren said to you?"

341

"Good God, isn't that enough? You sound as if you are pretty familiar with Warren Ellison." Michael had unlocked the door. We walked into a room with a floor-to-ceiling window wall that was one-eighth of the circular hotel building. Beneath us, Boston Harbor glimmered in the moonlight. Telling me that, personally, he thought Warren Ellison had an overinflated ego, and that he didn't care much for him, Michael didn't pursue the topic of our relationship. With me in his arms, he tumbled us onto the bed. A warm glow from the moonlight suffused the room. I could feel his hand under my dress, searching my body, and I was responding to his kisses as avidly as he gave them.

"No mother ever felt like you do," he whispered huskily. It occurred to me that his voice inflection was similar to my own. "Penny told me about you. A wild story, right out of the old-time science fiction that I read when I was a kid. You tried to convince her that you had been hibernated for sixteen years." Looking at me dubiously, he stood up and took off the jacket he was wearing. "I must admit that I have never been so attracted to a woman before." Even in the moonlit shadows I could see the warm smile on his face. "If it's filial attraction—so what? Every male likes to be mothered. Would you like some champagne? The management leaves a half-dozen bottles of the best California in the refrigerator. At one hundred and fifty dollars a night, it's part of the room rent."

"You're obviously a rich-ik," I said, amused.

"And you're obviously a leck." He sounded a little peeved. "It's too bad Morrow drew those battle lines."

"They've always existed. The haves and the have-nots. He's determined to change that."

Michael was pouring the champagne. I was already feeling a little giddy from the several glasses of it I had drunk at the table.

"He won't succeed," Michael insisted. "But he's made it more difficult for all of us to co-exist. Like now—why are we talking politics? First thing you know, you'll be angry because I'm a rich-ik—to use Morrow's terminology—and I can afford a room like this, and you probably can't."

I laughed. "I could if I married you. Then I'd be a poor little rich girl!"

I was torn between pursuing the discussion—asking Michael what he had done to deserve his good fortune—and wanting to hold him in my arms. I accepted the glass of champagne he handed me. A holding action. The physical attraction between us was hypnotic. My need to refashion my little boy from the Klausner mold was intermixed with maternal feelings. Memories of him climbing into bed with Karl and me when he was three or four, telling me that he loved me more than Daddy because I read to him, along with hundreds of other images of a tousled-haired little boy, busy with his own pursuits, flashed through my mind. But even while I was thinking these thoughts, I let Michael, the man, slip my dress over my head, and I was lying naked with him, sipping champagne and more conscious of myself as an excited, loving woman than as a mother. The moonlight and shadows softened the hard, clean lines of his body. Like Karl, except for a sandy bush of hair around his very erect penis, he had very few body hairs.

"I've had a strange feeling about you all evening." He was gently kissing my breasts. "I'm only vaguely interested in what motivated you to tell Penny that you were our mother, but you do remind me of her—or of her picture. I was only four when she died. I don't have a clear memory of her living face. Karl had a portrait painted of her when they were first married. I guess she must have been twenty-seven or eight. I used to look at her face and wonder what ghosts were haunting her mind when it was painted."

Michael was silent for a minute. His face lay quietly against my breast. "I had discovered that she was pretty mixed up psychologically. A manic-depressive. But I kept hoping that somehow she might walk out of that picture and tell me that she still loved me."

"Many men are attracted to women who remind them of their mother," I said. "Psychologists used to believe that the young male has a much more difficult time finding his personal identity than a young female—largely because the mother is forced to reject the male as the source of his love and protection. Young females don't have the same problem. Mothers can give them loving, touching affection that they finally have to deny their male children."

"I like making love this way." Michael's voice sounded dreamy. "I enjoy lying naked with a woman and talking to her. My mother used to romp around the room naked with Penny and me, and sometimes she'd tumble naked in bed with us. Then she'd read to us. We snuggled with her, and she didn't worry that she had no clothes on. My father didn't approve. We rarely saw him with his pants down."

343

Michael continued his loving search of my body. "My mother was very beautiful, too." He was silent for a long time, his lips on mine, his tongue timidly exploring mine, and then he laughed. "Christ, you'll be wondering if I have an Oedipus complex." He looked at me wide-eyed. "No way! Karl is a great guy. He loves money and women, in that order—and so do I! Karl and I see eye to eye."

"Especially politically." I couldn't help smiling.

"He would be as mad as hell if he could see me in bed with an admirer of Newton Morrow."

I wanted to add, "Who's also your mother," but before I could stop him—anticipating his intention, I was screaming, "Don't do it!"—I watched Michael pour his almost-full glass of champagne over my stomach and delta. As it dribbled into my crotch, he put his face between my legs and lapped it off, while his tongue searched my labia and clitoris. Then—too excited to heed my "No, please, honey, don't. You shouldn't!"—he was inside me moving in deep thrusts that I could feel to the edge of my uterus. Fully caught up in his own driving necessity, he climaxed almost immediately, and then he sobbed into my neck, "Oh, God, I'm sorry. I'm so sorry. I couldn't stop!"

"Mikey, Mikey," I whispered in his ear. "It's all right. I love you. I've always loved you."

A few minutes later, quietly holding me in his arms, a puzzled expression on his face, he said, "My mother always called me Mikey. Who in hell are you?"

"You may not be Oedipus," I told him, feeling only a little remorseful, "but I can assure you that I'm Jocasta."

"Will you hang yourself?" he asked, understanding my allusion, and delighted with the game.

I shivered. "God, no!" I leaned over him and kissed his lips. "But I will if you've gotten me pregnant!"

"Don't worry. I know how to protect myself against lecks and dreamy females who refuse to use the pill."

I cupped his reawakening penis and testicles in my hand, and I felt no guilt. A silly thought occurred to me, and I told it to him. "Many years ago, when I was studying psychology, I used to argue with my male professors that since the transition for the male, when his mother finally withheld physical love, was so shocking to his psyche, and, because most men grew up so inept and untrained in the enjoyment and the art of loving a woman, it might be a good idea if mothers taught their young male teen-agers how to make love—not essen-

344

tially for their own enjoyment, but as a gift to the females that their sons would ultimately marry." I smiled. "Unfortunately, my patriarchally conditioned male teachers couldn't accept the idea. They instinctively knew that if such a custom ever became a way of life, it would finally free the female forever from male dominance."

I slithered on top of Michael, and slowly kissed my way down from his face, across his chest and stomach, and took his penis in my mouth. Like all males, he luxuriated in the temporary ecstasy of female capture. When he was fully erect, I lowered myself over his moonlit shaft, and told him, "This time there's no hurry. Now you can learn kitsa with me."

"That proves it!" He laughed. "You can't be my mother."

"Why not?"

"Kitsa is Unilove—lecks preach that old Jesus crap—that money isn't important. They may be right, but Karl told me that while Christina would never admit it, her need to prove herself stemmed from her mother—who didn't have much money when Christina was little—and her father, who disappeared and left them penniless when she was very young. Christina tried to find her identity by becoming a celebrity, but even if she had become famous—fame without money is an empty bag."

On my elbow, leaning over Michael's face, I shook my head angrily. "That sounds like your father's words. He was wrong. I never gave a tinker's damn about money. And I certainly don't see what money has to do with kitsa."

Michael ignored my choice of pronoun. "It just seems to me that my mother wasn't the romantic kitsa type. Sex evidently didn't mean much to her. If it had, why did she make that porno movie?"

I was silent a moment, a little shocked, after so many years, to be confronted with the sins of my youth. "I don't know," I said, "maybe it was her way of telling her mother, and Karl, to go to hell—to leave her alone." I tried to smile, but tears were trickling down my cheeks. Again I spoke in the first person. "I guess I was a very rebellious young woman, but, nevertheless, I really wanted people to applaud me and love me. Anyway, I'm sure your mother never really felt guilty about her book, or the movie she made. There was no deviate sex—no sadism or masochism—in it. As far as she was concerned, men and women kissing each other's genitals

345

was a saner thing than killing each other, or hijacking planes, or blowing up buildings, or fighting religious wars."

Michael was lost in his thoughts, but finally he said, "Maybe if my mother had lived, we would have been good friends. Warren Ellison had a videotape of her movie. His son, Ted, found it, and ran it for me one afternoon. When I asked Karl about it, he just laughed, and told me to forget it. His theory was that if I ever found a woman like my mother, she'd put some seasoning in my life." Once again, Michael seemed to be speaking his inmost thoughts aloud. "But when I first saw that movie, I was thirteen or fourteen. Most of my friends and I had seen porno movies, but the women in them were some old whores—not their mothers!"

"I'm happy about one thing." My tear-wet cheek was slippery against his. "It didn't ruin you for life."

"What do you mean?"

"You seem to enjoy kissing and being kissed—all over!"

"Hell, I finally grew up." I knew Michael was enjoying the slow rotation of my pelvis, keeping his penis alive in me. "Anyway, you leck, you—you keep insisting that you're my mother, but you're making very erotic love with me." Laughing, he lay back. "You're in charge. You can hold me in your arms while I stay inside you the rest of the night." Then, still inside me, he rolled me on my side. I held his face against my breasts, and he tasted my nipples. He sighed sleepily. "Eventually, I'm going to convince you not to vote for Newton Morrow, but it will have to wait until morning—kitsa is much more fun than politics."

Hours later, thinking I was dreaming, I heard the click of a door opening, but it didn't come through into my consciousness that someone was actually slipping back the night latch on the room door. Then the dream turned into a nightmare. Before I could alert Michael, Warren Ellison, followed by two grinning waiters carrying a breakfast tray, burst into the room.

"You stinking son of a bitch!" Michael yelled, and jumped naked out of the bed. "Get the fuck out of my room!"

The waiters beat a hasty retreat, leaving Warren coolly surveying a naked, tousled me, while I belatedly clutched a sheet around myself.

"I'm sorry to invade your privacy, Michael." Warren refused to look directly at my face. "I can assure you, if it weren't me here, it would be Karl. When I told him this woman had arrived at our dinner party last night, and had seduced you into bed, he was ready to fly up here. We don't know what she's up to, but we suspect that she's working for Morrow. You know damned well that Kennedy wants you to join his confidential White House staff next January. Going to bed with a woman who claims to be your mother could make you the laughingstock of the country, and screw your future political career to a fare-thee-well. I suggest that the three of us have breakfast together, right here in this room, and perhaps we can convince this woman to tell us what she is trying to accomplish, and how we can resolve our little problems."

I looked at Michael, struggling to control the sobs that were racking my body. "There's really nothing to resolve, Michael," I said. "Eventually, all of you are going to have to face reality. I'm Christina Klausner. If Warren wasn't growing senile, he'd tell you that that is true. In fact, it would be very easy for him to confirm it in Washington. If he checks thoroughly, he'll discover that a top-secret hibernation project was authorized by the government more than twenty years ago."

I turned to Warren. "If I decide to insist that I've been a victim, instead of a willing conspirator, in the United States' little Belsen on Cape Cod, it could blow your precious government and Jason Kennedy into outer space. One thing I can assure you—what happened in this room is Michael's and my very private secret." I tossed the sheet aside, and stood up in front of them. "The last time you saw me naked, Warren, you were a lot more friendly. Whether you like it or not, I'm Christina—mole and all."

Although Michael was staring at me doubtfully, he was still furious with Warren. "Before I forcibly shove your ass out of this room," he said coldly, "I suggest you leave peacefully. You can tell Karl to get off my back, and to get off Christina's back. I don't give a damn whether she's my mother, or Talia, the Sleeping Beauty, I love her."

When I kissed Michael good-bye at the entrance of the Sheraton, I was sure he still wasn't fully convinced that I was his mother. Eating the breakfast with him that Warren had left—after his abrupt departure and nasty assurance that he most certainly would check out my story—I had told Michael that the fat was in the fire. Warren would tell Karl, and Karl would be enraged. He would hate me with a passion. While Karl had never been a very moral man sexually, I knew he would never believe that Michael and I making love together was a very special kind of rebirth for both of us. In 1996, some of the lecks might be very casual about incest, but I was certain that Karl wouldn't be.

"I should never have let it happen, Mikey." I hugged him. "It has to be the first and last time. A very special memory for both of us."

Michael was reluctant to let me open the door of the Tric. He held my hand. "I don't care whether you're a leck. It can't be the last time. I love you, Chrissy."

Tearful, as much because I was leaving him as for the strange coincidence that he had called me by Mory's name for me, I told him, "I love you too, Mikey. No matter what happens, please don't be angry with me." I was sorry that I hadn't managed to tell him about Mory, and that somehow last night, making love together, he had been the Newton Morrow of my previous life.

Telephoning Jennifer from the lobby of the hotel on a house telephone, I had a momentary feeling that a balding man, wearing a conventional ik-style summer suit, was watching me and not really reading the book that he held in his hand. It occurred to me that Warren might have noticed that I had seemed very friendly with Jennifer last night. Was he having me watched? Two hours had passed since he had burst into Michael's room. He'd had time enough to put me under surveillance.

I told Jenny that I thought I was being followed. "Don't worry," she said. "Just take the elevator to the twenty-third floor. Whoever is watching you can't get by my jailer."

An unconversational bespectacled man was waiting for me when I got off the elevator. He escorted me to the empty living room of Jennifer's suite and left immediately, closing the door behind him.

A moment later, a woman with bright blue eyes and leck-style blonde hair emerged from the bedroom, nodded at me, and locked the door leading to the hotel corridor. Then she turned, smiled at me, and said with a French accent, "Madame Manchester has to be careful. *Tout le monde la cherche.*"

I was nodding sympathetically, wondering why Jennifer

hadn't forced her maid or secretary to wear a different hair style, and then she yanked off the wig. It was Jennifer! "Hi, Sister Chrissy!" She laughed. "I'm happy to see my disguise still works—even with your sharp eyes." She popped out her contact lenses, and told me that we were completely alone in the suite. She had cleared herself with her staff—several secretaries and a campaign manager—who were on the floor below. She had promised to be back in Boston by Wednesday morning to fly to Chicago for a speech there. In the meantime, she was escaping for a no-questions-asked-or-answered long weekend. Tommy, the Secret Service man who had brought me to her room, was going to take us down the service elevator to the garage—and we'd be off.

"What about clothes?" I demanded. "I can't stay in this dress forever."

Jenny took me into the bedroom. Four See-Thrus in different colors lay on the bed. "We're still about the same size. Strip down. I'll give you one of my political dresses. We'll both leave Boston looking like conservative Republican matrons. Before we get to Topsfield, you can change to a pink See-Thru, and I'll wear a blue one. To complete the transformation, somewhere en route I'll put on my wig and contacts. Presto—an hour from now we will greet Mory, an aging leck mother and her daughter, faithful supporters of the United People's Party."

Finally, in a rented Tric, headed toward Topsfield, I asked her what she had told Mory about me. "Honey, I didn't. After all, I don't really know anything more about you than he does. He knew that you were married, and that you had presumably drowned. But you know Mory—in his Bellamy moods his realities are different from the rest of the world's. All I'm concerned about now is that Chuck Holmes, Mory's campaign manager, won't object to spending a few nights with an old lady."

I looked at her, puzzled. "I don't understand you."

"Me—I'm the old lady, Christa. I don't know about your reality, but I'm forty-nine. Chuck is about thirty-five."

Watching my expression in the curved Tric mirror, she grinned. "After Mory speaks tonight—tomorrow morning, at dawn, we're flying to a small island off the coast of Maine, near Vinalhaven, that Chuck owns. Chuck runs an oyster and lobster farm. There's an old farm house, barns, horses. There'll just be the four of us. I'm assuming that when Mory sees you, there'll be no doubt in his mind who he wants to tumble in the hay with."

I told Jennifer that she was moving too fast. I was sure that I couldn't jump into bed with a man I hadn't seen for twenty-three years, even if it was Mory. At the same time it occurred to me that I was becoming a sex maniac. Since my dehibernation, I had made love with five men, one of them my son, and all of it had seemed quite enjoyable and normal. "If I hadn't come," I told Jennifer, "Mory would have slept with you. What about his wife, Adar?"

Jennifer shrugged. "If Adar had been in Boston, she probably would have gone to bed with Chuck. If you haven't already been told, Mory's wife is the founder of Unilove. It's not a religion that requires you to forsake all others. Temporarily, Chuck is the bachelor member of their Love Group. His pair bond, a well-known actress, Sarah Masson, decided that her acting and Chuck's political life didn't mix, so she joined a Love Group that's involved in the theater. You have to understand that these partner changes in Love Groups are usually not acrimonious. Chuck and Sarah see each other occasionally and talk about their separate lives in bed together. They have one child, a boy, who is still with the group. Mory adores him."

Jennifer drove silently across the Mystic River Bridge. It was crowded with Trics heading for a Heli-bus port on the northern quadrant of the city.

"Actually," she said finally, evoking her thoughts, "Chuck wanted me to join the group as his pair bond. Last year I was Republican—Senator Jennifer Manchester from Connecticut. I knew damned well that at that juncture, I couldn't switch parties and join the UPA and still retain any political credibility. Then, when it looked as if I might get the Republican presidential nomination, Chuck and I decided that I might be more effective if I could draw votes from Jason Kennedy. As a result, I've been in a continuing juggling act—trying to run as a dedicated Republican and keep the party happy, without attacking Mory too much. It's been no easy job, especially because Jason Kennedy actually appeals to many of the conservative Republicans."

Jennifer smiled. "The other thing is that I have some old-fashioned hang-ups which don't seem to bother Chuck."

"Like what?"

Jennifer squeezed my hand. "I'm older than he is, and I'm not sure I could be the flexible kind of bed companion a

350

Love Group seems to require. I enjoy sleeping with Mory and Chuck." Jennifer giggled. "But I'm not too sure about old Henry Adams, or Carlos Gonzales, although he is very handsome. Anyway, at the moment, I'm married monogamously. Ted Byrnes is my second husband. I married Jerry Miner, the guy I was going with when we were in Cambridge, but Jerry and I lived in separate worlds. That's my problem. During the past fifteen years, I've been too busy to be a regular bed companion with one man, or to be the good wife who held my man's hand, as well as his prick, and soothed away his daily cares. A Love Group composed of politically motivated people may be the only sane solution for people like me. Enough of me. Tell me about last night. Did you actually go to bed with Michael Klausner? Is Mike really a carbon copy of his father? Is he really your son? It occurred to me that he might be a child by one of Klausner's previous marriages. Did you really make love with him, or did you just bunk with him?"

I sighed. "Michael's my son, all right," I told her. "But you'll have to forgive me, I really haven't come to terms with last night myself." I was in no mood for Jennifer's legal inquisition. How could I tell her, or anyone, the details of my lovely night with Mikey? There was no denying that he carried my genes. At certain times during the night, I had the weird sensation of seeing myself reflected as a male. The square-cut determination of his face, his pixieish sense of humor, the tone of his voice, all seemed to be a vague reflection of me. In a strange way, he seemed to be essentially the same kind of core person that I was, and maybe he would have been even more so had we grown together through the years in a natural mother-son relationship.

On the other hand, the thought struck me, maybe it was better that I had "died"; otherwise I might have created another me, searching for God-knew-what.

"Was he shocked when it finally penetrated his ik brain that you really are his mother?" Jennifer's mind was like a legal pencil sharpener, determined to achieve the sharpest point, even if it quickly broke under pressure.

"Really, Jenny," I said, "let's say that I'm old-fashioned, too. Without any further elaboration—I made love with Michael. It was a warm, affectionate, and caring night. Then, when that bastard, Warren Ellison, whom I also had slept with in my former life, invaded Michael's room and caught us, it was the end of the second act. I don't know what happens in the final act—but it occurs to me, because of my Klausner connection, I may be a very unwise companion for you to have along on this weekend. Especially since you're taking me on an even crazier excursion, to renew an even older acquaintance, with a man who's probably long forgotten me."

I thought Jennifer might be shocked, but she burst into laughter. "Okay, I won't probe, but I certainly would like to have seen Ellison's face. I'll be honest with you, I have no children, but if I had a son who was as handsome as Michael, and by some hibernation magic the age differential made it possible for us to be lovers, I most certainly couldn't have resisted."

Jennifer, who had put the Tric in computer control with the car in front of us, kissed my tearstained cheeks. "Stop feeling guilty, Christa, I'll defend you in court. At least you don't have my problem. I'm too old."

"I haven't absorbed all the facets of loving in 1996, but in Love Groups the age of the female doesn't seem to matter so much."

Jennifer agreed. "It's the beginning of the ultimate equality with the male. But keep in mind there's still millions of men and women who are not Uniloves. They live by the old rules. Their sex drives are fully repressed in their childhood. Finally, in mid-life, they become sexless. They substitute food or alcohol for human pleasuring of their bodies and their minds. Overweight and lethargic, they believe that sex and loving, and sheer enjoyment of another person's body and mind, is one of the seven ages of man. They have an everything-in-its-season mentality. Millions of voters who agree wholeheartedly with Mory's economics can't accept the humanistic sexuality of Unilove, or Mory's and Adar's blending of sex, work, and family into a total gestalt. Mory's sexual New Tomorrow won't happen until every youngster is brought up in a Unilove-style environment, and millions more of them are exposed to a new kind of premarital education that will integrate and blend the male and female from a very early age."

I knew that we'd be on the grounds of the Topsfield Fair in another fifteen minutes. I was suddenly wallowing in past memories. When Michael was four and Penny was five, I took them to see the farm exhibits, and the many livestock contests, where top breeds of cattle, sheep, goats, and pigs were displayed by their owners. Jennifer explained that the fair now attracted over four hundred thousand visitors, and more than fifty thousand were expected to hear Mory speak tonight, before the dog racing and the fireworks. Jennifer said that thousands of small commercial farmers were enthusiastic over Mory's corporate approach to farming. While individual farm-price supports would be eliminated, farm corporations, large and small, would, within certain guidelines, have their 10 percent profit requirements subsidized by the UPCC. A "Genesis Strategy" would be set up by a national planning commission to stockpile sufficient grain and basic crops against extended poor growing seasons. Beyond that, excess crops would be purchased by the government, and immediately exported at prices equal to the world market, or below them on a competitive basis, or they could be bartered with nations that had no credit balances for raw materials or intangibles.

"Intangibles?"

"Sure—in exchange for wheat and other basic grains, countries like India or Africa, or Third World nations, could provide housing and simple fare for people from this country who would like to travel and live with their people. Or we could accept native art, or live entertainers, and give credit for all cultural exchanges."

Jennifer suddenly turned off the highway onto a two-lane bypass road that hadn't been very well maintained. Dodging the ruts and pot holes, she parked alongside a thick growth of pine trees.

"Come on, Chrissy, it's time for our transformation," she said, and she took her suitcase out of the back of the Tric. "Mory's Heli-home is parked a few miles beyond the fairgrounds. We've got to meet Chuck first."

We were laughing like schoolgirls, momentarily naked as we shifted from Jennifer's conventional clothing to our pink and blue See-Thrus. I told Jennifer that she was in fine shape. Any man past puberty would be enchanted with her full breasts and her only softly rounded body. Giggling, she hugged me. "If all else fails, Christa, you and I can join a *konbi-konbi* Love Group. We never admitted it, but some of those times when we were both in bed with Mory, we were actually loving each other."

Back in the Tric, wearing her wig, her brown eyes lost behind the blue contacts, looking a little like one of those strange women one used to see on the covers of science fiction magazines, she explained that according to Chuck,

353

Mory's rented Heli-Home was surrounded by a protective fence enclosure that had been erected by the fairground's officials. Inside the enclosure, a tent had been erected for the various news-media reporters. At the fairgrounds, we would turn in our rented Tric. Chuck would meet us at the entrance gate. A couple of Secret Service men would drive us to Mory and get us past the reporters.

"Who are we supposed to be?"

"I told Mory that I was bringing one of my confidential secretaries along for Chuck. Chuck will tell anyone who wants to know that we're wealthy UPA contributors . . . friends of Adar's . . . Readers from local Unilove Churches."

"I wouldn't believe that. We look like camp followers. I still don't understand why you take such risks. You must love Mory very much."

"Of course I love him. But even if you weren't here, sex is not the driving force. I want Mory to win. There's only three weeks left. I want to coordinate my campaign, and particularly the last Presidential Conversation, with him. Somehow, during that encounter, I want to give Mory the margin he needs. Keep in mind, the betting odds shift back and forth between him and Kennedy."

"Another thing," Jennifer said. "While I love him, I don't swallow all his Utopian daydreams. Occasionally, I jar him back to reality. You're going to discover, Sister Chrissy, that Mory believes every damned thing he says. Even that he is some kind of essence of Edward Bellamy, returned to earth to complete his mission."

I laughed. "He always did."

"I keep telling him that it isn't good politics, but he doesn't pay much attention to me. If you really believe the bullshit you tell people, the next step is to believe that God has ordained you as mankind's savior. After that, you have no choice. To bring your plans to fruition, you ultimately become a *zaspi*—an evil one—whether you believe you are or not."

Joining the thousands of people walking toward the entrance of the fairgrounds, I had the strange feeling that I was two people. The Christina standing outside my body was telling me that I shouldn't worry. The third act would begin soon, and after all, it was only a play—if I fumbled my lines, it didn't matter. But the Christina walking alongside Jennifer was trembling and fearful of the ghosts of things past dancing in her mind. Sixteen years had passed, and I was still as young as many of the mothers with their children in tow. Sixteen years ago, I was buying cotton candy for the man I had gone to bed with last night. And now, in a few minutes, like Miss Ludington's sister, I would return in reality to haunt Newton Morrow.

"I wonder what Mory has told Adar about me." Once again I was close to tears.

Jennifer chuckled. "That he had three women in his life—and you'd always be one of them."

We had reached the gate. Chuck Holmes—lean, high-cheekboned, his black hair in a shorter male version of the leck Dutch boy cut—after a moment's hesitation swept Jennifer into his arms, while she kissed him enthusiastically. "Damn near didn't recognize you," he told Jennifer. "You look like one of the Newt's honey fugglers." He stared at me. "You, too."

Jennifer laughed. "Chuck enjoys confusing the news corps with old-fashioned slang. Honey fugglers are women who really adore their men. This is Christina Klausner. Where are Mory's keepers? Did Henry and Carlos arrive? Who else is with Mory?"

"There's a couple of bluebellies—Union soldiers—waiting for us." Grinning, he pointed to an eight-passenger Tric a few hundred feet away. "Our SS men are really northern WASPs and Irishmen. With the exception of Massachusetts, which has always voted for very liberal candidates, we're pretty sure Newt will lose New England. I've checked these momzers out. They claim to be for Newt, above and beyond the call of duty, but I'm not sure of them. They're in constant communication with Washington. They sure won't know who you are, Jennifer—and we damn well won't tell them. But Newt's being his usual careless self. This morning he was one of the honorary judges at a goat showing. I told him that there's a group of ex-CIA'ers who had an assignment—to see that Newton Morrow never becomes President. If he gets shushed, it's his own fault." Chuck suddenly looked at me again. "My God! You're not related to Karl Klausner, are you?"

I grinned at him. "So far as I know, he never bothered to divorce me. But he may start proceedings at any moment."

"Does anyone know that you're with Jennifer?" Chuck was obviously a little shocked. "I don't suppose that I have to tell you about the Invisible Hand Alliance." At my blank look, he explained, "It's a group of the chief executive officers of

355

most of the thousand top companies, plus the major bank and insurance company executives. It was organized by Karl Klausner. If Newt is elected, they have made a prior agreement not to cooperate with any government whose intent is to destroy private capitalism. Whose side are you on?"

"Christina hasn't been involved with Karl Klausner for many years," Jennifer told Chuck. "She probably thought that the Invisible Hand referred to a Mafia organization." Jennifer sounded a little impatient. "Actually, it's probably worse—and more powerful. The name Invisible Hand derives from Adam Smith's theory of supply and demand regulating itself in the marketplace." Jennifer shrugged. "We can bring Christa up-to-date later. Right now, I want to get out of the crowds."

"If you're for Morrow," Chuck said, as we walked toward the Tric, "you've got a lot of publicity value."

"More than you think, Chuck," Jennifer said. "Christa was hibernated sixteen years ago, and she's lived to tell about it. Chronologically, she's forty-nine years old."

Chuck whistled. It was obvious that his mind was churning. "God—it would be a neat ferly if you appeared on the rostrum tonight with Mory and spawled on your old man."

I couldn't help smiling. I might not know Loglan, but I knew that ferly and spawl—surprise and spit—were obsolete English words.

"Why not on the midway?" I asked him sarcastically. "You can ballyhoo the show. Charge admission. Step right inside and watch her strip. See the lady who returned from the dead! She'll prove to you that decomposition hasn't set in yet!" Chuck listened to me contritely. "Why don't we wait and see what Mory thinks?" I said.

"You sound as if you and Newt know each other. I thought she was your secretary, Jenny. What the hell is going on?"

Jennifer squeezed his hand. "Let's play it as it lies, Chuck." We were only a few yards from the Tric. "By the way, who do your SS friends think we are?"

"Honey fugglers—what else?" Chuck grinned at Jennifer. "When you were a kid, they called them groupies. They'd go to bed with anyone who had a gold record."

Ten minutes after we left the main entrance to the fairgrounds, the Secret Service men, who had kept watching us in the rear-view mirror of the Tric, drove up to a horse-corral gate that was monitored by several more security guards. A dozen men and women, some of them with television cameras, crowded around the car. Chuck told them not to waste their tapes—we were two local party contributors, come to say hello to the next President—Newton Morrow. We were finally cleared, and driven to a strange-looking helicopter parked a few hundred yards ahead of us. The rotor, flying mechanism, and pilot's cab were perched on top of a long fiberglass van. It was long and narrow, with windows like those in a mobile home.

"Jenny doesn't know it yet"—Chuck was speaking in a whisper, obviously not wanting to be overheard by our drivers—"but she and I are piloting this baby to my island in Maine—tomorrow morning at dawn."

I had seen the Heli-buses flying overhead. The Heli-Home was actually smaller, but I told Chuck that it seemed incredible to me that a helicopter could lift so much weight. "Not only can it lift that camper, but we could easily bring four more people along with us, too. It has a flying range of five hundred miles."

Jenny was frowning. "I thought this was a rented Heli-Home. Don't the owners provide a pilot? You know damned well that I don't know how to fly it."

Chuck's raised eyebrows and his gesture toward the Secret Service men who parked the Tric in front of the Heli-Home indicated that the discussion wasn't for their ears.

Boarding stairs were attached to one side of the van. As I followed Jennifer out of the Tric, my heart was pounding so hard that I was sure that I might faint, or, at the very least, I thought that I would wet the panties I wasn't wearing. Mory appeared on the top step waving at us, and Jennifer yelled, "Did you watch the telvi last night? We lighted candles for you!"

But Mory didn't answer her. He was staring at me, wide-eyed. Although he no longer was a boy, wearing a sheepskin coat and blue jeans, twenty-five years suddenly vanished. Was I still in my hibernaculum, dreaming past dreams, or was I in the Harvard Coop again? Was this really Topsfield, Massachusetts? Wherever I was, I was drowning in the love and recognition in Mory's eyes as he bounded down the steps and clasped me in his arms. "Chrissy! Chrissy!" he said, and his voice was tinged with wonder and joy, "you've come home again!"

Like a child who had lost her father in a crowd and then found him again, I was sobbing with sheer relief, enjoying the protection of his arms. Laughing and crying, I snuggled against his neck, and he picked me up and carried me into the van. "You've been a long time coming," he said quietly. "I've been waiting for you."

Inside the Heli-Home, he reluctantly put me down and introduced me to Henry Adams and Carlos Gonzales. I was still trying to assimilate his strange response. How could he have been waiting for me?

"This is Chrissy," he told them. "My first love. When I was a very much younger man, she was the first woman who believed in me. I told her then that I was going to be President." There were happy tears in Mory's eyes. "Way back in the seventies it took a lot of faith and courage to believe me."

I wanted to respond that Mory was overestimating me. I'd never really had faith enough. I should have married him and grown old along with him. Whether he became President or not wouldn't have mattered. But my self-accusations and Mory's amazingly blithe acceptance of me as Chrissy—still his woman after a quarter of a century—were for later exploration.

Mory was assuring Jennifer that the mobile home wasn't bugged, and he was marveling at her disguise, as were Henry and Carlos.

"It looks better than it feels. This damned wig is hot, everything I'm looking at has a pale blue cast to it, and these lens are irritating my eyes." Jennifer was surveying the Pullman-like quarters of the van. "The thought occurs to me," she said, grinning, "since it's only one-thirty in the afternoon and this place is scarcely big enough for two to stretch out, that I'd like some other place to relax. I want to stop playing politics and trying to be President, at least until Wednesday morning." She looked at Mory and me with raised eyebrows. "Actually, I want to give you time to be alone."

Henry Adams, an athletic-appearing, gray-haired man in his late sixties, stopped his silent study of me and told Jennifer that he had rented a suite at a former Holiday Travel Lodge a few miles away. He chuckled. "Of course, as you know, Jennifer, very few travelers use these highway motor inns any longer. I heard a rumor that a new chain was buying hundreds of them. They're going to rename them Tric Swive-Aways. Their slogan is going to be Enjoy belly bumping with a friend or neighbor in your own private Swive-Away." Henry was obviously teasing her. "Anyway, you're welcome

358

to join us. I have two bedrooms and a conference room. You can spend the night with Carlos and me."

Jennifer shrugged. "Great! I assume that your respective pair bonds aren't with you. I won't promise to swive with either of you—but if your bed is big enough, Henry, I might snuggle with you."

Chuck was enthusiastic. "It will give us all time to talk strategy with Jennifer. Henry and Carlos are flying to Boston tomorrow, and will meet us there on Wednesday. Tonight Newt has a dinner engagement with the local pols at six. He's speaking at seven-thirty." Chuck grinned at me. "That'll give Ms Klausner and Newt about three hours for paizogony."

I wanted to tell him that I didn't think that paizogony was in Webster's and that probably Mrs. Byrnes had made it up for her Dictionary of obscure words, but now Carlos was staring at me suspiciously. Chuck intercepted his unasked question. "I presume, Newt, that you know your Chrissy is married to Karl Klausner."

Mory smiled. "I had heard rumors to that effect—also, that she was dead. But here she is—alive and apparently ageless!" Mory seemed totally unconcerned about my past, or that both Henry and Carlos were a little agitated that they might be sheltering a Trojan Horse.

"I know this may scrump you, Newt"—Chuck nodded at me—"but Ms Klausner could be a three-way publicity gift. First, while I haven't had time to question her, she seems to be a leck. When a rich-ik turns leck, especially when she has a name like Klausner, that means something. It tells the hoi polloi that them who has everything are finally seeing the light. Second, according to Jennifer—and you no doubt will probe her story yourself—Ms Klausner has been hibernated for sixteen years, and was only resurrected a short time ago. So far as she knows, she's one of the first survivors. If that's true—and I haven't heard of any others—it's a major medical breakthrough. We both know that millions of people are very fascinated with all the wild stories and publicity about hibernation. Thousands can't wait to be hibernated. They hope to find a better life in some future world, or they're willing to be launched into intergalactic space. Some would just like to drop out for a while, and gain a few free years on their relatives and peers. Your constituency will be very sympathetic with Ms Klausner. Finally, Newt, if she would endorse you, and Adar would announce that she had invited your long-lost Chrissy to join our Love Group, it would be the love story of the century!"

Chuck knew that he was irritating Mory, but it was obvious that he was captivated by his own proposal. Scowling at him and shaking his head indignantly, Mory held my hand. "As you can see, Chrissy, my campaign manager is frightfully pragmatic. You can forget it, Chuck. Even if Chrissy were willing, I'm not interested in making a public spectacle of her."

Jennifer laughed. "Then you better hide her in your pocket, Mory. I'm sure that after last night her son, Mike Klausner, isn't going to let his mother disappear again." I wondered if Jennifer was going to tell Mory that I had slept with my son, but she just grinned at me. Before they all left for the motel, she hugged me. "Don't quit now, Christa. You've come this far, and for better or worse, you've got your Mory back. Chuck may be right. If you follow his scenario in the last act, the audience will be standing on their seats and cheering for encores."

Alone at last, sitting across from Mory in the narrow cabin of the Heli-Home, I grinned timidly at him, and I wondered if we could ever bridge the quarter-century gap. More than just a few years separated us from that idyllic year in Cambridge. I knew that like me, Mory and Adar had children. They were younger than Penny and Michael. Teen-agers. I had seen them swimming naked with Mory on a Life-a-Vision at the beginning of the Presidential Conversation. In addition, I was sure that after years of living in a Love Group, Mory was more sexually sophisticated than I could ever be.

While these and many other thoughts were chasing themselves through my head, and I knew that I was feeling just as dumbstruck and giddy and schoolgirlish and in love with Mory as I had ever been, he folded down one of the Pullman seats into a bed.

"Sister Chrissy"—he held my face in his hands and kissed me gently, as if I were an insubstantial apparition that was about to vanish before his eyes—"before you tell me the whys and wherefores of your life, take off your dress and lie with me."

Without waiting for my answer, he lifted the See-Thru over my head. He kissed my breasts and gently traced my mole with his fingers. "Chrissy still has her trademark," he said softly. "You are a miracle! You have defied time."

Responding to his kisses, sobbing my delight and fears, I told him that we were ill-fated. "First loves are dream loves, Mory. If we had married, or even lived together, eventually we would have awakened to reality." Watching him as he quickly slid out of his clothing and lay beside me naked, I told him sadly. "It's too late, Mory. You already have a First Lady."

He smiled. "Chrissy, I've always believed that when the time is ripe you pick it and mold it so it fits your own reality. Everyone is speculating what life in the White House will be like when it's inhabited by a Love Group, I'm sure that no one is going to worry if I have two First Ladies. You'll like Adar. You and Adar are skull sisters."

I shook my head. "You wouldn't have time for all of us. One of us would get jealous."

Laughing, and ignoring my worries, Mory rolled me on top of him, a favorite Unilove position for extended sexual blending. He was already deep inside me. I kissed his dear, time-marked face with a hundred little kisses. "I don't understand how you could be so sure of me," I told him. "What did you mean when you said, 'I've been waiting for you'?"

"Nearly a hundred years ago, I wrote a short story. I called it 'Blindman's World.'" Mory's eyes were twinkling, but his expression was dreamy, almost otherworldly.

"Oh, good Lord," I sighed, "I forgot—you're Edward, too!"

"Do you remember the story?"

"Very well—you read it to me while my ass was slowly sinking in mud in a swamp in Marshfield. Lying on top of me, you not only managed to hold the book of Bellamy's stories in one hand, but somehow you stayed inside me and maintained an erection the whole time!"

Mory laughed. "My differently time-oriented people lived on Mars. Of course, in the nineteenth century, when I was actually Bellamy, I didn't know that Mars was barren."

Suddenly what Mory was trying to tell me clicked into place. "I remember! Bellamy's Martians knew what would happen to them in the future—not all of it—just what was going to happen to them personally. As children, they knew whom they were going to love and marry—and when their loved ones were going to die."

"The past had no reality for them," Mory said. "They lived wholly in the present and in the future. They didn't believe that tomorrow belonged to God. All their tomorrows and their todays belonged to them. When they encountered people from Earth, who spent a large part of their lives dwelling on their past—people who believed that personal death was a grievous occurrence—the Martians couldn't empathize with them."

Mory was grinning with pleasure. He was like a father telling his daughter a fairy story, which he kept reassuring her was absolutely true. "I remember what I—Bellamy—had their spokesman tell a representative from Earth: 'Living wholly in the future and present with both the foretaste and actual taste, our experiences whether pleasant or painful are exhausted of interest by the time they are past. There are no tears at the bedsides of the dying . . . in contrast with those who live on Earth. It's the intercourse you have had with friends that is the source of tenderness for you. With us it is the anticipation of the intercourse we *shall* enjoy that is the source of happiness. . . . Suppose your life destined to be blessed by a happy friendship. If you could know it beforehand, it would be a joyous expectation. Instead your first meeting is often cold and indifferent. Long before the fire is kindled between you it is time for parting. We greet each other, at first meeting, not coldly, not uncertainly. We see our friends afar coming to meet us . . . smiling already in our eyes long before we meet. Love with us always wears a smiling face. With earthlings he feeds on dead joys, past happiness, which are only the sustenance of sorrow.' "

"Mory," I sighed, "I really think you are a Martian. You're still as beautifully weird, bewildering, eerie, and lovable as when I last knew you. Are you actually trying to tell me that you knew that one day in the future I'd be making love with you right here in Topsfield?"

"Not the exact place, or time or day." Mory was now using his penis to say hello again to my labia and clitoris in a tentative, very alluring way. His eyes were alive with enthusiasm, and it was impossible to tell if he was entirely serious. "But just as I'm sure that I am a continuation of the essence of Edward Bellamy, and that I would run for President, and that I would meet Christina North and love her, and probably lose her, I was confident that, like Bellamy, you are inextricably interwoven into my life . . . until death do us part, not just for this life but for the next time around."

I shivered. "If I had known, in advance, the kind of life I would live, I wouldn't have wanted to live it."

"But you didn't know, and you still didn't want to live."

Mory was kissing my breasts gently, adoringly, and I was so overwhelmed with emotion that I climaxed in a happy flood of tears. "Oh, *diprin*," I whispered, "on my second chance I want us both to live forever. I love you." And then a sad thought occurred to me. "If you know when you're going to die, make sure that this time I die with you."

Mory didn't answer and he seemed suddenly detached, as if his thoughts were wandering in the future and I was no longer there.

"My God," I demanded. "Do you know?"

A smile flooded his face, and he kissed me fervently. "Sweet Chrissy—if I do, keep in mind that I have lived fifty-three years. If I don't win this time, then, as any good Buddhist will tell you, I must return to try again."

Before Chuck returned I told Mory that I had decided. If I could help him win, it didn't matter how. I'd make love to him tonight while fifty thousand people watched. I wanted to really be a part of his life. If he wanted, he could introduce me as the wife of Karl Klausner, who had renounced the rich-ik way of life. When he was elected President I didn't care if I was his First Lady, but I really wanted him to be President. "And when you are," I told him, "you won't have to worry about me. You can hide me in a Washington back street—just so long as you visit me twice a week!"

———◆———

As I lay in Mory's arms the next morning in one of the pulldown beds in his flying boxcar, while Jennifer and Chuck flew it to Chuck's island off the coast of Maine, we watched a video recording that Jennifer had made the night before—she had purposely stayed in Henry Adams' suite, so as not to press her luck too far—of Mory and then me (yes, me!) addressing a cheering crowd of over fifty thousand people who had listened to us on a damp, misty, floodlighted night at the Topsfield Race Track.

Now, nearly twelve hours later, watching myself on the television screen as we flew over Massachusetts, I could only laugh in sheer disbelief and amazement. How had I ever summoned up the courage to talk to such a huge number of people? While it was true, I had told the startled audience, that I was Christina Klausner, I really felt like Alice in Wonderland after she chased the White Rabbit and fell down the rabbit hole. "How queer everything is today. Yesterday—in my Klausner life—everything went on as usual! Let me think, was I the same when I got up this morning? There were more than five thousand mornings I stayed in my hibernaculum and never got up at all. I almost remember feeling a little different. But if I'm not the same, the question is: who in the world am I?"

Remembering my talk, I was pleased and exhilarated. But accompanying my happiness was a growing apprehension about Mory's safety. As we had made love that first afternoon, while I tried to give him a summary of my six conscious years of life without him, I had discovered the scar of a bullet that had grazed his chest just a few months ago. Kissing the angry-looking red welt, I had told Mory that I was terrified that I might lose him again. A few inches to the left and the bullet would have gone through his heart.

"I'm beginning to think that you're the most dangerous radical that ever came within spitting distance of the presidency." I had pointed at a stack of pamphlets that I knew outlined the budget for the new United People's Government. "David Convita gave me one of those. I noticed that they were being handed out at the fairgrounds. It's truly unbelievable, Mory. You've not only planning to eliminate all the government agencies and departments that handle such things as social security, Medicare, welfare, housing and urban development, education, veterans' benefits, and most of the Internal Revenue Department and the Department of Labor—and God knows what other government functions—but you're planning to do away with life insurance companies, banks, finance companies, the stock market, investment brokers, and even labor unions. I've only lived with lecks so far, but I'm beginning to realize that millions of people must hate you, or are desperately afraid of you. You're almost an anarchist. Your life must be in constant danger."

Listening to me, but calmly kissing my breasts, Mory responded in a dreamy, faraway voice, "Actually, Chrissy, millions of people love me. The salvation of America is to simplify it. A productive society should be easily administered. Ours is overgrown and eroded with barnacles. Forward motion is impossible.

"Nearly fifty years ago, Louis Kelso and Mortimer Adler wrote a book called *The Capitalist Manifesto*. They proposed a new method of compulsory capital financing that would have eliminated the stock and bond markets as we know them today. They devised a program so that, over a period of fifteen to twenty years, the capital wealth of this country would be transferred from the upper-income people to the majority of low-income families.

"In 1977, Stuart Speiser wrote a biography of Kelso's activities in a book called *A Piece of the Action*, and he pleaded for what he called Universal Capitalism. Speiser detailed Kelso's Financed Capital Plan, which would have made it possible for low-income families to share in the capital wealth. If the plan had been underwritten by business and government, it would have finally created the kind of people's capitalism that I am advocating, and it would have ultimately diffused ownership of the productive capital of the United States to all of our forty- or fifty-million lower-income families."

Mory grinned at me. "Because of the basic refusal of the rich to face reality, twenty years later we have made little or no progress. But finally the time and the idea and the prophet have coalesced, and found fertile ground."

Ignoring my laughing attempt to salaam to him, Mory continued caressing my body sensuously as he rambled aloud. "No man gets to Mecca by himself, Chrissy. The seeds were planted long ago. People's capitalism is the natural outgrowth of these earlier theories for diffusing the capital wealth of the country. Nothing I have suggested will decrease the economic strength of the United People, or our productivity as a nation. My Capital Account approach, and the direct forced transfer of stock ownership, will leave most of the middle class exactly where they are dollarwise, but the purchasing value of the dollar will be greater.

"For the first time in American history, low-income people, and millions of Americans who exist below poverty levels, will have a minimum net worth, and an ongoing, assured earning power, both as workers and as citizens of the UPA. Their only fear is that I can't make the dream come true, but at least they know the truth—I'm trying to save what remains of capitalism from becoming a big-business-financed military dictatorship. Those who have net worth of over one million dollars will be forced to loosen their power grip on the country. They may hate me, but they shouldn't. If Jason Kennedy is reelected and continues with his blundering big-government socialistic dictatorship, we'll end up a second-rate nation. In the balance will be the possibility of a military dictatorship. I'm offering New Tomorrow—the alternative that deals the American people into the game!"

"I'm afraid that the game is too rough," I told him. "Millions of people not only don't have the education, but probably don't have the ability to handle their emotional lives. You're going one step further and insisting that they can handle their own money and provide for their own future."

"What you're implying, Chrissy, is that the average human being can't get by without a caretaker—a Big Brother. If this were 1496 instead of 1996, and Europe was just as well developed and industrialized as it is now, but Columbus, or some other adventurers, had only discovered America a few years ago, you can be sure that those who had the money and power would be saying the same thing. 'Give America to us! We have the divine right of power, and money!' Like the Romans—and the Americans centuries later—many of those who held the power would be promising to free some of the slaves. They would do anything to maintain the illusion that all men are created equal, but they would never admit that the reason most men can't stay monetarily equal is that we indoctrinate our children that the smart ones can take the money away from the ignorant ones. Americans have begun to wake up to reality. After good health, the only human differences are money, and education, in that order. In the New Tomorrow that I'm proposing, the monetary differences, and as a by-product, the educational differences, will be considerably narrowed. We will finally achieve the equality that the founders of this country envisioned in their Declaration of Independence, even though most of them, when they wrote it, didn't really believe it was possible."

"I still think that you're daydreaming," I told him. "The bad guys—those who have the money and power—aren't going to simply stand by and let you divide the American pie into smaller slices."

Mory laughed. "It may take a little longer than I am projecting in my campaign, but don't underestimate me. We will do it. I'm very confident that after election, most of Congress—and a good majority haven't sold out to the richiks—will go along with me, simply because they want to get reelected. When we get through, it won't be the same pie, anyway, and the slices for the large majority will be much bigger than they ever had.

"Don't worry." Mory kissed me reassuringly. "I haven't forgotten Machiavelli's advice: 'There is nothing more difficult to take in hand, more perilous to conduct, or more uncertain of success, than to take the lead in the introduction of a new order of things.' "

"One thing I'm sure of," I told him, as his penis once again came to life in my hand, and he blended himself with me, "if you are elected, you're going to be the most loving President who ever slept in the White House. But it still seems incredible to me that the American people no longer expect the President of the country to be monogamous, or to be a paragon of virtue."

"Some of them still do." Laughter was dancing in Mory's eyes. "But most Americans are incurably romantic. Since you seem to be willing to reveal who you are, if you wish, tonight I'll go the whole route, and not only tell the world that I love you, but that I'm sure that my wife, Adar, and all the others, will welcome you into our Love Group. Since Sarah Masson, Chuck's pair bond, left us, we have an opening. Tomorrow, millions of American women will wish they could trade places with you."

"Who says I want to marry Chuck or go to bed with him?" I demanded, grabbing Mory's naked behind and digging my fingers into it to emphasize my lack of enthusiasm.

"You don't have to marry him. You can be pair bonded in a Unilove ceremony, but only if you wish. Finally, if you don't adjust to each other sexually, it really doesn't matter. The key to Love Groups is learning how to be friends."

"Do people have to learn that?"

"Most of them." Mory grinned. "It requires a different kind of ego surrender than many people are capable of. As for Love Groups living in the White House, keep in mind that Jason Kennedy is divorced, and is occasionally seen with his first wife, as well as other single women, young and old. I'm more than willing to be accountable to the American people sexually, unlike most of my predecessors. Presidents who had extramarital sex lives didn't begin with Franklin Roosevelt, but he did have a mistress. It's been said that Eisenhower wanted to divorce his wife and marry his adjutant, and that when Jackie was out of town, John Kennedy not only had specific bedmates, like Judith Exner, but occasionally he filled the White House with loving women, and they all swam together naked in the swimming pool. Lyndon Johnson is said to have had at least one other woman besides his Lady Bird. Who knows, Nixon might have been a much better President if he enjoyed women as much as he did power. Jimmy Carter never strayed, but he revealed that like

367

most American males, he thought about sex, and could lust after women other than Rosalyn. Presumably, the average male thinks about sex four minutes in every waking hour. Most of our previous Presidents have greatly exceeded the average.

"There's strong evidence that the drive for political power, and the need for sexual conformation, are closely related. That's why so many congressmen and senators, who have tried to be monogamously faithful, haven't succeeded. The immoral thing is not loving, but concealing it. The American people know that I live in a Love Group. Since I do—though we've always made it a rule never to discuss our sex lives publicly—it should be obvious that I occasionally spend the night with Emily Adams, who is nearly seventy, and Maria Gonzales, who is just thirty, as well as with Adar, to whom, following the old custom, I am married legally."

Mory brushed my hair affectionately with his hand and kissed my eyes and nose. "After tonight, Chrissy, the American people will understand that I have another potential bedmate."

"What about Jennifer?" I asked, feeling a little peeved. I still couldn't fully comprehend how non-ownership sex, which obviously involved a great deal of interpersonal commitment among a small group of people, could work without jealousy raising its head.

"Jennifer and I will always love each other," Mory said, and I noticed tears in his eyes. "As you can see, Jenny is taking a great political risk. While she couldn't possibly win as a Republican candidate, she has already given up her senatorial position. Fortunately, under the New Constitution, I will be in a position to nominate her for the Senate."

Mory grinned at me. "I suspect what you're really asking about is jealousy. When Adar and I considered marrying, I told her about you and Jenny. Jenny wasn't interested in a ménage à trois, but if you had been available, I'm sure that Adar would have suggested that we form a Love Group of three. In those days, I was a little dubious. We most certainly would have been pioneers. Adar's theory was that mobile marriages like ours could embrace other people. We were both very busy with our own projects. She was devoted to establishing Unilove, and, of course, I was crisscrossing the country on political junkets. We were often separated. Years ago, they would have called it an 'open marriage,' but most of those relationships didn't work out well because the interpersonal and sexual commitment was too shallow. Love Groups like ours, composed of mobile people, create a larger center that holds us together."

Mory grinned at me again. "We've been on a non-stop talking, lovemaking kick. For the next half hour I just want to breathe your flesh and revel in the amazement of your existence. Next week, you'll meet Adar. She's been campaigning in California with Richie Marratt. I'm sure Adar will talk to you all night long about the futility of jealousy."

Later that first day, after Chuck had routed us out of bed and we were eating dinner with Henry, Carlos, and a group of fifty or more Essex County officials, local politicians, and sponsors of the Topsfield Fair, Mory introduced me as his good friend, Christina North. He hinted that tonight he was making a major speech, and he and Christina would make an announcement that would startle the world. But even then I'd had no idea I would actually stand up before an audience of fifty thousand or more people and tell them about my childhood and college years, and to try to interrelate my parental and social conditioning, and my anxieties as an overachiever, with the saner kind of world that 'my Mory' was projecting—a world where joyous living and loving, in a secure economic environment, were the basic goals of a happy life.

———◆———

Watching the video playback with Mory, as we continued our non-stop love reunion high in the sky, I told him that he must have hypnotized me along with most of the audience.

"Good companions," he had said, as the cheering crowd finally settled into their stadium seats, "on this Columbus Day, you and I are searching together for a new world. But we must never forget that the joy is in the search. Every finding should lead us into a new search and into the infinite mysteries of life here on earth and in the cosmos. Years ago Americans searched for their roots, but they never realized that we are all interconnected with the same root. You and I—living, loving, dying, and being reborn in a never-ending cycle, are simply God in search of himself."

To emphasize his words, Mory paused for a few seconds, his eyes scanning the audience. "Because nothing is so boring as to listen to a political candidate rehashing and repeating platitudes, or attacking the campaign promises and inadvertent political slips of those in the race against him, tonight, as in the past, I want to give you, and our video audience, some new ideas to think about. I want to tell you about the world *beyond* New Tomorrow. Before the year 2000, instead of trying to exist in a world where the value of your hard-earned money disappears before you can even put it in your pocket, instead of living, as millions of Americans do, in a world of pain, you and I can lay the groundwork for the twenty-first century—the Century of Human Fulfillment.

"These are not just campaign promises. Nor am I concealing, nor am I unwilling to discuss, any aspects of my proposals. With the cooperation of the Challenge Foundation, which is maintaining a round-the-clock-dialogue telephone service with the people of America, you can get specific answers to any question that may be bothering you about New Tomorrow." Mory laughed. "Even, if you should be interested, how a Love Group of eight adults and four children will manage to live together in the White House.

"Because I believe that a President should function as a generalist, and, in addition to resolving present problems, should conceive and project possible futures, and help lead the way to their actualization—tonight, I want to tell you about James Cooke Brown. Many of you know his name as the inventor of Loglan, that language which even now is teaching us to rethink our ideas. But twenty-six years ago, even before Loglan, with the essence of Edward Bellamy whirling in his brain, Jim Brown wrote this great Utopian novel, *The Troika Incident—The Coming of a Viable Human Society,* which I am holding in my hand. Like Bellamy, Jim Brown—who, I'm happy to say, is alive and healthy at seventy-eight—projected the world of 1970 a hundred years ahead to the world none of us has yet experienced, the world of 2070. While there is no time to cover the many aspects of the future that Jim Brown envisioned in his book, I am totally delighted that one of his inspirations was Edward Bellamy's concept of the Job Market. In this book, and others, Brown has fleshed out the Bellamy dream. He has visualized a complete reversal of the old concept of seeking a job. Instead of the nation's employers buying your labor, they would become the sellers of the jobs to be done, and you and I would become the buyers. Brown's creation is a Job Market, which would operate through nationwide computer-controlled regional centers. All the jobs available in this country, and in cooperating nations, would be advertised continuously. The Job Market would coordinate a future world that is within your grasp. Once we have established New Tomorrow, we can look forward to Job Market centers where employers all over the world would be *selling* their jobs. Each job would carry a work-hour credit rating. The buyer would know the job requirements and the length of the job. The credit-hour payment for a particular job would determine your income. Easy jobs, which require little skill, would have minimum credit hours. Difficult jobs, or unpleasant ones, are sold at credit hours commensurate with the demand. The Job Market would put productive labor in balance with manufacturing output and could eliminate inflation. On any one day, several million potential jobs would be for sale. When a true Job Market existed, those working in the Central Work Force in the world of New Tomorrow that I have projected, who wish to live a more creative life, could seek jobs especially designed to meet their particular skills or monetary needs. And, of course, any job that you would buy would automatically entitle you to stock ownership in a particular corporation selling a particular job.

"The Troika Incident not only introduces the Job Market, but covers all aspects of life and loving in 2070. The amazing thing is that it was written in 1970 and is proving prophetic. Already, in our world of 1996, millions of us are reacting sexually to each other just as Jim Brown described it in his lovely Utopian novel.

"Let me read you a small fragment. 'Even sex runs more creatively when it runs strong and free,' Brown wrote. 'In 2070, people have accepted the deep sexuality of their natures as well as their equally profound aggressiveness. . . . They fuck with the same spontaneous grace and ease as you and I might agree to swim across the bay together . . . or cast ourselves into some great work together. You see, there is *still* grace and majesty and mystery in the human person, and the wish to fuck another human being is to honor that mystery precisely by recognizing what is most spectacularly human in him/her and in oneself.' "

Mory smiled at his audience. "In 1996, that feeling is finally infiltrating most of our Western religions. As I have said many times, the kind and quality of our sex lives and our family lives and our economic and political lives are closely intertwined with the kind of equality we achieve for each other as Americans. The concept of kitsa—a Loglan word which was also invented by Jim Brown—involving the total genital and mental surrender, rather than a generalized word like fucking, a word which many of us have abandoned, is closely related to that kind of equality. Only when we have freedom from insecurity can we fully learn and enjoy our human mental and sexual potential in all of its dimensions.

"And now I want you to meet the woman who has been sitting beside me on this platform, a woman who has been hibernated for sixteen years, and has survived. Perhaps many of you are aware that I have been somewhat negative on the subject of hibernation and the wide attention that it has received in the news media. I prefer to accept my temporary death as a phase intrinsic to my next incarnation. I have no desire to sleep now, to awake in some future world. But aside from my personal feelings, I am proud to present living proof of a major medical breakthrough, and even more important, to let this lovely woman tell you in her own words a love story that has defied time."

Mory had extended his hand to me. I had no choice. Trembling, I arose. His arm around me for a moment, he said, "Meet the first woman I ever loved—Christina North Klausner." There was no choice. The crowd was roaring its approval. The telvi cameras were probing our faces, and projecting them five times life-size on a screen that hung over the platform. Like it or not, I was finally famous.

Lying naked in each other's arms in the Heli-Home, Mory and I floated backward in time. We shared thousands of tiny details of our lives—pieces of a jigsaw puzzle which, once we completed it, I knew we could glue together for life. And when I tried to recall the reasons for the deepening depression that had finally led me to David Convita, I realized that the larger, infinitely exciting world of Mory's dreams was more important to me than my ego fantasies had ever been.

Although we were flying over Massachusetts and Maine in a time frame of 1996, I knew time had stopped. We had never left Cambridge. Immersed in our discovery of each other, we were like children at the seashore after a long, dry summer, refusing to leave the water until our skin was puckered and we couldn't stop shivering. When neither of us stopped talking or philosophizing or trying to explain the devious byways of our lives, the other picked up the threads. Laughing, probing, hugging, tasting, sucking—almost in disbelief as we literally became each other's flesh: how erotic

372

my/your? skin and blood warmth are—we occasionally drifted into loving silence, and our lips together, our tongues touching, we luxuriated in the blending of our separate selves.

"I think you've given me a permanent erection." Mory surveyed his upright penis with amusement. Once again I had spread my legs over it, and felt my vagina suck him hard within me, and unable to control myself, had swiftly glided into another orgasm.

"How do you know that I'm not just responding to the changing scenery?" Mory asked.

"What do you mean?" I knew, because it had occurred to me, too, but I ignored the teasing tone of his voice.

"An old man with a new and young woman—discovering to his amazement that he can still get it up!"

"Don't you make love with Adar?" In truth, I was wondering how a man who had climaxed several times with one woman could repeat the performance the next night with another. But I didn't dare ask.

Hugging me, Mory answered my unasked question, "One of the theories of Unilove is that the more you love, the more you love, and the more you can love . . . until you're ninety, or even a hundred. Remember, Adar wrote the book!"

Chuck announced on the intercom that we were flying over the southern tip of Oyster Island. "In a few minutes," he said, "our scuddy passengers can pronken in the Atlantic Ocean—and freeze their asses and titties off."

Below us, I could see a heavily forested island with white sandy beaches on the ocean side. Further out to sea, a few yachts were cruising lazily by it, headed toward Bar Harbor.

"What does scuddy mean?" I heard Jennifer ask.

"Naked, honey," Chuck replied.

"Have you two been watching us down here?" I demanded. I knew that the pilot's cabin was connected with a two-way television.

"We tried," Jennifer laughed, "but you didn't turn your screen on. Never mind, we could hear you groaning and gasping occasionally."

Instead of pushing me away during this conversation, Mory continued to lie under me. He was still deep and hard in my vagina. Encouraged by his fingers exploring my breasts and perineum, I slowly rocked us both to a gasping climax. Then, as I was trying to catch my breath, I suddenly remembered Chandra's warning, and asked Mory if he had a T.R.

373

He looked at me, astonished. "You've learned a lot in a short time. Are you ovulating?"

"How would I know?"

"Evidently, you haven't learned everything. I should have told you to take a vaginal smear. There's a kit in the toilet."

"What if I had been?"

Mory hugged me. "Maybe I wouldn't have let you bring me to a climax. Maybe we would have just played with each other."

"Is it too late to tell now?"

"Probably not. But if you are ovulating, my sperm has probably found your egg already."

I giggled. "You sound like the birds and bees. I don't give a damn. Yesterday you told me that millions of women would jump at the chance to live in your Love Group. What will they think if you have to announce that I have a real live New Tomorrow kicking in my belly?"

"They'll love it. I think he'd be the first baby ever born in the White House."

It obviously was still a male world, but I was enjoying it!

<hr>

Chuck landed the Heli-Home in a meadow a few hundred yards from a large, weather-beaten New England farmhouse. Coming down the narrow circular stairway that connected the cabin and van, Jennifer was exultant. "I flew the damned thing, Christa! It's a cinch. Just think, a few hours ago we were in Topsfield. Now we're on a remote island five miles out to sea, off the coast of Maine."

"Jennifer has a great idea," Chuck said. "Next year, when you're President, we'll take over this island and run it as a hideaway for politicians. We'll even set up a special federal agency. The OPE—Orgies at Public Expense."

Chuck introduced us to Ned and Polly Schrank, a pleasant gray-haired couple in their late fifties, who were waiting for us when we walked down the landing stairs. "Ned and Polly run the oyster and lobster farms," he said, hugging them. "They believe in Mory—but not in Love Groups. Downeasters are still mostly monogamous."

Polly grinned at him. "The real reason is that Chuck's never asked me to go to bed with him." She stared at Mory as if she were about to curtsy to her first real live President.

374

"Of course, I'd prefer an invitation from Newton Morrow, our next President."

Laughing, Mory bussed her cheek. "I'd be afraid of raising old Ned." He shook her husband's hand. Chuck groaned at the old cliché, but Ned was obviously delighted.

Showing us the farmhouse, and the bedrooms with old-fashioned spool beds and huge feather mattresses, Chuck assured us that our disappearance was now complete. While their constituency might not approve, two of the presidential candidates had each dropped out of the world for a few sensible days of relaxation and lovemaking. "Today, tomorrow, and Tuesday are ours. We'll show you how we grow five million or more oysters, and a few hundred thousand lobsters, annually. We can sail together in an ancient wooden John Kennedy-style catboat, or plow around the coast in a Novi boat with a twelve-foot beam. We can make love in bed, on the beach, in the pine groves, or floating in the cold Maine water. Polly is planning to feed us our weight in oysters. They're bluepoints. *Crassostrea Virginica.* They only have about seven calories each. Tonight, we can experiment with their aphrodisiac and restorative qualities."

A half hour later, with a lunch of lobster sandwiches that Polly had packed for us, we ran naked along an endless white beach toward the oyster-and-lobster shipping pier. Ned had given us sun-deflector gowns and floppy hats, but we didn't have to wear them because the sky was overcast with light clouds. Chuck had brought along big jars of Desola, but none of us wanted to be blue people. "When you're flesh to flesh, it feels slimy," was Mory's only comment.

Raising the sail on the catboat, tacking toward Europe on a cool easterly that soon had us wearing woolen pullovers to cover the top halves of our naked bodies, none of us paid any attention to a lobster boat plowing through the waves about a half mile off our starboard bow. And we were so involved with each other that we ignored the boat Monday and Tuesday as well. Lobster boats were indigenous to this part of Maine, and unlike Chuck Holmes, who farmed his lobsters, many of the old-timers still set out traps. So what if they could see us naked through their binoculars? How could we have guessed that they weren't fishermen at all, but Mory's and Jennifer's ever-faithful Secret Service men—indirectly employed by Warren Ellison, the Secretary of the Treasury—who were watching us? If Warren wasn't worried about a

375

prime rate of 15 percent, at least he could claim that he was guarding the country's morals.

Jennifer's black hair was blowing in the wind. Tiller in hand, sailing on a reach, Chuck was entertaining her with sexual fantasies about the coming night. He told us that from his vantage point—sitting on the floor of the catboat, while Jennifer and I were sitting on the rail, he could enjoy the sight of our lovely "queynts."

"It comes from the old English word *acqueyntaunce* . . . it's also related to *quenchen*—to satisfy. Ultimately, it became quaint—strange. From there it was only a short step to cunt. Lecks use Loglan—*konbi*—and the English word is vulva, but I prefer queynts. Tonight, Mory and I hope to get re-acqueynted with your respective queynts."

Jennifer laughed. "Oh, lovely. It sounds as if we have an orgy coming up. Do we all tumble in your feather beds together?"

"Sure"—Mory grinned—"but only to talk. After four-way discussion has ceased, Chuck and you can enjoy kitsa together."

Jennifer pouted. "The master speaks. Is Mory making up your mind, Chuck?"

I wanted to suggest that maybe I was the intruder, and Mory and Jennifer should have some love time together. But I really didn't feel so magnanimous.

Chuck coolly dropped the sailboat's tiller and quickly kissed his way up Jennifer's bare thigh to her queynt. "You know damned well, Jenny, that I love you. Waffling and sarmassating with you invigorates my brain and makes me feel like Bacchus."

Mory cupped his hand against the saltwater rushing past the gunnel and tossed a handful over Chuck's head. "God Almighty, how can I ever make you presidential secretary? Even I don't know what in hell you're talking about most of the time."

Chuck laughed. "Before we waffle about anything else, it's time you listened to Jenny, and let her bring you up-to-date."

Her eyebrows raised at me, Jennifer flicked Mory's penis affectionately. It was dangling beneath his sweater. I couldn't blame her. Limp, it looked lonely. "Christa and Mory are like Chaucer's Monk and the Shipman's wife," she said. " 'In myrthe al night a bisy lif they lede!' They haven't time for politics."

Chuck approved. "I like that: sex with laughter. But we have to wake up to reality."

"My polling sources," Jennifer said, "are estimating that I'm going to take about five million votes from Kennedy, and three million from you, Mory. That will net you about two million. They're predicting you'll win by about two million votes. Whether you have swung those votes yourself or I aided you, no one will ever know for sure. One thing is certain. Last week, when the Dow inflation studies revealed that money invested in life insurance, even in variable annuities, lost its original purchasing power within ten years, the betting odds moved decidedly in your favor. I have it on good authority that a dozen top executives, and a couple of generals from the Pentagon who are associated with the Invisible Hand, want to meet with you and strike a deal to save the country. According to my sources, if you refuse, the combined wrath of the money gods, and the military gods of the Pentagon, will strike you down before you ever cross the threshold of the White House."

Mory shook his head. "I'm not meeting with them—before or after the election. There'll be no concessions. The only way to save the country now is to eliminate all the middlemen who control the flow of money. In combination with the legal profession, they have so obfuscated and misdirected the strength of the people that we've forgotten the prime purpose of money is a convenient way for people to exchange a product or a service. It's not a vehicle to sell a society into slavery."

"There's one thing that confuses me," I said. "Evidently, Kennedy and many other people believe that nuclear fusion will solve all the world's energy problems. Cheap power is presumably not too many years away. Then, everyone could not only have automobiles, but their own Heli-Homes, if they wish. Two billion Chinese and Indian people—not to mention the Africans and Russians—will all have high-powered hydrogen-driven automobiles. Not Trics, but automobiles like the old-time Cadillacs and Mark IV's. Eight-lane roads from Moscow to Siberia and Peking would be built, and they'll be dotted with hamburger and hot-dog stands, Pepsi-Cola signs and Russian Disneylands. It seems to me that you're the bad guy." I grinned at him, hoping that he knew I was teasing him. "You're depriving the world of all the fun!"

"Maybe I am,"—Mory's voice sounded a little harsh—"but even if we could create four billion more consuming idiots

377

to match the billion we already have—even if we could dig up the whole damned Moon and half of Mars and bring the raw materials back to Earth and turn them into plastic and metal junk, will anyone be happier?" Mory suddenly chuckled. "Sister Chrissy and Sister Jennifer, way back a quarter of a century ago I told you that someone, for good or bad, had to take the reins of the wild horses of capitalism in hand. We'll all be happier trotting to Nirvana than galloping there."

Three days and nights we talked, and we played and frolicked together. When our sexual needs dominated our explorations into economics and sociology and politics, or how Jennifer and Mory would handle the Third Presidential Conversation, or what made communities, and ultimately nations, loving and great—we separated. Sometimes only a few hundred yards apart on the white sandy beach, or hidden by the dunes, we made love together—I with Mory, Jennifer with Chuck. Naked, laughing, blended, ecstatic, and then in quiet awe and wonder, we floated in the sheer joy and amazement of our individual surrender.

And once, because it was right and happened very naturally, Jennifer embraced Mory, and Chuck embraced me. We were wandering along the beach, enjoying a warm summer southwesterly that was beginning to collide with an offshore easterly. Entranced by the slowly gathering fog, shivering a little, Jennifer and I climbed on our laughing men, occasionally switching as we played together, and scissoring them with our legs, and kissing them enthusiastically. Their hands clutched our bottoms. Their suddenly aroused penises quickly found homes in our vaginas. Plunging with their succubi into the cold ocean water, they tumbled and played together with us, and to our surprise, Jennifer and I received unexpected saltwater douches. When we finally came out of the water, their waving bamboos had shriveled so badly that we felt sorry for them, and laughingly mothered our little boys to life again with our mouths.

And Chuck showed his oyster beds and lobster corrals and told us about the many varieties of oysters, which, along with many varieties of shellfish such as clams and shrimps, were now being farmed all over the world.

"We're pumping ocean water from far out to sea—from
378

depths of hundreds of kilometers," he told us, as we ate oysters, together with lobster and homemade bread, washed down by cold, dry Meursault white wine. "The oysters thrive on it. It's rich in phytoplankton and other minute sea life. The oyster's cilia in turn pumps several hundred liters daily over its gills and much of its body. Thus, the oyster becomes a natural source of phosphorus and other sundry particles and chemicals that excite female genitals and help the male to rebuild his semen and ejaculate fluid!"

Not having been an oyster enthusiast in my previous existence, I was trying to swallow the bivalves without choking. Grimacing a little, I assured Chuck he had been reading old wives' tales. "The only reason that men believe oysters are an aphrodisiac," I told him, "is that they look like an open female vulva."

Laughing, Jennifer disagreed. "I think they look like the male testicles!"

"*Le huître*—oyster in French—is also slang for the female pudenda!" I argued.

But then, just as I was beginning to enjoy them a little, and had stopped thinking that I was some kind of cannibal, swallowing the poor things alive and into my stomach while their hearts were still pumping pale blue blood through their veins—Chuck pointed out that if you kept the *Crassostrea Virginica* oysters, which we were eating, in a temperature a few degrees above freezing, they'd remain alive for six months or longer.

I couldn't help it. My happiness, and the wine, conflicted with the tipsy realization that I had been a cryobiologist's dream girl. "I guess I was David Convita's oyster," I sobbed at Mory, who tried to change my mood by dropping a cold oyster on my breast and slurping it off.

My scream and pop eyes as I watched the slippery, shuddery thing oozing down my chest before Mory swallowed it, made Jennifer laugh so hard that she was gasping. But her laughter was short-lived. Chuck dropped one on her belly just above her delta. She clutched at it, but it escaped her and slid into her pussy hairs. She quickly acceded to Chuck's enthusiastic: "Don't touch it, Jenny. Just open your legs and I'll eat it off."

Captivated by this nonsense, I dropped one on Mory's penis and lapped it off. Then I remembered a quotation from Rabelais, which I had used in my movie. "A monk in a cloister is not worth an oyster."

379

After consuming about two hundred oysters among us, we continued playing sloppy scenarios from *Tom Jones,* with lobster juice dripping all over our bodies. Chuck proposed that Adar should write an Oyster Ballet for Unilove Churches—or better still, oysters should be imbibed at an especially created Unilove Mass. "The oyster is a perfect example of the androgynous quality of all life," he insisted. I was surprised that after so much wine he was still lucid. "The oyster begins life as a male, and when it is one or two years old, more than half of the males become females. Many European oysters shed their ova and become fully equipped males. American oysters alternate. Obviously, if the Unilove Participants imbibed an oyster in a Unilove Mass, it would have very lovely symbolism."

When we disputed such crazy yalk, Chuck unearthed an old book, *Lewd Foods,* by Robert Hendrickson, and read us the whole chapter about oysters. " 'The *Crassostrea Virginica,*' " he skip-read, " 'releases seventy million eggs in a single spawning, while her aggressive male counterpart extrudes a billion sperm each.' You can see, Chrissy—" he laughed at my astonishment—"you shouldn't feel like a cannibal when you eat them—especially in 1996. Today, we protect them from most of their natural enemies. If we didn't help eat them, we'd all be up to our asses in oysters."

———◆———

Wednesday morning, our tiny love vacation behind us, Chuck landed the Heli-Home at a rental agency in a Heliport on the northern quadrant of Boston. Jennifer had put on her wig and blue contact lenses, but when we opened the door of the van and saw a huge crowd of reporters and television cameramen waiting for us, we knew that Mory and Jennifer were up to their asses in the political scandal of all times.

"Take off your wig, Jennifer Manchester," someone yelled, as we stared at them, completely bewildered, from the doorway. Everywhere cameras were turning. "Tell us how you and Newt Morrow have wrapped up the 1996 presidential campaign—in bed together!"

Hundreds of questions and sexual taunts were being shouted at us, as Chuck, grasping the situation, pushed us back into the van.

"Some bed," I heard someone roar with laughter. "With all that beach sand creeping into Jennifer's and Chrissy's *konbis,* they must have sandpapered Newt's *pingu* into a new offensive weapon."

"The bastards must have bugged us," Chuck hissed. "Get back inside and I'll reconnoiter." Blocking the door, he shouted back at them, "What's all this crap about Jennifer Manchester? Newt's just returning from a few days with me and his Chrissy. We were all together on my island off the coast of Maine."

"Cut the crap, Holmes," was the response.

We saw Carlos Gonzales worming his way through the crowd and up the stairs. He pushed Chuck back into the van and slammed the door. "Have you listened to your radios?" He obviously was very, very agitated. He spoke rapidly to Mory, switching back and forth in an incomprehensible mixture of English and Spanish.

Finally Mory told him to calm down and speak slowly in English. Grinning at us, and shrugging helplessly, Mory summarized. "Carlos is trying to tell us that Chuck and I are the playboys of the Western world. Someone—he's sure that it was Warren Ellison—must have kept a tail on Chrissy. Then, because they were confident that more was going on than met the eye, one of my SS protectors must have bugged the 'copter with a signaling device. They followed us up the coast. For three days—evidently from those Novi boats that we kept seeing—they photographed us with telescopic lens. Our Oyster Island orgy is public information."

"You can't deny it!" Carlos said angrily. "They've run pictures of all of you, naked and screwing. They're showing them over and over again on all the news channels. They're even defying the telvi regulations and running clips from Christa's movie, showing close-ups of her back in the seventies with someone named Johnny Giacomo. They're comparing her oral technique with your Oyster Island pictures." Carlos stared grimly at me. "Fortunately, the 1996 version is not so clear. What are you going to do?"

For the moment Chuck and Mory seemed at a loss for words.

"We obviously can't deny it." Jennifer tried to speak calmly, but she looked a little pale, and her face suddenly seemed older and troubled. "I'm sorry, Mory. I should have listened to you and kept my distance until it was over."

Mory put his arm around her. "You probably shouldn't make your speech in Chicago tomorrow. Come to New York with us."

Jennifer grinned at him feebly. "When I'm running for the Senate again, and you're back trying to get reelected governor of Louisiana, we'll write a book about our rendezvous. But I can't quit now. No matter what, I've got to blunder on. I'm the Republican standard bearer."

Chuck suddenly came to life. "I agree with you, Jenny. First, we've got to size up the public reaction. America is a very loving country. After an election, presidential candidates always tell their constituents to forget their animosities and work together for the country's good. You and Mory were working in advance. A little happy screwing is an everyday occurrence. Maybe we can even convince them that presidential candidates should make love together."

"Mory didn't go to bed with Jenny," I reminded him. "He went to bed with me."

"Even Jenny and I don't know whether you continued to make love, or passed out from sheer exhaustion." Chuck shrugged. "But one thing is sure, at least, one of the days, we all had some unexpected fun on the beach. At the moment, our best bet is not to deny the known reality. Mory and Jennifer spent a few days in Maine together. Until we can figure out a good reason why, it's a no-comment situation." He laughed. "Maybe we can tell them that it was an anti-syzygy meeting."

Mory scowled at him. "What the hell does that mean?"

"A union of opposites!"

———◆———

A few hours later, after a flight to LaGuardia in a private jet that Chuck had chartered, we arrived at the Sheraton East Hotel, where Adar and Richie Marratt were waiting for us. Once again we were besieged by reporters and television crews, who were waiting in front of Mory's previously announced New York headquarters.

Before we flew from Boston, Mory and Chuck had decided that Jennifer should tell reporters that she had spent a few days with Newton Morrow to see if she could convince him, if he was elected, that he must moderate his eighteen-month Transition Period plan, and especially go slow on any attempt to liquidate the life insurance and banking industries. If necessary, she could spout the Invisible Hand Alliance propaganda, that life insurance and private banking was an American way of life that could be easily blended into a society

382

with greater capital diffusion. The Republicans would like that. She could tell the reporters that she had even threatened Newton Morrow. If he was elected without the Republican swing vote in Congress, his Utopian New Tomorrow daydream would go nowhere.

"For God's sake, don't be apologetic. Don't make excuses," Chuck had told her. "Tell them that you were in there pitching words, not your *konbi*. Tell them that even though the Republican vote is a minority vote, the GOP can still control Morrow, or Kennedy, whoever wins."

No decision had been made on the sexual aspects of our little holiday. "Most of the people in this country are no longer terrified by the thought of a highly sexed heterosexual President." Chuck was convinced that the day we had been screwing together outdoors was pretty foggy. If they *had* filmed our hilarious switch, it would weaken the Newton-Chrissy love story. Chuck assured Jennifer that once we'd all seen the film they were running on telvi, we'd have plenty of time to straighten out our stories. "If they just got pictures of Jenny and me together, and Newt and Chrissy together, no harm is done. It was an old-fashioned love reunion. All Jenny has to do is convince her husband that Chuck is a very innocuous lover."

We were all aware that Chuck was trying to roll with the punches. No matter what any of us said, no one was going to believe that Mory and Jennifer weren't lovers, or, from the obvious fact that she very probably had enjoyed sex with him, that she wasn't, in actuality, working for Morrow's election.

Stepping out of the Tric taxi at the hotel, Mory was amazingly cool and self-possessed. Waving at the reporters, he laughed aside some of the questions that were flung at him and responded to others. "Jennifer Manchester will make an announcement this evening from Chicago on the purpose of our meeting. I can assure you that Jennifer hasn't sold the Republican party down the river. She's doing everything in her power to get elected."

"Including screwing with the next President?" someone yelled.

Mory ignored that one and took my arm. "Yes, this is Chrissy. Christina Klausner. No, she hasn't met Adar yet."

"She will in a few minutes," a laughing reporter said. "Your wife and her brother-in-law, Richie Marratt, arrived twenty minutes ago."

383

"When Richie is Vice-President, will he sleep in the White House with the First Lady of his choice?"

Grinning, Mory fended that one. "Momentarily, Richie is a bachelor. Unfortunately, at the moment, we have no room for him in our Love Group."

Before the Secret Service cleared us through the lobby to the elevators, I was targeted and battered with questions. "Are you willing to share Morrow with his wife? Are you really only thirty-three? Will you join Morrow's Love Group? When are you going to meet your husband? Did you know that Karl Klausner announced this morning that he's delighted that you're alive? He says he'll never divorce you. You're the mother of his only children. He says that he looks forward to having you in his bed again."

At the same time, like locusts, they continued swarming around Mory. "What do you think of the Secretary of the Treasury's statement?—'Unless Jennifer Manchester has a plausible explanation for her conduct, she should withdraw from the campaign and let Robert Lee run for President in her place.' "

Chuck responded to that one. "Newt never comments on Democratic or Republican party interjurisdictional disputes. He'll make a general announcement later."

Finally, we were alone in the elevator. Mory hugged me. "Chrissy—Chrissy, you're trembling." Actually, I was in a state of shock. Behind me were the reporters. In front of me, coming up, were Adar and Richie. "Don't let them bother you, *diprin*," Mory said. "It's all part of the silly American hassle to elect a President."

Chuck grinned at me. "If Newt's elected, there'll be no more vastation. The President will be elected by Congress."

"What's vastation?" Mory seemed to enjoy playing end man to Chuck's verbal insanity.

"Purification by fire."

Mory grunted. "We never needed it. No matter how a President gets elected we don't need a saint in the White House."

Richie greeted us in the living room of the four-bedroom hotel suite. A great, hulking, brown-eyed, barrel-chested, snowy-haired man, he swung me in the air, booming enthusiastically: "So this is Chrissy! You're lovely. All America has fallen in love with you. They'll never forget the tears of happiness and love in your eyes when you told everyone that you were ashamed of your former self, and you were so proud

384

you'd be alive in 'Mory's New Tomorrow.' " Richie chuckled. "You're a star-spangled American girl. This morning, using the best political hyperbole, I told the media that you're a light shining through the blackness and despair of the past ten years! You've given proof 'that the stars are still there.' "

"Richie told reporters this morning that during the year 2000 we might return to the style of the first American flag." Carlos was obviously very pragmatic. He seemed a little calmer than he had been. "Fifteen stars for the fifteen new Commonwealths of the United People of America."

I smiled timidly at Adar, who was watching us. For a moment, I felt as if I were sinking into the warm, loving protection of her big brown eyes. Although I knew that she was nearly fifty-one, she had a startlingly youthful appearance. The pale orange See-Thru that she was wearing created an aura for her dark complexion and her gray-streaked black hair and madonna-style face; and it revealed glimpses of her lean, small-breasted body, and the strong, muscular thighs and legs of a ballet dancer. Her leck-style haircut completed her New Tomorrow image.

Instead of shaking hands, almost simultaneously we opened our arms and embraced each other. "I'm glad that Newt found you, Chrissy," she said without affectation. "Years ago, when I read your poetry and short stories, and your Sleeping Beauty novel, I knew that we were seeing the world in the same kind of loving focus."

Chuck interrupted us a little impatiently. "I'm sorry, you've got plenty of time for future meetings of your mutual admiration society. Right now, we've got to agree whether Newt and Jennifer were in Maine for a little friendly kitsa, or whether Jenny was actually selling the Republican party short."

Richie shook his head mournfully. "You've got another problem. Less than a hour ago, Jason Kennedy announced that he was withdrawing from the Third Presidential Conversation. He said that it's been obvious for some time that the Republicans and the UPA are involved in a nefarious coalition to win the election." Richie shrugged. "I warned you, Newt—you and Jennifer should have been much more discrete. The Big OIO, as they've dubbed your hegira, could cost you a lot of votes." Richie explained that OIO was either Oyster Island Orgy or Oyster Island Orgasm—take your pick.

I tried to protest that it was all my fault. Had I not been

385

with Jennifer, she and Mory would never have been discovered.

"It doesn't matter who's responsible," Richie said. "We've got to make up our minds whether the sex aspects of your escapade overshadow the political repercussions. Henry has our public-relations staff working on it. At the moment, the general public seems to be much more interested in the Newt-Chrissy love affair. Psychologically, many of the women identify with Chrissy. When they watch pictures of the two of you making love, they're not really voyeurs—they actually become Chrissy, finally making love with the man that she has loved for twenty-five years. There's a similar male identification with Newt."

While Richie was talking, Carlos dropped a tape cassette into the player, and larger than life size on a Life-a-Vision screen on the wall of the suite, Mory and I and Jennifer and Chuck were romping naked on the beach in hazy but clearly identifiable color. Fortunately, they hadn't caught us switching partners, but with Adar watching, I was embarrassed—especially at the extended sequences of Mory and me enthusiastically enjoying each other's genitals, or the cut-ins of me with Johnny Giacomo. Of course, our long, tender hours of kitsa were missing. Sex on film in 1996 was as one-dimensional as it had been in 1980.

When the fifteen-minute film, with a voice-over asking pertinent and leering questions, was finished, Chuck seemed a little relieved. The Newt-Chrissy love story was still intact, although, of course, the flagrant sexual life of Christina North, some twenty-three years ago, didn't aid the illusion.

Richie told us that Newt's staff, taking the bull by the horns, had tested public reaction on that too. For the most part, whatever Chrissy had done in her previous life was forgiven. Surviving through sixteen years of hibernation was suffering enough. Loving Newton Morrow for so long had completed my redemption. Richie insisted that this wasn't solely a leck response. The poor-ik reaction was sympathetic, too.

"You're bringing tears to my eyes. It's kalopsian." Chuck ignored Mory's grimace. "Kalopsia is a condition where things appear more beautiful than they are."

Mory laughed. "I knew I couldn't trust your weird English. Actually, Chrissy and I are more beautiful to each other than we can ever appear to the world."

After another hour of discussion and a phone call to Jennifer, who had arrived at her hotel in Chicago, the decision was made that since Jason Kennedy had announced that he would not appear on the final Presidential Conversation a week from today, on October 23rd, Mory and Jennifer probably wouldn't discuss the OIO—not unless public reaction made it necessary. In the meantime, they had a week's reprieve, and altogether about twenty days before Election Day—hopefully time enough to counteract adverse reaction, and make sure that the wind was still blowing on Mory's back.

Both Chuck and Mory were enthusiastic over Adar's suggestion that while Mory was taking a swing through the Midwest, and Richie was covering New York State, she and I should spend the next few days together. I could even accompany her on several telvi interviews that had been scheduled. Smiling at Mory, she told him, "Just keep in mind that a great many American women still aren't so liberated as your number one. They may not believe that Love Groups are possible—or that an older woman would ever want to share her husband with anyone as lovely as Chrissy, but it will reassure them to know that I love you, and that in my opinion you most certainly aren't promiscuous. You're a great, loving man."

She really meant what she said. During the following days, sleeping in a big double bed with Adar, wandering through New York stores together or buzzing back and forth across the city to special luncheons and dinners and television interviews (always with at least one Secret Service man in tow), I discovered to my surprise that while Adar really loved Mory, she was delighted that I loved him, too. "Loving can never be exclusive," she insisted. "I enjoy Chuck and Henry and Carlos—and yes, I love Jennifer and Emily and Maria." Smiling, Adar wrinkled her nose affectionately at me. "And Richie, too—my brother! He never should have married Alisha. A pleasant woman, but, unfortunately, she thought she could reform a Marratt."

"You must understand," Adar told a dinner gathering of the Associated Publishers of America the following evening, "that Richie, my stepbrother, and I were brought up by two loving mothers, Anne and Cynthia. They both loved Richie's father, Yale Marratt. Later, when Bob Coleman joined our family group and married Anne, Richie's mother, they continued to defy traditional monogamous possessiveness. From childhood, we were taught the sheer joy of living in an environment of expanded interpersonal commitment and caring."

I was sitting beside Adar as she spoke, and she extended her hand to me. "This is Chrissy, whom you've seen on the tclvi. She has joined our family. Next January, instead of one First Lady in the White House, we hope you'll have four. In order of age: Emily, Adar, Chrissy, and Maria!"

"What about Jennifer Manchester?" someone shouted.

Adar smiled. "Jennifer will always be a welcome visitor."

But Adar's cool poise and her ability to create and inspire a complete religious movement—paralleling Mory's charisma in politics—was never better than the Sunday she appeared at the Unilove Church in Times Square, a former Loew's movie theater. We took one of the electric trams—five cars in length, seating four people across and twenty people per car—that wormed their way slowly up and down the avenues between Park Avenue and Broadway. No Trics were permitted in New York City from 34th Street to Central Park or from Park Avenue to 8th Avenue.

Taking the place of a regular female Unilove Reader, speaking naked, under a stained-glass bubble roof, from a pulpit high above the packed audience, within a few moments Adar had several thousand people in the church-theater enthralled.

"As most of you at our Unilove gathering this morning, along with millions of our television audience, are aware, Newton Morrow believes, as I do, in continuous death-and-life cycles embracing strong elements of personal immortality. All life is simply a reflection of one unity that embraces the cosmos, or God—if you wish a name for the amazing and infinite mystery which continuously manifests itself in quadrillions of forms. Inevitably, and mathematically certain, we know the truth—that many of these continuously recurring forms duplicate one another. To the human eye, all leaves in a particular tree appear somewhat alike. If the leaves had conscious minds, the differences between humans might be indistinguishable to them, too. As human beings, we suffer needlessly because we fail to perceive that our true immortality, the essence of us, is continuous.

"If, like Newton Morrow, you use this lifetime to open your minds, you may, like him, discover not only present but former brothers under the skin. In the past week, I have been asked many questions about our Love Group—particularly whether I can accept Newton's love for Christina Klausner

388

without jealousy. In response, I'd like to read you what Newton, as Edward Bellamy, wrote more than a hundred years ago, in his novel, *Doctor Heidenhoff's Process*."

As she read, I'm sure that many of the audience were conscious, as I was, of the warm undercurrent of love and laughter in Adar's voice.

" 'In the strictest, truest sense, although it is hard saying, there is no room in a clear mind for jealousy. For the way in which every two hearts approach each other is necessarily a peculiar combination of individualities never before, and never afterward, duplicated in human experience. So that if we can conceive of a woman truly loving several lovers, whether successively or simultaneously, they would not be rivals, for the manner of her love for each, and the manner of each one's love for her, is peculiar and single, even as if they were two alone in the world. The higher the mental approaches of the persons concerned, the wider their sympathies, and the more delicate their perceptions, the more this is true.' "

Before the spotlight on Adar slowly faded, and she disappeared in the warm purple womb of the church, she concluded, "So, perhaps we should try a little harder to rediscover some of our empathy with the billions of lives that only seem to have vanished from this earth. In truth, they might be us. This morning the Church dancers will perform a lovely ballet, "Jealousy Revisited." We hope you enjoy it."

———◆———

Late the following afternoon, I was locked, naked, in the cabin of an old Egg Harbor-style motorboat that had been anchored somewhere on the Jersey side of the Hudson River.

"And it wasn't jealousy that got you into this predicament," were Karl's final words to me—indicating that he must have watched Adar Chilling on television. "It was just plain insanity."

The two men who trapped me in a unisex toilet in Bonwit Teller's had obviously been following Adar and me for days. Monday, before Mory returned from Wisconsin, Adar thought I might like to see some of the new styles in fall clothing. Not to purchase. Although the President now received five hundred thousand dollars a year, the cost of high-style women's clothing had skyrocketed to as high as three thousand to five thousand dollars for simple street dresses.

Most of them, as far as Adar and I were concerned, weren't as sexually attractive as the See-Thrus.

Followed by a half-dozen saleswomen who recognized us, we got involved with Georgy Illusi, who, I was quickly informed, was the famous Paris couturier. He had arrived in New York to promote his new fall Illusi fashions. Led on by Adar, who was obviously talking tongue in cheek, Georgy agreed with her that there was no reason why he couldn't redesign the basic See-Thru peasant-style dress and create unique See-Thru evening gowns for the Inauguration Ball.

Excusing myself because my bladder was bursting, I nodded to the Secret Service man, who ignored me, and found my way to the toilet. Having gotten used to the resocialized toilets, it didn't occur to me that in a women's store it was odd that I should be followed in by two men. They ignored the stand-up urinals and followed me into the side with stalls. The entire toilet was unoccupied, and this evidently gave them the opportunity that they had been waiting for. As I was pushing open the door of a compartment, trying to keep my mind off the incongruity of sitting down to piss within an arm's length of a man, they grabbed me, and before my gasp of indignation could turn to a scream, one of them snapped an adhesive bandage over my mouth. The other quickly fastened my arms behind me with handcuffs.

Hearing the outer door to the toilet open, they shoved me into the stall and closed the door behind us. While some unknown occupant of an adjoining stall urinated, wiped—it had to be a female—and washed her hands, I was crammed between two thugs. Both of them were ugly, with thick noses and lips and pockmarked faces. They pointed their stun guns at me and silently watched me with grim expressions on their faces.

When we were alone again, one of them told me not to worry, they were emissaries from my husband, Karl Klausner. "Since the pretty mountain won't come," one of them said, "we're bringing the mountain to Mohammed."

They assured me that if I acted like a nice lady, and did exactly what they told me to do, they wouldn't have to use their stun guns on me. They were going to remove the handcuffs and the gag. Then we'd walk out of the store together—in an opposite direction from where Adar was looking at Illusi's dresses. If I tried to escape anywhere on route, they'd stun-gun me, which they guaranteed would be a very unpleasant experience.

When I told them I had to urinate or I'd die on the spot, the grinning bastards watched me worm out of the light raincoat I was wearing, lift my dress, and release a flood into the toilet.

Ten minutes later, after a ride with my captors in one of the electric trams, I was shoved into a Tric rental on 9th Avenue and driven downtown to a deserted Hudson River pier. A motor launch, piloted by another seamy-looking character, was waiting for us.

While I had no idea what plans Karl had for me, I was certain that it wasn't going to be a happy confrontation. The only possible escape route—risking the stun guns, which I was sure they wouldn't use at this point—was to jump off the landing steps that they were leading me down.

Flinging my raincoat in the face of one of the men, I leaped past the other and plunged into the murky water. I swam furiously toward an opposite pier. To no avail. Within seconds, they were beside me in the motorboat. Still fighting, I felt my dress being yanked over my head. Letting it go, I swam away from them, naked. They continued to grab for me. When they finally landed their slippery fish, they revved up the launch and roared toward a long white yacht moored in the harbor. One of them examined my torn See-Thru and disdainfully tossed it into the water. None of them cared that I was a shivering, sobbing mess.

A tall, shrunken man, his skin yellowed and tight against his facial bones, watched me from the deck, a sardonic expression on his face, as I limped up the landing stairs, followed by my kidnappers. It was Karl. For a moment, I had a difficult time adjusting the reality to my memory of him. The powerfully built, well-nourished, craggy captain of finance, didn't match the present sick reality. But his cool, sarcastic manner hadn't changed. "Seems like old times, Christa," he said, a nasty smile on his face. "You always wanted to be a mermaid—even with Warren Ellison."

"We're sorry," one of my captors told him. "We didn't mean to deliver her bare-ass. A few minutes ago she started to act like a hellcat. We damned near lost her."

Karl shrugged. "I'm sure my wife doesn't mind. Millions of Americans have seen her lovely body in action. The three of you can wait in the stern," he told them. "The steward will make you drinks. I'll let you know whether I'll still need you."

Karl took my arm. Ushering me into the lounge, his hand

391

caressed my behind. I couldn't help shuddering. I suspected that he wanted a bed companion to share his coming rendezvous with death.

Still shivering, though it was warm inside the ship, I told him imperiously to get me some clothes. "Then you can tell your thugs to take me back to the Sheraton East."

"I want to talk with you."

"You could have telephoned, or even have come to the hotel," I said. "Really, Karl, I'm sorry for the bad years you had with me. It wasn't your fault. We simply had nothing to give each other. I should never have agreed to marry you."

Karl handed me a woolen shawl which just barely covered me. "I'm sorry, there's no women's clothes aboard. Grace took all her stuff off the ship when I left her in Villefranche in August." Karl stared at me a moment. "It really is unbelievable. You're more beautiful than you were sixteen years ago."

I was embarrassed by the tears and loving expression in his eyes, but at the same time I had an uneasy feeling that the old Karl, still alive in his brain, wouldn't hesitate. If he had had the strength he would have grabbed me and insisted on his long-delayed conjugal rights.

"I'm sorry about this unpleasantry," he said. "Ever since you arrived in New York, I waited for you to call me. Of course, I really was disappointed by your maudlin performance on television. I've been hoping that your brain wasn't damaged, and that you'd quickly rediscover where your bread is buttered. Newton Morrow is a dangerous man. Many of us think that he's working in close cooperation with the Russian government."

"This is a lot more than an unpleasantry," I told him angrily. I wasn't in the mood to argue politics with Karl. "You had me kidnapped. That used to warrant the death penalty."

Karl was amused. "As you can see, unless the treatments I'm taking bring a reprieve, I won't have to wait for the electric chair. Of course, there's always your friend, David Convita. I offered him five million dollars to hibernate me, but he refused. If I could last another ten or fifteen years they probably will be able to keep me alive until I reach one hundred and fifty."

"I don't think you'd enjoy hibernation," I said, "you'd be in some stranger's control for the first time in your life." I suddenly realized that David must have become quite famous, and was being deluged with requests like Karl's.

"After seeing you," Karl said, "I think I'll offer him ten million. I might even agree to endow his work."

"Just make sure that you don't give away my two million," I told him. "Those certificates you and Warren found in my safety-deposit box are mine. I earned the money myself."

"You'll have a hard time proving it." Karl laughed. "But you can have it back—and another one hundred and fifteen million or so to go with it." Karl spread his arms expansively. "All this can belong to you. Remember—you're still my wife. Any other women I've been involved with have been fully paid for services rendered. After election, I'm sailing for Majorca. I transferred most of my money out of the United States several months ago." He chuckled. "Newton Morrow is pretty naïve if he thinks his United People's Government is going to scoop off all the cream in this country."

"Please, Karl. Come to the point. What do you want from me? Why did you bring me here?"

"It should be obvious, Christa. I want to spend whatever time is remaining to me in the arms of my loving wife—the mother of my children. Michael and Penny will be delighted. It may not be so romantic as rediscovering your first love and becoming First Lady," he added sarcastically, "but it's a hell of a lot more realistic. This country has gone to hell, but there's plenty of sane places left in the world. There's major plans afoot and enough American money available to take over Australia or South Africa. We can transplant the American Dream."

I shook my head. "It has nothing to do with your health, Karl, or your age, or the fact that by some weird circumstance I'm still physically a young woman. I never loved you—or anybody, then. I would have screwed up Mory's life even more than I did yours."

"But you love Morrow now."

Tears in my eyes, I nodded. For a moment I really felt sorry for him, but then, as he had often done in the past, Karl stopped playing his I'm-really-a-good-guy role, and revealed his true motives.

"All right, Christa, I'm going to give it to you straight. Your unfortunate reappearance—and your cool nerve in using the Klausner name while you aligned yourself with Morrow—has become a great embarrassment to me. To be frank with you, when I thought you were dead, it was a great relief to no longer be saddled with a woman who never knew up from down—and apparently still doesn't. You were always involving my friends in embarrassing drunken situations. If it hadn't been for Grace's pleading that one day you'd straighten out, I'd have divorced you. Now, you're not only screwing around with Morrow, but you've completely fouled your own nest by making a mental case out of your daughter, and going to bed with your son and trying to corrupt him. If that wasn't enough, you go around wearing those nutty leck costumes and hair style, and you are obviously involved in that godless religion, Unilove." Karl paused. Now he was really angry, because I was clapping my hands and telling him that I was glad that he had finally taken off his sheep's clothing.

"There's no way that you can redeem yourself, Christa," he continued. "But you might be useful bait. Rather than immediately dumping you in the river, and making sure this time your disappearance is final, I'm going to offer Newton Morrow a very reasonable exchange. He gets you back unharmed, but he agrees to a pre-election, concession-making meeting with some of the country's top business and military leaders. It will be completely unpublicized and off the record."

"Mory won't do it. He's already stated publicly it's too late to do a patch job. Your meeting sounds like the Invisible Hand Alliance. They must be pretty sure that Mory is going to get elected."

Karl scowled at me. "Don't count on it. The Republican party isn't taking Jennifer Manchester's and your fuck festival lightly. You're a fast learner, but you haven't been around for quite a while. You don't know all the answers."

Maybe I didn't, but I also knew when *not* to ask questions. I didn't ask Karl what would have happened if I had agreed to return to his marital bed. Would he still have used me as a pawn to capture the King? But then, I didn't have to ask the questions, anyway. Karl rang a bell for his steward, and when my abductors returned, he just said, "Take her—get her the hell off my yacht."

They quickly made it obvious that they wouldn't hesitate to fit me to cement shoes should the necessity arise.

A day later—the day before the final Presidential Conversation, Mory held a press interview. Wrapped in a blanket, my only clothing, I listened to him on the radio. I was locked in the cabin of the motorboat where Karl's goons had left me. As I listened to Mory speak, I suddenly wondered if he had come to the conclusion that I was expendable.

"Christina—Chrissy—Klausner has been kidnapped," he said. "She's being held in incommunicado hostage by Karl Klausner." Mory's voice sounded harsh and angry. "I'm demanding that the New York Police Department immediately conduct a search of Klausner's yacht and his cooperative apartment. I'm sure they will find that she is being forcibly detained."

I shivered. Mory was underestimating Karl. If he was sure that I was being held by Karl, why hadn't he moved quietly and secretly to get me released? I didn't discover until later that the police had paid no attention to him. They weren't about to invade Karl Klausner's privacy, especially because they believed that one of Mory's women had jilted him and gone back to her husband.

Excited reporters demanded to know if Klausner had telephoned Morrow, and how Mory was sure that I was being held prisoner.

I gasped when Mory read them the note he had received. It had been typewritten on plain paper—" *'Christina Klausner requests the pleasure of Newton Morrow's company at a private, off-the-record meeting, with certain industrial business and military leaders, at a location to be given later, to discuss the probability of his election; and should it occur, to approve certain transitional approaches to his New Tomorrow concept that would cause the least social disruption. Christina Klausner will be present at the meeting and will rejoin Newton Morrow, if he wishes.'* "

The note was unsigned, but had an additional paragraph suggesting that the meeting could be held the following Saturday morning at a location easily accessible from New York City by helicopter. It also suggested that it was in the best interests of the American people, and all concerned, not to publicize the meeting.

The reporters jumped on Mory. Would this be a meeting with the Invisible Hand Alliance—a meeting he had previously refused? Would he make concessions on the avowed UPA platform promises? If this was actually an invitation from Chrissy, wasn't it possible that Karl wasn't holding her at all but that she was returning to her former style of life? After all, she had been—still was—the wife of one of the country's wealthiest men.

Mory insisted that Chrissy hadn't written the note. It was a last-ditch attempt of the IHA to force him into a pre-election deal.

"Wherever Chrissy is—if she can hear me, she knows that I have complete confidence in her. We are doing everything in our power to set her free, so that she can return to those who love her."

"If push comes to shove, will you meet with the IHA?" a reporter demanded.

"No!" Mory sounded very emphatic. "John Bream, president of Prudential Life Insurance Company, and Henry Kingsley, chairman of Metropolitan Life, as well as other members of the IHA, have continuously asked me to join in off-the-record discussions with them. I did that in the 1992 campaign, and proposed that some of the capital diffusion plans that had been envisioned in the late 1970s might be a good starting point, but they rejected them out of hand. Since then, it has become apparent that life insurance is no longer of any value in a new-style corporate America where *every* citizen will share in the total profit of this country, and has his own Capital Account to sustain him through his lifetime. By its nature, life insurance creates unnecessary monetary inequality. Originally, the poor couldn't afford it, and the rich used it to entrench themselves. Now, despite variable annuities, indexing, and other gimmicks to disguise the truth, low-income and moderate-class people are still trying to insure themselves against impossible inflationary odds. Even more vital to America's future are the billions of dollars controlled by these companies. The monetary flow of this huge wealth, must have better overall control."

Karl's response to Mory's "betrayal" of *my*—and only indirectly of his—off-the-record communication was cool amusement. "The police are welcome to search my yacht or my apartment. Christina visited with me yesterday, and asked if there wasn't some way she could help heal the country's wounds. Like millions of us, she's hoping to find a middle ground. I helped her draft the note. She indicated that she needed time to be alone. After years of hibernation, she's been through a very traumatic time. I have no idea where she has gone."

On Wednesday, the day the Third Presidential Conversation was scheduled, I was still an unattended prisoner on the motorboat. I wasn't sure whether Mory believed Karl or not, but I knew if Mory didn't concede, I was going to end up at the bottom of the ocean in a cement barrel. Karl had every right to detest me—and my final disappearance was the only cover left for his lie. He might even generously offer a huge reward for the return of his unpredictable wife. On the other hand, I couldn't blame Mory. A confidential meeting with the IHA, which they would obviously plan to leak to the media, *post facto*, could cost him the election. Sobbing, totally wretched, cursing my solitary confinement, I was sure that I was in a vise and God was turning the handle.

Puttering around the twilight darkness of the cabin, I was experiencing a new kind of conscious hibernation. The only light and air came from an overhead ventilator. I was nauseous and constantly seasick from the incessant bobbling of the boat on its mooring. I tried to use some of the silverware in the small galley to pry open the hatch door, but only ended up with bent forks and knives. In the distance, I could hear the horns of freighters, and occasionally a boat would seem to pass quite close, but no one ever heard my screams for help. A refrigerator, which evidently ran on storage batteries, was filled with cold meats and cheeses, and there were enough canned food, bread, and crackers to keep me alive for a month. A chemical toilet took care of my urine and feces.

Listening to Mory and Jennifer the night of the Third Presidential Conversation, when no mention was made of me during the first hour, I gave up hope. Mory evidently believed Karl's story that I had returned to my rich-ik past. At the beginning, Jennifer dominated the conversation. Her voice, husky with tears, she reviewed her political career and her changing political beliefs. She had known Newton Morrow for twenty-five years—initially at Harvard Law School, and later, when she was a senator from Connecticut, and he was governor of Louisiana. During the entire time she had been a staunch Republican. In the past ten years, while she had valiantly carried the Republican banner, it had become obvious that the United States was still basically a two-party country. The UPA was giving the voters of America a clear alternative to the mishmash of Democratic and Republican compromises. In her opinion, the only choice was between Democratic welfare socialism and Newt Morrow's new kind of Republican-Libertarianism, which restored individualism to America, and would force a drastic cutback in federal and state governments that were now employing more than nine percent of the population—twenty-four million people. The Republican sacrifice—a more equitable distribution of the

American capital and income—was far better than the Kennedy choice, which meant either living with high unemployment or risking insane inflation and impossible balance-of-payment problems as the result of stimulating domestic demand.

"Because of my very real concern that without Newton Morrow our country will continue its slide into oblivion," Jennifer concluded, "I'm frankly admitting tonight that while I will continue to faithfully carry out my responsibility as the Republican standard bearer, I am totally sympathetic with much of Newton Morrow's economic and political philosophy. On November fifth, if you're a Democrat, a vote for me—or better still a vote for Newton Morrow—is a vote for the kind of America in which liberal Republicans can survive and prosper."

It was a smooth political switch. Whether Jennifer and Mory would get away with it would be decided in the next two weeks. As the discussion continued between them, I was not only sure that Chrissy had been completely forgotten, but that it was probably just as well. Jennifer could fill the missing place in Mory's Love Group much better than I ever would have.

Then Mory—after telling Jennifer that he appreciated her concern at Oyster Island that he should moderate some of his Transition programs, and enter into an open discussion with the IHA, asked Jennifer's permission to involve the American people in a very personal problem.

"I am very worried about Christina North Klausner—Chrissy," he said. "Without implicating her husband in her disappearance, I am advising Karl Klausner in this broadcast, and through him the members of the IHA, and also in response to Jennifer's request at Oyster Island, that I will agree to meet with them Saturday morning. While I still am positive that the communication I received from Chrissy was not written by her, if she appears at the meeting, and the meeting is televised to the nation, or in lieu of that, the meeting is taped and recorded, so that, ultimately, all Americans, if they wish, can know where I stand, then, speaking for Chrissy and myself, we will not pursue the hows and whys of her disappearance."

Mory concluded with a brief discussion of our love vacation. "I'm really proud of the response of millions of Americans to the invasion of our sexual privacy on Oyster Island. No one associated with or sympathetic to the Unilove concepts, and the very positive return to God that the Unilove approaches imply, would look upon the films of Chrissy and me making love, or Jennifer and Chuck Holmes, as pornographic. If I weren't married to Adar Chilling, even as President I would be happy to go through a Unilove pair-bonding ceremony with Chrissy. I am only sorry that instead of the brief glimpses of us making love, the unknown photographers didn't make themselves known. Perhaps Chrissy and I would have invited them to photograph and record the joyous hours of kitsa we experienced. My deepest wish is that as a loving President I can set an example for the American people and establish a loving order of priorities that in the future all of you will have both the time and money security to emulate."

Mory and Jennifer had done it! Without making any concessions, thus far, they had turned the Oyster Island affair into a positive endorsement of Newton Morrow, politically and sexually. No one realized it better than Jason Kennedy, who blasted the Conversation the next day. It was an obvious attempt to subvert the moral structure of America. According to Kennedy, Mory was asking the American people to condone political trickery and the sick sexual behavior of satyrs and nymphomaniacs.

Thursday and most of Friday passed before Karl released me. His henchmen arrived late in the afternoon and handed me a note, handwritten on the yacht stationery, which was engraved with the wording *Fundamental IV* and a phony crest. *"The ship is yours tonight,"* it read. *"A 'copter pilot will pick you up Saturday morning at 8:45 A.M. for a short flight to the Tarrytown Executive Conference Center. You won't have to arrive naked. A friend of mine, Maggie Reardon, will be waiting for you on the ship with clothing. She'll be happy to help prepare you to meet the men who really run this country."*

Maggie was waiting on the ship's deck when I arrived. My captors, after depositing me on the landing platform, wrapped in a blanket, sped toward shore in their motor launch. A friendly, well-shaped, dyed blonde in her middle fifties, Maggie admitted that she often slept with Karl. "Mostly, he's not interested in sex. He told me once that if he should die in the night, he wanted to be able to crawl into the arms of a female and say good-bye."

Karl had been good to her. More than five years ago, he had financed a chain of Maggie Reardon Beauty Salons, and provided the money so she could market her own line of cosmetics nationally.

"He made me very rich, honey. I'm on his side. You should be, too." Maggie detested lecks and Unilove women. "Most of them wear See-Thrus, no makeup, and those crazy Dutch boy haircuts. All the leck men and women look alike. Worse than Chinese peasants. You can't tell them apart."

Maggie's interpretation of the Yang and the Yin was not based on androgyny. "The ancient philosophers knew that the Yin, the female half, carried a touch of temptation. That's why they labeled the Yang, the male half, 'the good.' Women finally have achieved equal rights," she told me, "but women know that the lure of female flesh and the female body keep the whole ball of wax in motion." In Maggie's opinion, See-Thrus weren't sexy. Being naked was never sexy. See-Thrus might have been seductive once—but not when millions of women were wearing them.

In the master stateroom, she held up an Illusi creation. "Georgy remembered you. He picked this one for you himself. It's an eight-thousand-dollar one of a kind." Dropping my blanket, I examined the outfit and Maggie whistled. "Believe me, that David Convita did a good job on you. You have the body to wear it."

Whether I did or not—and even though I was sure that Mory wouldn't be happy when he saw me in it—I had no choice. Even if there had been some way to go ashore, Maggie said she would refuse to buy me a See-Thru.

Before the helicopter arrived, I was wearing the Illusi pale green pantaloons, which were cut fore and aft on a diagonal, and bonded to some soft material that was completely transparent. Of necessity, since my leck-style haircut was in need of trimming and Maggie refused to do it, I was remodeled from head to toes into a rich-ik, ultra-sophisticated female.

My breasts were covered with a light purple jacket, and supported by individual quarter-bra cups which adhered to the skin underneath them with no pressure. Maggie pointed out that if the room was too warm, I could unbutton the jacket and reveal at least half of my naked breasts to match the rest of me. Front view, my midriff and the triangle of my pubic hair was bisected from my left hip with a transparent insert. Illusi even provided a merkin, in case the owner's pussy hair wasn't profuse enough. Rear view, from the top of my right buttock was a similar clear cloth, revealing the cleft of my behind halfway down. The gown came with no under-clothes. For the brisk fall weather, a knee-length outer coat matched the jacket.

◆

I was happy that the pilot of the helicopter, equipped with pontoons, that landed beside the yacht early Saturday morning, couldn't see the pantaloon suit that I was wearing.

When we arrived at Tarrytown twenty-five minutes later, I discovered that Karl had carefully prepared for my grand entrance, which had been planned not only to blow Mory's mind, but to leave a question in everybody's mind whether Christina hadn't shifted allegiances in an opposite direction, and thus Karl, in a minor way, would counteract Jennifer Manchester's betrayal of her party.

The Heliport was near the grounds of a one-hundred-room estate which had once been owned by Mary Duke Biddle, heiress to the American Tobacco fortune. At least sixty helicopters, with various company names and logos on their cabins, were lined up together on the landing field. A man who introduced himself as Jack Falk was waiting for me in a Tric. He explained that he was an employee of The Klausner Fund. Jack was obviously awed by the caliber of the men and women who had heeded Karl Klausner's summons. He pointed out an automobile parking lot near the estate, and for the first time, I realized that the very rich didn't drive Trics. Jack explained that the Mercedes, Bentleys, Jaguars, and Rolls-Royces, not to mention a few Cadillacs and Lincolns, had been converted to hydrogen.

"You're going to see the cream of the Invisible Hand Alliance," he told me. "There's more than five hundred top brass from Exxon, General Motors, Ford Motor, Texaco, Mobile, all the way down to companies like Times Mirror, which is two-hundredth largest, and Pabst Brewing, which finally broke into the billion-dollar sales category last year. In the retailing area, there are executives here from Sears Roebuck, Safeway, S. S. Kresge, J. C. Penney, and many others. In the transportation field, the bosses of TWA, United, Union Pacific, American Airlines, and many others have arrived. And, of course, the chief officers of the American Telephone, General Telephone, and a dozen top utilities are here."

Jack shook his head. "Of course, there's many more members of the IHA—over five thousand of them—but Mr.

Klausner tried to confine the meeting to about five hundred people. As you must know, the execs who are really worried are the heads of the banks and life insurance companies, and finance and investment companies. People from the major banks, like Bank of America, Citicorp and Chase Manhattan; and life insurance companies, like Prudential, Metropolitan, Equitable, and Aetna; and the loan companies, Household Finance and Beneficial Finance; and the major investment companies, from Merrill Lynch down to Bache, are here in force. Also, Major General Clayton Howell, Brigadier General George Clay, and many others from the Pentagon have arrived. They're afraid that Morrow and Alexi Lubayov have made some kind of undercover deal, and they're determined to stop Morrow from cutting the military budget to fifty billion dollars if he's elected."

Leading me into the building, Jack insisted on taking my coat, with which I parted reluctantly. It was nine-fifteen. The conference had already started. Jack took me backstage of the main conference room, and from the wings I could see Mory, Henry Adams, and Chuck sitting on the platform facing a packed audience.

Karl was already speaking from the rostrum and evidently trying to establish the order of business. Newton Morrow would listen to a counterproposal from Robert Guardala, President of the Bank of America, which would summarize the views of most of the members, and then Morrow could respond, and hopefully, before the conference was over a compromise could be worked out. Henry Adams thought that an immediate question-and-answer procedure would help to establish the areas of discontent, and by an overwhelming "aye" vote from the audience, they agreed to begin in this way.

At Mory's request, Karl told them the proceedings were being taped, but a compromise had been effected. The tapings wouldn't be shown until after the election. Karl pointed out, to cheers and applause from the audience, that if—as they all hoped—Jason Kennedy was elected, any tapes that were made today would find their rightful home in the Smithsonian Institution—a memory of the fateful day when America stood on the brink of communism, and pulled back just in time.

Before he finished speaking, Karl, who had obviously been waiting for my arrival, announced with perfect timing, "And now I take particular pleasure in welcoming Christina Klausner, Newton Morrow's friend, and I hope ours, to this platform."

Jack led me onstage, and when the audience of men and women executives, most of whom must have seen me on Life-a-Vision in my leck dress, saw me now, there was an audible gasp of astonishment, followed by enthusiastic clapping. On the surface, at least, I was dressed like one of them—a rich-ik female.

I saw Mory's look of total surprise, and I ran to him and hugged him. "It's not true, *diprin*, I'm on your side," I breathed in his ear. "Don't let the dress throw you." I didn't know how he was going to do it, but I prayed that somehow he could turn my flagrant rich-ik costume into a plus for our side.

Karl seemed unconcerned by my enthusiastic embrace of Mory. "As Newton Morrow can see, I have kept my personal promise to him," he said. "His Chrissy has been returned to him, no worse for wear, and somewhat improved in appearance." Grinning, he waved his hands at the enthusiastic applause. "Now, since we've agreed with Mr. Morrow's and Mr. Adams' approaches to this meeting, we'll take questions from the audience. Voice-Amps are available in the arms of all seats. Speakers will please identify themselves by company affiliation and executive title."

"Robert Guardala, President, Bank of America, speaking. The Bank of America wants to go on record as vehemently opposing any legislation that would eliminate the private banking system in this country. If the people are willing to surrender private control of their monetary lives, and personal privacy, which has been a continuing issue over the past quarter century, we've been in a position for years to introduce a cashless society, and operate it through a private banking system that will give the Federal Reserve System, and the President—hopefully a Democrat—practically instant information on the country's money flow through the banks of this country."

"I will respond to that," Henry Adams said. "As most of the financial community are aware, for many years I have been an advocate of a fiat money system, which is completely under mutual control of Congress and the President. Only with an agency such as the United Peoples Capital Corporation can the creation and the flow of money be controlled. In combination with FIST, the floating instant skim tax which Newton Morrow has proposed, and which, essentially, eliminates all other taxes, the UPCC can not only regulate the money supply, and control the rate of taxation from month to month, but keep both areas in balance with the productivity of the people.*

"The Federal Reserve System," Adams continued, "has always been in the partial control of private bankers, who are the directors of it, and who serve on the Open Market Committee. Since its beginnings in 1913, it has manipulated the nation's money supply, and though no one will admit it, it has often created inflation, as well as prosperity and depressions, for the benefit of bank profits and rich investors. Many years ago, in 1964, Wright Patman, Chairman of the Committee on Banking and Currency, wrote *A Primer on Money*, whose sole purpose was to acquaint the American people with the dangers inherent in their banking system. It's still good reading. Patman's attempt to integrate and coordinate our financial system for the benefit of the people was never achieved. Nor did Congressman Jerry Voorhis, and many others like him, who initiated legislation that would have given the people control of their banking system, get anywhere. The banks were, and are, still controlled by the super-rich, and the major corporations of this country, for their own benefit. Today, quite unnecessarily, except to profit the already rich, and prevent the rest of us from facing reality, we have a public debt of a trillion dollars, which requires nearly a hundred billion to support, and has made most of the people slaves to an outmoded economic system. Twenty years ago, the National Taxpayers Union estimated that Americans were on the hook of six and a half trillion dollars. Today the figure is close to twenty trillion."

"James Knowles, Vice-President, Citicorp, speaking: Mr. Morrow and Mr. Adams—your Utopian daydream can only have one ending. A dictatorship! May I remind you of the words of Baron Meyer Rothschild: 'Permit me to control the money of the nation, and I care not who makes its laws.' "

Mory was now standing beside Henry Adams at the rostrum. "We probably shouldn't batter each other with supposedly great insights from the past," Mory said, and he was smiling, "but Sir Josiah Stamp, once President of the Bank of England, paralleled that statement: 'If you want to remain slaves of the bankers, and pay the costs of your own slavery,

---

* EDITOR'S NOTE: Christina has compressed and only used sections from the transcript of this all-day meeting. The entire meeting is available as a Life-a-Vision transcription from most local libraries.

let them continue to create money, and control the nation's credit.'

"Far from becoming a dictator, as President my purpose will be to give this country back to the people—free from the dictatorship of federal taxes and federal bureaucracy, and free from the burden of debt. The United People's Capital Corporation's financial operations will be revealed daily, weekly, and monthly, in full detail, to its rightful owners—each and every citizen of this country. In addition, as their only tax, FIST, increases or decreases, they will understand why and how, as first-rate citizens in a cooperating national community, they can control their own taxation.

"It shouldn't be necessary to remind this audience of the unsavory history of private banking in this country. Thomas Jefferson, even before he was President, battled Alexander Hamilton, a New York banker, and attempted to create a sound monetary system. He lost. Later, Andrew Jackson won a temporary victory against bankers who tried to destroy him. Both men would have been appalled that the American people would have swallowed a Federal Reserve System which operates completely free of presidential and congressional control; is immune to income taxation; whose stock is in effect owned by private member banks; which issues its own currency, Federal Reserve Notes; which, in actuality, controls the interest rates and prices on all government securities, and ultimately determines the value of our national currency."

"Robert Keller, President, Chase Manhattan, speaking [in a very sarcastic tone]: I told Karl Klausner that this meeting would be a waste of time. Instead of listening to this insanity, all of us in this auditorium should be working night and day—in these last few hours—to elect Jason Kennedy President—and save the country!"

"John Bream, President, Prudential Life, speaking: Mr. Morrow, it seems to me that you've been very elusive in explaining just how you expect to manage the transition to people's capitalism without wrecking the country."

"Not really," Mory replied. "It is carefully outlined in *Looking Backward II*. Once the transition has been legally implemented, it will be quite simple. When all American citizens have registered and received their New Capital Account number—a process which incidentally will flush out and eventually eliminate illegal aliens—and when the regional computer centers of the UPCC are fully operational, an operation which will require the employment of many people now engaged in private banking, the UPCC will automatically take over all personal, corporate, and public bank deposits. All life insurance contracts will be canceled. In addition, all outstanding personal loans from banks, life insurance, finance companies, and other sources will be taken over by the UPCC and canceled. Existing corporate borrowings will be assumed by the UPCC and gradually liquidated by the earnings of corporations at a three percent interest rate. Each citizen over the age of eighteen will receive a Capital Account credit of thirty thousand dollars—to a maximum of one million dollars.

"Transition Day will not be announced until every aspect of the switchover is in place. Obviously, on Transition Day, the federal debt of one trillion dollars will cease to exist, since the UPCC will not owe the people's money to itself. Since the full purchasing power of the American people must continue without interruption, on Transition Day each and every citizen must be able to use his personal Capital Account credit card for all large purchases, and to obtain a *new* issue of paper money for small purchases. Paper money in circulation prior to Transition Day will be valueless, but all coinage in public possession will retail its former value."

Mory smiled at the grim faces in the shocked and silent audience. "Jennifer Manchester and Karl Klausner," he continued, "as well as many people assembled in this room, have asked me if there weren't some practical way to incorporate private banking, life insurance companies, and finance and loan companies as viable entities into people's capitalism. The answer is unequivocally no—unless they transform themselves, as many American businesses have done in the past, to new endeavors. We don't need these parasites in a sound economic system. Just so long as they exist, the flow of money, unnecessary credit extension, and the burden of uneconomic interest rates will continue in an uncontrollable crazy-quilt pattern. We could never guarantee the people that the dollars they save in their Capital Accounts won't, as they have in the past, lose their purchasing power, or be subject to the insane seesawing of preventable depressions and so-called stagflations.

"On the other hand"—Mory was smiling, but his voice had a teasing quality and he was grinning at me—"I'm prepared to make a concession that should intrigue the entrepreneurial spirit which I hope still exists among you, and hopefully will intrigue the officers and directors of those companies that will be phased out of existence. After your liabilities are canceled, most of your companies will have a significant net worth. The UPCC will be happy to help refinance your companies so that you can enter totally undeveloped areas of manufacturing and service industries which will boom in the coming years.

"For example, I expect that housing, once it is freed of the interest and tax burdens, and speculative elements placed on it by the present system, will become America's biggest industry. Companies like Prudential Life, Household Finance, *et cetera*, could switch into the manufacture and development of the hundreds of thousands of items that are necessary to transform America's outmoded housing. They could become the Prudential or Beneficial Home Corporations!

"Or, since education will be a new American corporate endeavor, with millions of people under twenty-five, and over fifty, pursuing educational goals, and the education industry will grow equal in size or larger than the housing industry, banks like the Bank of America or Citicorp could transform themselves into a Western and Eastern Education Corporation.

"Oh"—Mory was beaming at hundreds of disgruntled and angry faces that obviously didn't appreciate his humor— "thanks to Christina Klausner, a few moments ago I realized that, quite unintentionally on my part, many Americans may feel that See-Thru clothing is identified with New Tomorrow, and that it would be my intention to create a grim, dull gray, one-dimensional American society, with all of us thinking the same thoughts, or wearing the same clothes. On the contrary! While I'm not partial to the particular dress that Chrissy is wearing this morning, I firmly believe that achieving different identities, by the clothing and jewelry that one wears, is basic to human nature. Human beings have always enjoyed expressing themselves through self-adornment. The clothing industry could go all out to manufacture clothing from materials like cotton, linen, wool, silk, and leather, and probably could develop more synthetics, like the material used in See-Thrus, that don't require fossil fuels in their manufacture. Former life insurance companies could become Metropolitan Clothing Corporation, or the Equitable Clothing Corporation. They could quadruple the average American's wardrobe, and create billion-dollar industries without plundering our planet of basic raw materials."

During the remainder of the day, Mory and Henry Adams were questioned by executives from Litton Industries, United Technologies, and other billion-dollar-conglomerate companies on the various aspects of Mory's corporate-stock program. They reiterated that the people's government would no longer be interested in anti-trust actions. The people should have no fear of big businesses that had grown, or would grow vertically, that is by acquiring companies in the same basic industry. In any event, the workers would own these companies and share equally in their dividend distributions. The test of survival for any corporation would be whether it could achieve the necessary 10 percent profit on sale that would be a requirement of its continued corporate existence.

"It is probable in many cases," Mory told them, "that smaller corporations in the same industry would be better equipped to adjust to the changing environments. As for conglomerates, since all profits of individual, nonrelated companies and subsidiaries would have to be reported separately, the chances are that the conglomerates would gradually spin off companies that could not meet the federal profit requirements. Horizontal corporate growth would cease in the future."

Mory reminded his audience that the kind of business growth which created companies like Litton and United Technologies offered little improvement in the quality of life for the vast majority of Americans. Corporate growth of this kind simply had become a method of ego enhancement and pursuit of power for certain kinds of business leaders who would become obsolete in the coming years.

Mory was hammered by a majority of the executives who firmly believed that 90 percent of the people could not handle their Capital Accounts and would spend themselves into poverty or wouldn't work at all. He agreed that in many cases that would happen. But he insisted that when it came to money, Americans were fast learners. When they finally realized that they could trust the dollar as a sound equivalence for their initiative and their labor, and they realized that they no longer had a Great White Father in Washington to lean on, the vast majority would become enthusiastic citizens. For the first time in its history, a diverse nation of people would have a common purpose and believe in itself.

A few of the executives left the meeting feeling that the country might not collapse if Newton Morrow was elected President, but the majority, like Karl Klausner, felt that they had accomplished nothing. Newton Morrow hadn't deviated an inch.

Toward afternoon, Major General Clayton Howell insisted that Mory was in a conspiracy with Alexi Lubayov and the Russian government. He claimed that he had documentary evidence received from the Central Intelligence Agency to back up his charges.

"A cut in our military appropriations to fifty billion dollars is ridiculous!" Howell didn't speak, he roared. "Newton Morrow claims that Russia has been frightened for years by our military posture, and all along they've been willing to disarm and get rid of their nuclear power, but we had to do it first. I tell you, and our Chinese friends agree, it's a Communist plot! While I sympathize with you gentlemen, and I agree that our country is in danger of falling into the hands of a dangerous egomaniac, and our economic system will be destroyed by him even more frightening, if Newton Morrow is elected, is the very real danger of a direct Russian Communist take-over. America cannot afford to become a second-rate military power. This is a dangerous world. Our life as a nation is at stake!"

There was muttered agreement and cheering at Howell's concluding statement: "If you get elected, Morrow, our only hope is that some good American will respond in the Japanese kamikaze tradition and defend the honor of America—with his own life if necessary!"

———◆———

Someday I'll write another book. Maybe I'll call it *76 Days*. It will start on election night, November 5, 1996—when we finally passed out of the eye of the hurricane, and the sun came out, deluding us with a calm before the final storm. The book will end on January 20, 1997, when Mory and Adar were sucked into the whirlpool they had generated, and the Love Group that was left closed ranks and set the Bellamy-Morrow dream in motion.

In between would be a 76-day love story.

Mory was elected President of the United States with a popular vote of 41,265,840. Jason Kennedy received 39,523,-690 votes. Jennifer Manchester, for many voters a political heroine, received 8,785,250 votes. Candidates of other parties polled 1,742,150 votes. It was no mandate, and it was a long way from a 60 percent plurality of the 54 million popular affirmation vote that Mory had hoped to receive. The pundits were certain that New Tomorrow and the United People of America would be a long, long time coming. Millions of Americans seemed to be united in their determination to stop Newton Morrow's Utopian daydreams from ever being realized.

To my surprise, the entire suspense of Election Day coverage as I had known it, with the voting patterns being announced all night long from east to west, and the pollsters making early predictions, had been eliminated. Twelve of us—Mory's Love Group, adults and children—joined with Tom Morrow at the Morrow family homestead in Lafayette, Louisiana. At eleven P.M., when the returns were flashed before us on Life-a-Vision, revealing a neck-and-neck race between Mory and Jason Kennedy, we watched silently and prayed. Tom Morrow would permit no drinking unless Mory won. Finally, by twelve-thirty, with the western returns finally completed, particularly from the State of California, where Mory gained most of his plurality, we were sure. Mory had won by approximately 1,700,000 votes.

Elated, Tom Morrow hugged his son, and even conceded that some of the upright Old Testament characters had been bigamists, and he hugged and kissed all the First Ladies in turn. Then we gobbled a delayed midnight dinner of crayfish and several gallons of white wine, and we joined Mory in a torchlight parade led by thousands of students from the University of Southern Louisiana.

Congressional and gubernatorial victories from the eastern and midwestern states had been announced as they had been achieved—often within ten minutes after the computerized polls had been closed. Eight UPA governors—three more than in the 1992 elections—were elected. The Democrats still controlled the Senate and House of Representatives, but Mory insisted that a combination of radical Democrats and liberal Republicans, particularly those who would be seeking election two years from now in the fifteen new Regional Commonwealth governments, would eventually join together and activate a New Constitution.

While the transition to a United People of America and a corporate government might take anywhere from eighteen months to three years, Mory was sure that before the next presidential election, when the new President—it might not be Mory—was chosen by the Commonwealth's new House of

Representative—the United States would have become a profit-making government, owned by the people.

During the following weeks, right up to Christmas, while our Love Group and Mory's staff settled into a dawn-to-dusk discussion of the appropriate choices for Cabinet officers and heads of various government agencies—many of which would be gradually phased out of existence—Mory slept twenty-six nights with me and eleven nights with Adar, who was often away from our Love Group headquarters, in Carmel, California, overseeing various Unilove Church openings. In addition, he was with Maria eight nights, and spent five with Emily. On nights when he was missing, I joined Chuck or Henry or Carlos for hours of talk or kitsa.

Christmas Eve, in Mory's room, when I recited my "bed audit," he stared at me, astonished.

"No one else keeps track." He was choking with laughter.

"It's not that I'm jealous," I told him, "but I still haven't been able to figure out the pattern."

"There isn't any," he insisted. "It just happens or it doesn't. Obviously, Emily feels more at ease and comfortable with Henry than anyone else. All of the younger males have to reassure her that she's not too old—especially not for the mental stimulation of a younger lover. Maria is still basically monogamous, but she admits to Carlos that the widely different mental input from her various bed companions is very enjoyable. As for you and Adar, you catalyze each other, and me, so well that I'm thinking of having a special presidential bed made for the White House that will accommodate the three of us on occasion."

And, then, to his delight, when I told him that his real Christmas present from me was going to be delayed until next June, he awoke everyone in the house to share the news and to feel my only slightly protruding belly. Approximately June 15, 1997, his third child would be born.

We arrived in Washington on Sunday, the day before Inauguration Day, and Mory was immediately contacted by Chief Justice Robert Bynam. Would the oath of office have to be changed? Mory had not been elected "to preserve, protect, and defend" the present Constitution or, for that matter, "to execute the Office of President of the United States."

Mory disagreed with him. The President's responsibility didn't change—even if the Constitution did. As for the "Office of President of the United States"—that wouldn't disap-

411

pear until approximately three weeks after Bellamy Day—January 20, 2000!

Jennifer was waiting for us at Blair House, and while she and our Love Group explored our overnight quarters—the following night we'd all be in the White House—I had a long telephone reunion with David and Ruth, who were staying at the Washington Hilton. Mory had invited all of David's Love Group, including the children, to the Inauguration and to the White House afterward. In the meantime, Mory had disappeared behind closed doors to polish what he promised would be a history-making Inaugural Address.

The next morning, after a special one-hour service at the Washington Unilove Church, at eleven A.M. we were driven to the Capitol, where the platform had been erected for the Inauguration ceremonies. More than two hundred thousand people, many of them, men as well as women, wearing simulated zebra, leopard, tiger, and polar-bear fur coats, jammed the bleachers and overflowed the Capitol lawns. At Mory's request, the Marine Band was playing "Stars and Stripes Forever," symbolic of the fact that while the number of stars would change, the style of the American flag would remain.

To my surprise and delight, a few rows back on the platform, sitting with Adar and Mory's children, were Penny and Michael. Michael waved at me and his lips formed a quick "We love you!" Next to me, Mory brushed the tears of appreciation from my eyes. "I invited Karl and Grace too—personally," he told me—"but Karl refused and sounded grimmer than Jason Kennedy looks right now, and Grace is evidently an expatriate or still doesn't approve of me." I was happy that Adar was sitting beside Kennedy's wife, Debbie, and not me.

At his request, Yale Richard Marratt was sworn in as Vice-President by the son of an old friend of his father's, Richard Cohen, Speaker of the House. At twelve-fifteen, Chief Justice Bynam asked Mory if he was ready to take the oath of office. The famous George Washington Inaugural Bible was opened to Matthew 13:31, "The Kingdom of Heaven is like to a grain of mustard seed . . ." the verse that Mory had quoted to Sister Chrissy and Sister Jennifer so long ago. Adar held the Bible that Tom Morrow had used for years when he had been a famous southern evangelist, while Mory took the oath of office. Watching Mory through a blur of tears, I remembered him standing naked on our coffee table in Cambridge, saying "Sister Chrissy, when I'm

President of the United States, you're going to be my First Lady."

Then the band was playing "Hail to the Chief," and the Army fired its 21-gun salute.

Newton Morrow was President of the United States! But most of the words issuing from his mouth as he gave his Inaugural Address—as the news media would discover later—had been written by Edward Bellamy in his book, *Equality*, more than a hundred years before, and excerpted by Mory from the chapter called "The Transition Period."

"People of America," he said, and his voice was both melodic any hypnotic, "I thank you for your courage and the pioneer faith of your fathers which you have never lost, and your willingness to *dare* to experiment. I promise you from this day forward, we will stop drifting, and we'll begin the joyous task of creating a viable future for your children, and mine. As Ahab said: 'This moment was rehearsed by thee and me a billion years before the ocean rolled.'

"The most radical innovation in establishing economic equality is not the establishment of a reasonable level wage and income between the workers, but the admission of an entire population to a reasonable share of the national product. Now, for the first time since the original Revolution, the people of America have it within their power to gather into their hands the entire economic resources of their country, and proceed to administer them on the principle proclaimed in our great Declaration of Independence, but practically mocked by most of the ensuing governments of this nation—that all human beings have an equal right to liberty, life and happiness, and that governments rightfully exist only for the purpose of making good that right—a principle of which the first practical consequence must be the guarantee to all on *equal* terms of a sound economic basis.

"It is obvious that if private capitalism was right, then the New Tomorrow I have projected, and people's capitalism are wrong. If people's capitalism is right, then private capitalism becomes the greatest wrong that ever existed, and in that case it is the capitalists who owe reparations to the people they have wronged. For the people to have consented on any terms to buy their freedom from their former masters would have been to admit the justice of the former bondage.

"In taking possession of this country, and all the works of man that stand upon it, the people are but reclaiming their own heritage, and the works of their own hands kept from

413

them by fraud. But we must remember that perfect order cannot be achieved in a week, or a month, or a year. The personnel of any community is the prime factor in its economic efficiency, and not until the first generation born under a new order has received the highest intellectual and industrial training will the new economic order fully show what it is capable of. But in less than four years, the United People's Government will take all the people into employment on the basis of equal sharing.

"And even before that time, we will show results that will overwhelm the world. No previous experience will prepare the people of America for the prodigious efficiency of New Tomorrow. The difficulty under the previous style profit-sharing systems has been to avoid producing too much. The difficulty under a more equal sharing system will be how to produce enough. The smallness of demand has before limited supply, but supply has now set to it an unlimited task. Under private capitalism demand has been a dwarf, and a lame one at that, and yet this cripple has been the pacemaker for giant production.

"New Tomorrow will put wings on the dwarf! Henceforth, America's industrial and service giant will need all its strength to meet a new kind of demand that will enrich all our lives and will not plunder this planet.

"It is difficult to give you an idea of the tremendous burst of industrial energy to which a rejuvenated people will commit itself, and the enthusiasm you personally will discover with the joyful task of uplifting the welfare of all classes to a level where the former rich man will find nothing to regret in his sharing of the common lot.

"In the past there has not been work enough for the people. Millions—some rich, some poor, some willing, some unwilling—have always been idle, and not only that, but half the work that was done was wasted in competition, or in producing luxuries to gratify the few while the primary wants of the mass remained unsatisfied. Idle machinery equal to the power of millions of men, idle land, idle capital of every sort, mocked the needs of the people.

"But I can assure you that in the first full year that Congress implements and underwrites your and my New Tomorrow and makes it the law of this land, the total Gross National Product, a new and vital combination of goods and services, will *double* in the sound and relatively uninflated dollars of 1972. And in the second year the Gross National Product will double again!

"And just as important, the effect almost at once of universal and abounding material prosperity will become a matter of course for everyone. The greed motive in human nature, covetousness as to material things, will be mocked to death by abundance, and will perish by atrophy. The impulses of the economic world, and of each man and each woman, will be the joy of beneficence, the delight of achievement, and the enthusiasm of humanity.

"The main, often almost sole, business of governments has been the protection of property against criminals, a system involving a vast amount of interference with the innocent. This function of the state will soon become obsolete. Eventually, there will be a few disputes about property and the protection of property. Everybody will have all he needs, and as much as anybody else.

"Not so long ago we lived in a world where a great many crimes resulted from passions of love and jealousy. They were the consequences of the idea derived from immemorial barbarism that men and women might acquire sexual proprietorship in one another, to be maintained and asserted against the will of the person. Such crimes, still committed today, will cease to exist entirely when the first generation has grown up under the absolute sexual autonomy and independence that will follow from economic equality.

"It used to be a dream of the philosophers that men would be able to live together without laws. While we may never achieve that millennium, we are finally on the road that will lead us beyond New Tomorrow.

"One thing we can be sure of: Before we enter the twenty-first century the only government we will need is one that coordinates the profit-making activities of our associated industries—the profit-making corporations—owned by the people of America."

Mory concluded, "And the kingdom of heaven—and New Tomorrow—is like to a grain of mustard seed. . . ."

Following a luncheon in the Senate Office Building—during which Mory, in high spirits, insisted that Bellamy had been standing beside him whispering, "Thanks, Newt, I'm happy to be here today in your body"—Mory decided that even though it was a cold day and spitting snow, he would follow the precedent established by Jimmy Carter, and he and Adar, followed by his Love Group, would walk down Pennsylvania Avenue to the White House.

Mory had forgotten Major General Clayton Howell's warning. With no volunteers, Howell evidently had decided to be his own kamikaze agent. Even if the Secret Service had never been particularly devoted to Mory, it couldn't be blamed. Despite the message of Dr. Strangelove no one really believed that America was the kind of country in which a famous general would attempt his own private coup d'etat.

We had walked less than a quarter of a mile. Mory and Adar were about 10 feet in front of Chuck, me, and Richie. Behind us was Tom Morrow, with Adar and Mory's children. Henry and Emily were walking with Carlos and Maria and their children.

Then, suddenly, even before we realized what was happening, a military Tric, with Howell and a driver, edged slowly past the police. Presumably, they had an important hot-line message for the new President. I saw Howell lean out the window, his face grim and contorted, a vengeful god in uniform. Even as I saw the gun in his hand, and heard the repeated sharp ping-ping-ping, Richie tumbled me to the sidewalk and dropped on top of me.

Stunned crowds, which moments before had been cheering and yelling friendly comments as we passed them, shrieked and screamed their fear and dismay. I was vaguely aware that Howell was being dragged out of the Tric. If his driver hadn't swerved the car when he suddenly realized the nature of Howell's mission, all of us would have been dead. Howell was carrying three loaded six-shooters. But everything was peripheral to my cry of despair when I crouched over Mory and Adar. Both of them were flat on the pavement. Adar was dead—shot through the head, and Mory was bleeding from two gaping holes in his chest.

Minutes later, Mory was on a stretcher in an ambulance with Richie and me. He brushed aside the young doctors who were attaching IV's, and trying to give him oxygen and to stem his flow of blood.

"Don't cry, Chrissy," he whispered, when I put my face near his. His eyes were glazing as he spoke. "Our lives are comedy. In the universal, there is no tragedy. Individual experiences are too trifling for the dignity of tragedy." He stared vacantly at me for a moment, as if he was remembering something, and then he continued, his voice getting weaker. " 'Ask no heavens to open, nor firmament to dissolve,

416

that you may be left faced with God, and see the sum of things. Look into the well of your own life, and know the powerlessness of human tongues to express its endless depths . . . its boundless contents.' " Mory grinned feebly at me. "I wrote that in 1874, when I was Bellamy. I left a note that I hoped it would be read on my deathbed." He tried to brush the tears from my cheek, but his arm fell back. "I love you, Chrissy. Sorry you didn't get to be First Lady. Maybe next time around."

Newton Morrow was dead.

Sobbing, Richie kissed his immobile face. "Oh, God—the dream is over."

For a moment I had a strange feeling, as if Mory's thoughts were still reaching me telepathically, and I was speaking the words his silent lips could no longer utter.

"No, Richie," I said softly, and I put my arms around him and held his head against me. "Long before Mory, the dream was cast in the human mind. If only for a moment, Mory merged the dream with the reality. Like it or not, *you* are the President of the United States. It's up to you and me, now. Somehow we have to make this country the United People of America. We have to make Mory and Adar's dream the reality."

Bibliography

Because of many requests from readers of Christina North's autobiography, in this new edition of *Love Me Tomorrow*, published on January 1, 2000, in commemoration of Edward Bellamy's Great Revolution, and Newton Morrow's New Tomorrow, the publisher is pleased to present the following annotated bibliography. It not only includes reference material on all the books referred to by Christina (she and her pair bond, Yale Richard Marratt, are now in their second term as President and First Lady of the United People of America), but also lists an extensive and carefully selected collection of books which often anticipated the future, though they were written in the period 1950–1980, or are interesting commentaries on the manners and mores of that time.

While all references are to original publishers, twenty-first-century readers can call up most of the material on microfiche and Read-a-Film, or request a specific runoff on any book through their Central Computer Library Facility. While the annotations have been written from a 1980 perspective, it should be remembered that specific addresses applicable to the 1980s may have changed in the year 2000.

From the perspective of 2000, most of the predictions about the future made in the last third of the twentieth century will prove charmingly naïve. On the other hand, many of these books will provide interesting insights into the environment and minds of our grandparents and great-grandparents, who were the first humans mentally advanced enough to be concerned about a future that they would never live to see. Thus, in a very real sense, many of these writers, because they cared, actually made it possible for the world, as we know it, to exist.

It should be noted that the publication date of this edition, January 1, 2000, is the date for the achievement of Edward Bellamy's dream of a new, loving America. His vision of a Great Society emerging from our unique American individu-

421

alism was molded into a twentieth-century environment by Newton Morrow, and made a reality by his successors as the last President of the United States and the First President of the United People of America, Yale Richard Marratt.

Edward Bellamy and Other Utopianists, and Individual Futurists with a Perspective on the Twenty-first Century

Bellamy, Edward, *Looking Backward,* New American Library, New York, 1960. To understand how Newton Morrow has transformed the economics of Bellamy's vision to modern reality, this book and its sequel, *Equality,* are must reading for all politicians, economists, and pragmatic visionaries!

————, *Equality*: This is the last book Bellamy wrote before his death from tuberculosis at the age of forty-eight. It is a continuation of *Looking Backward* and written in the same captivating style. With much more detail, but an easily read, in depth analysis of Bellamy's proposals. A totally fascinating book when read in the perspective of the last one hundred years. Out of print. It can be obtained in a facsimile reproduction of the 1897 edition for $12.00 from A.M.S. Press, Inc., 56 East 13th Street, New York, N.Y. 10003.

————, *Doctor Heidenhoff's Process.* A delightful novel in which Bellamy anticipates Freud and modern psychology. Available in a facsimile reprint of the 1880 edition from A.M.S. Press, Inc., 56 East 13th Street, New York, N.Y. 10003. Price $17.60.

————, *The Blindman's World and Other Stories,* Garrett Press, Inc., New York. A reprint of the 1898 edition that has most of Bellamy's short stories, including "To Whom This May Come" and many other delightful stories. Available from MSS Information Corp., P.O. Box 978, Edison, N.J. 08817. Price $15.00.

————, *Miss Ludington's Sister, A Romance on Immortality.* This warm, loving, but eerie gothic story is waiting for someone to turn it into a television drama. A facsimile reprint of the 1884 edition is available from Gregg Press, 70 Lincoln Street, Boston, Mass. 02110. Price $10.50.

————, *The Duke of Stockbridge, A Romance of the Shay Rebellion,* Belknap Press of Harvard University Press, Cambridge, Mass., 1962. Samuel Morrison called this one of America's "greatest historical novels." A good story in which Bellamy examines the economic origins of the Constitution of the United States and gives a picture of United States history after the Revolution that's not available in most history books.

———, *Selected Writings*. Contains Bellamy's long essay, *The Religion of Solidarity*, which links him with Eastern philosophy. Available from Greenwood Press, 51 Riverside Avenue, Westport, Conn. Price $10.50.

Alexander, Thea, *2150 A.D.*, Warner Books, New York, 1976. Utopian science fiction with a completely built-in psychological and philosophical premise that doesn't have to wait for 2150 A.D. Thea even provides her address in the book if you wish to pursue her approaches.

Amosoff, N., *Notes from the Future*, Simon & Schuster, New York, 1970. An unusual and poignant novel by a Russian M.D. who wrote the famous *Open Heart*. Amosoff uses cryonics in a very detailed way to get his protagonist, a doctor dying of leukemia, into the twenty-first century. Excellent reading.

Brown, James Cooke, *The Job Market*. A fascinating unpublished book that takes Edward Bellamy's concept of the Job Market and develops it in detail into a social perspective that would eliminate inflation and depressions and expand the human work potential.

———, *Loglan, A Logical Language*, Price $7.80; *Loglan 4 & 5, A Loglan Dictionary*, Price $9.80; and *Loglan*, reprint of a *Scientific American* study, $1.50. Yes, Loglan really exists! If you enjoy languages, you should get acquainted with Loglan. An amazing creation of the man who invented the game *Careers*. The two basic books listed above give you both a grammar and dictionary. Along with tapes available from the institute, you can learn to speak it. Order direct from the Loglan Institute, 2261 Soledad Rancho Road, San Diego, Calif. 92109.

———, *The Troika Incident—The Coming of a Viable Human Society*, Doubleday, New York, 1970. One of America's great Utopian novels, which projects life in three different aspects in the United States in the year 2070. Out of print at the moment, and not widely known, perhaps because the title suggests it has something to do with Russia (it doesn't—*Troika* simply represents three astronauts who travel through the time dimension to the year 2070).

Callenbach, Ernest, *Ecotopia*, Bantam, New York, 1977. A great Utopian novel that takes place in the State of California, which has seceded from the United States to pursue saner ways of living.

Clarke, Arthur, *Imperial Earth*, Ballantine, New York, 1976. Clarke's novel is better than most of the science fiction written between 1950 and 1980. By 1996 Utopian novels had largely disappeared. Science fiction, flooding the market, relied on technological changes beyond human realization, and cared little about interpersonal behavior (unless it had to do with the interaction of robots à la *Star Wars*). It offered little to understand the human condition except escape, which was the order of the day.

Hayden, Dolores, *Seven American Utopias, The Architecture of Communitarian Socialism, 1790–1975.* A fascinating examination of the relationship between architecture and social groupings that allows the individuals in various communal groupings to evolve both as a group and as individuals. If you are interested in the potential of Love Groups, then don't miss this book!

Heinlein, Robert, *The Door into Summer,* New American Library, New York, 1957. Bob Heinlein is one of the few science fiction writers who present possible futures. This novel was written when publicity on cryonics and the freezing of humans was at its peak in the late 1950s and early 1960s. The sophisticated hibernation methods of Convita and Lebenthal and biological advances in lowered metabolism were still unknown.

Morgan, Arthur, *Edward Bellamy,* Columbia University Press, New York, 1944. This is the only biography of Edward Bellamy, written by a man who was President of Antioch College and Chairman of Franklin Roosevelt's Tennessee Valley Authority. Morgan's complete rapport with Bellamy is evident throughout this detailed analysis of Bellamy's life. Excellent reading! Available in a reprint edition from Porcupine Press, 1317 Filbert Street, Philadelphia, Pa. 19107. Price $19.50.

———, *Nowhere Was Somewhere,* Chapel Hill University, N.C., 1946. An interesting study of the origin of Utopias by the man who was Edward Bellamy's biographer, and though he only knew Bellamy through his writings (many still unpublished), loved him.

———, *The Philosophy of Edward Bellamy,* King's Crown Press, Morningside Heights, New York. Morgan examines the philosophy of Edward Bellamy in detail, based on unpublished manuscripts, letters, and Bellamy's novels and short stories. This paperback book, which contains Bellamy's *Religion of Solidarity,* is available from Community Service, Inc., Box 243, Yellow Springs, Ohio 14538. Price $4.50. Community Service also has Bellamy's *Religion of Solidarity,* $2.00, and Morgan's *Nowhere Was Somewhere,* $5.00, a very valuable study of Utopias, including Bellamy's.

Noyes, John Humphrey, *History of American Socialisms,* Dover, New York, 1966. Love Groups are a direct outgrowth of the original American experiments in communal living—especially Oneida, which, unfortunately, Noyes, its founder, didn't write much about in detail.

Pohl, Frederik, *The Age of the Pussyfoot,* Ballantine, New York, 1969. The hero of this novel gets projected into the world of the twenty-sixth century by being frozen for more than five hundred years. Naturally, it's an interplanetary world, but not quite so far out as *Star Wars* or *Close Encounters of the Third Kind.*

Reynolds, Mack, *Looking Backward: From the Year 2000,* Ace Books, New York, 1973. This book, plus a sequel, *Equality: In the Year 2000,* takes Edward Bellamy's characters, Julian West, Edith Leete, and Dr. Leete, and by hibernating Julian West in 1967, awakens him in the year 2000. Mack Reynolds' world of 2000 assumes that most of the 1970–1980 technological projections will be achieved. Interesting to compare with Newton Morrow's world. Unlike most science fiction writers, Mack has the potential to create an achievable Utopia.

Rimmer, Robert, *The Premar Experiments.* New American Library, New York, 1975. In the late 1990s, Premar-style education, growing out of the Harrad concept, has become a way of life for leck teen-agers. Premar is a complete proposal for a new approach to post-secondary education that would resolve the age-work gap that now exists for 50 percent of the American youngsters who don't have any further education after high school.

Roemer, Kenneth, M., *The Obsolete Necessity, America in Utopian Writings, 1888–1900,* Kent State University Press, Ohio, 1976. A brilliant analysis of Utopian writings and what they reveal about the period. Includes Bellamy, of course, and King Gillette, who not only invented the safety razor, but in his book, *The Human Drift* (1894), advocated a corporate society which would control all of America's production and distribution. Must reading. Contains an annotated bibliography of *all* American Utopian writings in this twelve-year period.

Swan, Christopher; Roaman, Chet, *YV 88, An Eco-Fiction of Tomorrow,* Sierra Club Books, San Francisco, 1977. A detailed blueprint for transforming the Yosemite Valley of 1988 into a place where the values of man and wilderness reinforce each other.

Theobald, Robert; Scott, J. M., *TEG 1994,* Warner Books, New York, 1975. Bob and "J. M." are a husband-and-wife team who are fully immersed in the future. This is a book that influenced Newton Morrow's thinking. In case the title bewilders you, TEG is a woman's name! Read it. You'll enjoy this world of tomorrow.

Weiss, Miriam Strauss, *A Lively Corpse, Religion in Utopia,* A. S. Barnes Co., New York, 1969. Utopias without religion. Impossible, and Miriam Weiss proves it in this fascinating excursion through the history of Utopias. She obviously would be intrigued by the 1996 reality of Unilove!

Alternative Futures, The Journal of Utopian Studies. Published quarterly. $8.50 subscription. Human Dimensions Center,

Rensselaer Polytechnic Institute, Troy, N.Y. 12181. Features material from the entire range of disciplines bearing on Utopian and future thinking. A fascinating amalgamation of two vital human areas.

Late 20th-Century Perspectives on
SEX—MARRIAGE—FAMILY—RELIGION

Allen, Anna and Ed., *Together Sex*, Grove Press, New York, 1976. The best book of its time to give a perspective and how-to on social sex and swinging. Contains a complete address listing of swingers groups and clubs.

Angus, S., *The Mystery Religions*, Dover, New York, 1975. Unilove services are both past, present, and future oriented . . . but the common denominators of sexual mystery and religion are one and the same. This is a good study of the early Greek religions.

Baba, Pagal, *Temple of the Phallic King, The Mind of Indian Yogis, Swamis, Sufis, Avantanas*, Simon & Schuster, New York, 1973. A good book from which to discover the meaning of the merger of Shakti, the active female principle in the world, with Shiva, the more passive male principle.

Bettleheim, Bruno, *The Uses of Enchantment, The Meaning and Importance of Fairy-Tales*, Alfred Knopf, New York, 1976. Turn off Life-Vision and rediscover the mysteries and wonders of enchanted worlds where love and adventure have magical dimensions. Storytelling reflecting on man's eternal quest for his own meanings is the key to Unilove services.

Blofeld, John, *The Tantric Mysticism of Tibet*, E. P. Dutton, New York, 1970. A good study of ancient Tantric meditation and ritual.

Brisset, Dennis; Edgely, Charles, *Life as Theater, A Dramaturgical Source Book*, Aldine Publishing Co., Chicago, 1975. Religion must become theater, too, with a final synthesis of life, religion, and theater for complete self-actualization. An excellent source book for both church and theater.

Bruck, Connie, *Professing Androgyny, Human Behavior Magazine*, October, 1977. A survey of the work of Sandra and Daryl Bern, who teach at Stanford, and their commitment to a gender-free, androgynous world. Sandra"s approaches to androgyny, however, might not accept the strong male-female sexual magnetism implications of June Singer's approaches and of Unilove, which derives from Eastern philosophy.

Byrne, Josepha Heifetz, *Mrs. Byrne's Dictionary of Unusual Obscure, and Preposterous Words*, University Books, Inc., New York, 1974. Chuck Holmes, Newton Morrow's campaign manager, enjoyed this book for bedside reading and to read to Christina and other women in his Love Group, when they made love in the White House!

Devi, Kamala, *The Eastern Way of Love, Tantric Sex and Erotic Mysticism*, Simon & Schuster, New York, 1977. At last, a joyously written "sex book" that separates elements of Tantric sex from the ancient ritual, and the Eastern mind, and makes it fully accessible to "human Western loving." Beautifully illustrated with drawings of Western lovers by Peter Schauman. This book, written by a woman, is required reading for Uniloves.

Dinnerstein, Dorothy, *The Mermaid and the Minotaur, Sexual Arrangements and the Human Malaise*. Excellent, thought-provoking reading for future-oriented males to gain a new perspective on the male-female dichotomy.

Duquesne, Jacques, *A Church Without Priests*, Macmillan, New York, 1969. A Catholic Church with married priests is a clue to the future of religion and a Western world that will embrace Unilove, even within the structure of the established churches and synagogues.

Farren, David, *Sex & Magic*, Barnes & Noble, New York, 1976. The missing word in the title is *Religion*. An easy-reading approach to the mystical aspects of life.

Guenther, Herbert, *The Tantric View of Life*, Shamhala Publications, Inc., 1123 Spruce Street, Boulder, Col. 80302. Good reading for Unilove adherents!

Hanna, Thomas, *Bodies in Revolt*, Holt, Rinehart, Winston, New York, 1970. Subtitled *The Evolution of 20th Century Man Toward the Somatic Culture of the 21st Century*. Hanna's contention is the brave new world is inside you, here and now—waiting to get out! Good reading for Uniloves.

Heilbrum, Carol, *Toward a Recognition of Androgyny*, Harper Colophon, New York, 1973. Excellent essays on our common sharing of the Yang and Yin, male and female principles that are active in both sexes.

Hendrickson, Robert, *Lewd Foods, A Complete Guide to Aphrodisiac Edibles*, Chilton Book Company, Rodman, Pa., 1974. No kitchen in 1980 or 2000 should be without this definitive book on "Sexual Cooking." Whether you try oysters like Chrissy and Mory, or more esoteric foods, the book is a delight to read from cover to cover.

Ippolito, Diane, *Erotica*: This is the complete poetry that Chrissy read to Mory that first day they met. The entire quality paperback volume, with lovely drawings, is worth owning. Order from Artists & Alchemists Publications, 215 Bridgeway, Sausalito, Calif. 94965.

Kiernan, Thomas, *Shrinks, Etc., A Consumer's Guide to Psychotherapies from Freudian Analysis to Sex Therapy*, Dell, New York, 1974. If you are lost in all the new, often faddish approaches to self-realization, this book is a valuable and humorously critical guide.

Kolenda, Konstantin, *Religion Without God,* Prometheus Books, New York, 1976. "The world matters only because each human life, yours and mine, matters first." A humanist approach to religion that permeates Unilove.

Kosnick, Anthony, *Human Sexuality, New Directions in American Catholic Thought,* Paulist Press, New York, 1976. Father Kosnick is not the author of this book. It was commissioned by The Catholic Theological Association of America to define new Catholic approaches to human sexuality. While the liberal conclusions divided church leadership in the 1980s, they point to the inevitability of a mystery religion, based on sex and human caring, either developing within the Church or separately, as Unilove.

McGlashan, Alan, *Savage and Beautiful Country, The Secret Life of the Mind,* Hillstone, New York, 1967. A delightful book that restores magic and myth to human living and loving.

Moffit, John, *Journey to Gorakhpur,* Holt, Rinehart & Winston, New York, 1972. Subtitled *An Encounter with Christ Beyond Christianity.* An excellent study of Hinduism by a Westerner who was a member of the order of Rama Krishna and is now a Catholic.

Mookerjee, Ajit; Khanna, Madhu, *The Tantric Way,* Art Science Ritual, New York Graphic Society, Boston, 1977. One of the guidebooks for Unilove, with many churches using material from this book in their church services. A beautifully designed and illustrated quality paperback. Must owning!

Needleman, Jacob; Lewis, Dennis, *Sacred Tradition & Present Needs,* An Esalen Book, Viking Press, New York, 1975. A good study of the mystical elements in various Eastern religions which are lacking in the Protestant and Jewish religions, but, as shown by Unilove, are basic to human needs.

Rajneesh, Bhagwan, *Only One Sky: On the Tantric Way of Tilopa's Song of Mahamudra.*
"And Tilopa says only then does Mahamudra appear.
The final, the utterly final orgasm with the Existence
Then you are separate no more."
Rajneesh is a Tantric Master. See Bibliographic references to him in Robert H. Rimmer's *Come Live My Life,* New American Library, New York, 1977.

Rawson, Phillip, *Erotic Art of the East,* Berkley Publishing Corp., New York, 1977. Rawson not only gives a comprehensive, fully illustrated study of Indian Tantra, but also a fascinating survey of ancient Chinese and Japanese eroticism, which permeated every aspect of life.

Schechner, Richard, ed., *Dionysus in 69,* Farrar, Straus & Giroux, New York, 1969. With her background in the dance and her experience with The Performance Group, Adar Chilling created Unilove. This book is the complete, fully illustrated adaptation of Euripides' *Bacchae*, with the nudity and sexuality that shocked audiences of the late 60s.

Singer, June, *Androgyny, Toward a New Theory of Sexuality*, Doubleday, New York, 1976. June's book is basic to an understanding of Unilove. She thoroughly analyzes the roots of androgyny in all religions and points the way to a new religion based on androgyny. Must reading! The book was highly influential on Adar Chilling's book, *Unilove*.

Sirjamaki, John, *The American Family in the Twentieth Century*, Harvard University Press, Cambridge, Mass., 1970. While social-science literature of the late 1970s is overwhelmed with studies of the family, this is a good summary with a look at the future. For a more extensive listing of books in the area of marriage and the family, see the bibliographies in Robert H. Rimmer's Alternate Life Style novels.

Skutch, Alexander, *The Golden Core of Religion*, Holt, Rinehart & Winston, 1970. Skutch's conclusion is that "loving care is the golden core of religion." An interesting examination of religion by a man whose specialty is botany.

Travers, P. L. *About the Sleeping Beauty*, McGraw-Hill, New York, 1975. This is the book Christina read to her daughter Penny. While sexual overtones of the Sleeping Beauty story are not accentuated by P. L., the magical wonder of the legend, which, almost Jung-fashion, has become a part of the female psyche, is revealed from many aspects.

Ward, Hiley H., *Religion 2101 A.D.*, Doubleday, New York, 1975. While Hiley fails to anticipate a religion similar to Unilove, which uses sexual loving to achieve transcendence, this book points the way. Good reading.

Watts, Alan, *The Essence of Alan Watts*, Celestial Arts, Millbrae, Calif. 94030, 1975. Nine beautifully illustrated paperback volumes covering Alan Watts' joyous approaches to God, Love, and Death. The seeds of Unilove were planted by Alan Watts. Listen to him on tape, also. Exciting selections from Alan Watts' lecturing and talking, in his inimitable manner, are available on many tapes from Alan Watts, Audio-Cassettes, M.E.A., Box 303, Sausalito, Calif. 94965. Write for listing and prices. Also The Electronic University, Mill Valley, Calif. 94941, offers audio courses by Alan.

Webb, Peter, *The Erotic Arts*, New York Graphic Society, Boston, 1975. A definitive and loving survey of eroticism in all the arts. Basic to an understanding of the remerger of sex and religion. A beautiful book worth owning.

Winter, Ruth, *The Smell Book, Scents, Sex and Society*, J. P. Lippincott, Philadelphia, Pa., 1976. Here's the book that will tell you all about pheremones and human loving. Maybe it's not really love at first glance—but a sudden rapport based on smell!

Wiseman, Jacqueline P., *The Social Psychology of Sex,* Harper & Row, 1976. Essays by well-known psychologists that point toward a new kind of interpersonal sexuality. Covers the search for variety in sexual relationships thoroughly. Good reading.

Young, Arthur M., *The Reflexive Universe, Evolution of Consciousness,* Delacorte Press, New York, 1976. A future-oriented merger of Eastern philosophy and Western science that makes the reader religiously "aware" in spite of himself.

Young, Michael; Wilmott, Peter, *The Symmetrical Family,* Pantheon, New York, 1973. An excellent British-based study of the family which has its feet firmly planted in the future.

At Home, P.O. Box 58, Rockaway, N.J. 07886. A beautifully illustrated magazine that exalts human sexuality, alternate life styles, and marriage and the family. Naked lovemaking is photographed joyously. Annual subscription $18.00.

The Androgyny Center, 1929 Cable Street, San Diego, Calif. 92107. Publishes *Androgyny Today*—four issues $8.00 annually. In their words, "The center proposes a range of choices by which people can identify themselves, secure that the masculine-feminine interaction within each individual is not only normal, but the dynamic factor in his wholeness." Obviously a precursor of Unilove.

Alternative Lifestyles, Changing Patterns in Marriage, Family & Intimacy. A present and quarterly future-oriented journal, edited by Roger Libby, published by Sage Publications. Annual subscription $30.00. Sage Publications, Inc., 275 S. Beverly Drive, Beverly Hills, Calif. 90212.

The A. A. Model. A fascinating book about an experiment in communal living and free sexuality which has been in existence since 1970. Fully illustrated, available in French, German, and English. Order from AA VERLAG, Hochstr. 23, D 8500, Nuremberg, Germany. Price approximately $8.50.

Lifestyle '77 Convention, San Diego, California, July 29–30, 1977. More than thirty 60/90 minute tapes from a unique assemblage of hundreds of people involved in alternate sex and marriage relationships. Including keynote speech by Bob Rimmer, *Two-Couple Sex as an Emerging Life Style* and Herb Otto's *The Growth Perspective on Interpersonal Relationships.* Plus many others. Order from Butterfly Dimensions, 8817 Shirley Avenue, Northridge, Calif. 91324.

Stan Dale Workshop, Not Forsaking All Others, Santa Rosa, Calif., November 12–13, 1977. Tapes that include Helen and Stan Dale, as well as their four boys, discussing their open marriage. Lonny Myers discussing *Compartment Four* relationships in marriage. Bob Rimmer on *Structured Two-Couple Relationships;* Persia Wolley on *Single Parenting;* and many others. Available from John Farmer, 68 Magnolia, Redwood City, Calif. 94067. $35.00 for six 90-minute tapes.

Understanding Human Behavior, An Illustrated Guide to Human Relationships. A twenty-four volume encyclopedia of Human Behavior that can become a source book and age-gap breaker between parents and their children. Easily understandable and comprehensive. Available under a monthly purchase plan of $4.98 per volume, from Columbia House, 1400 North Fruitridge Avenue, Box 1165, Terre Haute, Ind. 47811.

The Visual Dictionary of Sex, A & W Publishers, New York, 1977. A beautifully illustrated comprehensive dictionary— really a mini-encyclopedia of every aspect of human sexuality. Well worth owning.

20th Century Perspectives on
HIBERNATION—LONGEVITY—DEATH
—REINCARNATION

Ettinger, R.C.W., *Man into Superman,* Avon Books, New York, 1972. A fascinating survey of the possibility of living for centuries, by the man who has done more to publicize the possibilities of cryonics than anyone else alive. Bob Ettinger is still involved in the Cryonics Society of Michigan, and this book gives the addresses of other Cryonic Societies (a few of which are still active) around the world.

——, *The Prospect of Immortality,* Doubleday, New York, 1964. Perhaps the first book anywhere to introduce the potential of human freezing and low temperature hibernation.

Fennema, Owen R., and others, *Low Temperature Preservation of Foods and Living Matter,* Marcel Dekker, New York, 1973. Read this book and you may give up eating frozen foods. Based on present knowledge, ice formation in food fibers, as well as in human blood cells, does irreparable damage. Low temperature hibernation is the only route into the future for humans.

Harrington, Alan, *The Immortalist, An Approach to Engineering Man's Divinity,* Avon Books, New York, 1969. Alan's book is absolutely must reading to understand not only the basics of religious longing for rebirth, but the "we must have done something wrong" aspects of most religions. Among other things Alan even examines the Cryonics Underground. Unable to leave the theme, Alan wrote a novel, *Paradise 1,* Little Brown, Boston, 1978, about the world of 2007 when immortality becomes a reality. Funny, ferocious reading. Don't miss it!

Head, Joseph; Cranston, S. L., *Reincarnation: The Phoenix Fire Mystery,* Julian/Crown, 1977. If you are interested in reincarnation, and the many people, Thomas Edison, Albert

431

Schweitzer, Aristotle, Benjamin Franklin, and Lao-Tzu, who believed in it, you should own this book. Absolutely must reading if you are looking for one aspect of a new religion like Unilove.

Hubbard, L. Ron, *Have You Lived Before This Life?* Publication Organization Church of Scientology, Los Angeles, Calif. 90029, 1978. If you are interested in reincarnation, Ron Hubbard's total approach beginning with *Dianetics* is closely interrelated with the belief that one's body is inhabited by an immortal essence, a "thetan" that finds another body immediately after the death of the one you now inhabit. While this is not the concept advocated in Unilove or by Newton Morrow, it is an interesting approach with roots in antiquity.

Iverson, Jeffery, *More Lives Than One*, Pan Books, London, 1977. This is the fascinating story of Arnall Bloxham, one of Britain's leading hypnotherapists. Bloxham preserved more than two hundred tapes of people who regressed, under hypnosis, to their previous lives on earth, and gave accounts of their former lives that are so authentic that they can only be explained by the certainty of reincarnation.

Kostenbaum, Peter, *Is There an Answer to Death?* Spectrum Prentice Hall, New York, 1976. An excellent analysis of the illusion of death.

Kurtzman, Joel; Gordon, Phillip, *No More Dying, The Conquest of Aging and the Extension of Human Life*. An interesting survey of transplants, cloning, cryobiology, and genetic engineering, all converging on eventual life extension and hibernation.

Leek, Sybil, *Reincarnation, The Second Chance*, Stein & Day, New York, 1974. A good survey of the deep-rooted belief in reincarnation inherent in most religions—even Catholic Christianity which rejected it.

Lozina-Losinski, L. K., *Studies in Cryobiology*, John Wiley & Sons, New York, 1974. This translation will tell you where the Russians are at, in all areas of low-temperature preservation—including the freezing of humans.

MacGregor, Gedoes, *Reincarnation in Christianity*, Quest Books, 306 West Geneva Road, Wheaton, Ill., 1978. With a promise of afterlife in heaven or hell, can Christianity accept the doctrine of continuous rebirth? If you are interested in reincarnation, buy this excellent book direct from the publisher. Price $4.50. In addition, it has an excellent annotated bibliography.

Prehoda, Robert W., *Suspended Animation, The Research Possibility That May Allow Man to Conquer the Limiting Chains of Time*. Chilton Book Co., Philadelphia, Pa., 1969. An excellent survey of everything known in the 1960s and 1970s about cryonics and hibernation.

Restak, Richard, *Premeditated Man, Bioethics and the Control of*

Future Life, Viking Press, New York, 1975. One of the many books writtten in the 1970s that questions how far genetic engineering should proceed. Good reading.

Rosenfeld, Albert, *Prolongevity,* Alfred Knopf, New York, 1976. This is the book that David Convita and Max Lebenthal gave Christina to read. An excellent survey. Must reading if you have an ounce of curiosity about the quantum leap that biology is making into the future.

Segerberg, Osborn, *The Immortality Factor,* E. P. Dutton, New York, 1974. A thorough examination of every approach—past, present, and future—to extending man's life-span. But it will probably be the long shots—the unthinkables like Vitaleben—that will finally do it.

Shiffrin, Nancy, *Past Lives, Present Problems,* William Morrow, New York, 1978. A good survey of past-life therapy which assumes that traumas of your previous life (or lives) are influential on your present life. Past-life regressions are achieved by working with hypnotherapists. Keep in mind that Newton Morrow believed it isn't particularly important whether you can specifically identify *who* you were in a previous life, but that you can't "die" in the cosmic-energy sense.

Smith, Homer W., *Kamongo,* Viking Press, New York, 1932. A profound novel about the search for the African lungfish (Kamongo) which proved survival possibilities against all odds by hibernating! In 1978, lungfish were being flown to the University of Pennsylvania, where suspended animation, or estivation, as practiced by lungfish, was being studied to discover a way of lowering the metabolic rate of human beings.

Smith, Suzy: *Reincarnation for the Millions,* Sherbourne Press, Nashville, Tenn., 1976. An interesting survey of the continuing belief by many outstanding people, such as Thomas Edison, Benjamin Franklin, William James, and hundreds of others, in reincarnation.

Street, Noel, *Reincarnation, How to Recall Your Past Lives,* Lotus Metaphysical Center, Inc., P.O. Box 39, Fabens, Tex. 79838.

Stuphen, Dick, *You Were Born Again to Be Together,* Pocket Books, New York, 1976. Dick is director of an experimental hypnosis center in Scottsdale, Arizona, which uses regression into past lives on this earth to discover one's "real" self. Occasionally lovers have been reunited across the "death" barriers. Perhaps the world of 2100 will "discover" Mory and Bellamy again—and most certainly Chrissy!

Taylor, Gordon Rattray, *The Biological Time Bomb,* World Publishing Company, New York, 1968. Though partially outdated by recent developments, this very readable survey covers most of the fearsome aspects of the breakthrough in biological science. Taylor even examines "deep freezing" of human beings.

Vaux, Kenneth, *Biomedical Ethics, Morality for the New Medicine,* Harper & Row, New York, 1974. Among other things, Vaux considers the morality of immortality via freezing or anabiosis.

Watson, Lyall, *The Romeo Error, A Matter of Life and Death,* Anchor Press, New York, 1974. Death is an error of perception. The Romeo Error—thinking Juliet dead in her tomb— is all in your mind. Obviously, hibernation with life processes slowed nearly to zero is a new kind of bridge. Good reading.

The Committee for Elimination of Death, P.O. Box 696, San Marcos, Calif. 92069. A clearinghouse for every individual and group who believe that human beings can achieve immortality. As intermediaries, Stuart Otto, its founder, and all its members are kept in close touch with groups who are actively engaged in freezing human beings, hibernation, gerontology geriatrics, etc. As a member, you receive their newsletter and you become an Immortalist—"and choose life rather than death."

The *Cryonics Association* and the *Cryonics Institute* are both at 24041 Stratford, Oak Park, Mich. 48237. Both nonprofit. *CA* educational and scientific, associate membership $15, membership $50 yearly. *CI* contracts for services, membership $1,250 individual or $1,875 a couple; remainder of cryonic suspension package estimated in 1977 at $28,000. Without David Convita's Vitaleben, this is the only trip (nonguaranteed) to tomorrow!

The Cryonicist, 627 West Barry Street, No—3—V, Chicago, Ill. 60657. A complete directory of active cryonic (freezing) organizations and services available for those who refuse "to go gentle into that good night."

SUICIDE, DEPRESSION
Sylvia Plath—Anne Sexton

Books listed without annotation are for readers who may wish to explore in even greater depth the underlying causes of Christina North Klausner's inability to cope with herself, or the world, during her first thirty-two years.

Alpert, George; Leogrande, Ernest, *Second Chance to Live, The Suicide Syndrome,* DaCapo Press, New York, 1975. A half-million Americans attempt suicide every year. This is a deeply personal look at some of them.

Alvarez, A., *The Savage God, A Study of Suicide,* Random

House, New York, 1972. Alvarez is not just a commentator. He was there himself, and was a good friend of Sylvia Plath.

Butscher, Edward, *Sylvia Plath, Method and Madness,* Seabury Press, New York, 1976. The best biography of Sylvia Plath.

Fieve, Ronald R., *Moodswing: The Third Revolution in Psychiatry,* Bantam, New York, 1975. The story of lithium in manic-depression.

Flach, Frederick F., M.D., *The Secret Strength of Depression,* Bantam, New York, 1975.

Jacobson, Edith, *Depression,* International Universities Press, Inc., New York, 1971.

Knouth, Percy, *A Season in Hell,* Harper & Row, New York, 1975. Good writing by a man who was there and survived.

Kroll, Judith, *Chapters in Mythology, The Poetry of Sylvia Plath,* Harper & Row, New York, 1976.

Lester, Gene; Lester, David, *Suicide, the Gamble with Death,* Prentice Hall, New York, 1971.

Neary, John: *Whom the Gods Destroy, An Account of a Journey Through Madness,* Atheneum, New York, 1975.

Plath, Aurelia Schuber, *Letters Home by Sylvia Plath, Correspondence 1950–1963,* Harper & Row, New York, 1975. Interesting reading, but keep in mind, Christina North is a very different person from Sylvia Plath!

Plath, Sylvia, *Ariel,* Harper & Row, New York, 1965.

———, *The Bell Jar,* Bantam, New York, 1971.

Portwood, Doris, *Commonsense Suicide,* Dodd Mead, New York, 1978. The author argues the right to suicide for older people.

Reynolds, David; Farbgrow, Norman, *Suicide, Inside and Out,* University of California, Berkeley, Calif., 1976. A horrifying true story of a sane man, a trained psychologist, who purposely entered a psychiatric hospital.

Rubin, Theodore: *Compassion and Self Hate, An Alternative to Despair.* Ballantine, New York, 1975. Rubin's approach to self-hatred and self-anger are similar to Albert Ellis' more thoroughly defined Rational Emotive Therapy, which is a basic guideline for sanity in this or any world.

Sexton, Anne, *45 Mercy Street,* Houghton Mifflin, Boston, 1976.

———, *Live or Die,* Houghton Mifflin, Boston, 1966.

———, *Transformation,* Houghton Mifflin, Boston, 1971.

Sexton, Linda Gray and Ames Lois, *Anne Sexton, A Self-Portrait in Letters.* Houghton Mifflin, Boston, 1977. Fascinating insights into Anne Sexton's mind. Sylvia Plath and Anne Sexton knew each other. Anne's suicide may have been motivated by Sylvia's.

Schneidman, Edwin S. *Essays in Self-Destruction,* Jason Aronson, Inc., New York, 1967. *Can a Mouse Commit Suicide?* by Halmuth Schoeffer is included in this fascinating collection.

Schneidman, Edwin S., and others, *The Psychology of Suicide,* Jason Aronson, Inc., New York, 1976.

Steiner, Nancy Hunter, *A Closer Look at Ariel, A Memory of Sylvia Plath,* Harper Magazine Press, New York, 1973. Nancy was Sylvia's roommate.
Weissman, Myrna; Paykel, Eugene S., *The Depressed Woman,* University of Chicago Press, Chicago, 1974.

Late 20th Century
Technological Perspectives on
the 21st Century

Barash, David P., *Sociobiology and Behavior,* Elesevier, New York, 1977. Here are Edward Wilson's beliefs defined as sociobiology—that all living things behave in a way to maximize their Evolutionary Fitness—developed in a careful analysis of what altruism, courtship, and mating really mean. Hopefully, you may disagree! But it's worth thinking about.
Berhman, Daniel, *Solar Energy,* Little Brown, Boston, 1976. An excellent, readable book for the layman on every aspect of the future of solar energy.
Bova, Ben, *The Fourth State of Matter, Plasma Dynamics and Tomorrow's Technology,* New American Library, New York, 1971. Bova proves in this book why he writes good science fiction. You can't understand the technological potential of the future world until you've read this book.
Calder, Nigel, *Technopolis, The Social Control of Science,* Simon & Schuster, New York, 1970. How to mobilize scientific knowledge to prevent its own destruction. Calder's "Attitudes Toward Science, Mugs versus Zealots" is worth hanging on your bulletin board!
Clegg, Peter, *New Low-Cost Sources of Energy for the Home,* Gardens Way Publishing, Charlotte, Vt. 05445. A good survey of the many alternatives actually available or within our grasp. Many do-it-yourself alternatives for those who have gone back to earth.
Daniels, Farrington, *Direct Use of the Sun's Energy,* Ballantine, New York, 1964. Every aspect of the use of solar energy, including the use of the sun to produce hydrogen in fuel cells and internal combustion engines, as the most important source of fuel for centuries to come.
Dawkins, Richard, *The Selfish Gene,* Oxford University Press, New York, 1976. Is man a gene machine blindly programed to preserve its selfish genes? Dawkins is sure we are—but we rebel against destiny, too!
Doxiadis, C. A., *Building Entopia,* W. W. Norton, New York, 1975. Entopia, a place that can exist—to distinguish it from Utopia. This book is a must reading for all futurists!

—————, *Eucemenopolis, The Inevitable City of the Future*, W. W. Norton, New York, 1974. From the history of human settlements to the "rehumanized" city of the future. Doxiadis is essential reading for anyone interested in how societies live together.

Foley, Gerald, *The Energy Question*, Penguin, Nw York, 1976. A good survey of every aspect of energy and its particular potential for development.

Ford, Brian J., *Microbe Power, Tomorrow's Revolution*, Stein & Day, New York, 1976. Are you afraid of microbes? You won't be after you've read this fascinating study of the potential of microbes in the world today and tomorrow.

Freeman, S. David, *Energy, The New Era*, Vintage, New York, 1974. A good study of the complex energy questions and the many alternatives. Too few people are aware that how we resolve future energy needs will permeate every aspect of our lives, from sex to economics!

Gatland, Kenneth; Dempster, Derek, *Worlds in Creation*, Henry Regnery, Chicago, 1974. How the world and cosmos got here is almost as interesting as where it is going.

Gutnov, Alexi, and others, *The Ideal Communist City*, Braziller, New York, 1965. If you are interested in the future of the city, join the Library of Urban Affairs Book Club, which will keep you abreast of hundreds of future-oriented studies. This one is interesting because it envisions cities which would liberate individuals from group conformity.

Hilts, Phillip J., *Behavior Mod*, Bantam, New York, 1976. Ways of modifying human behavior all the way from drugs to the "operant conditioning" of B. F. Skinner. An easy-to-read survey.

Jastrow, Robert, *Until the Sun Dies*, W. W. Norton, New York, 1977. A poetic book that melds science and religion while Jastrow explains the mysteries of the origins of life and the universe. Must reading.

Jaynes, Julian, *The Origins of Consciousness in the Breakdown of the Bicameral Mind*, Houghton Mifflin, Boston, 1977. Did man only become conscious about three thousand years ago as a result of his growing culture? The implications for human beings today and tomorrow are intriguing.

Leontif, Wassily, and others, *The Future of the World Economy*, Oxford University Press, New York, 1977. An excellent examination of the world's economic future based on most imaginable scenarios—except Newton Morrow's *New Tomorrow!*

Lewis, Richard S.; Smith, Phillip, *Frozen Future, A Prophetic Report from Antarctica*, Quadrangle Books, New York, 1973. Science fiction and space travel can't compare with the reality of the great untapped and unexplored laboratory at our

437

feet. Good reading—if only to reveal how the nations of the world can work together.

Lovin, Amory, *Soft Energy Paths,* Ballinger Publishing Company, Cambridge, Mass., 1977. From now until nuclear fusion is a reality, and perhaps beyond, Lovin's theory, shocking to the industrial power complex, is the only sound way for free societies to go if they wish to retain their basic freedoms.

Ridpath, Ian, *Worlds Beyond, A Report on the Search for Life in Space,* Harper & Row, New York, 1976. This quality paperback makes science fiction look pale by comparison.

Rosen, Stephen, *Future Facts, The Way Things Are Going to Work in the Future,* Simon & Schuster, New York, 1976. Everything, from health and medicine to food, crops, construction, communication, human behavior, and play, that was on the "future drawing board" in the late 1970s.

Schneider, Stephen H., *The Genesis Strategy,* Plenum Press, New York, 1976. A practical approach to preserving world food supplies against unforeseen weather and climate changes. Unfortunately, not enough people are listening or *reading!*

Weizenbaum, Joseph, *Computer Power and Human Reason,* W. H. Freeman & Company, San Francisco, 1976. Are you afraid of the computerized world of the future? Read this book by the man who designed Eliza, a computer than can speak to you, and you'll lose your fears and wish you could return to the world in 2100.

Wilsher, Peter; Righter, Rosemary, *The Exploding Cities,* Quadrangle, New York, 1975. By the year 2000, more than half of mankind will be living in cities, and the world population could be more than 6 billion. A frightening look at today and tomorrow.

Wilson, Caroll, Project Director, *Energy Global Prospects 1985–2000,* McGraw Hill, New York, 1977. This Massachusetts Institute of Technology workshop study concludes that oil production will level off by 1985—and right now we should be deep in the transition to coal and nuclear power and renewable energy systems. Amazingly few people are listening.

Voegeli, Henry E., and Tarrant, John J., *Survival 2001—Scenario from the Future,* Van Nostrand & Reinhold, New York, 1975. A looking-backward approach with detailed drawing of solutions to our energy and ecology seen from the twenty-first century viewpoint. Great dreaming!

Economic Growth in the Future, The Growth Debate in National and Global Perspective. sponsored by the Edison Electric Institute. McGraw Hill, New York, 1976. The best survey anywhere comparing between the economic growth and no growth contenders—into the year 2000 and beyond.

Exploring Energy Choices, A preliminary report from the Energy Policy Project of the Ford Foundation, 1974. This pamphlet is an excellent survey of where the United States has been and where we'll go based on varying rates of national productivity.

Energy & Power, A Scientific American Book, W. H. Freeman, San Francisco, 1971. Articles from *Scientific American* that point the way to the future.

A Forecast for Space Technology, 1980–2000, National Aeronautics and Space Administration, Washington, D.C., 1976. If you really want to know where we are going, order this book from Superintendent of Documents, U.S. Government Printing Office, Washington, D.C.

Project Independence—Solar Energy. A blueprint for the development of solar energy prepared under the direction of the National Science Foundation for the Federal Energy Administration. $6.20 from the Government Printing Office. Interesting reading.

Selected Topics on Hydrogen Fuel, U.S. Department of Commerce, National Bureau of Standards. Edited by J. Hord. Economically produced hydrogen is the fuel of the future. This is a fairly technical survey available from the Government Printing Office for $2.80.

U.S. Economic Growth from 1976 to 1986, Studies of the Joint Economic Committee, Congress of the United States. 12 volumes—approximately $1.00 to 1.25 each, written by experts, on where the United States can or can't go in the coming years. Without Newton Morrow, of course!

Institute for the Study of Economic Systems, 111 Pine Street, Suite 1800, San Francisco, Calif. 94111. Publishes a newsletter, *The New Capitalist,* which promotes Louis Kelso's theories of dispersing capital ownership. Annual membership $10.00. Newton Morrow's version of stock ownership by individual workers has its roots in Kelso's theories, but carries them to their inevitable conclusion.

Late 20th-Century
Political and Economic Perspectives
on the 21st Century
SOCIALIST—LIBERTARIAN—COMMUNIST

Abt, Clark C., *The Social Audit for Management,* American Management Association, New York, 1976. In a corporate New Tomorrow society, all profit-making corporations would follow Clark Abt's proposal and submit an achievement balance sheet for men and women as well as a profit statement. An important concept.

Beter, Peter, *Conspiracy Against the Dollar, The New Imperial-*

ism, Braziller, New York, 1973. How those in control of the monetary power of various countries, including the United States, create the "stagflations" that the little guy must live with.

Bhaqwati, Joseph, Ed., *Economics and the World Order, From the 1970s to the 1990s,* Free Press, New York, 1972. In the time frame of its writing by a group of international economists, this book has a great deal of foresight.

Blair, John M., *The Control of Oil,* Pantheon, New York, 1976. Among other things, this book is conclusive evidence of the need for a populist government in control of the entire monetary establishment.

Braverman, Harry, *Labor and Monopoly Capital, The Degradation of Work in the Twentieth Century,* Monthly Review Press, New York, 1974. Note the wording, *Monopoly Capital.* People's capitalism isn't monopoly-controlled capital—neither is it Marxian communism or state-controlled capitalism. Good reading for a particular point of view.

Clarkson, Kenneth, Project Director, *Catalog of Research Issues for Understanding National Economic Planning,* University of Miami Law School, Miami, Florida, 1976. If nothing else, browse through this 1,750 page study showing, industry by industry, the insurmountable problems of centralized government planning.

Commoner, Barry, *The Poverty of Power,* Alfred Knopf, New York, 1976. Barry seeks the answers convincingly to a new kind of economics and politics to resolve our energy crisis. Thought-provoking.

Drucker, Peter, *The Unseen Revolution, How Pension Fund Socialism Came to America,* Harper & Row, New York, 1976. While Drucker tries to make a case that the pension funds of the top 500 companies constitute ownership of the companies, the fact remains that the control of these funds, via unions and money management firms, is a long, long way from the direct stock ownership proposed by Newton Morrow.

Frisch, Robert, *The Triumph of the ESOP,* Farnsworth Publishing Company, Inc., Rockville Centre, New York 11570. This book, along with Frisch's previous book, *The Magic of the ESOT,* gives you a here-and-now approach to Louis Kelso's Employee Stock Ownership Plans and Trusts in action—which must culminate in Newton Morrow's economic New Tomorrow.

Gray, Elizabeth; Gray, Dodson, and others, *Growth and Its Implication for the Future,* Dinosaur Press, Bradford, Connecticut, 1975. Graphs, charts, cartoons, all put together with a strong controversial text.

Groseclose, Elgin, *Money and Man, A Survey of Monetary Experience,* Oklahoma University Press, Norman, Oklahoma,

1976. If you enjoy your freedom, whether your prime interest is economics or not, you cannot afford to be ignorant of how money, in a wide sense, controls it. This book is easy and good reading.

Guttman, Daniel; Willmer, Barry, *The Shadow Government*, Pantheon, New York, 1976. Here's where your government really begins and ends in the powerful consulting organizations. A very important perspective on how the statistical American is put under a microscope and his lot in life planned—not by elected representatives either.

Harrington, Michael, *The Twilight of Capitalism*, Simon & Schuster, New York, 1976. Interesting, fairly difficult analysis, but too hooked to Marx (or Harrington's interpretation of Marx) with a reliance on socialistic big government. Total people's capitalism is more inspiring!

Hayek, Fredrich A., *The Road to Serfdom*, University of Chicago Press, Chicago, Ill., 1944. Must reading by a foremost Libertarian economist. Newton Morrow's only disagreement would be: who will finally own the capital or income-producing equipment and land of any society? The only answer can be "all of us" in a corporate society that still uses bottom-line profits as a driving force.

Hazlitt, Henry, *A New Constitution Now*, Arlington House, New York, 1974. Hazlitt argues for a British-style parliamentary system. Good reading for those who believe that our Constitution is part of the mythology of American democracy and can't be changed. Amazingly, Hazlitt ignores Rexford Tugwell, who has done a much more interesting overhaul in his book.

Heilbroner, Robert L., *Business Civilization in Decline*, W. W. Norton, New York, 1976. Given the world of the late 1970s and early 1980s, Heilbroner was on the right track. But New Tomorrow is a whole different way to loosen the bonds of a Big Brother, and still keep the society goal-oriented. All of Heilbroner's books are incisive and worth reading.

Heller, Walter, *The Economy, Old Myths, New Realities*, W. W. Norton, New York, 1976. Heller traces his own economic thinking through editorial conclusions that appeared in the *Wall Street Journal* from 1973. You can do this yourself, not just by reading Heller, but the weekly summary of the economy that appears in the *Journal*. You'll quickly come to the conclusion that the "big boys" have no answers, and, like it or not, Newton Morrow will get them eventually!

Henderson, Hazel, *Creating Alternative Futures, The End of Economics*, Berkley Windhoven, New York, 1978. A must reading collection of essays by a young woman who started as a small town activist and without college degrees educated herself so well that she could not only challenge top economists but project a new kind of world where we can

441

live lives on a more human scale. Hazel Henderson could succeed Yale Marratt as President, and she's young enough to do it!

Hospers, John, *Libertarianism, A Political Philosophy for Tomorrow*, Nash Publishing, Los Angeles, Calif., 1971. While Libertarians might not agree, Morrow's United People's Party and Libertarianism have a great deal in common. Hospers carries the libertarian philosophy close to anarchy, but is good reading.

Howe, Irving, *Essential Works of Socialism*, Yale University Press, 1976. Here between two covers are the essential writings of socialist philosophers from Marx to Martin Buber and beyond. Morrow's kind of people's capitalism is something else again.

Kahn, Herman, *The Future of the Corporation*, Marcom & Lipscomb, New York, 1974. While Herman is a "positive" futurist, (maybe too much so) the New Tomorrow solution never occurs to him.

Kelso, Louis; Hetter, Patricia, *Two Factor Theory, The Economics of Reality*, Vintage, New York, 1967. Once you've read Kelso, you'll understand Kelso's influence on Newton Morrow—also on Mark Silverman (for a detailed discussion of Employee Stock Ownership Plans, see Bob Rimmer's *Come Live My Life*).

Larson, Martin, *The Federal Reserve System*, and *Our Manipulated Dollar*, Devin Adair, Old Greenwich, Conn., 1975. To understand why a United People's Capital Corporation would resolve the inherent defects of our present monetary system, you should read this book.

Lerner, Abbe P., *Flation, What You Always Wanted to Know About Inflation, Depression and the Dollar*, Quadrangle, New York, 1972. One of many books published in the 1970s to try and explain the sad monetary world man has created where work is extolled, but money, the reward of work, loses its purchasing power faster than it can be earned. A good survey in its time frame. Check your library for many others.

Loebel, Eugen, *Humanomics*, Random House, New York, 1976. Loebel, who was Czechoslovakia's First Deputy Minister of Foreign Trade, is a much-neglected economist. Much of the roots of Newton Morrow's economics, including his FIST tax proposal, was nurtured by the brilliance of this book. Must reading.

Loebel, Eugen; Roman, Stephen, *The Responsible Society*, Two Continents Publishing Group, New York, 1977. Loebel's name is given first because this book ties in closely with his *Humanomics*. Amazingly, Roman is chairman of the board of the world's largest uranium mine. Together, the two men propose a completely new approach to government financing which has many parallels with United People's Capital Corporation. Absolutely must reading!

Low, Albert, *Zen and the Art of Management*, Anchor Press, New York, 1976. A 1970s approach, with the inevitable future in mind.

Moore, Truman, *Nouveau Mania, The American Passion for Novelty and How It Led Us Astray*, Random House, New York, 1975. While Truman might not agree, in New Tomorrow the existence, or nonexistence, of junk foods and junk products could simply be based on the profitability of their production. The enlightened citizen of the United People of America simply wouldn't buy much of any stuff that didn't offer reasonable life improvement. Good reading.

Ophuls, Williams, *Ecology and the Politics of Scarcity*, W. H. Norton, New York, 1976. If you want to understand the case for federal chartering of corporations, a fundamental function of the largest corporation in the world—The United People of America—then you must read this book.

Ophuls, Williams: *Ecology and the Politics of Scarcity*, W. H. Freeman, San Francisco, 1977. An important addition to the Schumacher kind of thinking. A prediction for a world of new values and steady state societies.

Oppenheimer, Ernest J., *The Inflation Swindle*, Prentice Hall, New York, 1977. This short book is a good guide to who benefits from inflation—and in all probability it isn't you!

Patman, Wright, *A Primer on Money*, You can buy this from the Superintendent of Documents, U.S. Government Printing Office, Washington, D.C. for 60¢. Read it and learn that America has been blessed with some great politicians, too. Patman wrote it for his colleagues!

Peters, Harvey W., *America's Coming Bankruptcy, How the Government Is Wrecking Your Dollar*, Arlington House, New Rochelle, New York, 1973. You may not have to read this to know that your money is not worth much, but this excellent book will reinforce you.

Rothman, Stanley; Mossman, Charles, *Computers and Society*, Science Research Associates, Inc., 1976. A good introduction to computers for the layman. Published by, who else, a subsidiary of IBM!

Rueff, Jacques, *The Monetary Sins of the West*, Macmillan, New York, 1972. Why the gold-exchange standard international monetary system doesn't work, by a famous advocate of a monetary system based directly on gold. Interesting to contrast with Morrow's guaranteed 1972 dollar, and a United People's Capital Corporation which could make the dollar, politically and economically, as sound as gold.

Sauvy, Alfred, *Zero Growth?*, Praeger Publishers, New York, 1976. Whatever else, Newton Morrow believes in accelerating growth . . . but based on a different kind of Gross National Product. The whole problem of zero growth and its implications for the less-developed countries who can't control their populations has the elements of a Greek tragedy.

Scott, Hilda, *Does Socialism Liberate Women?*, Beacon Press, Boston, Mass., 1974. The answer is no—but neither has capitalism, A.D. 1980. Good reading.

Silk, Leonard; Vogel, David, *Ethics and Profits, The Crisis of Confidence in American Business,* Simon & Schuster, New York, 1976. Why businessmen must search for a new system of ethics and social responsibilities. Good reading for the problems facing old-style private capitalism.

Solomon, Robert, *The International Monetary System, 1945–1976,* Harper & Row, New York, 1977. Subtitled, *An Insider's View.* Solomon was top economic adviser to the Federal Reserve. Not so difficult to read as it might sound.

Spencer, Charles, *Blue Collar, An Internal Examination of the Workplace,* Lakeside Charter Books, P.O. Box 7651, Chicago, Ill. Price $4.95. Worth reading. Written by a union worker and activist who would be an excellent man to have on the board of directors of *his* corporation in Newton Morrow's New Tomorrow!

Speiser, Stuart, *A Piece of the Action, A Plan to Provide Every Family with a $100,000 Stake in the Economy,* Van Nostrand, Reinhold, New York, 1977. Speiser, a Kelso enthusiast, has carried Kelso's theories to a fascinating and wholly achievable conclusion. Compare the modified diffusion of stock ownership with Newton Morrow's all-out approach. Absolutely must reading!

Tugwell, Rexford, *The Emerging Constitution,* Harper Magazine Press, New York, 1974. Tugwell's book was the catalyst for Newton Morrow's version of the New Constitution. This thoroughly fascinating book not only documents, in detail, the need for a New Constitution, but contains the last version of Tugwell's *Proposed Constitutional Model for the Newstates of America.* In the Center Magazine, September, 1970, an earlier version of Tugwell's *Model for a New Constitution* appears in full. Center for Democratic Institutions, Santa Barbara, Calif., 93103.

Von Mises, Ludwig, *Human Action, A Treatise on Economics,* Henry Regnery Co., Chicago, Ill., 1966. While Libertarians may not wholly approve of Newton Morrow's United People of America, Morrow's economics are a product of Libertarian economics carried to their logical extreme. Don't let the size of Von Mises' book discourage you. Use Doctor Eliot's "15 minutes-a-day—Harvard Bookshelf method" and you'll have finished it in a month and be a super-person!

Webre, Alfred L.; Liss, Phillip H., *The Age of Cataclysm,* G. P. Putnam, New York, 1975. After detailing numerous ways the world may end in the next quarter century, the authors conclude that if it doesn't, the United States must have a new political system *and* a New Constitution.

Weintraub, Sidney, *Modern Economic Thought,* University of Pennsylvania Press, Philadelphia, Pa., 1977. If you want to go all out, this 584-page survey will make you your own expert. Tackle a chapter at a time. It's not difficult.

Weisskopf, Walter A., *Alienation and Economics,* E. P. Dutton, New York, 1971. Weisskopf is one of the new breed of economists who is searching for a world where economics and human values merge. Good reading.

Young, George Park, *An American Alternative, Steps Toward a More Workable Society,* Crescent Publications, Los Angeles, Calif., 1976. An economist's proposal on how to restructure our economic system. Good reading.

Zaleznik, Abraham, and others, *Power & The Corporate Mind, What Makes People Tick, Organizations Run, and Executives Manage,* Houghton, Mifflin & Company, Boston, Mass., 1975. A good study of leadership for managers of any businss, large or small, which may be operating in 1980 or 1996!

Late 20th-Century
Social Perspectives on the 21st Century

Adizes, Ichok; Borgese, Elizabeth Mann, Eds., *Self-Management—New Dimensions to Democracy, Alternatives for a New Society,* Center for the Study of Democratic Institutions, Santa Barbara, Calif., 1975. A study of labor and management in Yugoslavia, Israel, and Norway that is must reading for those who would understand the potential of a total corporate society like the United People of America.

Aronson, Elliot, *The Social Animal,* William Freeman, San Francisco, 1976. Joyous reading on what makes you, *you*—both now and in 1996. Aronson should keep publishing new editions modifying and expanding his findings on human behavior.

Balzer, Richard, *Clockwork, Life In and Outside an American Factory,* Doubleday, New York, 1976. A good contrast of the present reality with the future potential life of working men and women whose working years in New Tomorrow would begin at twenty-five and end at fifty.

Bell, Daniel, *The Coming of Post-Industrial Society, A Venture in Social Forecasting,* Basic Books, New York, 1973. While Bell ignores Bellamy's *Equality,* his society of the future, in this careful analysis, has much in common with Bellamy's conclusions. Any study of equality versus inequality in a society raises the question of the various kinds of equality and whether individual merit can be rewarded other than by vast income differences—especially when those with the greatest incomes often contribute little to overall social good.

Bennis, Warren, *The Unconscious Conspiracy, Why Leaders Can't Lead,* American Management Association, New York, 1976. An excellent book on the quality of leadership needed now and in the future.

Berry, Adrian, *The Next Ten Thousand Years, A Vision of Man's Future in the Universe,* The New American Library, New York, 1974. Better reading and more awe-inspiring than any science fiction, by a positive "future-dreamer."

Boguslaw, Robert, *The New Utopians, A Study of System Design and Social Change,* Prentice Hall, New York, 1965. Valuable reading for the managers of industry in the computer-oriented world of New Tomorrow.

Bundy, Robert, Ed., *Images of the Future, The 21st Century & Beyond,* Prometheus Books, Buffalo, New York, 1976. A valuable collection of essays covering many aspects of our interpersonal lives in the future.

Burns, Scott, *The Household Economy, Its Shape, Origin, and Future,* Beacon Press, Boston, 1975. An exciting examination of the $212 billion (1968 figures) household economy which includes the value of women's *unpaid* labor of $124 billion. Note that Love Group Corporations pay for household labor as a part of their operating expense.

Chase, Allan, *The Legacy of Malthus, The Social Costs of Scientific Racism,* Alfred Knopf, New York, 1976. The "scientific" myths about race and ethnic groups that have been used by leaders in every country to convince the general public that a wide variety of social and racial groups are genetically inferior, and from this vantage point design our laws and public policy. Very mind opening!

Clark, Kenneth, *The Pathos of Power,* Harper & Row, New York, 1974. Seeking power to escape the fragility of the human ego was not Newton Morrow's motivation. But it is for many of our leaders. Good reading.

Clarke, Robin, Ed., *Notes for the Future, An Alternative History of the Past Decade,* Universe Books, New York, 1975. A collection of the best essays on the future, including *The Tragedy of the Commons,* by Garrett Hardin, among twenty others.

Cournand, Andre; Levy, Maurice, Eds., *Shaping the Future,* Gordon and Breach, New York, 1973. Is the future an inevitable extension of the present? Or can books like *Love Me Tomorrow,* and Newton Morrow's proposal (if enough people get the message) become a self-fulfilling prophecy? A good study of future forecasting.

Davie, Michael, *In the Future Now, A Report from California,* Hornish Hamilton, London, England, 1972. An English observer looking at California who believes that while the future may be revealing itself in California, it points to the cul-de-sac created by too much affluence in any society.

Day, Legrand, *A New Dimension of Freedom*, Mojave Books, 7040 Darby Avenue, Reseda, Calif. 91355. Price $4.95. A mind-boggling proposal to let each American choose the kind of government he would prefer to live under, and thus make government compete for its citizenry.

Dellinger, Dave, *More Power, The People's Movement Toward Democracy*, Anchor Press, New York, 1975. Good reading that gives you a sense of the strong undercurrents that are changing our world.

Dickson, Paul, *The Future File, A Guide for One People with One Foot in the 21st Century*, Rawson Associates, New York, 1977. A good survey of who is thinking what about the future.

Dickson, Paul, *The Future of the Workplace, The Coming Revolution in Jobs*, Weybright & Talley, New York, 1975. "Coming events cast their shadows before." Dickson's excellent study ranges the vast changes in the environment and style of work. Must reading.

Doughton, Morgan, *People Power, An Alternative to 1984*, Media America, Inc., Bethlehem, Pa., 1976. Here is the kind of people leadership, in all phases of each of our lives, that will make New Tomorrow a joyous place to live. Morgan anticipates an entirely new kind of Congress and the United People of America.

Ewen, Stuart, *Captains of Consciousness, Advertising and the Social Roots of the Consumer Culture*, McGraw Hill, New York, 1976. The essence of this fascinating analysis of industry is contained in Edward Filene's statement, "Mass production demands the education of the masses. The masses must learn to behave like human beings in a mass production world." Get in your auto right now (Sunday or not) and go buy something at the shopping center!

Fromm, Erich, *To Have or To Be*, Harper & Row, New York, 1976. This book encapsulates Erich Fromm's philosophy, and was obviously highly influential on Newton Morrow's religious and political thinking. Read this book and learn the crucial difference between "being" and "having."

Friedenberg, Edgar I., *The Disposal of Liberty and Other Industrial Wastes*, Doubleday, New York, 1975. A good look at our freedoms and lack of them in a society that rationalizes individual class exploitation as a way of life.

Fuller, R. Buckminster, *And I Came to Pass—Not to Stay*, MacMillan, New York, 1976. Bucky's philosophy and future predictions written as poetic essays. Must reading.

Gabor, Dennis, *The Mature Society, A View of the Future*, Praeger, New York, 1972. Good reading by the winner of the

1971 Nobel Prize for Physics. Interesting also to note, as with many other books in this bibliography, how rapidly "change" seems to negate the minor ripples, but not the gathering "seventh wave."

Garaudy, Roger, *The Alternate Future, A Vision of Christian Marxism*, Simon & Schuster, New York, 1974. A Christian Communist examines the revolution in progress in the world and the more joyous world it may presage.

Gheladi, Robert, *Economics, Society & Culture, God, Money and the New Capitalism*, Delta, New York, 1976. Gheladi is seeking a middle way between capitalism's alienating individualism and Communist and Socialist collectivism. Among other things, he contrasts Louis Kelso's economics with John Maynard Keynes'. Good reading to understand the corporate world of New Tomorrow.

Goldstone, Paul N., *The Collapse of the Liberal Empire, Science and Revolution in the Twentieth Century*, Yale University Press, New Haven, Conn., 1977. Are the new liberal philosophies and technologies in conflict? Good reading with some thoughtful answers.

Gorham, William; Glazen, Nathan, Eds., *The Urban Predicament*, Urban Institute, Washington, D.C., 1976. The problems of our cities are a top-priority problem that interweaves with the life styles of the majority of Americans. Must reading.

Gowan, Suzanne, and others, *Moving Toward a New Society*, New Society Press, 4722 Baltimore Avenue, Philadelphia, Pa. 19143, 1976. Price $3.75. Add this book to your library. The authors are members of the Movement for a New Society, a national communication network of groups seeking to build a new society based on maximum decentralization in both political and economic centers.

Greeley, Andrew: *No Bigger Than Necessary*, Meridian, New American Library, New York, 1977. While Father Greeley might not agree, his analysis of Catholic models of human nature evolving into "natural" groups anticipates Love Groups. Good future thinking in the area of human *inter*dependence.

Gullian, Robert, *The Japanese Challenge, The Race to the Year 2000*, J. P. Lippincott, Philadelphia, Pa., 1970. The Japanese industrial system is closely integrated with the personal welfare of the individual worker that denies some of the individualism of America, but eliminates insecurity in a patriarchal way. A corporate society paying dividends to its people—and thrusting initiative back on the people, has greater future potential. The United People of America could win the race. Read this book and others about Japan and decide for yourself.

Hardin, Garrett; Baden, John, *Managing the Commons*, W. H. Freeman, San Francisco, 1977. Understanding the "tragedy" of the commons is the jumping-off place for future studies. An excellent collection of essays on our planet's "unowned" resources.

Harman, Willis, *An Incomplete Guide to the Future,* San Francisco Book Company, San Francisco, 1976. Harman's tentative blueprint for New Tomorrow is the best of its kind. Don't miss reading this book. It will expand your horizons.

Heifetz, Milton, M.D.; Mangel, Charles, *The Right to Die,* Berkley-Medallion, New York, 1975. Among other things, this excellent and pragmatic book covers suicide as a human right.

Hirsch, Fred, *Social Limits to Growth,* Harvard University Press, Cambridge, Mass., 1976. "If everyone stands on tiptoe—no one sees better"—this is only one aspect of the limits that Hirsch studies in a fascinating, must-reading book for futurists.

Hubbard, Barbara Marx, *The Hunger of Eve, A Woman's Odyssey Toward the Future,* Stackpole Books, Harrisburg, Pa. 17105. When all women enjoy the hunger of Eve—the urge to learn and know more—we'll have one foot in the Golden Age. Good reading, by a dedicated futurist.

Kahn, Herman, and others, *The Next 200 Years, A Scenario for America and the World,* Morrow, New York, 1976. Herman and the Hudson Institute are the world's greatest optimists. Their scenario for 2176 is materialistically Utopian and upstages the fairy-tales of science fiction. Nice work if we can get it. But Kahn skips over interpersonal behavior in 2176 pretty lightly!

Karsk, Roger, *Teen Agers in the Next America,* New Community Press, Columbia, Md. 21044. An interesting examination of teen-agers raised in a closely knit community town, Columbia, Maryland. Good reading for futurists.

Kaufman, Walter, *The Future of the Humanities, A New Approach to Teaching Art, Religion, Philosophy, Literature and History,* Reader's Digest Press, New York, 1977. Kaufman shows how to make learning exciting, not for the dollar in your pocket, but for the sense of well-being that comes from knowing *all* your roots.

Keniston, Kenneth, *All Our Children, The American Family Under Pressure,* Harcourt Brace Jovanovich, New York, 1977. A vital analysis and proposal for a new society which would be resolved by Newton Morrow's economic proposal. Must reading.

Lasky, Melvin J., *Utopia and Revolution,* University of Chicago Press, Chicago, 1976. Is New Tomorrow a Utopian commitment that would require revolution or harsh government control? Read Lasky's provocative study of Utopias and find why New Tomorrow could be a "high middle-ground."

Leinwand, Gerald, Ed., *The Future,* Pocket Books, New York,

1976. Selections from various Utopian writers, including Bellamy. A good study guide to thinking about the future.

Marder, Jerry, *Four Arguments for the Elimination of Television,* William Morrow, New York, 1978. This is a must-reading book for a complete perspective on what television is doing to the human mind and culture. But Marder overlooks the possibility that television will eliminate itself as it has practically done in 1996 by too much of a good thing.

Mazlish, Bruce, *The Revolutionary Ascetic, Evolution of a Political Type,* Basic Books, New York, 1976. Can men like Lenin, Mao Tse-tung, and charismatic leaders like Newton Morrow love in the ordinary way? Mazlish's analysis of a new type of national leader is thought-provoking and scary.

Mayer, Martin, *Today and Tomorrow in America,* Harper & Row, New York, 1976. Good survey of where we are, where we are going, and which offers some cautious suggestions on what to do next.

Mendlovitz, Saul H. Ed., *On the Creation of a Just World Order, Preferred Worlds for the 1990s,* Free Press, New York, 1975. A must-reading book about relevant Utopias by leading American, Japanese, Indian, Chinese, and Latin-American scholars.

Merhabian, Albert, *Public Places, Private Spaces, The Psychology of Work, Play, and Living Environments,* Basic Books, New York, 1976. In the crowded world of New Tomorrow, better environments for living are the key to self-fulfillment. Don't miss this book.

Miles, Ian, *The Poverty of Prediction,* Lexington Books, Lexington, Mass., 1975. Good reading for futurists who might not be able to envision a New Tomorrow.

Morgan, Arthur, *The Community of the Future,* Community Services, Incorporated, Yellow Springs, Ohio. A study of communities, written in 1957, that has much validity for today, and derives from Morgan's great admiration for Bellamy.

Moshowitz, Abbe, *The Conquest of Will, Information Processing in Human Affairs,* Addison Wesley Publishing Company, Reading, Mass., 1976. Read this book to understand the changing distribution of power between the individual and society.

Olsen, Paul, *The Future of Being Human,* Dell, New York, 1975. An interesting view of our "damaged sexuality" from a psychotherapist's viewpoint.

Parker, Stanley, *The Future of Work and Leisure,* Paladin, London, 1972. The relationship of work and leisure is basic to a New Tomorrow based on a 25-year work life for most men and women. Good reading.

Pawley, Martin, *The Private Future, Causes and Consequences of Community Collapse,* Random House, New York, 1974. A good study of "individualism" and its destructive force on society. New Tomorrow and Love Groups will reverse the trend that peaked in the 1980s of 20 million single households in the United States.

Prehoda, Robert, *The Technophilic-Malthusian Perspective*, World Future Society Bulletin, September–October, 1977, World Future Society, 4916 St. Elmo Avenue, Washington, D.C. 20014. A fascinating, must-reading, middle-ground approach combining *negative* population growth, which ties in with Bob's *Principle of Optimization*, an article which appears in a previous issue of the *WFS Bulletin*. After you read it, Bob Prehoda would appreciate your comments. Reach him at P.O. Box 2402, Toluca Lake Station, North Hollywood, Calif. 91602. Bob Prehoda also wrote *Suspended Animation* (see listing under *Reincarnation*).

Poor, Riva, *Four Days in Forty Hours, and Other Forms of the Rearranged Work Week*, New American Library, New York, 1973. While Riva doesn't cover the New Tomorrows of a shorter working life, her book is necessary to an understanding of a different work ethic.

Reich, Wilhelm, *The Mass Psychology of Fascism*, Pocket Books, New York, 1976. Reich's theories of "work-democracy" and "sex politics" envisions a future society where men and women are not relieved of their social responsibilities, and love, work, and knowledge are developed organically. Many aspects of New Tomorrow are erected on Reichian foundations.

Rubin, Lillian Breslow, *Worlds of Pain, Life in the Working Class Family*, Basic Books, New York, 1976. Read this book to understand how the United People's Corporation, and a new kind of monetary security, can eliminate this kind of working and home environment that dominates the lives of millions of Americans, who, despite government income figures, *do not* live in an affluent society.

Schaller, Lyle E., *Understanding Tomorrow*, Abingdon Press, Nashville, Tenn., 1976. One of the best short overall perspectives on the world of tomorrow written in the 1970s. Must reading.

Scholes, Robert, *Structural Fabulation, An Essay on the Fiction of the Future*, University of Notre Dame, South Bend, Ind., 1975. "To live well in the present, to live decently and humanely, we *must see into the future*." Thus the necessity for future-fiction.

Schumacher, E. F., *A Guide for the Perplexed*, Harper & Row, New York, 1977. The author of *Small Is Beautiful* expanding his theories into a humanistic religion. Good reading, even though some critics think Schumacher is a male chauvinist.

Spring, Joel, *A Primer of Libertarian Education*, Free Life Editions, Inc., 41 Union Square, New York, N.Y. 10003. A good summary of alternate ways of educating human beings that go far beyond career and vocational education to create an environment for personal self-fulfillment.

Stavrianos, L. S., *The Promise of the Coming Dark Age*, W. H. Freeman, San Francisco, 1976. An excellent intimation of the future, presaging a New Tomorrow *without* Big Government, Big Unions, and Big Business. The promise is a world that has moved from subordination to self-actualization.

Stent, Gunther S., *The Coming of the Golden Age, A View of the End of Progress*, American Museum of Natural History Press, Garden City, New York, 1969. Was presumably written at the end of the hippie era. Stent anticipates Newton Morrow's world of the "iks" dominating all values. Even ten years later, scary reading.

Theobald, Robert: *An Alternative Future for America II*, Swallow Press, Chicago, 1970. In this book, Bob is thinking in terms of the emerging people power which culminates in New Tomorrow. Good reading!

————, *Beyond Despair, Directions for America's Third Century*, New Republic Book Co., Washington, D.C., 1976. Bob Theobald is America's outstanding futurist. Read this exciting book for challenging new perspectives, as we move from the industrial era to the communications era. If you are future-oriented, contact Bob Theobald's organization, Participation Publishers, Box 2240, Wickensburg, Ariz. 85358, for details of his Network-Linkage, designed to put highly skilled and committed people in touch with each other.

Theobald, Robert, Ed., *The Guaranteed Income, Next Step in Socioeconomic Evolution*, Doubleday, New York, 1967. Must reading. Guaranteed income is a direct outgrowth of Edward Bellamy's proposal for an absolute guarantee to "abundant maintenance." It was developed in a different framework by Louis Kelso with his Employee Stock Ownership Plans which would turn eighty million workers into capitalists—all of them owning a "piece of the action"—and takes on a new dimension with Newton Morrow's Capital Account for every citizen stockholder of the United People of America.

Tripp, Maggie, *Women in the Year 2000*, Arban House, New York, 1974. A collection of essays by well-known writers, many fanciful, some realistic, on women, sex, marriage in the year 2000. Unfortunately, Maggie was evidently unaware of Edward Bellamy's essay *Women in the Year 2000*, which makes him an equal rights prognosticator a hundred years before the event.

Tucille, Jerome, *Who's Afraid of 1984?*, Arlington House, New Rochelle, New York, 1975. An optimistic projection based on Libertarian economics. If you aren't acquainted with America's third largest party in 1980, you should be.

Turnbull, Colin, *The Mountain People*, Simon & Schuster, New

York, 1972. This is Newton Morrow's source for the "iks"—the dispossessed tribe of Ugandans who lost their nomadic existence to civilization. Must reading for members of, and voters for, the United People of America.

Citizen's Future's Organizations, Congressional Research Service, Library of Congress, Washington, D.C. If you are interested in working with Futurists, this 115-page pamphlet analyzes the activities of twenty-nine different groups throughout the U.S.

Congressional Clearinghouse on the Future, 3692 House Annex #2, Washington, D.C. 20515. An advisory committee to Congress, the Clearinghouse publishes a newsletter called *What's Next?* that keeps abreast of all organizations and individuals involved in future planning. The newsletter is available to anyone interested, at very small cost.

The Next 25 Years, Crisis and Opportunity, World Future Society, Washington, D.C., 1975. A stimulating collection of essays on every aspect of the future.

Liberty Press, 7440 North Shadcland, Indianapolis, Ind. 46250. A unique publishing company specializing in books that encourage the study of ideals of a society of free and responsible individuals. Many formerly out-of-print books such as Adam Smith's *Theory of Moral Sentiments, Popular Government,* by Henry Sumner Maine, are available. Write for their catalogue.

New Age, published monthly by New Age Communications, 32 Station Street, Brookline Village, Mass. 02146. Annual subscription $12.00. If you don't subscribe to *New Age,* you should! It not only publishes continuously fascinating articles on every aspect of the here-and-now future, which some people call the counterculture, but it is critically future-oriented, and editorially doesn't hesitate to sift the chaff from the wheat. The November, 1977 issue is an excellent overview and guide to *Death, Dying and Immortality.*

Rainbook, Resources for Appropriate Technology, Schocken Books, New York, 1977. The $7.95 this guidebook to a more fully realized life costs you will be repaid many times over. Presumably, it will (or should) be kept up to date. Buy it!

Interpersonal Support Network, 821 F Beverly Boulevard, Suite 5, Los Angeles, Calif. 90048. A network of independent adults sharing fun and friendship. The network is comprised of families or groups of twelve to fifteen people who meet on a regular basis. The network coordinates all families and sponsors social events, professional workshops, and personal development services. Expanding nationally.

What Do We Do When the Ship Goes Down?, Harper & Row, New York, 1976. Fascinating conversations with some top futurists, including Ian McHarg, Paolo Soleri, and others. If you're thirty-five or under, you may live to be aboard the

453

"ship" when it has 6 billion passengers instead of the present 4 billion!

Trend Analysis Reports, American Council on Life Insurance, Washington, D.C. An abstract of articles prepared by a team of life insurance executives who monitor everything being written that could represent new trends of significance to the future of business. Excellent reading. Probably available from your library.

World Future Society, 4916 St. Elmo Avenue, (Bethesda) Washington, D.C. 20014. Their free catalogue of *Resources* is the most complete listing of books in all areas written about the future. *The Futurist,* a monthly magazine, is available at an annual subscription price of $15.00. Also, *The Future, A Guide to Information Sources,* and *The Study of the Future, An Introduction to the Art and Science of Shaping Tomorrow's World,* are available at $17.50 and $9.50, respectively.

The Futures Group, 124 Hebron Avenue, Glastonbury, Conn. 06033. Ted Gordon, who heads up this organization, predicts the future in the only rational way as a direct outgrowth of the present and inevitable technological changes in the future. Write for a copy of his speech, "Life Style of the Future, Conspicuous Conservation." It's a classic.

American Association for the Advancement of Sciences, 1515 Massachusetts Avenue, N.W., Washington, D.C. 20005. *Shaping the Future of Our World, Electronics, Materials, Population, Food, Energy.* Five books dealing in different areas covering the problems of the future in which you may live—prices vary between $4.95 and $13.50 each, paperbound. Write for brochure. You may wish to join the AAAS and receive their magazine *Science.*

Social Indicators, 1976. U.S. Department of Commerce, published December, 1977. Available from the Superintendent of Documents, U.S. Government Printing Office, Washington, D.C. 20402. The second in a series. A 560-page publication, fully illustrated with colorful tables, an analysis of all aspects of American life that is a key to areas where we are and aren't achieving self-fulfillment and personal self-realization.

About the Author

Robert H. Rimmer has been called America's foremost chronicler of diverse forms of sexual relationships that soon may become a part of our daily lives. He is the author of many prophetic books about sex, the most famous being THE HARRAD EXPERIMENT. He is also the author of THE REBELLION OF YALE MARRATT, THE GOLD LOVERS, PROPOSITION 31, THURSDAY, MY LOVE, THAT GIRL FROM BOSTON, THE PREMAR EXPERIMENTS, and COME LIVE MY LIFE, among others.

Mr. Rimmer lives in Quincy, Massachusetts 02169.

Have You Read These SIGNET Bestsellers?

☐ **BELLADONNA by Erica Lindley.** (#J8387—$1.95)*

☐ **THE BRACKENROYD INHERITANCE by Erica Lindley.**
(#W6795—$1.50)

☐ **THE DEVIL IN CRYSTAL by Erica Lindley.**
(#E7643—$1.75)

☐ **THE GODFATHER by Mario Puzo.** (#E8508—$2.50)*

☐ **KRAMER VERSUS KRAMER by Avery Corman.**
(#E8282—$2.50)

☐ **JOURNEY ON THE WIND by Kay McDonald.**
(#J8547—$1.95)

☐ **VISION OF THE EAGLE by Kay McDonald.**
(#J8284—$1.95)

☐ **HOMICIDE ZONE FOUR by Nick Christian.**
(#J8285—$1.95)*

☐ **CLEARED FOR THE APPROACH by F. Lee Bailey with
John Greenya.** (#E8286—$2.50)*

☐ **CRESSIDA by Clare Darcy.** (#E8287—$1.75)*

☐ **DANIEL MARTIN by John Fowles.** (#E8249—$2.95)

☐ **THE EBONY TOWER by John Fowles.** (#E8254—$2.50)

☐ **THE FRENCH LIEUTENANT'S WOMAN by John Fowles.**
(#E8535—$2.50)

☐ **RIDE THE BLUE RIBAND by Rosalind Laker.**
(#J8252—$1.95)*

☐ **MISTRESS OF OAKHURST—Book II by Walter Reed
Johnson.** (#J8253—$1.95)

☐ **OAKHURST—Book I by Walter Reed Johnson.**
(#J7874—$1.95)

☐ **THE SILVER FALCON by Evelyn Anthony.**
(#E8211—$2.25)

☐ **I, JUDAS by Taylor Caldwell and Jess Stearn.**
(#E8212—$2.50)*

☐ **THE RAGING WINDS OF HEAVEN by June Shiplett.**
(#J8213—$1.95)

☐ **THE TODAY SHOW by Robert Metz.** (#E8214—$2.25)

*Price slightly higher in Canada

More Big Bestsellers from SIGNET

☐ **THE SERGEANT MAJOR'S DAUGHTER** by Sheila Walsh.
(#E8220—$1.75)

☐ **BLOCKBUSTER** by Stephen Barlay. (#E8111—$2.25)*

☐ **BALLET!** by Tom Murphy. (#E8112—$2.25)*

☐ **THE LADY SERENA** by Jeanne Duval.
(#E8163—$2.25)*

☐ **LOVING STRANGERS** by Jack Mayfield.
(#J8216—$1.95)*

☐ **BORN TO WIN** by Muriel James and Dorothy Jongeward.
(#E8169—$2.50)*

☐ **BORROWED PLUMES** by Roseleen Milne.
(#E8113—$1.75)

☐ **ROGUE'S MISTRESS** by Constance Gluyas.
(#E8339—$2.25)

☐ **SAVAGE EDEN** by Constance Gluyas. (#E8338—$2.25)

☐ **WOMAN OF FURY** by Constance Gluyas.
(#E8075—$2.25)*

☐ **BEYOND THE MALE MYTH** by Anthony Pietropinto, M.D.,
and Jacqueline Simenauer. (#E8076—$2.50)

☐ **CRAZY LOVE: An Autobiographical Account of Marriage
and Madness** by Phyllis Naylor. (#J8077—$1.95)

☐ **THE PSYCHOPATHIC GOD—ADOLF HITLER** by Robert
G. L. Waite. (#E8078—$2.95)

☐ **HEAT** by Arthur Herzog. (#J8115—$1.95)*

☐ **THE SWARM** by Arthur Herzog. (#E8079—$1.75)

☐ **THE RULING PASSION** by Shaun Herron.
(#E8042—$2.25)

☐ **CONSTANTINE CAY** by Catherine Dillon.
(#J8307—$1.95)

☐ **WHITE FIRES BURNING** by Catherine Dillon.
(#J8281—$1.95)

☐ **THE WHITE KHAN** by Catherine Dillon.
(#J8043—$1.95)*

☐ **THE MASTERS WAY TO BEAUTY** by George Masters with
Norma Lee Browning. (#E8044—$2.25)

*Price slightly higher in Canada